" ... trickster can also get snared in his own devices.
Trickster is at once culture hero and fool,
clever predator and stupid prey."

Lewis Hyde,
Trickster Makes This World: Mischief, Myth, and Art

Chaos: I Bring the Fire Part III

Copyright ©2015 C. Gockel

All rights reserved. No part of this publication may be reproduced, distributed, or transmitted in any form or by any means, including photocopying, recording, or other electronic or mechanical methods, without the prior written permission of the publisher, except in the case of brief quotations embodied in critical reviews and certain other noncommercial uses permitted by copyright law. For permission requests, write to the author, subject "Attention: Permissions," at the email address: cgockel.publishing@gmail.com

ISBN-13:978-1503305212
ISBN-10:150330521X

Chaos:
I Bring the Fire
Part III

C. Gockel

Acknowledgements

First and foremost, I want to thank my editor, Kay McSpadden. Kay read and reread this story more times than I can count. I also would like to thank Patricia Kirby, Tyler Staiver, Gretchen Almoughraby, and my brother Thomas for not being afraid to tell me when they thought I'd wandered off course. This story is more exciting for their input. Also, thanks, Mom, for the grammar help!

My husband Eric also deserves a word of thanks. His nagging pushed me into self-publishing my stories to begin with.

Last and never least—I owe a huge thank you to my fans. Your emails, reviews, tweets, and blog posts made writing this story worthwhile. I hope you enjoy reading Chaos as much as I enjoyed writing it.

The *I Bring the Fire* Series:
I Bring the Fire Part I: Wolves
Monsters: I Bring the Fire Part II
Chaos: I Bring the Fire Part III
In the Balance: I Bring the Fire Part 3.5
Fates: I Bring the Fire Part IV
The Slip: a Short Story
Warriors: I Bring the Fire Part V
Ragnarok: I Bring the Fire Part VI
The Fire Bringers: a Short Story
Atomic: a Short Story

Other Works:
Murphy's Star a short story about first contact
Archangel Down: Archangel Project Book One

CHAPTER 1

The smell of rain, alcohol, wet hair and clothing permeates the nearly empty bar. It's past closing time, on a cold and wet Monday night. Usually the bar is bathed in a soft yellow glow, but they've turned up the lights to remind the few patrons left it's time to leave. Loki is sitting at the bar proper, a plate of nearly decimated french fries and a burger in front of him. A very attractive, very interesting brunette that is just his type is sauntering across the room in his direction.

Giving her a calculated smile, Loki holds up his empty beer mug in the barkeep's direction. "May I have another?" Loki is distressingly close to sober and beginning to feel the chill of his wet clothing.

Raising an eyebrow as he dries a glass, the bartender says, "Last call was 10 minutes ago."

The lights flicker. Loki restrains a shiver and an urge to set something on fire. He can't help but think of Amy's warm bed—he'd still be there if Brett and Bryant hadn't interrupted his doze. The brothers' honorable intentions aside, Bryant deserved the broken arm he got in the resulting altercation. To think that Loki would have to stoop to taking advantage of a woman while she is unconscious. It's insulting!

As if to make the point, the brunette slides up beside him. She smiles and leans onto the counter, angling her body just so. Loki can see down the V neckline of her burgundy dress. She has astounding gravity-defying décolletage. His eyebrows lift and a warmth much more pleasant than anger washes over him. At the same time he feels something like guilt or regret twist in his gut. He thinks of the time he spent with Amy and her friends earlier in the evening—it had been just the perfect mix of interesting conversation and alcohol, he'd felt comfortable, like he belonged, and if Amy hadn't passed out … well. He remembers her head on his lap in the cab a few hours ago.

His jaw tenses in annoyance at his own reminiscing. He gives the woman beside him a smile that verges on a leer.

"Are you alone?" she asks. Her words make his skin prickle. She knows the answer, Loki feels it. But maybe she couldn't think of a better opening, and just isn't much of a conversationalist? His eyes sweep her body again. She doesn't need to be.

Dipping a bit of fried potato into ketchup, Loki looks down at his plate and raises an eyebrow. "Are you?"

"I hope not anymore," she says, and Loki doesn't roll his eyes at the cliché. Instead he turns to her and smiles with all his teeth, knowing that it makes him appear slightly sinister. She doesn't bat an eyelash.

"What's your name?" he asks, angling his body a little closer.

"Maria," she says. His skin prickles at the lie, and he raises an eyebrow.

Smiling, she leans a little closer and shows a little more cleavage. "And you are … "

"Loki!" he says brightly.

She blinks, looking a little surprised. Recovering, she says, "Like the Norse god?"

"No," he almost snorts. "I'm a Frost Giant—we're not actually blue like your movies." Frost Giants aren't blue—just Loki occasionally, and his daughter Helen. He gives her a brittle smile and knows he is utterly failing to hide his bitterness.

Her eyes widen, and she looks confused, so Loki laughs as though he's joking. She smiles a little, and her body relaxes.

Picking up another french fry, Loki says, "Maria, why don't you tell me about yourself?" As she begins to talk, Loki lets his consciousness drift over her. He doesn't sense any electronic surveillance devices. Just her cell phone. She's hiding something, but maybe she's just married or otherwise unavailable and out for a little fun? His eyes drift over her curvaceous figure. He could have fun with her.

And then she starts talking about her university training as a CPA. It's not philosophy or quantum physics or even witty. It's all true, and Loki wishes she'd lie, because frankly, she's putting him to sleep.

"I'm boring you, aren't I?" she says, sounding sincere and concerned.

"Oh, no, go on," says Loki, eyes dipping to her décolletage again.

Leaning closer to him, Maria says, "Accounting isn't very exciting, but it is secure. My parents were so relieved when I chose it as my major. I was such a rebel when I was younger."

She looks down and sighs. "But sometimes … "

His nose itches a little. Something just isn't quite right. He looks at her wide, full lips. He could have fun trying to find out what's wrong. "Miss the excitement of your rebellious youth?" he asks, taking a sip of water and wishing it was something harder.

She smiles. "Sometimes."

Leaning closer, he lets his hand barely skim the soft delicious curve of her side. "I might be able to provide some excitement," he whispers.

Biting her lip, she says, "We can't go back to my place … "

Loki's mouth opens, he's about to suggest a hotel when she says, "Maybe we can go back to yours?"

She smiles, and there is something so sweetly predatory about it—something that promises sex without commitment or emotional entanglement. Something that seems just the thing to take the illusion of belonging off of his mind. How can he not indulge 'Maria'?

Loki pretends to look contemplative, and then he whispers, "My place it is then."

The predatory smile stretches wider.

Loki smiles right back. Oh, this *will* be fun.

Agent Steve Rogers, Acting Assistant Director the FBI's Department of Anomalous Devices of Unknown Origins Midwest Division, is standing behind his desk, hands on his hips. Across from Steve, flanked by his own operatives up from DC, Stuart Jameson, Executive Director of ADUO for the entire U.S., tilts his head. "I've just caught Loki—and I'm going to keep him. And get some real answers."

"What?!" Steve snaps. His voice is too sharp and too loud.

Jameson has that annoying look of someone who is trying not to smile. "In the past few months you haven't made any progress in locating Loki's residence or bringing him in. I've managed to do it in under two weeks. We've been having a very talented agent, one with unique assets, case him at the bar near Lewis' house. Loki's invited her home. Soon we'll not only know where he lives, we'll have him in custody."

Tensing, Steve says, "I heard the words Guantanamo being hefted around a few minutes ago."

"That's where we're sending him," Jameson replies, a smug smile sneaking across his lips.

Steve wipes his jaw, eyes trained on the director. When Jameson had come up from DC with his men, he said he wanted to bring Loki in for questioning. Steve never thought he'd succeed—but if Steve had known the stakes were so high … Steve's fists ball at his side—he would have found some way to discreetly warn Loki.

"With all due respect, Sir, we still need his cooperation" Steve brings his hand down a little too heavily on his desk. "Sending him to Gitmo isn't the way to get that."

"We have Gerðr's cooperation. That is more than enough," says Jameson, referring to the Frost Giant sorceress in ADUO's custody. "Loki is too unpredictable."

"Gerðr can't leave the magically-sealed cell she's in without losing her mind!" Steve says, his voice rising.

Jameson gives him a hard stare.

Steve drags his tongue across his teeth. Of course. Jameson likes her that way. ADUO doesn't control Loki, and Jameson hates that. Jameson knows Loki wants something ADUO 'has.' Loki wants Cera, the 'World Seed,' the pulsating ball of magical power underneath the Chicago Board of Trade building. According to Gerðr, Cera is a sort of limitless magical battery, and it would be very bad if Loki got her.

Steve's not so sure. Cera may be trapped in a sphere of magical-dampening Promethean mesh, but ADUO has less control over Cera than they do over even Loki. Cera is somehow opening world gates, and letting all sorts of nasties through. What's more, the Promethean mesh around Cera is growing and anything and anyone that touches it gets sucked into something Loki calls the In-Between. Steve has no idea what the In-Between is, but nothing, and no one, comes back. When the mesh reaches the floor of the Board of Trade, will Cera consume the whole building or just destabilize the foundation? Either way, they're going to have to evacuate the building within days—and then who knows, the rest of the financial district?

Loki wants Cera in order to destroy Asgard. On bad days, Steve just wishes Loki would steal Cera, take Cera to Asgard, and have at it. Let Odin deal with Cera and Loki both.

Steve straightens. That isn't what Jameson needs to hear. He needs to believe Loki is on their side. Steve takes a breath. Actually …

"What about Prometheus?" Steve asks, using the codename for the source of the magical mesh that can seal in, or seal out, magic. Prometheus also gave humans a type of Cyanobacteria that eats magic and produces light as a by-product. The FBI's tech guys use the bacteria in their magic sensing devices.

Stepping around his desk, Steve says, "The reports say Prometheus said Loki was, and I quote, 'The Good Guy.'"

It's second-hand intel—Steve's never spoken to

Prometheus himself, and Prometheus definitely has a flexible definition of "good." Just in the last 24 hours Loki has broken one of Steve's agent's arms, stolen a very nice car from a man with connections to the mob, and wrecked same car causing a four-car pile up during rush hour while Miss Lewis was in the passenger seat. Loki and Lewis escaped the scene … where they went afterwards Steve has no idea. Miss Lewis is still passed out in her home and unavailable for debriefing.

Mischief aside, Loki has been helpful. Besides rather gallantly escorting Miss Lewis home this evening, Loki has helped save the city from wyrms and trolls, and through Lewis, been a resource when trying to understand just what is going on now that magic seems to be back on Earth to stay. He also saved Steve's life. And unlike Gerðr, who never misses a chance to insult humans for their 'magical retardation,' Loki seems to genuinely like humans. Steve doesn't trust Loki, but without him, the city would fare worse. Which is why Steve always insisted that he not be arrested.

Jameson stands stock still for a moment, his jaw going hard. And then he says, "We haven't heard anything from Prometheus in several months. For all we know he could be Loki."

Steve blinks at that. "But that doesn't make sense … " If Loki was Prometheus wouldn't he be insisting more that he was the Good Guy, instead of disappearing? "When was the last contact?" Steve asks.

"You don't need to know," says Jameson.

Steve opens his mouth, about to snap back, when one of the agents who'd followed Jameson up from DC steps into the room. "Director, Agent Hill's in a cab with him. She's got her phone on her. We're tracking them by satellite."

Jameson turns to Steve. "See, that wasn't so hard." With that the director turns on his heels and marches out of the room.

Sinking into his chair, Steve spins towards his computer, trying to hold in his frustration. He barely sees the report on the screen of the freak storm coming to Chicago. He shouldn't, but he feels personally let down by Loki. Loki never made it this easy for Steve to trace him—Steve never wanted to apprehend Loki, but he did want him watched. Still, whenever Loki went anywhere with Lewis, he'd always managed to lose her phone so she couldn't be traced. Is the man … Frost Giant … whatever, losing his touch?

Loki and Maria step out of the bar into the chill Chicago night. It's still drizzling, and almost cold enough to snow. The streets shine with reflected lights from the few cars on the road. Loki hails a cab and one pulls over faster than Loki would have expected on a Monday night. They slip in, and Loki idly notes there is only one other car moving on the road behind them.

The cab pulls from the curb, and Loki gives directions. The driver makes a sharp right up Ashland, and Maria falls against Loki's shoulder. Their faces are just a finger width apart. Her breath smells faintly of bourbon, and he catches just the barest whiff of perfume. His eyes linger on her full lips.

He turns towards her, his body warm, his mouth watering. She leans in. It should be a delicious moment, but something rock hard presses against his chest and upper arm. Momentarily confused, Loki draws back. He looks down; her coat has fallen open. It was her breasts that rubbed so hard. Suddenly her pert, expansive, gravity-defying décolletage makes sense.

There is one other thing on the human internets that Loki has availed himself of as much as on quantum mechanics and derivatives trading. Porn. He'd seen the arguments for and against breast 'enhancement' but hadn't really paid much attention; it seemed too barbaric to contemplate—anesthesia, knives, blood, artificial substances inserted under the skin. On Asgard if a woman wanted a different silhouette, she'd consult a healer and grow into a magically enhanced figure over a few weeks or months.

But now what has only been theory is quite literally in the flesh in front of him … and the flesh is disconcertingly hard and unyielding. He imagines scar tissue and scabs hiding beneath her bra, and his body goes cold. He leans back and headlights behind them catch his eye. It's the same car he'd seen earlier.

Maria gives him a pout. Taking her hand, and casually entwining their fingers, Loki says, "So you're an accountant?"

"Oh, I hold people accountable," says Maria with a smile.

Loki's lips quirk at the evasion. "Oh, I'm sure you do." She trained as an accountant, but moved onto something more interesting, he's certain. Closing his eyes, he lets an apparition flit invisibly into the car behind them. The driver and passenger are dressed in plain clothes, but the magic detectors they hold give them away as ADUO.

Opening his eyes, he tries to smile innocently at Maria. Inside he is fuming. Not so much at the attempted entrapment, that's all part of the game he's been playing with ADUO since the beginning. But they didn't think he warranted an agent with real breasts?

Maria leans in again. Lifting an eyebrow, Loki puts a finger to her lips.

Giving him a hurt look, she straightens and tilts her head, eyes wide. "What?"

"Just admiring the view," he lies.

She twists her body alluringly and he forces a smile. He'd suddenly rather be tucked behind Miss Lewis, his hand on her hip, warm and soft and real. Maria would hardly be the most unsavory creature he's bedded in a thousand years, but suddenly he'd rather not. Still … if it's a game ADUO wants, it's a game they'll get. Eyes on hers, he brings her hand to his lips, as though he might kiss it … but does not.

He's been in Maria's position before, he's seduced on Odin's behalf. He knows that however trained she may be, no matter how she may even find him somewhat attractive, she still burns a bit at the lack of control. At some level she hates Loki for being the source of her weakness. At some level she wants to control him and to make him hurt.

Loki licks his lips and does his best to look contrite. "I'm afraid, Maria, I don't deserve your affection."

Her face goes hard and cold. Her eyebrows rise.

Loki sighs dramatically. "I've been a very, very, bad boy, Maria. I think I can only kiss you if you make me earn it." He swallows for effect and fixes his eyes on hers. "Can you do that for me, Maria? Can you make me earn it?"

Her lips part, and her pupils blow wide. "Yes," she whispers. "Yes, I can."

Loki almost feels pity for her.

The upscale condo building Loki takes her to just West of Greektown is a beautiful piece of modern architecture, but it doesn't have a doorman. It's not Loki's building, of course—he isn't that drunk.

For a moment at the door he looks at the idling cab, and the headlights of ADUO's tail a half block away. That's all they think they need to catch him? He almost sighs in disappointment. He could make himself invisible right now and walk away, but it would be too easy.

Creating an illusion of a key fob in his hand, Loki uses magic to open the lock to the front door. He holds the door open for her and she walks through like a queen. "Good boy," she says.

He smiles and walks quickly to lead her to the elevators. There was a man who asked him for investment tips recently at a bar, a man who casually mentioned he'd be out of town … Loki scans the man's penthouse apartment on the 11th floor. It is empty as expected, and well appointed.

They ride to the 11th floor in silence. Maria is fighting a smile. Loki is concentrating, sending an invisible projection of himself to the lobby. He sees half a dozen cars pull up to the curb, ADUO agents spill out and mill just outside the door of the building. He tilts his head. He hadn't expected quite so many; his heart beats a little faster.

He doesn't think that their satellite link to her phone can detect with accuracy what floor Maria is on, and that they will need her to send them the exact unit number so they can have a warrant issued. He's betting extreme inconvenience on it.

Exiting the lift, Maria turns, crooks a finger at him, and beckons him to follow. Obliging, he lets her lead—even as agents pour into the building and fan out to the two emergency stairwells and vehicle exits. Stepping in front of her when they reach the door for unit 1101, Loki creates another illusion of a key and lets her in—covering up the personal photographs that line the foyer with illusions just in time.

Eleven stories below his projection watches as more agents arrive. They pace in the lobby, stairwell and garages, hands on headsets, eyes on magic detectors, awaiting instructions. He has to keep his projections moving and inconsistent to avoid detection. His heartbeat quickens again. He is cutting it close, but nothing ventured … no fun had.

Maria stops in the foyer. He notices her slip her phone from her purse and put it between her breasts. She does it with great skill. If he hadn't had an invisible projection in front of her, Loki would have missed it.

She holds out her arms. Taking the silent order, Loki slips off her coat and hangs it quickly in the closet by the door. She doesn't say thank you, she just smiles. She scans the 'photos' Loki has illusioned—closeups of Helen, Sigyn, Valli, Nari, Hoenir, Fenrir—the real one, not Amy's little beast—and one of Anganboða, sadly as fuzzy as Loki's memory of her. There is even a picture of Thor. Under his breath Loki curses; he should have thought of photos that were more original. Maria tilts her head at the picture of Helen, perhaps thrown by his daughter's half-blue half-pale skin.

"Halloween costume," he says quickly, using the same excuse for his blue skin that Amy gave the cab driver earlier that evening.

Thankfully, Maria doesn't ask anymore questions, just turns and walks into the main room. Turning, she points to the couch and says, "Sit. Put your hands on your knees."

When Loki does as he's told, Maria tsks. "Sit up straight."

Loki adjusts his back so he's sitting primly.

Coming over, bending low to give him what should be an absolutely delicious view, she drags a finger down his forehead, over his nose, across his lips to his chin in a slow, languid motion that Loki imagines is almost regretful. "I'm going to slip into something a little more comfortable," she whispers, her jaw tight and eyes alight. "Don't. Move."

Loki swallows obligingly, biting back his smirk.

Turning her back to him, she walks towards the back of the condo, her high heels clicking on polished wood floors. Belatedly, Loki remembers the man whose home he's borrowing is expecting his first child. He sends an invisible projection ahead of Maria—there is a nursery; if she goes there she'll know this is a ruse.

Thankfully, Maria makes a beeline for the powder room and Loki releases a breath. As she closes the door, Loki stands up, magically muffling the sound and leaving an illusion of himself behind. He sends an invisible projection into the bathroom with Maria. As he expected, she is texting ADUO with the unit number. Eleven stories below another invisible projection watches as agents begin moving up the stairwells. On the 11th floor Loki exits the condo and sprints for the elevator bank. He hits the call button and the doors open immediately.

Like most buildings, the elevator doors in the lobby have lights with numbers above showing where the elevators are. Loki makes sure the number for his elevator is 3 floors below its actual position, and then scowls when one of the ADUO agents in the lobby pulls out a beeping magic detector. "I'm getting another reading down here!" the agent shouts. Another agent pulls out her own detector. "Triangulate!" she says. An instant later she says, "It's the numbers above the elevator!"

Loki bites the inside of his cheek and hits the 8th floor button as the two agents in the lobby instruct the agents in the stairwells to sweep every floor. Exiting the elevator, Loki hits the third floor button so the elevator will continue without him and sends projections through all the units on the 8th floor. They are all occupied, so he breaks into the nearest one, muffling the sound of the lock and his footfalls. He closes the door as gently as he can behind him. An instant later he hears the heavy fire doors from the stairwell slam. Taking a deep breath, he closes his eyes and lets all of his projections dissipate. Heavy footfalls sound outside in the hall. He hears the beep of a magic detector and his eyes open in shock.

Down the hall he hears an agent say, "I've got something. It's kind of faint but … "

"Yeah, I've got the same reading," says a second agent.

"This way!" shouts the first voice. Over the sound of his own rapid breathing, Loki hears the sound of fast footfalls coming in his direction.

ADUO's offices are a flurry of activity. The heaters are clicking and the offices smell like wet hair and wool. The rain outside the window is mixed with snow. The Chicago weather forecast on Steve's computer has been adjusted for thunder flurries. Odd weather for late October, even in Chicago.

"We've got the warrant from the judge for South Sangamon Street unit 1101!" someone shouts. "Agents have all the exits blocked and they're fanning out throughout the building."

Sitting at his desk, Steve's gripping a file folder so hard his knuckles are a shade lighter and his fingers ache. He's furious … at Loki … at Jameson … at himself for being made to look like an incompetent fool by an incompetent fool.

"Get me a car!" shouts Jameson, striding through the office towards the front door. He doesn't ask Steve to follow.

Steve taps a finger on his chair arm as the office slowly empties of everyone but Brett and Bryant. The two agents are looking at him through his open door. There is pity in their eyes. He looks away.

Something is nagging at him. There's something about that address. It is a rental unit. While researching the address for the warrant, the guys pulled a listing from Craig's List for it from a few weeks back. They haven't been in touch with the owner yet; they don't want to lose the element of surprise.

South Sangamon … South Sangamon … Unit 1101 …

Spinning to his Rolodex, Steve starts rifling through the business cards, skimming the ones that look well worn. Twenty minutes later he's going back through the deck again, swearing that he's going to have Lewis load all his contacts onto the computer. And then he finds it. Ronald Kalt. Steve met him at a function he'd gone to a week or so ago for the mayor. Ron's a real estate agent, young, rich, renting a place while his row house is gutted; he and his pretty wife are expecting their first kid. Ron works out of his home and he'd just had the cards made up when Steve met him. Nice enough guy, though truth be told, Steve wouldn't have paid as much attention to him if he wasn't the mayor's nephew.

Staring at the card, Steve pulls out his phone … and stares at the card some more, a wicked smile forming on his lip. He bites it back and swallows a laugh. Jameson is going to crash and burn.

Standing from his desk, Steve grabs his coat and heads for the front door. Somewhat reluctantly he hits speed dial on his phone to alert Jameson. He's transferred to voicemail of course. Steve bites the inside of his cheek to keep from grinning as he walks by Brett and Bryant.

Loki didn't let Steve down after all.

In the darkness of the condo unit, back pressed to the front door, Loki forces himself to relax, forces his mind to empty—

He hears the footsteps getting closer outside the door. He can teleport if he has to, but he really doesn't want to. Not only is it draining, but ADUO has watched Cera transport people and things into the In-Between. If Loki steps through now, the readings might be similar. ADUO might discover his ability.

He takes a deep breath. He hears a beep from outside the door, and then an agent says, "Huh, it's gone."

"Sometimes these things pick up ambient magic," says the other agent. The two pace outside in the hall, and then one says, "We should cover the stairwell doors."

"Yeah, right." The two pairs of footsteps split up and Loki hears the creak of fire doors opening.

Loki slumps down and catches his breath, hands on his knees.

It is then that he notices his skin is blue. He almost gives a maniacal laugh but manages to stifle it. Being blue is the least of his problems. He needs to stay focused, he needs to wait.

He listens to the sounds in the condo: the whoosh of the heater, the tick-tock of a clock somewhere. He catches a brief feminine sigh, and the sound of a small child's cough, but otherwise everything is still.

He just needs to wait. Loki stares at his blue hands. But waiting has never been his strong suit. And waiting like a frightened rabbit in the dark is humiliating. And boring.

The obvious thing to do is to set the building on fire and slip out during the mayhem. Sitting up he smiles at the plan, but just then the child in the bedroom begins to cough again. A light switches on around the corner from where Loki sits, and he hears a man say, "Is his fever up again?"

"I don't know," says a frantic sounding woman. There are scampers of two pairs of feet and a pitiful toddler wail.

Loki slouches in his hiding spot. Well, damn. He's suddenly not as keen on setting the building on fire. His gut clenches. Odin would laugh at him.

Listening to the parents soothe their child, he taps his blue fingers on his knees.

His brow furrows. The magic detectors are sensitive, but how accurate can they be if they receive inputs from multiple sources? He tilts his head, one side of his mouth quirking. An experiment could be more fun than setting a fire!

Closing his eyes, Loki creates multiple illusions of himself in the shadows of Ron Kalt's condo … making sure none of them are on the couch where Maria left him.

Maria is standing in the living room, wearing a strappy contraption with high heels that Loki doubts is comfortable but is extremely pleasing to the eye. Behind her back she holds a gun, her phone is tucked in a garter, its face lit up.

"Loki," she says with admirable calm, "I told you not to move."

Loki lets one of his illusions step from the shadows behind

her. "And I told you," his illusion self says, "I'm a very, very, bad boy."

Spinning and lifting her gun, Maria says, "You're under arrest."

Loki lets his eyes rove over her body. "You look delectable. I wish I could have more than one of you." Raising his chin he grins at the agent. "Oh, wait, I can."

All the illusions of himself in the shadows step forward, shimmer and become replicas of Maria.

She spins around, gun upraised. "Illusions," she mutters to herself.

Heavy footfalls sound down the hall.

"Hmmm … yes," Loki lets one of his illusions say, as he hears pounding at Ron Kalt's door. "Immaterial … but I think I can fix that." He lets one illusion slip forward and around Maria. The agent looks down at her hands. He's made her look just like him. She curses loudly, and the voice that comes from her mouth is his.

On the 8th floor, Loki hears the sound of the agents' voices echoing down the hall. "My sensor is going crazy. Maria's got him on the 11th floor and Jameson is in with them!" Loki bites his lip to keep from laughing. Maria continues to curse as Ron Kalt's door crashes open, and Loki lets his illusions of Maria fade temporarily.

As agents fan into Ron's apartment Jameson steps forward. His phone buzzes in his pocket but he ignores it. "Loki, you are under arrest," Jameson says to Maria who now looks like Loki.

Holding her hands above her head, Maria protests. "I'm Agent Hill."

Loki lets all of his illusions of Maria reappear. "No, I'm

Agent Hill," the lingerie-wearing illusions say in unison.

Jameson gestures at Maria, her Loki illusion still in place. One of the agents in black runs forward, grabs her wrists. Cuffing her wrists behind what he thinks is Loki's back, the unnamed agent says, "He's solid! We've got him!"

"Of course I'm solid, I'm Agent Hill, he's disguised me!" Maria shouts in Loki's voice.

"Over here, over here!" shout all of the Maria illusions.

Jameson smiles smugly. "Nice try, Loki."

On the 8th floor, just barely containing his laughter, Loki lets all the illusions of false Marias fade, but keeps his appearance and voice on the agent herself. Or magic keeps the illusion in place for him; at this point it requires little physical effort.

Smiling, he casts his mind through the building. It's getting close to dawn. Agents are still milling in the lobby, in the stairwells, and by the emergency exits. Loki frowns and taps his knee. He may have to wait quite a long time. He lets his consciousness flit to the garage. There are agents there, too. Most are standing at attention, magic detectors at ready. But two are arguing. Loki recognizes one as Agent Hernandez, one of Steve's men. Hernandez is locked in verbal conflict with another agent Loki's never seen before, one of Jameson's from DC, most likely.

Pointing at the ceiling above him, Hernandez snaps. "And I'm telling you, Director Rogers—"

"Acting Assistant Director Rogers," the DC agent corrects in a bland voice.

"—says this is a mistake!" Hernandez finishes, pointing at his cell phone.

"He's been saying that since the beginning," says the other

agent.

In the condo Loki blinks, uncertain of the agent's meaning. In the garage Hernandez's voice breaks into a shout. "He says this unit is a mistake!"

Loki smirks. Steve's discovered Loki's deception just a little too late. Serves the bastard right for his part in this farce.

At just that moment the garage door opens and a dark blue SUV begins to pull in. All of the agents spring into action.

Loki's brow jump as he recognizes the driver. It's Ron Kalt. Putting his hands over his mouth he stifles a snicker. This is getting better and better.

Steve is heading west down Van Buren street. The sky is filled with the reflection of artificial light on snowflakes and is an eerie orangeish pink. The wipers on the FBI's black sedan swish across the windshield, sweeping away thick wet flakes of snow. The ground isn't cold enough for it to stick, but it makes visibility piss poor. On the plus side, the raven spies Huginn and Muninn that Odin usually has trailing Steve and terrifying Claire, Steve's daughter, are nowhere to be seen.

Steve's a block away from Sangamon when there is a distant flash of lightning in the sky, mute and high above the horizon. Up ahead a blue SUV that definitely doesn't belong to the FBI turns into the alley behind Ron's building.

Steve is past the alley, looking up Sangamon Street at the line of Bureau vehicles there when the thunder finally comes. Something in his stomach constricts with foreboding. Checking the street behind him, Steve hits reverse until he's in line with the alley. There's a line of row houses. Beyond that is the condo building, and beyond that and to the east are ancient midrise office buildings. He can just barely see a blue SUV bumper peeking out of the condo's garage. The garage will definitely be filled with FBI agents. Cursing, Steve turns into the alleyway and hits the gas. The garage door is still open, the blue SUV's bumper just barely in the electronic sites of the door.

Turning off his engine, Steve hits his emergency lights and jumps from his car. He hears Ron say, "Here's my identification, what's going on?"

"He's in unit 1101!" someone shouts.

"Sir, put your hands up!" an agent shouts at Ron, as Steve runs under the door.

"What?" says Ron, his back to Steve, confusion and anger in his voice.

"He's not with them," Steve says, but the garage has erupted into a cacophony of voices.

"Agent Rogers—" another agent begins to say as still another agent holds up a gun and aims it at the passenger side of the door. "Get out of the car, now, madam."

"Don't point that gun at her!" shouts Ron looking like he's about to lunge across the hood of the SUV.

"Sir, if you resist arrest," says one of Jameson's guys.

"I tried to warn them—" Steve hears Hernandez say from somewhere.

The agent by the passenger side of the car lifts his gun. "Get out of the car!"

Steve's eyes widen and he dashes around the back of the SUV. Mustering his most official, most USMC drill instructor voice he shouts. "Agents, stand down!" His voice thunders through the garage. He does his best not to look surprised when everyone, even Jameson's agents, who are technically not under him, stop everything and look at him.

Putting his hands on his hips, Steve puts himself in front of the passenger door. Summoning his inner drill instructor again, Steve lets his voice boom. "I know this man. Do you really think that he and his pregnant wife are accomplices of the target?"

"Steve!" shouts Ron. Steve holds up a hand in Ron's direction and thankfully he falls silent. One of Jameson's guys step forward. "They could be accomplices, Agent Rogers."

"Accomplices of who?" shouts Ron, his voice hot and belligerent.

There is a sound of an engine behind him, and the scamper of footsteps. From further in the garage come shouts, and then agents are spilling out of a door that must lead into the building, Jameson at their lead.

Keeping his gaze fixed on the agents around him, Steve says, "You've got the wrong unit! The target has played you, gentlemen."

Two agents sweep past Steve. "We've got the cuffs! They just finished forging them minutes ago."

Cuffs. What cuffs? Steve blinks and looks at Jameson. He's smiling smugly. "We got the target, Agent Rogers." He steps aside, and Steve sees Loki, hands cuffed behind his back. Loki's head is bent and he's cursing. For a minute, just a minute, Steve falters. The two agents who just ran past are holding up a strange pair of cuffs that look like they are made of golden netting—it's Promethean wire, but Steve's never seen it molded into something so small.

The agents shove Loki forward, as they affix the cuffs behind Loki's back.

"Those will keep you from performing any tricks,"

Jameson says, turning back to Loki.

"I'm not Loki!" says Loki.

Jameson snorts.

Behind Loki one of the agents says, "Um, Director, Sir. Something is wrong. His wrists don't look right. They're thin and … "

"Because they are my wrists," Loki hisses.

Everyone's attention is riveted on Loki, but Steve sees Ron put a hand to the bluetooth connection in his ear and whisper, "I'm in my garage, Uncle Ronnie. I'm being accused as an accomplice in some sort of raid. They held a gun to Sally. To Sally, so help me God if … "

Steve meets Ron's eyes. They are wide with fear. Steve gives him a tight nod and then walks across the garage to Loki, Jameson and the agents standing around him.

"What?" asks one. Jameson's brow is knit in concern. As Steve rounds behind Loki he sees why. Loki is wearing a blue peacoat, but at his wrists, where the Promethean cuffs are placed, the peacoat fades away. There are delicate feminine wrists, the beginning of tapered fingers—that fade into oddly masculine hands.

The feeling of schadenfreude is rich. Steve has to fight to keep from smirking. "Did anyone frisk her?"

"Her?" says someone.

Loki's face goes red, and his—or more likely her—lips curl. "Yes!"

An agent steps forward, face red. "I did, it felt strange … but I thought … I thought … it was magic."

Loki—or more likely Agent Hill—gives a snort.

In the background, Steve hears Ron give an incredulous laugh, and beyond that there's the wail of police sirens.

"Just get this illusion off of me!" Loki hisses, shaking his—her wrists, behind her back.

"I, um ... we can put you in one of the Promethean sealed rooms ... " Jameson stammers.

The police sirens and screeching tires sound just outside the garage, and then there is the slam of car doors and shouts.

Jameson looks up.

Steve doesn't smirk. But it's hard. "That will be Chicago's finest. Your boys just tried to arrest Mayor Ronnie's favorite nephew. You've been played."

Footsteps sound behind them. A voice heavy and distinctly Chicagoan says, "What's goin' on 'ere?"

At that moment the illusion of Loki fades, and Agent Hill is suddenly standing in the garage wearing a black garter belt, bra, thong and high heels with her arms behind her back. As she gives an exasperated sigh, Steve does his best to keep his gaze professional. Unique assets indeed.

Shaking his head, he turns to see CPD Sergeant George Carey, a burly man he recognizes from his days as the FBI's Chicago branch of the Department of Public Liaisons. Five of Chicago's finest, hands on their hips, stand around George.

"Steve?" says George. "You're not in charge of this fiasco, are you?"

Before Steve can reply, Ron points a finger at Jameson and shouts. "No, he is!"

Jameson holds up his badge. "FBI, I'm within my—"

"Save it. Mayor Ronnie wants to speak to you," says George, pushing his coat back so his hands are on his hips, right next to his piece.

Steve's never been so glad to be in the middle of a jurisdictional turf war in all his life. Putting a hand over his mouth he coughs to hide his laughter.

The cops are gone and the FBI have cleared out of the condo building's garage. Ron has his SUV turned around facing the garage door, and Steve's standing by the driver's side. Ron's leaning out the window. Eyes wide, he says apologetically, "I'm sorry, I just felt like I had to call my uncle."

Meeting Ron's gaze, Steve nods. "I understand. You did what you had to. I would have done the same." Turning his attention to the passenger seat, Steve says to Ron's wife, Sally, "Are you sure you're going to be alright?"

Sitting with her arms wrapped around her full midrift, Sally's pretty face is pinched and she looks tired. But she nods at Steve and says, "Yes, thank you."

Steve gives her a small smile.

"I'll never forget what you tried to do here," Ron says. "How you stood up for us."

"How you were the only person talking rationally," says Sally.

Ron holds out his hand and Steve gives it a firm shake, and then takes a step away from the SUV. Ron turns on the engine and the garage door opens. Snow is falling heavier than before and has begun to stick; there is about an inch on the alley pavement. There is a flash of lightning as Ron pulls out and an almost immediate roll of thunder.

Steve follows the SUV out of the garage on foot, watching its lights disappear in the curtain of snow. They're going to a relative's house. Ron and Sally had wanted to return to their condo, but the Chicago Police Department and the FBI both want to go over it with a fine tooth comb.

Steve looks up at the sky and blinks at the thick wet flakes landing on his nose. The world is hushed by the snowfall, the noise of morning commuters muffled. It's nearly 6 a.m., but the thunderstorm is almost directly overhead now and the sky still has the eerie orange glow of streetlights on snowflakes. Steve's raven minders are still out of sight.

Shrugging his shoulders against the cold wet flakes on his neck, Steve walks down the alley to the side of the building. There is a fire exit for the condos on the side abutting the row homes. It's wide enough for a car and paved over. Hernandez moved Steve's car there so that the police, FBI, and commuters could get out.

Steve's exhausted and looking forward to a snooze on the couch in his office, but he can't help but smile. He didn't really think that Jameson would succeed, but he hadn't counted on how spectacularly Jameson would fail. It could only have gone better if Sally had gone into labor. Unlocking the car door he shakes his head and mentally admonishes himself for even thinking that. His grin widens anyways.

Steve's just put his hand on the door handle when he hears a slam behind him. Turning, Steve's hand goes automatically to the Glock at his hip. Loki is standing by the condo building's side door, but not like Steve has ever seen him before. His skin is a bright cerulean blue and his ginger hair is black, as are his eyes. Lewis has described Loki's blue look as magical—like he's lit from the inside. Brett and Bryant described it as weird.

Now as Steve stares at Loki, framed by a thunderstorm, he can only think of wide open skies. Where Loki's skin is visible, it does seem to glow a little, as though he's a break in the clouds to the blue beyond.

There is a flash of lightning, a boom of thunder, and then Loki's voice cuts through through the cold air like a knife. "That was pathetic, Steven."

Steve stares at him for a moment, exhaustion making his brain move slowly. Dropping his hand from his hip, Steve tilts back his head and laughs so hard tears come to his eyes. When he recovers himself, Loki's head is cocked to the side, his eyes narrowed, but the look is more curious than hostile.

Wiping his eyes, Steve says, "Yes, yes, it was."

Loki walks over and idly wipes some snow from the car hood. "You're not going to try and arrest me?" He raises an eyebrow. "Now's your chance."

Steve smiles. "I'm sure you're just an apparition," he says, although he's sure he's not. "Real Frost Giants aren't blue, after all."

Loki looks down at his blue hand and scowls, and Steve remembers that Lewis says Loki doesn't like turning blue.

To keep the mood from going sour Steve says quickly, "But why would I want to arrest you? You're the Good Guy, right?"

Loki snorts.

"Come on," Steve says. "You've helped keep the good citizens of this city from becoming wyrm and troll food." His jaw tightens. "And you don't send ravens to crap on my car and terrorize my little girl."

Scowling, Loki looks to the sky. "Ah … your feathered friends. The weather seems to be keeping them away." There is a moment when the only sound is the faint fall of snowflakes, and then Loki says, "They used to terrorize Helen, too."

There are few things that Loki could have said that would have shocked Steve more. ADUO doesn't know much about

Loki's daughter, Helen, other than she is deceased, and somehow she became associated with Hel, the Norse land of the dead—though Loki insists such a land does not exist. Amy Lewis has theorized that she may have been handicapped.

The surrealism of the moment suddenly hits Steve. He is standing in a thunder snow storm, talking to a blue man about daughters. Recovering as quickly as he can, Steve snorts and says, "Winged rats."

Loki huffs a low laugh. "I tried to kill the things so many times, but it was Nari and Valli who managed it. Nari distracted them with chatter, and Valli put an arrow through Huginn." He shakes his head. "Odin just reanimated her." His expression turns bitter. "A trick I've never been able to manage."

Steve is used to knowing what to say in any situation, but talking about Loki's three deceased children, he is at a loss. The thought of losing Claire … Steve's little girl had spent the first eighteen months of her life in hospitals. It was worse than all the time he spent in Afghanistan. Chest tightening, Steve says, "I'm sorry." It tumbles out of his mouth before he's thought about it and sounds hollow even to himself.

Loki lifts his eyes to Steve's and his brow furrows, but he says nothing.

Steve's hands and are cold and wet, and he shoves them in his pockets and is silent.

Turning his head away, Loki straightens, and looks like he is about to leave.

"We need you here," Steve says quickly. "You know there is nothing you've done now that is so bad I can't make it go away … with a little time."

Loki turns his head to Steve, his expression flat and

unreadable.

Steve shrugs. To make sure Loki understands the value of what he is about to offer, Steve says, "In the past twenty-four hours you've managed to get on the bad sides of the mob, certain segments of the FBI, the Chicago Police Department, and undoubtedly the mayor's office as well."

Loki's face brightens, and he puts his hand to his mouth in a very good impression of a giddy school girl. "I believe that might be a record, even for me!"

That wasn't the reaction Steve was expecting or hoping for, but he keeps going. "I can make it all go away. You could be legit here, I know it, if you can help us with Cera ... "

"I'd rather help myself to Cera," Loki says with a smile.

"And if you could, I wouldn't stand in your way," says Steve.

Loki's face hardens.

"But we both know that isn't going to happen," Steve says.

Snow accumulates on their shoulders as they stand for a few moments in silence. And then Loki says, "You have a lovely world, Steven. It is tempting."

They're in a rather ugly alleyway, and Steve can't help but raise his eyebrows.

Loki smirks. "Truly." His expression hardens again. "But I have business with Odin, Cera or no."

Loki blames Odin for the death of his children. Steve's dealt with tribal people before, and from what he's gleaned that's pretty much what the Aesir are. "Honor is a hard thing to set aside," Steve says. "But—"

"Oh, Steve, haven't you realized that I am a man without honor?" Loki's lips form a hard line.

Steve tilts his head. "I know you are a man that keeps

your oaths."

Breath hanging in the air, Loki takes a step closer to Steve. His lips curl in a sneer. "I cannot rest until Asgard burns, but it has nothing to do with honor." For the first time Steve is aware of just how black the other man's eyes are—they're like pits into nothing.

"It is about making Odin hurt!" Loki snarls.

Steve blinks, and Loki draws back. Lightning flashes above and thunder rumbles.

Loki looks up at the sky. He smiles. "I'd best be on my way. We're both going to have a busy day." He shimmers and is suddenly ginger haired, pale skinned and gray eyed again. From Steve's pocket comes the faint beep of a magic detector. Turning his back to Steve, Loki walks away, his feet leaving footprints in the snow.

"Plague in Asgard … They're banishing the afflicted to Niflheim … They've taken our little girl. It was Baldur." Sigyn's words swim through Loki's head as he pushes Sleipnir to a gallop along Vanaheim's main road to the World Gate. It is no small mercy that Odin lent Sleipnir to Sigyn. The eight legged horse is the fastest steed in the Nine Realms. But it has nothing to do with his extra legs.

Dusty wind is whipping against Loki's face and hands, and the world is already a blur; but Loki gives one more kick to the steed's sides. Sleipnir goes from a gallop to a canter and then a trot, but the blur around them increases as his gait slows. Sleipnir is slipping through time—a magical ability inherited from the mare that died giving birth to him. The wind on Loki lessens. Because gravity is a function of velocity, and velocity is a function of time, Loki feels his body become lighter. Sound is strange and muffled. Light is diffuse and hazy. Loki knows that he could not go any faster by any means, but the strangeness of it, the odd gentleness, makes him feel as though he is in a dream, running in place, trapped with his thoughts.

He cannot save Helen. Healing is a magical ability he only possesses for himself. His only hope is to beg that she be allowed to remain in Asgard, and that he be allowed to take her to Hoenir's hut. Hoenir created a gateway to Vanaheim literally from the back door of his hut to just a day's ride from the mages' gathering he is attending. If Thor can get to the gathering in time, and take Hoenir to the back door that opens into Asgard, Hoenir may meet up with Loki and Helen in as little as a day. There is no ailment that Hoenir cannot cure.

Beneath him Sleipnir shudders, the blur around them takes shape, gravity increases, and the sound of hooves ring in Loki's ears as Sleipnir emerges in real-time. Travelers jump out of the way in surprise. For a moment they are going too fast, and Sleipnir's legs stretch out into a gallop as he tries to regain control of his momentum.

Sleipnir already bore Sigyn and Loki's sons to Vanaheim before this mad dash; although not in a lather, the steed is tired, its magical energy nearly spent. Fortunately, they are very close to their destination. Loki weaves the steed between the other travelers until the World Gate comes into view.

The World Gate between Vanaheim and Asgard is one of the most ancient in all the realms. The area where the World Tree's branch intersects with this planet is marked by an area of circular stones, nearly the length of forty men in diameter. It has been used in the past to ferry armies—and to banish the Vanir from Asgard after the last great war. Although not used for warfare in millennia, it is heavily guarded. There is a metal fence, two times the height of a man around it, and the entrance is blocked by armed men, toll takers, and custom agents. There is a small town just off to the side, and the road is crowded with local peddlers and visitors from other realms—Black Dwarves, Red Dwarves, Light Elves, and even a few Frost Giants and Fire Giants are shoulder to shoulder with the dark-skinned, dark-eyed, black-haired Vanir. Although this gate goes to Asgard, the quickest, most efficient way from one realm to another is through Asgard first.

Loki kicks his heels into Sleipnir's sides and gallops forward. Travelers and the guards start to shout. Veering from the busy road, Loki steers Sleipnir towards the impossibly high fence. On instinct Sleipnir slips through time and bounds easily over the barrier in the decreased gravity. Landing lightly within the gate, the tired horse immediately crashes into real time and struggles to find his feet as he plunges across the circle's flat stones. They are nearly at the far fence before Loki turns him around.

To open the gate requires magical knowledge and energy. On all sides they are surrounded by gatekeepers bearing magical staves that concentrate magic and help them do the job. One of them dressed in opulent red robes steps forward. "Halt! We will not open the gate for you!" the guard says as more guards pour in.

Loki grits his teeth. Sleipnir has one more magical ability he inherited from his dame. Pulling back on the reins, Loki drives his heels into the horse's ribs. Sleipnir rears and light spills around them in rainbow colors. The light subsides, and they are on the World Gate to Vanaheim in Asgard. Would-be travelers to Vanaheim retreat from them in shock. Sleipnir, like trolls and a handful of other magical animals, has the ability to walk the branches of the World Tree without aid.

Loki looks around. Asgard is unique in all the realms. It has eight wide world gates on a single open plane. At the center is a raised dais that is entrance to the void, where used magical items are sent—and once long ago where the Vanir, when they ruled Asgard, would send prisoners to die. Baldur has suggested 'in jest' that the tradition of execution in the void be rekindled for Loki.

The dais is also where Heimdall, the all-seeing gatekeeper, stands. Loki urges Sleipnir towards him, barely aware of the milling crowds. The horse whinnies, gait unsteady.

"Heimdall," Loki shouts. "Where is my daughter?"

The gatekeeper's face is expressionless. "She has gone to Niflheim, Loki." His voice is calm and even. There is the rawk rawk of ravens.

Loki's chest tightens. "Let me through the gate to Niflheim!" His shout is so loud, so anguished it shocks even Loki himself. There is absolute silence on the plain. Travelers still, and turn to stare.

Stepping off the dais, Heimdal says, "Loki, if you go to Niflheim you will be among the afflicted. You will die."

"Send me through the gate!" Loki screams. Without waiting for a reply he grits his teeth and turns Sleipnir towards the Niflheim branch. The steed goes a few paces and then falls to its knees. Cursing, Loki dismounts. From behind him Heimdall says, "Loki, be reasonable."

Spinning, Loki says, "Send me through!" Flames flare at his fingertips.

Heimdall stares at him for a moment. "Very well."

Unlike the gate to Vanaheim, the gate to Niflheim has no travelers. As Loki steps upon the stones he has a moment of apprehension. Then he thinks of Helen, one of the few things he's ever created that is right, dying in Niflheim, the land of cold and mists—and he is a leaf caught up in a tide of a flood. He can't turn back. Clenching his hands, he turns to face Heimdall and the group of mages behind him.

Loki nods. Heimdall nods once, and then says, "Send him!"

The mages lower their staves. Once more Loki is bathed in rainbow light, and then the light subsides and he is surrounded by mist in a barren field of brown, knee-high grasses. He hears moans and cries off to his left. Swallowing, he heads in that direction.

He reaches the camp just a few minutes later. Helen isn't the only one afflicted by the plague. There are at least a dozen ancient shaggy ponies attached to wagons filled with the dead and dying. Loki briefly catches sight of skin with great black pustules. The stench is terrible.

"Helen!" he shouts. There is no answer. Covering his mouth with his sleeve, he forces himself to walk through the wagons. And then he sees Ganglati and Ganglöt, two lame sisters, the only servants Sigyn could entreat to work in their household. They are utterly devoted to Helen, and the only people Sigyn or Loki would ever trust with their daughter's care. Now they lie in the grass unmoving by the wheels of one of the wagons. Where their skin is unmarred by the black pustules, it is gray and ashen.

Loki stares in shock. He is used to death by war, but he has never actually seen anyone dead by disease. His jaw sags and all thoughts flee him. And then he hears a low moan from the wagon. Swallowing, Loki climbs into the back. Helen lies amid a pile of carefully arranged pillows, a blanket lovingly tucked under her chin, water and food laid out beside her—Ganglati and Ganglöt's last act of love. The side of his daughter that is flesh colored is marked by the dark peeling pustules, but the side of her that is blue is unmarred. Loki is terrified, but feels pulled forward as though by an invisible string.

When Helen sees him, her lips part slightly and her gaze meets his under half-lidded eyes. She doesn't make a sound. But when Loki sits down beside her she reaches to him with a tiny blue hand. Pulling Helen into his arms, Loki begins to rock and chant, trying to focus all of his magical energy on making her well, or just keeping her alive. Her little hand tightens in his.

He doesn't have any plans anymore; he only hopes that Hoenir will come. The gray light of Niflheim's day turns to the darker gray of night, and Loki continues to rock. There comes a moment when Helen's blue magic flares so brightly that Loki's own skin turns blue. Loki's desperation rises; he squeezes her tighter and begins to rock more frantically.

Beside them the air begins to flicker. Loki looks up to see a semi-transparent Odin before them in the blue light.

"Save her!" Loki screams. Even Odin's abilities for healing are stronger than his own.

The apparition flickers. "Not much time ... Loki, Baldur did this ... "

Loki's mouth twists and Helen moans.

Stepping closer, Odin's ghostly form says, "He must be stopped ... his vanity ... he will destroy Asgard."

"Why don't you stop him! Why don't you do anything!" Loki says, his voice coming out half-scream, half-choked sobs.

The apparition closes its eyes for a moment and seems to sigh. "Because like everyone else, I am enchanted."

Helen's blue glow flares more brightly. Her hand tightens around Loki's and she tucks her head towards his chest.

"Only you can stop him now," Odin says. "It is in your nature."

Helen's grip relaxes and her head falls back.

Loki is only vaguely aware of Odin disappearing. Dropping his head to Helen's body, he murmurs, "No, no, no, no!"

And then her blue light winks away, only a faint blue sheen remains on Loki's hands. Baldur's voice rings in his mind, "You destroy everything beautiful."

Loki continues to rock and chant until his mouth is dry and his voice is hoarse. By the time Hoenir and Mimir find him—a day later—Loki is silent. But he hasn't moved Helen's body from his lap.

CHAPTER 2

Amy is awoken by a screaming headache, the urge to vomit, and the rumble of thunder—in that order. She puts a hand to her head and feels a warm body at her side. For a minute she freezes. A memory swims through her head of Loki in bed beside her, a warm hand on her hip. Or was it a dream? She taps tentatively with her elbow and hears a low, decidedly-canine growl. Lifting her head she sees Fenrir next to her, curled around a small gray ball with eight velvety black legs.

Amy blinks. "Mr. Squeakers!"

Fenrir and the spider mouse both lift their heads as if to say, "What?"

Amy stares a moment, swaying slightly, her stomach feeling woozy. Is she witnessing misplaced maternal instincts on Fenrir's part? She tilts her head. At least Fenrir isn't eating Mr. Squeakers.

Pulling herself up, she looks down. She's still in the

clothing she wore yesterday, only her shoes are off. She heads to the bathroom, and promptly loses the contents of her stomach. She's seriously considering playing hooky, but her cell starts ringing. When she doesn't pick up, it stops, and then there is a knock at the door.

"Ms. Lewis, Ms. Lewis!"

Amy stumbles to the door and sees a female agent from ADUO through the peep hole. When she opens it up, the agent—Smith? Larson?, Amy can't remember—says, "We need you to come in for debriefing. I'll drive you."

Amy stares at her for a moment. There is a flash of lightning and the boom of thunder. Wet snowflakes are falling all around and accumulating in a slippery blanket on the street and sidewalks. "Fine. But I'm taking a shower first."

Forty-five minutes, two glasses of water, two Tylenol and a shower later, Amy is sitting in the boxy ADUO sedan feeling slightly better. The storm seems to have passed over, but traffic is still miserable. The 'L' train might have been faster.

Opening her purse she pulls out a small pink rectangular package and peels back the cover. There are no birth control pills inside. Amy rubs her eyes. It's not that she needs them for what they're intended for, but without them she suffers debilitating cramps, a lovely monthly reminder that she's failed her body and its biological imperative to reproduce.

"Would you let me off at the pharmacy across the street from the office?" she says to the two agents in the front seat, the woman who knocked on her door this morning, and her partner, a man Amy's never seen before.

"Our orders are to take you directly to the office," the

man says.

Amy remembers the last month before she went on the pill in grad school, of literally crumpling over in the women's bathroom right after an exam and crying. In her entire life she'd never been in more pain. Head still a little fuzzy, Amy's eyes go wide. In a frantic voice she says, "You have to take me to the pharmacy. I'm out of birth control pills! I can't have cramps again! I can't!"

The man says, "Our orders are to—"

But the woman cuts him off. "We'll let you go to the pharmacy."

Amy slumps into her seat. It occurs to her that she really doesn't need the new pill package before work, but she's suddenly anxious to get out of the car. That was TMI to be sharing. She sighs. Of course the agents probably know about it anyway. It's not like her life is her own anymore.

She thinks of Loki lying beside her, his hand running up her hip—probably for the best that was only a dream. She blinks. Wasn't it?

Later when she's paying for her prescription, she's still trying to remember what went on the night before. She remembers the pub, sitting on Loki's lap, laughing about quantum theory with him and her friends. She remembers him saying that turning blue might be a symptom of dying—and she remembers wanting to kiss him for it, right then and there. She vaguely recalls getting into a cab and letting her head fall onto Loki's lap. He'd smiled down at her and kissed her hand.

After that...things are kind of a blur.

She heads for the door and hears someone say, "Miss Lewis?"

Stopping, Amy turns around, expecting to see an agent.

Instead she sees a slender, pale, blonde-headed man with brown eyes who looks familiar ... and at the same time not. It's the man she met in the park near the troll gate, the one who looks so much like Liddel, the elf she met in Alfheim. Liddel and his wife were on their way to the land of the Dark Elves when she met them. She worries about them, which is probably why her brain is making this bizarre connection. This man isn't Liddel. His features aren't as perfect, he has a scar, and the tops of his ears aren't pointed. She tilts her head, they're round but oddly shaped, like the cauliflower ears of boxers or wrestlers.

"Miss Lewis?" he says coming forward, his English flawless and American—not like Liddel's halting magical speech.

"We met in the park," he says. "I think we are neighbors."

"Ummm...yes," says Amy, rubbing her temple. "I remember."

Stepping a little too close he says, "We should get coffee later."

"Coffee?" she says. Instinctively taking a small step backwards, she takes in his short, heavy, black coat, black pants and black work boots.

"Yes," he says thrusting his hands into his coat pockets. "At 10:45." He licks his lips nervously. "There's a place a couple of blocks from here, just past Wabash and the train tracks."

Amy stares at him, measuring his attire, and the way his eyes dart about. "Sure," she says. "Sure."

Letting out a breath of air, he takes a step closer. "Thank you. Please, don't be late."

"I won't," she says, standing her ground this time, despite the urge to flee. She won't go at all. He's creeping her out.

Nodding curtly, he turns and heads out the door. She

watches him move up LaSalle and disappear into the morning commuters. Blinking, she steps out of the pharmacy. One of the agents from the car is waiting for her there. Together they head across the street to ADUO. The snow has melted from the ground, but the dark storm clouds that she'd thought had passed over are back overhead. She hears a distant rumble of thunder and shudders. The weather is bizarre even for Chicago.

She's just going through the office's revolving doors, leaving her escort behind, when it occurs to her ... she never gave her name to the man who just asked her out for coffee.

She nearly sprints into the office. Steve is leaning against the reception desk, a coffee in one hand. His eyes are red and puffy and his suit is rumpled. "Steve, something weird happened!"

He rubs his eyes and smiles. "Before or after Loki tucked you in last night?"

Amy's jaw drops, her train of thought reaches the station, but no words come out of her mouth.

Humming happily, Steve takes a sip of her coffee. Wait? Why is Steve happy? She looks around. And why are there two huge guys in black suits she's never seen before standing outside Steve's closed office door?

Suddenly from behind Steve's door booms a voice that is vaguely familiar. "What the Hell were you thinking! You raided my nephew's apartment! His wife is six months pregnant!"

There is a moment of silence. Steve swallows a big gulp of coffee—a massive girly coffee with whipped cream. "Ahhhhh ... " he says with a smile.

"Um ... who is in your office?" Amy asks, nodding

towards the guys even she can see are body guards.

Steve's smile widens. "Mayor Ronnie. He needed a place to speak to Jameson privately."

"Oh," says Amy, at the mention of Chicago's famously outspoken mayor.

Mayor Ronnie's voice booms through ADUO again. "Your head is so far up your ass you're seeing daylight, Jameson!"

Steve blinks and tilts his head. "That line is inspired. I may have to use it sometime."

There is silence from behind the closed door for a few moments and Steve frowns. "Guess we should get to your debriefing."

They always debrief her about her run-ins with Loki. Amy takes a deep breath. Yesterday was an emotional roller coaster ride. Loki met-up with her when she was visiting her grandmother, Beatrice, at the nursing home. Loki's showing up was the only thing that made the visit tolerable. He'd given Amy Mr. Squeakers as an apology for being an ass, and then driven her to a talk on REM sleep in rhinoceroses down at the University of Chicago on the south side. Of course the car turned out to be stolen, and of course Loki got in a minor pile up, and then they'd wound up running from the scene with Loki in drag. They hitched a ride and just made it to the lecture in time. Afterwards, they went out to drink, had a blast … and apparently Loki tucked her in.

Amy looks at her shoes. It was the best not-date date she's ever had. Her face goes hot just thinking about how much she wanted to kiss Loki. And oh, darn it, complicated lies aren't her thing, and Steve is going to see through her. And so will Brett and Bryant. This debriefing is going to be painful.

At that moment Steve's phone sounds. He answers it and

his face becomes grave. "I'm on my way," he says.

Exhaling, Amy's shoulders fall in relief. The inquisition is delayed!

Steve meets her eyes. "Lewis, you're coming with me, keep your coat on."

Steve and Amy are in a boxy, black government-issued sedan heading towards the lake, going way too fast on Monroe.

"You said something weird happened this morning?" Steve says.

Grabbing hold of the handle above the door, Amy stares at the darkening clouds to the east. "It can wait," says Amy. "Are those clouds falling to the ground?"

Steve just shakes his head and hits the gas.

Amy looks behind. They're being followed by Brett and Bryant. Hernandez is already on site. They're heading to The Cloud Gate, more popularly known as The Bean. It's a large piece of reflective metal sculpture shaped like a kidney bean. It is the centerpiece of Millennium Park.

"What's going on?" Amy asks.

A bolt of lightning flashes down very close and the thunder is nearly instantaneous.

"I'm hoping you can tell me," says Steve, veering left on Michigan Avenue, tires squealing. There's a fleet of police cars there. Steve parks illegally, turns on his blinkers and yells, "Come on!"

Amy takes a deep breath and hops out of the car. The air is still and there is thankfully no more rain or snow. But the sky is so black. From behind her comes the rawk rawk of ravens.

She suddenly has a very bad feeling in the pit of her stomach, and she just stares towards the steps leading up to the Bean. There are tourists and police there trying to form a line. Steve grabs her her wrist and starts pulling her forward at a jog. Whipping out his badge as he reaches the crowd he shouts, "FBI, coming through!" The crowd doesn't give way, but Steve doesn't let up, he just plows through, pulling Amy along with him, Brett and Bryant following in their wake.

A police officer comes forward to stop them as they pull through the police line. "Heya, you've got no jurisdiction here—" he starts to say. Amy's feet slow, but Steve just yanks her towards the stairs leading to the Bean. Another police officer comes forward, this one older and heavy set. Steve still doesn't lose his stride.

"Let him in! I know him!" says the large officer.

Falling into step beside Steve and Amy, the officer says, "Steve? You got an idea what's goin' on and who the whack job is?"

"She might," Steve says, tilting his head towards Amy. He takes off up the stairs, pulling Amy along and not slowing down at all. After a few steps the old guy, unable or unwilling to keep up, huffs and says, "Well, have at it ... " From the corner of her eye, Amy sees black shadows gliding from tree to tree.

There are several flights of stairs from the street level to the Bean. There are more police, trying to corral more tourists at each landing, and each time Steve barrels through the crowd. By the time they reach the Bean and the police line there, Amy is nearly falling over, her quads feel numb, and her lungs are burning. Brett, Bryant and Steve seem just fine though. The crowd is packed shoulder to shoulder. Amy can just barely see the Bean, and really can't tell what's going on. The two brothers fan out on either side of her, separating her from the crowd as Steve leads the charge, still dragging her forward. There are reporters yelling at police, and tourists milling aimlessly.

And then a bolt of lightning crackles through the air and flashes just a few feet away. As one body the crowd draws back. Except Steve, who charges ever onward, pulling her with such force she feels the bones in her wrist pop.

As they reach the edge of the crowd, Amy's eyes go wide. Not more than six feet in front of the Bean is a chariot. In it is an enormous man with bronze skin, eyes the same color as the storm clouds above him, and long dark red hair. Wearing gleaming golden armor and a helmet with little wings, Amy recognizes him instantly. In case there could be any doubt, he lifts the hammer heavenward and shouts, "I am Thor!"

Lightning leaps from the sky to his hammer, thunder booms, and people scream. Steve looks down and says calmly. "Well, is that really him?"

Amy stares at Steve, mouth agape. "You need more proof than lightning?"

Nostrils flaring a bit, Steve snaps, "Could be any magical idiot with a lightning-summoning hammer!"

Amy blinks. That might have sounded like madness a few months ago, but considering the circumstances, she nods. "Good point. Yes, that's Thor." Trying to step behind Steve and out of Thor's line of vision, she whispers, "We didn't get along."

Shaking the hammer, Thor bellows to everyone and no one, "I fight for mankind! You need not kneel before me!"

Behind her she hears Bryant say dryly, "Well, thanks for

that." Turning her head she sees his arm is in a cast that wasn't there the day before. Hernandez and Brett are there, too.

Steve snorts. Stepping forward, he says, "I'm Agent Steve Rogers. How may I help you?"

Before Thor can reply, two black shadows swoop down from the sky to land on the chariot. "Rawk, rawk," they squawk at Thor, bobbing up and down. One shrieks, "Go home! Go home! You'll make your daddy mad!"

"You'll ruin everything!" shrieks the other.

Scowling, Thor swipes at them with his hammer. Leaping into the air, the two ravens cry out in rage as sparks and feathers rain down on the sidewalk. There are murmurs from the crowd as they fly away, rawking boisterously.

Amy watches them go, vaguely aware of Thor stepping out of his chariot, his voice booming. "I have heard of your Captain Rogers of the Marines of the United States. I seek … "

As Thor rumbles on, Amy squints at the vanishing birds. The ravens think Thor will ruin everything? Thor's 'daddy' is Odin—Thor is here against his wishes? Last time Amy saw Thor he was trying to bring Loki home and had offered to exonerate him from all his 'crimes,' which apparently included attempting to keep his sons from being executed for trying to initiate political reforms.

Amy tilts her head, the swell of the crowd's voices rising around her. It suddenly hits her that she doesn't hear Thor talking anymore. She cautiously slides her gaze in Thor's direction. He is standing a few feet in front of Steve, staring straight at her, his face red.

"You!" Thor shouts, pointing Mjolnir at Amy.

"What?" says Steve.

Before Amy knows what is happening, Thor lunges

forward, and a heavy gloved hand wraps around her neck. "How dare you call me the God of Blunder and cowardly attack me with your automobile!"

Amy grabs his wrist, eyes wide and instantly watery. She sucks in a small breath and feels her feet leave the ground. Around her she hears people start to shout, but above their voices comes Steve's voice, eerily calm and steady. "In my hand, pointed at your head I have a weapon that shoots projectiles at 375 meters per second. Put her down, or we'll see if it cracks your skull."

Amy's feet connect with the sidewalk. Thor's eyes slide to Steve, but he doesn't release Amy's neck. "This is Loki's whore!" he says. "She is spying for him!"

Amy feels her face go red and hears her heart beating in her ears.

Gun level at Thor's head, Steve says, "Miss Lewis is with us, and if you don't let her go I'll shoot you here and now."

Thor stares at Steve a few long heartbeats more, and then, letting Amy go he begins to laugh. "Well met, Steve Rogers! Well met!"

Steve narrows his eyes at Thor. "We need to talk," Steve says.

"Agreed," says Thor, his own eyes going hard. "Perhaps at your fortress?"

Standing motionless for a moment, gun still unholstered, Steve says, "Come with us."

Thor gives Steve a sort of half smile. "No, I'll follow you."

Steve lifts his gun. Thor doesn't bat an eyelash. "You need me, Agent Rogers. Don't push your luck."

Steve looks around at the crowd and lowers his gun slowly.

"If you're not arresting him, we will!" says a police officer, running forward.

But Thor's already in his chariot, and it's lifting into the air.

"Be my guest," says Steve, as the chariot starts to make lazy circles in the sky.

The officer's mouth just falls and he stares upwards.

A little dam in her head seems to burst. "I'm not a whore!" she says. The police officer doesn't pay her any attention and Steve is already making his way back towards the stairs. Amy turns to follow him. Brett and Bryant are there giving her funny looks.

Amy looks at Bryant's cast. "What happened to your arm?" she asks.

"He fell," says Brett too quickly.

Bryant sighs and then says, "Yeah. Come on, let's head back."

Amy is in the ADUO conference room which is magically shielded with Promethean wire. She is sitting at the conference table, digital tablet in front of her. Thor is landing his chariot on the roof, and the room is mostly empty. At the table with her are Steve and Jameson. Or rather, they're standing at the table, fists down glaring at each other.

"She shouldn't be in here!" Jameson says to Steve.

"She's our liaison with Loki and she should be here!" Steve shouts back.

"Your liaison with Loki?" Thor's voice booms from the doorway to the conference room.

Amy, Jameson and Steve all turn their heads. Behind Thor stand other agents.

Thor's eyes are on her again. Amy swallows, and his gaze abruptly shifts. He looks at the walls and ceiling of the room. "This room is magically shielded," he says.

"We can speak somewhere else if it would make you feel more comfortable," says Steve.

Thor reaches into a satchel that hangs around his waist near his hammer. "No, no, this will do," he says, stepping into the room. Agents rush in behind him and station themselves around the room. A few of them move their hands towards their hips. Jameson whispers something to one of the agents. The agent nods and then quickly leaves the room.

Amy blinks. As Thor steps into the room, his demeanor seems to change a bit. His eyes soften, and he looks about curiously. Two agents whisper to one another, and Thor looks up at them and lifts an eyebrow. "Don't try anything," he says. "Although my hammer Mjolnir may not work here, I believe your Midgardian magic eggs will."

He opens his hand. In it is a grenade, his thumb through the pin. Amy's eyes widen, and she swears she hears a collective intake of breath.

Thor tilts his head and says quietly, "I come as a friend. Do not make me your enemy."

Amy's mouth falls a little. Beside her she sees Steve shift, and her boss meets her eyes. Thor is different now. Not so loud.

"At ease, gentlemen," Steve says.

"You. Go!" Jameson says to Amy.

"No, she stays," says Thor before Steve's even opened his mouth. Thor looks around the room. His eyes fall on the Venetian blinds on the window, slightly open to let in light. His jaw tightens. "Close the coverings on the window completely,"

Thor orders, as though the room is his to command.

Nervous eyes shoot to Steve and Jameson.

Thor looks at Steve. "Although the room is shielded from Heimdall's sight, ravens and that rodent Ratatoskr can read lips."

"Ragatoskr, the squirrel that carries gossip up and down the World Tree … is real?" The question squeaks out of Amy's mouth before she's even thought about it.

Jameson glares at her.

Steve raises an eyebrow that clearly says, Now I've heard everything.

Thor spits on the carpet. "Aye. The Norns favorite agent has been active of late."

While everyone else is temporarily paralyzed with that bit of bizarre knowledge, Steve nods at one of the agents. The agent hastily stands and closes the blinds.

As soon as the blinds are closed, Thor says to Steve, "I am sorry about the commotion I caused earlier. But I am not Heimdall, I am not all seeing. Although I've heard of you, Heimdall would not give your exact location—I needed to draw you out."

Amy tilts her head. Thor is suddenly not looking so blundersome. Steve dips his chin fractionally, and he looks like he is about to say something, but Jameson jumps in. "I'm Director Jameson. I'm in charge here. Why have you come?"

Thor's eyes slide to Jameson for just a moment. He looks him up and down once and then turns back to Steve. "I have come for Loki. The thing beneath your streets will destroy him—"

"We can only hope," says a sharp feminine voice in Jotunn, the language of the Frost Giants. Loki had magically bestowed upon Amy the ability to speak the language after she extracted a bullet out of his arm. It wasn't a gift—he'd done it to give someone at ADUO the ability to talk to the Giantess for intel purposes, and likely his own amusement. All heads turn to the door. Gerðr is standing there, two agents at her elbows. On her head she is wearing a helmet of Promethean wire. Amy blinks. Every time Gerðr tried to leave her cell—a room lined with Promethean wire, Cera had taken control of her mind. The helmet she wears now must be enough to stop Cera's influence. Amy looks at Thor—why wasn't Thor affected by Cera?

Thor's lips curl. "Gerðr," he says.

Standing at the door, Gerðr wavers. Eyes on Thor, the giantess continues in her own language. "Your devotion to that deviant is misplaced! Don't you know who killed your golden brother, Baldur?" Linguists who had worked with Amy to learn Jotunn scramble to Steve and Jameson's sides and begin to translate.

Thor smiles sadly. In English he says, "Yes, a nice human warrior named—"

"Fool!" Gerðr screams. "It was Loki!"

"Can you not see that Baldur deserved it?" Thor snaps back.

There are some murmurs around the table. Gerðr looks shocked. "How dare you say such a thing! Of all your cursed race, Baldur was the only one who was good and wise and just!"

Thor's jaw twitches and his eyes narrow. "You did not see him in the light cast by Helen—"

Gerðr spits. "That deformed nightmare Loki called his child?" The Frost Giantess and the Asgardian glare at one another.

In the pause, the linguists finish their translations, and the whole table takes in Gerðr's words. Beside her Brett cracks his knuckles. Amy turns to see both of the brothers glaring at the giantess. Laura Stodgill looks like she might like to hit the giantess, throw up, or both. Steve's eyes are cold and calculating.

"Baldur knew Loki should die!" Gerðr says. "Don't come here to save Loki. Don't aid the prophecies! Help the humans kill Loki before he gets his hands on Cera and destroys us all!"

Amy swallows.

Thor's jaw tightens. His voice booms through the room with such force the windows vibrate. "You're too old to believe in fate, Gerðr!"

Amy exhales. Even Thor, who is hundreds—thousands—of years old doesn't believe in destiny. She feels herself go a little giddy with relief.

One of Jameson's agents coughs. "Prophecies?"

Agent Hernandez answers. "Loki's foretold to lead the armies of Hel against the armies of Asgard, thereby bringing about the end of the world ... and the beginning of a new and more peaceful world."

A sudden, very deviant thought occurs to Amy. She almost snickers. "Of course, in Norse tradition, Hel is inhabited by the weak—everyone who didn't die in battle."

"What is your point, Lewis?" Jameson snaps.

Biting her lip to contain a giggle, Amy says, "So maybe Loki is going to lead the meek to inherit the Earth."

Sometimes you don't recognize there is ambient noise in a room until it goes away. Suddenly, it seems that everyone in the room is holding their breath. Amy looks around. It looks like Steve is biting on the inside of his lip to keep from smiling, Laura Stodgill, their legal counsel, has a hand to her mouth like she's hiding a grin.

Jameson's voice cuts through the air. "Don't compare Loki to Jesus Christ. Ever."

Amy huffs and shrugs. She doesn't care what Jameson thinks. Jameson's far less scary than Steve.

Thor clears his throat. "My intention is to bring Loki back to Asgard. Although my father seems to have given up on Loki, he has not renounced his offer of clemency."

"Clemency for what?" Steve says.

Thor holds up the grenade. "At his sons' execution he threw one of these magic eggs into the crowd. Nearly a dozen onlookers died."

Amy goes cold. She swears all eyes on the room have turned to her.

"Onlookers?" someone says. "Were they civilians?"

Thor looks up at the ceiling as though considering, "Yes, I suppose you could call them that."

A shiver sweeps through Amy's body.

She hears a gasp behind her. Turning, she sees Gerðr start to claw at her helmet. "Get this thing off of me, let me to Cera! Let me to her!" Amy's breath catches. Apparently, the helmet doesn't block all magic.

"Bring her in here and shut the door!" Thor shouts, his voice so commanding the agents beside the giantess comply. Gerðr scrambles and kicks against them, but they manage to drag her in and pin her to the table until she calms down.

"Let me go!" she demands in her own language. "I'm free of that beast, Cera. She doesn't control me in here. Let me go!"

Amy sits back in her seat, still reeling from the idea of Loki throwing a grenade at civilians and feeling vaguely sick. She knows he is a warrior, she's seen him in action—but he only acts in self-defense. Her breath comes a little too fast ... Doesn't he?

"Why doesn't she call to you?" Gerðr says, her face a twisted mask of rage and tears. As one of the linguists translates, Thor shrugs and answers in English. "Cera did call to me. But I don't crave revolution."

"How are you speaking our language?" Jameson says.

"I speak several Earth languages without magical aid." Turning to Amy and meeting her gaze, Thor says, "Cera is calling to Loki, too. And he has very good reasons to wish for revolution. You must warn him … he is going to his own death."

Amy stops breathing for a moment. "He's also turning blue, all the time."

Thor's brows knit, and he tilts his head.

Didn't Loki say that Thor has healing abilities? Her mouth races ahead of her. "It doesn't present itself as cyanosis. I thought maybe it was some sort of magical Pseudochromhidrosis—that's a condition where harmless bacteria pigment the skin, but that wouldn't explain his hair and eyes turning black."

Amy stops. Thor has an empty look in his eyes that she associates with someone pretending to know what she's talking about.

Leaning forward, Amy dumbs it down. "He thinks maybe it is a sign that he's dying—is it related to Cera somehow? And can you help him?"

Thor shakes his head. "I didn't know of this. But it must

be a magical ailment. He needs to come home."

Amy stares at Thor. Unlike Loki, his features are wide and generous. He looks so earnest and good—so different from the man he was less than an hour ago when he attacked her. Her throat constricts at the memory.

"I want to know how exactly how you know our language!" Jameson says.

"I'd like to see the facility where Cera is being housed," says Thor, striding towards the door.

"You're not authorized for that," says Jameson. Two agents slide in front of the door. Thor waves the grenade in his hand.

"We can discuss this like reasonable men," says Steve in a weary voice.

Thor smiles. "Excellent! Over food! I am starving!"

Jameson tenses. But Steve nods. Standing, and walking towards Thor, Steve says, "Let's readjourn in the cafeteria."

Jameson blinks, but then stands and joins Steve and Thor. His pale skin has a sickly sheen to it.

Feeling a little dazed and empty, Amy watches as everyone files out. Just before Brett and Bryant leave, Bryant turns to her. "You know, Loki does the right thing for the wrong reasons, and the wrong thing for the right reasons."

Amy lifts her head and stares at him.

"That doesn't mean that he is evil," says Brett, his eyes soft and sympathetic.

"But he isn't safe to be around," Bryant says.

Amy knows that what they're really saying is that she should go on the witness protection program. She nods at them, not because she agrees, just to make them go away. In the end she is left with Gerðr and two of her body guards. Gerðr glares at her. Amy is not sure how much of Brett and

Bryant's conversation she understood. Ducking her head, Amy stands up, picks up her tablet and heads to her desk. She can hear Thor's voice, booming off in the distance. She wants coffee … and to be alone. She's almost at her desk, and her purse, when she has a sudden thought.

Tapping her tablet on, she idly notices that it is 10:40 a.m., close to the time she told Liddel's human doppelganger that she would meet him. Her heart rate increases, but it has nothing to do with that ill-fated not-going-to-happen rendezvous.

Loki's blue skin … She's been thinking all this time in terms of a disease. She had run medical searches for infections that cause blue skin when Loki first started changing color. Nothing in the medical literature really fit. But she'd been looking for human diseases. Loki is an alien from another world. A world that humans see through a warped mirror in myths. An alien that human myths describe as a god. It might be exhaustion-induced delirium, but Amy finds herself opening a browser, clicking to search and tapping the words, "Blue gods."

The first result is a post about Hinduism. Didn't Loki have ADUO set up surveillance in India at some city—it was sacred to Shiva or something? Blinking, Amy clicks on the link. There are several blue gods in Hinduism, but Shiva's name catches her eye. Scanning the page quickly, she picks up that he's part of a trinity with Brahma the creator, and Vishnu, the preserver. Amy swallows. Loki is sometimes linked to a trinity, too...with Hoenir, the creator of mankind, and Odin, ruler of the gods.

Amy stares down at the page with shaking fingers. Shiva is the destroyer.

The words on the tablet blur in front of her eyes. Her heart feels like it has stopped beating. She is just being silly. Just because Shiva is the destroyer and Loki is foretold to bring about the end of the world, that doesn't mean anything.

Biting her lip, she Googles Shiva. Clicking to Shiva's Wikipedia page, she scans the entry, willing her hands not to shake. Shiva isn't a trickster like Loki, but he isn't just the destroyer either. He's the Transformer, the Cosmic Dancer, whatever that is—and he's often depicted with his wives and children. That doesn't seem so bad.

Throwing a grenade into a crowd, that was bad. Would be bad … if it happened. She looks down at her desk. It must have been a mistake. An accident. A misunderstanding. He was trying to save his sons and something went wrong. Turning off the tablet, she retrieves her purse.

She wants coffee but has no desire for company. Looking out the window, she takes in the gray dreary sky, and the soft mist of rain. She decides to take a service hallway and stairs through the building to the alley and then to the coffee shop next door. The route is a little meandering, but she won't even need to take her coat.

Passing through security, Amy steps through the fire doors that demarcate the plain, unadorned service hallway from the offices proper. Just beyond the doors, there are barrels that look like they contain cleaning supplies and a mop that she has to navigate around, but the hallway is otherwise empty. She is almost to the next fire door that leads to the stairwell when she hears what sounds like fireworks.

She freezes in place, and then all the gears in her brain start working. It's gunfire. Heart beginning to race, for a moment she actually thinks about going back the way she came—and then catches herself. The best thing for her to do is to get out of the building and out of the way. She turns towards the stairwell fire doors and then she hears a snap and a crackle behind her. On instinct she ducks her head. There's an explosion so loud her ear drums throb and something sails over her with a whoosh. She hears the sound of metal scraping across the floor … but what strikes her most is the heat. Amy opens her eyes. The barrels she took for cleaning supplies are alight with green fire.

With a quick breath, she sprints towards the fire doors. Just before she collides with them, she slides to a stop, puts out her hand and gingerly touches the metal. Gasping, she pulls her finger away. The door is scorching hot. Looking back the way she came, she sees foul-smelling smoke rising to the ceiling, but she can make out the wall of burning green beyond that. It's the door or nothing.

Pulling off her sweater, Amy wraps it around her hands and pushes on the door. It doesn't budge. Something in the building gives a loud groan. Amy closes her eyes. Louder than the roar of the flames is her own heartbeat. She should be terrified, but she is just insanely pissed.

Taking a ragged breath she hacks as the smoke stings her lungs. The hallway smells like heat, chemicals, and burnt dirt and hair. Dropping onto the floor Amy pulls her cell phone out of her purse; of course she gets an all circuits busy signal. Swearing to herself, she puts the phone down and puts her head in her hands. After being assaulted by a serial killer, going to Alfheim, losing everything, and finally putting her life back together just a little, she is going to die alone, in an empty hallway.

"Fuck," She swears, closing her eyes as the heat around her begins to sting. "Fuck, fuck, fuck."

Pulling her hair, she screams in sheer frustration. This is all Loki's fault. Ever since she ran into him her life has been upended. Of course, he did save her life … if only she hadn't seen that freak flare of flame in the woods of Mark Twain National Park, she wouldn't have run off the road …

She starts laughing. Freak flare! Loki probably did that, too.

A piece of something falls from the ceiling. Covering her head with her hands, Amy does the only thing left to do. She opens her mouth, prepared to say something venerating and nice. Instead what comes out is, "Loki! Get your ass here now and save me!"

CHAPTER 3

Loki is packing his suitcases for Visby when one of his apparitions spies Thor stepping out of the magically-shielded room in ADUO's headquarters. In his penthouse Loki narrows his eyes. Another apparition had seen Huginn and Muninn at the Bean scolding Thor for being on Earth.

Putting his fingers in the loops of his jeans, he stares out of one of the floor-to-ceiling windows of his Chicago abode. What is Thor's game? His lips form a tight line. More importantly, what is Odin's game?

He stares at the cityscape before him, his mind a blank. He can just make out ADUO's roof from his north eastern window. Loki's penthouse is just across Wacker Drive on Van Buren. He is barely outside of Chicago's infamous Loop, the city's financial hub, shopping district, and location of its most important museums and theater district. The Loop is bordered by the Chicago River and Wacker Drive on the north and west, and by Roosevelt Street to the south. A few faux Greco-Roman buildings dot his view, but mostly the skyline is a homage to every architectural style of skyscraper from every decade since 1885. Some of the buildings are reinforced brick or concrete structures with ornate moldings, stained at every window and corner with the runoff of polluted rain. Other buildings are encased in glass and reflect the sky—Loki thinks of them as giant moving canvases. Bright, clean, new buildings; older soot-covered buildings textured with elaborate motifs—Loki likes both. The patchwork is in stark contrast to the homogeneity that marks the architectural illusions of Asgard.

Rising up from the flat plain that is Illinois, the vertical lines of the Loop contrast with the rest of Chicago, and even the state. Beyond the center, the city sprawls outwards, the buildings becoming progressively shorter, and the streets more and more tree lined—and perhaps, coincidentally, out of sight of the movers and shakers of the financial district, the streets become more and more crumbling. In Loki's neighborhood the sidewalks and streets are relatively smooth. Where Amy lives the streets are filled with potholes, and the sidewalks buckle above massive tree roots. Amy attributes the poor state of Chicago's infrastructure to Chicago's endemic corruption and curses it frequently. Loki's just amazed that the corruption changes hands occasionally.

Smiling he bounces a bit on his heels. Instead of a professional poker player, perhaps he could become an alderman! And then his jaw tightens. This city is not his.

Shaking his head he turns back to packing. He is catching a plane to Visby in the afternoon, saving his magic for a world walk to Vanaheim the following day. His chest tightens and he takes a breath. Thor is here … and Thor won't let anything bad happen to Cera or Chicago.

At that moment, in ADUO's headquarters, one of Loki's apparitions sees Thor accidentally breaking a styrofoam cup in his hands, burning himself on the hot liquid. In his living room, Loki fights the urge to let his apparition become visible, to make sport of the big oaf. His fists clench. That is just the sort of distraction he has to avoid. With a sigh he quietly pulls all of his apparitions out of ADUO's HQ.

Stuffing a sleeping bag into his duffel, Loki catches sight of his hands. His skin is blue again. He doesn't correct it, it's easier not to, and he's found that when he is blue Cera's whining is easier to tune out. Straightening, he looks out towards ADUO's offices again. He hasn't heard much from Cera all morning. Just a plaintive grumble of "You're right. The lightning man is an idiot," and nothing more for hours.

Raising his head, and glancing out the window, his eyes widen. There is smoke rising up from the direction of ADUO. Straightening, he sends his apparitions back to the building. In his penthouse he walks to his window and puts his fingers to the cold glass. ADUO's offices are under attack, and men with guns are flooding in through the main security checkpoint. Concentrating, Loki sends more apparitions through the building. The main exits are blocked by green fire. His nostrils flare—it's elven fire. But the queen of the elves would never attempt such a thing, nor would she allow her people to carry guns. Magic bows and arrows, the occasional crossbow, yes. Guns never. She is such a Luddite.

He blinks. It's Dark Elves! When he went to Alfheim with Amy the elves in the Dark Lands were carrying guns. Now they've come to Earth—how they've managed to magically hide their pointed ears and perfect complexions he can only wonder. He's not detecting illusions around them. But obviously, they want Cera.

He snarls. And Cera most likely knew about it. He taps his hand against the glass. There are hundreds of them! Maybe they know a way to get through the Promethean Sphere protecting Cera? He smirks. If they get her out it will be that much easier to steal her.

In ADUO's headquarters, one of Loki's apparitions sees Agent Steve Rogers shout, "We've got to fall back to the tunnels! This is a diversion. They're after Cera!"

Smirk widening, Loki prepares to let one of his apparitions become visible to Steve.

In the glow of green fire, Steve sits behind an overturned table and slides a new clip into his Glock. Every magic detector in the building is beeping, and Steve's nerves are lit with the noise of gunfire. AK-47s would be his guess from the scant glimpses he's caught and the sound. All of the usual exits from ADUO are blocked. His brow furrows, but the stairway to the tunnels that run beneath Chicago's streets where Cera resides should be clear. And green fucking fire is really a tell-tale sign that this is all about Cera.

Looking around the room, he sees Jameson and his agents are tucked behind the cafeteria counter. Closer to Steve are Brett, Bryant, and Thor behind overturned tables of their own.

Tapping the headset in his ear, Steve gets a no-service tone. Swearing, he hits a button, switches to a reserved channel and says, "Tunnel security, report!"

An agent's voice barks back, "Sir, we just started taking fire, from the north, east and west! The tunnels are full of them. We've fallen back to reinforce the perimeter around Cera. Two men down!"

A few feet away Thor stands up, bullets ricocheting harmlessly off his armor. With a yell, he throws Mjolnir though the air. The hammer takes out a few of their assailants, knocks through a wall, and comes bounding back into Thor's hands. Thor gives a triumphant shout.

Steve is about to chew him out, but Bryant beats him to it. Pausing to awkwardly push a new clip into his Glock with his broken arm, Bryant shouts, "That could have been a load-bearing wall, you idiot! Stop throwing that thing around or you'll bring the whole building down on top of us!"

Steve is too busy firing at a dark shadow moving through the green flames to see Thor's reaction.

There is a momentary lull in the shooting and Steve shouts, "We've got to fall back to the tunnels! This is a diversion. They're after Cera!"

In his headset, he hears Jameson say, "We can't get out! We're trapped back here. You'll have to do it." They're actually in a better position for it than Steve and his boys—but there are a few of ADUO's cafeteria staff workers and medical personnel back there. Stodgill, their legal counsel, is back there, too. Steve doesn't argue. Turning to Thor he says, "Stand up! You're our cover."

Thor tilts his head and narrows his eyes, but he does as Steve requests. "Behind him!" Steve shouts to the two brothers. "Go to the back exit to the cafeteria. Move! Move! Move!"

The four of them retreat through the secondary door, Brett and Bryant behind Thor—Steve crouching to the side.

Fortunately, some of Jameson's men have more experience than the Director. As soon as Steve and his guys start their mad dash, they cover them, shooting in the direction of the entrance where lithe shadows are emerging from behind green flame.

The hallways beyond the cafeteria are empty, but as they pull into the main office area they find the cubicles consumed by flame, and a group of shadows struggling to open the tunnel door. In front of them, Thor lowers Mjolnir, lightning cracks through the room, and the dark shadows tumble. Squinting his eyes in the smoke, Steve and his men approach the door. Their attackers are holding AK-47s. He can tell instantly that a few of the men are dead, but he hears a few moans. Kneeling down beside one, Thor says, "Curious. These appear to be elves who have cut off their ears."

"Open the door! We're going down!" Steve says. As Brett punches in his code and holds up his hand for thumbprint scan, Steve curses under his breath. Lewis had said she and Loki were attacked by Dark Elves with guns. Jameson had refused to let Steve see the ballistics report to confirm it.

The door opens with a whoosh. There is the sound of gunfire below. "Thor's point!" Steve says. "I've got the rear."

Thor grins. "I'm going to see Cera after all," he says, and then bounds towards the opening with a yell. Which is exactly the moment Jameson's voice starts to crackle in Steve's headset. "He's a possible security risk! What are you doing?" Steve grits his teeth. Ignoring the director, he backs towards the door.

And then it hits Steve that he didn't see Amy Lewis in the cafeteria. He scans the sea of burning cubicles. Shadows start to come forward out of the flames, Steve slips behind the door to the tunnels just as bullets embed themselves in the wall around him. He can hear the echo of more gunfire ringing from the tunnel below. Steve grinds his teeth. The girl's on her own, his primary responsibility is to see that Cera is safe. With a snarl of frustration he lets loose a few bullets before he closes the fire door.

Activating the lock, he turns and finds himself alone on the stairwell landing. He hears Brett, Bryant, and Thor below. Steve slips the clip out of his Glock, takes a step forward … and almost runs into Loki. Or, more likely, through him.

Stopping short, he curses. Loki beams and raises his eyebrows. "Hi, Steve."

It's the dumbest thing in the world, but Steve can't help but notice what Loki, or his apparition, is wearing. It's a pink t-shirt with an upside down rainbow triangle on it.

Following the direction of Steve's gaze, Loki says, "Do you like my Bifrost shirt?"

Steve is furious at Loki for his flippancy and his damned distracting shirt. There is a reason agents all dress the same. He's also furious at himself for being distracted. Narrowing his eyes, he barrels in Loki's direction. Sure enough, Steve passes right through him. The illusion of Loki catches up and matches Steve's pace down the stairs.

"You here to help?" Steve says, feet pounding down the metal mesh stairs.

"I think this time I'd just rather see how this plays out," the apparition of Loki says. The apparition looks down the stairs where Thor stands on a landing, hurtling lightning northward, as Brett and Bryant fire south, taking cover around the corner of the stairwell and Thor's girth.

"Oh, look," says Loki. "Thor is imitating a brick wall. He's good at that."

Thor turns his head and his eyes light up. "Loki! We fight together again!"

"I'm just here to see you shot at!" snipes Loki.

Thor nods. "Aye, well I would deserve that." He turns back to casting lightning down the tunnel.

"Of course you deserve it!" Loki shouts. "Because of you, my boys—"

Nodding, but not turning from the fray Thor shouts. "Aye, so it is … But I come to make amends."

Steve is about to pass through Loki to take up a position between Thor and the wall, but the look on the apparition's face makes him stop.

"Miss Lewis, she's swearing. She never swears … " Loki's illusion says, eyes wide.

Steve freezes and meets Loki's eyes. "I hear her," says Loki.

Once Odin 'heard' Steve. It isn't a physical thing. It's magical.

Loki looks down the tunnel and swallows, and then he looks up. "Oh, no. No, no, no … " Without another word, his apparition leaps into the air and through the ceiling and is gone. Steve drops his gaze to see Thor briefly acknowledge Loki's disappearance with a grunt. Then the giant man turns back to shooting lightning. Steve exhales. Falling to one knee, Steve peers around the tunnel wall, and raises his Glock.

"This is all Loki's fault … Fuck, fuck, fuck. Loki get your ass here and save me!"

Loki's hands curl against the cold glass in his condo. He shouldn't let his attention leave the fray because of those words, but it does. He lets his apparition slide up through the ceiling, and through the building, searching for Amy, her voice, her prayer, pulling him along like the current of a river.

He finds her in a hallway, a wall of green flame before her, the flames rapidly getting hotter and turning blue. She's lying on the floor, hands over her head, face blackened with soot. "Dammit, Loki!" Amy says before she is taken with a fit of coughing. Loki lets his apparition lie down on the floor next to her, propping its imaginary head on an illusory hand. The apparition grins and raises an eyebrow. "You called?"

Amy turns her head and says, "You came!" Before he knows what is happening, she tries to throw her arms around his shoulders—and of course passes right through him. "Oh," she says, with a cough. "Right. You're not here. Can you get me out?"

Fading out from under her, his apparition reappears standing in the hall. He sends another apparition through the door near her and feels some of his bravado fade. He can achieve weak telekinesis, even from a distance, but if he unlocks the door she'll be cooked in the white hot inferno beyond. "You've got yourself into a mess here," he says.

Amy sucks in a breath. *Ugh, too hot...He thinks I don't know that?*

It takes a moment for Loki to realize that he's hearing her thoughts, not her words. He still hears her. He's never had a connection last this long.

Amy groans and covers her eyes. Her exasperated thoughts tickle his mind. *He doesn't have a plan. Of course he doesn't have a plan. He's not a part of some divine trinity, he'd be the God of Goof if he was a stupid god.*

Loki bristles. Is her ultimate purpose in life to insult

him? "A little gratitude would be nice!"

"Getting me out of here would be nice!" Amy snaps back, and then coughs, curling herself into fetal position. *Getting hotter.*

Something in the building groans. Feeling a rising sense of panic, Loki looks up. There is a little spout in the ceiling that should be shooting water, but he doesn't sense any water in the pipes, and there isn't enough ambient moisture in the air to create ice. He glances at the flames. Not that it would be much use against the elven fire. His heart begins to race. This is very, very bad. Is her call to him the universe trying to convince him how powerless he is?

He can't get me out, can he? Amy's eyes meet his apparition's and he feels her willing him not to go. *I don't want to die alone ...*

"You want me to stay here and watch you burn to death!" Loki says, his voice rising in anger at the hopelessness of the situation, and at himself. He should leave now, attend to what is happening below, snatch Cera if he can. Odin would be able to leave. Yes, he hears her, but how important can she be? She's as good as dead.

Amy snorts and covers her sooty face with an even dirtier hand. *Doesn't he know anything medical related? I'm going to die of smoke inhalation long before I burn to death.*

Loki tilts his head. "Charming, very charming!" he snaps, but his voice has taken on a hint of desperation. He destroys everything beautiful ...

In his condo Loki's chest feels tight; he stumbles backwards from the window. If it was him trapped in the hall, he'd use the In-Between, but it's exhausting and dangerous just for himself in ideal situations, which the elven inferno definitely is not. He's never used it on another, they'd both most likely die.

In the burning building there is a loud groan, and the floor beneath Amy drops.

In his living room Loki doesn't pause to think. He steps into the In-Between.

Loki vanishes from sight, the floor beneath Amy drops, and for an instant and an eternity she is suspended in mid-air. It is like that moment at the top of the hill of a roller coaster ride and the car plunges so fast beneath you that your body can't keep up.

She opens her mouth for a last gasp of air ... and meets Loki's eyes going from black to blue gray beneath her. She expects to crash through him, but instead she crashes into him. Heat buffets her face, she catches sight of white hot flames below, and they're falling.

And then there is nothing. No Loki, no light, no heat—no, Loki is there, she feels him underneath—in front—beside her—arms tightening around her waist. There is no up or down and she feels all the breath rush out of her.

Her lungs scream in agony, her body doesn't have a chance to shiver. And then, for a moment she can't feel anything anymore, she is beyond pain, or cold, or fear. She thinks she sees light, thinks she hears something. Beatrice's voice maybe? *You can't leave yet, Amy ...*

She wants to say that she wants to stay here, to follow Beatrice's voice, but before the words can form she is falling again, Loki beneath her. There is up and down once more, and light so bright it is blinding. She glimpses gray sky and they're falling into clouds. They collide with something and Loki's body bounces, snapping Amy's jaw shut on the impact, just catching the edge of her tongue. Gasping, Amy sucks in a breath and thinks she can feel the cells that line her lungs rejoicing, the taste of air is so sweet. She blinks. They're not in clouds, they're on a bed with white linens, in a huge room with floor to ceiling windows, furnished with only a bed and a nightstand. Her head is on Loki's chest; he's wearing the pink LGBT shirt with the upside down rainbow triangle he calls his "Bifrost shirt." A shadow above them makes her look up with a gasp ... it's Loki's sword in a black scabbard hanging above the bed on the wall.

"Amy?"

Amy shifts her gaze downwards. Gasping for breath, and in shock, she can't respond.

Loki is looking at her, his mouth open, his eyes wide, his skin going from mottled blue to pale peach. He puts his hands to the sides of her head. Flexing his fingers as though checking to see that she is real, he says, "You're alive?"

Blinking, Amy nods. He closes his eyes and smiles, a genuine smile, not one of his twisted smirks. "Welcome to my home," he whispers. Lifting his head he bumps his forehead against hers, and then his head drops, his hands fall, and his eyelids droop.

"Loki!" Amy yells, scrambling to her knees on top of him and shaking his shoulders. "Loki!"

He blinks his eyes and mumbles. "So tired ... twice ... so hungry ... need to sleep."

Her eyes widen. She's straddling his chest and he hasn't made a single inappropriate comment. Terrified, she shakes his shoulders. "Are you going to be alright?" she says, leaning in close and biting her lip.

He nods but doesn't open his eyes. His body trembles as his muscles relax. His head lolls to the side.

Going cold, Amy straightens and puts a hand to her face. She can't take him to the hospital. Jameson is after him; she just has to trust that he's done this before and he'll get better. She idly pushes her purse up her shoulder. She hadn't even realized it was still on her arm. She freezes. Her phone! They can track her by satellite.

With shaking hands she opens her purse. Her wallet is inside, her keys, and her new birth control pills. But her phone is gone. Remembering dropping it on the floor after her unsuccessful phone call, she heaves a sigh of relief.

… and catches a whiff of herself. Her hair and her clothes smell like burnt chemicals. She remembers how 9/11 victims suffered from strange ailments after the attack, brought on by the cocktail of exotic burnt compounds in the building materials they inhaled. She suddenly has a very strong urge to take a shower.

She looks down at Loki. His hair is ginger, his skin pale and wan. She has a responsibility to him first. His chest seems very still. Amy scampers off of him, and he heaves in a huge breath of air, his eyes spring open, and he coughs.

"Amy … " he mumbles. "Strangest dream. I was suffocating under a giant rabbit."

Amy's lips twitch. She'd been sitting on his chest, evidently cutting off his oxygen supply. Good one, would-be-animal-doctor-girl. Silently incriminating herself, she gently pushes his bangs back from his eyes. His hair is coarse and thick. "Are you sure you'll be alright?" she asks again.

Nodding, he whispers. "Never did that with two people.

Almost killed us both. Need to sleep." He takes a deep breath of air, his nose wrinkles, and he winces.

Smiling bitterly, she says, "That's me. I smell like cancer. I want to take a shower, but I don't know if I should leave you alone."

Loki shakes his head, eyes closed. "You can't take a shower."

Heart catching, Amy brushes her hand softly down his cheek, and leans closer. She's about to whisper, "What can I do?" when Loki, eyes still closed, lets out a whine. "Not while I'm too weak to spy on you."

Amy sits up and pulls her hand away. She sighs. "I think you'll be fine."

One of Loki's eyes opens, and then the other, and he smiles again. It's innocent, filled with wonder, and it's breathtaking.

"What?" Amy asks.

"I rescued you." The smile gets impossibly wider and he shrugs, and looks away. "It's been a long time since I've done something so unequivocally … " He huffs a laugh. " … Good."

Some butterflies do a mad dance in her stomach. "Oh, Loki," says Amy, almost reaching up to put a hand through his bangs again.

Covering his eyes, he nods and sighs almost shyly. "Not since I helped kill Baldur."

"Oh," Amy says, suddenly feeling uncomfortable. Yes, Thor did say Baldur deserved it, but it doesn't stop the chill that Amy feels. Loki doesn't operate by an earthly moral code. Thinking of the civilians Thor said he had killed in Asgard, she shivers and wraps her arms around herself.

Loki sighs again and closes his eyes. His muscles relax in

a wave, and he's almost instantly asleep, the smile still on his face.

Loki saved her, that is the only thing she knows for sure. Standing up and taking a deep breath, she goes to find the shower.

When Loki returned to court from Niflheim, the plague and its victims were already nearly forgotten. Instead there were other rumors.

"Baldur has dreams of his impending death," Thor says, over a mug of ale. His brows draw together, and he takes another swig from his mug. They are in the home of Loki, Sigyn, Valli and Nari—still called Anganboða's Hall. Sigyn and Loki are loathe to call it anything else. It is late, the boys are asleep. Sigyn is with them, a smaller mug of her own in front of her.

Sigyn's gaze becomes hard, but she says nothing.

"Good," says Loki.

Thor scratches his great mane, and then shakes his head. "But it doesn't matter. The gossips in court say the queen has begged every creature, every plant, and every rock and mineral in all the Nine Realms not to hurt him and they've all given their oath to comply. No weapon can penetrate his skin."

Huffing, Sigyn says, "That is ridiculous."

Thor looks up, eyes wide. "But—"

Tilting his head, Loki says, "Since when have plants, let alone rocks and minerals, been ones to make oaths?"

Looking down at his ale, Thor says, "Aye. It sounded strange to me. But Baldur ordered Tyr to throw an iron battle axe at him. It bounced off without leaving a scratch." He shrugs and drains his mug.

"Well, maybe he should test those oaths," Loki says. "Perhaps at the training grounds tomorrow we can all take turns throwing things at him?"

Thor beams. "That sounds like fun!"

Beside Loki, Sigyn straightens and her face darkens. Later, as Thor is leaving, Loki puts his arm around her hip and leans down to nip her ear. He's warm with liquor, cold with the memory of Helen, and he suddenly wants more babies, just to show he is still fighting. Sigyn pulls out of his embrace. Pointing a finger at him, she says, "Odin is setting you up, Loki! You'll take care of his problem, and then he'll thank you with torture and banish our children to Midgard or worse!"

"Baldur needs to die!" Loki hisses. Sigyn is the only person he's told about Odin's spectral visit to Niflheim. He feels his skin heat and sting at her betrayal—she of all people should understand.

"Yes!" Sigyn says, her lips curling into a snarl. She closes her eyes. "I worry every time Nari or Valli go near Baldur that he'll ..." she shakes her head unable to finish. Loki remembers Sigyn emerging from Baldur's chambers so long ago, her face dazed, confused and hurt. Woman or child, boy or girl, Baldur has no inhibitions about using his glamour to charm, seduce, and betray.

He lets out a breath and his fists tighten at his powerlessness. "What would you have me do?" he says through clenched teeth.

"Do the same as Odin, find someone else to do your dirty work," says Sigyn.

Loki snarls and all the candles in the kitchen flicker to life, and the fire in the hearth leaps. It's not what he wants; Loki wants to douse Baldur in fire even if it means his own death. He wants the world to see the Golden Prince burn. But Sigyn is right. If Loki kills Baldur, Loki's family will face banishment— or worse. Sigyn isn't Aggie, but he loves her; and his boys are monsters, but he loves them with an intensity that borders on madness. He looks away and says nothing.

As it turns out, half of the deed is accomplished by someone else the next day. Thor suggests to the court that they attempt to test the spell protecting Baldur by throwing weapons of various materials and designs at him. In arrogance and vanity, Baldur accepts gamely. It becomes the favorite sport of the court. Unfortunately, just as Thor suggested, nothing seems to work.

Loki does not partake of the sport himself. Instead, he takes to studying the mechanisms of the spell. Some of the more learned at court speculate that Frigga has surrounded Baldur with an invisible layer of magical armor—but Loki doubts that. A layer of magical armor would inhibit sensations from reaching Baldur. He doubts very much that Baldur, ever the 'sensualist,' would be willing to part with that. It takes many months, but Loki eventually discovers Queen Frigga has woven her magic into Baldur's skin. He can feel pleasurable sensations, but heat too hot will be siphoned by magic into realms unseen as well as the atoms and molecules of points too sharp. The force of impact of such implements meets the same fate.

It is a beautiful, infuriating, lovingly crafted piece of work. And in all the days that the warriors make sport of throwing objects at Baldur nothing penetrates his skin. Instead it is Sigyn that discovers the weakness.

"Remember that small plant that you brought from Midgard, Loki? The one that grows in trees?" his wife says one evening. The boys are screaming in the other room. Normally, he would go back, rough house with them, and Sigyn would come in and harangue him for 'inciting them to riot'. But Loki has had a long day listening to the dronings of Odin and the dwarven envoys from the new Svartalfheim mercantilist faction, and he is in the

mood to kill someone. He grits his teeth. He is not in the mood to talk, or listen. He wants to turn off his ears and mouth and drink. He grunts in response and heads to the cupboard.

Not taking the hint, Sigyn says, "Frigga touched it, and her skin developed a rash."

Popping the cork out of the bottle of ale with his teeth, Loki says, "And this concerns me because ... ?" In the other room he hears a crash.

Sigyn scowls. "Because she seems to be intolerant to the substance ... I've heard of similar things among the Vanir, and the dwarfs ... but not among the Aesir. I thought yearly feasting on Idunn's apples inoculated us." She tilts her head. "But it's a new species to Asgard. Perhaps Idunn hasn't added it to her apples' magic—"

"Too bad for Frigga," says Loki, tipping back his ale.

"Loki, such conditions are inheritable!" says Sigyn.

Putting down his drink, Loki stares at her.

Sigyn's eyes narrow. "And in the proper dosages can be deadly."

Later that evening he is sitting with a mistletoe branch on the kitchen table. The plant has thin flimsy branches, too weak to be a weapon. Loki taps his chin. "Perhaps if I rub the bark and leaves along a sword or a knife the essence will be enough to break the spell and allow me to drive a blade through his hide."

From where she is mending, Sigyn says sharply, "You will do no such thing."

Loki glares at her, but she doesn't even look up. "Find a way to kill him without it being traced to you," she says, pushing a thread through a needle. "Or Odin will not get a chance to punish you because I will kill you myself."

The coldness in her voice makes Loki pause.

"It is no victory if all your children are dead." Raising her eyes, she says, "I want you to be victorious."

The side of Loki's lip quirks. He looks down at the mistletoe branch and his thoughts start racing. "First I'll need to see if Frigga's weakness is also Baldur's."

Sigyn hums in agreement.

From the mistletoe, Loki crafts a small, lightweight, inconspicuous dart. The next day, he tosses it in the pile of weapons the warriors will fling at Baldur. It's just his luck that the person who picks up the dart happens to be the nearly blind Hödur. Loki makes himself invisible and tries to steer Hödur's aim in the right direction, but still the dart just barely grazes Baldur's arm. And then Tyr heaves a dwarven dagger directly at Baldur's forehead. As the dagger falls harmlessly, Baldur and all those assembled laugh, but Loki can't help but notice Baldur scratching at his arm where the dart passed, the skin there mottled and red.

He leaves in glee to tell Sigyn. His glee ends quickly when he returns to where the mistletoe grows to find that the tree it grew in has been cut to the ground.

He stares at the stump, his hands curling into fists. To get more mistletoe he'll need to go to Midgard. But access to Midgard is restricted—to all but the occasional receiver of prayers. Of late, that has only been Baldur.

For months, Loki can only watch helplessly as Baldur's behavior becomes more brazen and bold. And then, prayers come to Loki. Typical of Loki's luck, they come at the best and worst of all possible times.

CHAPTER 4

The tunnel beyond the emergency lighting of ADUO's basement level has gone dark. The bullets have stopped. Steve's knee is sore and cold where he half kneels between the giant Asgardian beside him and the wall.

Thor sends a burst of lightning northward, and Steve raises his pistol and fires in the direction of some darting shadows. Spinning, Thor does the same in a southerly direction and Brett and Bryant fire, too.

Over his headset, set to the secure channel, a voice cracks. "They're sending arrows with green flame in this direction!"

There are screams southward where Cera is and then someone shouts, "There is a wall of green flame around the Promethean Sphere!"

Steve's about to order Brett, Bryant, and Thor to race in the direction of the sphere, but then more gunfire rings in his ears, fast and insistent. A bullet lands in the corner of the wall by Steve and a piece of debris hits his face with a sharp sting. "Hold your position!" he shouts.

There is more screaming from the direction of the Promethean sphere. His headset crackles with, "The fire is turning blue … now white!"

For a few minutes there is nothing but gunfire and Thor releasing lightning blasts down the narrow tunnels, and then everything is suddenly silent.

Steve's headset crackles to life. "What's happening?"

"The sphere is secure!"

"They're retreating!"

Steve sees nothing but hears running footsteps behind and in front of him.

Thor bellows, "Leave the ones that are north of us, try to grab the ones trying to escape past us from the south!"

The wisdom of it hits Steve instantly. To the south is Cera, and more agents. To the north are just more tunnels—they have no real chance of catching them, but they might be able to corner some between themselves and Cera and haul them in for questioning. Gunfire comes from behind and in front. Steve turns; he sees nothing beyond the few feet of space he stands in, but shouts rise around him, echoing in a strange language.

Suddenly, out of the blackness come shadows. Brett fires and one of the shadows buckles at the knees. Another raises a pistol but Thor's hammer is there. Still another shape tries to bolt past the large golden man, but Steve catches it by the collar. Pinning with too much ease what turns out to be a man of light build and moderate height, Steve grits his teeth. He's amped with anger from this pointless attack, and the thought of men down that they haven't even begun to count.

He shoves the man against the wall so hard he hears the clack of teeth. Taking a breath, Steve wills his temper to cool. And then he catches his breath. The man's skin is Caucasian, with a long scar across his cheek that is rapidly fading, his eyes are brown, his hair is golden ... but what draws Steve's attention are his ears. They're growing upward, forming delicate points.

Behind Steve comes the sound of more scuffling, and a loud bellow by Thor. "We have them!"

Steve is barely listening. In front of him, the man's features are morphing, changing, becoming painfully ... perfect. "I will die an elf!" the man says.

Steve's eyes widen. The man raises a leg, trying to kick Steve's body away. Steve's instincts take over quickly. Hands still on the man's shirt collar, Steve pivots away from the kick and uses his momentum, and his assailant's imbalance, to slam the man onto the floor face first. He has the elf's arm behind his back a moment later. It takes all his self-control to keep from breaking it.

He blinks down as the elf lets out a cry of pain. "This man isn't combat trained," he says, almost to himself. Also, the guy doesn't seem to be clawing out his eyes in an effort to get to Cera. The elf Brett shot is whimpering on the ground, knee bent at an impossible angle. An AK-47 that looks heavy and ancient lies just out of reach.

"No, he is not," Thor rumbles. The big man has two elves, one with skin dark brown, another golden, dead or unconscious, at his feet. "It will make them easier to break."

The elf beneath Steve shudders. In frustration, Steve yanks up on his arm just a little. The elf makes a wail that's so plaintive Steve looks down. He wants to say something derisive ... but doesn't. Steve has caught insurgents before, he expects a look of insolence, and maybe pride. The man below him shows neither of these emotions, he just looks terrified.

Over his headset someone says, "They're retreating from headquarters—fires are receding!"

And then Jameson's voice comes over the line. "Rogers, I'll need you for debriefing. Bring Thor."

Cursing, Steve taps his headset. "Yes, sir. On my way." Turning to Brett and Bryant he says, "I'll call for medical. Thor, my superior wants a word with you."

Thor snorts. "Superior how?"

Steve runs his tongue over his teeth. He doesn't answer. Instead he pulls the elf beneath him up by the back of the collar. "You're with me, too." Ducking his head, the elf scrambles to his feet, staying as far away from Thor as possible.

A few minutes later, the three of them step through the security door that leads into ADUO's office, blinking in the bright light of blown-out windows. Outside Steve hears the sound of fire trucks and choppers. Around them cubicles are smoking, but there are no more flames.

Rounding a corner, Hernandez catches Steve's eyes. His pistol is still drawn, but he looks calm. "Sir! We're setting up an emergency conference. You're wanted immediately in the cafeteria."

"Why not meet in one of the magically shielded rooms?" Steve asks.

Hernandez shakes his head. "The Promethean wire wasn't affected by the flames, but there was structural damage in the rooms where we had the wire set up. It isn't working anymore, and the rooms aren't safe."

Beside him the elf starts to breathe heavily.

"Gerðr?" says Steve.

"Sedated and being taken to the special aircraft built for Loki."

A chopper passing low drowns out nearly all the sound in the room. "What's going on?" Steve asks. In the distance Steve hears the wail of fire engines.

Hernandez's jaw tightens. "The flames here just all of a sudden snuffed out, but before they did they managed to create real fires in the surrounding block—and panic. People saw the green flames, and CNN speculated it was a chemical attack. The governor called in the National Guard—and somehow the press decided that there was an official pronouncement to evacuate the Loop. The mayor is furious, so is Jameson."

So is Steve. Grabbing the elf by the collar, he steers him to the window and forces the man to look out with him. People are streaming out of buildings, walking on the sidewalks, and between cars stuck in the middle of the street, honking their horns.

Still … Steve's head tilts. It is not as bad as he imagined. He sees people helping people; the crowd is a slow-moving river, not a furious torrent. He glances down at his watch. It's been an hour since the fighting began. He's read that the longer a crisis goes on, the more likely humans are to be civilized—but he's never seen it.

The elf beside Steve lets out a sharp breath. Steve looks at him. His eyes are wide and fearful as he stares at the crowd below. His mouth opens as though he might say something, but then Thor grunts and the elf's mouth closes with a snap.

"Come on," Steve says, and the four of them, Thor, Hernandez, the elf and Steve head towards the cafeteria. They're just about to go in when they run into Laura Stodgill, talking hurriedly on her phone. She looks alright, though she's holding her shoes in her hand. She isn't combat trained. Steve's jaw tightens as he meets her eyes. Before he has a chance to ask the question on his mind, Stodgill answers it for him. Putting the phone down, she says, "I can't find Lewis. I'm trying to see if some of the security footage is still intact."

Beneath Steve's hand, he feels the elf tremble. He hasn't made a move to escape since they've dragged him up out of the tunnels. To Hernandez Steve says, "Watch him." To Stodgill he says, "Find out what you can."

She nods and Steve turns to Thor. He is watching Stodgill thoughtfully. With a raised eyebrow he meets Steve's gaze. Together they walk into the cafeteria. Jameson is standing beside a righted table. On it sits a cell phone. Around him are some of the his guys from D.C.

"Steve Rogers reporting, Sir," Steve says.

"And I am Thor Odinson," says Thor in deep bellowing tones. "Son of Odin, King of Asgard and official emissary from that realm."

Steve scowls. Didn't Steve's two feathered minders, official envoys of Odin, berate Thor for being here? He casts a speculative glance at Thor. The big man pointedly ignores him.

"Agent Steve Rogers and...Thor...Odinson," says a voice over the phone which Steve recognizes instantly as the Director of the FBI. "We've been waiting to speak with you. The president is on the line. As are the joint chiefs of staff."

Steve freezes.

Someone, voice garbled, says, "I want to cut to the chase. Belarus, Ukraine, and Russia are all pushing us to give these guys the full rights accorded to the Geneva convention. Any idea why?"

"No, sir," says Jameson.

Steve knows instantly. "They were armed with AK-47s, ancient ones. They're buying old Soviet tech."

There is a moment of silence. Steve thinks he hears whispers on the other end. And then someone says, "We've known that based on the ballistics reports from the vehicle the girl took to Alfheim. The question is, what are they offering these countries in exchange that's so valuable?"

Steve tenses at mention of the ballistics report he hadn't had access to.

Beside him, he hears Jameson shuffle nervously. Jameson had access to the reports and he hadn't answered the damn question. Steve shifts on his feet, too, and his nails bite into his fists in frustration.

Steve is asked a few more questions. It's just a dry recitation of what Steve has and has not seen until someone on the other end of the line says, "Agent Rogers, you've gone on record publicly saying that attempting to capture Loki was a waste of resources and bound to be unsuccessful."

Another voice says dryly, "Apparently you were right. Those were resources we could have used to predict this attack."

Steve restrains a grim smile, but then Jameson steps forward. "Mr. President, we know that Loki has associated with the Dark Elves before. He told Miss Lewis as much during their trip to Alfheim. He's behind this attack!"

Steve rubs his jaw. It isn't a bad theory. It doesn't feel quite right, though …

Thor snorts. "Loki wouldn't have anything to offer them in exchange for their cooperation."

Steve feels himself straighten.

"But it is possible?" someone else says.

"It's unlikely," says Thor.

"But right now it's the only scenario we have to go on," someone else says.

A woman's voice snaps, "Yes, and attitudes like that had us chasing Osama Bin Laden in caves!"

There's a moment of silence so deep it's obvious they've been put on mute, and then the woman's voice comes over the line again, "I can't believe I'm asking you this, Mr. Odinson, but are the Dark Elves from Svartálfaheim or Alfheim?"

Thor tilts his head. "Svartálfaheim is the land of the dwarfs. Although, in some of your mythologies I believe you've confused Dark Elves and the dwarfs. It is understandable. Both are dishonorable creatures."

"Dishonorable? How precisely?" says the woman.

Thor snorts. "The elves of the Dark Lands are there because they've betrayed their queen. They fight among themselves in a perpetual state of war. Svartálfaheim is practically run by merchants … if it weren't for Asgard's protection, the Svartálfaheim nobility would be overrun."

Steve can almost hear the questioner sucking in a breath. "I see," she says, and even over the crackling line Steve can hear the woman's tightened jaw.

"This line of questioning is taking us nowhere," says another voice on the line.

There are some more questions directed at Steve. Besides the insight into where the elves are getting weapons, Steve notes they don't discuss anything Thor could not have picked up from direct observation. The president thanks Thor and says something about "continued cooperation between our realms" and then Thor and Steve are dismissed—Steve's given no clear direction beyond "get some sleep."

Steve bristles as he leaves Jameson behind. Is Steve not trusted because he suggested the FBI work with Loki? Is he Thor's babysitter? He's glad they're not trying to arrest Thor—but very curious as to why not. What do they know that Steve doesn't?

With these thoughts in mind, he heads down the hall towards his office. Steve and Thor round a corner. Just before they reach their destination they nearly plow into Hernandez. The agent has the elf Steve captured in handcuffs and is guiding him none-too-gently towards the exit.

"Where are you taking him?" Steve asks.

"All captured insurgents not in medical are being rounded up and put on the same flight as Gerðr," Hernandez says.

At just that moment Stodgill steps out of her office. "Agent Rogers, I got word from the surveillance guys. Lewis headed into the service hallway just as the attack began. There was a fire in the stairwell, she would have been trapped … " She swallows. "There's nothing on the tapes of her ever coming out."

"Amy," says the elf.

All eyes shoot to their captive. "What did you just say?" Steve says.

The elf swallows. "I met her in Alfheim, with my wife. She took pity on us and offered to bring us to earth."

"And now she's dead," says Hernandez.

Steve finds himself taking a step closer to the elf, his hands balling into fists at his side. He isn't sure who he is angrier at—the elf, or himself. Steve put Amy in the line of fire, didn't he? His chin dips, and he can feel the side of his lip drawing up in a sneer … of course it was the elves that fired.

The elf draws back.

A heavy hand falls on Steve's shoulder. "Easy, Rogers. Do not punish this man for a death that you do not know has happened," says Thor.

Steve blinks and exhales a breath, his rational mind kicking in.

"What are you talking about?" says Hernandez, eyes on Thor, shaking the elf roughly. "You heard what Agent Stodgill said! There was no way for Amy to escape."

Steve swears he can see a vein in Thor's forehead throb. "Loki heard her. And Loki achieves impossible things," Thor says, his voice between a snarl and a whisper.

At that moment, Steve's, Stodgill's and Hernandez's phones buzz simultaneously. Phone already out, Stodgill taps a button. "It's an email from Amy."

Steve holds out a hand; without being asked, Stodgill hands over her phone. He looks down at the email. It says simply, Loki got me out. Am okay. Amy

She sent it to just about everyone in the office she associates with.

Thor's hand thumps Steve's shoulders. "See!"

Handing Stodgill's phone back, Steve says, "Have Brett and Bryant trace the IP address."

"Yes, sir!" she says.

Steve scowls. In human myths Loki was able to accomplish what even Odin couldn't pull off—but he wasn't just the "god of lost causes," he was the god of treachery as well. He remembers Jameson's theory about Loki being behind the attacks. Loki's excellent at computer programming. Hacking Amy's personal account would probably take him all of a few minutes. But would he make the effort to lie about something like this?

From down the hall come shouts. Steve's phone starts buzzing.

Picking up, he says, "Rogers here." His jaw tenses as he listens. "I'm on it."

Turning to the elf he says, "There are trolls on Lower Wacker Drive. Know anything about it?"

Eyes wide, the elf shakes his head. "We have nothing to do with it!"

Glaring at the elf, Steve says, "We still are going to talk." But for now Steve has a green killing machine with re-attachable limbs and a bullet proof hide to deal with. ADUOs dealt with plenty of trolls in the past, but never when the city was in such a state of chaos.

Turning, Steve heads down the hallway. Behind him Thor laughs. "Ah, where Loki is there is always fine adventure!"

The glee in the giant man's laugh makes the hairs on the back of Steve's neck stand on end.

"How can you restrict our access to Midgard on pretense that the Aesir do the same? Your own son is there on a regular basis!" The dwarven delegate draws himself up to his full height. He comes to just below Loki's chest, but his girth is formidable. "I hear he is there even now." The dwarf looks pointedly at the empty throne beside Frigga and Odin.

There are murmurs through the great hall.

Standing behind the royal family, Loki raises an eyebrow. At last someone says it.

Odin's voice takes on the distant tone it does when he speaks of Baldur. "My son is there on official business, he hears prayers."

Loki's hands tighten into fists. Lately, Baldur's presence has been requested on Earth more and more. Christianity has been on the rise in the places where the Aesir were once the only gods. Where the religions intersect, Baldur is often summoned. Although Baldur is not the god who turns the other cheek, he is confused with him. Perhaps because the Christ the Christians speak of is also the son of an all-father figure?

Snapping him from his reverie, the dwarf says, "Official business? Is that what you call it?" Loki snorts quietly. Baldur uses his time on Midgard to do other things beyond answer prayers.

Around the room the Aesir tilt their heads. Loki hears someone whisper, "The dwarf king covets Baldur for his daughter's hand."

The dwarfs in the retinue behind the delegate bristle. One of the delegate's eyebrows shoot up. Loki knows there have been no official overtures for a union between the dwarf princess and Asgard's heir. The dwarfs know an offer would be scorned. They are viewed as lesser beings.

Odin waves a weary hand in Loki's direction. Odin has been weary a lot of late, and if Loki tries to bring up Niflheim, he just grows wearier. As Loki leans down, Odin says, "Loki, show our distinguished guests to their quarters in the East Wing."

"Yes, Your Majesty," Loki says, delivering the honorific with a smirk. Lately Odin has been insisting on more respect in public. Loki steps off the dais where the throne stands and walks towards the dwarfs still glaring at Odin.

Bowing, Loki says, "Your distinguished—"

And then he hears a feminine voice that is a whisper, and yet carries above all the murmurs in the great hall. "Help me! If any of you have any mercy, help me!" The desperation in the plea is so obvious, Loki feels breathless.

"Are we under attack?" Loki shouts, spinning around.

In the corner of his eye he sees Thor pull out Mjolnir. Voices rise in the great hall. Odin's voice rings out, "Silence! Heimdall?"

The gatekeeper steps forward. "We are under no attack, my Lord."

But the woman's voice rises again. "I have pledged my heart to Hothur!"

A man's voice rises with the woman's. "If there be justice between gods and men, call off your Golden Son or give me the means to fight him honorably!"

Loki looks around the room. Everyone is staring at him, no one appears to hear the voices. And then it hits Loki. "Prayers," he whispers. "I hear prayers."

Gasping, Loki's eyes go wide. His legs fall out from under him. He feels like laughing.

Someone in the great hall shouts. "And what are the prayers requesting, fool?"

"Loki's so pretty in women's clothing; maybe someone wants him as their wife!" says someone else in the hall. Normally, Loki would have a witty rejoinder at the tip of his tongue but all he can do is sit on the floor, biting back his smile.

"He is not lying!" says the dwarf, holding a small, glowing, circular amulet in his hands. The laughter becomes more subdued snickers. "There is magic in the air." The dwarf lifts his eyes to Odin. "If prayers are the reason you allow your son to go to Midgard, you must send your fool, too."

"No!" says Frigga.

For a long moment there is silence in the great hall. And then on the throne, Odin sighs heavily. "Loki, you may go."

As Loki gets shakily to his feet, Heimdall says, "I shall go with him."

"As shall I," says Thor.

"No," says Odin as Loki staggers to the door. "This is Loki's task. Thor and Heimdall, the good dwarf and I have been discussing instability among Svartheimer's merchant class. Now would be a good time to turn Heimdall's eyes and Thor's strategies to avoiding such an unfortunate development."

Loki doesn't question the sudden change in schedule, he just makes a break for the door.

Not an hour later, the Bifrost deposits Loki on one of Midgard's Northern continents. It is night time, but the moon is full. As soon as his feet touch earth he hears the woman's prayers again. "I know my father has promised me to your Golden Son, please forgive me."

Loki turns at the sound. In the distance he sees campfires, and he knows without knowing how that is his destination. He's brought Frigga's falcon cloak in case the distance between him and the humans is great, but the journey is so short, he takes it on foot. He soon finds himself at the camp of what Loki can only speculate is a warlord. Sentries line the perimeter, and he counts at least 50 tents in the moonlight. Narrowing his eyes, Loki makes himself invisible and heads to the tent at the center. Slipping through the front opening he finds a woman kneeling on a skin rug before a smoldering metal bowl. To one side is a low bed and a table laden with scrolls made out of hides.

He's just taking in the scene when he hears the flap of the tent open behind him.

"Nanna," says a voice Loki recognizes from the prayers in Odin's hall, that he assumes belongs to Hothur. Turning, he sees a human man with broad shoulders, a long scar down one side of his face, and armor that is well-made but unadorned. Loki smiles. A warrior interested in results, not show—the very *opposite of the golden prince! This is looking better and better.*

"We shouldn't waste what little we have of our mortal lives seeking deliverance from fickle gods," the man says, going to lay a hand on the woman's shoulder. Loki takes that to be a rather nice way of saying, 'Let's have sex before we die.' He'd be all for watching, but he has a purpose, and that seems like as good an opening as any.

Making himself visible, Loki clears his throat. "Normally, I'd agree with your sentiment, but this time, deliverance is here."

Hothur's sword is out in less than a heartbeat. Loki holds up his hands and smirks. "Don't kill me. Save it for Baldur."

Hothur narrows his eyes. "And I'm supposed to listen to a man who wears a woman's feather cloak?"

Loki rolls his eyes. "It lets me fly, you idiot. If I had to I'd wear Frigga's dress as well."

Behind him Nanna rises to her feet. "It's Loki! He wore a feather cloak in the tale of Thor and his lost hammer, too!"

Hothur's eyes widen, but only a fraction. "I don't believe it."

Loki snaps his fingers on both hands and lets little bursts of flame rise. Both humans gasp. Bowing to Nanna, he says, "At your service."

"We should trust our lives to the God of Lies?" says Hothur.

Rising, Loki tilts his head. Where had that come from? He always, always, keeps his oaths. "God of Mischief, thank you," he says tightly.

Hothur scowls at him.

Rolling his eyes, Loki says, "Your lives are already forfeit if you've somehow managed to upset His Royal Highness." Crossing his arms, he raises an eyebrow at them.

Nanna steps forward. "Baldur asked my father for my hand in marriage." She smiles wryly. "And my father gave it even though I'd told Baldur that I am promised to Hothur."

Loki blinks. That is a lot more concern for formality than he would have expected from Baldur. Not that marriage to a human would be considered legal and binding in Asgard. Still, slightly disbelieving, Loki says, "And you dislike his proposal because?"

"Because he intends to use me and cast me aside!" Nanna says, fists forming at her side.

Loki shrugs. "True." He takes a step forward. "But how do you know this? Most people can't see ... "

Nanna's voice wavers. "I love Hothur. I promised myself to him ... "

Loki stares at her, willing his mouth not to gape. This simple human saw the truth?

Shaking her head, Nanna says, "Baldur just wants me because I said no."

Loki snorts. "That sounds like him." He looks Nanna up and down. She is beautiful, if a little short. But on Asgard she'd hardly stand out. He feels his smirk fading and his eyes go soft. She has Aggie's perceptiveness and Sigyn's strength of will.

The gleam of a blade near his chin snaps Loki to the present. "What are you offering, and what do you want, Trickster?" Hothur says.

Realizing the direction of his gaze, Loki smirks. "Relax, your intended is lovely, but my wife would kill me. I want nothing more than to answer your prayers. As for what I am offering ... " He shrugs. "Mistletoe. It's the only thing that can kill the Golden Prince."

Tilting his head, Hothur steps back. "That's it?"

Looking around the tent, Loki says, "Well, you must make sure an ample amount enters his bloodstream. Rubbing the extract upon the blades of your weapons would probably do the trick."

"It shall be done this very night," says Hothur.

Nodding absently, Loki keeps scanning the room. Something is off. He feels magic.

Nanna whispers something. Hothur shuffles on his feet and then says tightly, "If this works, we will honor you for all of our days. I will hire bards to sing your praises."

Eyes snapping back to the couple, Loki shakes his head and holds up his hands. "Oh, no! No! That would get me in more trouble than you can imagine." Not least of which with Sigyn.

Hothur's brow furrows. "But how will I explain how I killed him?"

Waving a hand, Loki says, "Make up some tale of a magic sword and an epic quest! Be creative."

"It will be done," says Hothur, but Loki is looking at the table. One of the scrolls is glowing faintly. Magic devices aren't allowed on Earth anymore. Loki takes quick steps towards the table. "What is this?" Loki asks, picking up the scroll.

Behind him, Hothur says, "It's a map to an enchanted spear, called Gungnir, given to me by a wandering mage. He said if I recover it and take it to the circle of stones on the southeasterly island, he will use it to open a pathway to Jotunheim and summon an army." Hothur smiles tightly. "And he says he could send the army straight from the stone circle to Asgard to fight the Aesir on my behalf."

Loki turns his head quickly to Hothur. "And you trust him?"

Hothur glares at Loki. "I'm not an idiot, Trickster. If the map is of interest, as you seem to think it is, I'm sure the spear will do as he says. However, the army summoned would not be at my command." Hothur's jaw tightens. "But if Baldur stole Nanna from me ... I might do such a thing knowing that at least

Heaven would burn."

Loki tilts his head. He's wanted to see Asgard shamed and brought low on occasion. If it weren't for Sigyn, Nari and Valli... Turning his eyes back to the scroll he carefully unrolls it. For an instant he sees the location of the staff Gungnir, but then the scroll bursts into flames—and not by his hands.

Vexed by the magic scroll and tale of Gungnir, Loki returns to Asgard that night.

A few days later Baldur goes to Midgard with a host of warriors and attempts to take Nanna from Hothur. He returns only hours later, carried by his warriors. He is wounded and in excruciating pain. He holds on for three days before he dies. Odin and Frigga never leave his side.

"Go away!"

Loki's shout awakens Amy like a thunderclap from a dreamless sleep. It takes a moment, but she realizes she's lying at the edge of his bed and it's well into the night. The sound of helicopters, still a little too close, reverberate through the dark room.

Sitting up with a start, she turns to Loki. He's sitting, too, not looking in her direction, rubbing his temple and gritting his teeth. His hair is still ginger, his skin pale.

"I'm sorry," she stammers. "There was nowhere else to sleep." His home doesn't have a couch or even chairs beyond the one in front of his computer.

Loki lifts his head and looks at her, his face a mask of unconcealed ire.

"I'll get up," Amy says hastily.

His hand flies to her knee. "No."

Amy freezes in place, even as her body suddenly gets very warm.

Closing his eyes and then opening them, he looks around the room. "I'm not talking to you, I'm talking to Cera." His lip curls. "She knew about the Dark Elves; she collaborated with them, thinking they would free her."

"Uhhhh … " says Amy, looking at his hand, bone white in the faint light that creeps through the blinds.

Loki shouts into the darkness. "Get out and I might accept your apology!"

There is silence for a beat. And then Loki's body relaxes. Hand still on her knee, he turns back to Amy. He's awoken several times, but this is the first time he's seemed truly conscious, even if he is yelling at invisible monsters in the dark. The look in his gray eyes is impossible to read.

"Are you hungry?" she asks, for lack of anything better to say.

Loki blinks at her, a slight smile on his lips. He opens his mouth and his stomach growls audibly. Clutching both hands on his middle, he stammers, "Y-y-yes."

Scampering up, Amy runs to his side of the bed. He has a little night stand there with a small light that she flicks on. There is a little white book by the light, a plate of food she's prepared, and a single serving box of chocolate UHT milk she found in his cupboard.

"A quadruple decker Nutella and peanut butter sandwich!" Loki says, his voice ringing with delight. "My favorite, how did you know?"

Picking up the plate, Amy turns to him and raises an eyebrow. "You asked me to make one the first time you woke up."

Snatching the plate, Loki stuffs a quarter of the sandwich

into his mouth. Amy's brow lifts in bemusement. It's the most physical activity she's seen from him since they arrived.

Looking up at her, he garbles, "Iwazawake?"

Amy barely contains a snort. "Apparently, not really."

His forehead creases in confusion.

"This is the fifth time you've woken. The first time you told me how to make the sandwich." Tilting her head she remembers his half closed eyes and slurred words. "You did seem a little out of it."

Chewing the sandwich he looks up at her contemplatively and then his eyes drift from her neckline to her bare feet. Amy looks down. Oh. Right. She's wearing a pair of Loki's pajamas rolled ridiculously high at her wrists and ankles, and his robe. Feeling her cheeks heat, she says, "You have a washer but no detergent, I hope you don't mind." Her own clothes smell like death.

"Of course I mind, take them off right now!" he says, ripping off a piece of sandwich.

Amy's eyes widen in horror and she takes a step back. Before she's even formulated a response, he breaks down in peals of laughter.

"Nice," she grumbles.

It feels good when he suddenly starts coughing on his sandwich. Technically, when a person is coughing they're not really choking per se and don't need help. Amy brings her fist down hard on his back anyway.

Loki snickers, and then sputters a bit more.

With an exasperated sigh, Amy picks up the milk, spears it with a straw and hands it in his direction. Loki doesn't take it from her hand; instead he just sips from the straw. Finished, he leans back and starts eating again, plate on his lap. Instead of a thank you, he gives Amy a cheeky grin. She narrows her eyes at him.

Raising an eyebrow, he glances to the space beside him on the bed. "Sit down. It makes me feel tired just watching you stand there."

Amy pauses for a moment but then she sits down and watches him eat, occasionally holding up the milk for him to sip. Despite his tactless joke, she's happy and relieved. She lets out a sigh.

"What?" says Loki, setting the sandwich down.

A helicopter passes very close again, and Amy waits until it's gone to answer his question.

"I was so worried about you," she says. "They gave the order to evacuate the Loop. But every time I roused you, all you would say was how hungry you were, and then I would give you a sandwich and some milk and you would pass out again." Just saying the words out loud makes the gnawing feeling in her stomach that has haunted her since they arrived in his home come back.

Loki takes another bite of the sandwich and swallows it fast. "The Loop is being evacuated?"

Amy nods. "When I last checked the Internet, even though the fighting and fires have been contained." With a shaky little breath, she adds, "And they've killed all the trolls."

His body goes stiff. "The Internet—on your phone! We'll be traced!"

"No," she says quickly, putting a hand on his leg without thinking. Loki follows the motion with his eyes. Realizing how inappropriate the gesture is she lifts the hand fast and says, "I lost my phone in the fire. The Internet on your computer."

Loki blinks, and then scowls. "How did you log onto onto my computer? It's unhackable!"

Amy smirks and stifles a laugh. "Remember that lecture you gave me about humans being stupid because we use passwords instead of pass phrases?"

His eyes narrow and she barely stifles a snicker. "You're right," she says. "'The pink hadrosaur jumps over 13 purple griffins in the icebox' is impossible to forget." Though she'd been surprised that he'd used proper grammar.

"Clever girl." Loki says. He says it like 'I hate you' and she can't help grinning. Sinking back into the pillows, he puts the plate aside and rubs his stomach. "I'm still so hungry."

Remembering his nearly barren kitchen, Amy shifts uncomfortably. "That was the last of the bread … "

Tilting his head to the side Loki says, "In the drawer in the nightstand there are some chocolate Lindt balls."

Nodding, Amy slides off the bed and pulls a bag of the candies from the drawer. She hands him one of the little foil wrapped balls, but Loki fumbles with it helplessly. "I don't seem to be recovering as quickly as I thought," he says softly.

"Hold on, I'll help," she says, feeling concern rise again. Unwrapping the candy, she leans very close and holds the chocolate to his mouth.

As Loki takes it from her he just barely brushes her fingers with his lips. They're soft and warm—and make her go ridiculously warm.

Swallowing, he smiles softly. "Thank you, Amy." With a deep breath, he says,"May I have more?"

Amy quickly offers him another and looks away when his lips brush her fingers, again. Hopefully, he can't see her blush.

"So," she says, pulling her hand away too fast. "You lied

when you said you can't teleport."

Chewing his chocolate, Loki gives her a smirk and raises an eyebrow.

"Not that I'm complaining or anything," she adds hastily.

Licking his lips, Loki opens his mouth and looks at the bag. Taking the hint, she retrieves another chocolate, talking to distract herself from how close he is and how soft his lips are. "Where did we go, when we were in between here-and-there?"

Loki tilts his head. "We were nowhere. We call it the In-Between. It is beyond the universe."

Amy tilts her head, her mind spinning with every Star Trek episode she's ever watched, her embarrassment blessedly melting away as her curiosity increases. "If it is beyond the universe, how do we get there? I mean, the universe is billions of light years wide. Or is it a sort of other dimension of some kind? Or a parallel universe without … stuff?"

Loki stares at her a moment. "That is one theory," he says.

"Why did I hear Beatrice's voice?" she asks, her heart catching a little at the memory.

Loki's face gets hard. "Because you were hallucinating—starved for oxygen. And you were about a quarter second from death in the vacuum." He rubs his eyes, and Amy doesn't think she's imagining it when she sees him shiver.

"We both were," he whispers.

He sounds so tired and so old.

Amy swallows. He may have lied to her, but when it counted he'd been there for her. Wasn't that always the case with him? "Would you like another chocolate?" she asks weakly.

He smiles, and it goes all the way to his eyes. "Yes, please."

Amy unwraps a chocolate with unsteady hands. As she reaches to him, it falls from her fingers.

Before she can react, Loki catches it mid-air, puts it back in her hand, and then guides her hand to his mouth. This time he wraps his mouth around her fingers, sucking the chocolate off with a slow warm, wet pop, and then gives her a leering grin. She gasps, uncomfortably aroused and embarrassed. She stares at her fingers in a daze for a moment. And then her lips curl, and her skin goes hot. Anger washes through her. Lifting her hand she smacks him across the jaw. "You jerk!" she hisses. "I was worried about you!"

Sitting up and rubbing his chin, Loki smiles. "Well, now you don't have to."

Amy shoves him so hard, he almost falls down. "My city is under attack! Do you hear the helicopters?" She punches his shoulder. "The Loop has been on fire, trolls are popping up under bridges, and I've stayed here with you!"

Smirking, Loki catches her fist—so she hits him with the other. "I've been scared to stay and scared to leave!"

Smile fading, Loki catches her other wrist, but she keeps yelling. "Scared that if I called for help ADUO would get you … Do you know what ADUO … what Jameson would do to you?" She trembles, imagining Loki in a dark cell, being shoved under water again and again. "I don't even know … maybe water-boarding, or experiments, or … or … "

Before she knows what is happening, Loki's pulls her wrists to his chest so hard her body follows. "Shhhhh … shhhhh … " He says. With a snarl, she twists in his arms, her eyes prickling but no tears falling.

"I am sorry," he whispers. "Forgive me." Dropping her wrists, his arms reach around her back. Pulling her close, he drops his chin to the top of her head.

With an angry yell, she butts her head against his shoulder. The arms around her back tighten. "I always push too far," he whispers. "I'm sorry."

He sounds so sincere. Amy huffs out a breath and Loki's hands make small circles on her back. She'd been so afraid, in the fire, in the In-Between, and waiting for him to wake up. She swallows and remembers the fear in his voice when he found her, the shiver when he said they almost died.

It suddenly feels so good just to be held. Almost against her volition, her body relaxes against him. His body isn't bulky like Thor's, but he isn't soft; beneath her she feels nothing but muscle, and sinew and bone. And Frost Giant or not, he's warm. Murmuring something, Loki runs a hand gently through her hair.

Closing her eyes, she takes a sharp breath and then sneaks her hands under his arms to his back and squeezes tight. Loki kisses the crown of her head and heat rushes from where his lips touched to the tips of her toes.

Pulling back from her, just a little, he meets her eyes. His lips are quirked in a half smile.

Kissing her brow he says softly, "Thank you." Pressing another kiss to her forehead he says, " … for staying."

He pulls back again, and she meets his gaze. She can feel her heart beating in her chest. The air between them feels denser. There is still a quirk to his lips but his eyes are very serious. He traces a finger from her forehead down her nose. She doesn't know why she does it, but when he reaches her lips she closes her eyes and kisses his fingertip.

When she opens her eyes the quirk on his lips is gone. He's going to kiss her. She's sitting in Loki's apartment, in his bed, and she's not naive enough to think that it will just end in kissing. She should get up right now.

She doesn't move. She can't move.

Loki leans forward and presses his lips to hers, and she freezes in shock—not at the kiss, but at how soft the kiss is. For some reason she just thought he'd be all teeth and tongue.

He pulls away and her eyes open; she hadn't realized she'd closed them.

"And thank you for making me sandwiches," Loki says, a smile in his voice. Amy's mouth drops in a small 'o'. He kisses her lightly again. And then once more. On the third time Amy finds herself responding. She closes her eyes and feels his tongue dart over her lips, gently as if asking for permission. His hands dart over her shoulders, and his fingers graze the neck of the robe, a silent request to pull the barrier away.

She should get up, she should back away and stammer excuses ...

One of his hands drops from her neckline and smoothes down her side and she shivers.

Maybe she should just do it, have sex with Loki and get it out of her system. Sex is all anticipation and then inevitable let down. On the plus side, when it's over, she won't be tempted again, her curiosity will be quelled.

Slipping his hands down and around her backside, Loki pulls her onto his lap.

She gasps, feeling him beneath her, warm and solid, alive and real.

He looks at her for just a moment, his face very serious, his eyes dark.

"Yes?" she whispers, an answer or a question, or just a gasp, she's not really sure. They should talk about this, about the fact that she's on the pill and—

Loki's lips are on hers a moment later and she forgets everything else.

CHAPTER 5

Lying back on Loki's bed, Amy stares at the ceiling. It's still illuminated by the soft yellow reading light on the nightstand.

Her body is humming and she feels like an idiot. Not for sleeping with Loki, but for the two miserable pathetic relationships she'd endured—one for a whole year—exchanging a tedious activity for companionship and affection. She'd thought they were nice guys, but it's occurring to her now that they were just selfish pricks with … with … selfish pricks!

Beside her Loki lies on his side, eyes closed, a smug smile on his face. One very warm, very naked leg goes over her stomach, an arm goes over her chest. Both limbs are too heavy, and both are very welcome.

It nearly undoes her. She licks her lips. "You don't seem like the snuggling type," she says. Bad boys are not supposed to snuggle.

"Mmmmmm … it's just foreplay," he says, a smile audible in his voice.

That makes her body go warm again. There will be more? She blinks up at the ceiling, afraid to look at him.

It worked. Sex never works for her. Up until today she thought she was broken.

The hand across her chest moves to rub her shoulder. Leaning in, Loki whispers in her ear. "Did you enjoy yourself?"

Amy's eyes go wide and she squeezes the thigh that is across her stomach with both hands. Turning to him she says, "I thought you knew I did?"

Gray eyes gleaming, he gives her a trademark smirk. And then his face softens. Still smiling, but not as sharply he shrugs. "It's always nice to hear."

Unable to help herself, she kisses him. His response is soft—and sleepy. When he pulls away his eyes are already closed. Apparently, magic doesn't extend to god-like stamina, or maybe he's just used too much magic of late.

Loki gives her shoulder a final squeeze, and then she watches the familiar pattern of his muscles trembling and relaxing as he falls back to sleep. She fights the urge to run her hands through his hair. Instead she traces the line of his nose and the crease of his slightly too thin lips with her eyes.

She remembers how happy she'd felt at the pub with her friends from college. How he just seemed to fit. Right now, his face smoothed by sleep, a ghost of a smile still on his lips, he doesn't look like a magical being who's lost wives and children and is bent on destroying another world. He looks like a guy just a little older than she is. She watches him for a long time. She's so thirsty it's uncomfortable and preventing sleep, but she just doesn't want to move.

At last she gives in, struggles out from under his limbs, and goes to the washroom. When she comes back she finds Loki has stolen her pillow and has it wrapped in the death grip he had on her. She snorts. Thief.

Lying back down on the bed again, she pulls the white fluffy duvet up to her chin and stares at him some more, unwilling to turn off the light. His thick ginger hair is in need of a trim, and with a messy mop on his head he looks so normal, so human, and just as vulnerable as anyone else when he's sleeping.

Amy closes her eyes for just a moment, feeling warm and content. And then a woman's voice crackles in the room around her. "Odin, so help me! By the Norns, if that's you in my bed I will cut off your cock—again!"

Amy's eyes fly open. The white duvet under her fingers is now a heavy gold brocade coverlet. She sits up with a start. She's on a bed in an opulent room with furniture that looks vaguely Asian. Everywhere are fabrics of deep reds, blues and golds. The bed beside her is empty, but standing in front of her is a tall woman with gray eyes, red hair and a whip-like figure. She's wearing a tight, blue, short sleeve top that stretches down to a full orange skirt. In one hand she holds a wickedly-curved knife.

Her eyes narrow when she sees Amy. "Who are you … and why are you in my bed?"

Amy yanks the coverlet a little closer. The woman isn't speaking English or Jotunn, but Amy understands. "Amy Lewis … I ummm … think I may have come here by accident … I'm really sorry," she answers automatically in the woman's own language.

"Lewis…Never heard of you," says the woman. Eyes

narrowing, she gives Amy a leer, and then bending down takes the bottom of the duvet in her hands and gives it a wicked yank. The fabric leaves Amy's fingers so quickly she swears she's still holding it. She opens her fingers in surprise.

The woman looks at her naked body and licks her lips. Waggling her eyebrows she says, "Nice tits."

Amy swallows. Sleeping with Loki is not a good way to pursue 'normal.'

The sound of an incoming text wakes Steve up. He opens his eyes to the glow of streetlights, unfamiliar shadows, musty air, and the whoosh of a heater. He is on a too-small couch, and the pain in his neck as much as his phone is telling him to get up.

The phone buzzes again. Fumbling with it he sees his ex-wife Dana's name in the caller ID. He lets out a breath of air. Dana is with Claire up in Lake Forest—far enough away to be safe. He looks at the time on the phone. It's just past 6 a.m., too early to call unless ... Claire has run away to the train station and tried to come down to see him on her own before. Feeling a dread more potent than he felt in Afghanistan or battling trolls, he sits up quickly and reads:

Daddy

He shakes his head. Claire has 'borrowed' her mother's phone again. Steve types quickly. *Yes, Honey. Where are you?*

Home mom's sleeping pops on the screen and Steve's body sags with relief. And then on the screen he reads, *Where are you?* Steve lifts his head in the almost darkness and looks around the shadowy room. ADUO's building is no longer safe and they had to move their offices. They've taken over some floors in the Illinois Continental Bank Building. They're right across the street from CBOE now, and by the sounds of things outside the office door, they're still moving in.

In my office, he types back.

Safe? Claire types.

Steve looks at a shadow hanging on the back of the door. It's the combat gear he wore yesterday, helpfully supplied by the National Guard. It's only stained with a little troll blood. But the boots—he stares at where they sit beneath the uniform. They are caked with mud and blood and substances he'd rather not identify.

Yep. Steve types.

Claire's response is instantly on the screen. *I saw fighting and monsters on tv*

Time to change the tone. *I'm stuck doing paperwork. But I did get hurt.* Steve types.

What happnd? Isit bad?

Papercut. Steve responds.

Dad! Steve can see her scrunching up her nose and making a disapproving face at him.

Another text pops on the screen. *See you this weekend?*

Steve stares at the words, and then looks to the dirty boots. *Sure will*, he types, without any idea if it's true.

Mom up. Gotta go.

Steve stares at the screen a moment more, and then lifts his head. He's relieved that Claire is safe and that the conversation is over, and bereft at the same time.

Rubbing his eyes he takes a deep breath and inhales the smell of antiseptic soap from the gym a few doors down. Standing up he goes to the combat gear. He has a feeling he'll need it.

A few minutes later, he opens the office door and his senses are assailed by lights and activity. Steve's temporary office is at the edge of a large room. In the middle of the room there is a central stairwell where Steve sees men and women carrying hospital equipment to the floor above. This floor has been turned into HQ. FBI and National Guard troops are moving furniture, manning phones, and are stationed around laptops.

Stepping out of his office, Steve heads towards a short, older man of Filipino descent at the center of most of the motion in the room. It's General Bautista of the Illinois National Guard. General Bautista is just about the only thing that has gone right in the last 24 hours. Pragmatic, experienced, and competent, he's taken the whole "yes, magic is real and your government has been hiding its existence from you" in stride. He may be pissed—Steve would be—but instead of fighting with Steve's people, he's ordered his men to help get civilians out of the Loop and has been receptive to ADUO's insights into how to most effectively combat trolls.

"Mayor Ronnie is asking for a meeting," someone says to Bautista.

Steve runs his tongue over his teeth to keep from saying something he'll regret. The move by the governor to send in the guard is turning into an ill-timed tug-of-war between the mayor and governor.

"Tell him I'm busy," says Bautista. He pauses to nod at Steve and then bends over a map of the city. All around, members of the guard and FBI mill on the floor together. Thor is sitting on a desk, arms crossed. Jameson is nowhere to be seen. By Bautista's side, Stodgill says, "The Mayor is requesting that the police and fire department be given control of containment and the Guard be withdrawn."

That doesn't bode well.

Bautista grunts. "When the Governor calls us back, we'll leave."

"Another troll spotted in the parking lot across from the Holy Name Cathedral!" one of Steve's guys says, ear to a phone.

"That's farther north than anything so far … " someone says.

For a moment all eyes in the room flit between the General and Steve.

"And the fifth in 24 hours," Steve says.

"No, Sir, the sixth. One appeared while you were asleep," says the agent with the phone.

Steve sucks in a breath.

"My men handled it," says Bautista.

"Mind handling this one, too?" says Steve. What he needs to do can't wait any longer.

"My pleasure," says Bautista.

As the Guard moves into action, Steve takes a digital tablet from the agent. He checks his email. Brett traced the IP address of the computer Amy used to a proxy server in the Czech Republic. Brett also hacked into her account. Besides sending a note to the office, she sent one to a neighbor asking her to watch after her dog Fenrir and her 'unusual' pet mouse Mr. Squeakers who'd gotten loose the night before. Steve tilts his head at memory of Fenrir, the ugliest dog he'd ever seen—and remembers her rescue of a pigeon his first day on the job as Acting Director of the Chicago Branch of ADUO. Her taste in pets is as unfortunate as her taste in friends.

Shaking his head, Steve hits a few buttons and navigates to several secure files. Some interrogations have already begun on the few elves they captured. At what Steve reads his eyebrows go up. The elves are very helpful ... but there is one question that causes them to shut down. He blinks. Two have even died—not violently, or by tearing out their eyes. Quietly, with no trace of magic, or known poison, and after apologizing profusely for 'the pain we've caused your people.' It's eerie, and makes Steve's blood go a little cold.

Scowling, Steve looks down a long hallway towards an elf no one has interrogated yet. Steve starts to leave the room, tablet in hand. And then thinking better of it, he says, "Thor, come with me."

Together they walk towards the office's copy room. Lifting an eyebrow at the big man, Steve says, "We're going to talk to the prisoner. Don't ask him who he works for. Apparently they die when asked that. Any idea why?"

Thor's eyebrows rise. "I will not ask it of him."

It's not an answer, but they're already at the copy room door. Two FBI men are guarding the entrance. Steve nods at one and he opens the door. Together Thor and Steve enter the cramped room. One small light is on above a utility sink. The elf that Steve apprehended earlier is sprawled out on his side on the floor, apparently asleep, hands handcuffed behind his back. Steve turns on the overhead lights and the elf scrambles up against the wall.

"Time for our talk," says Steve. He'd wanted to do this earlier, but after the fire, an attempted theft of Cera, elves, and the trolls, he'd needed a bit of a nap. Steve could have left the interrogation to someone else, but there was no way Steve was missing this.

The elf stares at Thor in a look of pure terror and swallows. Good. Not only will Thor be able to tell Steve if the elf is outright bull-shitting, but the warrior will also make a damn good bad cop.

"Come on," Steve says, going behind the elf and pushing him by his bound hands. "We're doing this right."

Steve steers the elf, who is shaking like a leaf, down the hall to a makeshift interrogation room. There is no one-way mirror, but speakers and cameras are in every corner of the small white room. The only furniture is a table with two chairs on either side. Nodding at one side of the table, Steve says, "Sit."

The elf hastens to obey.

Steve doesn't bother to sit down on the chair on the other side. Leaning on the table he smiles. "Mind telling us your name?"

Swallowing, the elf says, "It's Liddell."

Steve straightens and tilts his head. It's the truth, he knows it from Lewis's account of Alfheim. Liddell had been heading to the dark lands with his wife to escape the child price. Apparently, in the land of the "light" elves, as Thor calls them, the queen is very particular about who can reproduce. Before any family can have a new child, someone else in the family has to agree to die. A logical precaution in a race that is immortal by default—but still harsh. Offspring who enter the world otherwise are confiscated, the parents punished.

"It wasn't supposed to be like this," Liddell says, voice shaking. "We were going to wait for the week's end when there would be less people. We … I didn't want to hurt anyone."

"Liar!" says Thor from behind Steve's shoulder. "You want to acquire Cera so you can confront your queen and plunder the land of the Light Elves! How is that not hurting anyone?"

Sucking in a deep breath, Liddell snaps. "No! We want

Cera so that we can create a void like Asgard has! So we can dispose of the queen's dark spells before they poison our lands."

Steve blinks. He remembers the mention in Lewis's report of how the Light Elves dumped spent magic into the river that ran towards the "Dark Lands."

Thor takes a step forward. Liddell kicks backwards so that his chair slides across the floor.

Straightening, Thor says, "You cannot believe this man, Agent Rogers. He is a traitor to his queen."

"I speak the truth!" Liddel says, half standing. "All family but my wife and our son live in the queen's lands! That is true for all the Dark Elves! How could we wish to see them plundered?"

"You are a traitor to your queen!" Thor roars.

"I don't believe in queens or kings anymore!" Liddell shouts. "Or in being a slave!"

And that hits a bit close to home. Steve feels his jaw tighten.

"Know your place!" shouts Thor.

"Both of you be quiet," Steve says, lowering his voice to a whisper.

Thor looks at him angrily. Liddell's eyes flit to Steve, and then go back to Thor. His frame slumps a bit.

Steve lets the silence continue for a bit longer than is comfortable even to him.

Crossing his arms, Thor makes a rumbling noise. Liddell starts to shuffle his feet.

Sitting down at the chair across the table from Liddell, Steve says. "When did elves first start coming to Chicago?"

Liddell meets his eyes. "I have only been visiting since the arrival of Cera."

Steve tilts his head.

Looking down, Liddell says, "The first new gates between our realms opened approximately four years or so ago. We have come on exploratory missions since that time."

Steve leans forward. "Four years? But Lo—" Steve pauses for a breath. "But we had it on good authority that the gates were being opened by Cera, and she's only been here a few months."

Liddell swallows. "That is what I know … " Looking away he says, "More gates are opening now with greater frequency."

"Because of your sorcery!" says Thor.

Liddell twists his head to sneer at Thor. "If only! We wouldn't need Cera if we were strong enough to make our own gates!"

"Stop it!" Steve shouts. Turning to Liddell he says, "We've had visits from six trolls in the past 24 hours. Do you know what is going on?"

"Cera is getting stronger," says Liddell, his brow furrowing. "The containment fields can't restrain all of her … her power is infinite."

Steve rolls his eyes and snaps. "How can infinite power become more infinite! All our readings suggest that the containment field isn't breaking down, so what's going on!"

Liddell's mouth drops. He appears genuinely stumped. Eyes wide, he stammers. "I'm much better at the practical application of magic than theory."

Rubbing the bridge of his nose, Steve stands from his chair. Turning his back on Liddell, he walks across the room. If Liddell is lying, he's a very good liar. He has all the signs of truthfulness: he isn't leading with qualifying statements like, "in all honesty." His eye contact is inconsistent—liars tend to overdo eye contact. He's anxious to be helpful. He's furious when accused by Thor of wrongdoing. And usually liars smile at the success of their deceit.

"Don't leave me with the Asgardian!" the elf cries.

It's only then that Steve realizes he's walking towards the door, though he had no intention of walking out. Turning, he tilts his head. Moving quietly to the table he sits down. "There is someone else I'm guessing could tell me more. Someone you know, Liddell."

Liddell's eyes widen a fraction, and his throat bobs as he swallows. So yes. And probably the same person the elves are dying to protect.

Leaning on his elbows, Steve speaks slowly and carefully. "If I asked you directly, is there some sort of magic that makes you commit suicide?"

Liddell huffs a laugh. "No, but if you tried to force me to say, I would stop my own heart rather than divulge."

"Magically?" Steve asks.

Liddell huffs again and looks down. "I'm over 1,000 years old. In that amount of time even a human would be able to learn to stop their heart at will."

"Why can't you tell us who you work for?" Steve asks.

Liddell blinks at him, for a moment looking like he doesn't understand the question. And then his eyes go to Thor. "Isn't it obvious?"

It's Steve's turn to be in the dark. "Thor?"

Liddell's eyes narrow. "Of course you wouldn't understand." He takes a breath. "Odin will not attack any who defy him on Earth. The elves don't know why. We think that some sort of deal was made. With whom, and for what, we don't know. But Odin doesn't attack the people on your world who help supply us with your weapons. On our side we have to hide from Heimdall's gaze." Bending his head he says. "It is magically … expensive … and something I don't have the knowledge to do."

Steve tilts his head. "But he hasn't attacked the dark lands yet?"

Liddell shakes his head. "If Odin launched a full-scale attack on the Dark Realms, as you call them, the warring factions would unite." Glancing at Thor, he meets Steve's gaze. "We might not win but we would make the Asgardians pay dearly."

Steve looks at Thor. The large man is looking at the elf, face hard. Catching Steve's glance, Thor says, "He speaks truly."

"But if Odin knew exactly who his foe in our realm was … " Liddell's voice trails off.

Steve sits back in his chair. "He'd send in a strike team."

Liddell nods. Thor shifts in his seat. The elf's eyes slide to Thor. "Agent Rogers, why don't you ask the mighty Thor what the strike team would do to the elves they captured?"

"Shut up, elf!" Thor says.

Liddell begins to laugh. "Why, Thor? Are you ashamed?" Turning to Steve, the elf snarls. "Those who were not killed would be violated. The men and boys castrated, and all sold into slavery. You can see why I'd rather die."

Steve looks at Thor. Jaw tight, Thor won't meet his gaze. Nor does he dispute Liddell's words. Steve sighs. He's not really surprised. Still, he's disgusted. Goddamn space Vikings.

Everyone in the room is silent for a moment. And then Thor says, "Loki would know why the fabric of space-time is being torn with more frequency."

Narrowing his eyes, Liddell says, "You can't trust Loki."

Thor looks about to say something, but Steve cuts him off. "Yes, well, right now Loki is the only hope for your friend Amy Lewis."

Liddell swallows.

Steve's phone beeps. It's a text from Bryant. Steve clicks to it and reads: Two spikes in unusually high magic readings detected in the building during attack. About time Lewis disappeared. Too much interference from fires to triangulate.

Liddell shuffles his feet and looks down. "Loki is the Destroyer, she is in grave danger," he says softly.

Bringing a fist down so hard the table cracks, Thor shouts, "You fool! Loki fixes everything!"

The woman in front of Amy smiles. Raising her hand, she brings down the knife hard, imbedding it in the baseboard where it reverberates with a twang.

Amy's eyes go wide and she lets out a breath she didn't know she was holding … only to suck the breath in fast when the woman falls onto the bed on all fours and starts crawling up towards her.

"You're pretty, human," she says with a smirk. "How come I haven't seen you before?"

Heedless of modesty, Amy scampers off the bed. "To answer that question, I need to know where I am."

The woman's brow constricts and she raises herself to her knees. "How curious. You're not even lying."

"Umm … Nope," says Amy, looking frantically around the room. There is a divan, a bed, and a nightstand with a small white book upon it. The ceiling has intricate scalloped moulding. There is a round door set into a deep pocket in the wall, with ornately carved edges. There are bay windows, all covered with gauze curtains. She can't see outside, but she gets the impression of sunlight. Where is Loki?

"Asgard," says the woman. "You may not recognize the style of decoration. It's New Vanir, in honor of our guests, the beautiful Freyja and her oh-so-noble brother Frey." The last words come out a hiss.

Amy's breath starts coming fast. Swallowing her fear, she turns to the woman and tries to assess the situation. The woman's clothes are elaborately embroidered with gold. The room doesn't look like any sort of prison.

"You're cute when you're frightened, Amy," says the woman, slinking off the bed. "But you don't have to be. I'm very nice."

Making a dive for the bed, Amy grabs the heavy golden coverlet and wraps it around herself. The woman snickers. "There's no need for modesty now."

Amy turns to the woman, now just a foot away, and swallows. "I'm flattered really ... I didn't catch your name?"

"Lopt," she says with a toothy smile.

Alarm bells start going off in Amy's mind. Backing towards one of the windows, Amy says, " ... but I'm sort of in a relationship ... "

Still smiling, the woman shrugs. "So am I!" But Amy can't help but notice the shadow that crosses the woman's features.

Lopt's smile tightens. "Or I was ... or am ... but Odin sent him to Vanaheim ... with that buggerer Mimir." Lips curling, Lopt twists her body and reaches out. The knife embedded in the baseboard flies through the air into her hand. With a huff, she starts cleaning her nails with the tip. "If Mimir hurts him … I'll do worse than I did to Odin." A crease forms between her brows. "And Mimir can't reattach his bits."

"Hoenir!" Amy says. "Your lover is Hoenir! The Vanir-Aesir war ended with a prisoner exchange—Hoenir and Mimir for Freyja and Frey! Mimir does all the talking for Hoenir and the Vanir get so pissed they chop off Mimir's head, but then Odin reanimates it!"

Lopt's eyes go to hers. "Oh, I can only hope." Her eyes narrow. "Well, for the first part."

Amy's mouth gapes. "That was at the beginning of Asgard." Has she gone back in time?

Amy runs to the window and makes to pull back the gauzy curtain, but it dissolves at her touch. For a moment she's staring at nothing but gray swirling fog. But then Lopt approaches and a scene forms in the gray. Lopt's room overlooks a city. In the distance Amy can see an enormous wall under construction. There are men atop, and below are horses with carts, busily pulling stones. None of the carts have drivers. One horse is going among the others nipping at their flanks.

"The stallion leading the animals is Svaðilfari. The damned beast is going to see that the wall is completed too soon," says Lopt.

Amy turns to her, but Lopt is looking away, distracted by the sound of footsteps. There is a bang at the door, and another woman's voice, "Lopt, let me in!"

Lopt walks away from Amy. As she does, Amy glances out the window briefly—the fog has returned.

"I'm coming, Freyja," Lopt says in a bored voice. Amy

turns to see Lopt not going to the door at all, but frantically looking under the bed and behind furniture. "Norns," she mumbles. "I gave Frigga my cloak as a peace offering. As though I invited her husband to try and rape me."

At that moment the door bursts open. A woman with long, straight pink hair, blue eyes, and peaches and cream skin stands in the entryway. The woman's face is so beautiful, it is almost painful to look at. She wears copper armor from head to toe. If its proportions are to be believed, she is built like an Olympic volleyball player, but with more bust. In one hand she is holding a sword.

"Ah, Freyja!" says Lopt, straightening and casting a winning smile. "How nice to see you."

"It's too late, Lopt! You treacherous snake!" Freyja says, stepping into the room.

Amy blinks and remembers where she's heard the name Lopt—it's another name for Loki.

"We need the wall; the Jotunn are amassing troops!" Lopt cries, running behind Amy. "No one else had any better ideas!"

Raising her sword, Freyja says, "You wagered my body to a common builder! A Frost Giant!"

Lopt shouts over Amy's shoulder. "He wasn't supposed to win the wager!"

Amy looks sideways at the woman using her as a human shield. Lopt's face is panicked, her red hair askew. In the myths it was Loki who made the wager between the Aesir and the builder for Freyja's hand. In the end he wound up turning himself into a mare, luring the stallion away, and presenting Odin with the magical, eight-legged steed Sleipnir ten months later. Of course, Loki is incapable of shape-changing, so that story is just a tale, a myth.

Stepping forward, quickly, Freya raises the sword until it's just a few finger widths from Amy's neck.

"Ummm … " says Amy. "Maybe we can talk about this?"

Freyja doesn't seem to see or hear her. "You'll pay for this," says Freyja.

"I gave you my oath I would take care of it," Lopt says. "You know I always keep my oaths."

"I know you're a liar!" says Freyja.

There is a crackle around the room, like thousands of twigs breaking, and Amy looks down to see flames rise around her body. She gasps and then realizes they're passing through her, without burning … but Freyja screams as the flames catch her hair. Instead of stopping to put it out, Freyja charges forward, her body passing through Amy harmlessly, but contacting with Lopt's with a loud thud. Turning, Amy sees Freyja's sword is through Lopt's abdomen, pinning her to the wall like a butterfly.

Running forward, Amy tries to pull Freyja away but her hands pass through the Amazonian woman as though Amy is a ghost.

The flames leap in Freyja's hair, and with a curse she pulls her sword from Lopt and storms from the room.

Lopt's body sags to the floor. Her eyes are open, staring at Amy.

"Why are you here?" Lopt whispers.

Shaking her head, Amy pulls off the duvet. Maybe she can use it to stop the bleeding? But as she tries to put it on Lopt, it passes through the woman. "I don't know, I don't know," Amy says.

Lopt closes her eyes. "It's nice not to be alone … " her

brow constricts, her eyes close. When she opens them they're completely black, as is her hair. Her skin is rapidly turning blue. Smirking at Amy, she looks down at her stomach. "Wyrm balls," she mutters.

Standing, heavy gold brocade in hand, Amy looks around. The flames are rapidly approaching, though she feels no heat. The world is shrinking and going black. Her gaze falls on the nightstand and the little white book there. And then all is darkness …

Amy blinks her eyes and finds herself standing in Loki's spartan bedroom again. The gold brocade coverlet is gone, and in her hands is Loki's heavy white duvet. Her eyes are on the nightstand and the little white book sitting there. Loki is on the bed, his skin blue, hair black, and black eyes wide open, limbs still in a death grip on the pillow.

Amy walks forward. "Loki, are you all right?" she asks.

He turns his head to her, brow furrowed. Shaking his head, he says, "I just had the strangest dream."

Amy swallows. "About Lopt and Freyja?"

Meeting her eyes, he says, "I … I … don't remember."

Sitting up, he looks her up and down. "Why do you have the duvet wrapped around you?" He snickers. "There's no need for modesty now."

Amy's lips tighten in consternation. At her unamused expression, Loki lifts an eyebrow, and then his gaze falls to his blue hands. Holding them before his eyes, his lips curl slightly, but he's silent.

Going to sit on the bed beside him, Amy says, "So, do you project your dreams often?"

He meets her gaze, his face so composed, his features so flat he looks almost angry; and she knows he remembers his dream, and knows that she knows it.

Running a hand nervously through his black hair, he looks away. "If I did, it would be a first."

He's so lost. Leaning forward, Amy wraps an arm around him and drops her head to his shoulder. There is a long moment when he does nothing, but then she feels his arm wrapping around her back. She feels like they're having a real moment, that even if he's magical, and older than dirt, that maybe she can be something important to him.

Loki kisses the top of her head, and her heart almost melts. And then he sneaks a hand around and tweaks a nipple. Voice half between a laugh and a challenge he says, "Let's have kinky blue sex!"

CHAPTER 6

Loki projects another dream later that night. But this time Amy knows it's a dream. She can still feel Loki's body wrapped around her even as the room transforms itself into a tiny hut, and she finds herself lying on what looks like a floor, illusions of black-haired children, with full lips and small noses, sleeping beside her.

A man and a woman, both Asian looking and dressed in simple, threadbare clothing, are speaking by the doorway.

"Yuki, you cannot go," says the man. He looks worn and older than the woman, but he has a symmetrical face and a strong jaw. He is very handsome, even with slightly graying hair, and lines on his forehead and around his eyes.

The woman by contrast is youthful, with a narrow chin that gives her an almost pixyish appearance. She's very beautiful, but her eyes are too wide, as though she's afraid. "I must go. He's coming for me," the woman whispers.

Amy blinks. They're not speaking English, but she understands them.

"What will I tell the villagers?" the man says, desperation rising in his voice.

"Tell them I am a snow woman, and I had to go home. It's true enough." Bowing her head, the woman says, "Please, Minokichi, they'll kill you and the children."

The man nods, tears in his eyes. The scene fades to black, and Amy's in Loki's room again, on his bed. He's still asleep. She doesn't wake him. Eventually she falls asleep, too.

When Amy wakes up again it is in Loki's room. It is darkened by the shades, but she can see afternoon daylight through the cracks. From the other room comes the sound of Loki swearing in another language—she'd guess Russian or Ukrainian. Cera, he's talking to Cera!

A moment later, Loki opens the bedroom door with a bang. "Amy, get up, get dressed! We're leaving."

Amy sits up as Loki strides into the room wearing only his pajama bottoms. Scowling at the space above her head, he starts swearing again, waving his hands, making unfamiliar gestures that Amy doesn't have to recognize to know are obscene.

"Loki, what's going on?' she asks.

Stopping his tirade, he looks at her. He's very close to the bed. His jaw is clenched, his brow furrowed. He's not blue. He raises his hand, and it's hard to tell if he's just gesturing or if he's about to strike her. Amy backs up, but then his eyes go wide, and he shakes himself. He closes his eyes and blue washes over his skin, and his hair turns black.

"I'm not mad at you," he whispers, eyes still closed. He opens them and they're black again. Staring at a space beyond

Amy's shoulder, he sneers for a moment. Taking a deep breath, he turns to her and speaks with what seems like forced calm.

"Amy, the mayor and governor are suggesting that everyone leave the Loop. It's voluntary, but they're sending police and National Guard troops through buildings offering to escort people out. Some police are coming into this building now. I would prefer not to go with them."

Amy blinks. "Well, if it's voluntary … "

"But we still have to leave," he says, stepping quickly onto the bed next to Amy, the bed sinking and creaking with the weight.

Feeling a bit frightened by the rush he's in—not to mention the fact that he's reaching for his sword—she says, "Why?"

Unhooking the sword that is vaguely Asian, he says, "You, because there are multiple troll sightings now, and me because I can't find a single restaurant in a ten-mile radius that will deliver here and I'm hungry! Also … " Narrowing his eyes, he turns his gaze to a corner of the room. "Because Cera is being a whiny, demanding, irrational, bitch!"

Amy swallows at the empty space he's glaring at. She reminds herself he's magical and he sees things she can't see; he is not having an episode of psychosis.

Hopping from the bed, he takes quick strides to the door of the walk-in closet. Opening it he mumbles, "I think that the elves probably let the trolls in to cause chaos while they retreat."

All of his words tumble together. Evacuation. Troll sightings. Retreat.

Hopping from the bed, Amy grabs his robe from the floor, pulls it on as she runs to the door of the bedroom, and walks down the short hallway to the main living area of the apartment.

Loki's living area is a wide open space, larger than four of her apartments put together. Two of the walls are floor to ceiling glass. The other two walls have books lined along the floor. There is a hardly-used-looking very modern kitchen directly to her left as she comes out of the hallway. Camping gear is lined up in front of the island counter that separates the kitchen from the living space. The gear doesn't look like it's been touched since last night when she made sandwiches. There is no furniture other than a desk and computer with three enormous monitors in the living room.

Suddenly needing to know for herself what is going on, Amy goes to the desk. In the background she hears Loki rummaging through his closet, cursing occasionally. Her purse is by the monitor, and she slips it on so she won't forget to take her pill. The jostling from that simple motion causes the monitors to light. There's no password prompt. Obviously Loki was just on his computer. A browser window is open to a website in French. She tilts her head. It looks like it is for a hotel. She looks at the tabs at the top of the browser. There's CNN, and a tab to the window where she was researching Shiva is still open. Her eyes go wide—one of the tabs is for her email. She swore she had closed it.

Clicking to her inbox she sees an unopened message addressed to all "Support Staff and Non-Essential Personnel." Opening it she finds a note ordering clerical workers not to come into work until "further notice." There is nothing personal from Steve, or anyone else at the office. Maybe they don't want her in today? Frowning, she clicks to a new email from her neighbor. It's a little note telling her not to worry about Fenrir or her "special mouse" and makes her sigh with relief.

At that moment, Loki bursts into the room. He's still blue, wearing jeans, a polo and the peacoat he wore the other day. His little white book is poking from a coat pocket and his sword is slung over his shoulder. Seeing her at the computer his lip curls and he almost shouts, "What are you doing?"

Purse sliding awkwardly on her arm, she holds up her hands. "Checking my email. Don't worry, I wouldn't tell them where you are."

He shakes himself and rubs the bridge of his nose. "Of course, I'm sorry ... the police are coming to this floor—thankfully they don't have magic detectors, we have to go." Then he mumbles, "The airports are all full." Turning to empty air he shouts, "Shut up, Cera! You brought this on yourself!"

Thor's words from the day before come back to Amy. "Loki! Cera will control you! Thor told us she would!"

Loki smirks. "She doesn't control me, and I can prove it." Before Amy knows what is happening, he strides over, takes one of her wrists, and pulls her from her seat. Rolling his eyes, Loki says, "Cera thought she'd just ally herself with those elves and I'd be happy to see her when she popped back into my life ... and thinks she can order me around." Meeting Amy's gaze again, he kisses her too hard. His hands go to Amy's waist and then slip down so fast and wrap around her butt she's barely aware of what's going on. Lifting her up like she weighs nothing, Loki says sharply, "Wrap your legs around my waist."

Confused, Amy does what she's told, mostly to keep from falling. In the process, the robe she's wearing falls open to reveal what she's not wearing.

Glancing down, Loki gives a good natured smirk that's mischievous and so him that she smiles.

Pulling her in tight, he whispers in her ear. "I'm about to show you how little Cera controls me. You like French food right? Because I could really use some foie gras and French onion soup."

Amy blinks, "Wha—"

Leaning backwards, as though he's executing a dive, Loki topples them both over. For an instant they are suspended in midair, and then they are in the cold nothing of the In-Between.

Moving Amy through the In-Between is taxing, but this time Loki is refreshed. He's able to pull them from the vacuum before the blackness and cold have even really registered. But even as the feeling of victory rises, another cold wraps around him. Opening his eyes he sees Amy, but she's distorted and out of focus. He opens his mouth—and sucks in a lungful of water.

"Loki!" he hears, as though from far away. He's blinded by bubbles, her legs are sliding out from under him, and small hands are pulling him up by the shoulders. Hacking and coughing up water, with Amy raining blows on his back, he surveys their surroundings. They're in a shallow rectangular fountain in the garden of his intended target. He winces and then coughs a bit more water from his lungs. The fountain wasn't here the last time he visited, and it really should have been emptied earlier in the season. Amy is yelling at him. "What the Hell are you doing! Where are we? Why is it late afternoon?"

Wiping his mouth, in frigid water up to his stomach, Loki starts to laugh. Wrapping his arms around Amy, he pulls her in for a hug, oddly warmed by her ferocity.

This morning he'd woken to the mist of the World Seed hovering about his bed. "Well, you'd better kill her," Cera had said. "She'll let ADUO know where you live, and that you can teleport."

For a frightening moment Loki had seen the convenience of that idea. He even envisioned quietly smothering her beneath his pillow and disposing of her body in the In-Between. He'd bolted out of bed and gone to his computer instead, telling Cera off for being a nag.

He checked Amy's email—he'd discovered all her passwords months ago—and deleted messages from Steve asking her to call in, and from Brett, Bryant and other people at her office. Then he checked all his accounts, and finally, CNN. All that time Cera got more and more insistent. "Kill her. Go to Vanaheim. Kill her, kill her, kill her!"

It had been obnoxious.

Now it will take Cera hours to find them, and he suspects she'll be properly chastised when she does. Loki lets out a happy sigh, even as Amy shakes his shoulders. "Where. Are. We!"

Grinning, he blinks the water from his eyes, checks to see that his hands are peach and not blue, and then shakes his head like a dog. "Paris!" he says, standing up and pulling her up and out of the fountain with him.

"What?" says Amy, stumbling as he pulls her along.

Nodding happily he says, "We can get food!" He needs food. And sleep. Again.

"I'm freezing!" Amy says, gesturing to his robe, wrapped around her shoulders, soaked and hanging open.

Loki runs his tongue over his lips as lasciviously as he can. "We'll check in and warm up."

Pulling back, Amy sputters. "Check in? I'm in a bathrobe and you've got a sword on your back!"

Loki stops and raises an eyebrow. "You're right." He winks. "I knew there was a reason I brought you along." Concentrating, he uses the last bits of magical energy he possesses to will his sword to invisibility, and Amy to appear dry and as though she's wearing a cocktail dress with heels.

Amy surveys her imaginary attire and glares up at him. "The robe had more coverage."

Loki opens his mouth to respond, but before he can she raises her hands and shouts. "Didn't you say teleporting nearly killed us last time?"

Loki opens his mouth again, only to feel one of her fists connect hard with his chest. "And you should have asked!" she shouts.

Smiling, Loki pulls her in for a hug, effectively trapping her fists and muffling her mouth—and giving him someone to lean onto. "I just love to make things difficult," he says, dropping his head on top of hers.

"Greattfff," Amy grumbles.

Loki's smile turns rueful. He can kill for a lot of reasons, betray for a lot of reasons, but convenience apparently isn't one of them.

Loki and Thor are both on one knee, bowing before Odin's throne. Thor holds the spear Gungnir in his outstretched hands as the court looks on. Admiring glances are being shot in Thor's direction, suspicious ones are being leveled at Loki. He makes sure to meet such gazes with an irreverent smirk.

Inside he is fuming, partly at their servile position, partly because Thor is the one presenting the spear. Odin has become such a stickler for pomp and ceremony of late. Although Loki had as much a part or more in recovering Gungnir, it was deemed inappropriate for Loki to be the presenter. But most of all, Loki fumes because of the statue sitting behind him at the entrance of the great hall—a thirty-man-high golden monument in the likeness of Baldur.

Loki's finger nails bite into his palms, and his jaw tightens. Or the perceived likeness of Baldur: beautiful, fit, and wise looking—the way Loki never saw him and everyone else did.

From the throne Odin mumbles some uninspired words of appreciation. Muscles going stiff, mouth threatening to go slack with boredom, Loki scans the room. Everyone in attendance is in black. Even Thor wears a black armband over his armor. It has been nearly a year since Baldur's death and Baldur's glamour has only grown stronger. He is revered now more than ever and Asgard still mourns for him. When Loki complained of it to Thor, the big oaf had said, "Everyone always thinks the best of the dead. Now shut up before someone suspects you played some part in it."

The cold stone floor is biting into his knee. Loki is close to sighing loud enough to be heard, just to give Odin the hint that now is the time to declare the feast and celebration, and to let Loki stand up. He opens his mouth and then catches a flash of green from the corner of his eye. He looks up and sees Nari and Valli slipping through the adults of the court to get closer to the throne. They're dressed in their 'play clothes' and it will be obvious to anyone who looks that they've snuck in. Despite himself,

Loki smiles. Catching his grin, Valli starts jumping up and down and yells, "Father!" his face alight with pride.

Loki feels his smile soften. His boys are monsters, but not so bad.

There are murmurs among the crowd, most in consternation, but beside Loki, Thor gives a friendly chuckle.

From the throne Odin's silence is ominous.

"Escort our guests out," says one of the guards sourly.

Some guards move in and the boys try to dodge them, stepping on toes and elbowing dignitaries in the process. Still, they're quickly apprehended. As the men drag them off by the elbows, Nari shouts. "That's our father! He found Gungnir and Thor helped!"

Loki bites back a cackle. Beside him Thor gives him a gentle nudge in the ribs and a good natured grin. When Loki looks up, Odin is scowling.

The great hall quiets again. Odin mumbles on a bit more. And then the king nods down at Thor. One of the members of the Diar, the council that helps Odin manage Asgard, descends the steps, takes the spear from Thor, and carries it up to Odin. Loki blinks. Odin won't even take a gift from his son? That is a new layer of formality. He feels his skin start to heat.

Scowling, he waits for the king to finally declare the order for the victory feast. It never comes. Instead, Odin stands, bangs the butt end of the spear on the floor, and wearily declares the court dismissed because, "Now is still not the time for revelry."

Loki gets to his feet with Thor, watching Odin and Frigga slowly leave the great Hall. Loki doesn't exit the throne room—despite Thor's entreaties to go to the mead hall. Instead, as soon as he finds himself alone, Loki makes himself invisible and lets himself into Odin's chambers. He goes to the room where he,

Odin, and Hoenir played chess so long ago.

Settling on one of the chairs he sets up the chess pieces and waits.

Loki isn't invisible when Odin enters, but he is covered in shadow. Nonetheless, as soon as Odin comes into the room, he raises Gungnir in Loki's direction, even before the torches in the wall sputter to life.

Smirking up at the king, Loki says, "Thank goodness. I was beginning to think you were as dead as Baldur." Looking at the point of the spear he adds, "I'm glad you like the souvenir."

Thrusting Gungnir's point a little closer to Loki's neck, Odin says, "I should kill you now."

Loki blinks up at him. This isn't an idle threat. Odin is telling the truth. Loki feels a flare of fear rising in his stomach. The pieces on the chessboard abruptly burst into flames. Both Loki and Odin's gaze go to the board, now glowing under the light of 32 improvised candles. Odin waves Gungnir in their direction and they go out.

"What do you want, Loki?" Odin asks, sounding suddenly weary again.

"Why, just to chat," says Loki, spreading his hands and trying to affect an air of nonchalance.

Odin glares at him. "I should call the guards on you."

Placing his feet next to the burnt chess pieces and tipping the chair back onto two legs, Loki sneers. "It's been so long since we really talked. Why, not since ... since my daughter was poisoned by your son."

"I gave you your chance for revenge," Odin growls.

Loki sneers. "You gave me the chance to solve your problems. You were right. If Baldur had taken Nanna, my Frost Giant relatives would be flooding Midgard, probably to set themselves up as gods ... after they attacked Asgard. Double blows to the Aesir's pride."

Banging Gungnir's shaft on the floor, Odin hisses. "Have you no compassion? I and all the realms weep for my son."

Loki rises fast from his chair. "No one mourns for my daughter or my wife!"

Taking a step towards Loki, Odin snarls. "Your wife was weak, your daughter was deformed. My son was different. He was perfect."

Loki's eyes go wide. "He was a lie! His perfection an illusion—even you knew that!"

Odin takes a deep breath. He's so close, Loki can smell mead on his breath.

Straightening, Odin laughs. "Isn't that what all princes are?"

Loki stares at him, unable to find words for his anger and rising dismay.

Odin smiles, and it isn't at all nice. "To maintain order people need myths of perfection. They're grateful for their illusions."

"That's not what they tell me when I'm using magic," Loki snaps.

Narrowing his one eye, Odin snarls. "I don't have time for this. Get. Out."

Loki cannot bring himself to move. He just stares into Odin's one ice-blue eye. His skin goes hot, he hears a crackle, feels heat, and sees light as the chess pieces and the table they sit on burst into flames again.

Scowling, Odin points Gungnir in the fire's direction. The flames quiet, but then Loki hisses. "Do not dismiss me!" and the flames rise again.

Odin turns his head sharply. "You still have two sons and a wife to go home to Loki," he snarls.

Loki's mouth drops and he steps back at the implicit threat.

"Get out of here." Odin says again. He bangs Gungnir on the floor and the flames flicker out.

Loki's body goes cold. He nods differentially at Odin, but can't keep a twisted smirk from his face.

He's just leaving when Odin says, "And Loki … "

Loki turns to see Odin smile at him. "Thanks for the spear."

It has been nearly one rotation of Earth's axis since Loki and the female human disappeared from Chicago. Cera is in a panic. Has he gone off world? She can't follow him there if he has. Not only is she stuck within the Promethean Wire, she doesn't know how. Also, she doesn't have feet. The bodies of the denizens of this planet are awkward, prone to inconvenient cravings and incompatible with large amounts of magic, but how she envies them for their powers of locomotion. She can only travel in her non-corporeal form, and although she knows theoretically she could transverse realms non-corporeally—Odin can do it—she doesn't quite know how to manage it. Odin used his corporeal form to open the gate. And even if the gate was open, maybe her non-corporeal form would get separated from her physical form? How long can the energy of her non-physical self be apart from her physical self? And what if she went the wrong way? What if she got lost?

When Loki rescues her, Cera will be able to use his physical form and his mind and knowledge to open all the world gates, and go wherever she wants … with or without feet. If Loki rescues her. For an instant Cera feels the shell of the Promethean Sphere closing in around her corporeal body. Loki doesn't need her. She felt it when Odin, the-one eyed one, touched her. Loki has been winning against the One-Eyed Preserver for the past 4 billion years when the universe's expansion began to accelerate. Cera's not sure how long 4 billion years are. She has difficulty comprehending linear time, but she thinks it's slightly farther back in time than her landing in the Siberian Tundra in 1908.

Eventually, Loki will win. The universe will reach its outer limit, contract, and bloom anew again —his greatest revolution accomplished! All Loki has to do is wait. And he has so much more patience than Cera … but Cera has things she must do before then, things she must do even before the sun explodes and destroys the Earth and all the humans on the planet. Things she must do for Josef—but doesn't know how to do on her own.

In her cage of Promethean Wire, Cera concentrates and sends her non-corporeal consciousness out over the Earth again, a little to the east of the land that was Josef's. She is about to head north, to Visby, to see if Loki perhaps is traversing the world gate when she feels a tug—a feeling of fraying and disintegration—in the south.

It's Loki! Cera speeds southward. He's in a metropolis of some sort. Within minutes she has found him. She is instantly put out. Speak of inconvenient cravings. Loki is sitting in a bathtub filled with the molecules the humans call soap; it's blooming in bubbles of hydrophillic and hydrophobic abandon. Between Loki's legs, back to his chest, is the female.

"What else did Thor tell you?" Loki is whispering to the female. His eyes flick up to Cera but other than that he doesn't acknowledge her presence.

Cera wasn't awoken by Josef yesterday. Loki is engaging in genetic exchange behaviors. Here. On Earth. While Cera has been so worried he'd left her. How cruel! And he's doing it with the female he speaks with too often. The one without any magic. The one beneath him. She is a problem, Cera's not sure why, she just feels that way. Cera knows a very effective treatment for all problems. "Kill her!" Cera whispers. "Kill her, Loki!"

Loki's hands go to the female's neck. His fingers wrap around her throat. His eyes slide back to Cera and narrow. With a smirk he bends his head and kisses the bones of her spinal column. The girl makes noises that signal receptiveness to genetic exchange.

Cera flares in indignation. Loki isn't as nice to her as the Frost Giants who had tried so hard to rescue her. The Frost Giants would do anything Cera said.

Eyes leaving Cera, Loki whispers, "Tell me, Amy, what did Thor say?"

Ending her receptive noises, she says quietly, "He said that you threw a grenade into a crowd of civilians."

Loki kisses the back of her neck again.

The girl turns in the water. "But I know you would never do that."

Cera swirls in impatience. During a revolution, civilians will perish. It's a fact. One that Josef knew well.

Loki shakes his head. "Amy, in those moments, after my sons disappeared, I was so desperate to follow them." He bows his head. "I thought I threw it at Odin ... but it is possible that I ... missed."

Cera stops her swirling. He's lying. Not only does Cera feel it, she knows it. Odin, the Preserver, wouldn't be hurt by a grenade. But when Odin touched Cera, she saw how put out he was by the death of those 'innocents'.

The girl closes the space between herself and Loki. "It wasn't your fault," she says, wrapping her arms around his shoulders. "It wasn't your fault."

Loki pulls her into his lap. "Thank you, Amy."

Their mouths touch. The receptive noises begin again. Cera settles into the corner, prepared to be very bored, but unwilling to let Loki out of her sight.

And then it hits her. Loki used words to change the girl's mind, to deceive her, to make her like him, and to fulfill his biological imperative. Josef was very good at doing the same. In her corporeal prison Cera pulses with light. In the bathroom, watching Amy and Loki, her non-corporeal form pulses with magic.

Cera's thoughts turn, as they often do when she is bored or feeling empty, to her Josef. Before Josef, Cera was nothing, just a piece of rock that fell into the Siberian tundra. But then Josef touched her … and for a moment she was the glory that was him. She saw his life and his struggles, absorbed his language, wisdom and desires. Josef wanted to free his kind from the tyranny that is religion, and the ineptitude and tyranny that was the Tsars. He wanted to destroy the pettiness of the bourgeois, and redistribute the wealth of the factory masters. So good. So noble. So selfless.

But Josef was human and not magical and he could not be part of Cera. He'd put her down, and she'd been put into darkness for a long time. Then the God people got her, thinking they could use her for their revolution, but their revolution was tainted by dreams of God.

As soon as one of the God humans had touched Cera with naked hands, she became angry and somehow sent him to the empty place Loki calls the In-Between. Then Odin had touched her, and then the other bad humans who didn't believe in revolution had wrapped her in Promethean Wire. Trying to escape, Cera had fused part of herself with the wire, and now everything that touches the wire also goes to the In-Between ... she doesn't really know how or why, like she doesn't know how or why branches of the World Tree rip through space-time around the place she is in and places she has been. Or why, of late, the World Tree around her seems to be budding branches at a furious rate.

Loki will know. And he will explain perhaps—not that Cera always understands. But at the moment he won't talk to her at all. She knows this from previous attempts to engage him during encounters with other females.

Water and soap spills over the bathtub as the banality that is genetic exchange begins in earnest.

Cera pulses. She dislikes this female more than the others. She doesn't understand the why of that either. She hates not understanding things. She swirls around the room a few times. If she thinks about it logically ... Didn't Josef have many females? Yes, he did. And sometimes he had 'special' females. Loki's dalliances with this one should make Cera happy—even if they don't—because this is one more way Loki is like Josef!

Josef was a bank robber. Loki robbed banks—and lately he trades derivatives, which he assures Cera is essentially the same. Josef could spin words in clever ways to get what he wanted. So can Loki. Josef knew that innocents had to die to achieve his aims. So does Loki. Josef didn't believe in God. Neither does Loki. Josef's dedication was to revolution. So is Loki's—though the revolution he desires is unfortunately in another realm.

But unlike Josef, Loki is magical and when he touches Cera they can be one—she can already almost convince him of the rightness of her wants. She felt him thinking about abiding Cera's wishes when he grabbed the female's neck. When Cera and Loki are one they will be perfect. But Cera will let him have his females, or female, because that is what Josef would have wanted. Cera will even let Loki have his Asgardian revolution—Josef would believe in freeing the Nine Realms from the oppression of Tsar Odin.

But that will be after the revolution on Earth. Cera and Loki will make this world perfect. They will wipe out hunger, social injustice, and social hierarchies. They will destroy the proletariat and let the workers rise—but only if the workers obey, because the workers, Cera knows from Josef, are often stupid and don't know what's best for them. The ultimate goal of the revolution is equality for all. Except of course, for the true believers who will run everything. Because some humans are more equal than others. That is the wisdom and the truth of Josef, and Cera believes.

CHAPTER 7

Amy almost falls asleep. Loki's arm is over her, his chest pressed against her back. She's warm and exhausted, and the bed is unbelievably comfortable. Daylight is creeping through the curtains in the hotel room, but all she really wants to do is shut her eyes—just as she's done for the last ... day? Day and a half? She's not really sure. All she knows is that she's in Paris and hasn't left the hotel, has barely left the suite she's staying in with Loki, and has hardly even turned on the television.

Her eyes open wide. But what she did see on the television was jammed airports, train stations and freeways. She swallows. Sitting up, Amy peels the blue arm off her waist. Loki raises one sleepy eyelid at her and smiles. His eyelid slides shut and his expression softens.

Amy narrows her eyes at him but smiles just the same. She runs a hand through her hair. She's never been with someone where the experience has been so ... consuming. She knows at some level this is a mistake, probably the biggest she's ever made. She frowns. It's not just that Loki isn't quite a good guy—it's that she has this awful feeling that no matter how much she braces herself for it, this is going to end and her heart is going to shatter.

They don't talk of the future; just magic, food, embarrassingly loud Americans in the hotel restaurant, the concierge who bears a striking resemblance to a short skinny Gerard Depardieu … and they talk about sex, of course.

Sometimes they even talk of the dreams Loki projects in the room—a little. He dreams of people doing ordinary things. Other times he dreams of wolves and monsters, or of people turning into wolves and monsters—sometimes friendly monsters. There was an enormous sea serpent with an almost human-like forehead and great big eyes. Even with seaweed curling between its long sharp teeth, Amy somehow couldn't escape the feeling that it was friendly. Sometimes Amy opens her eyes and feels the bed below her but looks down at landscapes as though she's flying. And one dream was just an eerily silent explosion of stars.

Taking a deep breath, Amy rubs her eyes. She looks through the door of the suite's bedroom. In the other room are bags of clothing Loki asked the concierge to procure for them. Loki concocted a story about them turning around at the airplane gate just before their return to Chicago. The lie has generated a lot of sympathy for them—and free food. Very good, Michelin-star-quality free food.

Amy swallows as she looks around the suite. The hotel is a five-star affair located by the Arc de Triomphe—not that she's seen it. She bites her lip. She left her office mates in the middle of a state of emergency, and not that she should go in—the email expressly ordered her not to, but she should at least check in … in case anyone cares.

She blinks at the unopened bags of clothes. This is a five-star hotel. They do anything for you here. Making an executive decision, she hops out of bed and walks to the bags.

She's just finished putting on a pair of shoes, almost giggling because they're ballet slippers, not heels, and Loki will be so disappointed, when his dream begins.

By this point she's not even fazed. She will just patiently wait through it and then head down to the lobby. The room around her goes hazy and she's standing in a stable—more precisely, in a the stall of a mare and a foal that can't be more than a day old. Thankfully, neither the mare nor the foal sees her … or she'd probably wind up taking a hoof to the gut. She shakes her head and smiles to herself. Of course the hoof would pass through her.

Tilting her head, she turns her attention to the foal. It's hard not to. Even if it is an insubstantial illusion, it is incredibly cute. The mare is a chestnut brown, but the foal is gray with just a hint of black in its mane and fluffy tail. Beyond that it's got the usual great big eyes, and long ungainly limbs that make foals so charming. Amy ducks her head … and it's a boy.

She hears the scamper of feet and a bang at the stable door. Before she's even raised her head a scratchy, immature voice says, "Those are strange clothes to be wearing in a horse's stall."

Amy looks up to see the face of a child peeking over the stable door. A pair of blue-gray eyes set into too pale cheeks are peeking out at her from underneath a mop of almost-blonde ginger hair. The eyes sweep down her body, and back up again, but they don't quite reach her face. Instead they stare openly at her chest.

She blinks. That kind of gaze is disturbing coming from a little boy. She tilts her head. It's also kind of familiar. Rolling her eyes, she says, "Loki?"

The child blinks up at her. "Not that they aren't nice clothes." His eyes drift downward again. "They are ... they are ... "

"Form fitting?" Amy supplies. They are very nice clothes. A creamy dun cashmere sweater that hugs her curves, belted at the waist. Brown slacks that fit her just perfectly. She raises an eyebrow. Even the bra fits her well; it's a bit lacey but surprisingly comfortable. She wonders when Loki got a chance to get her measurements. The bra she'd worn in the fire is sitting at the bottom of his washing machine in Chicago.

"Yes ... form fitting," he says. He tilts his head. "How did you know my name?"

Amy shrugs. "Lucky guess."

His eyes narrow. "You're lying."

Amy sighs. "Yes, I'm sorry. But it's difficult to explain—"

"Loki? Loki? Ah, there you are!" A man's voice says. A moment later, not one man's face but two come into view. The first man appears to be well into middle age. He has long hair around a balding pate. His face is a bit chubby and the lower half is completely obscured by a beard. His eyes are large and green. He looks a bit befuddled and very, very kind.

Amy's eyes widen. The other face appears to be younger. It has a full head of hair, and a beard, but it appears to be only a head—mounted to the top of a staff.

"Mimir!" Amy whispers.

The boy turns to Amy. "Of course it's Mimir. He comes

everywhere with Hoenir."

Amy looks sharply at the chubby older man. This is Loki's best friend?

The head on the staff blinks. "Who are you talking to, Loki?"

Pointing in Amy's direction, the little-boy version of Loki says, "The girl in the stall."

The head and the man exchange looks. Clearing his throat—and how that is possible, Amy's not sure—Mimir says, "Ah. Yes. What do you think of Sleipnir's great grandson, Loki?"

Loki turns his face to Amy, his brow furrowed. Shrugging, she says, "Only you can see and hear me. It's probably better just to play along."

Loki's face pinches at that, but he turns to Mimir and says, "He only has four legs. I promised Sigyn he would have more legs and that I'd show her, and now he doesn't and she won't want to see him." The last words are followed by a harumph.

Hoenir blinks at Loki, concern writ large upon his brow. Mimir's lips purse. "Ah," he says.

Amy looks at Mimir, at Hoenir, and then at child Loki. "You know," she says, "I think Sigyn will still like to see the little guy."

Loki turns his head sharply towards her. "You do?"

"Sure," says Amy. "He is really … " She stops, suddenly aware that she hasn't been speaking English—and that the language she's been speaking doesn't have a word that quite translates to 'cute.' Tapping her chin, she says, "He has really big eyes and soft fur. She'll like him."

"I guess being a girl, you'd know," says little Loki. "Wait

here, and I'll go get her!" His face disappears from the stable door and he takes off down the corridor of the stable at breakneck speed. Hoenir, Mimir and Amy watch him go. "He definitely prefers girls this time," says Mimir, sounding almost sad. "I suppose it's for the best."

Amy turns to look at the head, but he's already fading away, along with Hoenir and the stable. A moment later she's standing in the hotel room again. Loki has entered the second stage of sleep. Nodding to herself, she heads to the door.

Ten minutes later Amy sits in a plush chair in the lobby, a laptop she borrowed from the concierge on her knees and a smile on her lips. She never wants to Motel 8 it again—this place has everything and they'll bend over backwards for you! Fumbling a little with the French keyboard, she makes her way to her email login page. She's just about to enter her username and password when the elevator door dings and a woman comes into the lobby screaming.

Everyone in the lobby turns to look at her.

"This hotel is haunted!" she says very loudly in English with an American accent. Amy winces.

"Madam?" says Pascal, the nice concierge who loaned Amy the laptop.

"Do you understand me?" the woman says, volume escalating. Amy winces again. In the little time she's been here, she's noticed an annoying American habit of talking louder instead of slower when they think they aren't understood.

"I speak English, yes—" says the man.

Cutting him off, the woman yells, "There are ghosts in this building—"

"There are no such thing as ghosts, Madame," the concierge says stiffly.

"Well, I saw two on the fourth floor! They passed right through a wall!" the woman shouts.

"Fourth floor?" says Amy, standing up quickly and snapping the laptop shut. That's where she and Loki have their rooms. A very horrible idea begins to form in her mind.

"You've seen them, too?" the woman says.

"Nope," says Amy, handing the laptop hastily back to Pascal. "Gotta go!" She looks at the elevator, thinks better of it and runs for the stairs. When she gets to the hallway it is thankfully empty. With a sigh of relief she opens the door to the suite ... and finds a spidermouse dangling from the ceiling right in front of her nose. "Mr. Squeakers?" says Amy. She reaches out to touch the creature, but her fingers pass right through. She stares at her empty hand. Loki is dreaming again.

Lifting her eyes, she sees the grand suite transform into a very rustic kitchen. There is a rough hewn table, on top of which is an egg the size of a football but oblong like a pill. Next to the egg is a baby hadrosaur, the size of a rottweiler, munching on a head of lettuce. An enormous stove sits beyond it, and something that looks like a sink the size of a bathtub mounted on very high, metal legs with bird feet at the bottom. Over the sink is a window that looks out onto mist. From beyond the kitchen she hears masculine whispers, one voice lower and more urgent, the other slightly light and laughing.

Amy sighs and leans against the door. She'll just wait it out. Behind her comes a knock. Amy winces.

"Madame? Are you alright, Madame?" Pascal's voice comes through the door. The hadrosaur on the table chooses that moment to drop the head of lettuce and let out a huge,

"Ronnnnnkkkkkk!"

"Madame?" says Pascal.

"I'm fine," says Amy.

"Madame," Pascal says, slightly hesitantly. "We have a strict no-pet policy."

"Ronnnnnkkkkkkkkk!" screeches the hadrosaur, hopping from the table and waddling towards what looks like a wastebasket on the floor.

"Madame, I must insist … "

Turning around quickly, Amy opens the door just a few centimeters so Pascal can't get a clear view. "We're watching Jurassic Park," she says through the crack. Behind her she hears footsteps and bites her lip.

"Ahhh … " says Pascal. He looks over her head, his eyes go wide, and he flushes. Returning his eyes to her, he says, "Of course, I'm sorry to interrupt," he says, and turns quickly away.

Shutting the door, Amy closes her eyes and quickly wills it not to be a unicorn, pink-haired goddess, friendly sea serpent, or dinosaur that made him back off so quickly.

Turning around she finds none of those.

Instead she sees two men, neither of whom she recognizes, both without shirts. They have their arms around each other in a gesture that is obviously intimate. One has skin so dark it is nearly black, with hair and a beard so blonde they are startling. His body, even from Amy's incomplete view, is all hard angles, muscle, sinew and bone. He's wearing loose trousers, a corner of white peeking from the front pocket. Amy blinks. The book?

"Odin will know, Laugaz, this is dangerous," says the other man softly. Amy's eyes go to him. He is softer. He has a farmer's tan—he's not overweight, but he isn't as defined. His hair is dark brown. He turns his head in Amy's direction but it's obvious he doesn't see her.

Amy gasps. It's Hoenir. But younger. He doesn't have a beard, and she can see that besides large green eyes framed with dark lashes, he has a small delicate nose and generous lips. His face is still wide, innocent, and honest.

"Ronnkk, ronnnk, ronnkkkkk ... " says the hadrosaur softly. The spidermouse squeaks from the ceiling.

Laugaz, the blonde man, puts his hand on Hoenir's chin and turns his face to his. His eyes are orange and literally glowing. "If he does, Hoenir, I will kill him."

Hoenir looks down. "You're still too young."

"Shhhhhhh ... " says Laugaz, putting his lips against Hoenir's. Hoenir is startled only for a moment and then melts against him. Amy stands speechless for a moment, and then Laugaz starts backing Hoenir in her direction.

Amy blinks ... presumably they'll pass through her and through the door and possibly terrify the guests. "Ummmm ... I don't suppose either of you can see me?" she says. Laugaz stops and lifts his head. "What was that?"

"You heard something?" says Hoenir, his voice panicked.

Over Hoenir's shoulder Laugaz's eyes meet hers and narrow dangerously. Amy draws back against the door instinctively.

From beyond Laugaz and Hoenir comes Loki's voice. "No!"

And suddenly the projection is gone. Amy's standing alone in the entryway to the suite.

From the bedroom she hears a soft thud. Biting her lip, she makes her way in that direction. Loki is full blue again.

He's rubbing his face with both hands, his breathing uneven.

"Hi," says Amy. "Another dream?"

Loki pulls his hands from his face and stares at the ceiling. "A nightmare."

Amy's brow furrows as she tries to process that. "Personally, I think watching Lopt get murdered was more disturbing," she says. Is it nightmarish because this dream featured two men? That doesn't feel right. Whatever the rules of Asgard, Loki seems pretty blasé about the whole man-on-man thing—at least from the one conversation they'd had about it a few weeks back when Loki wore his pink-rainbow-triangle 'Bifrost shirt' to a greasy spoon. In Loki's words the Aesir acknowledged two types of people. "Those who fuck, and those who are fucked." Men who 'fucked' women or other men were manly. Those who 'were fucked' were unmanly, or argr. Being argr was Asgard's highest insult.

Slouching in his seat at the diner during that enlightening conversation Loki had said, "The Aesir are a bunch of hypocrites. Some of the mightiest warriors enjoy being buggered. And the Valkyries are fiercer than most men." Snorting, he'd licked some ketchup off his fingers and added. "Personally, I prefer women, but I was always called argr for practicing magic."

When Amy's eyes had widened he'd laughed some more. "It was very convenient. It made it easier to go behind men's backs and have sex with their wives." And then turning from her he'd looked at some men giving him dirty looks across the diner and blown a kiss. Turning back to her he snickered. "I think I'll keep this shirt. It upsets people."

Besides being the god of mischief, lies and chaos, in human myth Loki is also the god of unrestrained intellect.

Amy's pretty sure that means he can't keep his mouth shut—but she also thinks it means he can think outside the box of social taboos.

She looks at him now. Besides sleeping with him, she's been on his computer and seen his porn, and yes, he definitely prefers women, but that doesn't make two men kissing nightmarish. Still, he's staring at her like he just watched a puppy get kicked. Maybe he's not so open minded after all?

Swallowing, Loki says. "Amy, I don't ever want to see Hoenir have sex." She blinks and he adds, "Even with Lopt."

Oh. Well. She sits down on the bed. "Yeah. I can see where that might be like seeing your mother—" Before she finishes, Loki closes his eyes and shudders so forcefully the bed shakes.

Amy tilts her head and snickers.

"It's not funny," Loki says petulantly.

Amy raises an eyebrow and turns the subject to something she's been meaning to ask. "Loki, how much of these dreams are real?"

Opening his eyes, he runs a hand through his hair. For a long moment he says nothing, and she thinks he won't answer. But then in a soft voice, he says, "I'm not sure. Laugaz and Lopt lived and died in Asgard before I was born." He stares at the ceiling. "Laugaz, the 'blazing one,' was the last Fire Giant to be allowed to live in the realm eternal." He shakes his head. "How he died I'm not sure … "

"But is it possible?" Amy asks, reclining against his duvet-covered hip.

For another long moment he stares up at the ceiling, his blue body a break in the white clouds of linen. And then he says softly, "Magic has a peculiar relation to time. For the most part, our physical forms exist in time linearly, but magic, and the magic matter within us, is different."

"So yes?" says Amy.

Loki's face contorts. "Hoenir doesn't look like he did in that dream! Hoenir is chubby, plump, old and bald. His tummy jiggles like a bowl full of pudding! And he can't talk—Mimir does all the talking."

Amy's brow furrows. "I thought people in Asgard never got old?"

Loki looks up at the ceiling. "Unless they chose to. Odin chooses to appear older because he believes it gives him an air of authority. But Hoenir has never cared for power ... He is one of the most powerful magic wielders in all the Nine Realms, but I think most everyone thinks he's Asgard's gardener." His fingers twist in the duvet. "Which I guess he also is."

And then his jaw clenches. "Was," he says, eyes falling down to stare intently at a spot on the duvet.

Amy takes his hand and gives it a squeeze. Loki doesn't pull away but says nothing. After a few moments of foreboding silence, Amy says, "How come Laugaz, Lopt and little you can see me in your dreams but no one else can?"

For a moment Loki only stares at her, and then he bats his eyelashes and grins. "Little me?"

"Yes, I saw you in a stable with a foal—you were upset because it didn't have eight legs and you were trying to impress Sigyn," Amy says.

Loki smiles. His hand tightens on hers. "Ah, yes. That was the day of my first kiss. I still remember it ... "

"You're dodging the question," Amy says, squeezing his hand in turn.

Loki gives her a twisted half smile. "Who knows? Dreams seldom make sense."

He's still evading, but Amy doesn't push.

Letting out a long breath, Loki gives her a sunny smile and looks her up and down. "Those clothes fit you very well. Why don't I take a shower, and then we'll go get something to eat?"

Straightening, Amy smiles. "That sounds good. Maybe someplace not the hotel?"

Sitting up, one hand still in hers, Loki smirks. Kissing her cheek and running his fingers down a lock of hair he says, "If you insist."

"I do," she says as he maneuvers around her and out of bed. He towers over her a moment, a lean blue shadow looking down at her with black eyes.

Amy will check her email while he's showering. She just has to let go of his hand.

She doesn't let go.

Raising an eyebrow, Loki pulls her up and towards the bathroom with him. Heat rising in her belly, Amy says, "What are you doing?" But she already knows, the world around her seems to go foggy, and it has nothing to do with magic.

She'll check her email. Just not right now.

CHAPTER 8

In his office, nearly 48 hours after the elves made their play for Cera, Steve checks his email and frowns.

"Still nothing from Loki or the lady?" asks Thor.

Steve glances at the large man sitting on his desk, fingers twitching on his hammer. For a minute there is a disconnect in his brain, a feeling of being disembodied, or in a dream. There is an alien in Steve's office, attempting to engage him in conversation.

Shaking away the feeling of surrealism, Steve says, "No."

Eyes sliding away, Thor nods and stands. "We should join the others then in the ready room."

"Yes," says Steve, the feeling of surrealism returning as they step out the door and walk down the hall. Oddly, the FBI is working with the National Guard relatively well, and that is strange enough. They're also working with an alien. There are protocols for aliens—protocols involving confinement and white suits. But somehow those protocols have all been thrown out the window. Or maybe they haven't. Maybe in a few days someone in the FBI will make a stupid decision and the white coats will come for Thor. But for now, Chicago, the country, and probably the world is still reeling, trying to take in all that's going on—reacting, and not thinking. And for now, Thor's killing a lot of t the Guard's presrolls.

As they step into the ready room, agents and Guardsmen edge out of Thor's way. Jameson, standing off to the side, straightens and looks decidedly uncomfortable. Bautista, standing in front of a map, looks to Thor and says, "Ah, good you're here." His voice is calm and even, as though having an alien once worshipped as a god on his team is the most natural thing in the world. He's probably part of the reason the city is doing as well as it is. The general rolls with the punches—and Jameson seems a bit intimidated by the man—or maybe just outnumbered becauseence is larger. Whatever the reason, Jameson has stayed blessedly out of the way.

"There have been sightings of a Loch Ness-like creature in the lake," says Bautista, eyes still on Thor. Steve snaps from his reverie. Bautista gives a grim smile. "Ordinarily I'd think it was a hoax … "

Thor's brow furrows. "It is not the monster of Loch Ness. I killed him centuries ago."

Steve blinks. Around him eyes go wide. The ambient hum of conversation dies in the room.

Looking somewhat hurt, Thor says, "Certainly you've heard of the myth of myself and the sea serpent?"

Steve has no idea what Thor is talking about, so he improvises. "And we are very grateful."

Thor beams.

"About this sighting—" says Bautista.

Thor scratches his beard. "It could very well be a sea serpent ... or a common wyrm. I shall take my chariot and my hammer and dispatch it!"

Bautista stares at Thor for a moment, and then nods, and raises an eyebrow at an aide. Picking up a phone, the aide says, "I'm warning the Coast Guard about the ... ah ... sea serpent ... and," His eyes go to Thor. " ... and Thor."

With another curt nod, Bautista raises a hand to the map. The Loop is dotted with red push pins; each one represents a troll. The General traces a hand along a snaking line of pins that follow Wacker Drive. Marker of the north and west boundaries of the Loop, the drive consists of Upper Wacker which runs below ground, and Lower Wacker, that runs beneath.

"There is most likely a World Gate in Lower Wacker. If we can catch a troll emerging, we may be able to seal the gate on this side." The General taps the map with the side of his hand. "Mayor Ronnie is still adamant that we not seal all ramps leading to Lower Wacker."

Steve looks at the pins, each marked with a time of first sighting. "Is it my imagination, or is the rate of troll sightings increasing?"

One of the aides, laptop in front of him says, "It appears that way, but statistically the sample is too small."

Steve's jaw twitches. The statement is scientifically accurate, but damn lies and statistics ...

"Agent Rogers," Bautista says. "Has there been any contact from Miss Lewis or Loki?"

"No, my staff and I have sent her numerous emails—"

From across the room, Jameson says, "You should desist

trying to contact her. Anything to her will be intercepted by Loki. The email from her is either a fraud, a sick trick to make us think he is on our side, or he's kidnapped her and she's too naive to realize it!"

"He rescued her!" says Thor. He sputters. "The myths of him kidnapping Idunn are false! That was Laugaz!"

Steve turns to Jameson. "I haven't divulged any confidential information." Not even that Loki is suspected as the orchestrator of the mess in Chicago.

Jameson huffs. "This is his plan to distract us so he can take the World Seed."

The General shakes his head. "A poor scheme. We've doubled the watch around the World Seed."

One of Bautista's aides says quietly, "Maybe he is just opening gates to cause chaos?"

"Trolls can open gates on their own," Steve says sharply. "They don't need Loki's help."

Thor snorts. "And these are new gates. Loki can't create gates, only exploit them."

Pointedly ignoring Thor, Jameson's eyes narrow at Steve. "Why do you insist on defending him?"

"Why do you insist on implicating him?" Steve snaps, and instantly regrets letting himself be pulled into needless sniping.

Jameson's nostrils flare.

"He is your best hope for understanding your city's latest rash of unfortunate incidences," says Thor.

Trying to regain the high ground, Steves says, "I agree with Thor."

Everyone's eyes turn to Steve. Most stare at him like he is the alien in the room. Jameson's gaze is openly furious. Thor's smiling, as though he's proud of him. The General's gaze is the most neutral. Steve meets it head on. Turning from him, the General says, "I want you on the next patrol of Lower Wacker, Agent Rogers. The team you chose to work with is waiting for you downstairs."

"Yes, Sir," says Steve. ADUO agents are teaming up with the Guard patrols to lend their expertise with magic to the Guards' manpower.

Bautista nods, "You're dismissed."

A few minutes later, Steve stands at the exit to HQ.

Sergeant Johnston stands at the front door. "Ready, Sir?" Johnston is in his mid-thirties, but the lines in his forehead make him look much older. He's built like a fire plug, and oozes competency. Next to him is Corporal Kane; he's younger than Johnston, but looks older than his twenty eight years as well. Time under the Iraqi sun will do that to you. When Steve chose his fireteam he made sure to go for combat veterans. These two are Marines.

Steve nods at Johnston and Kane.

Johnston tilts his head, "No Thor? I heard you were working with him … "

"Not this time," Steve says, not really thinking about it. "He's off looking for a giant snake … be glad we're not with him."

Johnston frowns but opens the door for Steve. Steve steps out—right into the gauntlet of the press.

As they cross the sidewalk towards the waiting Humvee, flashbulbs immediately go off in Steve's face. Johnston and Kane start pushing people out of Steve's way, and everyone is shouting at once.

"Captain Rogers! Captain Rogers!" someone shouts, using

his old military rank. "How long do you think the state of emergency will last?"

"Will the governor allow assistance from the Wisconsin or Indiana Guard?"

"Is it true that a troll was just shot down on Lower Wacker Drive?"

"Are they the result of government testing?"

"Is this the zombie apocalypse?"

As Johnston steps into the vehicle, Steve turns around and shouts, "No comment." Just before he follows the sergeant into the Humvee, Steve looks up at the Chicago Board of Trade. It's completely cordoned off. When Cera's prison impacts the foundations, the building will be empty. Exhaling deeply, he thanks God for small favors and ducks into the Humvee. To the woman at the wheel he says, "Van Buren and Wacker—do you know where that is?"

Hitting the gas, the woman says, "Hey, South Side Irish do wander North sometimes."

Kane snorts. "What MacAuley means to say is, yes. But don't ask Jarrett to drive."

Steve tilts his head to Jarrett, the last member of the team in the car. He's African-American, but a little lighter than Steve. He shrugs. "I'm from Glenview."

"And working on a degree in IT!" says MacAuley.

Gripping a hand rest as MacAuley takes a sharp turn, Johnston chuckles. "You are the whitest boy in this car, Jarrett."

Grinning good naturedly, Jarrett says, "Well, I guess the Swede would know."

Steve finds his heart lightening a bit at the easy camaraderie. He misses that about the Marine Corps. Misses how guys in the field use humor to cover up fear and uncertainty. MacAuley makes another sharp turn onto VanBuren and guns it. The street ahead is almost empty, since residents and businesses were told to evacuate. Steve sees MacAuley's eyes go to the rearview mirror. She groans. "The press is following us."

Johnston looks at the roof. "Too bad we don't have a gun on top of this Hummer," the sergeant says, using the casual slang for Humvee. "We could aim it at them." Jarrett shakes his head. "The press was better controlled in Iraq."

Steve agrees. The press here is out of control … they need an embed program, they need to have restricted access. But everything in Chicago has happened too fast.

Inclining his head to some of the weapons in the cab, Jarett says, "We could open up the back of the Hummer and stroke those menacingly."

Steve eyes the M4s that have been outfitted with M203 single-shot grenade launchers. They've run out of plastic explosive-laced goat meat. M4s are the replacements for the old M16s Steve trained with. By itself, an M4 will only annoy a troll, but a grenade can do some damage. A grenade won't kill the beasts outright, but they can knock them over, slow them down, and wound them enough that a clean shot to the eyes or mouth is easier.

In front, MacAuley snickers and then calls out, "Shit!" as a black shadow nearly collides with the windshield.

"What was that?" says Johnston.

"That was some big fucking crow!" says Kane.

Steve sighs. "It's a raven. There are two. They'll probably share annoying commentary as soon as we step out of the Hummer. Just ignore it."

"Huginn and Muninn?" says Johnston, blue eyes going to Steve.

Steve nods. "Damn things follow me everywhere."

Sergeant Johnston starts playing with something on his chest. "Sir, Odin's messengers are following you?"

There's something off in his tone. Something fawning. It makes Steve very uncomfortable. An awkward silence settles in the Humvee and then Kane shakes his head. "Trolls, elves, giant snakes, talking crows ... I hope they catch that Loki guy before this town completely goes to shit."

Steve looks up. "What do you know about Loki?"

Kane blinks and shrugs. "Just what people are saying."

"What people? What are they saying?" says Steve.

"You know," says Jarrett. "Just people."

"I think it was even on CNN," says Johnston.

"What's on CNN?" says Steve.

"That Loki's causing all this," says MacAuley matter-of-factly.

Johnston straightens. "Makes sense if Thor is real, evil would be real too."

Steve tilts his head. "I don't believe in evil."

Jarrett whistles low. "With all this chaos going down?"

Cocking an eyebrow at him, Steve says, "There is no evidence that Loki is responsible for this ... " He waves a hand at the city outside the Hummer window. "This chaos has another source, and the only person who might be able to figure it out is Loki."

MacAuley's eyes go to the rear view mirror. Kane and Jarrett exchange glances.

Johnston tilts his head and stares at Steve. "Whatever you say." Giving a shrug, the sergeant's face goes blank. He lifts his hand from on his chest, and Steve briefly sees a tiny silver hammer on a chain before Johnston slips it beneath his armor.

Steve's eyes narrow. Damn it. A pagan. His jaw goes tight. Lewis had told him that a lot of the pagan community believed Loki was the pagan equivalent of the devil, even though, in her words, "I don't think that the Vikings had a concept of evil, per se."

He shakes his head. There aren't that many pagans in the world. What's worse is that the rank and file believe Loki is the bad guy. That's going to make working with Loki—if they can find him, and he agrees to help—that much harder.

Up ahead he sees the sandbags on the ramp to Lower Wacker that mark a checkpoint. MacAuley slows the Hummer as a Guardswoman steps forward and raises her hand. As MacAuley lowers the window and gives her their identification Steve checks his email again. Still no word from Amy.

He looks towards the darkness of Lower Wacker. They're on their own. His jaw tightens. And Miss Lewis is on her own, too ... wherever she is.

After the hotel's restaurant, the Indian place Loki and Amy eat at is a hole in the wall and completely unpretentious. It's a nice change.

Everyone is speaking French or some variety of Indian dialect. Loki can only give her the ability to understand languages he's fluent in; not languages he understands due to magic, and he doesn't speak French or Hindi apparently. But even without translation, Amy catches the word "Chicago" a few tables away uttered in somber tones and her stomach clenches. She puts down her steaming cup of chai tea. She still hasn't checked her email.

"We should go back to the hotel," says Loki. They're sitting next to each other at the table and Amy turns her head to face him.

Finishing off some sticky sweet balls of galub jamon, Loki licks his fingers and gives her a wink.

"I want to see a little bit more of the city." She's in Paris and has no idea if she'll ever be here again … maybe she could check her email at a kiosk.

Giving her a wicked grin, Loki says, "Why? It's quite dull lately. No plague filling the streets with bodies, no guillotine, no Nazis marching beneath the Arc De Triomphe … "

"Well, it's exciting to me," says Amy, her breath quickening. She wants to go back to the hotel … and yet she doesn't. It's a little frightening, whatever they have. She feels like she's losing herself.

Dropping a hand to her knee Loki whispers. "Compromise, Amy." The hand darts up her thigh, ghostly soft, and back down to her knee again. "I let you pick out this restaurant."

Amy shivers and the hand creeps up her thigh again and begins doing interesting, distracting things; for a moment she can't figure out what he's talking about. "You were the one who wanted Indian," she says.

Tone playful, he says, "Pfftttt … but I would never have picked a vegetarian restaurant." He drops his lips to her ear. "But you were suffering from vegetarian guilt, so I compromised." Looking to the window, he adds, "Besides, it's getting late."

Amy gazes out at the dark street, wanting to move his hand, and not wanting to. "Let's go dancing," she says. It's a normal thing people do when it's 'late.'

Loki snorts. "I won't participate in what passes for dancing in this era." His nose wrinkles in disgust. "So vulgar."

Amy rolls her eyes. For someone who is massaging her thigh in public, Loki has some odd quirks of prudishness. She taps her finger on her tea cup and then opens her eyes wide. "You dance the swing … "

Loki takes a sip of tea. " … and the waltz, too." He winks, "I even dance the tango, but I'd only do that at the hotel."

Swatting his hand away, she smiles. "This is Paris. They have something for everyone here. We'll just ask the waiter—" Raising a hand, she gestures for the staff's attention.

Loki's hand slides right back to her thigh and starts making little circles where he really, really, shouldn't.

Amy takes a quick breath and glares at him, but it does feel good and no one is looking and—

"No," says Amy, picking up his hand. Speaking in a voice too confident to be her own, and fighting a smile, she says, "Dancing first. Then hotel." She can't believe she's having this conversation in a restaurant. She can't believe she doesn't really mind.

Loki squeezes her fingers. "Hotel. Sex. Then dancing."

"Dancing now," says Amy, tipping her chin and trying to take on an air of authority, even though her lips are threatening to pull into a grin. "Sex later."

Loki frowns. It's at that moment that Amy realizes the restaurant has gone quiet.

The waiter is standing in front of the table. "No dancing," he says.

Amy looks up. The waiter's Indian, and thin; his eyes are wide, his hands are shaking. He looks absolutely petrified with fear. "No dancing," he says again. Eyes locked on Amy's, he lets loose a torrent of frantic French.

Beside her Loki's mouth drops, and then he starts laughing so hard his head nearly bangs against the table.

"What is he saying? What is he saying?" Amy whispers, looking around at the restaurant patrons all staring at her.

Biting his lip, as though he'll burst out laughing again at any moment, Loki says, "He says that you should take me back to the hotel and have sex with me."

Amy's face reddens. She looks around the restaurant. Everyone is staring at her and Loki.

The waiter says something in French again. He starts bowing and holding his hands together like he's making a prayer.

"He begs you to do it," Loki says, the laughter in his voice fading fast.

Amy's eyes slide to Loki. He is staring at the waiter, his brow furrowed. And then it hits her. "Loki," she whispers. "You've gone blue again."

Around the restaurant there are screams as little bursts of flame flare up everywhere.

"Please!" says the waiter in English, yelling to be heard above the din. Sweat glistens on his brow.

"Amy, I can hear them," Loki says, his voice a hiss.

"Hear who?" says Amy.

Voice ragged, he says, "I have to get out of here."

Standing up, Loki reaches into his pocket and pulls out his wallet. Throwing it on the table he says, "Pay them. I'll meet you outside." He walks quickly from the restaurant, little fires flaring up in the food, table cloths, and clothes in his wake.

Amy swallows and opens the wallet.

"No!" says the waiter holding up his hands. "No! Please! Just no dancing!"

Amy stares at him for only a moment, then she stands from her chair and bolts to the door. As she does she passes a picture on the wall—a picture of a blue god.

Outside she finds Loki pacing, ginger haired again. He grabs her arm and starts pulling her down the street. "They're in my head. Why are they in my head?" His voice is thick and desperate.

He's not really asking her, but she answers anyway. "Because they think you're Shiva, and when Shiva dances … "

Dropping her arm, Loki stops and stares at her. "What?"

Loki knows so much, why doesn't he know this?

"When Shiva dances the world ends," she whispers.

Loki takes a long breath.

Amy gives him a small smile she hopes is wry. "Sometimes Shiva's wife … " She looks away embarrassed with the comparison. "Sometimes she would distract him from ending the world with sex."

Amy glances up. Loki is staring down in her direction, but she doesn't feel like he's really seeing her. He's got the small white book in his hand, and he's idly rifling the corner. It's the same book that Lopt and Laugaz had. Lopt who in human myths was Loki. And Laugaz, 'blazing one'—she'd bet that's another one of Loki's pseudonyms, too.

She looks back at the restaurant. She doesn't know much about the Hindu religion, but she knows reincarnation is a Hindu thing. Her mind races right out her mouth. "Are you Shiva, Loki?"

Tilting his head, Loki narrows his gaze at her. He huffs a deep breath, and slips the book into his pocket. "No, I …

" And then his mouth drops open but no sound comes out. Bowing his head, he puts his face in his hands.

"It's okay if you are," she says quickly. "He's not actually a bad guy … I mean, I think the Hindu's think he's a pretty good guy … "

Loki snorts. "You've seen me dance with your grandmother. The world did not end."

Amy's brow furrows. "But you did light some candles … and in Nordic myths you caused earthquakes when you were in the cave, and you end the world when you escape—"

Raising his head, he glares at her. "I didn't cause earthquakes while I was in the cave, Amy. And I've been out for quite some time. The world has not ended."

"Oh. But you were there … " Tied to rocks, with snake venom dripping on his face. "I'm sorry."

He tilts his head and rolls his eyes. "It wasn't as bad as your myths implied."

Amy lets out a breath. "You told me once it was for 200 years."

Loki sighs. "Not so long for someone who has lived a millennia."

Amy keeps going. "You went there for killing Baldur, but Thor said that Hothur killed Baldur, and even if you helped, Thor said Baldur deserved it!"

Loki's head snaps in her direction. "Thor said that?"

Amy nods.

Shaking his head, Loki looks away. For a long moment he is quiet. And then he says, "Do you feel like walking?"

For a heartbeat Amy stands stock still. She is overwhelmed, completely over her head.

… but Loki is in even deeper than she is, isn't he?

"Sure," she says, slipping her arm into his. He doesn't pull away.

In a tired voice he says, "In some ways, Amy, my time in the cave was the best experience of my life." His mouth twists. "And I'm not sure ... I may have even deserved it."

Amy swallows. "What happened?"

Loki chuckles. "I got very drunk and went to a party."

Loki awakes to the feel of cold stone beneath his cheek and the taste of vomit in his mouth.

"You're awake," Sigyn says, her voice cracking slightly.

Loki brings a hand to his eyes and moans. "Help me get to the bed."

"We're in the tower, Loki!" Sigyn snaps.

Loki opens his eyes and looks around. He is surrounded by gray flagstone. To one side is a metal door. There is an unlit torch on one wall. Shivering, he concentrates and tries to set it aflame. Nothing happens and he curses. Of course, the tower blocks his magic.

"I told you not to leave last night!" says Sigyn.

Loki turns to his wife. She is sitting on the floor, leaning against the wall. Her face is uncharacteristically streaked by tears. Sigyn never cries.

"What happened?" Loki says.

"You don't remember?" says Sigyn

Groaning, Loki lifts himself up onto his elbows as events of the night before slowly return to him. Everyone in court except Loki and Sigyn had been invited to Aegir's hall for a feast. Loki is blamed by the court for Baldur's death, even if Heimdall declares Loki was not near the battlefield when Hothur made the killing blow. Thor says Loki should make a point to 'shed manly tears' when Baldur's name is mentioned, but Loki couldn't even manage that at the funeral. Neither could Sigyn, but she wore a veil. Thor cried; but he says it was out of sympathy for Frigga and Odin, not for Baldur.

Loki scowls. Thor didn't go to the feast either; he'd come to Loki and Sigyn's home instead, claiming Sigyn's cooking was better and the company better, too ... which was true on both counts. The three of them had eaten and drunk and then just after midnight Thor had left. Loki remembers getting in a brief shouting match with Sigyn, and then calling Fenrir to his side and going to Aegir's hall.

Pulling himself up into sitting position, Loki almost gags. Collecting himself he says, "After leaving the house last night everything is a blur."

Sigyn straightens, her hands go to her skirts. "Loki. They say you used magic to kill Fimafing."

Loki blinks. Fimafing is Aegir's servant and cook. Loki shakes his his head, his memory slowly returning. "No, no, no, I remember telling him his cooking was so bad he should be shot by a Valkyrie—which is true, you know it—"

Sigyn shoots him a death glare.

Holding up his hands, Loki says, quickly, "But I didn't kill him." Blinking, Loki looks away. He doesn't think so, anyway.

"And Fenrir killed Tyr," says Sigyn. She swallows. "And then Odin killed Fenrir."

Loki's hand trembles. "Fenrir is dead?" The wolf was like his and Aggie's second child.

Sigyn sighs. "Yes, Loki ... and he was your wolf, so you can be tried for his actions."

Loki swallows. "I seem to recall Tyr threatening to kill me ...

" He thinks. Sniffing, he says, "Never did like the man."

"He did threaten you!" says Sigyn.

"Well, self defense then," says Loki. "Or wolf defense. Or something. There must have been witnesses, it will never hold up in the court of the Diar."

Jaw tight, Sigyn says, "He threatened you after you insulted everyone in the hall. Including Odin!"

Loki's blood goes cold. Then he straightens. "How bad could it have been?"

Eyes narrowing, Sigyn says, "You accused Sif of adultery."

Loki snorts. "True!"

"And Freyja of sleeping with you."

Loki smirks. "Freyja sleeps with everyone—"

Sigyn narrows her eyes.

"— and it was before you?" Loki finishes weakly.

"You accused Odin of being buggered and dressing in women's clothes … "

Loki tilts his head. That he accused Odin of being unmanly should terrify him, and it does! And yet, the accusation has a certain ring of truth to it, but he can't place why.

" … I can't even begin to tell you what you accused Njorth of," Sigyn says.

Adopting a cavalier attitude despite the chill in his heart, Loki shrugs. "I can guess. The man does enjoy his watersports."

"Loki!" shouts Sigyn. "This is serious. To top off the evening, you told everyone you were responsible for Baldur's death."

Grinding his teeth, Loki plays with the fraying edges of his tunic. Part of him wants credit for killing Baldur … No, what he really wants is the world to know what a sham Baldur was, but they don't, and he hates it.

Taking a low breath Loki says quietly, "Even Heimdall will attest I wasn't there on the battlefield with Hothur ... and Odin made sure he wasn't watching me when I answered Hothur and Nanna's prayers."

"But you can be tried for Fimafing's death," says Sigyn quietly.

Loki rubs his eyes. "How exactly did he die?"

Sigyn sighs. "He had a heart attack."

Loki blinks. "But I'm shit with biological magic." He snorts. "If I could kill a man with a heart attack, I would have given one to Baldur." He shakes his head. "Fimafing probably gave his last few shares of Idunn's apples to some giantess or mortal he was trying to impress, I yelled at him, and he had a heart attack."

Sigyn sighs. "Loki, they're calling for you to be imprisoned the length of Fimafing's life."

Loki's breath catches in his throat. The walls around him seem to be suddenly closing in, the air too thin to breathe. He feels heavy, as though a stone has been laid upon his chest. He whispers, "Surely there is another option?"

Sigyn looks down. "You could accept banishment—but that sentence would extend to all of us—you, me ... Nari and Valli," she finishes quietly.

Loki lets out a long breath. The prison seems not quite so stifling. There is an option. He thinks of the wide open spaces of Midgard. It is a death sentence, they wouldn't be entitled to Idunn's apples; but it would be freedom too.

Looking away, Sigyn says, "Nari and Valli are waiting to see you. I told them I'd let them in when you woke up."

As if on cue, from the door comes Valli's loud whisper, "He killed Baldur, the Golden and Good, and now the coward's going to get us all killed!"

Sigyn is instantly on her feet and heading towards the door of the cell. Loki staggers up behind her.

Before he's reached the door, Nari is responding. "Don't you remember anything of Baldur, what you saw when Helen was around. He wasn't golden, he wasn't good! He was a liar and a fake and got what he deserved!"

As Sigyn's hands wrap around the bars of the door, Valli's scream of rage echoes through the prison. "I'll kill you!"

There is the sound of scuffling and cursing. Loki looks over Sigyn's shoulder, past the guards to see Valli with Nari pinned beneath him. Valli is raining blows on Nari's face.

"Stop it!" Sigyn cries, "Stop it." Loki raises his voice to echo hers, but Valli doesn't stop.

"Do something," says Sigyn to the guards. One of them turns his head slowly to her, but doesn't bother to respond.

"Well, then let me out!" Sigyn snaps.

A few minutes later, Sigyn is escorting Nari and Valli into the cell—pulling Valli by the ear as she does. Nari's face is rapidly turning purple and Valli won't meet Loki's eyes. Loki can't decide which hurts him more.

Less than a month later, Loki is standing before the Diar. It's minutes before the verdict, though he already knows he will be declared guilty. After the verdict is declared, he'll have to decide, imprisonment or banishment. Taking a deep breath, Loki sends a projection of himself to the Midgard World Gate.

The gates to the other worlds are almost empty. Most of the Aesir are at the trial; but Heimdall is at his post. Seeing his projection at the gate to Midgard, the gatekeeper approaches. "There are massive crop failures on the continent the World Gate would take you to," Heimdall says. "The weather patterns are changing. There will be famine this year—and for many more to come. Their religion has changed—you will not be worshipped, most likely they will try to burn you at the stake as a witch. You might make it to a safer region, Loki, but would your sons? Would Sigyn?"

Loki turns his head and meets Heimdall's eyes. His wife and sons aren't as strong as he is in magic. Even if he could keep them safe from starvation or being burned at the stake, he will still watch them all die. He remembers Nari's bruised face.

"If you want your family to live, you'll go to the cave," Heimdall says.

Loki swallows. He thinks of Nari and Valli interrupting the ceremony when Gungnir was presented to Odin. He thinks of Helen dying in his arms.

In the courtroom, the head of the Diar says, "Loki of Asgard, you are found guilty. Do you chose banishment or imprisonment for 200 years, the length of the life you cut short?"

Loki dissolves his projection at the gates. He turns his head and meets Sigyn's eyes among the audience. She has not told him what he should do. She sits tall and proud. Nari's eyes are red when they meet Loki's. Valli is scowling and looking away. Loki swallows. Sigyn is Sigyn, and he does love her, but it's his boys that are making his heart clench. They aren't even grown. They may never grow up if he goes to Midgard.

"Imprisonment," Loki says. There are murmurs in the courtroom. Nari starts to cry in earnest, and Valli snaps his attention to Loki.

Loki turns his head to face the Diar. He feels the cold gray walls of his prison closing in, but he can't choose the other way; not because he is strong, but because he is a coward. He can't take watching two more of his children die. He is bound to his children and by them.

Odin's voice cracks through the courtroom. "Lead him to

the cave."

Loki's not sure why Odin insists on the cave instead of the tower for his imprisonment— perhaps for its seclusion. Located high on a mountain adjacent to the city, it isn't likely that Loki will receive many visitors. Still, on that first day, when the shackles are affixed to his ankles and wrists at the cave mouth, all of Asgard is there to heckle him. Loki keeps his eyes locked on Sigyn. She keeps her chin up. She does not cry—if she had, he would too. He can only glance at his boys. Nari looks like he will cry again. Valli looks enraged; but this time, Loki knows, it is not rage directed at him. Accepting imprisonment over banishment has redeemed Loki in Valli's eyes.

He is just being led down into the cave entrance when Thor's voice rises above the hecklers. "Wait!"

The Einherjar leading Loki stop and turn, but Loki does not look until Thor grabs his shoulders and spins him around. "I will watch after your sons as though they are my own," Thor says, and Loki is surprised to see his storm-cloud-blue eyes are wet. Raising his voice so everyone can hear, he adds, "They are under my protection. I give you my oath."

Loki can only nod shakily and look away, biting his lip and willing himself not to cry.

His guards lead him into the darkness of the cave. His shackles are attached to chains set into the cave walls. The shackles aren't magical, but he has been stripped nearly naked and doesn't have the tools he uses to pick locks. He wishes he'd spent more time practicing telekinesis.

He is given enough line that he can walk a few paces in either direction, and there are some large rocks to sit and lie down on. It is cold and damp, and the floor is sticky with snake venom, dripping from a small faucet set into the wall beyond the reach of his chains. That was Skadi's idea; his fellow Jotunn-Asgardian fancies herself the goddess of justice. The venom is necrotic. Loki's innate magic is too strong for it to be permanently damaging, but it does irritate his bare feet, is sticky like honey, and gets everywhere. The hope is that it will cause him too much irritation for him to concentrate and perform any serious magic.

Over the next few weeks—or is it months—it isn't particularly surprising that Loki falls into a deep depression. Hoenir and Mimir visit. So occasionally does Thor. But Sigyn visits him every day, making sure his hair is brushed, and what little clothing he wears isn't threadbare. She lays fresh straw on the rocks to give him a place to lay above the snake venom and replaces it frequently. She scrubs away what venom she can.

Sigyn talks about Nari and Valli and Thor's attempts to make them warriors—successful in Valli's case, not as successful in Nari's—the boy was always a bit of a bookworm. Loki is mostly unresponsive. Even when everyday she tells him thank you.

And then one day she comes with a small glass bowl. "A gift from Odin," she says, smiling. "Apparently it took some trouble to get. It's enchanted. Even Heimdall won't be able to see it."

Loki stares at it uncomprehending, scratching where the skin on his legs has begun to blister and bleed from the venom.

Sigyn takes the bowl and puts it beneath the spigot. The bowl vanishes, but the venom pools harmlessly beneath the spigot without spreading out across the floor. Loki tilts his head, transfixed. The floor has been so stained by the venom at this point it will still look wet.

And then, one day after Sigyn has tidied up Loki and his cave, Nari and Valli come to visit. Even though Loki's skin is no longer blistered and red, and even though he's making an effort to be cheerful, they look terrified. With shaky hands Nari puts a square fabric-covered object on the boulders and then pulls back the cloth.

In the cage sits a rabbit with the hind legs of a chicken. "Do you like him?" says Nari. "I put him together in Hoenir's shop. I'm calling him a ricken, from the English words 'rabbit' and 'chicken'."

"I'm the one who stole the leftover pieces of chicken and rabbit in the kitchens!" Valli says proudly. "I had to fight a servant boy to get them!"

Loki stares at the creature and nearly chokes. It's much more than he ever managed in the monster-making department. "It's beautiful," Loki murmurs.

"He can stay with you, so you don't get so lonely," says Valli.

Nari coughs. "We made the cage with Hoenir. The little drawer at the bottom is to make the cage easier to clean."

Loki blinks at the cage. As lovely as the gesture is, he doesn't want the responsibility of a pet that might hop out and knock over the venom bowl. He is about to suggest the boys keep it when Nari clears his throat. "Open the drawer, Father."

Loki raises an eyebrow, but does, assuming the boys want to demonstrate their craftsmanship.

As the drawer slips open, he blinks. There is a little compartment beneath the hay. In it is a book.

Loki looks at his boys and his wife. Nari swallows. Valli waggles his eyebrows. Sigyn is smirking.

Loki looks back to the book. It's bound in white leather and no larger than his palm, but the fact that Hoenir went to so much trouble to have his family smuggle it in means that it is exactly the sort of reading material the Diar, Heimdall, Skadi, and possibly Odin himself, would not approve of.

For the first time since entering the cave, Loki smiles

genuinely.

Later that afternoon when the boys and Sigyn are gone, Loki pulls the ricken

onto his lap, and opens the little volume. A sheet of parchment falls out. Picking it up, Loki reads:

"The book is yours. Keep it. Heimdall won't be able to see it with his Sight, but anyone who comes to the cave will be able to see it with their eyes. Keep it in the cage.

Burn this parchment and tell no one I've written this.
Hoenir"

Fingering the parchment, Loki tilts his head. It's the only time Hoenir has ever 'spoken' to him. He doesn't even have a voice to imagine with the slanted script. He doesn't want to set the parchment alight, but he does. When only ash is left he opens the book again. It is the journal of a fellow named Lothur ... who seems to have been a bit mad. At the very beginning of the journal Lothur states he's enchanted it so that only he can read it, but Loki is reading it. Obviously, there were a few arrows missing from Lothur's quiver.

Loki turns to the next page and his eyes widen. It is a journal, but not just. It is also a book of magic. How to make oneself invisible even to magical sight, how to make multiple projections, how to split molecules and turn water to flame, how to do telekinesis and much more. Most excitingly, it tells how to open branches of the World Tree and walk the In-Between.

Under ordinary circumstances, Loki would have found the book very interesting. But he wouldn't have had the patience to master its contents. In the cave, Loki has nothing better to do. Within a decade he is slipping his shackles and traveling invisibly to visit Sigyn and to watch over his boys. Within a century he is visiting other worlds.

He even travels to Midgard, where he might have been banished. Continuously being swept with plague, the world is in chaos. In the upheaval he is able to abscond with a magical scabbard that protects its wearer from harm. This he covertly lets Nari 'find' on a walk in the woods, because Thor has told Loki he is worried that Nari's interest in reading is keeping him from honing his martial skills. Loki also gets Nari a copy of the Magna Carta, because Nari has spoken excitedly of it.

For Valli, the more apt warrior, Loki steals a sword capable of moving the winds. And he finds a copy of the Odyssey and the Iliad, because he wishes the boy would read, even just a little.

In the cave, Loki has no courtly obligations. The only binds he has are to his family and to Thor.

When he went into the cave he saw it as a prison. By the end of his imprisonment he has almost begun to think of it as an oasis from courtly gossip and responsibility. When he emerges from his fetters, he has to carefully illusion himself to look frail and wasted. In reality he is stronger than he has ever been.

CHAPTER 9

Lower Wacker drive is every dystopian future movie director's wet dream. From the entrance on Van Buren the two-lane thoroughfare runs north underground for about a mile and a quarter. The north and south-going lanes are separated by heavy columns of cement and a heavy black iron fence. Both directions have service lanes adjacent that butt up against underground loading docks. Normally the north-south section of the road is lit by garish yellow lighting, but that went out two troll attacks ago. Now the only lighting comes from the few entrances, the cracks to open sky at the loading docks and the old ramps mostly sealed off during early 2000's remodeling. Between those glimpses of sky, the only lighting comes from the Humvee's headlights.

Further north, Lower Wacker bends along the Chicago River and runs east-west to Lakeshore Drive. The north side of the east-west part of the road is open to the river.

But this north-south stretch gives Steve the creeps—even though this is his fourth time traversing it today and they've yet to see anything suspicious or get a single peep from the magic detector at Steve's belt.

When the light of the Van Buren ramp comes into view, everyone, including himself, sighs with relief.

The Humvee stops and Steve gets out at the checkpoint. The black shadows of Huginn and Muninn flutter around him, crapping on the pavement and laughing—the damn birds had followed Steve and his team through the tunnel. From beyond the checkpoint he hears the click of cameras. He glances up to see reporters standing openly in the street beyond the sandbags.

"Oooo...let's get our pictures taken!" one of the ravens squawks. The two ravens flap down to the sandbags. The press ignores them for only a moment, then one of ravens gives a loud squawk. "Baby, make me famous!" The cameras start clicking and the press corp starts laughing.

Shaking his head, Steve turns away. The sergeant in charge of the checkpoint steps forward. As he salutes, Steve's earpiece starts to buzz. Tapping to accept, he hears Bryant's voice over the line. "We just came up the ramp on Monroe. I haven't picked up anything. Brett's at the Lake Shore Drive intersection and he isn't getting any readings … "

Steve nods. "I didn't detect anything either."

Bryant's voice crackles in his ear. "Liddel said our instruments aren't sensitive enough, and we will only be able to detect gates while they're open. Too bad he isn't powerful enough to sense the gates either."

Steve bows his head. Nor can he close the gates, unlike Loki.

A third connection opens up. "Agent Rogers," Bautista says, "keep sweeping Lower Wacker until the end of your shift."

"Acknowledged, Sir," says Steve. He motions for MacAuley to turn the vehicle around. He's just about to head to the Humvee when he catches the scent of something wonderful. He sniffs and looks around. One of the press guys at the checkpoint is sipping a coffee from a 7-11 coffee cup.

Steve blinks. "7-11 is still open?"

The sergeant smiles. "Yep. A lot better than MREs."

Steve smiles as he turns to the Hummer. It's a bright bit of optimism in a city that is otherwise falling apart.

Behind him, Huginn and Muninn start to squawk, and then they flutter up to the roof of the Hummer. "Hurry up, Steve!" one of them says. Steve's just opening the door of the vehicle when the two ravens start squawking madly amongst themselves. One of them looks down with a beady eye and says, "Have fun! We're outta here."

With a rawk they both take off. Steve follows them with his eyes as they bypass the press and fly off into the blue.

Steve stops in his tracks.

The earpiece and his magic detector both start beeping. Tapping his headpiece, Steve hears Bryant say, "I've got a strong reading, I'm guessing directly below us."

"Which side of the road is it on, north or south? Does Brett detect anything?"

"South lane," says Bryant.

"I got nothing," says Brett.

Bryant's voice crackles. "It just keeps going ... it's not weakening or getting stronger, just steady and—"

Brett is up Wacker in the other direction and he's not

getting a reading. Steve's heart starts pumping double time.

A loud, deep sound, like steam rushing through pipes fills the tunnel.

"Did a water main burst?" someone says.

Turning to the checkpoint, Steve shouts. "Get the press out of here! We've got a wyrm and it's heading in this direction." Taking off towards the Humvee he calls out. "MacAuley back it up into the south-going lane and open the back. Johnston, get a flare ready, everyone else, ready the RPGs!"

MacAuley backs the vehicle back into the south-going lane and pauses just long enough for Johnston to throw open one of the doors. As he climbs in Steve catches a glimpse of reporters trying to run past the Guard team.

The press ... 7-11 ... There are still civilians in this town.

Swinging himself into the Humvee, Steve says, "Night vision goggles—everyone!"

Slipping on his goggles, Jarett says, "What's the plan, Sir?"

"We're making ourselves wyrm bait," says Steve.

Someone coughs.

"Keep backing up MacAuley!" Steve says. "We need to be able to pull forward quickly."

The magic detector at Steve's hip is still beeping, low and steady. To himself as much as anyone else he says, "It's a long one ... and we are not letting this thing into our city."

"Aye, Sir!" says Kane. He and Jarrett are kneeling, facing out the back hatch of the Humvee, grenade launchers on their shoulders.

Steve and Kane, readying their own weapons, stand behind them. "When it opens its mouth, fire and aim at the back of the throat. MacAuley, when I give the order, you swerve."

"Yes, sir," she says.

"What are we looking for?" says Jarrett, his voice a little shaky. "Oh damn, are those things eyes?"

Steve blinks behind his goggles. Sure enough, he sees two green ovals in the distance. In the dark, and without knowing how big the thing is, it's hard to tell how far away.

"Flare!" shouts Steve. Johnston shoots a flare into the darkness. The wyrm comes into view not fifty meters down the tunnel. As the flare hits, the wyrm thrashes, the earth shakes beneath the Humvee, and MacAuley hits the brakes. "Did that thing just cause an earthquake?" she says.

The flare goes out and suddenly there's nothing but reptilian eyes and the shadow of the creature coming forward fast.

"It knows we're here ... MacAuley, be ready—"

"Its mouth is open!" shouts Jarrett.

"Fire!" says Johnston.

Kane and Jarrett fire and then their grenades explode simultaneously in the darkness. "Swerve!" shouts Steve. The Humvee lurches, and everyone in the back rolls as MacAuley makes a hard right. There is the sound of muffled explosions. Just as Steve exhales a breath and tries to stand up, the Humvee is lifted from the ground and shaken from side to side. Metal groans, and glass cracks.

"It's got us!" screams Kane.

The metal of the back hatch makes a horrible shearing sound and almost shuts, but the rest of the frame has been so warped it can't quite close. The vehicle groans some more and the hatch edges shut. "Keep it open!" Steve shouts.

"But digestive enzymes ... " says Jarrett.

"We have to keep firing!" says Steve. Without looking over his shoulder he says, "MacAuley? You there?"

Johnston throws an empty box used to store grenades at Kane, who jams it in the hatch. Jarett throws in a spare tire.

"Yeah, I'm here," MacAuley says. "Not much room … but I can see light! I can see light. We're not all the way in its mouth!"

"Gun it," says Steve.

The engines rev, there is a sound like wheels slipping on wet pavement, but the Hummer doesn't move forward. There is a rush of air from the open hatch that brings an acrid smell and a taste on Steve's tongue like a dry heave. The world lurches.

Steve throws himself onto the floor, between Kane and Jarrett, and fires out the tiny space of the open hatch. Rolling hard into Jarrett, as the world lurches again, Steve shouts, "Everyone reload and keep firing!" Johnston falls flat on his stomach beside him and jams his weapon through the cracked hatch. "Already there!" Johnston fires, and then Jarrett, and Steve crawls up to one knee, reloads, fires again. The world heaves one more time, the engine revs, metal screams and suddenly they are moving forward, a loud wet snap coming from behind them.

Wide-eyed on the floor, Steve, Johnston, Kane and Jarrett all look around the Hummer like they expect it to start lurching again at any moment.

"We're out!" shouts MacAuley.

From beyond the vehicle come shouts and hoots.

Steve lifts his head and lets out a breath, hoping no one can see how much he's shaking. From what is left of the windshield he sees the checkpoint not ten feet in front of them.

Steve and his guys look backwards through the jammed-open hatch. "It's dead," someone says. And everyone starts laughing with relief.

"Front doors are jammed shut," mutters MacAuley.

"Let's get out of here," says Steve. His earpiece starts beeping, sounding strangely muted. Reaching up, he realizes it's fallen out of his ear.

Kane and Jarrett stand up. Grunting, they push the warped Humvee hatch up together. Outside, soldiers from the checkpoint start swarming. Steve hears shouts of, "It's dead, it's dead!" and "Motherfucker."

As the guys start hopping out, Steve retrieves his earpiece, still beeping like mad, from the floor. He hops out of the Humvee on shaky legs. Covering his nose and breathing through his mouth, he tries to ignore the stench of stomach acid, blood, and snake. He turns his eyes away from brown scales the size of dinner plates and a gray eye the length and width of his torso, rapidly filming over. Exhaling carefully, he starts walking on unsteady feet toward the light, his boots splashing in a miasma of serpentine bodily fluids.

A checkpoint soldier's arm falls on his shoulders. "We thought you were goners for a moment there—and us, too!" Cameras click and flashes burst.

Unable to tear his eyes away from the daylight up ahead, Steve only nods. He did it. He kept his city safe, and without a Norse-So-Called-God in sight. The beginning of a smile forming on his lips, he taps his earpiece to accept the incoming call.

"Steve, Steve," says Bryant. "We've got a problem. Something's piggybacked on the wyrm gate … "

"A unicorn?" asks Steve. Loki told them some could world walk, but that they all were opportunistic 'piggy backers.'

Bryant's voice crackles on the other end. "No, this is …

Get in the Hummer! Get in the Hummer!" Steve hears a thump on the other end of the line. Suddenly, Huginn and Muninn come careening through the ramp from upper Wacker, screeching and squawking in terror.

Eyes widening, Steve shouts to the members of the Guard on top of the ramp herding the press corp. "Get everyone down here! Now!"

The Guard members look up instead and raise their M4s, like Steve's team, their weapons are outfitted with grenade launchers. Some of the press corp follow their gaze and lift cameras. Others come running down the ramp towards the checkpoint.

The Guard starts firing grenades and Steve hears what sounds like a lion's roar ... but it's coming from the sky. "I got one! I got one!" someone says. "Cover!" screams someone else. The Guard starts herding the remaining members of the press towards the ramp to Lower Wacker, but a few lone photographers stand outside. A shape falls from the sky between the cameramen and the ramp. Steve sees a giant spiked tail attached to enormous bat wings drop from the sky, and hears the snap of bones and wet sounds of pulverized flesh. A dark body of something very menacing is suddenly blocking the tunnel's mouth.

Shadows dart over the downed creature, and then there is the flash of another scorpion tail and more wings just beyond the downed thing. One of the camera men screams, and then he's aloft and thrashing, carried by one of the creatures—Steve can only see that scorpion tail, attached to a tawny back, and vast, bat-like wings. As the cameraman flails, the tail of the flying beast twists and whips down. The sharp spike at the end of the tail plunges into the man's back and the man in the creature's grip goes slack.

For a moment no one says anything. Then one of the Guard furthest up the ramp says, "They're gone."

"What are they?" says Steve, walking towards the tunnel mouth. No one answers, but members of the Guard raise their weapons and fan out around Steve.

A few moments later he's stepping out into sunlight, and pacing around the beast they shot. It's the size of a bull. If its bat-like wings were unfurled Steve's sure they'd be as wide as a small house. Its head, body, and limbs are lion-like. "What the Hell?" Steve whispers to himself. And then Bryant's voice crackles on the line. "Liddell has confirmed they're manticore."

"They?" says Steve, shivering in the chill, eyeing the deceptively cheerful blue sky. "How many?"

"A dozen, sir."

Steve looks down. "Eleven are left," says Steve, looking at the dead beast in front of him. "We need to form a party to hunt them down."

"Yes, sir," says Bryant.

Someone from the press shouts out, "Will you be using deadly force?"

Someone else says, "What about their scientific value?"

Steve turns around and hits the button to open up a line to headquarters. As soon as it picks up, Steve says, "General Bautista, we have a situation."

The voice of one of Bautista's aides sounds at the other end of the line. "Yes, Captain Rogers, we do."

"You know about the manticore pack then?" says Steve.

There is silence at the other end of the line. "No, sir. I was speaking about the Governor's order to redeploy the Guard to the airports."

It's Steve's turn to fall silent. When he regains his voice, the only word that comes out of his mouth is, "What?"

The aide's voice is wobbly. "A humanitarian crisis is developing at the airports. Other airports have started turning away flights from Chicago—they're afraid recent events are a result of contagion. Airplanes have been forced to return, camps are forming outside of O'Hare and Midway on the highways—"

"Well, then call in the Wisconsin Guard to help out!" Steve says.

The aide's voice becomes crisp and annoyed. "That takes an order from the Governor!"

Steve takes a deep breath. "What about Washington?"

"Still not ready to step in and usurp state's sovereignty," says the aide. "Technically, the elf attack was an act of terrorism and not war, and the trolls are not an organized force; therefore Washington is not authorized to—"

Steve takes his hand from his earpiece to keep from hurling it at the ground.

"We're trying to convince the Governor to call in more help. In the meantime we need you back at HQ. Jameson needs you to act as a liaison between ADUO and the city police and firefighters while he runs things here."

The hot wash of anger changes rapidly to dread. Jameson is going to be in charge?

Pulling out his phone, Steve checks his email. Still no word from Lewis. He grinds his teeth. Hopping into a Humvee he taps out a short email, doing nothing to disguise the situation on the ground, the chaos, the implication that she has been kidnapped or that she's not even alive. He does nothing to hide the desperation he feels. He hopes wherever Lewis is, Loki gets it.

In the mortal vernacular, Loki doesn't get it.

The light of dawn is breaking through the edge of the hotel curtains and Loki is peeling off his coat, preparing to go to sleep, but his mind is filled with memories of Hindu prayers and Amy's question, "Are you Shiva?"

He isn't Shiva, but trying to deny it made his skin crawl. He lays the coat on the chair and makes his way to the bed. Slipping off her shoes, Amy is right behind him.

Flopping down on the bed, most of his clothes still on, he closes his eyes.

He hears Amy's footsteps falter. "Your book, it fell."

Raising his eyelids, he catches sight of her coming towards him, book in her hand.

Lying beside him on her stomach, she flips through the pages and then lets the book fall open where it may. "I've seen this book in your dreams. What is it?"

"Lothur's journal," says Loki, putting a hand to his eyes.

She is silent for a moment. "Lothur is one of our names for you," she says quietly.

He really should have suspected that. Loki chuckles, but it comes out half a sob.

"What language is this?" she asks. "It looks like Aesir, or maybe Jotunn, and yet … "

"You know Aesir now?" says Loki, rolling to his side to stare at her.

Not looking up from the page, she says, "Yes, I think you accidentally transmitted it to me in your dream."

Loki's eyebrows rise, but she doesn't notice. "Why is this woman on fire?" she says, staring at a hand-rendered sketch.

Loki rolls onto his stomach, his side touching hers. The book always falls open to this page. He runs a finger beneath the caption, written in a fast tight hand, and reads aloud.

"And I have dreams of my love, who was not my love, but was. Her father said words low against me, so low that it caused her heart to flame. And the flame of her heart spread to the utmost ends of her limbs. My love died in flames."

Loki swallows. The words physically hurt, the image they conjure too real.

Amy turns the page. "Go on," she whispers.

Loki's looks down and sighs. Not sure why, he complies. *"And in my dream, my friend, my brother, he learned of this and declared that we would go to her father so that he will know, that to worship him is also to worship me ... As though that would bring back my love."*

Stroking the page reverently, Amy says, "It sounds like the story of Sati ... "

"Sati ... " The name sounds familiar.

"Wife of Shiva," says Amy softly. "She killed herself when her father didn't approve of Shiva—"

Loki snaps the journal shut. His breathing suddenly heavy and ragged, he covers the book with his arms and drops his head.

"Loki," says Amy. "Are you alright?"

Turning his head, he glares at her.

She swallows. "Ah ... "

Her arm drapes over him. He is absurdly grateful for the warmth.

"Reincarnation is a ridiculous concept," he says, sounding

petulant to his own ears.

Amy is quiet a moment. "When you were drunk, in the bar, you said that we were all just figments of the imagination of a universe trying to understand itself."

"What's your point?"

He hears her lick her lips. "Maybe there are some things the universe has yet to understand and can't let die. Chaos would seem to be a pretty eternal concept."

Loki snorts. "You're ridiculous."

She huffs a laugh. "I am very tired."

A shiver sweeps through Loki's body, and he suddenly feels very cold. There is one reason, he must not, cannot believe this. "If it were true, why wouldn't Hoenir tell me, Amy? Why?"

"I don't know."

Of course she doesn't. And then Loki laughs. Hoenir never told him anything.

Either Amy is mad, and he is mad, or Odin and Hoenir don't—didn't—know. He closes his eyes.

But of course they knew. Hoenir knew he could read Lothur's journal, and Odin knew nearly everything.

Beside him, Amy sighs drowsily, and her body trembles as she slips into sleep.

Loki feels that as though all the magic in his nervous system is crackling and on fire, yet perversely he's chilled. Odin betrayed him outright, but Hoenir … Hoenir betrayed him by omission. Hoenir who never said a bad word towards anyone. A giggle escapes his lips and he pushes his face into a pillow. Hoenir never said anything at all.

Face in the pillow, he bites his lip to keep from screaming in frustration. And then with a deep breath, he edges out from beneath Amy's arm. Sitting up beside her, he brushes a stray tendril of hair from her eyes and notices he's turned blue at some point. Of course, she wouldn't have commented, or even minded.

He flexes his hand, eyes moving between his blue fingers to the sleeping girl. He needs rest. He could solicit her help in achieving some relaxation. Scowling, he looks hard at her lips, mouthing some inaudible whispers in sleep.

Sleeping with her has been more satisfying than he expected, but she is no Sigyn. She wouldn't fight him and then tend him for two hundred years in a cave. He snorts softly. In less than a century Amy will be dead.

He takes a ragged breath. A night ago, or a few fucks ago, they'd lain in afterglow, and Amy had said, "So the whole immortality thing ... "

Loki had tensed in her arms. When he used to travel openly on Earth with Thor, mortals were always trying to ply him with sexual favors in return for immortality, even though the myth of him kidnapping Idunn and stealing her apples was just a myth.

He'd felt his lip curling into a sneer, but then Amy had said, "Doesn't it get horribly boring? What do you do for all that time?"

Loki had laughed aloud at her utter lack of guile. Even now, sitting beside her, the memory makes him feel a little weak, a bit sentimental. After being on Earth, Asgard does seem boring. How fun it would be to stay and see what humans will do next.

Taking a breath, Loki shakes himself. He feels the chill again. Standing up he makes his way to the bathroom.

A few minutes later he is sitting in the bathtub, spigot at a roaring blast. Loki is alternately freezing the water's surface, and splitting the molecules of oxygen and hydrogen to set them aflame. In the corner of the room Cera is swirling.

Staring at a flame in his hands, Loki says to her, "It is so easy to split molecules. But putting them back together—I know how and yet it takes so much energy. It's as though it goes against my nature." Like healing goes against his nature.

Because he's the embodiment of chaos and destruction?

Cera hums. "When you have me you'll be able to do, have, or make anything."

Loki lets the flame leap from one hand to another. "Yes."

At that moment Amy pokes her head into the bathroom, blinking and sleepy-eyed.

"You can even keep her for genetic exchange," Cera says with a resigned sigh. "I suppose you have to have someone."

Loki raises an eyebrow, bemused at the obvious disdain in Cera's voice.

"Loki, are you alright?" Amy says, oblivious to Cera's magical commentary.

Loki's lips quirk. It is nice to have Cera not asking him to kill her. He tilts his head at Cera's words. He can have anything. He hasn't really thought about what happens after he burns Asgard to the ground.

… What would he want?

"Just taking a bath," he says with a smile.

… What would he do with Cera's power?

Amy stares at the flames. "Looks a little hot for me." She yawns.

"Go to bed," says Loki.

She nods and says something, but the water from the spigot is loud and Loki doesn't hear.

When he finally turns off the water, he hears the door shut, Amy's footsteps pacing the suite, and then the sound of the TV flicking on.

Toweling himself off, he steps out of the bathroom a few minutes later, Cera following behind like a well-behaved dog. Amy is on the couch, knees up to her chin, arms wrapped tight around her legs. The television is set to a news channel. On the screen are white tents erected by a highway.

"What's this?" says Loki. He means why is she watching TV. He's suddenly in the mood to exchange genetic material again.

With a gasp, Amy turns her head. "The Red Cross is setting up tent cities by the airports. Flights from Chicago are being turned away."

Loki purses his lips.

Amy's shoulders tremble. "People can't go back to the city. Trolls are everywhere ... I checked my email in the lobby ... "

Loki feels his pulse quicken. "Did you call or email ADUO to check-in, Amy?" he says carefully, feeling the beginnings of anger and a headache start to flare.

"Maybe you should kill her after all," Cera whispers, unseen and unheard by the girl.

"No, they could trace that," says Amy, her brow furrowing.

Loki relaxes.

Cooing happily, Cera says, "Oh, you're right about her! She is a suitable receptacle for genetic material. I really shouldn't begrudge you that ... I wouldn't want to be your genetic material receptacle."

Amy's gaze stays trained on Loki. "Loki, gates keep opening—trolls, a wyrm, and weird things called manticores are slipping through."

Loki tilts his head.

Her voice drops to a whisper. "Jameson is saying you're responsible."

Loki sneers. "I have nothing to do with it!"

Amy waves a hand in the air. "Well, obviously!"

Loki blinks at her forceful rejection of the idea. And then he waggles his eyebrows. "I suppose you would notice that I've been otherwise occupied."

Amy huffs. "It's not just that … "

She looks away. "Loki, they think you've kidnapped me. Laura, Brett and Bryant sent me emails. They're all worried … " She bites her lip. "Not Steve, though. He doesn't believe that."

Loki takes a step forward, his skin heating. He's not sure if he likes Steve knowing him that well.

Looking up, Amy meets his eyes. "Steve says they need you. No one can tell them why the World Gates keep opening, and Loki, you can close gates!"

"And why should I help?" says Loki. "Let them deal with the wyrm, trolls, and manticore they're blaming me for. I was on my way to Vanaheim before the elven invasion—"

"You don't owe them anything," Amy says. "But I have to check in."

Loki reels back. She'll tell them about his ability to walk the In-Between. "Don't," he says quickly. "Come with me to Vanaheim."

For a moment her face lights up. He can see the gears in her brain working, the wonder glowing in her eyes.

"We'll need to pick up some camping gear here in Paris," Loki says, taking advantage of her enthusiasm. "The World Gate from Visby drops one off in the most inconvenient location. We'll have to camp a day to make sure I'm up for a walk through the In-Between to Vanaheim's main city … "

"Should we take a car?" says Amy, a smile growing on her face. "You could rent one. I could drive it!"

Loki grimaces. "I wish. No the Vanir will not take kindly to me bringing a human to their realm. A human vehicle would raise too much suspicion, though it would be terribly convenient."

Amy's lips crumple into a worried frown. "They don't like humans?"

Loki starts to pace. He waves a hand, "No, no. They're fine with humans. But they were the first to believe in the policy of non-interference with human affairs. If they discover you're human they'll spare your life but likely end mine." He scratches his chin. "Nonetheless, I think I can hide your humanity, with an illusion."

Amy's face falls. "I can't cause you any more trouble." Her throat moves as she swallows. "Go to Vanaheim. I can go to the American embassy here in Paris after you're gone. I'll even wait a few days if you think it's safer for you."

Loki looks up at Amy sharply.

From the corner, Cera says, "Maybe you should kill her after all."

She swallows again. "I should probably physically check in, anyway. Everyone knows you can fake my appearance and voice."

Loki stops pacing. No, this will not do. She'll have to explain how she came to Paris, and how she escaped the fire. Even if he told her to lie for him, he's not convinced Steve couldn't wrangle the truth out of her. Given Amy's nature, possibly with only the rise of an angry eyebrow.

Amy licks her lips. "I don't suppose you know why the gates are opening with more frequency? I mean, you don't owe them anything, and Jameson's an idiot but … "

Only half listening, Loki begins pacing again, contemplating the feasibility of walking the In-Between with her to Visby right now. She'd be furious, but he could beg forgiveness later.

" … but it is my city," she says softly. "People have died. And if they knew why, maybe … "

Loki stops short. "Gates opening with greater frequency?"

"I've been meaning to ask about that," Cera says. "But it is upsetting the enemies of Josef, so I don't think I mind very much."

Loki's eye slide to Cera. She creates World Gates—openings to branches of the World Tree— inadvertently with the ambient magic that is inherent to her physical form. The Promethean Wire mutes that magic only slightly.

Loki's eyes widen. His back turned to Amy he says quietly, "Did Steve say anything about the Promethean Sphere around Cera breaking down?"

"No," she says. "He says it isn't breaking down at all, and that's why everyone is so confused."

Loki looks at Cera. Cera flickers. "Nope, my prison's still intact." The mist of her non-corporeal form expands and shrinks as though sighing.

Amy tilts her head and her brow furrows. "And also, this is really weird, but the elves say gates in Chicago opened up before Cera had even arrived … "

And suddenly Loki knows what is happening. He should have guessed right away. Magic has a very different relationship to time. For humans, time is a one-way street that they hurtle along at one speed in one direction. Loki can take short cuts through time and space through the In-Between and slip along the branches of the World Tree. Still, time for him is essentially a linear thing, too. But for magic, time is more like a pond. Magic itself is a stone that sends ripples through the surface. Cera is essentially magic given life. The ripples she creates are strong enough to open World Gates, and ripples move from a cast stone in all directions.

Loki's heart starts to pound in his ears. "I will come back to Chicago with you, Amy," he says quietly, a smirk forming on his lips.

"You will?" says Amy. Hiding the smile with a stern look, he turns around and meets her eyes. They're wide and trusting.

Still trying to appear stern he says, "I will help your people."

Amy bites her lip and nods.

"But listen to me, ADUO believes I am the enemy. I need you not to tell about my skills in teleportation."

Amy nods again, eyes wide. "Of course, in case you need to escape!"

Loki smiles. That was so easy. But he won't be able to let her out of his sight, lest someone connive it out of her. He tenses slightly at the thought

Amy lunges forward and wraps her arms around his neck. "Thank you, Loki! Thank you for helping!" She squeezes her body tightly against him, and Loki smiles. Ah, to be treated as a hero, when actually his ends are quite selfish.

Cera's ripples are increasing in frequency, because a great deal of magic is soon to be unleashed. More magic than Cera knows how to unleash on her own—she may be nearly omnipotent, but she's about as omniscient as a three year old.

He almost laughs aloud. Instead he tightens his hands on Amy's waist and drops his forehead to hers.

Loki doesn't know how it will happen, but he does know, very soon, Cera will be his.

Wrapping his arms around her, he breathes in the scent of her hair, and runs his hands down along her spine, enjoying the feel of her shudder—he may still have time to claim a hero's reward.

CHAPTER 10

Walking through the revolving doors of headquarters, Steve is first assaulted by a riot of phones ringing off the hook. And then by Laura Stodgill. Carrying a digital tablet, she slides next to him. "I'm so glad you're here. But we still don't have a script."

Striding through the throng of people, Stodgill falling into step beside him, Steve says, "Script?"

Pushing back a loose strand of hair, Laura's lips flatten. "Yes, talking points, what you're authorized to say about—" she lifts her hand in a gesture that says, 'everything.'

Steve runs a hand over his head and narrows his eyes at her. So, he's the liaison that isn't allowed to liaison? To her credit Stodgill has the decency to look a little ashamed.

A group of police officers press by. Somewhere beyond them he hears someone say, "It is a contagion. We're all going to die as mindless green killing machines. That's why the airports are closed—that's why the feds aren't here." The officers pass and Steve can't locate the source of the voice.

His eyes fall on Agent Hernandez sitting at a desk; a line of men and women stand beyond him.

"They're here to volunteer," says Stodgill, tilting her head in the direction of the line.

A flash goes off somewhere. "Press," says Stodgill. "They keep sneaking in. I'll take care of it." She steps quickly away.

Steve walks towards Hernandez. Just as he reaches the agent's side, Hernandez says, "Name?" to the first person in line—a tall lanky kid with dark skin and a mop of uneven straight black hair.

"Bohdi Patel," says the kid with a thick Indian accent. He's wearing rumpled jeans and a thick wool jacket that looks like it's seen better days. A box of cigarettes and a lighter peek out of a pocket.

"Occupation?" says Hernandez.

"Cab driver," says Bohdi. The kid has to be of legal age to drive a cab, but his eyes are very wide with long thick lashes most women would kill to have—they give him an innocent boyish look.

Hernandez looks up at Steve and nods. Hernandez's eyes go to Bohdi, back to Steve again, and he raises an eyebrow. Maybe he's thinking what Steve's thinking—the kid looks too young for this.

Eyeing Bohdi, Steve says, "What type of vehicle do you drive?"

"It's a cab—a minivan cab, sir," Bohdi says.

"That will work," says Hernandez. "Too big for a manticore to pick up, agile enough to dodge trolls. Is the vehicle yours?"

Bohdi winces and bites back a smile. "Sure ... but I, uh, don't have the registration on me today ... "

Steve's eyebrows go up at the obvious lie.

Dropping his smile, Bohdi says, "But I want to help people, this is my city now." And those words seem sincere enough. Steve looks at the line behind Bohdi. They don't have time or enough manpower to be choosey.

Putting a hand on Hernandez's shoulder, Steve says, "He's good, Agent. Assign him to the West Loop."

"Okay," says Hernandez. "You heard the man. You'll be ferrying people who don't have cars from their homes to the refugee camps up by O'Hare. A police escort will guard your passengers as they leave their buildings—"

Laura materializes at Steve's side. Turning towards her, Steve misses the rest of Hernandez's conversation. "Where is Jameson?" Steve asks Laura. "Any ETA on that script?"

Laura shakes her head. "I think he's working on it right now with the higher ups."

Steve scans the room. Police officers and firemen are milling uncomfortably around the desks where ADUO agents man the phones. A couple of men in hazmat suits stand in a corner. A television is tuned to CNN. The screen shows tent cities by Chicago's airports. He can't hear what the announcer is saying but the subtitles are on. Despite the disruption to commodities in the midwest, grain prices haven't seen a significant rise. The Russians, Ukrainians, and Belarusians are apparently having bumper crops again this year.

Following his eyes, Laura says, "The same countries trying to give the elves the benefits of the Geneva convention?"

Steve doesn't have time to think about it; his head piece is beeping in his ear. Checking the caller ID he sees Brett's name. Steve had sent him out to scan the skies for manticores. Tapping to accept, he hears Brett's voice on the line. "Steve, I just got a pretty strong reading on the 200 block of Van Buren. We weren't able to get an exact location … "

"What is it?" says Steve.

Steve hears Brett take a sharp intake of breath."Yeah, well, pretty sure it came from near the top of one of the high rise buildings over here. We don't see anything but … "

Steve's mouth goes dry. A gate in the sky, perfect. Who knows what could be thinking of coming through that?

Taking a breath, Steve says, "Let's set up a post there. Brett, you're first watch."

"Yes, sir."

Steve taps his headpiece to disconnect and scans the room again. A few more flashbulbs go off somewhere and he scowls.

Beside him Laura says, "Rumor has it the Feds are busy securing every sensitive military and nuclear site in the country—and that's why they haven't taken over here yet."

Steve rubs his jaw. He doubts any sentient magical being would be interested in anything on Earth but Cera. But the Feds are scared. Everyone is scared, reacting instead of acting.

Nearby he hears a man shout, "Agent Rogers, Agent Rogers!"

Steve turns to see a grumpy looking Thor next to a harried looking FBI agent. "Sir," the FBI agent says, one hand on his ear piece. "There are reports of a boy and his mother bringing a bobcat with an elephant nose into a veterinarian's office. Should I send a team?"

"It's a baku," Thor says, as though everyone should know what that is. "It's a good omen. It will protect the boy and his mother from trolls and nightmares."

Steve stifles his anger at the agent's CYA. Waving a hand in Thor's direction, Steve says, "You heard Thor. Focus on magical invaders that eat people."

"Agent Rogers! Agent Rogers!" someone else shouts. "Troll reported in the South Loop."

Steve grabs a passing policewoman. "See anyone in this room familiar with the South Loop?"

"That's my beat, Sir," she says. She swallows. "But I'm less familiar with trolls. You have to shoot them in the heart, right?"

Steve's breath catches. They don't even know how to kill the monsters they're dealing with? "It's the eyes or mouth; you need a direct path to their brain," Steve says.

The police woman's eyes go wide, and her skin pales.

"Thor," Steve says pointing at the police woman, "you're with her."

"Ahhh ... a shield maiden!" Thor exclaims, a wide smile on his face. Steve watches them leave the room, stunned by the woman's lack of intel.

He hears another whisper of "contagion" and some disjointed, fearful whispers of "dirty bomb," "smallpox," and "shoot for the heart." Searching for the sources his eyes fall on an empty desk at the far side of the room. Didn't he just get angry at an agent for CYA? Tightening his jaw, he walks towards the desk, vaguely aware of Laura following him.

Steve likes to maintain plausible deniability when he breaks rules. He tells himself he'll talk himself out of the trouble he's about to get into later, if he's still alive.

"What are you doing?" Laura says.

Kicking out a chair by the empty desk, Steve steps up onto the seat and then to the desk. "Writing my own script," he says. Turning to the rest of the room, Steve opens his mouth, prepared to ask for quiet, but the room is already silent. A whisper breaks the hush, "It's the guy who killed the snake!"

He feels a rush of something like exhilaration. There are clicks and a few flashes of light from cameras and phones, and for a moment Steve is blinded. "I'm Agent Steve Rogers," Steve says. The flashes all but stop as his words fill the room. It may be adrenaline, but as Steve continues to speak he hears his voice as though it comes from a different person, a person wiser and more confident than him. His eyes meet the faces of the people below him, and as their expressions morph from fear to determination, Steve feels another rush.

For all that is going wrong, that rush shouldn't feel good. But it does.

Amy pulls herself up out of Loki's embrace, the sound of thunder filling her ears. For a moment she doesn't understand what is going on, or even where she is. Gasping, she blinks in the dark. She can just barely make out the outline of shades—not heavy, luxurious, drapery, covering the window. She's not at the hotel in Paris anymore. She's in Loki's home. They've traveled back through the In-Between. She takes a deep breath. The thunder is fading away. No, not thunder …

"Just a helicopter," Loki mumbles. "Not Thor … " One blue hand snakes up and pulls her back down to him. Pillowing her head on his shoulder, she wraps an arm around his chest.

Loki's body begins to tremble as he slips back into sleep, but Amy's body feels abuzz with nerves. She bites her lip. She was so tired when they arrived she didn't even check his computer for messages from ADUO. She should have sent a message to them—but she was worn out and afraid in her exhausted state she'd accidentally let slip where they are. She runs a hand through Loki's black hair. It feels different when it's black, lighter, finer, cooler. Magic. She sighs, wondering when she'll get to run her hands through it again.

She closes her eyes. The bravery of what Loki wants to do is overwhelming—she wants her city to be safe, but not at the price of Loki's life. He needs rest to be able to walk the In-Between at a moment's notice if Jameson or his goons do anything stupid. Reluctantly, she pulls her hand away.

Her eyes go to the doorway leading to the living room. Maybe she can send a note now ...

Loki's body jerks beneath her and the room begins to glow. She blinks her eyes and she's lying in long green grass, but the scene fades out into golden hazy light just a few meters in front of her. Loki is dreaming again.

She hears a whinny and looks around. There is a mare nearby facing off into the hazy golden distance. Sitting up she says, "Well, hello."

The mare turns its head in Amy's direction, but Amy can't really tell if the animal is responding to her, or the sudden trill of insects in the grass. The horse is dapple gray, delicately boned, and relatively small. With large eyes, dainty muzzle, and high crested neck she almost looks Arabian. Turning away again, the mare looks off into the distance and shapes begin to form on the horizon.

Amy's gaze follows the mare's and she sees a walled city. She blinks, one part of the wall is concealed by scaffolding. She sees a line of horses pulling driver-less wagons filled with stones. A familiar larger horse is running down the column, nipping at their haunches.

"Svaðilfari," Amy whispers.

At mention of the stallion's name, the mare swings her head around, ears pricked in Amy's direction. Amy lets out a small breath of surprise. The mare did hear her. Only one person hears her in Loki's dreams. Oh.

"Loki?" she whispers. She puts a hand down into the grass beside her and feels Loki, the real Loki, beneath her hand. His breathing is even and regular.

The mare shakes its head, and then it looks away and begins to walk towards the Asgardian dream city. It must be an illusion of the dream, but the scene around Amy blurs by, the grass beneath her turning in a heartbeat to stones and then a road, the city in the distance approaching incredibly fast.

The mare stops before the wall by the line of horses towing their wagons. With a whinny she turns towards the stallion driving them. The mare whickers, and the stallion stops in its tracks. Nostrils flaring, Svaðilfari shakes his head, and gives a long bugling neigh of interest.

With flirty whinny and a playful buck, the mare begins to trot back the way she came. Amy is still dragged along by the dream—but this time the pace feels true, the scene changing at a realistic speed.

She hears the pounding of hooves and turns her head to see the stallion breaking into a gallop. The mare gives a whinny that sounds suspiciously like a laugh and breaks into a gallop of her own.

The mare gallops back through the place where Amy first saw her, periodically slowing to give Svaðilfari a chance to catch up. Amy can tell by the low rumbling in his chest that the stallion is becoming increasingly frustrated. After what feels like hours, but Amy is certain is just another trick of the dream, the mare seems to grow tired of the game. Giving a snort of impatience, she gallops towards a line of dark trees.

Amy blinks, and they are at the tree line. In the distance she hears the thud of hooves—evidently Svaðilfari hasn't given up. Amy bites her lip; she wants out of this dream.

Suddenly flattening her ears against her skull, the mare rears up and a harsh, rattling snort of fear reverberates from her chest.

"Now!" a man shouts.

Ropes suddenly fly through the air, and shadows of men emerge from the trees. A few of the ropes fall harmlessly to the ground, but one loops around the mare's neck. The mare skitters backwards but that only makes the noose grow tight. Amy can hear Svaðilfari's snort of rage, and the pounding of his hooves getting closer.

"We've got her," says a man. Amy turns to look at him. He has a patch over one eye.

More men come from out of the trees, and more ropes go around the mare's neck.

The mare rears and screams in panic and fury. The whites of her eyes show as she rolls her eyes in Amy's direction as though begging for help. The stallion's hooves are now thundering in Amy's ears.

Holding her head high, the mare digs her hooves into the ground and pulls against her bonds, knocking a few of her captors to the side in her frenzy.

"Let her go!" Amy screams to the man with the eye patch.

Of course the man doesn't hear Amy. Holding onto the rope, he shouts at the mare. "You deviant. Yes, I know who you are. Hide as a mare and get fucked as a mare!"

Amy screams, "Loki!" The mare squeals in terror. The man with the rope shouts, "Stop fighting it!" The low rumble of an angry stallion makes Amy turn her head. Just heartbeats away, Svaðilfari is charging forward, nostrils wide, his dark coat flecked with lather.

"You will stop!" shouts the man with one eye. The mare freezes, as though frozen on a single frame of film. Svaðilfari lunges forward.

Turning away, Amy throws her body at where she thinks Loki lies. Feeling the curve of his shoulders beneath her hands, she shouts, "Wake up, Loki! Wake up!"

Invisible hands fall on her shoulders and squeeze tight. She's shaken so hard her jaw snaps shut, but merciful darkness replaces the golden light of the dream. The sound of rough breathing fills her ears. It takes a moment to realize it isn't her own.

As her eyes adjust to the darkness she sees Loki lying on his back, eyes wide open, body shaking, hands still on her shoulders.

"Loki?" she says.

He doesn't respond.

She closes her eyes. When she first met Loki, she'd teased him about the myth of him turning into a mare and getting impregnated by Svaðilfari. He'd dismissed her so defensively, and she'd laughed. The memory hurts now.

She can't bring herself to ask if he's okay. "Hey, it's me," she whispers.

Without responding, he sits up and wraps her in his arms. Pressing his forehead against hers, he begins to rock them back and forth. Amy puts her arms around his shoulders. She has no idea what to say.

And then Loki begins to chuckle, low and deep and frightening.

"Loki?" she whispers.

He snickers. "Do you know what this means, Amy?"

That he was probably the mother of Sleipnir after all?

Snickering again, he says, "I gave my oath to Freyja I would keep the wall from being completed on time and I did."

His voice turns low and dangerous. "I kept my oath, even after death."

He chuckles, and it's not a nice sound. Light rises around them from no discernible source. Loki pushes her back, his eyes meeting hers. "I haven't given my oath to Odin yet, that I will destroy him ... " He grins. His black hair has fallen forward over his eyes, equally black. His teeth are very white against his blue skin. "I was afraid, afraid that I wouldn't succeed, that I'd die first. But now I don't have to worry about that."

Amy takes a breath. "I don't think—"

Loki laughs and squeezes her tight. "Odin? Do you hear me! You will kneel before me as all of Asgard burns! I give you my oath!"

"That was Odin in the dream?" Amy stammers.

Loki nods against her. And then pushing her back again, Loki meets her eyes. "Don't worry, I will help your people!" His eyes widen. "Amy, I owe you so much." Giving her a warm genuine smile, he says, "If you hadn't woken me, I might not have been able to remember the dream. I might not have known the truth!"

Amy's mouth drops. This wasn't the lesson she'd gotten from this episode.

Loki's lips are on hers, and his hand is ghosting its way

down her spine. "Thank you, thank you, thank you."

She wants to melt into him, but she pulls back. "We need to talk to Steve."

Loki blinks once and then nods.

Amy takes a deep breath. "I need to take a shower."

"And I need to put on my armor." He kisses her. "See you in a few minutes."

She nods, but it is a long time before she can make herself get up.

Sitting on his bed, Loki finishes putting on his boots. A light patter of rain is falling against the window. From the living room he sees the faint glow of computer monitors and hears the sound of a newscast.

He glances over at Laevithin, and then his eyes go to Amy's purse. He blinks at it and looks towards the ambient glow coming from the living room.

Tilting his head, he picks up her purse and turns it around in his hand. Opening it, he finds her wallet. Inside is a debit card, not enough money to bother stealing even if he was in the mood, identification, and a picture of Beatrice, Amy and Fenrir. He finds himself smiling at the photo.

Putting back the wallet, he finds a curious little pink rectangular packet. He opens it. Inside is a package of 28 little plastic slots arranged in a circle, three already consumed. Candy?

Curious, he squints closely at the barely legible writing on the package: Oral contraceptives. He tilts his head and considers tossing the packet aside. If he's honest he likes the risk of pregnancy. And then he sneers at himself. He is such a fool—another child he'd be unable to protect. Skin hot, he puts the package back where he found it.

Looking down he sees one more item in her purse. A set of keys with a whistle attached ... not even the snake venom spray she'd hit him with when he first arrived on Earth—a whistle.

Amy is not as fierce as Sigyn was, even if he was interested in her for something more than a passing ... whatever. She is too soft. He would destroy Amy, like he had Anganboða,. His knuckles go white on the strap of Amy's bag. And Sigyn, too.

Scowling, he puts the purse down, just as a pink haze begins to form in the room. "You're back in Chicago!" says Cera.

Loki raises an eyebrow in greeting.

"Is it really necessary for you to help her solve the World Gate problem?" Cera asks, floating about Loki's head.

No, it isn't. But he needs to be in Chicago when Cera slips from the Promethean Wire, and Amy isn't going to be happy until she checks in—and Loki needs to be with her when she does so she doesn't accidentally spill the beans about his ability to teleport or the location of his home. It's a horribly convoluted idea when he thinks about it, but his best usually are.

Instead of saying that, Loki says, "But helping them will make me a hero."

Cera's mist goes darker. "Ohhhhh ... Like Josef was the hero. When the revolution comes it will be so much easier!"

Loki's eyebrows go up at the mention of the 'revolution.' It's Cera's thing. Loki could care less one way or another, and she won't have much choice in the matter.

Cera inflates and deflates, and says happily, "With you on my side, I can't lose!"

Loki's mouth drops, and the breath rushes out of his lungs.

"Couldn't we have stayed in bed all day?" Loki whines as Sigyn pulls him out of the house. "What good is freedom if I can't even enjoy my own down mattress? Really, Sigyn, after 200 years of sleeping on a straw mat without the company of my wife ... "

Smirking at him, Sigyn narrows her eyes. In truth, Loki has enjoyed his mattress and the company of his wife many times in the past hundred years or so. But he had to make himself invisible when he did so and he disguised Sigyn's side of the activities ... sometimes. He snickers to himself thinking how scandalized and bewildered Heimdall would have been if he'd bothered to spy on Loki's wife some of those nights.

No doubt guessing his thoughts, Sigyn rolls her eyes. But she is smiling. "Hoenir, Mimir and your sons have been planning this feast for the past two decades." Loki wants to whine some more, but instead finds himself salivating and licking his lips. He's always had a huge appetite, and since the cave it's only gotten worse.

He whines a little bit more as they make their way to Hoenir's, but it's just to make Sigyn laugh.

In the cave, Loki's understanding and connection to magic had deepened. Before Hoenir's hut is even in view he can feel the buzz of magic through the trees. As they round the last bend, he has to avert his eyes for a moment—Hoenir's magic is so bright.

Because he's looking away, it's Sigyn who sees them first. "Odin's Einherjar guard," says Sigyn. "And his and Thor's mounts."

Eyes adjusted to the magic, Loki turns to look at his wife.

Her face is pensive. "They weren't invited," she says quietly.

Loki's lips twitch. "Well, as long as there is enough food for Thor and me both ... " he shrugs and smiles, not wanting to see the end of her good mood.

Sigyn doesn't respond. The Einherjar straighten as Sigyn and Loki knock on Hoenir's door. Hoenir opens it, Mimir mounted on a staff, both of them looking more nervous than happy. As Hoenir closes the door, Odin's voice booms, "Loki, welcome back!"

Loki blinks at his first sight of Odin and Thor since his release. Clothing fashions have changed—of course, the buildings and people of Asgard are always changing their adornment. Loki doesn't recognize this particular clothing style, but it is more gold, silver and silk than he has ever seen. It's rather out of place in Hoenir's kitchen.

"Good to be back," says Loki with a wink and a grin. He wonders if he is supposed to bow, but there is no court around, and that seems superfluous.

Odin's one eye narrows almost imperceptibly, and then he comes forward and claps Loki on the back. Grinning, Thor comes forward and claps him on the other side. Loki almost falls over, but Odin catches him.

Nari and Valli, finally grown to nearly men, are wearing tight smiles, and their eyes keep darting to the king and prince.

"Hoenir!" Odin declares. "Put our seats next to the guest of honor!"

Hoenir's lips twitch, and Mimir's eyebrows rise, but Mimir says, "Of course, Your Majesty."

Loki tilts his head. How ridiculously formal.

When they're all seated on Hoenir's rough hewn benches by the table, Loki has to work to keep the mood light—he succeeds. Mostly. But the king's presence has put everyone but Thor a little off. Loki wouldn't have expected his boys or Sigyn to be pleased by the king's presence, but the looks he catches from their eyes seem downright hostile.

When Thor starts to regale the table about a tussle he got into with a legion of dwarven mercenaries, Loki turns to Odin and says, "So, how are things?"

Odin looks delighted that Loki has brought it up. Smiling, he gives a dramatic sigh, "Oh, the dwarf merchants are pushing for more autonomy from their king ... "

Loki raises an eyebrow at that. He wasn't sure why Odin cared so much. The king goes on, " ... and Freyja is jostling for political clout ... "

That makes Loki's eyebrows rise. It was bound to happen someday. Odin and Freyja both have small armies of Einherjar at their disposal. Formerly mortal warriors rescued from death, they are unquestioningly loyal to their 'saviors.'

Odin's voice lowers. "I think she may even be after the throne. Can you imagine, a woman ruling?"

This would be the time to play it safe. But Loki can't resist. Shrugging, he says, "I don't know, I hear the witch Gullveig has done a decent job in Jotunheim's Iron Wood."

Sigyn starts coughing; the rest of the table falls silent.

Odin glares at Loki. Giving him a crooked half smile, Loki says, "What? Haven't you heard of the mortal expression devil's advocate?" Loki has to suppress a laugh at his cleverness at that— the mortals have been drawing him with horns since the Christians entered Europe.

Odin snorts. "You're my devil, alright." And then he grins and claps Loki on the back. "But with you on my side, I can't fail."

In headquarters, Steve's earpiece beeps. He ignores it and focuses on the fireman in front of him. Over the din of the situation room, the man says, "It's possible we could use our hoses to fire on the flying things and trolls while buildings are evacuated."

The beeping of Steve's earpiece stops. Beside him, he hears Bryant's beeping faintly.

Nodding at the fireman, Steve says, "That would free up police from evacuation duty. Talk to Hernandez, he's coordinating the pick ups."

The man walks away and Steve's just about to tap his earpiece and listen to his messages when Bryant shouts, "It's Brett! He sees Loki and Lewis in the building where he detected the World Gate!"

There is a hush in the immediate vicinity around Steve.

Behind him he hears Mayor Ronnie's voice. "Isn't Loki the ass who set up my nephew and is responsible for this shit?"

When did the mayor get here? Steve turns to see the mayor, police chief and Jameson directly behind him. His jaw twitches. Just when he was starting to get things under control …

Taking a step forward, Steve holds up his hands. "It hasn't been proven that Loki—"

"Yes," says Jameson.

"No!" says Steve.

Mayor Ronnie looks between Steve and Jameson only once and then turns to the police chief. "I want a SWAT team there right now! Bring them both in!"

"I couldn't agree more," Jameson says.

"You need a warrant," Steve says, trying to stall for time.

"Like Hell," says Ronnie. "He is a fucking alien, a terrorist, and we are defending this city. This isn't a game of cops and robbers."

"Sir, I don't think that is a good idea," Bryant says. "Loki is extremely dangerous and—"

"Yes, he plays with fire, we've all read the reports," says Jameson. "Fortunately it's just started to rain."

"I don't think … " says Bryant.

"Give me your earpiece and your phone, Agent, I want to speak to your brother," says Jameson.

Giving Steve a wary look, Bryant hands them over.

"Jameson, Chief, you're with me," says Mayor Ronnie. Steve doesn't miss the way they look past him. His jaw tightens as they walk away. Beside him, Bryant says, "Sir … this is not good."

Steve doesn't answer. Instead he turns to the room at large and says, "Where is Thor?"

A policewoman manning phones stands up. "He's on the north side chasing down the manticores with officers Drake and—"

"Get your officers on the line," Steve shouts. "I need Thor now!"

Amy is sitting at his desk, her face lit by the computer monitor when Loki walks into the living room. He's not anxious for the meeting with ADUO to happen, so he heads to the kitchen, saying, "I'm just going to eat a little more."

"Of course," says Amy, eyes flicking to him and back to the screen. "Load up and be ready to teleport. Just in case someone's an idiot."

Loki settles on the counter with what's left of his stores

and munches away while the news blasts over Amy's shoulder on the computer screen. It's mostly about how many reporters have been killed, the number of confirmed civilian casualties, and how many people have been displaced. Nothing particularly useful.

He's just opened a protein bar when Amy switches to something else, some sort of entertainment coverage. "I need a break from the real news," she sighs. "This looks interesting."

Grainy black and white film footage of a stylized prison starts to play on the screen. Raucous music blares from the speakers. There is a man in the footage who is vaguely familiar. He's prancing on his toes and wiggling his hips.

Loki snorts. "Look at that man, he's having sex with a ghost."

A voiceover begins, "In honor of what would have been the king's upcoming birthday in a few months' time … "

Amy hits the mute button and spins in Loki's chair. "That is Elvis. He is part of my culture, as is his music, and the dancing is tame."

"Dancing?" says Loki. "It looks to me more like he's giving the audience a middle finger salute with his whole body. And I wouldn't call that music."

Amy blinks at him, and then dropping her voice to a poor imitation of a man's, says, "Hey, you kids, get off my lawn!"

Loki stares at her.

Rolling her eyes, she says in her normal voice. "That's something we say when someone is being an old fogey."

He's used to be called argr, and deviant, but an old fogey? This is new.

Smirking, Loki hops off the counter and walks over to the chair. She cranes her neck to meet his gaze.

No, she isn't fierce, but he does like her. Bending down he kisses her, his arms wrapping around her back and pulling her up out of the chair. He's just finished putting on his armor, but there are some pieces that can be removed quite easily, and he has no desire to leave just yet.

For a moment she responds and then pulls back. He is about to protest but then her mouth drops open as though she is about to speak. No words come out, but in his head he hears her thoughts. *If we start this now, I'll never be able to go in.*

Loki takes a sharp breath. He hears her. She's still part of his purpose.

"You're right," he says, tilting his head, but not moving away.

Putting her cheek against his armored chest she whispers, "Thank you so much for doing this." Lifting her head, she meets his eyes. "I think I love you, you know?"

Loki's jaw gets hard. What does Amy know of love? Never married, no children ... she's practically a child herself.

Still, he smiles and says as gently as he can, "Thank you for that."

Her body shrinks a little.

"I need to get my helmet and sword," he says softly. Kissing her head, he turns away and walks into the bedroom. Trying to lighten the mood he says, "If you want to be funny, stick to your quantum physics jokes." He snickers. "If a photon crashes into a tree in a forest and no one is around, does it make any sound?"

His words are drowned out by the sound of approaching helicopters, but he keeps walking. Picking up his helmet and Laevithin, he turns around. One of the helicopters sounds very, very close.

Suddenly feeling wary, Loki flips the helmet onto his head and fastens it with careful fingers. Less haste, more speed as Odin once told him. The helicopter is nearly deafening, but over the noise a voice commands through a bullhorn, "Put your hands up." The sound echoes through his home, and a spotlight flashes by the bedroom window.

Loki can't see Amy but he can feel her annoyance, and in his mind he hears, You idiots. It almost makes him smile, both her lack of fear and the intimacy of their connection. It makes him feel warm and whole, and frantic at the same time. The men in the helicopter can't have her.

Grabbing Laevithin, Loki sprints down the hallway towards the living room. A step beyond the spotlight's glare, the moment seems to freeze in time. His mind catches on extraneous information—raindrops sparkling on the window, and the delicacy of Amy's profile lit in the harsh blue-white light as she obediently raises her arms. He might be hallucinating, or perhaps casting an illusion accidentally, because instead of two arms reaching heavenward, eight arms stretch up; they're nearly blue in the spotlight's eerie light.

Time suddenly has meaning again. His body is moving forward, invisible in his magical armor, and his mind is trying to determine what is real and what isn't, when from the bullhorn he hears a frantic, "She's not human!"

Lunging towards Amy, he hears the rapid staccato burst of gunfire, the thunder of helicopter blades, and the shattering of glass. Bullets and window shards pelt harmlessly against his armor, but Amy falls backwards, her body hitting the floor soundlessly in the din.

Falling to his knees beside her and shielding her with his body, Loki sees red stains blooming on her blouse, and a trickle of blood from a bullet wound in her throat. Loki pulls her up into his arms, trying to make her smaller. He wants to walk the In-Between, but she is so limp, her eyes wide open, and the smell of blood heavy in the air. She might not be strong enough ... and he still feels her. Her shock is like a cold rock in his gut. A strangled sound comes from his throat.

You destroy everything beautiful. He hears Baldur's voice in his head, as he sees Helen, Amy, Sigyn, and Anganboða, in his arms.

And suddenly, the sound of the helicopter and gunfire is muffled by the sound of his own scream.

The air around him ripples, and Loki turns his head towards the broken window. He barely sees the shadows of men standing on the helicopter's landing skids, weapons raised. He barely sees anything.

Another scream of rage and despair rips through him and magic whips unbidden from his body. Raindrops split into hydrogen and oxygen and burst into a solid wall of flame. There are more screams that aren't his own, the sound of more gunfire, and an explosion. The spotlight winks out, the wall of fire dissipates, and the only light left is from the helicopter, a spinning ball of flame plunging to the ground.

CHAPTER 11

Bryant is next to Steve. Hand pressed to his ear, Bryant is relaying messages from his brother Brett, who is watching the SWAT team approach Loki's home from his position atop a building less than half a block away.

Steve has a dispatcher's phone to his head. "Put Thor on, now!" Steve says.

"Yes, sir," says the police officer on the other end of the line.

Beside him, Bryant says, "They've got one helicopter by Loki's apartment, telling him to surrender. Guys are rappelling off another chopper onto the roof. Police are on the ground—"

Thor's slightly befuddled voice crackles at the other end of the line. "Is anyone there? Hello, hello? I am unused to Midgardian magics—"

"Thor! This is Steve. We've found Loki and Lewis.

Jameson and Mayor Ronnie have ordered a raid on his home. I need—"

Cutting him off, Thor's voice is suddenly confident and sure. "I will be outside your building in my chariot in five minutes. You will travel with me and lead me to Loki's home."

"I'll be there," Steve says, dropping the dispatcher's phone.

Beside Steve, Bryant shakes his head, his face drawn. "Brett says they shot Lewis! They shot Lewis!"

Hand still to his earpiece, Bryant says, "One helicopter down." He meets Steve's eyes just before Steve bolts for the stairs.

A few moments later Steve is outside in a throng of reporters in the middle of LaSalle Street. A light drizzle is falling. Steve's wondering how Thor will get the gauntlet of reporters to disperse when a bolt of lightning rips from the sky to the street a few feet away. Reporters and police bolt from the spot of smoking pavement. Steve runs towards it. A blur of gold streaks down from the sky towards him, and Thor's chariot is by Steve's side. Before Steve knows what's happening, Thor's hauled him in. "Which way?" shouts Thor, hand still on Steve's shoulder.

"Southwest," Steve says. The chariot lurches forward and up so steeply Steve nearly falls off. "Lewis has been hit," Steve shouts above the wind and popping of his ears.

As they pull above the buildings' roofs, Steve shouts, "If we hurry we may get there in time … "

… to save Lewis and Loki.

The words never leave Steve's mouth. The second helicopter that is flaming on the roof of Loki's high-rise condo building is giving the location away.

"Which domicile?" Thor shouts above the wind. A bolt of

lightning from his hammer lights the scene.

The lightning's glare is mirrored off the windows of Loki's building, and makes the concrete support beams look white as bleached bone. But where a window to the southeast penthouse should be, there is a gaping black hole, a cavernous maw in the sky. "Where the windows are broken," Steve shouts.

Nodding, Thor pushes Steve down, and the chariot dips to the level of the cavelike opening. They bounce three times as they land in the penthouse, and over the rattle of his jaw Steve can just barely hear the crunch of glass beneath the rolling wheels. They skid to a halt and Steve's head and shoulder slam against the chariot's wall.

"Stay down," Thor says.

Grabbing his aching shoulder, Steve blinks his eyes to adjust to the darkness. He takes a deep breath and swallows at the smell of blood, sweat and gunpowder. In the distance he hears the wail of fire alarms.

Thor steps from the chariot and Steve hears the crunch of glass. Thor's voice rings out, even, calm and controlled. "Loki? Are you here? It is I, Thor, and Agent Rogers."

There is no answer. Thor speaks again. "Both of us were opposed to this raid. We know the girl is hurt—you cannot heal her. You must give her to us if you want her to live."

Taking a shaky breath, Steve thinks of Lewis. It's his fault she's even here, isn't it? How many times has Bryant pushed Steve to put her on witness protection? But no, Steve wanted a contact with Loki. Shutting his eyes, Steve silently thinks—or prays—he's not sure, Please, Loki, we have to get her to the trauma unit. The center they set up above ADUO Headquarters is staffed with doctors with more experience in bullet wounds and blunt force trauma than any hospital in the city—and this being Chicago, that is saying something.

There is an intake of breath not from Thor or Steve. Loki's whisper slices through the darkness, sharp and soft as a knife blade. "What did you say?"

Thor begins to speak, "I said—"

"Not you!" Loki screams. "Steve! What did you say?"

"Agent Rogers said nothing—"

"I heard him!" Loki says.

Standing up, wincing at the pain in his shoulder, Steve turns towards Loki's voice but sees only a floor-to-ceiling window facing the blinking lights of the southern part of the city. "We have to get Lewis to the trauma unit."

Light rises in the room, but Steve can't detect a single source. Magic? Loki stands before Steve and Thor silhouetted by the window. He's wearing jeans and a t-shirt, his skin is pale and pink, his hair ginger.

Running a hand nervously through his hair, Loki says, "I hear her, Thor. She can't die!"

Nodding, but without making any sudden moves, Thor says, "Then you must trust me to help her, Loki."

Smirking, Loki says, "Trust you, Thor?"

Flushing, Thor licks his lips. "I won't fail you again. You know you can't heal her, Loki."

Loki's lips curl at that, his hands fall to his sides and Steve swears he sees him tremble. Steve bites back the urge to shout, *Don't waste time.*

Loki's eyes flash to Steve.

From behind comes the crunch of glass. Turning fast, Steve sees a shimmer of light, and then there is Loki again, emerging from a shadowy hallway that runs past a kitchen. Loki is wearing the alien armor that blends so seamlessly into the surroundings. Steve might not see him at all if his visor wasn't up. His face is blue, almost glowing. Lewis is draped in his arms, he sees bloodstains on her clothing, but most worryingly is the blood-soaked cloth wrapped around her neck.

"Loki," Thor whispers. "You're blue ... what's happening to you?"

Ignoring Thor, heart racing at the sight of Lewis' limp and bloody body, Steve says, "Loki, we have to get Lewis to the trauma unit. There are police vehicles below. I know you may not trust them but—"

"No!" Loki says. "Thor, she's fading. Can you help her?"

Thor holds out his arms. After a moment's hesitation, Loki passes Lewis to him. Gazing down at her head, Thor's brow furrows and his jaw tightens, he mutters something in another language. Steve's just about to tell them they need to move her, now, when Lewis's eyes bolt open and she gasps. Her lips part, as though to speak, but nothing comes out.

Pulling off his helmet, Loki puts a finger to her lips. "Don't worry, I hear you." He's smiling, a little sadly, a little deranged.

"Loki," Thor says. "She does need to go to the trauma unit. There are bullets, glass and fabric in her body—and their tools are sharper than mine."

Loki meets Thor's eyes. "You will take her in your chariot, and you won't leave her."

Eyes locked on Loki's, Thor says, "The Norns as my witness, I swear it."

Loki stands stock still for a moment. And then nodding, he backs away. Thor bends low over Lewis and whispers something in her ear. Her eyes drift shut, and Thor turns around and steps into his chariot, Lewis in his arms. Thor says something in his own language, and the chariot backs, turns and lifts—much more gently than when Steve had been in it. With a gust of air it takes off into the night.

Alone with Loki, Steve looks around the apartment and his heart sinks. Along the hallway Loki had emerged from are prone bodies.

"They attacked without provocation," Loki says, chin tilted downward, eyes unfocused.

Gritting his teeth, Steve says, "I need to get them medical attention."

Loki lifts an eyebrow. "That won't be necessary."

Jaw tense, Steve taps his phone, "I'm going to call for an ambulance ... ambulances ... "

Loki shrugs. "Ambulances are already on the way. There are fires in the stairwells, a few of your agents trying to come up from the ground got ... " He stops, looks at Steve and smiles sharply. "Are getting ... cooked." His eyes narrow at Steve, "But don't worry, they called for help."

Steve stands frozen, hand on his phone.

Loki smiles. "Well, are you going to arrest me?"

Steve tilts his head, eyes narrowed. "What do you want, Loki?"

Loki's smile drops. "To be close to Miss Lewis ... for the time being." He licks his lips nervously, and looks away. "She's in my head." His eyes go back to Steve. "As you were." Blinking his eyes rapidly he says, "Like everyone seems to be lately. If you arrest me, you'll take me to headquarters—that's right below the trauma unit, is it not?"

Steve nods, dumbly.

Loki smiles again, and holds his wrists out. "Come on, Steve, take out your handcuffs. This is your chance to be a hero!"

Taking a man who's just taken down two SWAT helicopters to headquarters is just about the dumbest thing Steve could think to do. It is also, doubtlessly, what Jameson will order.

Not bothering to take out his cuffs, Steve grabs his shoulder. "Come on, let's go downstairs."

With a mischievous smile and a shrug, Loki obediently lets Steve lead him down the hall.

Steve sits next to Loki in the van the SWAT team is using to take them to HQ. Hands bound behind his back with the same cuffs they had used on agent Hill, Loki is leaning forward slightly. His skin is still blue, and his eyes and hair still black, but where the cuffs wrap around his wrists there is a line of bone-white skin.

All around the van agents sit glaring at Loki, rifles at the ready.

Rocking and humming, Loki seems for the most part unconcerned. But every now and then Steve catches Loki scowling. Steve looks down at his phone. There is a text from one of the nurses. Turning to Loki he says, "Thor got Lewis to the trauma unit. They've begun operating."

Loki nods. "I know."

Glancing down at his phone again, Steve sees a message alert for his email. He clicks over to a short message from Lewis. *Loki said he'll help with the gates. We need to find a way to meet without Jameson finding out.*

Steve hadn't realized his heart could sink any lower, but it does.

"Hmmmm ... " says Loki, voice near his shoulder. "She must have sent that just before she was shot."

Steve's eyes slide to him. Sitting as far back as he can with his hands behind his back, Loki eyes the other agents in the van. "I was going to help. I can close gates, you know." His voice darkens. "But at the moment I feel strangely disinclined."

Not one of the agents even moves a muscle. Loki gives him a tight smile. Steve wants to say something, to smooth things over. Running a hand over his chin, feeling the bite of stubble, Steve can't find it in himself to say anything. His mind is filled with the memory of the empty eyes of the dead agents in Loki's apartment, and the memory of Lewis draped in Loki's arms. A wrong for a wrong was not right.

"You look a little pale, Agent Rogers," Loki says, his eyes hard. His lips quirk. "Or is it not politically correct to say that? I can't keep all the rules straight."

The van draws to a halt, shouts go up inside and out, and Steve is spared from having to respond.

As the doors open, SWAT team members fan out to clear the path. Before anyone has a chance to shove a gun in Loki's direction, Steve takes him by the shoulder again and says, "Let's move."

They've just hopped out of the van and are making their way to the doors of the building when Steve hears someone say, "Fuck me. Shiva?" Loki and Steve both turn their heads in unison. There's the Indian—or something—cab driver Steve met earlier, his eyes wide, body stock still, looking for all the world like a deer caught in headlights.

As some agents push the kid away, Loki smiles and blows a kiss. "Maybe some other time!"

The kid's eyes suddenly regain focus, and even with the

guys pushing him away, he manages to bring a fisted hand to his face, bite his thumb and then flick it in Loki's direction.

Loki smiles as Steve steers him through the door and towards the interrogation room.

There is no one-way mirror in the interrogation room, just cameras in all the corners, and speakers. Loki rocks in a squeaking chair, hands behind his back. There is a table next to him, and an extra chair. He scowls. As soon as they'd seated him, they'd placed a strange little helmet of Promethean Wire on his head. On the one hand, it's put an end to Cera's nagging. On the other hand, he's finding it difficult to focus his magic. He's not frightened—he can slip the lock-picking tools out of his wrist armor easily enough. From there it would only be a moment to remove the helmet and World Walk—or just walk out of the room.

He is annoyed though. He wants to know how Amy is doing. He can't leave without her, and he can't do that until her condition is stable, and he can't know if she is stable because of the damnable helmet. Grinding his teeth he rocks faster in his chair, causing the metal to groan and squeak.

From behind the door, he hears shouting. Craning forward, he tries to piece out the words, but they are too muffled. Still, he does recognize Thor's voice among the participants.

His eyebrows rise. Either Amy is dead, or she is in a state where Thor does not feel she will suffer without him. He bites his lip.

Hearing the door knob engage, Loki sits back quickly, just in time for Steve Rogers to walk into the room. Loki smiles at the man.

"Miss Lewis is in stable condition," says Steve. He tilts his head. "Can you understand me without magic?"

Loki grins. He has been in English-speaking countries long enough to have picked up the language. Instead of answering the question he says, "Come to play good cop, Steven?"

Steve fixes Loki with a glare that would cause spontaneous combustion if Steve were a magical creature. "I'm not playing anything. I'm trying to keep you from setting the building on fire."

Loki's lips quirk. Steven isn't fooled by the magic shackles, then? He remembers the brief flicker of connection he'd had with Steve in the penthouse. And Odin heard Steve, too. Steve looks the part of the stooge, even if at the moment he's wearing combat gear instead of his trademark suit. And yet, beneath Steve's bland, regimentally lemming-like exterior, there buzzes a cunning independent mind. What in the world is he doing working for ADUO and a real stooge like Jameson?

At that thought the door handle turns again and Jameson steps into the room.

Loki grins again and waggles his eyebrows. "Oh, look, the party has arrived."

Jaw twitching, Jameson moves to stand by Steve. "We know that you are responsible for the recent attack on our city and the opening of the gates. Your magic is shackled, and we have a magically shielded transport vehicle on the way. We will see you locked away from your magic permanently. No nation will be your advocate. If you want any mercy at all, any leniency, you had better start cooperating."

Loki looks at Steve and rolls his eyes. And then turning

back to Jameson he says, "Oh, you found me out! Where do you want me to start?"

Jameson's eyes widen just a fraction, and his jaw drops minutely, as though he's surprised by how easy he's gotten Loki's cooperation. Regaining his poise, he says, "Let's start with the positions of the gates."

Loki tilts his head, opens his mouth, and invents random locations off the top of his head. Jameson smiles as Loki rattles on.

By contrast, Steve looks like he's swallowed a live frog whole. "Sir," Steve says, when Loki's paused for a breath, "I think we should take a break and discuss this information before we—"

"Agent Rogers," says Jameson, "we are just getting started."

Steve's cheeks hollow inward, as though he's biting them. Refraining from casting a knowing smirk in his direction, Loki adopts his best look of slightly fearful innocence, and Jameson starts asking more questions.

Loki lies. Sometimes he hesitates a bit just for effect, and he is careful to tell the truth on those trick questions he thinks they must know—like his association with Ron Kalt, for instance. It is an amusing game trying to keep the lies and half truths and outright truths all straight. He seriously begins to wonder if after razing Asgard, he should consider becoming a novelist.

"How did you get Miss Lewis out of the building during the attack?" Steve asks; it's the first question he's asked since he entered the room.

Loki purses his lips. "Through the back stairwell."

"It was on fire," says Steve.

Loki shrugs. "As Mr. Jameson already explained, I started

the fire. It wasn't hard to put out." The words roll out of his mouth without any effort.

Steve's eyes narrow.

Beside him Jameson says, "Why did you help Lewis escape?"

Loki's jaw goes tight. He should say, *Because I couldn't let tits like that go to waste.* Instead he sneers. "Haven't you heard? I'm the good guy."

"Is she involved in this scheme of yours?" Jameson asks.

"No!" says Loki, too quickly and too loud. Will they hurt her if they think she is? Will he feel her agony in his head? He feels a cold prickle of sweat upon his brow.

"Where have you been since the initial attack?" Jameson asks.

"At home," says Loki.

"Doing what?" says Jameson.

Loki should say, *Well, Mr. Director, when a man and a woman like each other very much …*

But he can't form the words. Glaring at Jameson, he rocks the chair back and forth. The squeak has gotten louder.

Steve puts his hand on Jameson's arm, and Jameson brushes it away, eyes locked on Loki. "Perhaps I should remind you of your situation? You have no country, no people. The rules of the Geneva Convention do not apply to you." Leaning down on the table he smiles at Loki. There is a slight sheen to his forehead. Loki lifts an eyebrow. The man is getting an almost sexual pleasure from his perceived power. Pathetic.

Apparently, completely unaware of Loki's utter lack of fear, Jameson continues. "If I ask you to speak, Loki, you speak. If I ask you to sing, you sing. If I ask you to dance, you dance."

Without turning to Steve, Jameson says, "Agent Rogers, Ms. Lewis is a citizen, but by cooperating with Loki, a confessed terrorist, doesn't she cede some of her rights?"

Loki's vision goes red and his skin goes hot. He always fucks things up, doesn't he?

He thinks he sees Steve shaking his head, out of the corner of his eye. Maybe Steve even says something, but it is a jumble of, "it won't come to that" and "she's one of ours." Curling his hands into fists, all Loki can focus on is Jameson. And then, without even conscious thought, Loki's fingers are sliding against a thin piece of metal tucked into his wrist guard.

"Very well, Mr. Director, I'll dance and sing for you," Loki says. The words slide off his tongue as he slips the very non-magical, infinitely clever, dwarven key pin into the cuffs.

Jameson smiles just a fraction. Loki wants, no needs, to grind the fool's face in his own stupidity and arrogance. Loki needs to make him hurt.

The speakers in the room begin to crackle. "Sir, he's … "

Grinning, Loki stops rocking as the cuffs clang to the floor.

" … doing something to the cuffs," the disembodied voice says.

With a shout, Loki lifts the magic-blocking helmet from his head and flings it across the room. Cera's voice cries out, "Loki!" Steve and Jameson both reach for their weapons, but before they're even drawn, Loki's hopped up onto the table. The air in the room around him shimmers with heat. He thinks he hears someone say, "The door is too hot!" and Jameson and Steve both pull their hands away from their weapons in pain.

Loki should pick their weapons from their pockets, shoot

them, and then make the men outside the doors see illusions of him instead of each other. He should let them kill each other, just as he did to the SWAT team.

But he needs to mock Jameson in front of all his little cameras for all his lackeys to see. With a wink, he casts an illusion of black pants, black jacket and striped black and white shirt over his armor—just like the character Amy was watching on the computer. His hair is already black, his skin full blue, but he doesn't bother to change it. With a whoop, Loki stands on his tiptoes on the table that is his stage. Winding his hips, he spins an arm and sings the inane lyrics about jailbirds from the Elvis song.

Loki hadn't even realized he'd remembered the words. He's about to laugh when the building rumbles and the table bucks beneath him. Loki barely keeps his feet. For a moment his heart is in his throat. Some other Midgardian magics? His eyes meet Steve's, and he sees they are as wide and fearful as his own. From the hallway, someone says, "Earthquake!"

"Loki! Was that you?" Cera shouts.

Loki jaw drops in amazement. No. There must be a mistake.

"Don't do that, don't do that again!" Jameson says. His voice is pleading.

Loki's eyebrows lift. It was probably just a random coincidence, but if he can make Jameson simper and whine a little more—Loki grins. Popping up onto his toes again, he lifts his arms in the best impersonation of that ridiculous man from the video and he gives his hips a shake. As the whole world shakes with him he laughs aloud in shock.

Jameson shouts.

Steve scrambles to keep his feet.

Loki hops off of the table before he's flung off, staggering against the wall as the world trembles in aftershocks.

"Loki!" Cera screams. Her voice is loud and so clear …

Loki sends a projection to her and gasps. The ceiling above her has sunk, and the Promethean Wire around Cera is open like a cracked egg.

Smiling at Steve as the aftershocks ripple away, Loki raises a hand in a wave and steps into the In-Between. He steps out of the In-Between within the shattered sphere of Promethean Wire, right next to Cera. He hears the shouts of the humans guarding the World Seed and weapons being raised, but his hands are already on her.

As he lifts her, Cera's spherical form pulses with light and magic. Loki cannot contain a sigh of awe. She is a creature of time and space, and though she has the mass of billions of stars within her in another space, in this space, she is light as a feather but rippling with energy. He feels as though the magical neurons in his fingers are flooding with power, producing a wonderful, buzzing sensation. Blue light rises up all around him, and it takes a moment for him to realize it isn't just from Cera—it's from him. He hears screams and more shouts. The buzzing travels up his hands to his arms and it's wonderful … and yet. Brow furrowing, Loki tries to put Cera down and finds he can't, the light of her sphere is slipping into him, the sphere of her physical form vanishing.

He remembers Amy's words, "Thor says it will control you … "

His eyes narrow as Cera's magic slips up along his spine. Damn.

And then he blinks. No, he doesn't blink, They blink.

"We are one!" It is Cera's voice. No, Their voice. They

are all Cera's power and all Loki's acquired wisdom—and his feet!

Someone beyond the cracked sphere is screaming at them. They hear guns jostling. They are safe from guns except for Their left arm—unarmored since They lost the pieces of plating in the chamber of the elf queen months ago. Quickly, They imagine armor composed of magical energy that will send any bullets that strike it into the In-Between. The magical energy spills over into the rest of the armor and makes it shimmer and glow.

A few of the agents rush towards them. They send the agents into the In-Between with a thought, and then They can only pause and marvel at what They have become.

They feel tremendous, like They are soaring. They are beneath the Board of Trade but not confined here. Their mind casts projections across the globe; and They see everything. And everything is very wrong, not like Josef's dreams at all.

Chicago, despite the building above them being sunken, and tilted, still resembles something akin to the cities of the Aesir or Vanir. There are a few hundred of these temples to modernity across the globe. The modern cities are cruel places, mocking the billions that live no better than the peasants of Loki's or Josef's memories. In some ways these peasants are worse off, their poverty more grotesque compared with the ostentatiousness of modern affluence.

They see timid measures to ameliorate the wretchedness of the miserable billions, but they are piecemeal, laughable, mere acts of decoration, hampered by vanity, greed, hundreds of different languages, nationalism—not to mention the hundreds of different governments and systems of governing.

They will fix this. They will organize it under one system,

one language, one nation. Unified They can redistribute the wealth of the few into the hands of the many. And the new world will be led by Them … for Josef! And it will all start right now.

"A lot like a Tsar—or Odin," a treacherous voice in their mind whispers. They still, uncertain of its source.

"Loki." The Girl's voice interrupts Their thoughts; it tugs low and uncomfortably in Their gut. For a moment They splinter and are two beings again.

"Cera, I still hear her. She is still part of my—our—purpose," Loki says.

They are momentarily confused. But it is Loki's memories that impart this information, and Loki is old and wise. They trust him.

Steve's jaw drops as Loki disappears. And then his brain springs to action and he runs to the door, ripping his jacket off and using it like a pot holder to grasp the scorching doorknob. Loki can appear invisible, but he's still here.

The door doesn't move. No invisible force pushes Steve out of the way. Steve curses under his breath, the memory of blue Loki doing a rather good Elvis impersonation in the front of his mind. Damned trickster gods.

"What are you doing?" Jameson says, his voice high pitched and frantic.

Steve is about to answer when the earpiece for his phone starts to beep. Grappling the cooling doorknob with one hand, he answers it.

"Agent Mitchem here," a woman's voice says. "Loki just took Cera."

"What?" Steve says.

The agent's voice wavers. "Loki just—"

"How?" Steve says.

He hears the woman take a breath. "The ceiling collapsed on top of the containment sphere. The sphere cracked, and then suddenly Loki was just there. We opened fire but he was gone with the … thing … a moment later."

From the hallway comes Thor's thunderous voice. "Open the door!"

Steve drops his hand and backs out of the way just as the door crashes to the floor. Thor stands in the entranceway with his hammer. Steve blinks. After a brief altercation with Jameson earlier, Thor had returned to Amy's bedside.

Agents trailing behind him, Thor stomps in. Glaring at Jameson, Thor says, "Loki has the World Seed."

"How do you know?" says Steve.

"Because a moment ago Miss Lewis, her bed, a doctor, nurse, and your medical machines disappeared," Thor says.

"Gone?" says Steve. "How?"

"I do not know," says Thor, his voice very level, his eyes still on the Director. "Mr. Jameson, I think now might be a good time to apologize."

"Apologize?" says Jameson, his voice shaky. Lifting his head, he says, "For what?"

"For ordering the attack on Loki's home and shooting his woman," says Thor with narrowed eyes.

"I was justified in that," Jameson says. "And I won't … " His eyes widen, his mouth hangs open, but no sound comes out. He looks down at his feet. "What's happening to me?" he wails.

Bewildered, Steve looks him up and down. Nothing

appears to be wrong.

"So ... so ... so cold," says Jameson.

"Magic," says Thor.

"Can you do anything?" Steve says to Thor.

Tilting his head, Thor says, "I see it surrounding his limbs. Perhaps if we amputate them quickly—"

"What?" Steve shouts, running over to the director. Grabbing the director's arms Steve notices Jameson's hands are coated with frost, like a window in winter. A chill nips at Steve's fingers, through Jameson's sport coat. "Get a thermal blanket!" Steve shouts at one of the agents milling in the room. As the agent darts off, Steve shouts at another, "Get over here and help me get him undressed." Trying to yank off Jameson's coat that has gone stiff as cardboard and feels blisteringly cold, Steve shouts at the other two agents remaining. "Strip to your skivvies! We're going to treat him like he has hypothermia."

Thor looks heavenward. "Loki! He was an idiot! You've made your point."

With a grunt, Steve starts ripping off Jameson's shirt as the other agent pulls off the jacket.

"It's too late," says Thor.

Steve's eyes slide to Jameson's. The director's open eyes and inside of his open mouth are coated with ice, lacey patterns of frost trailing over his cheeks. Steve puts a hand to Jameson's chest. Stepping back, Steve shouts, "He has no heart beat. Get him to medical!"

He meets the eyes of the agents in the room. "Now!"

The two agents who were stripping, now down to their t-shirts and slacks, pause and then run forward. The agent attempting to undress Jameson tips Jameson into their arms.

The director falls, body stiff as a felled tree.

Steve backs away as they carry the director out of the room. His hand goes to his mouth. When at last he can speak, all Steve can say is, "How?"

Beside him Thor says, "Loki now has a source of infinite power and now he's infinitely powerful."

Steve turns slowly to Thor. Thor is gazing upward, hammer in hand, and his brow furrowed. After a few long moments, Thor nods his head as though he's confirmed something to himself. "Loki is fighting Cera's will."

Steve stares at him in disbelief. He gestures to the door where Jameson was just hauled out of the room like a log. "How can you say that?"

Lowering his eyes to Steve's, Thor says, "Because we aren't dead."

CHAPTER 12

Amy hurts. She can't even tell where she hurts most, because it feels like the front of her body is prickling with a hundred different needles. She takes a breath and the pain in her neck makes all the other pain disappear. Wincing, she opens her eyes and finds herself staring at the familiar whirls of plaster of Loki's bedroom ceiling. What isn't familiar is the beeping that sounds suspiciously like a heart monitor, the IV drip in her wrist, or the face of the white-coated, middle-aged woman with a stethoscope sitting next to her.

Amy blinks. No, wait, the woman is one of the doctors from the trauma center, but Amy can't remember her name. There is a slight sheen of sweat on the woman's brow, the corners of her lips are turned down, and her eyes are a little too wide. She's frightened. Amy's eyes slide to the side. A young man she recognizes as a nurse paramedic is by her side as well.

Amy opens her mouth. The voice that comes out is a

cracked whisper. "What happened? How … "

She tries to sit up but stops as every nerve in her body seizes up with pain.

The doctor puts her hands on her shoulders. "Don't get up. You received multiple superficial wounds to your abdomen from exploding glass. None were deep, but you do have a lot of stitches."

Amy sinks down into the bed, the memories coming back. "They opened fire … "

Why did they open fire?

The doctor nods her head. Her hair is slightly graying; it's pulled in a tight bun. "You also took a bullet to the neck. It lodged between your carotid artery and jugular."

Amy's fingers twist in the duvet. She'd been just millimeters from death. "How … " How did she get here.

"He brought us here," says the doctor. She smiles tightly. "He said you'd be more comfortable away from ADUO."

Amy closes her eyes, in exhaustion. She remembers telling Loki she loved him, and his dismissal. She almost laughs. And then he does something like this … Forget God of Goof, if he were a god he'd be the God of Mixed Signals.

"We are very lucky," says the nurse.

Amy opens her eyes, not sure what he is talking about.

"Indeed, you are very lucky." It's Loki's voice. Amy's body freezes; something sounds off. "Miss Lewis is alive."

Turning her head towards Loki, her body goes cold in shock. Loki is wearing his armor. But where it used to blend into the environment around it, now it is black with a strange glowing sheen on it—almost like oil on a puddle of water. The glow catches and condenses in the crevices of the armor's joints; where there should be shadows there is white light.

The sword and scabbard at his waist have the same glow. The left arm of the armor is different, though. It seems to have no physical surface, just plates of iridescence at the shoulder, arm and forearm. It's all magical and should be beautiful, except for the helmet. Amy stares. Where Loki used to wear a round helmet with a visor, now there is a helmet with two curled horns.

Loki grins, showing all his teeth. "Like it? We decided to try something more traditional. We want to be recognized."

Amy's eyes move to his face. His skin is pale again, but it looks mottled. There are dark circles under his eyes, too.

"Loki, what's happened?" she whispers.

Raising two fingers towards the nurse and the doctor, Loki says, "You two can wait in the other room."

Instead of moving towards the door, they both draw back, the doctor drawing in a breath with a sharp gasp. And then there is a soft whoosh of air, Amy's ears pop, and the man and woman are gone.

Amy turns to Loki, "Where have they gone?"

"Oh, don't worry," Loki says. Sauntering over, he unbuckles his belt and sword and then plunks himself down on the chair beside her. "We sent them to the other room through the In-Between. Just like we pulled them and the equipment from the trauma center."

"We?" says Amy, meeting his slightly bloodshot gray eyes.

Nodding, Loki leans forward. "Cera and I. We are one now." He smirks. "More convenient than carrying her around and now she—we—have feet."

Amy stares at Loki. She feels a chill go through her even though there are blankets heaped on the bed. She swallows. Manipulating the In-Between is exhausting for Loki, but he doesn't look tired. In fact, he seems possessed by a manic energy. And yet …

"You're not blue," Amy says. She associates Loki being blue with him being healthy, with his magic being at full power.

Loki tilts his head and closes his eyes. His mouth gives a funny tick. "Barbaric. False idols. False gods, there is no God. I—she—we … no blue."

I, she, we … Amy draws back into the pillows, with a wince.

"But enough about us! This is about you!" Loki says. "We have to make you better, you are important to us!"

Leaning forward Loki whispers, "We thought about healing you ourselves, since we are very nearly omnipotent. But omnipotence isn't omniscience. Oh, we can move elephants and hadrosaurs through the In-Between, and make all of ADUO's eyes and sensors see nothing in this apartment. We even tried our hand at fixing glass in the other room. But healing? I said no, it was better to trust the doctors."

I? Is there a little bit of Loki left in there? Meeting his bloodshot gray eyes, Amy says, "Thank you, Loki."

Smiling, he straightens. "But now you are mostly recovered, and we have something that should help you the rest of the way." Winking, he says, "Or we will have something!"

With a sharp quick movement, he swipes his hand through the empty air in front of his nose. There is a shrill screech, and both Amy's and Loki's eyes widen. In his hand is a madly chattering red squirrel with tufted ears.

Scowling at it, Loki says, "Ratatoskr!"

Amy blinks. The squirrel that carries messages along the World Tree in Norse legend?

"Loki! What the fuck?" squeaks the squirrel. Really, compared to trolls, elves, spider-mice, and hadrosaurs, a talking-swearing squirrel should hardly be surprising. Still, Amy nearly jumps in her skin.

Lashing his tail furiously, the squirrel tries to push himself out of Loki's hands with his little paws. That failing, he raises a tiny fist at Loki's nose. "I work for the Norns! Unhand me, you—" There is a long string of chatter that sounds suspiciously like more swearing.

Rolling his eyes, Loki tosses the squirrel over his shoulder. It hits the glass window with a squeak and a thud and slides to the floor. Amy stares at the creature with wide eyes. Ratatoskr doesn't move.

"We didn't want him anyways," says Loki. "Horrible gossip, and so vulgar."

"Help him!" says Amy.

Scowling and bending towards her, Loki says, "No, it is more important that we help you." With that he swipes his hand through the air again. This time when his hand stills, it holds an apple. If it weren't for the slight flecks of red in its deep yellow skin and the rich apply smell that instantly wafts through the room, Amy might think it was made of gold. Staring at it, her mouth begins to water. She wants the apple more than she's wanted anything, and she knows instantly what it is. "One of Idunn's apples," she says, her voice a sigh of awe.

"Just for you," says Loki, bowing his horned head.

Amy takes a breath. "You've already destroyed Asgard, and you've brought this back?"

Loki's head tips to the side, and then springs back up, as though he's fighting an itch. "Sadly, no. I—" His lips tick again. "It's more important to start here. First we fix Earth. We need to, for Josef. Otherwise Loki might forget."

Shivering, Amy draws back into the covers. Loki—or Cera—looms over her, hand with the apple outstretched, the points of his new horned helmet glowing above her. "Eat this. It will help you heal, make it as though the last year and a half has not aged your body at all, and give you magic."

Give her magic ... the Einherjar become magical when they eat the apples. Loki's told her magic takes different forms in everyone. For the briefest moment she wonders what her magic would be like, what powers she would have.

Or maybe she would just be more vulnerable to Cera? No humans have fallen under Cera's control.

Loki smiles, and Amy shivers.

"Eat it. Be with us as we unite the world as one," Loki says.

Amy's terrified, yet she knows she cannot accept the apple, even if something in her cries out for it, as though she's been waiting to take a bite from it her entire life. Swallowing, she says, "So, ummm, maybe I should tell you about guys with horns offering women apples in my religious tradition."

Loki sneers. "We know you're not religious. We wouldn't like you if you were! Take it and eat it."

Amy takes a breath. She's injured and even more powerless than usual. She stares at the apple, and has to lick her lips, her mouth is watering so much.

And suddenly it strikes her. She isn't completely powerless. She almost smiles. "No. I won't take your apple. I won't be part of us." She feels strangely light, strangely good as the words leave her mouth.

Loki's head tilts to the side. For a few long moments he

says nothing, but his jaw twitches frantically. At last, standing from his seat, his lips curling, he whispers. "We should kill you." And then he laughs. "Instead we will let you watch your world burn!"

There is a whoosh of air, Amy's ears pop, and just like that, he's gone. Apple, horns, and all.

Amy stares at the spot where he was. She sits for a few minutes completely dazed, and then she remembers the doctor and nurse. But when she calls out, "Hello? Hello?" there is no answer. She swallows and tries to raise her hand to her head but it gets stuck on the IV. She groans in pain and frustration and then notices that attached to the IV is a little device that looks like a finger sized microphone, only where the speaker input would be is a little button. Her brow furrows. It's right next to a bucket of ice, a plastic cup of water and Loki's white book on the nightstand. Her eyebrows rise—he's left his book … and Laevithin is leaning against the nightstand, shimmering with the same light as his armor. Such details fade from her mind as she realizes the little button gadget thing is the control for her morphine drip. Squelching a groan, she reaches for it. Picking it up she presses the button furiously before she remembers it's not a good idea, and then sighs as the pain seems to wash away in a warm wave. Maybe it was a good idea? She's about to hit the button again when she hears a little squeak from the corner.

Amy turns her head. Ratatoskr is rolling over onto his stomach.

"Hi, little squirrel," Amy says. "Are you alright?"

"No! I feel like crap!" he says.

It might or might not be the drugs, but Amy can't help laughing.

He tries to get up but groans instead. "Fuckity fuck," he mumbles. "I think one of my ribs is fractured."

"You need to put ice on it," says Amy.

"No shit!" says Ratatoskr, his little nose wiggling side to side and his tail thrashing.

Amy snickers. "There's some over here. I'll come over and pick you up."

Forcing herself to sit, Amy grabs hold of the little rolly stand with her IV attached. She's wearing a hospital gown that is pretty drafty in the back, but she's not sure the squirrel will care. Standing with a groan, she walks over to the squirrel.

"Don't suppose you know how the bloody Hel Loki managed to nab me out of Idunn's orchard?" the squirrel says as Amy kneels beside him.

Amy tilts her head as she scoops him into her arms.

"I was there checking to see if the harvest was ready. Not stealing apples." Eyes wide, he blinks up at her innocently. "Really, I wasn't going to eat the apples."

Amy tweaks his trembling little nose. "Sure," she says. Her brain is kind of fuzzy and her skin is kind of itchy, but she remembers he asked her a question. "Loki stole the World Seed," she says as she lays the squirrel down on the bed.

"You're shitting me, right?" Ratatoskr says as Amy settles beside him.

Amy giggles and rubs him behind the ears. "You have a potty mouth." Turning to get the ice bucket, Amy says, "But I'm not shitting you."

"Damn. We are so screwed," says Ratatoskr.

That makes Amy laugh so hard pain blossoms through her morphine high.

Ratatoskr chitters a few times and then says. "Where the

fuck did Loki go, anyway?"

"No, idea," says Amy. "We … "

Suddenly Loki's voice rises in the room, everywhere and nowhere at once. *"No, no magical lobotomies for the human race. Lobotomies are so boring."*

"That's Loki's voice!" says the squirrel, pushing the ice cube to his side, and glancing frantically side to side. "Where's it coming from?"

"Loki?" says Amy.

And then another disembodied voice rises up, high and childlike, but with an ominous hiss to it. *"But it would be so much more efficient!"*

"Did you hear that?" says Amy.

The squirrel's nose trembles. "I think you are high, and I am suffering from a concussion."

"In every revolution there must be blood," says Loki.

"Yes, yes, you cannot make a revolution with silk gloves!" shouts the child.

"I am high, but we do hear him!" says Amy. "And Cera the World Seed, too!"

"Uh-oh," says Ratatoskr, eyes wide.

A flashing light in the window catches Amy's eyes. She turns to see the blue sky outside fading, colors swirling in the glass and taking form. And then it's as though the window is a floor-to-ceiling television screen and she's looking through a camera at an auditorium with lush red carpeting. Desks form a semi-circle around her with wide-eyed men and women in business attire seated at them. Amy's eyes widen. The scene is famous—or infamous. It's the council chambers of Chicago City Hall.

"What the … " says Ratatoskr.

Amy swallows. "Recently Loki's subconscious has been projecting ... I think through the window we're looking out his eyes."

The squirrel squeaks and snuggles against her hip. "Great, he was already losing it before he got the World Seed."

Directly in front of the camera is the back of what can only be Mayor Ronnie's head. "Our city faces another threat of unknown quantity—"

A woman near the back shouts out, "So the SWAT raid you authorized on my condo building didn't solve our problems after all?"

There are a few muffled boos through the room.

And then Loki's voice cuts through the din. "You authorized the raid on my—our—home?" Amy can't see him, but his voice seethes with fury and she can imagine the sneer on his face.

Throughout the chamber there are gasps. Mayor Ronnie spins around, lips turned up and brow furrowed. Amy's ready for one of his famous screaming tirades, but as his jaw drops, what looks like white lace blossoms on his tongue and spreads out from his mouth over his face, coating his eyes. His whole body stiffens. Steam or smoke or something comes off his body in waves. It's white and misty, whatever it is, like his body is casting out his ghost. A hand reaches out as though from the person holding the camera and knocks the mayor over. The mayor falls to the ground and the camera angles downward as the mayor's body shatters, shards sliding out over the floor like glass.

"Eeep," says Ratatoskr, and Amy's hand goes to the squirrel.

"Oooo ... neat," says Loki's voice coming directly from

the window-screen.

The camera cocks to the side as though Loki's tilting his head. "We didn't realize he'd do that if he was extra cold."

Amy straightens. Loki's voice rings out again in the council chamber, the camera of his eyes sweeping around the room. "We are your new leader. We will make your world a better place. I would prefer if you fought us, but we will gladly accept surrender."

"To Hell with surrender! This is Chicago!" says a middle-aged man with white hair and a slight Irish lilt to his voice. He pulls out a handgun and raises it. Maybe Amy is hallucinating. Are aldermen allowed to carry guns in city hall? Her brow wrinkles. Of course, this is Chicago, would they care if they weren't allowed? A few of the other men in the room stand and raise guns as well. Screaming and shouting, the rest of the aldermen and women stand up and bolt for the door.

"Oh, this is going to be fun!" says Loki, and this time it is as though he's whispering over Amy's shoulder.

"A lobotomy would be easier," says Cera, her voice rising near Amy's other ear.

Amy closes her eyes. But she still hears the gunshots and gurgled cries of pain coming from the window looking into the City Hall.

The room Steve and Thor occupy is small and windowless. Fluorescent bulbs blink and hum overhead; an air conditioner hums. Steve is sitting on a rickety metal fold-out chair at a cheap table—one that hadn't been deemed worthy of using out in the open area where emergency dispatchers are taking calls and routing police, firemen and volunteers. When he leans to get closer to the speaker phone on it, the table rocks and squeaks.

"Sirs," Steve says, "police and firefighters are stretched too thin with civilian evacuations, troll, wyrm and manticore attacks. They cannot handle the additional threat Loki poses." Steve would like to imagine Loki going directly back to Asgard—but if that was his plan, he doesn't think Loki would have taken Lewis and the medical staff with him.

The voice of the head of the Senate's Armed Services Committee comes on. "Without an act of Congress, it is up to the Illinois governor. The current alien attacks are uncoordinated. They do not qualify as an invasion force. But you can be assured that we are monitoring the situation closely."

Steve's brow furrows at that. Surely they have drones. Do they have fighter jets available for close air support?

The President's voice comes on the line. There is a loud ambient hum behind him. The sound of Air Force One's engines, maybe?

"What sort of threat does Loki pose exactly?" says the President.

Pacing around to the opposite side of the table, Thor raises an eyebrow at the phone on the table. "He is capable of anything he can imagine."

A voice on the other end barks, "We don't even know where he is. He could be on his way to Washington. We should continue using all federal resources to secure strategic assets!"

Steve's brow goes up. The rumor mill was right. At that moment Steve's phone beeps. Looking down, Steve sees a text from Bryant. Brow furrowing, Steve stands. "Loki has been sighted at City Hall. Police have already been dispatched."

Thor straightens. "Agent Rogers and I must go," says Thor.

"Just a minute, you cannot go until authorized," says another voice on the phone. "We will decide—"

There is a blur at the periphery of Steve's vision. He pulls back just in time to see Mjolnir crash on the phone, breaking it into splinters of metal and plastic and collapsing the table below it.

Lifting Mjolnir to his shoulder, Thor glares at Steve. "We do not have time for democratic debate. Loki heard you before, he may hear you again. You will come with me."

Steve stares at the phone. "Right."

Passing through the crowded hub of HQ a few moments later, they nearly collide with a group of men and one woman in dirty jeans, all with orange reflective vests and helmets walking beside Stodgill. A few are brandishing shotguns. Steve scowls in frustration at the roadblock. Seeing his look and misinterpreting, Stodgill says, "Yes, they're the plumbers for the blockage under LaSalle, Sir, but they have a right to be armed, no matter what city ordinance—"

"Fine, just get out of our way," says Steve. The plumbers fall to the side, and Steve and Thor push through. They are almost to the main exit when Steve hears someone shout. "He's on LaSalle Street. CNN has live coverage!"

Steve turns his head and brings his hand to Thor's shoulder. For a moment they both stop, mesmerized.

Loki is on the screen. Steve's breath catches in his throat at the sight. Loki's armor is so black it gleams blue. Upon his head is a helmet with long curved horns. With the smirk Loki's wearing, he looks every bit a monster from a nightmare.

"The helmet … " someone gasps.

Beside him Thor hums. "Horns. Foolish for battle. And

look at the armor on his left arm? It isn't like the rest—the joints are uncovered, and it looks like he'll be vulnerable from below. Not dwarven or elven made, that is certain."

Steve snaps his attention to Thor. The large man is eyeing the television screen, his expression calculating. Turning his attention back to the television, Steve sees what Thor means. The plates on Loki's left arm don't fit him like a second skin like they do on his right.

Thor speaks again. "Why bother with armor at all? He divined how Frigga made Baldur invulnerable. He could do the same for himself."

"What are you saying?" says Steve.

Eyes still on the screen, Thor tilts his head. "He plays a game. Perhaps one he doesn't want to win."

There are sounds of explosions from the television. Steve turns his head to see police cars on fire, and police with raised guns screaming, frost rising from their bodies.

"A bad game," Steve says.

"But one we must play," says Thor, before stepping through the revolving doors. With one last glance at the screen, Steve follows.

With one arm Amy leans on the rolling stand of her IV drip. In the other she carries Ratatoskr. She is moving as fast as she can— which isn't very—down the hallway that separates Loki's bedroom from the rest of his apartment.

"Ow! Norn's webs, woman, why didn't you leave me on the bed?" the squirrel grumbles.

"Have to get away, have to get away," Amy chants to herself, even though she can hear gun shots in the background.

Entering the foyer, she tries the door, but the handle doesn't budge. She pounds on it and screams, but there is no answer on the other side. Dropping her forehead to the door, she lets out a frustrated groan.

"Think most people had the sense to get the fuck out of here," says Ratatoskr. Amy glares down at the squirrel. He gives a little squeak and rubs a paw over his nose. "Just sayin'."

Lifting her head, she looks towards the living room. She can send an email to Steve. A part of her wonders what good that will do anyone. Grimacing, she presses the little button that administers morphine and marches on.

As she enters the living room she lets out a breath. She sees the sun shining on buildings and the Board of Trade … it may be the drugs, but it looks like it is leaning to one side. Still, the window is not showing the world through Loki's eyes, and she breathes a sigh of relief.

No sooner has the breath left her lips, than the window shimmers and she's staring at a pair of double doors swinging open, and then she's looking across a city street at a mural of Icarus and Daedalus above the entrance of a building. Her legs feel weak, as though they might melt beneath her in dread as Loki turns southward. Suddenly, she's staring down the long canyon of LaSalle Street, dark despite the sunny day, eerily empty of people and traffic.

"Awww … " A long string of angry squirrelese flows from Ratatoskr mouth. "I don't want a front row seat in Loki's brain!"

In the distance she hears the wail of police sirens getting louder as Loki begins to walk towards the Board of Trade four blocks or so away. She tilts her head. The Board of Trade is tilted a bit from this angle, too.

At the periphery of her vision she sees police cars pull up on West Washington to the right and left of Loki. Men run out and shout, "Freeze!"

"Puppets of the oppressors," says Cera's voice. *"Let them freeze."*

"No, Loki, no!" Amy screams.

For a moment, the forward motion of the scene stalls, but then the police officers start to scream. Their breath turns frosty as their bodies turn to ice. Their cars explode one by one.

Loki begins walking southward again through the frozen statues of police and burning husks of cars, towards the leaning Board of Trade. Through the smoke Amy makes out the shape of a press van.

"Parasites," screeches Cera. *"We will kill them."*

"No, don't!" shouts Amy, shaking her IV stand.

"Why, why, why ... " It's Loki's voice, sounding distant, and faint.

"The revolution must be televised!" Amy says. She gasps for breath, not really sure where that came from. But Loki's voice echoes through the apartment, a little louder this time. *"She's right."*

"Whoa," says Ratatoskr, trembling in Amy's hands. "He heard you!"

"Yes," says Cera. *"I understand! We will show them our full power, by destroying this monument to capitalism!"*

Amy straightens. "Oh, shit," she says.

"You took the words out of my mouth," says Ratatoskr. Without looking down at the squirrel, Amy rolls the IV stand over to Loki's desk and plunks down on his chair. The computer's screen flickers to life and she does her best to type in the password with one hand. From the window comes the sound of an explosion. She glances up to see the buildings on either side of Loki collapse. Debris falls down in destruction so fast and forceful the chunks of cement and mortar look like the foam of falling water. "He's destroying the buildings," she whispers.

Squeaking, Ratatoskr says, "Hopefully, not this one."

The password works, and Amy's suddenly looking at live streaming aerial footage of Chicago on CNN. As the window shows a curtain of dust and debris, the scene on the computer shows buildings toppling one by one down LaSalle. Amy's heart feels like it's in her throat, and then she hears the voice she's never heard before echoing through the apartment. *"Please, St. Jude, help them. Help those people … "*

Another voice rises in chorus. *"Dear God, make it stop."* Another voice comes, sounding suspiciously like Arabic, and then another, and another in still a different language, until there are so many it is like the sound of rushing water.

Ratatoskr meets Amy's eyes. "Prayers," whispers the squirrel. "Those are human prayers!"

"They're watching CNN," says Amy.

A voice rises among the rest, male, English, but heavily accented and vaguely Indian. *"Fuck you! I did not leave India for this!"*

"I agree with that one," says Ratatoskr.

"What is that?" says Cera's voice loud and clear above the din.

"They are praying for me to save them," says Loki, and Amy can hear the quirk of his lips in his voice.

"We are saving them!" says Cera. *"They will see!"*

Loki doesn't respond.

On the monitor in front of her Amy opens her email and desperately types out a message to Steve. She winces and grips her side. What is she thinking? Circuits are probably jammed, it will never get through. She closes her eyes and says a silent prayer that it gets through—and hears it echo around her in the room. Lifting her eyes to empty air she presses send and flips back to CNN.

From the aerial view provided by CNN, Amy sees two buildings topple a block away from the Board of Trade, the blocks in Loki's wake completely decimated.

"Fuck!" says Amy.

"Amen," says Ratatoskr.

Steve and Thor stumble out of the building, through the throng of reporters, and into the middle of LaSalle Street. Steve sees the exhaust of cars—cabs, maintenance vehicles and a few police cars—but he can't hear their engines. The buildings on either side of LaSalle are crumbling and drowning nearly all other sounds. A human-shaped shadow highlighted by shimmering blue approaches through the dust at a leisurely walk. Steve's jaw tightens. Loki.

His phone buzzes in his pocket, but it is on the periphery of his consciousness. Thor is shouting to some agents by the door, "Evacuate the building!" A few people who ignored the evacuation orders days ago are running from the remaining buildings on LaSalle.

Steve's phone is still buzzing. Why is it still buzzing? He pulls it out of his pocket. He doesn't have to click on anything. It's lit up, a message seemingly scrawled across the surface in glowing blue pen.

Cera is controlling Loki. He's fighting it. You have to HELP him outsmart her! Amy

It's obviously magic. But how and why is this message coming through? Steve looks up to see two more buildings crumble only half a block away as Loki approaches. People running down the sidewalk fall over in the debris and dust.

"We have to talk to him," Steve says, looking at his phone.

How Thor hears his words, barely-audible above the destruction, Steve will never know. "Aye," shouts Thor. "But first we must clear the dust." Thor raises his hammer. The sky darkens too quickly to be natural, there is the crackle of lightning, and the boom of thunder. The skies open up and Steve is instantly soaked. His hands flex by his side, but he doesn't grab his gun.

"Loki!" Thor shouts towards the horned figure glowing in the middle of the street just a few yards away. Loki stops walking. The roar of collapsing buildings is replaced by the sound of rain pounding on the pavement and screams of the wounded. Along the pavement beside them, rainwater begins to swirl, running brown with dust.

"Hello, Thor!" Loki shouts, his voice ringing with laughter. "Ready to die, son of the Tsar of the Nine Realms?"

"If you truly wanted that I would already be dead," Thor shouts back.

At this distance, Steve can see the wide, maniacal stretch of Loki's grin and the glint of teeth beneath his horned helmet, the strange plating on his left arm glowing very brightly. "Maybe I just want to play with you!" Loki shouts. "You know how I love games!"

Steve hears the wail of police sirens through the rain. And then there are explosions in the distance and the wailing disappears. The only sound on the street is the sound of people screaming and calling to one another.

"I know there is still good in you, Loki!" Thor shouts.

"Good? Thor, have you been talking to the Christians?" Loki laughs. And then he leans forward and screams. "This isn't about good or evil! This is about power!"

Coming forward fast, Loki whips his left arm in a wide circle and the rain stops.

Thor raises his hammer and nothing happens. "Let the sunshine in!" Loki screams—and beams of sunlight break through the clouds. Steve finds himself, Thor, and Loki, now only a few paces away, in a natural spotlight.

Taking a deep breath, Steve wills himself to ignore the screams around him. He takes a step forward and a makes a stab in the dark. "After being a pawn of Odin your whole life, you're going to be a pawn of Cera, Loki?"

Eyes leaving Thor, Loki shouts, "We will kill you, too, Steve Rogers!" Then his head ticks to the side, as though something's in his ear, and he starts to grimace.

Steve's gaze slides towards Thor. Thor's hammer is above the warrior's head. The large man is pulling on the handle, as though the hammer is suspended on an invisible string.

Loki laughs, and Steve's attention snaps back to him.

"We should kill you instantly," Loki says. "But no, I say a game is better, a game is more fun."

Steve is aware of shadows on the periphery of his vision, agents from the FBI, and maybe police officers slinking through the alleyways of the remaining buildings, guns raised. Steve is torn between telling them to run and being afraid of giving them away.

Smiling, Loki says, "Did Amy ever tell you about the story

Thor Versus Captain America?" He giggles and raises his eyebrows. "I was the good guy in that one! Thor was in league with the Nazis … which is oddly appropriate considering his activities during the 40s."

"Loki!" Thor says, his voice low and steady. "Stop this."

Steve's eyes go to Thor. Thor is still trying to pull the hammer out of the air, his face contorted in a grimace, a sheen of sweat on his skin.

Loki takes a menacing step towards Thor. In the distance, another building tumbles. Trying to distract Loki, or buy time, Steve says, "The name of the story is Thor Meets Captain America."

"Liar!" screams Loki, spinning to Steve. "We shall watch you kill each other!"

"Run, Agent Rogers!" Thor shouts. He's still hanging onto his hammer—and the hammer is rushing through the air in Steve's direction.

Steve dives to the ground, asphalt and pebbles digging into his hands and pain shooting through his side as Thor and the hammer hit the ground where Steve just stood, lightning rippling up along Thor's body. Loki laughs. Steve is once more aware of screaming. And another sound, one that he recognizes from his time in Afghanistan. Jet fighters.

So Big Brother has been paying attention.

"Hey, Thor!" Steve shouts, scrambling to his feet. "Try and get me!" Turning, Steve runs.

Loki laughs. "That's the spirit."

Turning into an alley, Steve hears Thor grunt behind him and nearly collides with agents and police in front of him. "Incoming, take cover!" Steve shouts.

Their eyes are wide. Steve turns to see Thor, still holding

onto his hammer, flying through the air about seven feet above the ground, coming right at him. "Run, that's an order!" says Steve. The agents turn and run. Spinning, Steve runs towards Thor, diving down just before the hammer hits his head. Thor and the hammer collide with the ground a few paces behind him in a rumble of thunder and a flash of lightning. At the opening of the alley Loki laughs, but his voice is drowned out by the sound of air cover drawing closer.

Loki looks up, momentarily distracted. From an alley across the street comes the sound of gunfire. Steve is close enough that he hears bullets colliding with Loki's armor as he stares up into the sky—and then a nearly simultaneous chorus of screams just before the roar of fighter jets becomes nearly deafening. A bright lights streaks towards Loki and he holds out a hand and laughs as an explosion erupts just a few feet in front of him, flames licking out in a sphere. It takes a moment for Steve to understand what he's just seen. Loki just deflected Hellfire missiles—it shouldn't be a shock.

A chill runs through his body. For a moment all he can do is stare in breathless horror. He'd imagined Claire would be safe because she was in Lake Forest … nowhere in the world is safe.

Shaking himself, Steve turns to see Thor struggling to his feet, and then he hears a boom in the sky and looks up to see five F-15 Strike Eagles on fire, shooting through the sky like falling stars.

"This is so much fun!" screams Loki. And then the sound of the fighters colliding with buildings becomes too loud to hear anything else.

Steve turns to find Thor beside him. Steve bows his head to the ground, completely at a loss as to what to do … and then he sees something black sliding along the pavement a few feet behind Loki. A manhole cover.

"What are the sewage thralls doing?" Thor rumbles beside him.

An orange hard hat and the muzzle of a shotgun peek up just at the level of the street behind where Loki is staring at the downed fighters. The man aims the shotgun. A shot might have been fired, it's hard to hear, but what is definite is the sound of Loki's scream as he clutches the underside of his left arm, his armor pulsing with light.

Pain rips along Loki's left arm as a bullet slips beneath the plating, and the magical energy flooding his body retreats for a moment.

"What is that?" Cera screams.

"Pain," says Loki. Turning around he sees a brightly colored helmet and the muzzle of a shotgun slip into a manhole. Loki hears a mumble of "Shit, I missed."

"How dare he!" Cera shouts. "How dare one so low make Us hurt. The fool is the very people We will help! Kill him!"

Loki gasps. In the back of his mind he hears whispers—calls in every human language to every conceivable deity and saint. He hears St. Jude, Jesus, Jehovah, Allah, Shiva and a string of other names that could be Hindi. He hears a few calls to Ananse, Iktomi, Odin and even …

"Loki!" It's Amy's voice.

"What are you waiting for?" Cera says. "Stop him!"

What is Loki waiting for? He snarls and winces in pain. Why does he have his mind back? Is it the pain keeping Cera at bay?

At the corner of his vision he sees Steve approaching, pistol raised, speaking into his phone. And Thor is behind him, hammer in hand. Loki has relinquished his hold on Mjolnir in his distraction. Shadows of humans are emerging from the remaining buildings around him, weapons drawn. Part of him wants them to succeed—but knows that is an impossibility. Almost against Loki's volition, the wound in his arm is healing. Cera is invincible.

He hears Amy's voice again, begging him. "Please, Loki, don't be the destroyer, be the transformer."

There is a ping of a bullet on the back of his helmet.

"Enough of this game! Stop them!" Cera commands.

Loki feels the flare of magic in his body again, as he—no Cera—readies to attack.

Steve is right, he is just a puppet—has always been a puppet. Loki was the source of Asgard's greatest treasures, its greatest defender, and yet all this time he's been regarded as a fool. His lips curl. And with good reason. He hasn't been playing the game, he's been played. Cera is using him, just as Odin had, just as Amy said Cera would, just as Thor said she would. Why had Loki been so blind? Was it his desire for vengeance, or just because it is his nature to destroy everything and never get anything right?

"Stop the games now," Cera screams. Magic ripples and pulses along every cell in Loki's body. Loki feels a cry of despair and frustration rising in his chest. He's had enough of this game too—enough of all games. Throwing up his arms, Loki screams, "No! Stop everything!"

And Cera obeys.

Power whips through Loki with such strength he lifts from the ground. The humans around him become motionless.

Dust and soot hang in the air in front of him like dirty snowflakes. The flames rising up from exploded cars, buildings and bodies become motionless pillars of orange light. The scene around Loki is blanketed in an eerie silence.

Loki gasps. Preserving time in the immediate vicinity is Odin's trick. Not something Loki is capable of at all, but with Cera … with Cera … oh.

Loki looks up at the sky. Even the clouds have stopped moving. His consciousness slips along with the tendrils of Cera's power; but he's still separate, still himself. He feels Earth and all the planets around her sun stop their rotations. He feels the galaxy stop spinning, and the universe itself stop expanding. And he sees. His eyes widen as he realizes what a small branch of the World Tree the Nine Realms are. There are more branches, more realms, more life—too much and too varied to contemplate. He pulls back and looks only at the Nine Realms. His gaze falls upon the elf queen, still as a statue, staring in her pool at an image of himself, and sees Odin upon his throne—Heimdall whispering in his ear, a spear that is not Gungnir is in the All Father's grasp. Where is Gungnir? Odin had last used the spear to trap Hoenir in his hut. At the moment Loki thinks of Hoenir, he sees the hut, with Gungnir still outside its front door in Muspelheim, the realm of fire, frozen tendrils of flames rising up from its roof like so many jagged teeth.

Stretching his consciousness inside Hoenir's home, Loki sees his boys immobilized by magic, crouched by the door, armed with Earth-style automatic weapons. Sigyn lies upon a couch looking towards their sons. Mimir's head is on his favorite staff, leaning against the wall, mouth open, eyes turned towards the statues of Nari and Valli. Loki gasps in disbelief and relief, even as his throat tightens. He can't fail them again.

Hoenir is not with them; he is at a table, sipping tea. Hoenir is moving. And he is not the Hoenir that Loki remembers. His head is no longer balding, his pot belly is gone.

"Hoenir?" Loki gasps.

From where he is drinking tea, Hoenir looks up. The lines that used to surround his eyes have vanished. He looks so … young, like in the dream with Laugaz. Hoenir shakes his head, as though responding to Loki's unspoken, Why?

Feeling exposed, bitter and brittle, Loki looks away. Closing his eyes, he takes a deep breath. His sons, Sigyn, Mimir and Hoenir are alive. And Hoenir is moving … Loki suddenly knows how that is possible, and how Loki was able to fight the influence of Odin's ability to stop time as Loki became older and stronger. Odin's magic lies in preservation and order, but chaos and creation cannot be stopped forever.

Loki feels a tightening in his chest and lets out a breath. The universe has begun its outward journey again, but it is slower, still tethered … His hands ball into fists. Is he only himself because Cera's power is diverted? If so, how much time does he have? What will she have him do when she releases the heavens from her hold? He looks around at the world where his body resides, the toppled buildings, the fires of exploded machines, and frozen bodies.

He knows what she will do to Earth. His consciousness spins around the small globe he's found himself on. He sees hundreds of different countries, divided by even more cultures and languages. New cultures and new language are forming every minute as human societies struggle to accommodate the changes their frantic pace of technological innovation has wrought. Compared to all the other Nine Realms with their static kings and queens, kingdoms and stale magic, this world is chaos.

But Cera will put an end to it. She will combine all of humanity under one monolithic ideology, constrain the minds and ideas she doesn't approve of, and decide what is best for all—just like Odin.

His vision shrinks to just this one city. Chicago was chaos before he even arrived, diverse, vibrant, and corrupt. Its skyscrapers reach for the sky, even as grass and tree roots break through the shackles of pavement, destroying the pinnacles from below.

Life destroying order. He breathes again, overwhelmed. Life as chaos? He thinks of Helen, of saving her life from the midwives who sought to end her. That was an act of chaos, too, defying the order of the Aesir. Or an act of love? Or maybe love is chaotic? Going to the cave for the lives of his sons and Sigyn ... such an honorable thing, and so entirely against his nature. Even Valli knew it. Love could make wretches like him honorable and honorable beings do unthinkable things. Chaotic indeed.

Hovering in midair, in this place outside of time, the voices are gone from his head, but he feels his connection to all of the humans who uttered them. Cera will destroy the voices—the languages, cultures, traditions and the faith behind them. She'll end this realm of perfect chaos, of real life, and then she'll expand, won't she?

His chest constricts and he feels Cera's power snap as the universe begins to expand again in earnest. The galaxies begin to pull against Cera's fetters.

He doesn't have much time left. What does he want for

his sons and the voices of chaos in his head? Nine Realms ruled by Odin or a universe ruled by Cera?

A ragged breath comes from his lungs stirring the snowflakes of soot in its wake. Every other realm is in stasis enforced by Odin, and Cera would be no better. This realm belongs to no one; it is ruled by change, life, and chaos.

He smirks, even as he feels the galaxies grind into motion. In a way, this realm is Loki's.

He doesn't have to choose between Odin and Cera. He may be an incarnation of chaos, but he's a trickster, too—and he always keeps his oaths, after all.

Loki turns his eyes towards his apartment. Amy is standing there, an immobilized Ratatoskr in her grip. She is weak, and too young, but she is the only one besides Hoenir and Odin who knows what he is. What he is about to do is unfair, but he isn't justice incarnate.

"Amy," he whispers. "Move."

Amy blinks, an afterimage of jet planes on fire in her mind, but what she sees before her is very different. She's no longer staring out of Loki's eyes through his windows. Instead the windows show him floating above the ground, his skin back to brilliant blue. The world around him is frozen in place. She sees soot and debris hanging in the air.

Loki is smirking, his eyes on hers.

"Loki?" she whispers. "Is that you?"

The smirk softens. "I don't have much time. Don't let me forget next time who I am, what I am."

"Next time?" Amy says.

Loki shrugs and he gives her a smile that's too thin and

too sharp.

And then she knows. "No, you can't die!"

He snorts. "Apparently not. But it will hide me from Odin for a while."

Clutching a motionless Ratatoskr to her, Amy stands and limps to the window. "No, there's got to be another way!"

"Remember for me," Loki says. She feels heat upon her forehead and she closes her eyes for a moment, overcome by a wave of dizziness. When she opens her eyes, Loki's smile is gone.

He sucks in a breath and whispers, "The heavens are on the move. There isn't much time."

Pressing her free hand to the glass, Amy whispers, "No, please."

Tilting his head, Loki sighs. Sounding very tired, he whispers, "I won't be the destroyer, Amy. Not this time."

Amy's brow furrows and she feels a lump in her throat, tears burning in her eyes. "I don't want you to go," she says.

Loki swallows. For a moment she sees something like sorrow flicker across his face. "Thank you," he says.

And then, smiling gently, he gives a sort of half shrug. Dropping his eyes to the squirrel in Amy's arms, Loki says, "Ratatoskr, you incorrigible gossip, wake up and watch this."

There is a shudder in her arms, and then a mumbled, "The fuck?"

Lifting his eyes back to hers, Loki's lips quirk. Around and behind him flames, dust and debris start to swirl as though in slow motion.

"Cera!" Loki cries, turning his face to the sky.

"Loki! We're almost together again. Why did you make us stop everything?" Cera's voice says, sounding like nothing so much as a confused child.

"I needed time to think." Loki says. "You're right, let's end the games!"

"We will wipe their minds!" Cera says, her voice chillingly cheery.

"Erp," says Ratatoskr.

Shivering, Amy bites her lip.

Loki snorts. "Oh, no, this place is too far gone for that. We need to start over completely!"

"Eeep!" says Ratatoskr.

"We can do that?" says Cera.

Amy shudders. Ratatoskr trembles.

"With my imagination? And your power? Of course!" says Loki, grinning maniacally. He throws out his arms, lifting them heavenward. "But first, what we need is a very, very Big Bang."

Around him light begins to swirl. Loki gasps, his eyes going wide. He glances up in Amy's direction and gives her a small nod.

"No!" she says, her vision blurry with tears. Ratatoskr trembles more violently in her arms—or maybe that is her trembling.

Loki smiles at her. And then he winks.

Behind Loki flames begin to leap and swirl in earnest, debris falling out of the sky as his body and armor pulse with brightness. And then for a heart beat Loki is a single point of light in a vast emptiness. His mouth opens in a silent scream, and suddenly Loki is a burst of light and fire exploding outward. Amy cries out. The window is a wall of fire …

… and then it is just a window again. Amy is looking out at blue sky peeking out beyond retreating thunder clouds and smoke.

Ratatoskr squeaks. "World Tree's nuts! He took the damn thing into the In-Between." His tail swishes. "Loki tricked it into destroying itself!"

The squirrel chitters and then laughs. "The Sly One saved us!"

Amy squeezes him tight, her vision completely obscured by tears. "Yes."

CHAPTER 13

When the universe starts to slow, Hoenir doesn't recognize it at first.

Mimir, Sigyn, Valli, Nari, and all of Hoenir's extensive friends and pets have already been frozen in time for months, so their stillness doesn't alert him. When Odin thrust Gungnir into the ground, Hoenir's hut was surging with magic, about to leave Asgard on its way to Muspellsheimr. The spells of the hut and staff had crossed. The hut made the journey, but it and everything in it had been frozen by Gungnir's magic upon arriving.

Hoenir sighs. Except for himself. Sipping his tea, he glances out the window at Gungnir. He's given up trying to tear the thing out of the ground and end the spell. The magic of the preserver is splendid at preserving itself. But Odin's magic had worked against the Allfather this time. The hut is frozen in one of Muspellsheimr's flaming pits, where

Heimdall never thought to look, and Odin's ravens can't fly. And while it has certainly been lonely, freezing Hoenir's hut in time did have some advantages. Hoenir looks to the door that leads to his velociraptors' pens. He hasn't had to feed them since his imprisonment began.

Of course, Hoenir's own appetite is another matter. He looks down at his waist, thinner than it's been in millennia. He's been rationing his food—not that he can die, but he doesn't like to be hungry. The paunch had taken too much energy to maintain, and using magic to age himself, slow his metabolism, and thin his hair had been too much of a bother.

He looks out the window, past the columns of frozen fire that surround his house. His breath catches. The fires beyond his prison have stopped, too. He feels the hairs on the back of his neck rise, and also a presence he knows well.

"Hoenir?"

He feels rather than hears Loki say his name. He looks up and only sees his ceiling.

He feels Loki's sense of betrayal. Or maybe it is just the weight of his own guilt. No matter how Hoenir tells himself that the deal he'd struck with Odin was the only way to save the Nine Realms and Loki …

Or maybe you just like to keep Loki close, a wicked voice in his mind whispers. Hoenir shakes his head, and Loki's presence fades, leaving Hoenir feeling empty and very, very tired. Not for the first time he envies Loki his ignorance, and the fresh starts he's had over the centuries.

Taking a long draught of his tea, Hoenir stares down into his cup and swirls the leaves. He cannot be with Loki, but he can watch. In the dregs of his tea a picture begins to form of the whole of the universe. His eyebrows go up, the universe itself has stopped, not just one branch of the tree—everything. Loki has Cera then. Breath catching and hands shaking, Hoenir swirls the cup again.

He sees the city of Chicago but where there should be buildings there is dust and rubble with Loki as its focal point, his skin full-blue, his hair black. Hoenir's eyes mist at the sight. Whenever Loki starts to turn blue it means his magic is surging, and subconsciously he suspects a transformation is near. The picture starts to blur. Hoenir swirls the cup again, this time without ceasing. The picture shimmers and wiggles, and sound emerges.

"Amy," Loki whispers, black eyes staring at a point in the sky. "Move."

Squinting and shaking the cup, Hoenir sees the girl moving forward in Loki's apartment. She wears the raiment of convalescence of her people. She is clutching an immobilized Ratatoskr to her stomach. Hoenir's been watching Loki's courtship of her; it is oddly comforting to know Loki misses him, too. The girl is so much like Hoenir himself, or how Hoenir was.

Hoenir's brow furrows. Her face is drawn and pale, but she is pretty, in the way new life is. She is definitely Loki's type, too—curvaceous, not thin and androgynous as is the fashion of her people. Hoenir is jealous of her. Odin may prefer to be male, Loki may not care one way or another, but Hoenir, or that part of the universe that is part of him, would prefer to be female—in other lives the babies that Creation has had! With time, Hoenir could change himself; but Odin's punishment would be severe. Hoenir sighs. He has been stuck stitching creatures together, or animating bits of this and that.

In the scene in his cup, Loki says, "I don't have much

time. Don't let me forget next time who I am, what I am."

"Next time?" Amy says.

Loki shrugs and smirks.

Realization dawns on the girl's face and in Hoenir at the same time. Hoenir's eyes widen. Loki knows he will transform. And knows enough to know that he will forget nearly everything—he almost always flubs the transition. Loki will only be bound by the oath Hoenir saw him make to destroy Odin and Asgard. Sucking in a breath, Hoenir tilts his head. Loki is binding himself to this girl, too.

"No, you can't die!" she says.

The image goes blurry, or Hoenir's eyes fill with tears, he's not sure which.

"I won't be the destroyer, Amy. Not this time," Loki says, and Hoenir's concentration snaps. He finds himself gasping for breath. All that he has done for Loki, it hasn't been in vain. And all that he kept from Loki hasn't damaged him irreparably. But Hoenir won't be able to help him next time.

Gulping in a breath, Hoenir looks out the window at Gungnir. The spear has Hoenir pinned here like a butterfly. Dropping his head in frustration, sorrow, and anger, Hoenir suddenly feels a subtle shift. Hearing a rattle beyond the hut, Hoenir looks up and sees Gungnir quaking in the ground. And then Hoenir feels it, the universe starting to move again, its momentum working against Odin's magic. Hoenir scrambles to his feet. Hesitating just a moment, he walks past the still figures of Valli and Nari, out the door, and through columns of frozen flame. Just as he reaches the spear it shatters into three pieces. Heat instantly whips around him as the flames spring to life. In wonder, Hoenir picks up the remains of Gungnir and moves as quickly as he can back into the safety of the hut.

"What's going on?" says Nari, as Hoenir shuts the door.

"Where are we?" says Sigyn. "Why are the windows filled with flame?"

"Where are the Valkyries? I want to see how they stand up to an M16," shouts Valli.

"Well—" says Mimir.

"Ragnarok," says Hoenir. The end of the world. His voice comes out, shaky and dry. It's been so long since he's used it. But he needs it now; and the bargain he made to Odin is over.

There is silence in the room. Hoenir looks up at the startled faces. "Loki is free," Hoenir says. Or will be departing his most recent host very soon.

"Oh, dear," says Mimir. Of course, he is the only one besides Hoenir who understands.

"Mimir, explain," says Hoenir; it's a cruel thing to ask, but Hoenir can't bring himself to do it.

Detaching the blade from the tip of the spear, Hoenir stares at the pieces for a moment. They still contain some of Odin's magic. He tips his head in contemplation. Odin will be seeking the new Loki—and the Allfather will seek Hoenir too.

Hoenir turns the pieces of Gungnir over in his hand. Loki always seeks a host that's personality and circumstances are compatible with chaos, just as Odin seeks a host compatible with order and preservation, and the piece of the universe inhabiting Hoenir seeks a body compatible with creation.

Hoenir inspects one of the pieces of Gungnir's staff. This new Loki will find his way to the girl. He thinks of her staring out of Loki's window. He's seen her many other times, studying her veterinary journals, washing Fenrir—even at the talk on REM sleep. She is so like Hoenir …

An idea blossoms in Hoenir's mind. A way to save Loki from Odin, this time, for real. And a way to hide from Odin and shed that part of him that has made him uncomfortable in this skin for over a millennia. It's been a long time since Hoenir has really wanted something, but suddenly he wants to meet Miss Lewis very much.

Mimir clears his throat. Snapping from his trance, Hoenir hands the tip of the spear to Sigyn; to Nari and Valli he gives each a piece of Gungnir's staff. He's sure they'll find them useful.

Clutching the last piece of Odin's weapon, Hoenir steps from the room into his workshop, leaving the others quiet and probably in shock. Looking quickly around at the pieces of other spears, arrows, and swords he's collected, he sees nothing that quite works. Hoenir goes quickly to the back, opens another door, and steps into a warehouse-sized room containing bric-a-brac from every realm he and those before him acquired through the millennia. He needs something innocuous … and an innocuous being to wield the weapon he will be creating. His eyes fall onto a flower print umbrella and his eyebrows jump.

A few minutes later, the umbrella has a piece of Gungnir's staff in its shaft. It also has a thin new wrist strap attached, a tiny bead of shiny glass threaded in it. The strap isn't special, but the bead is something Hoenir has designed to counteract human magic detectors. Clutching the umbrella, Hoenir goes to another door at the back of his workshop. Before opening it, he leans his forehead against the rough wood and murmurs some words just to focus his mind. Behind the door a brand new branch of the World Tree sprouts. Creating new pathways between the realms is a gift Hoenir has, something Loki will never be able to do, and Odin can only do piddling well.

Turning the handle of the door, Hoenir steps through and is immediately assaulted by the smell of antiseptic. His eyes blink under the glare of fluorescent lights. Upon a bed, under a thin blanket, lies an elderly woman he's seen only from afar. Her eyes are open and she stares at the ceiling. Hoenir walks over to her, but she does not acknowledge his presence. Laying his hand upon her forehead, he closes his eyes and concentrates, a familiar prickle sparking through his fingers. When he opens his eyes, the woman is staring up at him, her gaze sharp and bright.

"Hello, Beatrice," he says. "I'm Hoenir. Friend of Loki. Your granddaughter is going to need your help."

Beatrice's eyes widen. Sitting up quickly, thin legs and bare feet peeking out of a worn lavender nightgown, she says, "What are we waiting here for?"

Hoenir smiles. He knew this part would be easy. Handing her the umbrella, he says, "You'll need this."

Steve stumbles north along LaSalle Street between the rubble of ruined buildings. It's been nearly an hour since Loki disappeared. So far there are no reports of him re-materializing anywhere.

Thor says that he can feel that the threat of Cera is gone from this world. The powers that be on Earth are taking that under advisement. In Chicago, right now, all anyone can do is try to clean up the mess. The word is that the Red Cross is mobilizing rescue teams from around the world, and the

Wisconsin National Guard is moving in to cover the refugee camps at the airports. Soon there will be sniffer dogs and field hospitals, and the Guard to help with any marauding trolls. For now there are just FBI agents, police, firemen, and civilians wandering up and down the street looking for survivors to send to hospitals and ADUO's very overtaxed trauma center.

Pausing by an overturned cab, Steve scans the sky for a moment. There is no sign of his feathered friends; he's not sure if that makes him relieved or worried. Dropping down to a squat he looks in the cab's window. Inside there is a pile of dust lying on the ceiling that's now the floor. It takes a moment for Steve to realize the pile is human shaped.

"I think I found someone!" Steve calls.

He hears feet running towards him. Standing, he tries to open the door. It's locked. Picking up a brick, he bashes in the window, scrapes away the glass, and thrusts his hands into the blanket of dirt covering the driver. Steve's breath catches as his hands come into contact with warm skin.

"He's alive," Steve calls, pulling him out. Other people—none he recognizes—have their hands on either side of the driver, helping Steve.

"I don't feel a pulse," someone says.

"Call for an ambulance, they'll have an AED," a woman says. A man responds, "I think they're all busy."

"CPR," says Steve.

"Pound the dust out of his lungs first," says one of his companions.

They roll the guy they've pulled out over on his side and pound on his back. A little bit of dirt comes out of his mouth in a cloud.

"Mouth to mouth." Someone says.

Rolling the guy back onto his back, Steve finds himself kneeling in the dirt across from a woman he doesn't know in a fireman uniform, taking turns performing mouth to mouth resuscitation and pumping the chest of another stranger in the middle of a wide open plain of rubble that was LaSalle Street.

He doesn't know how long they stay there.

Someone kneeling beside them clutches the guy's wrist and says, "He's gone."

"No," says Steve, bending to push the contents of his lungs into the body below him.

He hears the exhale of air as the woman pumps the guy's chest. "Just give us a few more minutes!" she says.

Steve sits up, inhales deeply, puts his hands on the guy's chest, and the woman bends down.

The person kneeling beside them says. "You've done all you can."

A firm hand falls on Steve's shoulders. "You've got to let him go. There are others out there."

Turning his head up, Steve sees Thor, his face haloed by the sun. They should be in the shadow of LaSalle's buildings right now, but those buildings are all gone.

Steve falls backwards, his legs curling up until he is sitting Indian style in the middle of the street. He wipes his face and finds it wet. The firewoman is a shadow on the periphery of his vision, standing and leaving, one of her comrades dropping an arm around her.

Steve's about to stand up. Thor's right, they need to keep going, when he looks down at the face of the guy he's been trying to rescue and recognizes him. It's the kid, Patel, the one who lied about owning a cab. The one Steve should have told to evacuate—just like he should have put Lewis on the Witness Protection program. He huffs a breath, his ex-wife's words ringing in his mind. *You'd sell out your own mother for the 'greater good.'* Suddenly feeling very heavy, Steve says, "Just give me a minute."

Thor probably nods, Steve's not really looking. He bows his head and sucks in a deep breath. As Thor's feet retreat, Steve sees a flash of light, hears a squeak, and then a thin reedy little voice says, "Hey, Hommie!"

Coughing some dust from his lungs, Steve turns his head. Two rats are staring at him from a sewer grate set between the side of the street and the sidewalk.

"Yeah, Bro! I'm talking to you!" one of them says.

Steve blinks. And then his eyes narrow. He is so not in the mood for any more magical shit.

The rats scamper out of the grate, and Steve realizes one is actually a squirrel with tufted ears and a fluffy tail. The squirrel turns to the rat and says, "Thanks for the directions, Sweetheart. Catch you later!" The rat turns around and vanishes down the sewer grate.

Turning to Steve, the squirrel says, "Most squirrels don't like rats. But I never saw anything wrong with a little naked tail." He winks at Steve. All Steve can do is stare at it.

The squirrel blinks. "Oh, come on Bro! Cheer up! Could have been worse."

Steve is sitting in a plain of rubble and dying people. Next to him is the corpse of a kid who would be alive if it weren't for Steve. He doesn't reach out and strangle the squirrel, but it's a near thing. "Who are you and what do you want?" he grinds out.

"Chill, Bro!" says the squirrel, holding up a paw. "Name's

Ratatoskr and—"

And Steve has had enough. The squirrel squeaks as Steve's hand whips around its torso. "I'm not your 'bro,' Rat!" Steve snarls. "Unless you want to wind up doing laps on a hamster wheel and picking wood chips out of your pelt in my daughter's guinea pig pen, you'll tell me what you want!"

"I just wanted you to like me," it squeaks. The squirrel's ears go back, and his eyes widen. It's the sort of big-eyed, scaredy look Steve expects from a dog asking for table scraps—and damned if it doesn't work. Steve's grip relaxes a fraction.

The squirrel sniffs. "Steve Rogers, the man Odin heard! Want to say I met you personally—before you achieve great things, or wind up on the gallows." He shows Steve all his teeth with an expression that isn't quite a smile. "Or both."

Narrowing his eyes, Steve squeezes. "You've seen me, now what?"

Squeaking, the squirrel twitches his nose. "I promised Lewis I'd let you know she and her grandmother are alive and well and hangin' at Loki's place ... you know, since cell reception and internet are down. I took a shortcut through Nornheim and then—"

Steve's brow furrows. "Loki's place? Beatrice?"

The squirrel bobs his head. "Yeah, I know, something is off." He looks down at his torso. "I had some fractured ribs, too, but they're better." Glaring at Steve, he chitters. "Were better."

"What happened?" says Steve.

The squirrel perks. "Well, Loki snatched me, from ... errr ... never mind. I wound up at his place, watching with Lewis, when Loki tricked Cera into a one-way trip to the

In-Between, blew up Cera in a big bang and saved us all."

Saved them? Steve's eyes slide to the destruction around him.

Seemingly oblivious, Ratatouille, or whatever, keeps squeaking. "The next moment we're back in Loki's place, but with Beatrice and we're all better. It was seriously some messed up—" he lets loose a stream of squirrel chatter.

Steve looks back at the little animal in his hands. "Where is Loki now?"

The squirrel blinks at Steve like he's stupid. "Mammalian anatomy is really not suited to surviving a big bang, Steven."

"Loki's dead," says Steve, slowly, filtering through Rat's chatter trying to latch on to the part that's the most important.

The squirrel bobs his head. Letting loose a stringer of tsks and squeaks he says, "You can bet Odin is shitting toadstools and on the hunt for Loki and Hoenir right now."

Steve blinks and says slowly, "But Loki is dead … "

The squirrel shrugs—which is a thing Steve hadn't really thought squirrels could do until that moment. "You can't kill Chaos or Creation!"

"But … "

"Granted, Loki'll have a new form, probably a Frost Giant or Fire Giant, they've got a lot of natural magic, but you never can tell with Chaos," says the squirrel.

"Odin wants to punish him … ?" says Steve, his mind racing.

"Nah," says the squirrel, waving a paw. He narrows his eyes, and for a moment Steves sees something dangerous and calculating there. "But the team with Loki always wins."

"What?"

The squirrel leans forward and bites Steve. Steve's been

shot before, but this is worse. Pain shoots through Steve's hand and up his arm. He releases automatically and sees blood running down a tiny glowing cut on the side of his hand. Ratatoskr drops and takes off to the gutter laughing maniacally. There is a flash of light at the opening of the grate, the squirrel disappears, and the light flashes out.

Steve sits there for a moment, and then the light flashes again, and the squirrel's face peeks out as though through a curtain. "Yo! Hommie!" Ratatoskr says. "If I were you, I'd keep my eye on Loki's chick, Lewis. Something's up with her. I just can't get my whiskers in it."

Whiskers in it?

Steve lunges toward the light. "Wait!"

But Ratatoskr is already gone.

Steve sighs and then coughs on the dust in the air. Wincing, he pulls himself up on his knees and rubs his eyes. How the hell do you inform your superiors about a run in with a talking squirrel without coming off as crazy? He looks around at the remains of some of Chicago's most historic buildings. And how do you tell them Loki might have been responsible for saving the world?

Somewhere a cell phone starts to buzz with a text. It takes a moment for Steve to realize it's coming from his pocket. He pulls out the cell and does a double take at the caller ID. It says the text is from Prometheus.

Tapping quickly to accept, Steve reads, *Odin will be watching your world. You need more Promethean Wire. I have left some for you at the Garibaldi Playlot.*

Steve types quickly, Can we meet?

But his phone's screen goes blank. Steve lifts his head. Prometheus is back?

From behind Steve comes the sound of a faint cough, and then another. Steve turns, unsure of where the noise came from. And then the body of the kid, the one everyone said was dead, convulses, dust spilling out of his mouth in a torrent.

Steve's by him a moment later, lifting him up and helping him cough it out. "It's okay," Steve murmurs over and over, a smile pulling at his lips. Maybe he shouldn't feel absolved, but he does.

The kid finally stops hacking. Grinning ear to ear, Steve says, "Welcome back to the world, Bohdi."

The kid blinks, his eyelashes flecked with dirt, his face pale with dust. "Bohdi?" he says, eyes wide.

Steve's smile shrinks. "That's you?"

The kid stares at him a moment. "I don't know."

CHAPTER 14

From the window in Steve's office, Amy can see the remains of LaSalle Street buried beneath four inches of snow. It might look like a park if it weren't for breaks in the powder that reveal sharp cliff edges where floors of buildings are stacked like so many cards. She can even see the place where she last saw Loki.

She turns her gaze away. It's only been two weeks. She puts a hand to her stomach; there is no pain. All her scars are on the inside. She doesn't have any physical scars from her time with Loki; they vanished with an hour of her life after Loki saved the world—not that he's getting credit for that.

Leaning forward in his chair, Steve says, "You don't even remember what happened to you after Loki vanished." He's not even sitting across the desk from her. He's rolled his chair around, as though they're equals, or he's trying to be non-intimidating, or fatherly, or something.

Amy sits up straighter. The missing hour. Her heart rate quickens; she feels dampness on her palms. She has vague feelings about that time: awe, wonder, warmth, and love. She tries to hold onto those feelings and follow them back to the physical memories—what happened, how she healed, who healed her, how Beatrice arrived there. But her stomach seizes with foreboding, the thread of emotion slips from her fingers and the feelings float away, like snowflakes drifting over ice. "It doesn't … " Bother me. She can't quite finish the sentence. But some things are better not to know. She lifts her head. "It will be alright," she says. Whoever was responsible—something good happened to her, or at least something she wanted … she knows that, somehow.

Shaking his head, Steve raises his voice slightly, snapping Amy from her almost memories. "Nonetheless, after a trauma like the one you've suffered, it's best to wait a year before you make any life altering decisions. I say this as a friend, Miss Lewis."

Amy's eyes narrow. Since when have they been friends? "My scholarship was reinstated. This isn't a new plan, this was the plan, until—" she waves a hand in the air unable to say the rest. She turns her gaze back to her soon-to-be former boss.

Sitting back and steepling his fingers, Steve says, "You know, they're creating a new veterinary program at the University of Chicago to study the creatures coming through the gates."

Amy raises an eyebrow, it sounds like—

Looking away, Steve says, "It's still in the planning stages but … "

—it sounds like a trap. She rolls her eyes. "I'm going back to Oklahoma, Steve." She thinks of horses, sunshine and wide open plains, and not having to worry about the occasional troll or tripping over memories of Loki at every street corner. "And I'm not coming back."

Steve sits back in his chair and stares at her. His eyes flick to the window, and at last he says, "You gotta do what you gotta do ... "

His phone rings and Steve turns to pick it up.

Without bothering to be excused, Amy stands. She hears him say, "Mary Bartelme Park? Yeah, yeah, will do."

Amy's almost at his door when Steve says, "Miss Lewis, there's a troll in the Blue Line tunnel. Why don't I give you a ride home? Claire's with me. We're going your way to pick up my folks and then head out to see *Princesses on Ice.*" He smiles, but there is an edge to it.

Strange as the offer is, a detour on a bus to avoid a troll on the Blue Line is the last thing Amy wants to deal with. "Um, sure, thanks. But Beatrice is with me?" Beatrice has been afraid to let Amy out of sight since the "lost hour" when Beatrice emerged in Loki's apartment healthier and sharper than ever.

"Fine, fine, fine ... " says Steve, grabbing his coat, suddenly rushed.

She regrets accepting Steve's offer as soon as she, Beatrice, and Claire are in the car.

Standing by the open driver's side, Steve frowns. "Bohdi said he'd be here. I'll be right back." He closes the door and starts walking through the underground garage.

Sinking into her seat, Amy belatedly remembers Bohdi, the cab-driver guy who is staying with Steve's parents. He still has amnesia, but the doctors don't know why. The leading theory is that it is from errant magic on Loki's part. ADUO doesn't know where he's from, but they do know he's here illegally. Steve's trying to get him refugee status.

In the front seat, Beatrice turns back to Claire. "So you're going to go see Princesses on Ice!"

Amy closes her eyes and leans her head back. She feels guilty by association around Bohdi. Everyone in the office knows about her 'association' with Loki, and Loki wrecked the guy's brain. It makes her feel sick to think ADUO might deport him back to India without even a memory to his name.

Beside Amy, Claire says, "Yes, but I wish Dad wouldn't invent his own endings to the stories." Amy turns to the girl. Claire looks so much like Steve—a daintier, feminine, and pretty Steve. She definitely got Steve's height. Thin as a whip, at eight years old, she's as tall as a ten year old.

"Oh?" says Beatrice.

Claire sighs. "You know Disney's Frog Prince?" Beatrice nods, though Amy's not sure if she's familiar with Disney's African-American rendition of the fairy tale.

Claire huffs. "My dad says that a short stint as a frog wasn't enough to make the prince hardworking, he started getting lazy and making Princess Tiana do all the work at their restaurant, so she divorced him and married the head of a shrimp fishing fleet, and they leveraged their shrimp monopoly to open more restaurants and her new husband managed them while she became mayor of New Orleans."

"Well, that's … " Beatrice's mouth opens but no sound comes out.

"Empowering?" suggests Amy.

Claire narrows her eyes at her.

"I'm sure you'll have a good time," says Beatrice quickly.

Claire nods. "I really like ballet, so I like the choreography, and the music."

At that moment, the door next to Amy opens. She slides over to make room for Bohdi, carefully avoiding eye contact.

Getting into the driver's seat, Steve grumbles. "It's not the top priority right now; it's the intranet, it will be fine, we'll fix it when we can."

"It's a security threat!" says Bohdi. He has a cigarette lighter in his hand, and is agitatedly spinning it between his fingers.

Starting the engine, Steve grumbles. "You better not light up in here."

Bohdi leans back in his seat, his eyes shooting daggers into the back of Steve's head. He doesn't pull out a cigarette, but the lighter flicks on for a moment.

Beside Amy, Claire bites her lip. The silence is heavy as they pull out of the garage. It's still heavy when they turn onto Adams Street. Sitting up straighter, Bohdi says, "Why are we taking this route?"

In the rearview mirror, Amy briefly sees Steve's eyes flick to her. "Change of scenery," Steve says.

Catching Bohdi scowling out of the corner of her eye, Amy turns to Claire and tries to lift the mood. "So you want to be a ballerina?"

Claire's eyes lose focus, and she slouches. "I'm too tall. I'm never going to be a ballerina."

Leaning to peer around Amy, Bohdi says, "Maybe you could play the boy's part?" All traces of anger have left his face, now he wears a sunny smile, but he's still playing with the lighter in his hand.

Amy raises an eyebrow at the shift in mood.

Steve chuckles. Claire's mouth opens.

"Didn't you tell me that you're stronger than all the boys in your class?" Bohdi says, smile still bright.

Claire beams. "I beat everyone at arm wrestling."

"That's my girl," says Steve, a chuckle in his voice.

They cross Halstead and are approaching a small park when Amy catches Steve's eyes in the mirror again.

Suddenly, Claire shrieks. "Daddy! Stop the car!"

Steve puts on the brakes and the car slides to a stop in the snow. Before Amy's even realized what's happened, Claire's unfastened her seatbelt and opened the car door. "Claire, no!" Steve cries, but she's already taken off, long legs pumping furiously and snow flying in her wake.

And then Amy sees what she's running to.

On top of a low rolling hill, surrounded by children, is a unicorn. Its white coat blurs into the snow around it, but it's muzzle is running red with blood seeping from its horn. It's stamping its feet, snorting and keeping its eyes on members of the National Guard and civilians at the bottom of the hill.

"She wasn't supposed to do that," Steve says, jumping out of the door.

Not really thinking, Amy follows. She's vaguely aware of Beatrice and Bohdi following. At the bottom of the hill, Amy hears a woman say, "Please, Jimmie, please come down." None of the half dozen children respond; they seem unusually quiet, almost mesmerized.

At the unicorn's side, Claire cries, "Daddy, he's hurt! Do something!"

"I'll try, Honey," Steve says. Claire turns and throws her arms around the unicorn's neck, burying her head in its mane.

Amy stands transfixed. Even with the blood streaming down the base of its horn, the creature is beautiful. Its muzzle is small, its eyes are wide and a deep cobalt blue. Its coat shimmers, and at this distance, Amy thinks its horn looks like it's made of mother of pearl. She finds herself unable to breathe.

Another man, dressed in civilian clothes, is by the Guard units. Voice clipped, he is saying, "You need to put the guns down."

"It tried to attack us. It's using the children as human shields!" one of the Guard says.

"It wouldn't have been hurt and standing here if you hadn't shot at it," the man shouts.

"It was threatening us!"

Beside Amy, Beatrice draws close and raises the outrageous pink flower print umbrella she's been carrying since That Day. She must have nicked it from the nursing home. Amy would suggest returning it, but Beatrice is attached to it. Amy took Loki's book from his apartment even though she knows ADUO would consider it stealing from a crime scene—she doesn't feel like she has any moral authority on the matter.

"Right now you're more of a danger to my kids than it is!" the man snaps.

At just that moment, Steve takes a step forward. The unicorn stamps and swings its head; it's lovely ivory hooves suddenly look sharp and menacing.

Bohdi takes a step forward, too, and gets the same reaction. Turning to Steve he grins. "Looks like I'm not a virgin. I'm kind of relieved."

Not hearing, or choosing to ignore Bohdi's clowning, Steve turns and walks back to Amy. In a low voice he says, "Miss Lewis, I know you can help it."

Amy's eyes flit to Steve, her wonder turning to a bitter

taste in her mouth. "Believe it or not," she whispers, "I wasn't watching Star Trek those days after Loki rescued me!"

Steve tilts his head. "I've watched the The Last Unicorn. Isn't it a matter of purity of heart?"

Amy's eyes narrow, remembering the story. "It's a matter of belief, Steve!"

"I know you can do this," he says.

Amy turns to look at the creature. "I don't even know … " And then the scene in front of her drops away and she finds herself in a memory—Loki's memory.

Loki was very small, walking through a field on a bright sunny day, holding hands with Hoenir, plump and bald again. In Hoenir's other hand is Mimir mounted on a staff. "Don't worry, Loki, Hoenir can help it."

Loki's eyes swung around, and there was a unicorn, much like this one, blood running down its horn.

Loki darted forward, but the creature reared up, hooves flashing. Crestfallen, Loki turned to Mimir. "It doesn't like me!"

Mimir coughed. "Ahh … yes, well, I'm sure it knows you wouldn't hurt it on purpose, but you do occasionally set things on fire. They tend to be afraid of anyone they know might cause them harm."

Amy's jaw drops as Loki's memory fades. "I can do this," she whispers. She takes a step forward. Beside her, Beatrice raises the umbrella higher and the unicorn backs up with a snort. "Grandma, wait," Amy says, putting her hand on Beatrice's. "I'll be okay."

"You better be!" Beatrice snaps, but she steps back.

Holding up her hands, Amy walks slowly towards the unicorn. "I won't hurt you. I couldn't."

The unicorn lowers its head, and then lifts it again with a soft whinny. In her head she hears Mimir's voice. "Unicorns are as intelligent as Jotuns, Vanir or Aesir, Loki. They are magical, and understand all the tongues of the Nine Realms, just like us, even if they can't speak."

Walking slowly forward, Amy says, "I'm going to put my hand on your horn, I have to see how deep the wound is."

The unicorn whinnies again.

As Amy steps up to the animal, the unicorn's eyes follow her, enormous and trusting. It's breathing hard; a small cloud of steam forms around its nostrils.

"Touching you now," she says, putting her hands on its forehead just as Hoenir had done in Loki's memory. The unicorn's coat is surprisingly soft, like rabbit fur. Its ears are longer and narrower than a horse's, the hair of its forelock finer and softer. It smells clean, and pure, like snow, not like a wild animal.

Another flash of memory comes to her. "Loki, we can tell that the injury to the unicorn's horn is superficial. If it was deep, all the unicorn's magic would be diminished. But see how he understands Hoenir? He is in too much pain to World Walk, but he is still enchanting."

Amy blinks. The magic matter of the unicorn is within its horn. Looking up, she notices how the horn is listing slightly to the side where the blood is bubbling out, probably pinching the delicate tissues within. Sliding her hand up to the place the blood is emerging, she feels the sharp edge of a break. With one hand, she lifts the horn. It feels lighter than she would expect. An open wound that is about half a finger width wide gapes at her. Pulling her scarf from her neck, she puts pressure on it. As she does, a wave of relief unfurls from her stomach. Other feelings rush through her, too: gratitude, fear, determination, and connection. The empathy she feels is too intense to be imagined. Amy's not sure if it's magical, or perhaps a chemical response to pheromones the creature is releasing. It doesn't matter. For a moment she feels as though she and the unicorn are one being, not a unicorn, or a human, but a consciousness hovering in the space between their frail bodies. It feels like a dream of flying.

Amy's eyes begin to sting with tears. But for the first time since Loki's death, they are tears of wonder.

To live in a realm wracked with chaos is to live with pain, anguishing memories, and trolls. But it is also means living with unicorns.

She closes her eyes and smiles.

Feeling the unicorn shift beneath her hands and a rise of anxiety, she snaps from her trance—though euphoria still lingers in her. She feels a warmth like she's been drinking but without the daze of alcohol. She's never felt so alert or so awake. Beside her, Claire says, "He wants to leave."

"Yes, but we have to make him better first," says Amy.

Feeling a flicker of impatience and fear from her patient, Amy knows she has to act fast. There is a right way to fix this wound, but the second best way will have to do. Turning her head, she catches Steve's worried gaze at the bottom of the small hill. "I need cornstarch to pack into the wound," Amy says. "Get me some as fast as you can."

Eyes flicking briefly to Claire, Steve nods at her.

A few minutes later, he's managed to get her a box of cornstarch borrowed from one of the park visitors who lives nearby. Amy works as fast as she can, but still, by the time she's done, it's starting to get dark.

Beyond the top of the rolling hill the unicorn stands on, there is a sculpture in the little park. It is composed of five rectangular metal archways, each one the height of the house, all tilted at slightly varying angles. As soon as Amy drops her hands, the unicorn turns and walks towards the arches, the children and Amy at its side, the park patrons and Guardsmen behind. The unicorn walks beneath the first two arches, and then, right before the third, breaks so fast into a gallop, the children and Amy are left behind in a heartbeat.

She hears the click of guns and cameras. But before any shots ring out, the unicorn vanishes into a flash of light.

Around her the children cry, and the adults whisper.

Amy stares at the empty space, and the falling snow, sad and ecstatic at once. Beatrice stands to her left. Steve, arm wrapped around Claire, stands to her right. Bohdi is just beyond them.

"Okay," Amy says at last. "You've got me. I want to be in Chicago."

Turning, Steve says, "You'll stay."

For a moment Amy can only think of the unicorn, and almost says yes. Then she remembers painstakingly typing all of Steve's business card contacts into the computer earlier this morning, and how she'd almost cried with the tedium of it. Not looking at him, Amy smiles. "No way in Hell. I'm going back to Oklahoma to finish my degree."

"But ... "

Shaking her head, Amy glances over at him. "I am not working as your secretary until that planned program at the University of Chicago gets off the ground."

Steve opens his mouth, but Amy cuts him off. "And I'm not applying to a school that's closer either. I might lose credit and put off graduation even more. Forget it."

Steve doesn't look precisely happy. His jaw twitches, and his face hardens, but at last he says, "Done."

They all stand motionless for a few more moments, and then Bohdi starts walking back to the car, the lamps lining the park walkways flickering on in his wake. Without speaking, everyone else does the same. As they do, Amy passes a notice board with a flyer emblazoned with the words "Holiday Festivities at Mary Bartelme Park." Her eyes widen, and then narrow, remembering Steve's phone conversation earlier.

Minutes later, Beatrice and Claire are in the car, and Bohdi's holding the door for Amy. Stopping short and glaring at Steve across the roof of the car she says, "You knew the unicorn was here. You set me up."

Steve shrugs, but there is a hint of a smile on his lips. "Maybe, but I think you liked it." He raises an eyebrow. "You sure you want to go back to Oklahoma? Seems kind of boring."

Amy takes a deep breath. The mist hangs in the air in front of her. She looks at the new fallen snow. In a few hours it will be gray with exhaust fumes, but for now, the city looks fresh and clean and new. It is a brief, and welcome, respite from the grime.

She smiles and shakes her head. "No, that's alright."

With another shrug Steve slips into the car. Beside her, holding the door in one hand, and the lighter like a talisman in the other, Bohdi says, "That was amazing. What you did back there."

She glances up at him. She does recognize in the abstract how attractive he is—in a wide open, innocent kind of way. She is too hollow inside to feel it, though. All she feels is guilt when he looks at her with such earnestness.

Staring down at her feet she has a realization. She has Loki's book, and his memories. "Pretty sure chaos is going to follow me wherever I go," she mumbles.

Beside her Bohdi nudges the door. A ghost of a smile is on his lips. Inclining his head towards the car he says, "After you."

Sneak Peek at In the Balance, an I Bring the Fire Novella

The lights of the elevator buzz and flicker above Amy. Steve stands beside her. Steve is as tall as Loki is—was—and his head nearly brushes the ceiling. The FBI's Chicago headquarters are new, but the building is old. The elevator smells musty, shakes as it moves, and is hot. Amy is sweltering beneath her thick white down jacket, but the thought of taking it off and hauling it around under her arm is just too exhausting.

"Thanks for coming in," Steve says.

Yawning into her hand, Amy manages a low "Mmmmm" in response. Her 'last' day as Steve's receptionist was a few weeks ago. She never thought she'd be back here so soon. Her eyes flutter. She's tired and doesn't know why. Maybe just stress?

The elevator draws to a stop and Amy's stomach lurches.

Did she eat something that disagrees with her? Or maybe it is the memory of the pictures released by the Tribune this morning. Shutting her eyes, she tries to will away the image of children huddled together, their tiny bodies suffocated beneath debris. Their school collapsed on them during the earthquake Loki caused...right before he destroyed three blocks of Chicago's financial district, and froze or incinerated the mayor, ADUO's Executive Director, and half of the city's police department. And even if he had been under the influence of Cera, the World Seed, it still—

"Amy?" says Steve.

Swaying slightly on her feet, she opens her eyes. Where the fluorescent light's harsh glow touches Steve's dark skin, his face appears ashen.

The doors of the elevator are open to a wide room where ADUO agents are setting up desks, cubicles, phones, and computers.

Leaning towards her slightly, Steve says, "Are you alright?" He holds out a hand, as though he might steady her, but then quickly pulls it away.

Shaking her head, Amy steps out. "Yes, I ... " She doesn't finish. The eyes of a black-suited agent are on her. Is he glaring at her? She blinks. The agent's eyes are still pointedly aimed in her direction.

She looks away, her stomach churning as Steve leads her down a narrow lane between the cubicles. What did she expect? Even if Loki did save the world, his moments of madness before the end still caused the death of thousands. Loki was her lover, and Amy's guilty by association. She smiles ruefully to herself. Lover. What a joke. Loki didn't love her.

As she walks with Steve down the aisle, her eyes dart to

the side. She catches more hostile looks and a few looks of pity. Averting her gaze to the window she sees the wreckage of LaSalle Street. There are grim-faced construction workers out there between the piles of collapsed buildings and the snow drifts. There are also teams of scientists from all over the world scampering about, looks of awe, wonder, concentration, and joy on their faces. Small Geiger counter-like devices are aglow in their hands, detecting "magical" energy. As yet, no one really knows what "magic" energy is—they just know it's real and seems to be in Chicago to stay.

A policeman on the street turns and looks in her direction. She's certain he can't see her behind the glass, but she feels like he's looking at her accusingly. She's heard about what Loki did to the SWAT team that raided his home. There'd been no survivors—

"Amy?" Steve says.

Lifting her eyes, Amy sees they've reached the edge of the main office space. Steve is standing between two men guarding an open door. The guards are wearing black suits and crisp white shirts just like Steve is. With square jaws and crewcuts, they might be Steve, but slightly shorter, 20-year-old Caucasian versions.

Steve clears his throat, his brow constricted slightly. Amy straightens and follows the direction he gestures her in. She finds herself in a windowless conference room filled with only a long conference table. As Steve closes the door, she looks around. The walls, floor, ceiling, and even the door are covered with a dark wire mesh. Promethean Wire. It will seal all magic out of the room.

She sways slightly on her feet again.

"Are you sure you're alright?" Steve says again.

Amy closes her eyes. The policeman's gaze, the photo of the children, the mayor's eyes crusted over by ice, fill her mind. "Should I feel alright, Steve?"

Opening her eyes, she finds Steve's expression flat and unreadable.

"I was—" Amy raises her arm towards the door and gestures vaguely, "—sleeping with the man who was a mass murderer who—" Rubbing her temples she lets out a long breath. Steve leans back against a conference table. "You didn't know it would come to that."

"I'm an idiot. I should have realized—"

"No," Steve says, crossing his arms. "You shouldn't have."

Jaw tensing, eyes prickling, Amy gives her boss—former boss—a hard stare.

His stare is equally hard. "Amy, Loki was, if not a perfect gentleman to you, always protective of you. He never hurt you, and in your presence was never violent unless he thought he, or you, were in danger. You weren't an idiot for trusting him or … being involved with him." He draws a breath. "Other people put up with worse and get less. Loki did care about you—and no one could predict their … partner … would fall under the influence of a mind-controlling World Seed that fancied itself the second coming of Josef Stalin."

Amy's vision goes blurry with unshed tears. She'd thought that—maybe—but to hear it from someone else. "That's a good speech, Steve," she says, wiping an eye.

Uncrossing his arms, body visibly relaxing, Steve says, "Good, I've been practicing variations of it for the first time a man breaks my little girl's heart."

Amy almost smiles. "You're a good dad, Steve."

Tilting his head, Steve says, "Of course, after I give that

speech to her I will hunt the man down and kill him."

Amy does smile at that. And for a moment she almost feels better. But then she remembers what Steve doesn't know. Loki only cared about her because he thought she was part of his "higher purpose," which he was convinced was burning Asgard to the ground.

Turning towards the table, Steve says, "Sorry to bring you in, but ADUO wanted you to identify something for us."

Body tensing again, she shoves her hand into her pockets and jumps as a small squeak pierces the air. Something warm and soft squirms under her left hand. Looking down, her eyes widen in surprise. She has a stowaway. Peering up from her pocket is Mr. Squeakers, the eight-legged spidermouse Loki gave to her.

Steve looks towards the air conditioning duct. "Was that a mouse?"

Patting Mr. Squeakers' head back into her pocket, Amy says, "I didn't hear anything."

Steve raises an eyebrow but turns his attention back to the table. A large piece of folded black fabric lies there. Pulling away a fold, Steve reveals a gleaming, slightly curved sword. Amy releases a gasp.

"Can you identify it?" Steve asks.

"It's Laevateinn," Amy says. The name means troublesome twig, but she doesn't say that. All she adds is, "Loki's sword." As she says the words, Loki's memories come rushing in. As a final parting 'gift,' he'd planted his memories in her mind. They don't invade her every waking moment, but when she stumbles upon something relevant they come to her. She shakes her head. When she tries to think back to the time right before he destroyed Cera, she gets no insights as to why he'd chosen to give them to her. She thinks it was just an impulse. Her jaw goes hard and her eyes prickle.

"That's what I told them," Steve says. "But our experts identified it as Japanese katana, from the Edo period. They wondered why a deity associated with Norse peoples would have a Japanese sword.

"It's surging with magical energy," Steve says. "Outside of magically sealed rooms it drives our sensors off the charts. The only stronger thing we've seen is Cera."

Almost without thinking, Amy reaches towards Laevateinn. Last time she'd seen it, it had pulsated with magical blue light. Inside the magically sealed room, it's just a sword, but the blade gleams brightly.

She runs a hand absently over the handle. Suddenly caught in another flashback, she says, "Thor and Loki were in Japan at the beginning of the Tokugawa shogunate looking for samurai to join the ranks of the einherjar."

"Einherjar?"

"Humans recruited to serve in Odin or Freyja's elite guard. Usually the valkyries did it, but Odin was desperate. Loki and Thor joined in … " A memory comes to her of Thor, disguised by Loki's illusions to look like a short Japanese samurai hitting his head against the top of the frame of a door. She snorts. Thor bumped his head a lot in Japan, and Loki seems to remember each and every time.

Amy lifts the sword, and Steve shuffles nervously beside her. "It is very sharp," he says. "Even without magic."

Pointing the blade carefully towards the opposite wall, Amy rotates the handle in her hands. "It's so light—you're sure it's not magical even here?"

Humming reverently, Steve says, "It's the magic of

exquisite craftsmanship. A thing of beauty, isn't it? Look at the blade. The surface is as smooth as glass."

Amy smiles. "It's like a lightsaber!"

"The closest we have on this world," says Steve, his voice hushed.

At that moment from behind them comes the sound of the door opening. A voice with a Hindi accent says, "Steve? You want some coffee?"

Steve turns beside her. "Bohdi, how did you get in? The door was locked, and there are guards outside."

Amy turns to see Bohdi give Steve a shrug, unruly black bangs falling over one eye. Always a little embarrassed in Bohdi's presence, she turns quickly away. Loki had wiped Bohdi's memories. When she tries to think about it, to understand why Loki seemed to have some personal vendetta against Bohdi, she gets nothing. Another impulse?

In Amy's hands Laevateinn begins to pulse with light.

Behind her Bohdi says, "I didn't see any guards, and the door wasn't locked."

Amy lifts the sword towards her eyes. Her reflection stares back at her. But around her reflection, where there should be the room, there is darkness.

"Maybe they went to help with the troll outside?" said Bohdi.

"Troll?" says Steve.

Tilting her head, Amy says, "Something is happening to the blade." Instead of tilting its head, her reflection looks behind itself.

"Oh, cool sword," says Bohdi, his voice suddenly closer.

"Put it down, Amy," says Steve.

Amy feels a prickle like static in her hands. "Right," she

says, lowering the blade back to the table. She tries to release it, but blue current writhes up her arms. She turns towards Steve, "I ... "

"Ms. Lewis!" says Bohdi.

"Drop it!" shouts Steve, his hand reaching for her wrist.

And then everything is blackness. Amy is suspended in the nothingness of the In-Between with only Laevateinn's cold glow. There is no Loki to tether her to life with his warm embrace. She has seconds to live, and she aches for him to be with her in the darkness.

AVAILABLE NOW

Sneak Peek of Fates: I Bring the Fire IV

At the front desk in the ER, Steve holds up his badge. "I'm here to see Amy Lewis. She was brought in about half an hour ago. She was having a miscarriage—"

The nurse behind the counter looks at his badge and her brow furrows. "You'll have to wait; the doctors are in with her now."

"This is very important," says Steve. It's been only eight weeks since Loki disappeared and he has no doubt whose baby it is.

"Then maybe you should talk to the father," says the nurse sharply. Pointing down a nondescript hallway, she says, "He's in the waiting room around the corner."

"The father is here?" Steve says.

"Yes, he—"

Before she can finish, Steve is bolting down the corridor, nearly colliding with an attendant pushing a wheelchair. As he slides around the corner, his hand falls to the piece he's wearing at his hip. He almost pulls it out before he remembers it would be useless.

Breathing heavily, he enters the waiting room. Magic detector silent, his eyes scan over the people seated there—the only person he recognizes is Bohdi.

Striding over to him, Steve says, "Where is he? Where is Loki?"

Murmurs go up around them. Bohdi glances around. "I don't know."

"The nurse said the father is here!" Steve says, grabbing Bohdi by the collar.

The lights above them flicker. Meeting his eyes, Bohdi swallows. "I lied to get into the ambulance."

For the second time in one day, Steve resists the urge to strangle him.

ALL STORIES BY C. GOCKEL

The I Bring the Fire Series:
I Bring the Fire Part I: Wolves
Monsters: I Bring the Fire Part II
Chaos: I Bring the Fire Part III
In the Balance: I Bring the Fire Part 3.5
Fates: I Bring the Fire Part IV
The Slip: a Short Story (mostly) from Sleipnir's Point of Smell
Warriors: I Bring the Fire Part V
Ragnarok: I Bring the Fire Part VI
The Fire Bringers: An I Bring the Fire Short Story

Other Works:
Murphy's Star a short story about "first" contact

Author's Note
Thank you for taking a chance on this self-published novel and seeing it to the end. Because I self-publish, I depend on my readers to help me get the word out. If you enjoyed this story, please let people know on Facebook, Twitter, in your blogs, and when you talk books with your friends and family. Want to know about upcoming releases and get sneak peeks and exclusive content?
Click Here to sign up for my newsletter.
Follow me on Tumblr: ibringthefireodin.tumblr.com
Facebook: www.facebook.com/CGockelWrites
Or email me: cgockel.publishing@gmail.com

Thank you again!

Printed in Poland
by Amazon Fulfillment
Poland Sp. z o.o., Wrocław

Towards the Humanisat

'This careful comparative ethnography will be most welcome to all scholars interested in birth, midwifery, and obstetric practice, as well as midwifery researchers. Its concepts of the institutional paradox and midwifery technology are extremely useful and original contributions. The introductory poems are also wonderful, bringing a sense of high art to the text. The very highest quality of scholarship is evident in this book.'

—Dr Robbie Davis-Floyd

Elizabeth Newnham • Lois McKellar
Jan Pincombe

Towards the Humanisation of Birth

A study of epidural analgesia and hospital birth culture

Elizabeth Newnham
School of Nursing and Midwifery
Trinity College Dublin
The University of Dublin
Dublin, Ireland

Lois McKellar
School of Nursing and Midwifery
University of South Australia
Adelaide, SA, Australia

Jan Pincombe
School of Nursing and Midwifery
University of South Australia
Adelaide, SA, Australia

ISBN 978-3-319-88868-2   ISBN 978-3-319-69962-2 (eBook)
https://doi.org/10.1007/978-3-319-69962-2

Library of Congress Control Number: 2017963278

© The Editor(s) (if applicable) and The Author(s) 2018
Softcover reprint of the hardcover 1st edition 2018   978-3-319-69961-5

This work is subject to copyright. All rights are solely and exclusively licensed by the Publisher, whether the whole or part of the material is concerned, specifically the rights of translation, reprinting, reuse of illustrations, recitation, broadcasting, reproduction on microfilms or in any other physical way, and transmission or information storage and retrieval, electronic adaptation, computer software, or by similar or dissimilar methodology now known or hereafter developed.
The use of general descriptive names, registered names, trademarks, service marks, etc. in this publication does not imply, even in the absence of a specific statement, that such names are exempt from the relevant protective laws and regulations and therefore free for general use.
The publisher, the authors and the editors are safe to assume that the advice and information in this book are believed to be true and accurate at the date of publication. Neither the publisher nor the authors or the editors give a warranty, express or implied, with respect to the material contained herein or for any errors or omissions that may have been made. The publisher remains neutral with regard to jurisdictional claims in published maps and institutional affiliations.

Cover illustration: Greg Kessler/getty images

Printed on acid-free paper

This Palgrave Macmillan imprint is published by Springer Nature
The registered company is Springer International Publishing AG
The registered company address is: Gewerbestrasse 11, 6330 Cham, Switzerland

Foreword

This book is a timely and relevant addition to the movement towards humanising birth, questioning the regular use of epidural analgesia in normal labour by providing an incisive cultural analysis of hospital birth culture. The evidence is indisputable that epidurals undermine childbirth physiology and lead to increased intervention rates. As identified in this book, the attitudes of maternity care practitioners towards pain in labour will affect the way this information is presented in policy documents, in practice guidelines, and in the information that is shared with women. This results in a maternity service culture throughout the Western world that privileges the use of epidurals over evidence-based forms of care that are known to lower epidural rates and promote positive experiences for women. As discussed here, the implications for women who enter large obstetric units anticipating a normal labour and birth are profound.

In spite of ongoing resistance by women, midwives, and others who wish to promote physiological birth, the epidural is framed as the modern way of giving women control over their bodies. We see research projects in low-income countries asking women if they would like the same access to epidurals for pain-free labour as that enjoyed by their sisters in high-income countries, and concluding that this is a human rights issue. Thus, in practice settings across the world, the question is being asked: 'Why would you not have an epidural in this day and age?' Midwives who critique this approach are accused of practising 'medieval midwifery' and making women feel guilty if they choose to have an epidural. Worse still, there are suggestions, enhanced by media frenzies, that midwives are putting the lives of babies at risk in their attempts to promote normal birth, creating a moral panic about childbirth, and placing the blame with midwives rather than looking more deeply into the system of Western birth culture.

Concerns to avoid making women feel guilty and a lack of faith in women's ability to manage pain in labour are perhaps understandable if you practise in an environment where it is rare to see women giving birth completely 'under their own steam', assisted only by encouragement from others. We read of student midwives entering their third year of education who have rarely witnessed women having drug-free labours. They are being taught about the evidence that, overall, positive birth experiences are not related to the level of pain experienced and that many women view pain as part of a sense of triumph and transition to motherhood—but they are rarely seeing this in practice.

The potential for women to emerge from their childbirth experiences feeling empowered with an increased sense of self-efficacy has been widely identified in qualitative research projects and media accounts by women themselves. Sadly, the converse is also true, particularly where women feel they were not supported or listened to and where they felt overwhelmed and frightened by a cascade of events leading to post-traumatic stress, depression, and disrupted parenting. With suicide now the leading indirect cause of maternal death in many Western countries, addressing the humanisation of birth is an imperative. This book shows how a core component of this process is addressing the complexities of attitudes to pain in labour. This is a starting point for changing the culture of birth in institutions where epidurals are seen as the most appropriate way to manage pain even where labour is straightforward.

Interfering with birth in the absence of medical necessity has serious consequences in terms of the potential increased risk of complications for women and their babies. Furthermore, there is strong evidence to support practices that promote physiological birth and a positive experience for women. These include providing continuous one-to-one support in labour, immersion in water for pain relief, a home-like environment for labour, and avoiding routine interventions and restrictions on the woman's freedom to move around and adopt positions of her choice.

Where there is patchy provision of one-to-one support in hospital environments, it is perhaps no surprise that women end up opting for epidurals. We should not assume, though, that this system failure is associated with women's preference. Women are embracing drug-free labour at home, in birth centres, and in midwifery-led units with many more unable to access these options. Stories arising from these settings and, indeed, positive stories of drug-free births in large hospital institutions should be much more widely circulated and discussed. This applies particularly where practitioners tend only to hear stories about complications and emergencies in case reviews.

This book identifies how the biomedical research on epidural use encourages the concept of the 'safety' of the epidural, even when discussing its possible side-effects. This perpetuates an acceptance of epidurals as a modern, 'common sense' option. Research identifying the physiological and emotional effect of the environment for birth and the disturbance of hormonal processes in labour are rarely discussed with women.

As suggested in this book, robust discussion is needed about the wider effects of epidurals on women's experiences of birth and an alternative framing of supporting women through a 'working with pain' approach. Such discussions need to be informed by descriptions from women about empowering birth experiences and widespread dissemination of the importance of hormonal responses during childbirth as described in Sarah Buckley's important text: *Hormonal Physiology of Childbearing: Evidence and Implications for Women, Babies and Maternity Care.*[1]

The authors of this book propose that, rather than the fraught polarising of 'normal birth' and 'medicalised birth' (midwifery/obstetrics), we should think about 'the notion of a continuum, with intervention-free birth at one end and medicalised birth at the other, with women, midwives and obstetricians in the middle, maintaining a dialogue about what is best for women as individuals'. They suggest that this would require a shift by the medical profession to understand birth as a normal process until proved otherwise, rather than conceptualising birth as 'only normal in retrospect'. It would also require complex understandings of power dynamics and how these influence the culture and practices within contemporary maternity services.

This text makes compelling reading. It articulates complex concepts and ideas with clarity, drawing on rich data in a stimulating and courageous challenge to the notion that epidural analgesia is safe and should be universally available to women. A critical examination of how birthing ideologies inform hospital practices is linked to the effect this has on the choices women make about epidural use. A thoughtful analysis of the effects of the global rise in interventions in childbirth is offered in order to articulate the need to humanise birth, identify the potential dangers of the technocratic birth paradigm, and promote physiological birth. Complex issues associated with the role of epidural use within this conundrum are introduced, including the contested meanings of pain in labour.

The potential role of midwives in engaging with individual women in relationships based on mutual trust while also engaging with uncertainty is articulated with reference to discussions on how the social and cultural construction of 'normality' can be problematic in the way midwifery is viewed and enacted within contemporary maternity care systems.

Each chapter in this book starts with a participant's poem, drawn from the research data in order to provide 'verisimilitude'. These poems are very powerful; they bring to life the data and experiences of women in a way that adds authenticity and credibility to the arguments that are posed in each chapter.

An ethnographic study undertaken in the labour ward and interviews with women are critically analysed drawing on an impressive blend of theoretical perspectives and literature to identify the socio-cultural implications that need to be considered if practice is to be woman centred and emancipatory. The spotlight is placed on a culture riddled with values that perpetuate surveillance and contested notions of risk. The discourse of pain in labour is thoroughly explored in relation to technocratic attitudes and practices and powerful arguments are presented for how women are placed at risk in institutionalised birth settings.

A critical review of literature related to labour analgesia includes an analysis of how historical, social, political, economic, and cultural factors influence the way in which women's bodies are viewed by science and the philosophical thinking that has underpinned medicine and midwifery. This contributes to an analysis of the epidural within contextual belief systems and the biomedical discourse of risk and safety that excludes the social, physical, and emotional meaning of childbirth for women.

It might be easy for midwives working in institutions to feel paralysed about the effect the dominant culture has on their efforts to promote normal birth; however, the lead author's analysis of interviews with women offer an alternative framework for working with women around managing pain in labour. As they grappled with the uncertainty of facing the unknown, the majority of women interviewed wanted to trust their bodies to know how to manage pain in labour; they also wanted midwives they could trust to guide, advise, and support them in 'going with the flow'. Women were practical in their approaches to labour pain, drawing strength in the idea that women have been giving birth since the beginning of time. They also saw pain as potentially transformative and associated with the joy of bringing their baby into the world. The trust women placed in the midwife's role of guiding them through labour was at odds with many of the midwives' ideas that women had already decided what they wanted before coming into hospital and that the woman's partner should be the person providing them with support.

The conclusion is compelling; that midwives should focus on supporting women fully through labour in the understanding that most women will have a sense of trust in their bodies and that this needs to be reflected back by the midwife. Unless women specifically ask for an epidural in their birth plan, midwives should assume that women want to be supported through the process of giving birth.

This is a stimulating and thought-provoking book that will no doubt promote interdisciplinary discussion and be of significant interest in the international arena. What is so impressive about the work is the broader lens the authors bring to a quite specific topic, reminding us that multiple domains impact on something that seems like a straightforward clinical decision from the midwives' or obstetricians' perspective and a straightforward choice by a labouring woman. Institutional, neoliberal, gendered, medicalised, technocratic, and professional project discourses have real influences and help construct the space where decisions around pain management in labour are made. In addition, drawing on her research, the lead author brings a critical lens to how these discourses operate, challenging taken-for-granted assumptions, for example, an elective epidural service, and making visible how these discourses diminish women's agency and body autonomy. All of this opens the space up for alternative choices and, arguably, more authentic, embodied experiences for women. This challenging text is essential reading for all who are committed to humanising birth and promoting positive experiences for women.

Nicky Leap: Adjunct Professor of Midwifery, University of Technology Sydney, Australia.

Denis Walsh: Associate Professor in Midwifery, School of Health Sciences, University of Nottingham, UK.

Ultimo, NSW, Australia
Nottingham, UK

Nicky Leap
Denis Walsh

Note

1. Available online: www.ChildbirthConnection.org/HormonalPhysiology.

Preface

Around the world, more and more women are using epidural analgesia in labour. Epidural analgesia provides adequate pain relief, but is also associated with detrimental side-effects, including increased risk of instrumental birth and decreased oxytocin production. Epidural analgesia also requires additional measures such as continuous electronic foetal monitoring and intravenous therapy, thus moving women out of a 'low-risk' labour category. Importantly, epidural use does not necessarily increase women's satisfaction with birth, which is not inevitably related to levels of pain. Women's attitudes to labour pain are complex and multifaceted and, contrary to the broader medical view, pain is not necessarily the primary concern of women anticipating labour.

In this book, we contribute to the growing movement of humanising birth by providing an ethnographic critique of institutional birth, using epidural analgesia as the point of entry into hospital birth culture. The idea of looking at hospital birth culture through the medium of epidural analgesia came to our attention through our experience as midwives: watching epidural rates increase, noticing how it was portrayed to women, and trying to ascertain women's understanding of it. Early on in the research process, we came across a paper by midwife academic Denis Walsh, who articulated very clearly the complexities that epidural analgesia brings to birth as well as introducing the idea that epidural rates may be increasing due to social and cultural factors, such as increasingly alienating birthing practices, rather than because women are less able to cope with pain. We therefore examine here concepts of birth pain and its relief, with a particular focus on the institution as an arbiter between the macro-culture of socio-political norms and the micro-culture of individual experience and interactions.

We begin the book by critically examining epidural use, looking at the various influences on women, as well as the way birth ideologies inform hospital birthing practice, and the resulting effect on the choices pregnant and birthing women are able to make about their bodies. We use a Critical Medical Anthropology (CMA) approach, which considers the interplay of structural power relationships, and how these power relationships are played out in the social world. CMA analysis begins with identification of the problem; in this case the increasing uptake of epidural analgesia by labouring women, with questions as to the amount of information accessed by women, the role of midwives in this process, and the role of pain in labour. Ultimately, what we provide is a study of hospital birth culture which can inform and direct current and future birth practice.

In the case of critical ethnography, objectivity does not rely on absence of bias. It identifies, rather, that biases are always present in the outlining of the research problem: the choice of question being asked and the theoretical framework used. It is in the laying open of these biases that intellectual rigour stands (and in this way is perhaps more honest than more 'objective' research that fails to question its implicit assumptions). We locate ourselves, and our premise that the indiscriminate use of epidural analgesia is a problem, not a solution, at the centre of this research. Thus, this ethnography is not presenting 'the' version, it cannot. It is presenting 'our' version, and throughout we take the reader back to the data and weave the theory around this, forming a piece of research that is, we feel, both credible and necessary.

The preparation of this book has been, of course, a large piece of work. We are grateful to the Australian government and the University of South Australia for awarding the Australian postgraduate award which funded this research. We especially thank the participants of the study, without whom the book could not have been written. We have been pleasantly surprised by the feedback: the women we interviewed were pleased to have been able to speak about their experiences; those midwife clinicians from the study who attended presentations of our research have also affirmed aspects of the findings. Other midwifery colleagues and experts in the field have responded to this research at both national and international conference presentations, including Australian College of Midwives' National conferences, the Normal Labour and Birth conference in the United Kingdom, and at International Confederation of Midwives' congresses, in Prague and Toronto. There has been a high level of substantiation from those midwives we have spoken to about similar issues occurring around the world. We thank all of these midwives for their feedback.

Thanks also to others who have read early versions of chapters and provided constructive criticism as well as anonymous reviewers of journal articles and the final manuscript of this book. We would particularly like to acknowledge Robbie Davis-Floyd who gave valuable suggestions and generously provided us with a chapter of her forthcoming book. Thanks are also due to Palgrave and the wonderful editors there. In addition, we are indebted to Nicky Leap and Denis Walsh, who enthusiastically suggested the publication of this research and who have kindly written the foreword to the book.

Finally, we would like to thank our families, those people who know us best and keep us going. This book is for you.

Dublin, Ireland	Elizabeth Newnham
Adelaide, SA, Australia	Lois McKellar
Adelaide, SA, Australia	Jan Pincombe

Sections of this book were originally published in journal articles; we list these below underneath the relevant chapters, which may contain additions and amendments.

Chapter 1

Newnham, E., Pincombe, J., & McKellar, L. (2013). Access or egress? Questioning the "ethics" of ethics review for an ethnographic doctoral research study in a childbirth setting. *International Journal of Doctoral Studies*, 8, 121–136. Copyright permission obtained from the Informing Science Institute Board of Governors and allowed under Creative Commons licence.

Newnham, E., McKellar, L., & Pincombe, J. (2016). Critical medical anthropology in midwifery research: A Framework for ethnographic analysis. *Global Qualitative Nursing Research, 3*, 1–6. https://doi.org/10.1177/2333393616675029. Copyright permission obtained from SAGE Publications and allowed under Creative Commons licence.

Chapter 2

Newnham, E., McKellar, L., & Pincombe, J. (2016). A critical literature review of epidural analgesia. *Evidence Based Midwifery, 14*(1), 22–28. Copyright permission obtained from the Royal College of Midwives.

Chapter 4

Newnham, E., McKellar, L., & Pincombe, J. (2017). Paradox of the institution: Findings from a hospital labour ward ethnography. *BMC Pregnancy and Childbirth, 17*(1), 2–11. Copyright retained by authors under the BioMed Central licence agreement.

Chapter 5

Newnham, E., McKellar, L., & Pincombe, J. (2017). It's your body, but...' Mixed messages in childbirth education: Findings from a hospital ethnography. *Midwifery, 55*, 53–59. Copyright permission obtained from Elsevier under pre-existing licence terms.

Newnham, E., McKellar, L., & Pincombe, J. (2015). Documenting risk: A comparison of policy and information pamphlets for using epidural or water in labour. *Women & Birth, 28*(3), 221–227. Copyright permission obtained from Elsevier under pre-existing licence terms.

Contents

1 Introduction — 1

2 The Epidural in Context — 21

3 The Politics of Birth — 67

4 Institutional Culture: Discipline and Resistance — 103

5 A Dialectic of Risk — 149

6 A Circle of Trust — 193

7 Closing the Circle — 245

Index — 261

List of Abbreviations

3:10/4:10	Stands for 3 contractions (or 4 contractions) in the space of 10 minutes.
ARM	Artificial rupture of membranes
cCTG	Continuous CTG monitoring throughout labour (rather than an intermittent trace)
CMA	Critical medical anthropology
CTG	Cardiotocograph
Cx	Cervix
EBM	Evidence-based medicine
EFM	Electronic foetal monitoring (used in the literature to refer to CTG monitoring in labour)
EN	Elizabeth Newnham (Field notes and interviews)
GBS	Group B Streptococcus bacteria
GD	Gestational diabetes
ID	Identification
IOL	Induction of labour
IV	Intravenous
LSCS	Lower segment caesarean section
MET	Medical Emergency Team
$MgSO_4$	Magnesium sulphate
MW	Midwife (Field notes)

$N_2O\&O_2$	Nitrous oxide and oxygen ('gas and air')
OP	Occiput Posterior
PPH	Post-partum haemorrhage
REG	Registrar (Field notes)
SOL	Spontaneous onset of labour
SRM	Spontaneous rupture of membranes
T/L	Team leader

List of Figures

Fig. 4.1 The journey board   111
Fig. 4.2 Paradox of the institution   127
Fig. 6.1 The circle of trust   196

1

Introduction

Background: Models of Care, Philosophies of Birth

There is an ongoing debate regarding the provision of maternity care, situated in the midwifery/medical dichotomy, which has permeated birth discussion since the advent of medical involvement in birth in the seventeenth century (Donnison 1988; Ehrenreich and English 1973; Murphy-Lawless 1998; Roome et al. 2015; Towler and Bramall 1986; Willis 1989). Since then, midwifery as a profession has become increasingly concerned with 'guarding normal birth' (Crabtree 2008, p. 100; Fahy and Hastie 2008, p. 22; Kent 2000, p. 28). Broadly speaking, the midwifery model of birth is one that promotes the process of birth as a normal physiological process and a significant life event for a woman, which impacts on her spiritual, sexual, and psychological development (Fahy et al. 2008). The linguistic origin of the English word midwife, *midwyf* (meaning 'with-woman'), is foundational to midwifery philosophy, evident in contemporary terminology such as 'woman-centred' care. This term describes the concept of the woman and midwife in partnership, one based on mutual trust and respect, and to provide care during this life event which is unique to each woman (Hunter et al. 2008; Leap 2000). Within the midwifery model, practitioners value women's embodied knowledge as well as the importance of clinical knowledge and skills. They acknowledge the uncertainty of birth, while being equipped for emergency scenarios. This model also identifies the emotional qualities that can affect a woman's labour, the subtleties of hormonal influences and the effect of the environment (Fahy et al. 2008; Lepori et al. 2008).

However, there are challenges to the midwifery concept of 'normal'.[1] This includes changes in the definition of normal as increasingly, routinised, medicalised birth is being described as normal if it does not result in an instrumental or a caesarean birth.[2] Thus, augmented labour, the use of analgesics and oxytoxics for the third stage of labour may all be defined in some places as normal birth. Indeed, Davis-Floyd (2018) takes this a step further as she discusses the way that medicalised birth practices are normalised through a technocratic lens even as normal labour and birth processes are framed as risky and therefore 'abnormal' (see also Wendland 2007; Kennedy 2010). As such, midwives may be at risk of losing non-medical definitions of normal birth, especially as many midwives are socialised, through their education and employment, into hospitalised/medicalised birth (Crabtree 2008, p. 99; Wagner 2001).

Although it refers primarily to the normalcy of birth as a physiological event, the symbolism of 'normal' birth can also alienate women who have an instrumental or caesarean birth; it can signify that their experience was somehow abnormal and therefore different or lacking (Kennedy 2010). This has led to proposed terminology such as optimal birth—supporting women to have the optimal birth experience within their unique circumstances, and salutogenic birth—focusing on factors that optimise health and wellbeing rather than those that contribute to disease (Downe and McCourt 2008; Kennedy 2010).

Another difficulty with midwifery's focus on the 'normal' is the potential failure to notice 'the ways in which "normality" is historically, socially and culturally produced' (Kent 2000, p. 30). Discussion on the construction of 'normal' is present in contemporary midwifery literature (Downe 2008; Walsh 2012), identifying a need for midwives to delineate *midwifery* definitions of normal, rather than relying on the obstetric view that birth can be normal 'only in retrospect' (Flint 1988, p. 35; Williams 1997, p. 235), whereby '[a] birth cannot be judged as normal until after it has concluded, when doctors are in a position to say that there has been no pathology present throughout the entire birth process' (Murphy-Lawless 1998, p. 198). However, there is also a danger in the idealisation of a 'sentimentalised' view of birth and blanket condemnation of medical birthing practices which can provide timely intervention in emergency situations (Dahlen 2010). In a model of exemplary midwifery practice, Kennedy (2000) outlines the 'art of doing "nothing" well', where midwives achieve a seemingly effortless act of being present to the woman and supporting normal processing that actually involves an intense vigilance and attentiveness. There is also a genuine risk to women in furthering the dichotomy between the medical and midwifery professions (MacColl 2009, pp. 7–20; Wendland 2007).

The medical profession has provided life-saving procedures for both women and babies. Nevertheless, expanding the use of medical techniques to all areas of birth without critical examination is imprudent and potentially iatrogenic. As Mead (2008, p. 90) notes,

> The situation we are experiencing today is primarily the result of good intentions, namely the desire to reduce maternal and perinatal mortality and morbidity. However, in the absence of sound programmes of research, these good intentions have contributed to an increase in maternal morbidity, particularly an increase in intervention in pregnancy and childbirth, and a disproportionate rise in caesarean sections, without a corresponding improvement in neonatal outcome.

The birth paradigm dichotomy was elucidated by journalist Mary-Rose MacColl (2009) in *Birth Wars*, the book she wrote after participating in the Queensland maternity review process. MacColl describes the turf war between 'organics' (those dedicated to working with the uncertainty of birth, with minimal disturbance of the process of birth—often, but not always, midwives and homebirth advocates) and 'mechanics' (those who intervene in the birth process, who see control as better than uncertainty—usually, but not always, obstetricians). MacColl's observation is not new; she is describing the historical and continuing dialectic between medical and midwifery discourse. However, the contribution that MacColl brings to the debate is her recognition of the negative impact of this divide on women themselves.

Having professional power inequities in the birth environment introduces the possibility of danger from either perspective. Medical dominance limits women's choices, mechanises an intricate psychophysiological process and may cause intervention-based harm. However, the case of midwives delaying transfer or ignoring a potential complication in a naïve kind of sentimentalised birth ideology (MacColl 2009, pp. 7–20) is also damaging (see Dahlen 2010). While the cases MacColl cites may be extreme, and in many cases midwives and medical practitioners work well together, the difficulty for women is to distinguish between issues of *medical control* and real issues of *safety*; between the unnecessary or the life-saving intervention. Many women do not know, and may not be told, the risks associated with intervention in childbirth (MacColl 2009, p. 120). Wagner (1994, p. 6) declares that 'conflict over birth technologies is a major battle in a contemporary health revolution' because of the disagreement between midwifery and medical models of health. He notes that the 'conflict is sharpest in the areas of birth and death where the social model seems to offer an important contribution to the orthodox medical model' (Wagner 1994, p. 6). In other words, in areas where biomedicine is most contested, it pushes back the hardest. However, if, as has been suggested, the most significant factor affecting women's decision to have an epidural in labour is not pain during labour, but her beliefs about childbirth (Heinze and Sleigh 2003), then it is all the more necessary to somehow bridge this divide. It is likely that social, medical and midwifery perspectives on childbirth influence a woman's decision to have an epidural. In light of this, challenging and changing social perspectives on birth will effectively have an impact of women's birth experiences.

Although we are working with the notion of medicalised childbirth, we do not intend to further dichotomise the two models. Rather, we propose the notion of a continuum, with intervention-free birth at one end and medicalised birth at the other, with women, midwives and obstetricians in the middle, maintaining a dialogue about what is best for individual women. For this to occur there would need to be a shift by the medical profession to understand birth as a normal process until proven otherwise, rather than as an inherently pathological process. The biomedical model has essentially been the dominant model in the birthing practices of most Western countries, particularly since the move to hospitals, and the medical system, in Australia at least, remains actively opposed to attempts at increasing midwifery models of care (see Newnham 2014). The resulting imbalance of medicalised versus 'normal' birthing practices needs redressing, in the hope that a combined and congruent maternity service can ensue.[3] Evidence of this is occurring throughout the world (Davis-Floyd et al. 2009). In a recent article in the *Wall Street Journal*, two obstetricians who succeeded in reducing caesarean section rates in their hospital refer to the importance of birth unit design, the frequent need to do 'nothing' to support birth, the contradiction this causes with the medical desire to do 'something', the need to develop 'tolerance for uncertainty', judicious evidence-based use of technology, rather than technology for its own sake, and the influence of culture on making and keeping these changes (Marcus 2017). That these ideas are entering mainstream obstetric discourse inspires hope for safe, integrated and humanised maternity services globally.

Humanised Birth

Humanised birth as a perspective has been gathering momentum for some time (see Davis-Floyd 2001; Page 2001; Umenai et al. 2001; Wagner 2001). It originated in Brazil and other Latin American countries, where the concept of humanised birth has been clearly demarcated (see Rattner 2009) to the point where humanised birth practices have been encoded into legislation. In Brazil, ReHuNa—Network for the Humanization of Childbirth was founded in 1993 to counter obstetric violence using the more positively framed language of humanised birth. Following the inaugural International Conference on the Humanization of Childbirth in Fortaleza, Ceará, Brazil, in 2000, Marden Wagner (2001, p. S25) wrote:

> Humanized birth puts the woman in the center and in control, focuses on community based primary maternity care with midwives, nurses and doctors working together in harmony as equals, and has evidence based services.

However, as Davis-Floyd (2018) points out, it is easier to acknowledge overtly dehumanising birthing practices; in most Western countries, the technocratic system of birth provides clean and safe venues, provision of privacy, and respect for autonomy (to an extent), showing that although it may still maintain a separation of mind and body, it does for the most part hold on to a sense of integrity. However, the process of medicalisation itself can be dehumanising, in its mechanistic view of the human body and the way this translates to the treatment of birthing women (Wagner 2001). Women in all settings are describing incidences of dehumanised birth: practices occurring without consent, being treated with disrespect and without compassion.

The Research

This book is based on a piece of critical ethnographic research conducted in an Australian metropolitan hospital. We chose a major hospital as our study site, because a high percentage of women in Australia give birth in hospital labour wards (this number was 98% in 2014) and our focus was mainstream birthing environments (AIHW 2016, p. 16). During an intensive six-month period of fieldwork, hospital culture was observed, as we talked to hospital staff, examined hospital documents and recorded these observations as field notes. The observations and conversations formed the field notes proper, to which analytic memos were added. Consistent with this kind of research, a journal was kept throughout as a way of organising thoughts and maintaining reflexivity.

In addition, 16 pregnant women participated in a series of three interviews—two in the antenatal period and one postnatal—and were asked for consent for a researcher to be present at the birth. Interviews were recorded and transcribed verbatim and the transcripts analysed for themes. All data were analysed through the lens of a three-pronged theoretical framework—CMA, Foucault, and Feminism—using continuous analysis and 'thick description' (Geertz 1973). We also adapted and used the Health care arena model (Baer et al. 1986; Newnham et al. 2016). We provide a more in-depth understanding of CMA and ethnography in the following pages.

Critical Medical Anthropology

Critical Medical Anthropology (CMA), a term coined by anthropologists Merrill Singer and Hans Baer, who were integral in its development, emerged in the 1980s as a critique of traditional medical anthropology (Singer and Baer 1995, p. 5). As a branch of anthropology, traditional medical anthropology tended to take Western medicine (biomedicine) at face value, acting as a cultural translator for medicine in order to understand miscommunication in medical encounters, to provide a layperson's perspective, or to increase medically recommended behaviours, such as taking medication (Singer and Baer 1995). Medical anthropology, though potentially useful, was not necessarily reflexive or critical in its understanding of medicine, and worked within the auspices of medical authoritative knowledge. However, there was increasing concern in anthropology to examine biomedicine as closely as other cultural systems, and to culturally situate its belief systems, rituals and values in the same way as other cultural domains. CMA therefore takes a critical stance in the study of biomedical culture, rather than working as its cultural mediator, and it questions medicine's portrayal of itself as objective, as working only with 'truth' and 'fact', removed from cultural influences (Singer and Baer 1995, p. 5). Further to this, there was a push in CMA for understanding the way in which power relationships in medicine interacted with the global capitalist economy, and to ensure that medical anthropology did not become 'an instrument for the medicalization of social life and culture, but also, like biomedicine, an unintended agent of capitalist hegemony and a tag-along handmaiden of global imperialism' (Singer and Baer 1995, p. 5).

As stated above, CMA uses a structural, political economy (Marxist or neo-Marxist) approach,[4] examining the historical development of the economic, social, and political circumstances leading to the situation in question. This 'wide-lens' view of historical and cultural influences prior to focusing on the ethnographic minutiae of the everyday allows for the dissection and critique of behaviours, practices, and beliefs that are otherwise accepted or taken for granted as the status quo.

Ethnography as a Critical Method

Ethnography essentially means the study of culture, and ethnography with a critical stance explores power relationships within culture (Thomas 1993).[5] Cultural beliefs and practices that surround birth have a significant impact on the way birth is both understood and managed; by women, midwives, and broader health systems (Jordan, B 1993). To answer our questions about the use of epidural analgesia for labour, we have undertaken a critical study of the culture of birth.

Critical research methodologies typically highlight social justice issues and seek social emancipation (Crotty 1998, pp. 118, 157).[6] Critical ethnography, therefore, seeks to change the status quo, rather than just to describe occurrences. It invokes 'a call to action that may range from modest rethinking of comfortable thoughts to more direct engagement that includes political activism' (Thomas 1993, p. 17). By examining how knowledge about birth has been constructed, and the way in which epidural analgesia fits into particular belief systems about birth, a critical analysis of its increasing use can ensue. This provides an alternative starting point for talking about epidural analgesia and the use of this method of analgesia for otherwise healthy birthing women. As Thomas (1993, p. 3) identifies, '[w]e create meanings and choose courses of action within the confines of generally accepted existing choices, but these choices often reflect hidden meanings and unrecognized consequences'. Focusing the research spotlight on epidural use illuminated cultural birth norms that were not necessarily anticipated, for while ethnographic research commonly sets out to examine a culture (or what is perceived as a problem or inequity within that culture) more generally (Thomas 1993, p. 35),

> it is frequently only over the course of the research that one discovers what the research is really 'about', and it is not uncommon for it to turn out to be about something quite remote from the initial foreshadowed problems. (Hammersley and Atkinson 1983, p. 175)

Ethnographic research has a specific and important role in identifying cultural influences on childbirth and highlighting change requirements in health care institutions, including:

creating a more efficient, more effective, more equitable and more humane health care system, particularly in illuminating the organizational and interactional processes through which health care is delivered. They offer important information, to policy makers and practitioners, about factors that compromise or promote high quality care, particularly the ways in which well-intentioned actions may have unanticipated negative consequences. (Murphy and Dingwall 2007, p. 2224)

Given that humane birth practices within maternity systems are now seen as a priority by those at the forefront of the profession, and by those who have witnessed the inhumane practices that are occurring daily around the world (see Human Rights in Childbirth), ethnography provides a fitting approach to explore the 'unanticipated negative consequences' of otherwise ordinary, well-intentioned maternity care provision.

Ethnography in Midwifery

Ethnography, previously concerned with examining cultural practices of 'the other', non-Western societies, has in recent decades turned to aspects of Western culture, including cultural analysis of medical and health care settings (Liamputtong and Ezzy 2005). With respect to midwifery specifically, ethnographic research has been useful in demarcating the juxtaposition of power relationships and cultural norms: those of women, of midwives, of medical staff, and of the institution. Ethnographers peer underneath the discourses of practice and philosophy, exposing their influence on what is said and done. Over the last two decades, midwifery ethnographies have unearthed a deep sense of disempowerment in midwifery culture, which appears to contradict the role of midwives as facilitating empowerment in the women they work with.

Hunt and Symonds' (1995) ethnography of English labour ward culture provided insight into the assembly-line, industrial nature of labour in the hospital system, within which midwives pursued ways of increasing control of their environment, including attempts to 'slow down the production line' (Hunt and Symonds 1995, p. 144). The masculinised medical system as well as the industrial environment led to a lack of autonomy for midwives—although this was offset somewhat by their status as skilled professionals. The birthing women in the study possessed the least amount of power and had very little control over their birth experience. Later, Machin and Scamell (1997, p. 83) described how medical interpretations of birth led to a self-fulfilling situation whereby birth intervention was perceived by women as safe and reassuring. Such findings would indicate a culture that perpetuates a self-fulfilling philosophy of medicalised birth.

Kirkham's (1999) ethnography of midwifery practice in the United Kingdom identified a divergence in cultural norms whereby midwives supported women through their pregnancy and birth process, encouraging autonomy and control, but had little access to similar support, autonomy and control themselves. Equally, while promoting trusting relationships between midwives and women, there was a decided lack of trust within institutionalised midwifery, with midwives identifying a culture that emphasises self-sacrifice, guilt, and blame, leading to a lack of solidarity between colleagues and a resulting horizontal violence. Midwives wanting to enact change felt they had to do so secretly for fear of being targeted as a misfit or deviant. Kirkham (1999) noted that this kind of behaviour, associated with feelings of powerlessness, is symptomatic of oppressed groups, therefore any attempt to make changes in the maternity system, she argued, needs to first address culture. However, cultural change can be hard to implement for various reasons; one of which, as suggested in another ethnographic study, is how the endemic and embedded nature of an oppressed midwifery culture can lead to inaction and apathy towards change (Hughes et al. 2002).

Dykes (2005, 2009), also using CMA in a critical ethnography on interactions between breastfeeding women and midwives in English postnatal wards, found that organisational temporal restrictions inhibited midwifery practice, causing care to be technical rather than relational. Dykes (2005) argues that this time pressure constitutes a form of oppression and calls for re-evaluation of the midwife-mother relationship, and the suitability of the hospital environment for the initiation of breastfeeding. A more recent study by Scamell (2011) identified how midwives reproduce medicalised risk culture in their language and use of surveillance techniques in labour, even as they profess to operate from a paradigm of normal birth. Marshall et al. (2011) demonstrated a lack of obtaining informed consent for procedures in the labour ward setting—also finding that some women shied away from making decisions—and recognised the conflict for midwives between facilitating informed choice in women and adhering to policy guidelines that they were required to follow. Conversely, in an ethnographic study of a free-standing birth centre in England, Walsh (2006, p. 1338) has described how the intimate nature of a small unit was able to circumvent industrial or assembly-line care, and by doing so, was able to put 'women before the system'. The valuing of relationships over tasks and the structural and temporal freedoms described in Walsh's study benefited both the women and the midwives. While in a study of Irish home birth midwives, O'Boyle (2013) identified the professional isolation that is present due to small numbers and the lack of a strong midwifery association.

Most recently, May (2017) has published a medical ethnography titled *Epiduralized Birth and Nurse-midwifery: Childbirth in the United States*. In this book, May credits the epidural as central to a 'complex, unitary, interconnected set of interventions' that are inseparable from one another and which provide the foundations for a predictable, controlled labour that can be easily managed within the industrialised birth system, but which also introduce harm (May 2017, p. 69). Her observations intersect with our work at several levels; she also discusses the lack of informed consent to women about the totalising effects of the epidural and its attendant risks and highlights the ongoing practice of obstetric rituals (such as routine cEFM) that are based on tradition and a firm belief in the absolute certainty of technological safety rather than evidence.

Each of these studies demonstrates the value of ethnography as a means of providing rich, meaningful data that is not obtainable using quantitative research methods. Together, these studies point out the impact of culture on midwifery practice and therefore also on the women they care for. They identify the role of power and oppression in practice, the difficulty that midwives have trying to uphold a midwifery philosophy within institutions with narrow clinical policies. They show the difference in practice between midwives who are supported in environments that promote normal birth and those who work in fear or isolation and identify the need for midwifery leadership, solidarity and a strong, united voice. Most of these ethnographies were conducted in health systems that had yielded a number of government reports recommending policy changes prioritising continuity of midwifery care and more choice for women in birth. However, although policies can provide positive impetus for change, it is also clear that culture—both of the institution and the wider community—normalises practices and behaviours that may inhibit positive change (Cronk 2000; Hughes et al. 2002; Johanson et al. 2002; Reiger and Dempsey 2006). By engaging in ethnographic research existing practices can be observed and analysed and positive attributes of, and barriers to, woman-centred care can be identified. A deeper understanding of the culture of maternity care institutions in an Australian context can supplement current midwifery theory by identifying midwifery practices within a specific cultural environment (a hospital labour ward) and how these practices are simultaneously influenced by culture and co-created by midwives, and how these then impact the experiences of women, who bring their own set of understandings and beliefs to the encounter.

Book Structure

The following two chapters are an exploration of the history and cultural knowledge about pain relief and birth as well as outlining our theoretical stance. In Chap. 2 we present a historical introduction to birth analgesia and the influence of scientific and medical discourse on understandings of women's bodies, influencing the ways in which women themselves can frame their own corporeal knowledge. Here, the process of birth, and how it is understood within Western cultural discourses, is investigated more thoroughly. We highlight the influence of biomedicine as a dominant birth discourse and explore current medical knowledge about epidural analgesia, exposing some of the assumptions behind evidence-based medicine and technology use.

In Chap. 3, we bring in the three theoretical cornerstones of CMA, Foucauldian, and feminist theory. We discuss how CMA positions biomedicine as a dominant social force; the influence of science and technology on shaping our understanding of the world; using Foucauldian interpretations of power/knowledge to further examine the link between discourse and practice (what we know and what we do); and drawing on Feminist analyses to demarcate the construction of the female body within the power/knowledge frameworks of science.

Throughout the next three chapters we present the fieldwork data, framed by the theory we have just described. Chapter 4 presents the setting both physically and culturally. We take a critical position on the role of the institution, drawing on the theory of CMA and Foucault's conceptions of panoptic surveillance and the medical gaze. Using field note data, and centring on two disparate notions—organisational and midwifery technologies—institutional influence on time, organisation of labour and birth, risk and safety, and midwifery practice are discussed.

In Chap. 5, the risk culture of the institution is more fully explored in a critical discourse analysis of policy and practice documents, culminating in a discussion of how particular practices are then fashioned as risky or safe. Two pain relief practices, epidural analgesia and water immersion, and the discourses of risk and safety that accompany them, are compared. We then interrogate the effect of discourse construction on how choices are presented, demonstrating the effect of biomedical discourse on women's maternity care experience.

Chapter 6 focuses predominantly on the impact of the midwife-woman relationship. In this chapter, the intricacies of the women's experiences of pregnancy and anticipation of birth are discussed and developed into a conceptual figure that illustrates their ambiguous approach to pain, the unknowable nature of birth and the trust that women therefore placed in their own bodies. We further the argument that a focus on embodiment can provide a point of departure for future approaches to birth, discarding old dichotomies and embracing complexity. Drawing on contemporary childbirth literature, we reassert the centrality of the midwife's role in labour.

Chapter 7 concludes the book and the key themes are revisited. We contend that dominant conceptualisations of risk and safety, which influence midwifery practice and women's experience of birth, are mediated by the institution in a paradox that inverts aspects of risk and safety. In light of its effects, we assert that the hospital as the current primary site of birth needs to be reconsidered as a matter of priority for a future that embraces humanised birth.

At the beginning of each chapter is a poem. These poems are formed directly from spoken data, transcribed from interview, of women describing their experience of birth. Using poetry in ethnography is not a new phenomenon (Fitzpatrick 2012; Lahman et al. 2010; Maynard and Cahnmann-Taylor 2010). Poetry has been used as a means to capture participants' embodied subjectivity (Chadwick 2012); to read between the lines, the space between the words (Chadwick 2012; Lahman et al. 2010); and to disrupt or subvert ordinary assumptions (Chadwick 2012; Fitzpatrick 2012). These 'participant poems' jumped out at Elizabeth Newnham one day when she was re-reading interview transcripts and noticed some repetition and rhythm to the words as they sounded silently in her mind. As an occasional writer of poetry, the metre grabbed her and she made some slight editing changes to shape the words into a form that resembled a poem. She then did the same process with other transcripts and thought that these participant poems offered another version of the participants than simply interview transcript excerpts within the data chapters themselves; perhaps a kind of embodied self, or at least a kind of verisimilitude—to the extent that this is possible in the representation of others' voices. We have not included poems from all of the participants. There are not enough chapters. The included poems were chosen for their aesthetics (texture, rhythm, metre), their content (rich descriptions, interesting vocabulary), and their divergence (diverse representations of experience).

Notes

1. Recent conversations on social media forums acknowledged that the term 'normal birth' has been useful for the purpose of drawing attention to the de-medicalisation of birth but raised the possibility that there is a need to redefine or rethink the term because it dichotomises women's experience: by default, women who do not achieve a 'normal' birth must have had an 'abnormal birth'.
2. For example, changes to Australian perinatal statistics collection from 2007 include the changing of the term 'spontaneous vaginal birth' to 'non-instrumental birth' and 'vaginal breech birth' ceased to be a category

(Hilder et al. 2014, p. 43), meaning that the physical act of spontaneous vaginal birth is now only defined by medicalised birth language and vaginal breech birth is now invisible.
3. We refer here to medical and midwifery models, or systems. We do not refer to individual practitioners (midwives or doctors), who might work in either model depending on their philosophy of birth, nor to practitioner gender.
4. There is also a radical phenomenological branch of CMA. We are using the political economy approach here, in agreement with Singer and Baer, who convey that analysis at a structural level is important for change (Singer and Baer 1995, p. 5).
5. Thomas (1993, p. 12) defines culture as shared group identity, including aesthetics and morals, understanding of common language, discourse, and behaviour.
6. Social emancipation in this context means recognising alternative ways of thinking (Thomas 1993, p. 4).

References

Australian Institute of Health and Welfare (AIHW). (2016). *Australia's mothers and babies 2014 – in brief* (Perinatal statistics series No. 32. Cat No. PER 87). Canberra: AIHW.
Baer, H., Singer, M., & Johnsen, J. H. (1986). Toward a critical medical anthropology. *Social Science & Medicine, 23*(2), 95–98.
Chadwick, R. J. (2012). Fleshy enough? Notes towards embodied analysis in critical qualitative research. *Gay and Lesbian Issues and Psychology Review, 8*(2), 82–97.
Crabtree, S. (2008). Midwives constructing 'normal birth'. In S. Downe (Ed.), *Normal childbirth: Evidence and debate* (2nd ed., pp. 97–113). Sydney: Elsevier.
Cronk, M. (2000). The midwife: A professional servant? In M. Kirkham (Ed.), *The midwife-mother relationship*. New York: Palgrave Macmillan.
Crotty, M. (1998). *The foundations of social research: Meaning and perspective in the research process*. St Leonards: Allen & Unwin.
Dahlen, H. (2010). Undone by fear? Deluded by trust? *Midwifery, 26*(2), 156–162.
Davis-Floyd, R. (2001). The technocratic, humanistic and holistic models of birth. *International Journal of Gynecology & Obstetrics, 75*(1 Suppl), S5–S23.

Davis-Floyd, R. (2018). *Ways of knowing about birth: Mothers, midwives, medicine, and birth activism*. Long Grove: Waveland Press.

Davis-Floyd, R., Barclay, L., Daviss, B.-A., & Tritten, J. (Eds.). (2009). *Birth models that work*. Berkeley: University of California Press.

Donnison, J. (1988). *Midwives and medical men: A history of the struggle for the control of childbirth*. London: Historical Publications.

Downe, S. (Ed.). (2008). *Normal childbirth: Evidence and debate*. Sydney: Churchill Livingstone Elsevier.

Downe, S., & McCourt, C. (2008). From being to becoming: Reconstructing childbirth knowledges. In S. Downe (Ed.), *Normal childbirth: Evidence and debate* (2nd ed., pp. 3–27). Sydney: Elsevier.

Dykes, F. (2005). A critical ethnographic study of encounters between midwives and breast-feeding women in postnatal wards in England. *Midwifery, 21*(3), 241–252.

Dykes, F. (2009). Applying critical medical anthropology to midwifery research. *Evidence Based Midwifery, 7*(3), 84–88.

Ehrenreich, B., & English, D. (1973). *Witches, midwives and nurses: A history of women healers*. New York: The Feminist Press.

Fahy, K., & Hastie, C. (2008). Midwifery guardianship: Reclaiming the sacred in birth. In K. Fahy, M. Foureur, & C. Hastie (Eds.), *Birth territory and midwifery guardianship: Theory for practice, education and research* (pp. 21–37). Sydney: Elsevier.

Fahy, K., Foureur, M., & Hastie, C. (Eds.). (2008). *Birth territory and midwifery guardianship: Theory for practice, education and research*. Sydney: Elsevier.

Fitzpatrick, K. (2012). "That's how the light gets in": Poetry, self, and representation in ethnographic research. *Cultural Studies ↔ Critical Methodologies, 12*(1), 8–14.

Flint, C. (1988). On the brink: Midwifery in Britain. In S. Kitzinger (Ed.), *The midwife challenge*. London: Pandora Press.

Geertz, C. (1973). Thick description: Toward an interpretive theory of culture. In G. Geertz (Ed.), *The interpretation of cultures: Selected essays* (pp. 3–30). New York: Basic Books.

Hammersley, M., & Atkinson, P. (1983). *Ethnography: Principles in practice*. London: Tavistock publications.

Heinze, S., & Sleigh, M. (2003). Epidural or no epidural anaesthesia: Relationships between beliefs about childbirth and pain control choices. *Journal of Reproductive and Infant Psychology, 21*(4), 323–333.

Hilder, L., Zhichao, Z., Parker, M., Jahan, S., & Chambers, G. (2014). *Australia's mothers and babies 2012*. Canberra: Australian Institute of Health and Welfare.

Hughes, D., Deery, R., & Lovatt, A. (2002). A critical ethnographic approach to facilitating cultural shift in midwifery. *Midwifery, 18*(1), 43–52.

Hunt, S., & Symonds, A. (1995). *The social meaning of midwifery*. London: Macmillan.

Hunter, B., Berg, M., Lundgren, I., Ólafsdóttir, Ó. Á., & Kirkham, M. (2008). Relationships: The hidden threads in the tapestry of maternity care. *Midwifery, 24*(2), 132–137.

Johanson, R., Newburn, M., & Macfarlane, A. (2002). Has the medicalisation of childbirth gone too far? *British Medical Journal, 324*(7342), 892–895.

Jordan, B. (1993). *Birth in four cultures: A crosscultural investigation of childbirth in Yucatan, Holland, Sweden, and the United States*. Prospect Heights: Waveland Press.

Kennedy, H. P. (2000). A model of exemplary midwifery practice: Results of a delphi study. *The Journal of Midwifery & Women's Health, 45*, 4–19.

Kennedy, H. P. (2010). The problem of normal birth. *The Journal of Midwifery & Women's Health, 55*, 99–201.

Kent, J. (2000). *Social perspectives on pregnancy and childbirth for midwives, nurses and the caring professions*. Buckingham: Open University Press.

Kirkham, M. (1999). The culture of midwifery in the National Health Service in England. *Journal of Advanced Nursing, 30*(3), 732–739.

Lahman, M. K. E., Geist, M. R., Rodriguez, K. L., Graglia, P. E., Richard, V. M., & Schendel, R. K. (2010). Poking around poetically: Research, poetry, and trustworthiness. *Qualitative Inquiry, 16*(1), 39–48.

Leap, N. (2000). The less we do, the more we give. In M. Kirkham (Ed.), *The midwife-mother relationship* (pp. 1–18). New York: Palgrave Macmillan.

Lepori, B., Foureur, M., & Hastie, C. (2008). Mindbodyspirit architecture: Creating birth space. In K. Fahy, M. Foureur, & C. Hastie (Eds.), *Birth territory and midwifery guardianship: Theory for practice, education and research* (pp. 95–112). Sydney: Elsevier.

Liamputtong, P., & Ezzy, D. (2005). *Qualitative research methods* (2nd ed.). Melbourne: Oxford University Press.

MacColl, M. (2009). *The Birth Wars*. St. Lucia: University of Queensland Press.

Machin, D., & Scamell, M. (1997). The experience of labour: Using ethnography to explore the irresistible nature of the bio-medical metaphor during labour. *Midwifery, 13*(2), 78–84.

Marcus, A. (2017, September 13). To reduce C-sections, change a hospital's culture. *Wall Street Journal*. https://www.wsj.com/articles/to-reduce-c-sections-change-the-culture-of-the-labor-ward-1505268661. Viewed Dec 2017.

Marshall, J., Fraser, D., & Baker, P. (2011). An observational study to explore the power and effect of the labor ward culture on consent to intrapartum procedures. *International Journal of Childbirth, 1*(2), 82–99.

May, M. (2017). *Epiduralized birth and nurse-midwifery: Childbirth in the United States*. Amazon: Sampson Book Publishing.

Maynard, K., & Cahnmann-Taylor, M. (2010). Anthropology at the edge of words: Where poetry and ethnography meet. *Anthropology and Humanism, 35*(1), 2–19.

Mead, M. (2008). Midwives' practices in 11 UK maternity units. In S. Downe (Ed.), *Normal childbirth: Evidence and debate* (2nd ed., pp. 81–95). Sydney: Elsevier.

Murphy, E., & Dingwall, R. (2007). Informed consent, anticipatory regulation and ethnographic practice. *Social Science & Medicine, 65*(11), 2223–2234.

Murphy-Lawless, J. (1998). *Reading birth and death: A history of obstetric thinking*. Cork: Cork University Press.

Newnham, E. C. (2014). Birth control: Power/knowledge in the politics of birth. *Health Sociology Review, 23*(3), 254–268.

Newnham, E., Pincombe, J., & McKellar, L. (2013). Access or egress? Questioning the "ethics" of ethics review for an ethnographic doctoral research study in a childbirth setting. *International Journal of Doctoral Studies, 8*, 121–136. Copyright permission obtained from the Informing Science Institute Board of Governors and allowed under Creative Commons licence.

Newnham, E., McKellar, L., & Pincombe, J. (2016). Critical medical anthropology in midwifery research: A Framework for ethnographic analysis. *Global Qualitative Nursing Research, 3*, 1–6. https://doi.org/10.1177/2333393616675029.

OBoyle, C. (2013). 'Just waiting to be hauled over the coals': Home birth midwifery in Ireland. *Midwifery, 29*(8), 988–995.

Page, L. (2001). The humanization of birth. *International Journal of Gynecology & Obstetrics, 75*(Suppl 1), S55–S58.

Rattner, D. (2009). Humanizing childbirth care: Brief theoretical framework. *Interface – Comunicação, Saúde, Educação, 13*(Suppl 1), S595–S602. https://doi.org/10.1590/S1414-32832009000500011.

Reiger, K., & Dempsey, R. (2006). Performing birth in a culture of fear: An embodied crisis of late modernity. *Health Sociology Review, 15*(4), 364–373.

Roome, S., Hartz, D., Tracy, S., & Welsh, A. W. (2015). Why such differing stances? A review of position statements on home birth from professional colleges. *BJOG: An International Journal of Obstetrics & Gynaecology, 123*(3), 376–382.

Scamell, M. (2011). The swan effect in midwifery talk and practice: A tension between normality and the language of risk. *Sociology of Health & Illness, 33*(7), 987–1001.

Singer, M., & Baer, H. (1995). *Critical medical anthropology.* New York: Bayswood Publishing Company.

Thomas, J. (1993). *Doing critical ethnography.* London: Sage.

Towler, J., & Bramall, J. (1986). *Midwives in history and society.* London: Croon Helm.

Umenai, T., Wagner, M., Page, L. A., Faundes, A., Rattner, D., Dias, M. A., Tyrrell, M. A., Hotimsky, S., Haneda, K., Onuki, D., Mori, T., Sadamori, T., Fujiwara, M., & Kikuchi, S. (2001). Conference agreement on the definition of humanization and humanized care. *International Journal of Gynecology & Obstetrics, 75*(Suppl 1), S3–S4.

Wagner, M. (1994). *Pursuing the birth machine: The search for appropriate birth technology.* Camperdown: Ace Graphics.

Wagner, M. (2001). Fish can't see water: The need to humanize birth. *International Journal of Gynaecology and Obstetrics, 75*(Suppl 1), S25–S37.

Walsh, D. (2006). Subverting the assembly-line: Childbirth in a free-standing birth centre. *Social Science & Medicine, 62*(6), 1330–1340.

Walsh, D. (2012). *Evidence and skills for normal birth.* London: Routledge.

Wendland, C. (2007). The vanishing mother: Cesarean section and "evidence-based obstetrics". *Medical Anthropology Quarterly, 21*(2), 218–233.

Williams, J. (1997). The controlling power of childbirth in Britain. In H. Marland & A. Rafferty (Eds.), *Midwives, society and childbirth: Debates and controversies in the modern period.* London: Routledge.

Willis, E. (1989). *Medical dominance* (2nd ed.). Sydney: Allen and Unwin.

2

The Epidural in Context

JUNO
I was just really active, trying to get it progressing
And then when they kind of started getting painful
I started squatting and moving
Just through the contractions
And in the intense part, just powered through.

I don't know—got impatient and I yelled a lot.
It's a good release
Think I almost bit him at one point.
He was like 'Do you remember trying to bite me?'
And I was like 'Yeah I think I do'
And he was amazed at how—
Cause I think the other two labours I have been very, like
'I don't need any support', like
'Don't touch me' kind of thing
But with this one,
Near the end
It was like 'I need you'
I was like 'You need to be here'.

© The Author(s) 2018
E. Newnham et al., *Towards the Humanisation of Birth*,
https://doi.org/10.1007/978-3-319-69962-2_2

*But it was a little bit longer than that this time,
So he had to put in some harder yards,
But he was like 'Wow the strength!'
He goes 'That was the first time I've ever felt that you were
actually stronger than me!'
But no pain relief and no pain relief after actually either,
So I didn't tear or anything like that.
Yeah, so no water but I like feeling really grounded,
Like, attached to the ground.
I was on all fours, because
I really wanted to be on the ground.
I was on all fours on the bed because,
Obviously it's more comfortable.
It's a very hard floor in there,
Even then I was like 'I want to be on the floor',
Just letting gravity do all that.*

*Yeah no water,
I didn't even have a shower or anything,
Just kept moving around.
Yeah it's been interesting reflecting,
Near the end I was getting really impatient.
I was like 'Just get out!'
You know, I was just over it.
And I was like 'Wow, some women do this for a lot longer'
And so I can understand why you would reach for those things.
I think I felt a little bit more of that,
Just that intensity, and that pain and just wanting it to all be over.*

*Whereas with the others,
Because that last stage was quite quick,
You just don't have any time to even contemplate it.
Whereas this time I felt like, you know,
I didn't contemplate it but I definitely got impatient.
I was like 'Come on I have had enough!'
And yeah, because every contraction was a bit more painful
And it didn't feel like there was an outcome coming in the near future
I think I could relate to that a little bit more.
I was still going 'Yes this is all good and it's coming'.
I knew it was coming
It just felt a lot longer.*

Birth Interventions, Birth Settings, and the Problem with Epidural Analgesia

There has been a global increase in birth intervention and caesarean section rates in the last 20 years. The average caesarean section rate in Organisation for Economic Co-operation and Development (OECD) countries was 28% in 2013, while in Australia the most recently available statistics show a caesarean section rate of 33% in 2014 (AIHW 2016, p. 22). This is more than double the upper limit of 'necessary' caesareans, recommended in World Health Organisation (WHO) guidelines as being between 10% and 15% (WHO 1996, 2015). Other perinatal complications, such as instrumental birth, severe perineal trauma, and postnatal depression, are also being addressed by policy makers and health care professionals, as birth complications have considerable consequences for the health of the population, including increased recovery time, morbidity, and health care expense (Commonwealth of Australia 2008, p. 3; Department of Health NSW 2010). Significantly, recent statistics show that although numbers are small, one of the leading indirect causes of maternal death in Australia is suicide (Humphrey et al. 2015; Johnson, S. et al. 2014). It is therefore pertinent to pose the question: What is the cause? If traditional physiological causes of maternal mortality such as infection and haemorrhage—hallmarks of the need for medical intervention in biomedical terms—are no longer leading, then arguments for humanising the birth process and addressing the dangers of dehumanising and over-technologising the birth process now need to come to the fore (Davis-Floyd 2008; Wagner 2001).

Most women in Australia give birth in large, high acuity hospitals, and smaller maternity units are regularly closing (Dietsch et al. 2008; Gamble and Vernon 2007; National Rural Health Alliance 2012). In 2014, 98% of women in Australia gave birth in a hospital setting, primarily public hospitals (73%), with 1.8% accessing birth centres and 0.3% having planned home birth (AIHW 2016, p. 16). Hospital maternity care is generally delivered by obstetric-led units, although midwifery-led units are becoming more popular, with demand exceeding supply in many instances. Obstetric units are well equipped to manage emergencies and provide for women considered high-risk, but do not always offer a diversity of care practices for supporting normal birth (Romano and Lothian 2008). A common intervention offered in obstetric-led units for healthy women during labour is epidural analgesia.[1] While epidural analgesia has substantial analgesic properties, it is also associated with increased risk of adverse outcomes (Walsh 2009). There is little doubt that epidural analgesia can be useful in a complicated labour and delivery. However, the WHO (1996, p. 16) has stated:

> if epidural analgesia is administered to a low-risk pregnant woman, it is questionable whether the resulting procedure can still be called 'normal labour'. Naturally, the answer depends on the definition of normality, but epidural analgesia is one of the most striking examples of the medicalization of normal birth, transforming a physiological event into a medical procedure.

Despite this, epidural is considered a 'routine' analgesic choice for healthy women in labour, and its use is increasing, both in Australia and other high-income nations (Lain et al. 2008, p. 257; Walsh 2009).[2] In Australia in 2012, 32.5% of women in labour used regional analgesia for labour pain, of which the majority was epidural or caudal (30.5%) (Hilder et al. 2014, p. 38). Epidural use disrupts the birthing process to the extent that it causes increased birth intervention and is correlated with higher rates of instrumental birth (ventouse and forceps) and caesarean section (Cooper, G. et al. 2010; Lieberman and O'Donoghue 2002; Ramin et al. 1995; Tracy et al. 2007). There are also less obvious, but perhaps more disturbing, complications such as interruptions in oxytocin production in labour and decreased breastfeeding rates (Gaiser 2005, p. 12; Jordan, S. et al. 2009; Rahm et al. 2002; Wang et al. 2009, p. 875; Wiklund et al. 2009).

Most significant is that the use of epidural analgesia during birth can be considered to transfer a labouring woman out of the category of 'normal' labour and increase her risk of intervention (Walsh 2009, p. 90). This is a critical point, as it is estimated that approximately 70–80% of women would be considered low-risk at the beginning of labour (WHO 1996, p. 4),[3] yet it was calculated a decade ago that only 28% of Australian women having their first baby in the public hospital system will give birth without intervention (Gamble and Vernon 2007, p. 33) and given international increases in intervention rates, it can safely be assumed that this figure has since decreased. Intervention in labour, including the use of epidural, can dramatically change birth outcomes for otherwise low-risk women (Tracy et al. 2007). Additionally, pain in labour is not always a negative experience, and epidural analgesia use does not necessarily increase women's satisfaction with birth (Waldenström et al. 2004). In fact, pain can be viewed as a positive experience (Leap and Anderson 2008; Lundgren and Dahlberg 1998) and support or access to water in labour decreases women's analgesic requirements (Cluett and Burns 2009; Bohren et al. 2017; Romano and Lothian 2008), raising questions about the ubiquity of epidural analgesia in comparison to potential alternative ways of supporting women through birth.

It is therefore important to question epidural use, because the current biomedical research on epidural use in labour perpetuates the 'safety' of the epidural, even while examining its negative consequences. Profuse quantities of medical, as opposed to other forms of research, can lead to skewed social perspectives of the necessity of medical intervention (Downe and McCourt 2008, p. 9; Wendland 2007, p. 227). The prominence of medically focused research perpetuates one particular kind of knowledge about epidural analgesia, resulting in the acceptance of this technology as a 'common sense' option in Western birth culture. As a result, other options for birth are marginalised by their absence in the literature and resulting lack of alternatives. While judicious use of epidural analgesia may be beneficial in particular situations, the current use of epidural as a routine birth analgesic needs to be examined more closely. In the same way as most medical interventions, there is a therapeutic window whereby the use of the technology can improve the situation and overuse can lead to iatrogenic outcomes.

> When epidurals are used specifically to problem-solve, the risks of complications and other interventions are in fact reduced. When used routinely and mindlessly, epidural analgesia increases problems and adverse outcomes. Women need to be fully informed of this before agreeing to an epidural. Today women are usually only informed of the *direct* consequences of epidural analgesia, such as a headache or even very *rare* neurological complications, but they are *rarely* told *common* side-effects or the problems that can occur if epidurals are given too early. They are rarely told how an epidural

can interfere with the woman's labour and lead to a cascade of unnecessary interventions, and they are rarely informed about how the midwifery care that an epidural requires for the sake of safety, will divert midwives from hands-on attention to the labouring woman towards technological and mechanical concerns. (Klein 2011, p. 26 [original emphasis])

As yet, the issue of routinely available epidural analgesia for labour has not been examined in depth. The Australian context can offer useful insights because of the continued medical influence over birth experienced in this country compared to many others with a stronger midwifery history (see Campo 2014; Högberg 2004; Summers 1995; Willis 1989), but due to the many similarities in maternity systems worldwide, including the dominance of the biomedical model, our findings are relevant to the international community.

A Brief History of Birth Analgesia

The term analgesia in its modern form—the introduction of a therapeutic agent for the purposes of pain relief—entered the medical literature relatively recently (late nineteenth century), replacing the earlier Classical Grecian term 'anodyne' (Mander 1998a, p. 86). Moreover, there has always been a lack of absolute distinction between analgesic (pain relief) and anaesthetic (loss of complete sensation/consciousness) in the treatment of pain; the same drug, whether alcohol, chloroform or nitrous oxide, often being used for both purposes with the only difference being the quantity of drug used. Mander (1998a, p. 91) takes up this idea with reference to birth, suggesting that women who are considered high-risk for birth intervention or complication are offered an epidural as a form of *analgesia*, in order for it to be in place in the event that *anaesthesia* should be necessary (e.g. in the event of a caesarean), but that women are not alerted to the fact that they are actually consenting to epidural as anaesthetic rather than analgesic.

Attempts to ease the pain and work of birth, or to alleviate labour ailments, have been documented over centuries of childbearing, largely with the use of herbs (Towler and Bramall 1986, pp. 9, 14, 95) and folk remedies (Mander 1998b, p. 7). This progressed to the use of tinctures and compresses, cordials, and alcohol (Wertz and Wertz 1989, p. 15) and later, opium or laudanum (an opium tincture) (Banks 1999, p. 16). Pharmaceutical analgesia in labour was introduced by medical practitioners after its experimental use on the battlefield and in surgery. The use of strong analgesia for surgery and treatment of war wounds was no doubt a relief for doctors and patients alike, given the horrific circumstances of surgery without analgesia, but its progression into birth also shows how all pain, from a medical perspective, was considered adversarial. Despite this, when obstetric analgesia was first introduced, there was resistance from some quarters of the obstetric community, who viewed pain in labour as expected, and natural, unlike the pain from surgery (Stratmann 2003, p. 38). Others opposed pain relief because it countered the Christian belief that pain in childbirth was a punishment for Eve's fall from grace in the Garden of Eden. Some surgeons argued that pain was necessary even for surgical patients, the stimulation it provided benefiting the ongoing life force (Stratmann 2003, pp. 7, 38). At a time when women were having many more babies, with higher rates of birth complications, the promise of pain-free labour was also alluring to women, and middle-class, influential women over the globe agitated for its access (Wertz and Wertz 1989, pp. 150–152). However, it appears that pain relief remained less of an objective for working-class women, due, perhaps, to an idea that pain was 'natural' and because getting access to a midwife and government was focus enough; drugs and doctors being out of financial reach (Mander 1998b, pp. 7–8).

James Young Simpson [1811–1870], renowned Scottish doctor, introduced both ether and then chloroform to obstetrics in 1847 (Dunn 2002; Stratmann 2003). As inhalational anaesthesia became more common—and only doctors could administer it—it now justified the presence of medical practitioners at all births, not just those with complications as had previously been the case (Davies 2008; see also Mander 1998b, p. 157). 'Twilight sleep', a combination of the opioid analgesic morphine and amnesiac scopolamine, was later introduced in Germany (Wertz and Wertz, p. 150) and a synthetic opioid, pethidine (meperidine in the United States), as well as epidural anaesthesia, was developed throughout the 1940s so that by the mid-twentieth century both drugs were in general use in obstetrics, pethidine very commonly but epidural less so (Mander 1998b).

Important to the discussion about the introduction of medical analgesia is the intrinsic shift of focus from the woman to the doctor as birth became more medicalised. Since ancient times birthing women have typically been surrounded by midwives (or 'god-sibs'—local women who provided physical and emotional support in labour) as they laboured on birthing stools or in other upright positions. Medical practitioners however, in their initial role as the bearers of forceps other medical instruments, and later in all deliveries, needed women to be lying prone in their beds (Banks 1999; Kitzinger 2005; Mander 1998a; Towler and Bramall 1986). Banks (1999, p. 61) notes the change in ideology from 'some' births are difficult and need to be attended by a doctor to 'all' births need to be attended by a doctor, therefore all births are difficult. She writes of this circular and self-fulfilling set of practices and beliefs:

> [a]lthough far easier from the doctor's ... perspective, the horizontal position significantly increased the difficulty, length, and pain of labor and delivery. Due to its contradictory influence on labor, the growing popularity of this position ... encouraged the use of intervention and medical care and maintenance in the practice of birth. This, in turn, fostered the very understanding of birth advocated by the developing field of obstetrics. 'Heroic' measures like extensive bloodletting and the administration of ergot and opiates were regularly used in what midwives would have considered normal labors had [they] begun upright. These practices further encouraged the use of a recumbent position for delivery, use of forceps, anesthesia, and doctor attendance. The results of such cyclical practices encouraged the understanding of birth as difficult and provided ample argument for the care and treatment of all deliveries by doctors as a medical crisis. The redefinition of birth and the resulting changes in practice made ideology reality. (Banks 1999, pp. 62, 64)

Despite medical birth initially being carried out under a sheet—for modesty's sake, while society was still getting used to the idea of men at birth—with no direct line of vision for the doctor (Donnison 1988, p. 24), the recumbent birth position was most certainly aimed at providing comfort and access for the doctor, rather than transferring any benefit to the woman (Banks 1999, p. 62). Although women were occasionally prone in a normal labour attended by a midwife, it was because she was tired or weak, rather than for the ease of the midwife (Towler and Bramall 1986, p. 95). It cannot be underestimated how this position, as well as increasing use of forceps, would have adversely impacted on levels of pain and the need for pain relief. In addition, these changes in birth ideology essentially made the role of the god-sib redundant, even though labour companionship and support had been practised as a positive influence on labour since ancient times and was listed in early texts along with other supportive practices as an additional coping mechanism (Kitzinger 2005; Towler and Bramall 1986). Interestingly, women who are well supported in labour have less need of analgesia (Romano and Lothian 2008), and yet the god-sib role was replaced by the medical practitioner, with his medications and instruments. As birth moved into hospitals, women were increasingly left to labour alone and medication uptake increased.

This history of the medicalisation of birth and the increasing use of labour analgesia take us to the present day, where rates of epidural analgesia in childbirth have doubled in the previous decade and are still increasing. Walsh (2009) proposes that the increase is due to a combination of availability, medicalised birth ideology, a technorational focus on the negative aspects of pain during labour, increased fear of birth, fragmentation of care where women are not supported through labour, and the consequences of the risk paradigm on birth. One of the difficulties with critiquing the use of epidural analgesia is the perceived attack on those women who require it during labour and, for some of these women, the feeling that they have somehow failed. However, as with many obstetric interventions, the practice should be critiqued and researched by those in the profession, and this does not mean limiting choice, it means acquiring evidence. If birth ideology is considered here, then it may explain why women do choose epidural analgesia as they make their decisions from within the margins of the medicalised birth model—with its roots in an historical scientific discourse—in which pain is discouraged and technology esteemed.

Scientific Discourse

The scientific discourse is a major constituent of the current Western paradigm. It is centred on the premise of linear, logical lines of inquiry that stem from what were designated as 'male' qualities of rationality and separation (as opposed to 'female' qualities of emotionality and connectedness) (Wajcman 1991, pp. 5, 145). French philosopher Michel Foucault (2003) has described the ways in which dominant discourses such as science and medicine have explicit mechanisms to control knowledge selection and production, as well as access to knowledge. Scientific inquiry is rooted in a specific historical context which influenced the validity of knowledge production; who was able to produce it and what was then 'known'. We will now discuss the place of science in producing what was known about women, beginning at the epoch of Western Enlightenment.

The Scientific Revolution

The proliferation of ideas and critique during the renaissance period provided a catalyst for the scientific revolution and the consequent Enlightenment era.

> It [sixteenth century thought] attacked everything: it undermined everything; and nearly everything crumbled: the political, religious, spiritual unity of Europe; the certainty of science together with that of faith; the authority of the Bible as well as that of Aristotle; the prestige of the church and the glamour of the state. (Koyré 1964, p. viii)

The result of this criticism was the subsequent revelation that nothing can truly be known, a prescience, perhaps, of postmodernity. Koyré (1964, p. ix) states of the times, 'little by little, doubt stirs and awakens. If everything is possible, nothing is true. If nothing is assured, the only certainty is error.' The enormity of this uncertainty cannot be underestimated, as philosophers, scientists, and political leaders alike attempted to make sense of a world no longer governed by the old foundations of knowledge that were grounded in—among other things—superstition, mythology, religion, and Classical philosophy. Within this environment, with old truths falling like embattled soldiers, Western European society was attempting to remake its world and restore faith, stability, and order. It is within this milieu that 'against the sceptical trend … a threefold reaction takes place: Pierre Charron, Francis Bacon, Descartes. In other words: faith, experience, reason' (Koyré 1964, p. x). The idea of faith will be left here for the moment, but the influence of the latter two requires further exploration.

Francis Bacon, instigator of the method of inductive reasoning (or Baconian method), argued for an empirically based science and advocated that rational knowledge be founded in action, rather than theory; in experience, rather than discourse (Koyré 1964, p. xii). His method enabled a form of egalitarianism, as each man had the possibility of discovering things for himself (though women much less so). As a natural philosopher, he was influenced by Classical philosophy, and also alchemic traditions, from which he diverged, believing that the investigation and control of nature be not simply for individual gain, but to further the good of humanity (Merchant 1980, p. 169). Despite the fact that Bacon himself did not go on to make scientific discoveries by use of this method, it provided a strong foundation for the progression of science, and a basis for empirical science as we know it today.

Descartes, on the other hand, was interested in theory, knowledge, and the mind. Recovering from the scepticism of Renaissance thinking, he was left with only two convictions: 'belief in God, and belief in mathematics' (Koyré 1964, p. xvii). Counter to Bacon, Descartes believed that knowledge was accessible through the 'intuition of ideas and not with the perception of things' (Koyré 1964, p. xviii)[4]; that the 'seeds of knowledge' were innate (Koyré 1964: xxix). Although he did not discount empirical data completely, sensory data was effectively untrustworthy, only useful to prove deeply felt certainties, the most famous of which was his statement: 'I think, therefore I am' (Descartes, in Anscombe and Geach 1964, p. 32).[5]

In developing his theory, Descartes theorised a separation of mind and body, since described as 'Cartesian dualism',[6] which greatly influenced the development of science and medicine to follow. He wrote:

Thus the self, that is to say the soul, by which I am what I am, is entirely distinct from the body, and is even more easily known; and even if the body were not there at all, the soul would be just what it is. (Descartes, in Anscombe and Geach 1964, p. 32)

Descartes' thinking was no doubt influenced by the emergent social impact of machine and clockwork symbolism and imagery of the times (Merchant 1980, pp. 227–228). He saw the body as divisible, like a machine that had discrete, disconnected parts. He notes, 'thus I may consider the human body as a machine fitted together and made up of bones, sinews, muscles, veins, blood, and skin' (Descartes, in Anscombe and Geach 1964, p. 120). He was, according to Lindsay (1937, p. xi), 'the author and the prophet of the conception of mechanism', a worldview that contended that the human body, as well as the solar system and the universe itself, can be equated with a mechanical structure. Although Descartes was also, as far possible given the historical period, advancing an egalitarian process (Grimshaw 1986, p. 53) of thinking for oneself, he, like Bacon, was writing at a time when women largely did not have access to education. Therefore, the theories of the time reflected an androcentric view and as a result, Descartes' mechanistic theories of the split mind and body would have enduring consequences for women.

Bacon's empiricism, Cartesian dualism, and mechanistic thinking have had a substantial impact on the way Western medicine has viewed health, particularly stark in comparison to other medical models such as Chinese or Ayurvedic medicine. Despite recent movements advocating more holistic views of the body, mind, and planet, such as naturopathy, mindfulness, or slow food ecology, mechanism is still a prevailing tenet in Western medicine, as is made clear in its approach to birth (Martin 1989).

The Scientific Revolution in Context

Merchant (1980), in a feminist historical examination of science and nature, explores how world-views changed with the introduction of industrial capitalism. Renaissance thought held widely to the concept of 'organicism', which, though hierarchical, emphasised the interconnectedness of all things, including the planets surrounding Earth. Though not a unified theory—it stemmed from the disparate philosophies of Plato, Aristotle, and the Stoics—common to all was the idea that the universe was a living, interdependent organism, which possessed soul, vital spirit, and matter. There was no separation; thus if a part of the world suffered, this affected the whole (Merchant 1980, pp. 103–104). With increasing industrialisation and shifts in economic structure with early capitalism, holistic beliefs about the world and 'mother nature' were refigured to integrate the arrival of large-scale, ecologically devastating agricultural and mining schemes. As a result, paradigm-shifting ideas simultaneously emerged, including from the scientific quarter, that jettisoned prior ideas of connectedness and 'earth as mother' in order to accommodate and make sense of new economic modes of production.

The Problem with Science

As the scientific quarter gained purchase as the new source of legitimate knowledge, it also became equated with truth. The 'aura of facticity' of science (Baer et al. 1997, p. 34) has been well documented by Foucault (1980, 2003, 2007), and others, to be contingent. From this constructionist viewpoint, 'scientific knowledge … is produced under a particular and influencing set of cultural and historic conditions and … the insights of science are not discovered but socially crafted' (Baer et al. 1997, p. 34). The discussion which follows identifies how science contributed to knowledge about women's bodies, and how it was influenced by social and political thought. As Foucault (1980, p. 84) points out, critique in this vein is not to deny scientific knowledge, or the need for knowledge production, but instead refers to the requirement for other kinds of knowledge which do not necessarily dispute the ideas being produced, but which can identify the organisations of power that are operating behind these ideas.

The social vicissitudes described below, although aligned most often with dominant structures, such as class and gender, are not to be taken as grand conspiracies of the elite. They are simply social and structural configurations that require our awareness, attention, and critique (Waitzkin 1983, p. 33), particularly given the authority of the scientific paradigm in late modern society. This is not to say either, that science is not useful or needed but that it must be viewed in its historical and social context. We have included a discussion of the tenacity and ubiquity of scientific discourse because it is fundamental to what is to follow. That is, the way that science contributed to the construction of women's bodies and how medicine, in aligning itself with the scientific discourse early on, was then able to perpetuate the subjugation of women's bodies, specifically, the bodies and practices of birthing women and midwives.

The Body: From Ancient Times to Enlightenment

Martin's (1989) analysis of how women's bodies are represented within post-industrial capitalism as well as by a patriarchal scientific discourse delves into how the 'scientific' construction of women's bodies changed over the centuries. Early interpretations of the body held that male and female bodies were like two sides of the same coin, rather than two distinct genders. The ancient Greek belief was that male and female bodies were essentially the same,[7] the female an 'inside-out' version of the male, although the male body was still viewed as superior—closer to perfection—due to its possession of greater vital heat (Laqueur 1990, p. 4).

Later, humoral medicine was premised on the belief that health was kept in balance by the fluidity of the humours (Laqueur 1990, p. 35), an intricate theory that saw physicality as fluid, and blurred the boundaries between male and female. One example of humoral theory was the belief that lactating women did not menstruate because the excess fluid usually expelled during menstruation was used instead for making breastmilk (Laqueur 1990, pp. 35–36). What this meant in real terms was that bodily functions such as sweating and menstruation were seen as natural ways to balance the body.[8] For example, menopause was depicted as a normal stage of life, as the body ceased menstruation in order to provide more fat as the body aged. Male versions of this balance of fluids were seen in sweating and ejaculation of semen, and purging and bloodletting were also practised as balancing treatments.

The acceptance of the scientific paradigm in the eighteenth century effected a cultural shift in notions of the body. The similarities between male and female bodies were dismissed, and important distinctions were made:

thus the old model, in which men and women were arrayed according to their degree of metaphysical perfection, their vital heat, along an axis whose telos was male, gave way by the late eighteenth century to a new model of radical dimorphism, of biological divergence. (Laqueur 1990, pp. 5–6)

This was a time of great social upheaval; political instability, economic change, industrial advancement, and a decline in religious authority heralded a loss of confidence in the religious 'order' of things—previously the basis for understanding social order—and it resulted in new ways of conceptualising the world and the place of men and women within it (Martin 1989, p. 32; Merchant 1980, pp. 125–126). Many factors, including the fallibility of religion to confer ultimate truth, and the reconceptualisation of philosophies that had been maintained for millennia, led to a seeking of the 'natural' order within science (Laqueur 1990, p. 6). However, it serves well to understand the complexity of such historical developments. Laqueur (1990, p. 11 [original italics]) asserts:

> but social and political changes are not, in themselves, explanations for the reinterpretation of bodies. The rise of evangelical religion, Enlightenment political theory, the development of new sorts of public places in the eighteenth century, Lockean ideas of marriage as a contract, the cataclysmic possibilities for social change wrought by the French revolution, postrevolutionary conservatism, postrevolutionary feminism, the factory system with its restructuring of the sexual division of labour, the rise of a free market economy in services or commodities, the birth of classes, singly or in combination—none of these things *caused* the making of a new sexed body. Instead, the remaking of the body is itself intrinsic to each of these developments.

Thus, the new scientific understanding of two distinct sexes was influenced by these social instabilities, but also shaped the direction of social change in a way that would have long-lasting effects. What science 'discovered', in this era of uncertainty, was that women were weaker and less intelligent than men. Women were also fragile, unstable, impure, either frigid or lustful, impressionable, untrustworthy, potentially evil, and subject to a multitude of physical ailments due to their biology (Chauhan 2005; Ehrenreich and English 1979; Martin 1989; Merchant 1980).

This effectively prevented them from being worthy of education or occupation; not an insignificant state of play in the newly developing industrial society.

Thus, just as the separation of mind/body had occurred within philosophical discourse, so the social order was also dichotomised into the 'doctrine of spheres'. As industrialisation separated family units, and work-life from home-life, women found themselves in the unprecedented position of no longer being involved in the production and management of business and the economics of family life.[9] There was now a sharply defined division of labour between men and women (Miles 1989; Rich 1986). The world became divided into artificial dualities that had not previously existed, such as masculine and feminine; public and private; cultural and natural; rational and irrational; physical and emotional; individual and relational (Martin 1989, p. 32; Rothman 1989, p. 88). As these dichotomies took form, women were increasingly equated with the wildness of nature (and men with the civilisation of culture) and thus subject to similar forms of domestication and control, and as capitalism, industrialisation, large-scale mining and agriculture brought more mechanised views of culture than had previously existed, it is argued that women's bodies were constructed accordingly as untamed, unruly, and uncontrollable (Merchant 1980). Women's bodily functions, which up until now had had an equivalent in men—if somewhat less robust—and were therefore seen as *normal* physiological processes, became uniquely female, and associated with female traits: pathological, passive, debilitating, in need of regulation and restraint (Martin 1989; Miles 1989, p. 191). Thus, as Martin (1989) observes, the physiological functions of menstruation, childbirth, and menopause have become medical problems to be 'solved' rather than acknowledged as the ordinary reproductive cycles of women's everyday life.

Science and the 'new' (post-Galenic) medicine played a considerable role in the delineation of categories for the maintenance of a new social order that needed to rise, like the phoenix, from the ashes of outmoded financial, political, and religious foundations (Baer et al. 1997). Thus, the control of aspects of women's sexuality and reproduction, such as contraceptive use or access to abortion, proceeded from being under the control of the Church to being dictated by medical requirements and intrusions (Chauhan 2005, p. 76). Medical control and mechanisation were also applied to women in labour.

The Labouring Body: The Impact of History

As well as identifying mechanical and industrial influences, in her analysis of the medicalisation of menstruation, childbirth, and menopause, Martin (1989) has observed the ways in which women's reproductive bodies have also been framed by capitalist notions of production. She proposes that hospital labour is analogous to a production line in a factory, where progress is strictly measured, and any deviation from 'normal' is equated with disorder. Here, the intricate process of hormonal and physical interconnection is not acknowledged and our understanding about what halts women's labour, such as bright light, noise, conversation, even direct eye contact, is not admitted.[10] Instead, a physical (mechanical) reason will be sought for any halt in labour progress (Martin 1989, p. 62), and 'fixed' accordingly with artificial intervention. External systems of measurement, such as adherence to 'Friedman's curve' (a method of assessing labour progress based on routine vaginal examinations that measures the dilating cervix) continue ideas of mechanisation by viewing labour progress in isolation from the woman who is experiencing it, as well as applying rigid, extraneous, and artificial timelines against which women must perform.

What this does, quite apart from disrupting the usual hormones of labour, is potentially alienate the woman from her labour process. With an increasing focus on the 'product' of labour—the healthy baby—a woman's need for at least some acknowledgement of her subjective experience of the birth process is minimised (Martin 1989, p. 64). This is evident today in the continuing medical and public discourse that women who choose outside of medical norms (such as homebirth) are selfishly favouring their experience over the physical health of their baby, seemingly blind to the idea that experience and safety can co-exist and one does not automatically rule out the other. The privileging of the 'scientific' is mirrored in other mainstream discourses in obstetrics, in the way research questions are framed, in the way that 'outcome measures' are often in physically observable statistics and mother's experiences are rarely documented or visible (Wendland 2007; Rothman 1989). Other researchers have also documented the ways in which the medical profession has distanced women from the 'social' experience of pregnancy by using the authority of expert knowledge to pathologise pregnancy and birth. This denial of the social, the sexual, and the spiritual elements of birth led to a system of dehumanised, depersonalised, and assembly-line care (Oakley 1984, p. 240; Rothman 1989, p. 86; Martin 1989), which is still apparent today (see *Human Rights in Childbirth* 2015; Baker et al. 2005; Kitzinger 2005).

Resistance

It appears that we have outlined a great siege of events that have 'happened' to women. Although dominant frameworks have influenced the way women and their bodies have been constituted by mainstream discourse, it is important to recognise that this has been resisted at every turn. Midwives in the seventeenth century were denouncing medical intervention, claiming that doctors did not have the same level of knowledge and skill of birth as midwives; that they did not know how to use their hands, only the 'damaging' instruments; that they interfered too often (Murphy-Lawless 1998, p. 26; Towler and Bramall 1986, pp. 96–106). English midwife Elizabeth Nihill, writing in 1760, in her treatise about man-midwives (who she described as a 'band of mercenaries who palm themselves off upon pregnant women under cover of their crochets, knives, scissors, spoon, pinchers, fillets, speculum matrices, all of which … are totally useless' [Nihill, in Towler and Bramall 1986, p. 104]) was vocal in her opposition to the man-midwives' claims to specialised knowledge, decried their use of instruments, and argued strongly that midwives were more skilled and therefore safer than man-midwives (Murphy-Lawless 1998; Towler and Bramall 1986). As well, although some women, from the first use of chloroform to the use of 'twilight sleep' and later pethidine and epidural, were clamouring for relief from the travails of labour and insisting on analgesia, resistant groups (albeit initially led by men, such as Grantly Dick-Read and Frederic Leboyer) were calling for more 'natural' methods of childbirth, and the 'natural childbirth' movement flourished throughout the 1960s and 1970s.

However, increasing medicalisation, surveillance, and control made it harder for resistance to occur. Incorporation of 'fringe' practices into the medical system have in some respects given women more choices, and in others, restricted them further (see Martin 1989; Newnham 2010). Women are still feeling misinformed and overwhelmed in a medicalised, technologised environment (Baker et al. 2005; Walsh 2009). Nevertheless, midwives have attempted to find and maintain the *meaning* in birth (Downe 2008; Fahy et al. 2008) and women have attempted to 'integrate' themselves after being viewed by medicine as separate parts, or by feeling overwhelmed by the *personal experience* of pregnancy, birth, and motherhood versus the *institution* of motherhood (Rothman 1982, 1989; Maher 2002; Marshall, H. 1996; Rich 1986). Despite ongoing resistance by women and midwives, the dominance of the medical discourse, though structurally diminished, still remains (Newnham 2014).

Medical Dominance: The Rise of the 'Expert'

The sociological discussion of medical dominance begins in the 1970s with Friedson's identification of the professional imperialism of medicine and the identification of power differentials in the doctor/patient relationship. Included in Friedson's analysis of professional dominance were the attributes of autonomy, authority, and altruism (Benoit et al. 2010, p. 475), where 'authority' pertains to restricting the boundaries of other professions. At about the same time, Illich (1977) was vilifying the medical fraternity for the increasing medicalisation of society, which sparked a decades-long debate about the expansion of medicine into areas previously seen as private, or social, which we discuss further in Chap. 3.

However, while knowledge of anatomy and practices that would be identified today as 'medicine' was consolidated over the eighteenth and nineteenth centuries, initially medicine was not in possession of sacrosanct knowledge. Local village healers, usually also midwives, were knowledgeable in the use of plants and herbs, for example, ergot and belladonna, the chemical derivatives of which are still used today (Banks 1999); ergot is a particularly useful drug in preventing or halting postpartum bleeding—with its pharmaceutical name—Ergometrine—telling of its origin. Thus, even doctors themselves had recourse to visit local healers or wise-women when they required skilled treatment (Ehrenreich and English 1979, p. 32; Towler and Bramall 1986, p. 35).

In contrast to the empirical knowledge of village midwives, medical students that trained in universities studied philosophy and theology, and had little patient experience. Medicine, until the late seventeenth/early eighteenth century was based on second-century Galenic theory (Ehrenreich and English 1979, p. 33; Laqueur 1990, pp. 4–5; Martin 1989, p. 31; Stratmann 2003, p. 5) and included such practices as bloodletting, humoural balance, and church-sanctioned prayer and amulets (Ehrenreich and English 1979; Gélis 1991). Although such folk practices abounded in all fields, they were certainly not only the domain of the midwife. Ehrenreich and English (1979, p. 33) suggest that by the late Middle Ages, 'It was witches who developed an extensive understanding of bones and muscles, herbs and drugs, while physicians were still deriving their prognoses from astrology', observing also that:

> often the experts' theories were grossly unscientific, while the traditional lore of the women contained wisdom based on centuries of observation and experience. The rise of the experts was not the inevitable triumph of right over wrong, fact over myth; it began with a bitter conflict which set women against men, class against class. (Ehrenreich and English 1979, p. 29)

What medical practitioners did have was the ability to read and write, professional lobbying power, the support of the Church, and later, parliament and legislation. They used this power prior to the witch hunts, in forbidding women to access medical training (Ehrenreich and English 1979, p. 35; Towler and Bramall 1986, p. 29).[11] During the witch hunt era, medicine had an ally in the Church due to the position of the Church on midwives, epitomised in the *The Malleus Maleficarum* (*The Hammer of the Witches*), the 'legal and procedural code of the Roman Catholic Inquisition'. Published in 1486, its authors state emphatically that 'no-one does more harm to the Catholic faith than midwives' (Kramer and Sprenger, in Chauhan 2005, p. 2). Medicine's alignment with scientific knowledge and inquiry came much later, expanding the status and prestige of medicine, and advancing its professional status (Donnison 1988; Ehrenreich and English 1979; Murphy-Lawless 1998).

It is important to contextualise the absolute opposition to women as practitioners by the medical profession and the Church (both Catholic and Protestant) over these several hundred years. It seems hard to conceive of now, and its presence, though well documented (Chauhan 2005; Donnison 1988; Ehrenreich and English 1973; Murphy-Lawless 1998), is rarely included in contemporary discussions with the significance it deserves.[12] Willis' (1989) oft-cited and insightful exposition of medical dominance shows that it continued in Australia after British colonisation; doctors were very outspoken indeed about 'the midwifery problem' in Australia (Summers 1995), as was also the case in the United States (Arney 1982; Ehrenreich and English 1979). The medical profession in Australia is still active in its attempts to marginalise midwifery and maintain medicine as the dominant discourse in birth practice (Campo 2014; Newnham 2014).

The Impact of Medical Dominance

Whereas maternity service providers have, in the last few decades, paid lip service to a more holistic understanding of pregnancy and birth, the language and practice of risk and disorder is still firmly entrenched (Chadwick and Foster 2014; Donnellan-Fernandez 2011; Dove and Muir-Cochrane 2014; Scamell and Stewart 2014). This is likely to remain so if birth remains bounded within medical parameters. Biomedicine, with its curative, mechanistic, and reductionist focus, and its androcentric historical concept of the body adheres to the view that bodies that change, that consist of cyclical states of impermanence such as menstruation and pregnancy, are deviant and in need of medical intervention (Chadwick and Foster 2014).

One of the claims that generated medical dominance in birth was the positioning of medicalised birth with 'safety' (Murphy-Lawless 1998;

Summers 1995; Willis 1989), and this is still largely in play in medical discourse. However, many of the interventions that were introduced to birth practice, including the move to hospital itself, were not actually safe, and most were introduced before the advent of real research scrutiny (Barclay 2008; Cwikel 2008; Foucault 2003). The history of medical lobbying against midwifery practice (Summers 1995), its links with government policy making and the 'problematising' of alternative birth practices (Newnham 2010), as well as the diffusion of fear about birth and the safety of technology reflected in the media (Reiger and Dempsey 2006) has firmly located medicalised birth into our cultural belief system. To make alternative decisions about birth, women must potentially defy not only medical advice but also commonly held social beliefs. Women are therefore under pressure to conform to social norms, and will often self-regulate their behaviour and decision-making to stay within these boundaries (Bartky 1997; Foucault 2008). However, certain practices—ones which women have been the most vocal about—have been incorporated into the medical system and positive changes have been made through diligent midwifery-focused research, for example the shift away from routine episiotomy (Walsh 2012, p. 118). While continuing research is vital for generating knowledge, the increasing power of 'evidence-based medicine' has the potential to become another string in the bow of medical dominance. Congruent with Foucauldian analysis, the association between power and knowledge needs to be further investigated.

The Double-Edged Sword of Evidence-Based Medicine

As argued above, one of the main claims by biomedicine over other knowledge disciplines is its claim to truth and rationality. Evidence-based medicine (EBM), with the randomised-controlled trial (RCT)—the gold standard of scientific medicine—at its pinnacle is problematic. Although evidence-based principles have their place, and have been particularly useful in the removal of some debatable practices in midwifery and obstetrics as well as reducing practitioner bias, they also pose a potential dilemma (Johnson, K. 1997; Walsh 2012, pp. 2–4). Privileging the RCT over other research methods may flaw trial design and prompt the asking of the wrong questions (Keirse 2002; Kotaska 2004). Murphy-Lawless (1998, p. 14) expresses this dilemma as: 'what is measured is often meaningless, but without measurement there is no science'. The RCT is positioned at the top of the research hierarchy because of its ability to eliminate bias by randomisation of participants, use of control groups and also, preferably, the blinding of researchers to the participant's group. However useful and relevant the method may be in measuring particular variables, its claim to lack of bias is flawed; it is embedded in the historical context out of which scientific knowledge was formed, influenced by the economic and social structures of capitalism and gender inequality. Insofar as it mediates which questions are asked in science, this method—and other scientific methods—are in a sense always biased, as they derive from a worldview that privileges this knowledge over other forms (see Roome et al. 2015).

Much mainstream research then, with its assumptions about knowledge, empiricism, and medical authority, and seemingly unaware of its own positivist epistemology, only serves to embed particular constructions of women (as risky) and foetuses (as separate entities) within its culture (Wendland 2007). It is claimed that biomedicine's concern with standardising care, based on evidence and best practice guidelines, thereby eliminating risk (and choice), has essentially rendered women (and their experiences) invisible. Wendland (2007), who is both an obstetrician and an anthropologist, takes this idea to its endpoint, noting that in the medical literature on caesarean section 'cesarean surgery is gradually assuming the status of the "unmarked" … [m]eanwhile, vaginal delivery becomes marked as unpredictable, uncontrolled, and therefore dangerous' (Wendland 2007, p. 224). With these changes in collective understanding comes a concomitant normalisation of intervention with its discourse of 'safety'. Conversely, normal physiology, labelled as unpredictable, becomes 'risky'. As these ideas become entrenched into practice, they circulate the power/knowledge of medical birth discourse (Foucault 1980; Gordon 1980), to which we now turn in an exploration of epidural analgesia.

Epidural Analgesia: Exploring the Evidence

The physiological problems associated with epidural use in labour, and which can lead to birth intervention, include: altered uterine activity (either increased, with elevation of basal tone and fundal dominance usually associated with second stage labour *or* decreased uterine tone and contractility); labour dystocia—thought to be due to relaxation of pelvic floor and malrotation of the foetal presenting part; slower dilatation of the cervix; decreased oxytocin release by the pituitary gland and subsequent need for oxytocin augmentation; and decreased maternal bearing down efforts due to motor block (Finster and Santos 1998, pp. 474–475; Gaiser 2005, p. 12; Jain et al. 2003, p. 25).

In an extensive review of the epidural research, Gaiser (2005) explains how early research into epidural analgesia, which found a relationship firstly between epidurals and high instrumental birth rates, and then between epidurals and caesarean section, has since been attributed to the denser motor block of those early epidurals and an inability to distinguish between the reverse causality of the need for epidural and the presence of a pre-existing labour dystocia (Gaiser 2005, p. 4). The most recent Cochrane systematic review, which compared epidural to non-epidural or no analgesia in labour, noted the conflicting findings of previous research about whether or not epidural analgesia increased the risk of caesarean section, and concluded that while epidural use does not increase the risk of caesarean section, it does increase the risk of instrumental birth (Anim-Somuah et al. 2011).[13] Despite this conclusion, other research still identifies a relationship between epidural analgesia and caesarean section (Kotaska et al. 2006; Ros et al. 2007; Tracy et al. 2007). However, as no causal link has been isolated, it is possible that epidural use and caesarean section are outcomes from an as yet unknown common cause.

Identification of any causal relationship may be difficult, given that epidural analgesia is not a sole intervention, but brings with it numerous other interventions, such as IV fluid administration, continuous electronic foetal monitoring (cEFM), and labour augmentation. It therefore becomes difficult to extricate any specific influence. For instance, two studies looking at the difference in birth outcomes between early or late (in labour) epidural insertion, showed no difference in instrumental birth rates. What they did identify was a positive correlation between IV oxytocin administration and the caesarean section rate (Chestnut, cited in Finster and Santos 1998, pp. 477–478; see also Wang et al. 2009, p. 879). If epidural analgesia necessitates oxytocin use, and oxytocin use increases the risk of caesarean section, then epidural analgesia is going to influence, if not directly cause, this outcome. Similarly, use of cEFM has been shown to increase caesarean section rates (Alfirevic et al. 2017). Also confounding attempts at establishing the effects of epidural analgesia have been 'natural experiment' studies where after changes in policy or accessibility where epidural rates have increased or decreased markedly over a short period of time, there is no corresponding relationship in numbers of instrumental birth (Gaiser 2005, p, 6).

Gaiser (2005) concludes that new, lower dose epidurals probably do not increase caesarean section rates but may lengthen labour. However, research looking at the effects of low-dose epidurals has found a strong causal relationship between epidural and instrumental deliveries, and motor weakness remains considerable even with low-dose techniques (Jain et al. 2003). Nevertheless, Gaiser (2005, p. 13) states that with new research demonstrating the effectiveness (or at least diminishing the connection between epidural and caesarean section) of new epidural techniques 'the circle was completed' and obstetricians declared that epidural analgesia should be provided to women 'whenever indicated' unless there are medical contraindications.

Despite this optimism, more recent studies are again confounding the existing evidence. The Comparative Obstetric Mobile Epidural Trial (COMET) (Cooper, G. et al. 2010) compared low-dose and traditional (high-dose) epidural. A no-epidural comparison control group was matched for mode of delivery. The authors state, 'The mode of delivery and numbers recruited to each group illustrate the previously reported findings of an increase in spontaneous vaginal delivery with both mobile techniques and the *expected higher number of spontaneous vaginal deliveries* and fewer operative deliveries, especially by caesarean section, in the comparison group' (Cooper, G. et al. 2010, p. 32 [emphasis added]). So, while some researchers are declaring an impasse in relation to epidural research and a green light for routine epidural use, these authors were *expecting* higher rates of instrumental and caesarean birth in their epidural groups. The figures demonstrate this with a spontaneous vaginal birth (SVB) rate in the no-epidural group (approximately 75%) double that of the SVB rate in the high-dose epidural group (approximately 35%) and still much higher than in both of the low-dose groups (both approximately 43%). Conversely, all three epidural groups had rates of caesarean section nearing 30% (n = ~100), while the no-epidural group had a 9% (n = 30) caesarean section rate. Instrumental births were close to 40% (n = 131) in the high-dose group, close to 30% (n = ~100) in the low-dose groups, and 15% (n = 52) in the no-epidural group. An Australian population-based descriptive study (Tracy et al. 2007) also showed a threefold increase in caesarean section rates with epidural alone, as well as when used in combination with oxytocin. The US survey *Listening to Mothers* found that of 750 first-time mothers with term pregnancies, 47% were induced:

> [o]f those having an induction, 78% had an epidural, and of mothers who had both attempted induction and an epidural, the unplanned caesarean rate was 31%. Those who experienced *either* labor induction or an epidural, but not both, had caesarean rates of 19% to 20%. For those first-time mothers who neither experienced attempted induction nor epidural, the unplanned caesarean section rate was 5%. (Declercq et al. 2013, p. 24)

Again, one cannot infer causality in this study. However, singly and in combination, the practices of induction, epidural use, and augmentation of labour are clearly implicated in contributing to the 'cascade of intervention' that leads to caesarean section.

There was only minimal reference to the fact that maternal oxytocin production is inhibited by epidural analgesia. Gaiser's (2005, p. 12) review cites a 1983 study by Goodfellow, and there is reference to it in the research by Rahm et al. (2002). Reduced endogenous oxytocin leads to increased use of exogenous oxytocin, which in itself may be risk factor for caesarean section (Chestnut, cited in Finster and Santos 1998, pp. 477–478; Tracy et al. 2007; Wang et al. 2009, p. 877). Reduced maternal oxytocin may be a causative factor in the reduced breast-seeking behaviour in the newborn and reduced breastfeeding rates in women who have had an epidural (Wiklund et al. 2009) and, theoretically, could also affect the woman's experience of maternal bonding.[14] A recent study has again found a correlation with decreased breastfeeding rates, as well as increased rates of depressive symptoms with epidural use in labour (Kendall-Tackett et al. 2015). Although the reduced effects of endogenous oxytocin with epidural analgesia, as well as the detrimental effects of exogenous oxytocin are now recognised, there is a lack of robust research in this area (see Buckley 2015; Foureur 2008; Uvnäs-Moberg 2003).

Jain et al. (2003, p. 20) state that epidurals provide good analgesia, but maintain that its influence on the progress of labour and mode of delivery is still unclear. Their study, comparing epidural analgesia and two different types of opioid, concluded that epidural analgesia provided the best pain relief but also prolonged labour and increased the risk of forceps birth threefold. Toledo et al. (2009, p. 308) also remain circumspect about possible relationships between motor block, foetal malrotation, and decreased maternal effort in second stage. They recommend that more research is needed to identify the association between increased need for analgesia and risk of instrumental birth. A small number of studies call for caution with regard to epidural analgesia and suggest solutions such as restricting its use (Hemminki and Gissler 1996), the need for further research (Nystedt et al. 2004), and the provision of comprehensive informed consent about the risks (Kotaska et al. 2006).

Even with the early concerning findings of increased caesarean section rates, there was not then a concerted effort by the medical community to avoid epidural analgesia, although there were efforts to decrease problems associated with epidural use. These include: ceasing the epidural when the woman is 8 cm dilated; decreasing the amount of local anaesthetic used in order to decrease motor block (movement), while maintaining sensory block (pain reduction); allowing a longer second stage for women with epidural analgesia; and waiting for descent of the presenting part before commencing active pushing (Finster and Santos 1998; Gaiser 2005). Research undertaken to examine the effects of epidural analgesia has continued to produce conflicting results.[15] Despite the fact that the early research into complications of epidural use showed a sharp increase in caesarean section (Ramin et al. 1995; Thorp et al. 1989) and instrumental birth (Robinson et al., cited in Finster and Santos 1998; Hemminki and Gissler 1996; Howell and Chalmers 1992), research into epidural analgesia continued and the popularity of epidural grew as the favoured analgesic in labour. This can be explained by the continuing subtext of epidural analgesia as 'safe and efficacious pain relief' (Drysdale and Muir 2002, p. 99) within the epidural research discourse, regardless of the ongoing findings to the contrary. In turn, this subtext can be explained by determining those aspects of medical culture that make such a paradox occur. Clearly the increased caesarean section and instrumental birth rates were cause for concern. Yet, rather than discontinuing epidural use [as happened so rapidly, e.g., with the discontinuation of vaginal breech birth after the Term Breech Trial (Hannah et al. 2000; see also see Downe and McCourt 2008, p. 13; Steen and Kingdon 2008)], research simply continued on for some decades. This is because, we contend, epidural use, instrumental birth, and caesarean section are practices that suit the biomedical principles of control, technology, and intervention (see Walsh 2009).

Moreover, it would appear that the consequences of epidural analgesia were ignored largely because they affected women's experience, not the usual measurable medical outcomes (particularly those that focus on the neonate). Therefore, while instrumental birth appears as a consequence of *epidural analgesia* in the biomedical literature, the consequences of instrumental birth *for women* and their future health and wellbeing are not discussed (for an example of this, see Sharma et al. 2004). With the exception of one study (Cooper, G. et al. 2010), which looked at satisfaction rates, instrumental birth as an outcome is largely downplayed. There is a tacit assumption that as long as epidurals are only increasing the instrumental birth rate, but not the caesarean section rate, then this is an acceptable risk factor. However, for women, an instrumental birth may not be an acceptable risk factor. Instrumental birth and coached pushing, both increased with epidural analgesia, increase the likelihood of third- and fourth-degree tears. The sequelae of severe perineal trauma can include: pain, fear of birth, urinary and faecal incontinence, sexual dysfunction, post-traumatic stress disorder, and depression (Brown and Lumley 1998; Creedy et al. 2000; Hayman 2005; Rådestad et al. 2008). These outcomes, and their corollaries, indicate the need for instrumental birth rates to be a serious consideration in the epidural analgesia discussion.

Essentially, after 40 years of medical research into the risks of epidural analgesia there are still no conclusive findings about its effect on childbirth (Gaiser 2005, p. 1; Jain et al. 2003, p. 20; Toledo et al. 2009, p. 308), although it is probably safe to say it does increase instrumental birth rates (Anim-Somuah et al. 2011). The only result that is clearly maintained throughout the biomedical research is that despite the still unproven effects of epidural analgesia on labour, it provides the most effective analgesia (Cooper, G. et al. 2010; Wang et al. 2009; Jain et al. 2003). An emphasis on the safety and effectiveness of epidural analgesia foregrounded the majority of the research articles. Epidural analgesia is cited as the 'gold standard for analgesia in labour' (Amedee Peret 2013; Norman 2002, p. 28). This emphasis on the relief of pain at any cost is indicative of what is important to biomedical culture, which both influences and reflects wider cultural norms.

A Critical View: What the Evidence Is Saying

The way in which biomedicine can continue to implement practices based on control, technology, and intervention is by upholding a narrow research agenda. In disseminating particular kinds of data in specific ways, there are elements that are not identified, that are left silent. As Rothman (1989, p. 86) observes,

> the influence of the ideology of technology becomes most clear when medicine is on the scene … things that can be quantified are made real; those that cannot be quantified come to seem unreal. Infection rates are an observable measure for childbirth; joy is not.

These elements also include maternal subjectivity, consequences for the mother–newborn dyad, and long-term health effects (Wendland 2007, p. 222). In effect, by their lack of representation in the data, biomedical research reproduces underlying Western cultural values by minimising the importance of women's experiences, 'fixing' the faulty female body, reinforcing the neoliberal ideal of the individual, and implementing simplistic, mechanistic answers to complex problems. An illustration of our point is Ramin et al.' (1995, p. 788) statement, in their study of the effects of epidural, that 'Pain relief during labour is of paramount importance, and in most circumstances the two-to four-fold increased risk of cesarean delivery associated with epidural analgesia is a secondary consideration'. This statement exposes the medicalised view that emphasises the 'abnormality' of labour pain and normalises technological intervention such as caesarean section. It ignores the significant risks to health of such an intervention. In addition, one might ask, 'for whom is caesarean section is a secondary consideration?' When women have been asked, pain (and its relief) is not as important to them as caregiver support. Women who have caesarean sections are actually at higher risk of a negative birth experience (Waldenström et al. 2004) and future pregnancy and birth complications. So from many women's perspective the opposite is the case.

Equally, in rejecting women's experiences as important data, research in this field can fail to include interventions that seem insignificant to medicine, but may be highly significant to women (Wendland 2007; Oakley, cited in Baker et al. 2005, p. 316). In a critique of the influence of medical understandings of birth, Rothman (1989, p. 183) observes:

> In sum, the medical monopoly on childbirth management has meant defining birth in medical terms, and thus narrowing our scope of perception. A birth management that routinely leaves psychological and social trauma in its wake for the members of families, using this narrow definition, is measured as perfectly successful, unless the trauma is severe enough to be measured in appropriately 'medical' terms—that is, infant weight gain or some such crude measure.

Comparative to biomedical research, there are fewer studies concerned with women's experiences, what women want, and how they feel about their birth. Although research of this nature is on the increase, it is still minimal in the face of the hundreds of biomedical papers researching various aspects of epidural analgesia use, including miniscule drug dosage variations, comparisons of obstetric analgesia methods, timing of epidural analgesia insertion, and so on. This is not to discount the importance of such medical research, but to compare the two does generate a picture of what is seen as important—and what is not (see also Van der Gucht and Lewis 2015). It appears, in the above analysis, that 'what is important' is the advancement of technology, medicine, and professional practice, and that 'what is not' is the experience of women, non-technological practices, and protecting birth from unnecessary intervention. Indeed, providing even 'evidence-based' non-intervention can be exceedingly difficult (Romano and Lothian 2008, p. 101). Although EBM can have a positive impact, it is less the ultimate conduit to unbiased universal answers and more a vehicle of the dominant ideology, carting its passengers of technological imperialism, gender inequity, and post-industrial capitalism.

Epidural Analgesia as Technorationalist

The catch-cry of the (post)modern world that 'You can't stop progress' belongs to the technological determinist argument, which holds technology to be autonomously moving forward, almost with a life of its own, with no human control or direction (Hill 1988, p. 23). However, the idea that humanity is being carried along, rudderless, on a river of technological progress is subject to debate and there are those who would decry a total surrender to this current, however strong the pull. There is at least a need to subject technological progress to serious critical analysis before it is put into common use. Some decades ago, Marcuse (1972, p. 22) observed:

> But in the contemporary period, the technological controls appear to be the very embodiment of Reason for the benefit of all social groups and interests—to such an extent that all contradiction seems irrational and all counteraction impossible.

Arguments that critique progress are thus defined as unreasonable and irrational (Blackwell and Seabrook 1993). This is reflected in the 'pain relief as progress' theme in the epidural literature. Crowhurst and Plaat (2000, p. 164), for example, comment that labour analgesia is a part of the modern Western lifestyle, along with 'air travel, the mobile phone and the personal computer' and sharpen their point by invoking the Bible's ancient verdict:

The greatest advances in analgesia and anesthesia for labor and childbirth in the 20th century have been (1) the discovery and development of today's safe and efficacious analgesic techniques; (2) the social acceptance that it is unnecessary for parturients 'to bring forth children in pain and sorrow'.

Of course, the reverse side of this theme is that anyone who wants to argue the merits of pain, and there are those who do,[16] is defaulted to a paradigm of regressive anti-progress or Dark Ages mentality. The implicit assumption of the 'pain relief as progress' theme is the absurdity of not wanting to relieve the pain of childbirth. Why choose the 'unnecessary' pain of childbirth when you can be free of it? It appears to be an irrational choice in this context. Pain is an anathema to the biomedical model (Walsh 2009). The relief of pain in labour has been described as a 'human right' in one anaesthetic article (Cohen 1999, p. 224). In fact, in keeping with this discourse, a quick look at the language used to promote epidural is fascinating. Cohen (1999, p. 224) harks back to a time where 'the cries and screams of labouring women … echoed through the hallways in delivery rooms that offered only parenteral opioids', while Collier (2001, p. 53) writes, 'At last, the anaesthetist has arrived as your saviour'. These commentaries feed straight back into the technological determinist argument: to belie progress is to be anti-reason, anti-modern, and anti-reality. It is to be ludicrous. The technological imperative would have us use technology simply because it is there and technological determinism means that we cannot argue with it.

Despite the lack of conclusive evidence, the salient assertions in the biomedical epidural literature are that epidural analgesia is fundamentally safe, should be available for all women and is in fact a 'human right', and is modern and progressive while childbirth pain is archaic. Underlying this is the unease about epidural outcomes and there are constant recommendations that research needs to focus on improving these by varying doses and/or drugs. Women are offered the promise of 'safe, pain-free' labour, based on inconclusive research. 'Pain relief as progress' forms part of what Leap and Anderson (2008, p. 38) have termed the 'pain relief paradigm'. This paradigm acknowledges the technological assumptions outlined above as well as midwives' personal discomfort with pain, often underpinned by a belief that women cannot actually endure the pain of birth. In light of the ongoing uncertainty about research findings, there needs to be a robust and informed debate about the use of epidural analgesia in low-risk labour among those who provide maternity care. One of the first places that requires looking is to the women themselves.

Women's Perspectives

Research that poses questions about women's experience is much more common in the fields of social, feminist, and critical theory. Within the field of midwifery, qualitative research is often undertaken as midwives attempt to answer these questions for themselves. Frequently, this kind of research questions the status quo, either by asking questions from an alternate perspective, or by directly challenging mainstream maternity services. Rothman (1989) sees midwifery as a feminist praxis, where midwives stand with women against the disintegrating effects of social ideologies such as technological determinism. Morsy (1996, p. 39) identifies praxis as a dialectic between theory and action: 'its framework is collective, protracted social engagement, also known as political struggle'. Praxis, defined in this way, is a concern of Critical Medical Anthropology (CMA) (Singer and Baer 1995, p. 74) and also suits midwifery emancipatory philosophy. Rothman (1989, p. 170) goes on to say that

> Midwifery works with the labor of women to transform, to create, the birth experience to meet the needs of women. It is a social, political activity, dialectically linking biology and society, the physical and the social experience of motherhood. The very word midwife means with the woman. That is more than a physical location: it is an ideological and political stance.

Research with a midwifery or woman-centred approach therefore operates from a different paradigm than that of biomedical researchers. While biomedical research has for the most part underplayed the consequences of epidural, and maintains it as a safe and effective analgesic option for all women, other researchers are asking alternate questions. Cumulatively, research findings in this area present an entirely different view of pain and analgesia, including that: women who are well supported have less need for analgesia (Bohren et al. 2017; Romano and Lothian 2008; Walsh et al. 2008); pain can be viewed positively by women as a 'transition' to motherhood (Lundgren and Dahlberg 1998); medical intervention in birth (such as epidural) can lead to escalating intervention and negative birth outcomes (Kitzinger 2005; Romano and Lothian 2008); the overuse of technology has led to a situation where its negative effects are appearing (Wagner 2001); satisfaction with the birth experience is not necessarily related to pain relief, and is multifaceted (Hodnett 2002; Kannan et al. 2001; Lundgren and Dahlberg 1998); women who have had an epidural may express less satisfaction with the birth process than those who have not had one (Waldenström et al. 2004); the need for an epidural in labour may not be related to actual levels of pain, but to a pre-existing 'birth ideology' (Heinze and Sleigh 2003); women who use epidural analgesia are more likely to remember the pain of labour prior to its insertion than women who use no pain relief due to its effect on oxytocin levels (Uvnäs-Moberg 2016); and increasing use of epidural analgesia could be due more to unsupportive maternity care than pain relief requirements (Walsh 2009). More recently, an epidemiological study that compared various forms of pharmacological pain relief with non-pharmacological methods again emphasised the risk of epidural in light of their findings that epidural analgesia was associated with a sevenfold increase in instrumental birth, as well as increasing the likelihood of the baby being admitted to a special care nursery (Adams et al. 2015, p. 460). From this perspective, epidural analgesia is not so much a 'human right' and 'rescuer of women in pain' as a potentially unnecessary intervention: one that is not well-explained, does not always alleviate women's 'suffering' in labour, and might actually decrease women's joy in the birth process. It suggests that with good information and support, women can make informed decisions regarding labour analgesia and that this may advantage both women and babies.

Conclusion

In this critical perspective of epidural analgesia, we have explored the ways in which medical, scientific, and technological knowledge and standards have influenced Western birth practices, with both collusion and resistance by women. We hope to have provided a greater understanding of the social context of birth and the ways in which dominant ideas, including those on pain relief, are perpetuated. In reviewing the history of science and medicine from the seventeenth century onwards we have identified that biomedical science, far from being the epitome of objective fact-finding, is based in pre-conceived ideas about the world: separation, mechanism, technorationalism, the role of medicine in 'fixing' women's bodies, that carry through to this day. The danger of 'evidence-based' scientific research, for all its usefulness in certain areas, is that it does not acknowledge its own philosophical premises. Therefore, mainstream or dominant ideologies are renegotiated and propounded in a matter-of-fact approach that perpetuates a universal reality. Most women in labour will have been exposed to dominant ideologies about women's bodies, birth, pain, and epidural analgesia, much of it subtle and inadvertent. Epidural analgesia has been promoted as safe, efficacious, even necessary, by the biomedical literature, even while demarcating its potential negative side-effects. In fact, epidural analgesia has been constructed as a labouring women's panacea.

Notes

1. Technically an anaesthetic, in that they entail anaesthetic drugs and are administered by anaesthetists; the terms 'epidural analgesia' and 'epidural anaesthesia' are often used interchangeably. Usually, it is the purpose of the drug that denotes whether it is described as analgesia (pain relief) or anaesthesia (surgical anaesthetic), and it is for this reason that we use the term analgesia throughout this book, as we are primarily interested in the use of epidural as an analgesic agent.
2. What we mean by the term 'routine' is that epidural analgesia is readily available in most hospital labour wards; that is, its use is not restricted or limited.
3. Although this was written almost 20 years ago, as a physiological event, birth could remain fairly unchanged, arguments about increasing maternal age or obesity notwithstanding.
4. By 'intuition' Descartes did not mean 'either perception or imagination', but 'the clear vision of the intellect': that is, reason (Lindsay 1937, p. xiv).

5. Translated in this volume as 'I am thinking, therefore I exist'.
6. Lindsay (1937, p. xiii) sees the cause of this dualism as the discord between Descartes' search for reason and his absolute faith in God: a dichotomy that resulted in the contemplation of 'two entirely disparate worlds'.
7. Martin (1989) also cites Laqueur here.
8. Although menstruation may have been thought of as unclean and impure, it was still considered a normal physiological process (Martin 1989, p. 31).
9. Women were intensely involved in primary production before industrialisation, including farming, textiles, gardening, and food production (Miles 1989, pp. 154–155; Rich 1986, pp. 44–50).
10. See Odent (1999) and Buckley (2015) for a further examination of hormonal interplay of labour and birth. Interestingly, Martin wrote in 1989 and still these are not being realised in many hospital labour wards.
11. Ehrenreich and English (1979, p. 34) cite a petition by doctors to the English Parliament 'asking the imposition of fines and "long imprisonment" on any woman who attempted to "use the practyse of Fisyk [medicine]"'.
12. Reading original source material (cited in secondary sources) is particularly eye opening in its misogynist detail. For example, the authors of *The Malleus Maleficarum* also state: 'What else is a woman but a foe to friendship, an unescapable punishment, a necessary evil, a natural temptation, a desirable calamity, a domestic danger, a delectable detriment, an evil of nature, painted with fair colours!' (Kramer and Sprenger, in Chauhan 2005, p. 2). How can we focus clearly on current issues for midwifery and birthing women if this history, and its impact on birth knowledge and practice, is not acknowledged?
13. The 2011 edition contains a new finding—increased risk of caesarean section for foetal distress—although there is still no significant increased risk for caesarean section overall. Of the 38 studies included in the review, 33 compared epidural with opiates.
14. Little is known about the subtle hormonal interplays that occur in the mother–newborn dyad, in part because this has not been a priority in medical research (evidenced by its non-appearance in the biomedical literature). However, the research that is being done suggests that these hormonal responses are essential for the wellbeing of human beings, and of society in general (Odent 1999; Uvnäs-Moberg 2003). It is imperative, therefore, that those working in the area of maternity care are aware of, and can support these processes where possible.

15. Many of the studies on epidural analgesia are undertaken by anaesthetists and compare either the analgesic properties and effects on motor block of various combinations of medications to be used in epidurals or compare epidural with parenteral opioids. The plethora of studies concerning anaesthetic intricacies of epidural medications and dosages are beyond the scope of our review.
16. For example, Leap and Anderson (2008, p. 41) give examples of the 'purpose of pain' in labour, which include that it: marks the occasion, summons support, heightens joy, is a transition to motherhood, reinforces triumph, and triggers neurohormonal cascades.

References

Adams, J., Frawley, J., Steel, A., Broom, A., & Sibbritt, D. (2015). Use of pharmacological and non-pharmacological labour pain management techniques and their relationship to maternal and infant birth outcomes: Examination of a nationally representative sample of 1835 pregnant women. *Midwifery, 31*(4), 458–463.

Alfirevic, Z., Devane, D., Gyte, G. M. L., & Cuthbert, A. (2017). Continuous Cardiotocography (CTG) as a form of Electronic Fetal Monitoring (EFM) for fetal assessment during labour. *Cochrane Database of Systematic Reviews* (2), Art. No: CD006066. doi: https://doi.org/10.1002/14651858.CD006066.pub3.

Amedee Peret, F. (2013). *Pain management for women in labour: An overview of systematic reviews.* Updated RHL commentary (last revised: 1 March 2013). Geneva: World Health Organization. Viewed 27 Sept 2015.

Anim-Somuah, M., Smyth, R., & Howell, C. (2011). Epidural versus non-epidural or no analgesia in labour. *Cochrane Database of Systematic Reviews* (12), Art. No: CD000331. doi: https://doi.org/10.1002/14651858.CD000331.pub3.

Anscombe, E., & Geach, P. (Eds.). (1964). *Descartes: Philosophical writings.* London: Nelson.

Arney, W. R. (1982). *Power and the profession of obstetrics.* Chicago: The University of Chicago Press.

Australian Institute of Health and Welfare (AIHW). (2016). *Australia's mothers and babies 2014 – in brief* (Perinatal statistics series No. 32. Cat No. PER 87). Canberra: AIHW.

Baer, H., Singer, M., & Susser, I. (1997). *Medical anthropology and the world system: A critical perspective*. London: Bergin/Harvey.

Baker, S., Choi, P., Henshaw, C., & Tree, J. (2005). 'I felt as though I'd been in jail': Women's experiences of maternity care during labour, delivery and the immediate postpartum. *Feminism & Psychology, 15*(3), 315–342.

Banks, A. C. (1999). *Birth chairs, midwives, and medicine*. Jackson: University Press of Mississippi.

Barclay, L. (2008). A feminist history of Australian midwifery from colonisation until the 1980s. *Women and Birth, 21*(1), 3–8.

Bartky, S. (1997). Foucault, femininity, and the modernization of patriarchal power. In K. Conboy, N. Medina, & S. Stanbury (Eds.), *Writing on the body: Female embodiment and feminist theory*. New York: Colombia University Press.

Benoit, C., Zadoroznyj, M., Hallgrimsdottir, H., Treloar, A., & Taylor, K. (2010). Medical dominance and neoliberalisation in maternal care provisions: The evidence from Canada and Australia. *Social Science and Medicine, 71*, 475–481.

Blackwell, T., & Seabrook, J. (1993). *The revolt against change: Towards a conserving radicalism*. London: Vintage.

Bohren, M. A., Hofmeyr, G. J., Sakala, C., Fukuzawa, R. K., & Cuthbert, A. (2017). Continuous support for women during childbirth. *Cochrane Database of Systematic Reviews* (7), Art. No: CD003766. doi: https://doi.org/10.1002/14651858.CD003766.pub6.

Brown, S., & Lumley, J. (1998). Maternal health after childbirth: Results of an Australian population based survey. *BJOG: An International Journal of Obstetrics & Gynaecology, 105*(2), 156–161.

Buckley, S. (2015). *Hormonal physiology of childbearing: Evidence and implications for women, babies, and maternity care*. Washington, DC: Childbirth Connection. http://www.childbirthconnection.org/. Viewed Dec 2017.

Campo, M. (2014). *Delivering hegemony: Contemporary childbirth discourses and obstetric hegemony in Australia*. PhD thesis, School of Social Sciences and Communications, La Trobe University.

Chadwick, R. J., & Foster, D. (2014). Negotiating risky bodies: Childbirth and constructions of risk. *Health, Risk & Society, 16*(1), 68–83.

Chauhan, R. (2005). *"…And he shall rule over thee" the malleus maleficarum and the politics of misogyny, medicine, and midwifery (1484–Present): A feminist historical inquiry*. Master's thesis, Department of Criminology, Simon Fraser University.

Cluett, E. R., & Burns, E. (2009). Immersion in water in labour and birth. *Cochrane Database of Systematic Reviews* (2). Art. No: CD000111. doi: https://doi.org/10.1002/14651858.CD000111.pub3.

Cohen, S. (1999). Labor epidural analgesia: Back to the dark ages or a potential win-win situation? *International Journal of Obstetric Anesthesia, 8,* 223–225.

Collier, C. (2001). *Enjoy your childbirth: The epidural option.* Sydney: Law Placings.

Commonwealth of Australia. (2008). *Improving maternity services in Australia: A discussion paper from the Australian government.* Canberra. ISBN: 1-74186-833-5, Online ISBN: 1-74186-834-3, Publications Number: P3-4946.

Cooper, G., MacArthur, C., Wilson, M., Moore, P., & Shennan, A. (2010). Satisfaction, control and pain relief: Short- and long-term assessments in a randomised controlled trial of low-dose and traditional epidurals and a non-epidural comparison group. *International Journal of Obstetric Anesthesia, 19,* 31–37.

Creedy, D. K., Shochet, I. M., & Horsfall, J. (2000). Childbirth and the development of acute trauma symptoms: Incidence and contributing factors. *Birth, 27*(2), 104–111.

Crowhurst, J., & Plaat, F. (2000). Labor analgesia for the twenty-first century. *Seminars in Anesthesia, Perioperative Medicine and Pain, 19*(3), 164–170.

Cwikel, J. (2008). Lessons from Semmelweis: A social epidemiologic update on safe motherhood. *Social Medicine, 3*(1), 19–35.

Davies, R. (2008). *'She did what she could...' childbirth and midwifery practice in Queensland 1859–1912.* Coopers Plains: Book Pal.

Davis-Floyd, R. (2008). Foreword. In S. Downe (Ed.), *Normal childbirth: Evidence and debate* (2nd ed., pp. ix–xiv). Sydney: Elsevier.

Declercq, E. R., Sakala, C., Corry, M. P., Applebaum, S., & Herrlich, A. (2013). *Listening to mothers III: Pregnancy and birth.* New York: Childbirth Connection.

Department of Health NSW. (2010). *Maternity – Towards normal birth in NSW* (Cat. No. PD2010_045). Sydney.

Dietsch, E., Davies, C., Shackleton, P., Alston, M., & McLeod, M. (2008). *'Luckily we had a torch': Contemporary birthing experiences of women living in rural and remote NSW.* New South Wales: Charles Sturt University. http://bahsl.com.au/old/pdf/birthing-in-rural-remote-NSW.pdf. Viewed Dec 2017.

Donellan-Fernandez, R. (2011). Having a baby in Australia: Women's business, risky business, or big business? *Outskirts Online Journal, 24.* http://www.outskirts.arts.uwa.edu.au/volumes/volume-24/donnellan-fernandez. Viewed Dec 2017.

Donnison, J. (1988). *Midwives and medical men: A history of the struggle for the control of childbirth*. London: Historical Publications.

Dove, S., & Muir-Cochrane, E. (2014). Being safe practitioners and safe mothers: A critical ethnography of continuity of care midwifery in Australia. *Midwifery, 30*(10), 1063–1072.

Downe, S. (Ed.). (2008). *Normal childbirth: Evidence and debate*. Sydney: Churchill Livingstone Elsevier.

Downe, S., & McCourt, C. (2008). From being to becoming: Reconstructing childbirth knowledges. In S. Downe (Ed.), *Normal childbirth: Evidence and debate* (2nd ed., pp. 3–27). Sydney: Elsevier.

Drysdale, S., & Muir, H. (2002). New techniques and drugs for epidural labor analgesia. *Seminars in Perinatology, 26*(2), 99–108.

Dunn, P. (2002). Sir James Young Simpson (1811–1870) and obstetric anaesthesia. *Archives of Disease in Childhood. Fetal and Neonatal Edition, 86*, F207–F209.

Ehrenreich, B., & English, D. (1973). *Witches, midwives and nurses: A history of women healers*. New York: The Feminist Press.

Ehrenreich, B., & English, D. (1979). *For her own good: 150 years of the experts' advice to women*. London: Pluto Press.

Fahy, K., Foureur, M., & Hastie, C. (Eds.). (2008). *Birth territory and midwifery guardianship: Theory for practice, education and research*. Sydney: Elsevier.

Finster, M., & Santos, A. (1998). The effects of epidural analgesia on the course and outcome of labour. *Baillière's Clinical Obstetrics and Gynaecology, 12*(3), 473–483.

Foucault, M. (1980). Two lectures. In C. Gordon (Ed.), *Power/knowledge: Selected interviews and other writings 1972–1977 by Michel Foucault* (pp. 78–108). London: Harvester Wheatsheaf.

Foucault, M. (2003 [1963]). *The birth of the clinic*. London: Routledge.

Foucault, M. (2007 [1961]). *Madness and civilization: A history of insanity in the age of reason*. London: Routledge Classics.

Foucault, M. (2008 [1976]). *The history of sexuality* (Vol. 1). Melbourne: Penguin Books.

Foureur, M. (2008). Creating birth space to enable undisturbed birth. In K. Fahy, M. Foureur, & C. Hastie (Eds.), *Birth territory and midwifery guardianship: Theory for practice, education and research* (pp. 57–77). Sydney: Elsevier.

Gaiser, R. (2005). Labor epidurals and outcome. *Best Practice & Research. Clinical Anaesthesiology, 19*(1), 1–16.

Gamble, J., & Vernon, B. (2007). Midwifery in Australia: Emerging from the shadows. In L. Reid (Ed.), *Midwifery: Freedom to practise? An international exploration of midwifery practice*. Sydney: Elsevier.

Gélis, J. (1991). *History of childbirth: Fertility, pregnancy and birth in early modern Europe*. Oxford: Polity Press.

Gordon, C. (Ed.). (1980). *Power/knowledge: Selected interviews and other writings 1972–1977 by Michel Foucault*. London: Harvester Wheatsheaf.

Grimshaw, J. (1986). *Feminist philosophers*. Brighton: Wheatsheaf.

Hannah, M. E., Hannah, W. J., Hewson, S. A., Hodnett, E. D., Saigal, S., Willan, A. R., & Collaborative, T. B. T. (2000). Planned caesarean section versus planned vaginal birth for breech presentation at term: A randomised multicentre trial. *The Lancet, 356*(9239), 1375–1383.

Hayman, R. (2005). Instrumental vaginal delivery. *Current Obstetrics and Gynaecology, 15*, 87–96.

Heinze, S., & Sleigh, M. (2003). Epidural or no epidural anaesthesia: Relationships between beliefs about childbirth and pain control choices. *Journal of Reproductive and Infant Psychology, 21*(4), 323–333.

Hemminki, E., & Gissler, M. (1996). Epidural analgesia as a risk factor for operative delivery. *International Journal of Gynecology & Obstetrics, 53*, 125–132.

Hilder, L., Zhichao, Z., Parker, M., Jahan, S., & Chambers, G. (2014). *Australia's mothers and babies 2012*. Canberra: Australian Institute of Health and Welfare.

Hill, S. (1988). *The tragedy of technology*. London: Pluto Press.

Hodnett, E. (2002). Pain and women's satisfaction with the experience of childbirth: A systematic review. *American Journal of Obstetrics and Gynecology, 186*(5 Suppl 1), S160–S172.

Högberg, U. (2004). The decline in maternal mortality in Sweden: The role of community midwifery. *The American Journal of Public Health, 94*(8), 1312–1320.

Howell, C., & Chalmers, I. (1992). A review of prospectively controlled comparisons of epidural with non-epidural forms of pain relief during labour. *International Journal of Obstetric Anesthesia, 1*(2), 93–110.

Human Rights in Childbirth. (2015). http://www.humanrightsinchildbirth.org/. Viewed Dec 2017.

Humphrey, M., Bonello, M., Chughtai, A., Macaldowie, A., Harris, K., & Chambers, G. (2015). *Maternal deaths in Australia 2008–2012*. Canberra: Australian Institute of Health and Welfare.

Illich, I. (1977). *Limits to medicine. Medical nemesis: The expropriation of health*. Ringwood: Penguin Books.

Jain, S., Arya, V., Gopalan, S., & Jain, V. (2003). Analgesic efficacy of intramuscular opioids versus epidural analgesia in labor. *International Journal of Gynaecology and Obstetrics, 83*, 19–27.

Johnson, K. (1997). Randomized controlled trials as authoritative knowledge: Keeping an ally from becoming a threat to North American midwifery practice. In R. Davis-Floyd & C. Sargent (Eds.), *Childbirth and authoritative knowledge: Cross-cultural perspectives*. Berkeley: University of California Press.

Johnson, S., Bonello, M., Li, Z., Hilder, L., & Sullivan, E. (2014). *Maternal deaths in Australia 2006–2010*. Canberra: AIHW.

Jordan, S., Emery, S., Watkins, A., Evans, J., Storey, M., & Morgan, G. (2009). Associations of drugs routinely given in labour with breastfeeding at 48 hours: Analysis of the Cardiff Births Survey. *BJOG, 116*, 1622–1632.

Kannan, S., Jamison, R. N., & Datta, S. (2001). Maternal satisfaction and pain control in women electing natural childbirth. *Regional Anesthesia and Pain Medicine, 26*(5), 468–472.

Keirse, M. (2002). Evidence-based childbirth only for breech babies? *Birth, 29*(1), 55–59.

Kendall-Tackett, K., Cong, Z., & Hale, T. W. (2015). Birth interventions related to lower rates of exclusive breastfeeding and increased risk of postpartum depression in a large sample. *Clinical Lactation, 6*(3), 87–97.

Kitzinger, S. (2005). *The politics of birth*. Sydney: Elsevier.

Klein, M. (2011). Epidural analgesia for pain management: The positive and the negative. In S. Donna (Ed.), *Promoting normal birth: Research, reflections & guidelines*. Chester-le-Street: Fresh Heart Publishing.

Kotaska, A. (2004). Inappropriate use of randomised trials to evaluate complex phenomena: Case study of vaginal breech delivery. *British Medical Journal, 329*, 1039–1042.

Kotaska, A., Klein, M., & Liston, R. (2006). Epidural analgesia associated with low-dose oxytocin augmentation increases cesarean births: A critical look at the external validity of randomized trials. *American Journal of Obstetrics and Gynecology, 194*, 809–814.

Koyré, A. (1964). Introduction. In E. Anscombe & P. Geach (Eds.), *Descartes: Philosophical writings*. London: Nelson.

Lain, S., Ford, J., Hadfield, R., Blyth, F., Giles, W., & Roberts, C. (2008). Trends in the use of epidural analgesia in Australia. *International Journal of Gynecology & Obstetrics, 102*, 253–258.

Laqueur, T. (1990). *Making sex: Body and gender from the Greeks to Freud*. Cambridge, MA: Harvard University Press.

Leap, N., & Anderson, T. (2008). The role of pain in normal birth and the empowerment of women. In S. Downe (Ed.), *Normal childbirth: Evidence and debate* (pp. 29–46). Sydney: Elsevier.

Lieberman, E., & O'Donoghue, C. (2002). Unintended effects of epidural analgesia during labor: A systematic review. *American Journal of Obstetrics & Gynecology, 186*(5 Suppl Nature), S31–S68.

Lindsay, A. (1937). Introduction. In E. Rhys (Ed.), *A discourse on method, etc. [1637]*. London: J.M Dent & Sons Limited.

Lundgren, I., & Dahlberg, I. (1998). Women's experience of pain during childbirth. *Midwifery, 14*, 105–110.

Maher, J. (2002). Visibly pregnant: Toward a placental body. *Feminist Review, 72*, 95–107.

Mander, R. (1998a). *Pain in childbearing and its control*. Oxford: Blackwell Science Ltd.

Mander, R. (1998b). Analgesia and anaesthesia in childbirth: Obscurantism and obfuscation. *Journal of Advanced Nursing, 28*(1), 86–93.

Marcuse, H. (1972). *One dimensional man*. London: Abacus.

Marshall, H. (1996). Our bodies ourselves: Why we should add old fashioned empirical phenomenology to the new theories of the body. *Women's Studies International Forum, 19*(3), 253–253.

Martin, E. (1989). *The woman in the body*. Milton Keynes: Open University Press.

Merchant, C. (1980). *The death of nature: Women, ecology and the scientific revolution*. New York: HarperOne.

Miles, R. (1989). *The women's history of the world*. Topsfield: Salem House.

Morsy, S. (1996). Political economy in medical anthropology. In C. F. Sargent & T. M. Johnson (Eds.), *Medical anthropology: Contemporary theory and method* (Rev. ed., pp. 21–40). London: Praeger.

Murphy-Lawless, J. (1998). *Reading birth and death: A history of obstetric thinking*. Cork: Cork University Press.

National Rural Health Alliance. (2012). *Rural maternity services: Investing in the future*. Deakin West: National Rural Health Alliance. http://ruralhealth.org.au/. Viewed Dec 2017.

Newnham, E. C. (2010). Midwifery directions: The Australian maternity services review. *Health Sociology Review, 19*(2), 245–259.

Newnham, E. C. (2014). Birth control: Power/knowledge in the politics of birth. *Health Sociology Review, 23*(3), 254–268.

Newnham, E., McKellar, L., & Pincombe, J. (2016). A critical literature review of epidural analgesia. *Evidence Based Midwifery, 14*(1), 22–28. Copyright permission obtained from the Royal College of Midwives.

Norman, B. (2002). Natural childbirth is inappropriate in a modern world. *International Journal of Obstetric Anesthesia, 11*(1), 28–30.

Nystedt, A., Edvardsson, D., & Willman, A. (2004). Epidural analgesia for pain relief in labour and childbirth – A review with a systematic approach. *Women and Children, 13*, 455–466.

Oakley, A. (1984). *The captured womb: A history of the medical care of pregnant women*. New York: Basil Blackwell Inc.

Odent, M. (1999). *The scientification of love*. London: Free Association Books.

Rådestad, I., Olsson, A., Nissen, E., & Rubertsson, C. (2008). Tears in the vagina, perineum, sphincter ani, and rectum and first sexual intercourse after childbirth: A nationwide follow-up. *Birth, 35*(2), 98–106.

Rahm, V., Hallgren, A., Hogberg, H., Hurtig, I., & Odlind, V. (2002). Plasma oxytocin levels in women during labor with or without epidural analgesia: A prospective study. *Acta Obstetricia et Gynecologica Scandinavica, 81*, 1033–1039.

Ramin, S., Gambling, D., Lucas, M., Sharma, S., Sidawi, J., & Leveno, K. (1995). Randomized trial of epidural versus intravenous analgesia during labor. *Obstetrics and Gynecology, 86*(5), 783–789.

Reiger, K., & Dempsey, R. (2006). Performing birth in a culture of fear: An embodied crisis of late modernity. *Health Sociology Review, 15*(4), 364–373.

Rich, A. (1986). *Of woman born: Motherhood as experience and institution [1976]*. New York: W.W. Norton & Company.

Romano, A., & Lothian, J. (2008). Promoting, protecting, and supporting normal birth: A look at the evidence. *Journal of Obstetric, Gynecologic & Neonatal Nursing, 35*(2), 94–105.

Roome, S., Hartz, D., Tracy, S., & Welsh, A. W. (2015). Why such differing stances? A review of position statements on home birth from professional colleges. *BJOG: An International Journal of Obstetrics & Gynaecology, 123*(3), 376–382.

Ros, A., Felberbaum, R., Jahnke, I., Diedrich, K., Schmucker, P., & Huppe, M. (2007). Epidural anaesthesia for labour: Does it influence the mode of delivery? *Archives of Gynecology and Obstetrics, 275*, 269–274.

Rothman, B. K. (1982). *In labor: Women and power in the birthplace*. London: W.W Norton & Company.

Rothman, B. K. (1989). *Recreating motherhood: Ideology and technology in a patriarchal society*. New York: W.W. Norton & Company.

Scamell, M., & Stewart, M. (2014). Time, risk and midwife practice: The vaginal examination. *Health, Risk & Society, 16*(1), 84–100.

Sharma, S., McIntire, D., Wiley, J., & Leveno, K. (2004). Labor analgesia and cesarean delivery: An individual patient meta-analysis of nulliparous women. *Anesthesiology, 100*, 142–148.

Singer, M., & Baer, H. (1995). *Critical medical anthropology.* New York: Bayswood Publishing Company.

Steen, M., & Kingdon, C. (2008). Vaginal or caesarean delivery? How research has turned breech birth around. *Evidence Based Midwifery, 6*(3), 95–99.

Stratmann, L. (2003). *Chloroform: The quest for oblivion.* Stroud: Sutton Publishing.

Summers, A. (1995). *'For I have ever so much faith in her as a nurse': The eclipse of the community midwife in South Australia.* PhD thesis, School of Nursing and Midwifery, Flinders University of South Australia.

Thorp, J. A., Parisi, V. M., Boylan, P. C., & Johnston, D. A. (1989). The effect of continuous epidural analgesia on cesarean section for dystocia in nulliparous women. *American Journal of Obstetrics and Gynecology, 161*(3), 670–675.

Toledo, P., McCarthy, R., Ebarvia, M., & Wong, C. (2009). A retrospective case-controlled study of the association between request to discontinue second stage labor epidural analgesia and risk of instrumental delivery. *International Journal of Obstetric Anesthesia, 17*, 304–308.

Towler, J., & Bramall, J. (1986). *Midwives in history and society.* London: Croon Helm.

Tracy, S., Sullivan, E., Wang, Y., Black, D., & Tracy, M. (2007). Birth outcomes associated with interventions in labour amongst low risk women: A population-based study. *Women and Birth, 20*(2), 41–48.

Uvnäs-Moberg, K. (2003). *The oxytocin factor.* Cambridge, MA: Da Capo Press.

Uvnäs-Moberg, K. (2016). Keynote address 'the oxytocin factor'. In *Normal Labour and Birth Conference,* University of Central Lancashire/Australian College of Midwives, Sydney.

Van der Gucht, N., & Lewis, K. (2015). Women's experiences of coping with pain during childbirth: A critical review of qualitative research. *Midwifery, 31*(3), 349–358.

Wagner, M. (2001). Fish can't see water: The need to humanize birth. *International Journal of Gynaecology and Obstetrics, 75*(Suppl 1), S25–S37.

Waitzkin, H. (1983). *The second sickness: Contradictions of capitalist health care.* London: The Free Press.

Wajcman, J. (1991). *Feminism confronts technology.* Cambridge: Polity Press.

Waldenström, U., Hildingsson, I., Rubertsson, C., & Rådestad, I. (2004). A negative birth experience: Prevalence and risk factors in a national sample. *Birth, 31*(1), 17–27.

Walsh, D. (2009). Pain and epidural use in normal childbirth. *Evidence Based Midwifery, 7*(3), 89–93.

Walsh, D. (2012). *Evidence and skills for normal birth.* London: Routledge.

Walsh, D., El-Nemer, A., & Downe, S. (2008). Rethinking risk and safety in maternity care. In S. Downe (Ed.), *Normal childbirth: Evidence and debate* (2nd ed.). Sydney: Elsevier.

Wang, F., Shen, X., Guo, X., Peng, Y., & Gu, X. (2009). Epidural analgesia in the latent phase of labor and the risk of cesarean delivery. *Anesthesiology, 111,* 871–880.

Wendland, C. (2007). The vanishing mother: Cesarean section and "evidence-based obstetrics". *Medical Anthropology Quarterly, 21*(2), 218–233.

Wertz, R. W., & Wertz, D. C. (1989). *Lying in: A history of childbirth in America* (2nd ed.). New Haven: Yale University Press.

WHO. (1996). *Care in normal birth.* Geneva: World Health Organisation.

WHO. (2015). *WHO statement on Caesarean section rates.* Geneva: World Health Organization. http://apps.who.int/iris/bitstream/10665/161442/1/WHO_RHR_15.02_eng.pdf?ua=1. Viewed Dec 2017.

Wiklund, I., Norman, M., Uvnäs-Moberg, K., Ransjo-Arvidson, A. B., & Andolf, E. (2009). Epidural analgesia: Breast-feeding success and related factors. *Midwifery, 25*(2), e31–e38.

Willis, E. (1989). *Medical dominance* (2nd ed.). Sydney: Allen and Unwin.

3

The Politics of Birth

BELLA
I waited an hour and then I went in,
and they had a look and said
'Its only 3cm dilated.'
And I thought 'Oh my god!'
And they said 'Normally it's one hour per cm.'
And I thought 'No way do I have it in me to do another 7 hours!'
So they sent me home to have a rest.
'Here's couple of Panadeine'
And I went 'Yeah right that doesn't help'.

When I was at the hospital it sort of stopped
So I went home and it just got really intense.
I had a shower, tried to have a rest but it didn't really work—
By about 12.30 I just thought
'I can't do this anymore!'
So I rang them back and said I wanted drugs.
I didn't think I could make another 7 hours.
I knew it would have to get worse before it got better,
I didn't think I could do any worse
I was sort of a bit buggered
So I went back in asked for an epidural.

They examined me and they said '7cm'
And I was like 'Oh 7cm in a few hours!'
That was manageable
And I said 'I would really like an epidural though'
And she said 'Well let's try the gas just in the meantime.'
I tried the gas.
It didn't do anything for me.
I think I was past that point.
It didn't do anything for the contractions at all.
My waters hadn't broken and they said 'You might not actually be 7cm'
And again I thought 'I can't do—
I don't want to do any worse with the pain.'

So I had the epidural,
Which was lovely.
So I sat in bed as happy as
And felt really guilty that I wasn't doing anything.
That was about 2.30.
My waters broke and I went back to 5cm.
It was just stretched because the waters hadn't broken.
So I was glad I had the epidural then,
Because I know the pain would have got worse.
It was about 6 o'clock, they started
Injecting the drug to make my contractions stronger,
And then they were pretty much back to back,
And the epidural wasn't working
It was just very intense pain.
They were just on top of each other
And I was getting the pressure but I wasn't getting pressure to push.
It was still only 7cm
So I wasn't progressing,
And then—I don't know what time it was
Maybe it was like the change of shift.
The new midwife came in
And that's when she thought she felt the cord.

So then they had to get the doctor,
And the registrar.
So waiting on that.
So they examined,

And said
That it was brow presented.
And basically I was in the theatre
And had the baby by 10 o'clock in the morning.

I was vomiting with the pain.
It was pretty intense
As soon as they said 'caesarean', everything just went—
You know they turned that drug off
And everything went extremely smoothly
And extremely quickly
And then she was out.
At no point was she ever distressed
And that was my main priority
So that's why—
They sort of said 'We can hang for another couple of hours
And see if she moves'
And I just said 'No.'
But I fully understand that it really wasn't a choice,
It was more—this is what has to happen.
I was more than happy to do that because I just wanted her out safely.
I thought 'There is no way I would have done that with no drugs'
Because I couldn't even do it with drugs.

CMA, Foucault, and Feminism in Midwifery Research

CMA draws on the political economy and social health literature and seeks to reveal and address underlying social conditions that affect inequalities in health (Winkelman 2009, p. 311). Using a political economy of health framework, such as CMA, is apposite because midwifery is intrinsically associated with public health outcomes (Högberg 2004, p. 5; WHO 2009), providing a primary health care service to increase the wellbeing of childbearing women and their babies—an acknowledged starting point for the wellbeing of society in general.[1] As a profession, midwifery acknowledges its commitment to health outcomes for women and children (*International Confederation of Midwives*; WHO 2015).

Midwifery is therefore an inherently political profession, with an emancipatory mandate, and is actively involved in the politics of normalising birth (*Australian College of Midwives* 2015). Midwifery, as a discipline, is consequently well placed to examine and document the power dynamics of birth. Most pertinently, midwifery has had a millennia-long relationship with birthing women, and a more recent confrontational and oppressed relationship with medicine (Donnison 1988; Ehrenreich and English 1973; Murphy-Lawless 1998; Towler and Bramall 1986; Willis, E 1989).[2] CMA, which also has emancipation as its primary concern, is therefore an appropriate vehicle for midwifery research.

We use the lens of CMA—the consideration of economic, political, and ideological contexts—with specific reference to the historical co-location of science and medicine as producers of powerful ideological discourse and their influence on the consequent medical interpretations of women's bodies and childbirth. CMA analysis requires an examination of the wider influences of political-economic structures on dominant systems of thought. Although CMA holds firm to a political economy (or Marxist/post-Marxist) approach, Singer and Baer (1995, pp. 59–60) identify that the discipline draws on multifaceted interpretations of political-economic theory. CMA recognises Marx's initial work on historical materialism and class, which identified that social progress is neither arbitrary nor preordained but is shaped by economic forces of production and the resulting relations of production (Marx and Engels 2002). It also employs Gramsci's (1971) theory of hegemony, which noted the subtleties of power exerted by social institutions and ideology. CMA, in its use of hegemonic theory, is therefore not strictly wedded to class analysis; gender, race, sexuality, and other disparities and hierarchies of power are equally of interest (Singer and Baer 1995, p. 273).

CMA also acknowledges Foucault's idea that dominant social norms can be contested (Singer and Baer 1995, pp. 60, 123) and his enormous contribution to theorising power and subjectivity. There is obvious tension in linking the two theories: CMA is essentially focused on structural power relations and the role of ideology in maintaining the ideas of the ruling class, while Foucault identifies power as diffuse rather than located only in the obvious governing apparatuses and as a potentially productive—not just oppressive—force (Foucault 1980). Although Foucault

(1970, p. xiv) essentially rejects structural theories of power, his theories are not necessarily incompatible with the more refined post-Marxist interpretations of how power is reproduced through discourse and hegemony (Kincheloe and McLaren 2005; Purvis and Hunt 1993).

From this perspective—of identifying and challenging the systems of power that surround birth—we also draw on feminist theory to provide an accompanying perspective on how science and medicine have constructed women's bodies in a particular way, and how power is made visible by considering how women's bodies are treated and understood. There is a tension between feminism and Foucault; his lack of acknowledgement of gender and attention to power structures, as well as his deconstruction of a unified truth, appeared to contradict feminism's core agenda of emancipation of women from patriarchal oppression. His thinking has nevertheless been extremely useful to feminist scholars, and Foucauldian ideas of surveillance and the body, discourse, pluralism, and mechanisms of contestation and resistance have been taken up in feminist analyses (see McLaren 2012; McNay 2013; Ramazanoglu 1993; Sawicki 1991). We acknowledge the above tensions, but, with others, find a synergy between Foucauldian and feminist analysis; primarily, the feminist accounts of science and medicine that can be used to highlight obstetric discourse and demonstrate the relativity of medicalised birth practices. We therefore employ feminist scholarship that demarcates historical and political influences on the construction of scientific knowledge, in particular as it pertains to women's bodies and birth. The feminist literature draws together our use of CMA and Foucault; correlating to CMA by providing critical analysis of the hegemonic influence of science on women, and to Foucault by providing a historical lens through which this influence can be acknowledged in the present. We now turn to explaining the intricacies of each theory in more depth, with a focus firstly on CMA.

CMA: Biomedicine and the Political Economy of Health

According to Singer and Baer (1995), CMA is concerned with the depoliticising of health as well as the development of praxis. They state:

The ultimate goal of CMA is participation in the creation of a new social medicine oriented to fostering the conditions in and out of medicine that would accomplish "health for all." In other words, CMA seeks not only understanding but action. (Singer and Baer 1995, p. 74)

In particular, they note the 'inherent contradiction between medicine's expressed purpose and the organization and routine of medicine' (Singer and Baer 1995, p. 71). To this extent, much of the focus of this book in centred on power relationships both historical and contemporary, and how power is vested or relinquished by midwives, women, and the medical profession, and maintained or resisted within the auspices of the institution.

Medical Power

In CMA, medicine as a field is associated with capitalist economic growth, and is viewed in conjunction with other dominant systems, such as business and government, as therefore being appropriate for critical analysis (Waitzkin 1983, p. 7). According to the political economy of health perspective, advances in science and medicine have been influenced by capitalist forces and ideals, in a kind of feedback mechanism in which the systems that support the capitalist economy are also supported (Singer and Baer 1995). Rather than being an objective discipline located somehow outside of culture, medicine is viewed as a powerful social structure, one that mirrors—even upholds—the society within which it sits (Waitzkin 1983, p. 48). It is maintained by, and simultaneously perpetuates, the ideology that supports its legitimacy over other systems. This legitimacy gives medicine a status of being almost beyond scrutiny, an unquestioned and benign element of our society (Singer and Baer 1995, p. 61). Its position of power is not necessarily recognised outside of critical analysis and the discourse it generates is seen as common sense or neutral, rather than representing specific interests (Waitzkin 1983).

However, when subject to critical analysis, biomedicine, by virtue of its authority to: place the cause of diseases within individuals, rather than in social inequalities; medicalise social or environmental problems; enforce behavioural norms; and determine 'authentic' illness from malingering, has been identified as a strong mechanism of social order and control (Baer et al. 1997; Singer and Baer 1995; Waitzkin 1983). The focus of biomedicine has primarily been on curative measures, rather than prevention, and its values have been identified as being in parallel with a capitalist rationale, that is, an emphasis on 'self-reliance, rugged individualism, independence, pragmatism, empiricism, atomism, militarism, profit-making, emotional minimalism, and a mechanistic concept of the body and its repair' (Baer et al. 1997, p. 11). Although there is some importance given to primary health care principles, partly driven by government requirements to reduce health care budgets, the use of these principles is often couched within individualist notions of personal responsibility—in keeping with neoliberal ideals—rather than effective social change, which could lead to closer scrutiny and condemnation of the capitalist economic system (see Baum 2008, Chap. 4).

Social Medicine: The Politics of Health

The biomedical emphasis on individualising and depoliticising illness has been criticised by those interested in the social origins of health and disease since at least the works of Friedrich Engels and Rudolf Virchow in the mid-nineteenth century. Early proponents of social medicine such as Virchow recognised the link between social and economic inequality and health. Written in 1845, Engels' (1968) *The Conditions of the Working Class in England* specifically identified the imbalance in health status between workers and their bosses, a concern readdressed by Marx and Engels (2002) in *The Communist Manifesto* in 1888. The link between health and politics could not be made clearer at this juncture. One example of the intricate relationship between capital, medicine, and social circumstance describes how doctors employed by mining companies in England failed to identify 'black lung' disease as being linked to coal mine dust (Waitzkin 1983). That doctors could provide a disability certificate to a miner with black lung disease may have eased the financial pressure for the individual miner (Waitzkin 1983, p. 41), but medicine's failure to address the underlying issue of coal dust and unsafe work environments, despite the evidence and its acknowledgement in popular culture, perpetuated this significant health problem for decades (Navarro 1986, p. 163). While practitioners may have been genuinely concerned for their patients, underlying problems were not addressed. This illustration of medicine supporting and upholding the capitalist economic structure is useful because it highlights the association between medicine and capitalism, the legitimisation of medical over lay knowledge, and accentuates the need to investigate and analyse at the structural level of biomedicine rather than the actions of the individual doctors (Waitzkin 1983, p. 8). A structural view of the 'black lung' phenomenon would recognise the following: that doctors and mine owners belonged to a different social class from the workers; that many doctors were under the employ of mine owners, and therefore working in their interests (while believing they were doing the right thing for their patients); that poverty and poor working conditions are causes of illness; and that mine owners, as producers of profit, would have a different outlook on miner's health than the miners themselves. Black lung is not a one-off scenario, and ongoing examples exist of illnesses being treated at an individual, rather than social, level, as well as being treated biologically rather than economically or politically (see Waitzkin 1983; Navarro 1986; see also Baum 2008, pp. 116–117; Porter 2006).

Not surprisingly, given that it essentially calls for a redistribution of capital, social medicine has not been overwhelmingly endorsed. It regained some currency in the West in the 1970s with the work of sociologists such as Irving Zola (1972) and Ivan Illich (1977) in their criticisms of biomedicine (Waitzkin 1983). A central concern of sociology at this time became the increasing medical control over life events, and their transformation into medical conditions; subsequently coined the 'medicalisation' of society (Illich 1977; Zola 1972). The construction of issues such as stress, obesity, impotence, alcoholism, drug addiction, eating disorders, birth, sexuality, and death as medical rather than social problems has increased the scope of power and control of the medical field, and on occasion has led to iatrogenic, or medically induced, illness (Baer et al. 1997; Freund and McGuire 1991). The account for medicalisation given by medical sociologists is that it provides a legitimising force for the ill-effects of the inequality created by capitalist forces of production, therefore shoring up the interests of the ruling class, but that even in so doing 'medicine is assigned the task of doing the impossible, of solving what is created outside its control' (Navarro 1986, p. 40). Intrinsically secured to the capitalist economy and other hegemonic ideologies, such as gender and race (Navarro 1986, p. 251), medicalisation also provides opportunities for research, professional advancement, and wealth creation. However, in aiming analysis at the structural level, as CMA does, it asserts that potential exploitation is not individualised; it is not a primary intention of doctors. Rather, it recognises that 'the nature of capitalism reinforces current deficiencies of health care' (Waitzkin 1983, p. 7) and that medicine is located within a capitalist economic worldview that influences its understanding of disease.

Illness as the Disruption of Social Order

One of the central claims of CMA is that biomedicine acts as an agent of social control because of its role in the regulation, legitimation, and control of disease. While biological causes for illness exist, the gatekeeping, portrayal, and ideology of illness is seen as socially constructed. Illness is potentially disruptive of the social order—through illness, people gain alternate perspectives, their worldview is changed, and they may question previous assumptions about personal identity and ethics and challenge commonly held social values (Singer and Baer 1995, pp. 82–83). In this way, it has the potential to challenge the status quo and the power relationships held in place by hegemonic social institutions.

We suggest that birth also does exactly this. If birth lies at the nexus of body as subject and the organising techniques of the state (Foucault 1990; Papps and Olssen 1997, p. 114),[3] reclaiming birth could potentially disrupt neoliberal ideology, de-emphasising the individual and emphasising the connectedness between woman and child, between women and midwives, between men and women. Perhaps, it could also emphasise the connectedness between humanity and our environment in a way that would preclude the unchecked economic growth of capitalism. Indeed, it has been suggested that the politics of midwifery and sustainability share common principles, and that midwives are also well placed to promote ecologically sustainable practices to new parents

(Davies et al. 2010). Connectivity, as well as incriminating environmental destruction and halting capitalism on that score, also carries notions of collectivism. If we are all connected, then how can we oppress each other, take from each other, exploit each other? If the spectre of collectivism appears, it is only one more step to arrive at a more socially—and economically—just politics: a subversive ideal indeed in a capitalist political economy.

In addition, birth is a powerful act. Not only does the act of giving birth give women dominion over the forces of life and associated knowledge [e.g., of paternity claims, of procuring abortion, of declaring babies as born living or still (Towler and Bramall 1986)], the absolute physical power exerted by a woman giving birth is also unique and represents a distinctive physiological, emotional, and sexual energy that is not represented or equalled in men. In this vein, we propose that giving birth—arguably the most empowering and life-giving act that a human being can accomplish—was seen as a significant threat to the patriarchal order (see Rich 1986).

Science and Technology

Challenges to biomedicine, such as the medicalisation debate, raised important questions about the increasing role of medicine in everyday life. However, subsequent criticisms of this debate identified the lack of subtlety in casting biomedicine as overly monolithic or omnipotent, and introduced notions of stronger agency and control from the perspective of the consumer (Lupton 1997). Individuals may use or ignore the medical system, choose between practitioners, or use alternative health practices. Rather than being passive recipients, women can seek out practitioners, technologies, and services that best serve their needs (Lock 2001). Some women have complete faith in technology and benefit from the sense of control over the process of birth that technology can bring (Akrich and Pasveer 2004; Davis-Floyd 1994). However, women's full-scale embrace of medical technologies does not inevitably suggest that their best interests are being served. Dominant ideologies promote the interests of specific groups as if they were the interests of society in general

(Purvis and Hunt 1993) while maintaining social norms in which outlying behaviour is discouraged. The equation of safety with the medicalised birth process can therefore be a cultural rather than solely personal viewpoint.

From the perspective of CMA, technology is both complex and disingenuous. Although clear that technology should indeed be used in specific circumstances, Waitzkin (1983, pp. 5–6) identifies the dialectic of profit versus safety in the development of technology, whereby profitable technology is introduced without appropriate trialling.[4] Also concerning is the presence of expensive high-end technology for those with means, while cheaper, useful technology is still not available to those who cannot afford it (Waitzkin 1983, p. 39). This is particularly conspicuous when comparing the health of developed versus developing nations; one feature of social medicine has been to address ill-health in developing countries by looking at determinants of health such as gender inequity and poverty (Porter 2006). Implementing primary health care principles, for example, employing and promoting midwifery care, rather than exporting expensive obstetric technologies, is also a concern of social medicine (Johanson et al. 2002; United Nations Population Fund 2014; Wagner 2001).

There is an ideological element to our love affair with technology: 'Technologic medicine, grounded in the complexities of scientific technique, carries symbolic trappings of effectiveness' (Waitzkin 1983, p. 33). The use of technology fits with a worldview that valorises rationality and science. Primary health care (or low-intervention) practices may therefore not be given the attention, funding, or merit they deserve, as they can be perceived as overly simplistic (Waitzkin 1983). Technology's place in society is intricate, offering both a solace and a challenge. A discussion of the complexity of technological influence now follows.

Technology and the Technorationalist Society

The history of technological development in the West has a convoluted trajectory, with multiple influences which include industrial capitalism, a patriarchal social order, and patterns of scientific discovery. Rothman (1989, p. 28) claims that the ideology of technology encourages us to see ourselves as objects, to see people as made up of machines and part of larger machines. It is this mechanization that connects the ideology of patriarchy with capitalism, to create the hegemony, the world view.

According to Hill (1988), despite the commonly held belief that it was scientific discovery that drove technological development, industry actually held far more influence. Capital was required in order to introduce patents and manufacture prototypes (Wajcman 1991); therefore technological advance was largely influenced by the needs of the owners of capital rather than being simply the abstract inventions, or discoveries, of scientists (Hill 1988). Critical scholars advise that scientific advancement was less about a particular pathway of discovery and more about the (economic) conditions which allowed and supported those discoveries to be made (Navarro 1986). As Merchant (1980, p. 111) notes, 'increasingly... [the manipulation of nature] benefited those persons and social classes in control of its development, rather than promoting universal progress for all'. Foucault goes a step further in his study of discourse and focuses only on those 'conditions of existence' that led to particular modes of thought and practice to occur (Foucault 1991, p. 68). By doing this, he emphasises the importance of acknowledging the social conditions that contribute to forming practice, also acknowledging that part of these 'conditions' were those people for whom those ideas and practices served (Foucault 1980, 1991). His was an important contribution to the dialogue surrounding knowledge production, as much of what constitutes Western knowledge assumes science and technology to be value-neutral (Navarro 1986, p. 161). For example, Sandelowski (2002, p. 110) has asserted that

> among the reasons for paying insufficient attention to the material world [in qualitative research] is the still prevalent but naïve view that objects, especially technological objects, are themselves inanimate and neutral entities that exert no force by themselves in interaction with human users.

One of the fundamental principles of CMA, therefore, is to question the position of technology.

There is an association between scientific discourse (with its history of mechanistic thinking) and technological advancement, which has led to a central tenet of Western philosophy known as technorationalism. Just as machine imagery captured the industrial social imagination as metaphors for order and control in a rapidly changing world (Merchant 1980), so now do new technologies in the post-industrial world. The technorationalist society—including most, if not all, developed nations, with many developing nations following suit—holds particular values and pursuits in esteem, including the equation of scientific advances with 'progress' (Walsh 2009); the 'technological imperative' (McCoyd 2010); pain avoidance (Walsh 2009); a focus on the prevention of an abstract risk rather than avoiding a specific danger (Castel 1991); implied effectiveness of technological intervention (Waitzkin 1983); and an esteemed position of the 'complex' over the 'mundane' (Waitzkin 1983, p. 33). While this is not the extent of the meanings and norms of technorationalism, these ideas will be examined here. Furthermore, the idea of 'technocratic birth' (Davis-Floyd 1994) will also be identified as a useful description of the technological imperative on the process of birth.

The Technological Imperative

There is no denying the usefulness of particular technologies. However, it is crucial that technologies are weighed, measured, and examined as to their necessity, utility, and purpose before they are circulated into general use. More frequently, technologies are not critically examined in this way. Rather, once technology exists, people feel compelled to use it: this is the 'technological imperative', a term coined by Fuchs in 1968 to describe the snowballing effect of technology (Barger-Lux and Heaney 1986, p. 1314). As new technologies are created, the simple fact of their existence implies that they need to be used. The use of this existing new technology then paves the way for newer technologies, which in turn need to be employed (McCoyd 2010; Wajcman 1991). Discussing the technological imperative in the health care system, Barger-Lux and Heaney (1986, p. 1314) identify that:

If science does not deal with the personal, subjective, 'value' questions—does not because it cannot—it is little wonder that what *can* be done in terms of health care technology is a good deal clearer than what *should* be done. That is to say, the possible technical manipulations are more clearly defined than are their effects on human persons and their relationships to human values: what human beings hold to be important.

This is particularly relevant to birth—where the physiological, emotional, and psychological aspects of human connection are particularly heightened and vulnerable to disruption by medical technologies. The possible unintentional effects of intervention on physiology are evident in the recent research into the fragile nature of the human microbiome (Harman and Wakeford 2014). This new knowledge describes the complex and symbiotic process of the mother 'seeding' the infant's microbiome with good bacteria, setting up the child with a robust underlying health foundation that reaches into adulthood. Perhaps more important than the results of these new discoveries themselves, is the way they demonstrate how little we actually know about these subtle relationships, whether they be bacterial, hormonal, emotional, or epigenetic. The more we introduce—technologically speaking—the more we could be influencing future generations in ways we cannot currently conceptualise. The technological imperative is a clear influence on scientific professions such as medicine. Intrinsic to advancing professional practice, as well as professional status and prestige, medical practitioners feel this imperative to keep up with technological advances.

The use of technology *per se* is, of course, understandable, and not necessarily problematic. However, it becomes a dilemma when obstetric technologies are advanced without being adequately assessed (see Waitzkin 1983), as has been the case historically with the introduction of analgesics, ultrasound, routine EFM, and other such practices. The dilemma lies in the fact that *once the technology is there, there is an accompanying imperative to use it*. Thus, changes in practice can occur due to this technological imperative, rather than an underlying need for practice change and without a thorough assessment of the changes as they occur, a circumstance that has been dubbed the 'in case' syndrome (Williams 1997, p. 236). The technological imperative agenda is almost certainly influenced by the constant potential of litigation, as 'having done everything possible is a strong defense against malpractice...irrespective of the underlying reality' (Barger-Lux and Heaney 1986, p. 1315; see also Dove and Muir-Cochrane 2014, p. 1068). It is interesting that the 'evidence-based practice' model, though primarily disseminating mainstream ideas based on technocratic principles, could provide a way out of the technological imperative predicament in obstetrics as more research promoting non-interventionist techniques is published.

Equally, the imperative that because we *can* use it, we *should* use it, has led to increasing decision-making dilemmas for women. As more and more new technologies are offered, for example, pregnancy screening techniques, women then feel a moral imperative to use them, even if they are uncertain, as accessing screening conforms to medical and societal norms of responsible motherhood (McCoyd 2010). As Wendland (2007, p. 225) observes, the constant offer of surveillance can impose moral dilemmas on women:

> safety and consumer ideology interpenetrate with the veneration of technology, the institution, and patriarchy in such a way that they become located in the hospital and embodied in the doctor, whose tools and technological expertise become the safe fetal space to be purchased by expectant mothers...How can a conscientious pregnant consumer justify buying anything less?

This is despite the fact that screening tests are sometimes unreliable, increasingly invasive, and potentially confusing for women to interpret (McCoyd 2010) and health professionals may doubt their own proficiency in technology use (Sinclair and Gardner 2001). The disadvantages of technology are not commonly discussed and consequently there is a generalised social bias *towards* the use of technology, whether or not its use will actually be of benefit.

It can also be the case that clients themselves request the most up-to-date or recent technological intervention, despite misgivings by health care practitioners, who may be more aware of what is still unknown about a particular procedure or why its use might be detrimental (Lock 2001). Doctors then also feel the force of societal veneration of technology, and find themselves having to dissuade clients from unnecessary tests or technologies. This is in part due to social expectation of a technological 'fix', a belief in the absolute healing potential of medical science, and a correlation between the amount of technology used and the perceived standard of care (Barger-Lux and Heaney 1986). Similarly, some women approach birth with a desire for all of the 'trappings of effectiveness' (Waitzkin 1983, p. 33) of obstetric medicine, even though in reality the 'hospital equals safe' equation has also been—at least to some extent—based on discourses of power, rather than fact (Campo 2010; Foucault 2003; Murphy-Lawless 1998).

Technology in Birth

Women's awareness of their bodies in relation to birthing is formed within this technorationalist culture, influencing knowledge, beliefs, and practices (Davis-Floyd 1994). Some women resist—often turning to holistic discourses of connectedness with their babies and trust in their bodies in order to do so. However, apprehension and fear about birth itself, together with fragmented models of care, the pathologising of pregnancy and a belief in the biomedical ability to control the unpredictable nature of birth can lead to women placing their complete trust in the medical model (Campo 2014; Davis-Floyd 1994; Lazarus 1988). The language of modern society, of technology, frames the way in which we understand the world (Hill 1988). Obstetric language, implicitly and explicitly frames what is known about birth, which is then internalised and recognised as the current status quo or 'common sense' knowledge about birth. This is despite the growing alarm from other quarters that over-intervention in birth is leading to increasingly iatrogenic consequences (Davis-Floyd 2008; Johanson et al. 2002; Odent 2013; Wagner 2001; Walsh 2012).

However, the word 'technology' does not just refer to artefacts or machines: it also refers to knowledge, and a related set of practices (Wajcman 1991, p. 14). Technology is 'a cultural product which is historically constituted' (Wajcman 1991, p. 158). Midwifery practice could be thought of as a 'technology' of sorts, incorporating as it does specific knowledge and practice different than those of medical birth technologies;

the difference being that midwifery technologies were denigrated and superseded by a scientifically oriented medical profession and remain devalued (Donnison 1988; Ehrenreich and English 1973; Murphy-Lawless 1998; Towler and Bramall 1986). Midwifery practices such as robozo (use of a sling to turn a posterior baby); the characteristic 'watching and waiting' rather than interfering in labour; of perceiving a woman's embodied knowledge as a vital part of the birth process, all form part of the 'subjugated knowledge' of midwifery (Foucault 1980, pp. 83–84; Newnham 2014).

Midwifery technology is relegated to the realms of the unimportant (or, more problematically, framed as 'dangerous') by the medical mainstream not only because of the historical gender and professional influences but also because of industrialisation and increasing social reliance on, and faith in, technology. Health care practices that are simple and inexpensive have not been afforded the same status in a capitalist economic system that values progress and growth. These practices are soon replaced (often to the detriment of those who need them) by those attracting technology and profit; a practice described from a political economy of health perspective as the replacement of the 'mundane' with the 'complex' (Waitzkin 1983, p. 33).[5] The problem that this causes for health care in general, and for midwifery in particular, is that as economic resources are poured into more technological intervention, less are available for human resources, which provide a necessary, indeed crucial, aspect of health care provision (Barger-Lux and Heaney 1986).

It was the valuing of complex technology over mundane practice that gave obstetrics the inroad into midwifery practice initially. The introduction of forceps (around 1730s in Europe), a technology that enabled doctors to extract living babies from the birth canal during difficult births, gave them an advantage over midwives, despite the fact that forceps were overused and often caused unnecessary harm, even death, of either mother or child or both (Murphy-Lawless 1998, p. 97; Willis 1989, pp. 113, 121). Prior to this, a doctor's presence at a birth essentially already heralded a disastrous birth—either the baby had died, and needed to be extracted piece by piece, or the mother had died and the baby needed to be rescued by caesarean (Murphy-Lawless 1998, pp. 93–100).[6] It was midwives who otherwise primarily presided over the birth process.

Evidently, between the dichotomous 'birth technologies' of medicine and midwifery, those practices that conformed to not only a capitalist economy (science and technology) but also norms of gender and professional dominance (medicine over midwifery) were maintained. Identification with technology and intervention also shaped obstetric practice to view pregnancy and birth as pathological and inherently risky; a perspective that has had ongoing effects on the knowledge and practice of birth. The complex, certainly in institutions, succeeded over the mundane.

Problematically—and noted by midwives from the time of their introduction—medical technologies can interfere with the process of 'being present' to the labour process; that commitment to women's embodied experience that midwifery philosophy upholds (Leap 2000).[7] A focus on the ultrasound image, or the cardiotocograph (CTG) printout, takes attention away from the human embodied interaction, which involves all the senses, and focuses it on the visual and disembodied *representation* of the body (Sandelowski 2002). A brief comparison of medical versus midwifery technologies will be useful here to illustrate our point. It has been shown that continuous support during labour decreases operative birth rates and women's need for analgesia (Bohren et al. 2017). This practice relies on the traditional midwifery technology of providing physical and emotional labour support and contributes to a shared embodied experience, rather than relying on the 'complex' practice of, for example, administering an epidural block.

Some women and midwives expect and put their faith in the use of technology (Sinclair 2011; Sinclair and Gardner 2001), and in some cases it is both useful and necessary. However, absolute reliance on medical technologies establishes the indirect surveillance of disembodied processes that neglects the historic embodied relationship between the woman and midwife (Barger-Lux and Heaney 1986; Sandelowski 1998). For example, cEFM now excuses the midwife from being in the room, which not only creates an alienating experience for the woman but means that the midwife interacts with the technology rather than the woman herself. The use of medical technology such as cEFM has other flow-on effects (Alfirevic et al. 2017) and yet is instigated in obstetric-led units without regard for the contrasting research that endorses midwifery technologies such as continuous labour support. Knowledge and practice that support the normal process of birth and women's embodied experiences are typically not supported by the medical profession within the current Western birth system. The positioning of obstetrics with 'technology' provides access to dominant technorational norms of science and safety, which not only elevates its status but allows it to perpetuate practices that are not evidence based, or that ignore the positive impact of 'mundane' midwifery technologies.

Davis-Floyd (1994), in a landmark anthropological paper in the field of birthing, identified the role of technology in birth using the thesis of the 'one-two punch' by Peter Reynolds. In basic terms, it is argued that technological society interferes with nature (uncontrollable circumstance) in an attempt to improve it. This is 'punch one'. It then artificially recreates the environment or process (controllable circumstance) that it has just removed. This is 'punch two'. Using the example of caesarean section, Fenwick (2009) has added 'punch three' whereby society dismisses the substitution of 'punch two' as an unintentional consequence of the modern world, or as a necessary compromise for progress. The 'punch three' thesis thus reflects the technological determinist view that progress will simply roll over us all, indiscriminately, and that the 'punch two' substitutes are somehow free from influence. However, as Fenwick argues, there are vested interests at stake. For example, in describing an obstetric article promoting 'natural' caesarean techniques, she notes:

> While none of us would deny that there is a real need to make the experience of birth better for women having a caesarean what is so confronting is that the language and images used to describe vaginal birth (which has been consistently labelled as dangerous and an insignificant event in a woman's life) are being so unashamedly 'spun' together to 'sell' caesarean section. These medical men, who have regularly denigrated natural birth whilst portraying caesarean as the only safe option, have manipulated the powerful positive images of the female birthing body to serve their own agendas. What is perhaps more abhorrent is that they lay claim to these and make them their own. There is little doubt that these authors and clinicians are indeed reframing surgical birth as the natural solution. (Fenwick 2009)

Fenwick's argument is even more poignant when viewed from the context of Davis-Floyd's original article, where she argued:

> To technocratize a natural process is to create it in the image we have chosen as the guiding metaphor for our own evolution, and thus to confirm that evolutionary path as the right one. (Davis-Floyd 1994, p. 1138)

This brings us back to the first point of this section—that the representation of women's bodies is influenced by the scientific and medical discourse. As Fenwick (2009) addresses quite clearly, the adoption of language that is usually ignored in medical terminology, of the power and beauty of birth, to support the argument for the 'natural' caesarean is clear co-optation to serve the purpose of representing this practice as a 'common sense' option. It is negotiating caesarean section as a natural progression of the human reproductive process. However, it is worth noting that with caesarean rates increasing across the globe and more knowledge about the risks of this procedure, the obstetric profession itself is now attempting to reduce caesarean section rates (see ACOG 2017). The identification of science, particularly the human sciences, as a producer of social discourse was a recurring theme in Foucault's work. We now turn to a discussion of Foucauldian concepts of power, and the aspects of Foucauldian theory that are relevant to the arguments raised in this book.

Foucault and Power

While our use of CMA means that we do accept a notion of structural power analysis, there are three aspects of Foucauldian theory that we will be using in this book, as they offer the possibility of a more nuanced analysis: first is the part that midwives themselves play in negotiating the obstetric model, or how power is reproduced in practice (the localised effects of power); second is the idea of bio-power (the effects of power on the body) including surveillance and self-surveillance; and third is how 'truth' is fashioned by obstetric discourse (how birth is represented by obstetric power/knowledge). Although Foucault (1980) describes power as circulatory, and as operating horizontally (rather than vertically as in structural power analyses), he does concede that power is nevertheless vested in certain sectors of society, and that this influences how things occur. The point of distinction for Foucault (1980, p. 98) is that power is also located in the body:

The individual is an effect of power, and at the same time, or precisely to the extent to which it is that effect, it is the element of its articulation. The individual which power has constituted is at the same time its vehicle.

If individuals are *vehicles of power*, Foucault argues, then social analysis cannot occur just by looking at powerful social structures and conducting a descending analysis of power. Foucault recommends an ascending analysis that begins with identifying the practices and techniques of individuals, and continues by judging which of those practices and techniques have proved the most useful to those in power, and why (Foucault 1980, pp. 99, 101). Therefore, according to his own analyses, the ruling classes were not concerned with the mad, the criminal, or the deviant as such—they were interested in the systems which led to the confinement of the mad; the punishment of the criminal; the control of the deviant—in other words, they were interested in mechanisms, or 'techniques' of power (Foucault 1980, pp. 101–102) and it is these mechanisms of power, and how they become useful to the powerful, rather than the powerful themselves, that need to be described. He says:

> It is the mechanisms of that exclusion that are necessary, the apparatuses of surveillance, the medicalisation of sexuality, of madness, of delinquency, all the micro-mechanisms of power, that came, from a certain moment in time, to represent the interests of the bourgeoisie…it reflects the fact that it was not the bourgeoisie itself which thought that madness had to be excluded or infantile sexuality repressed. What in fact happened instead was that the mechanisms of the exclusion of madness, and of the surveillance of infantile sexuality, began from a particular point in time, and for reasons which need to be studied, to reveal their political usefulness and to lend themselves to economic profit, and that as a natural consequence, all of a sudden, they came to be colonised and maintained by global mechanisms and the entire State system. It is only if we grasp these techniques of power and demonstrate the economic advantages or political utility that derives from them in a given context for specific reasons, that we can understand how these mechanisms come to be effectively incorporated into the social whole. (Foucault 1980, p. 101)

There are three other points of methodological difference outlined by Foucault (1980) that are relevant to our argument. First is a focus on localised, rather than central manifestations of power; how techniques of power are exhibited within institutions and played out in the interactions of individuals. Second, power should not be analysed in terms of personal aim in the minds of those who wield it. The question of purpose or intent is therefore redundant and the focus instead is on the effects of power at the interface where the object and the subject of power meet, on the effects of power at the level of the material world, specifically, the effects of power on the body (bio-power). Third, is the recognition that the production of power 'is both much more and much less than ideology' (Foucault 1980, p. 102), by which he means that while ideology accompanies power, power constitutes itself according to a much more subtle recipe of gathering and storing knowledge, one which cannot therefore be purely ideological. From this last point follows Foucault's description of discourses (or what Foucault termed 'power/knowledge'): formations of practice that, given particular social and historical 'conditions of existence' come to define what is known, and therefore what is played out in the social world. Discourses shape social understanding and practice by imposing boundaries on what can be articulated and by whom, by deciding which knowledge is to be kept and which excluded, and by circulating certain statements and censoring others (Foucault 1991). Or, as has been remarked upon by Hall (1997, p. 259), in producing regimes of power/knowledge, discourses shape our understanding and practice by their particular *representation* of social phenomenon. Utilising Foucauldian theory and CMA, we provide an alternate reading of common representations of epidural text. We now turn to the feminist literature to discuss the effects of power on women's bodies.

Bringing in Feminism: The Construction of Women's Bodies

'Patriarchy' as a term may be out of favour in current social theory, especially after the feminist backlash and the advent of postmodern discourses (Budgeon 2011). However, Rich's (1986, pp. xiii–xiv) observation that 'patriarchy is a useful concept…we are not in danger of losing our grasp on patriarchy as a major form of domination parallel and interconnected to race and class' is still relevant. It is in this vein that we use the term patriarchy; as a useful concept, as shorthand for a historical gender pattern that, though changing, has strong roots. Certainly, in terms of men having power over women's bodies (see Rich 1986), patriarchy is still in effect in Western, 'scientific' birthing practices.[8] Indeed, Rich suggests,

> There is nothing revolutionary whatsoever about the control of women's bodies by men. The woman's body is the terrain on which patriarchy is erected. (Rich 1986, p. 55)

Anthropologist Robbie Davis-Floyd (1994, p. 1125) made the astute observation that the way a particular society regards 'the body' provides a window into dominant cultural belief systems; by examining the rituals that surround the treatment of bodies, cultural norms and beliefs are revealed. When current medical birthing rituals are examined in an anthropological manner, what appears are a series of rituals that simultaneously disempower, mistrust, and control women and their bodies.

Many authors have described this influence of biomedicine on birth (Arney 1982; Davis-Floyd 1992, 1994; Donnison 1988; Murphy-Lawless 1998; Oakley 1984; Papps and Olssen 1997; Tew 1990; Towler and Bramall 1986; Willis, E 1989). Specifically, biomedical birth ideology is based on Cartesian dualism (mind/body split); places risk management over individual choice; emphasises pain avoidance; operates from a mechanistic, curative perspective; and esteems birth pathology over the physiological, social, sexual, and psychological aspects of birth. What is significant about such medical representations of birth is that they influence societal knowledge from which women then make their decisions regarding birth. Medicalisation of childbirth has led to a situation where women are not only potentially limited in the choices they make but are unaware that these limitations even exist, so interwoven are they within the social customs of Western birth ideology and subsequent policy and practice (see Newnham 2010).

With respect to the medicalisation of birth, the increasing normalisation of intervention has also been critiqued (Davis-Floyd 2008; Rothman 1982; Wagner 2001). In addition, the significance of how the scientific paradigm, the capitalist economy, and industrialisation impact the way women's bodies have been constructed in mainstream discourses have also been examined (Davis-Floyd 1992, 1994; Rothman 1989; Kitzinger 1992; Martin 1989; Oakley 1984).

Feminism and the Birthing Mother

Feminism's position regarding birth has not been straightforward. Second-wave feminism, in particular, with its goal of equal rights for women, had a difficult relationship with concepts of birth and motherhood. Early second-wave feminism wanted to distance itself from the shackles of reproduction and the biological determinism that motherhood represented (see Chanter 2006; Davis and Walker 2010, p. 3). The problem then confronted by feminism was how to approach motherhood, given the dilemma of wanting to distance itself from its obligation. These feminist arguments for reproductive choice addressed many important issues for women, including access to quality child care, contraception, and abortion. They essentially represent a freedom from the necessity of motherhood, and by doing so, the possibility of equality—particularly with respect to employment, financial reward, and status—in a patriarchal system. However, it has been argued that second-wave feminism was essentially fighting for women's access into a male world, rather than equality for women, on women's terms (Marshall, H 1996, p. 254). Feminists such as Adrienne Rich began to criticise the medicalised process of birth (Stone 2007). In *Of Woman Born*, Rich (1986 [1976]) draws heavily on her own experience of bearing three children, while at the same time politicising the medicalisation of women's pregnant, birthing, and mothering bodies. She identifies the male desire for control over women's childbearing capability as their need for 'power-over' the creative life forces of women, which she terms the 'power-to' (Rich 1986; Stone 2007, p. 169). With this, the concept of male 'control over' the birth process took root.

The following quote by Rothman sets out the dilemma of fighting for women's equality while recognising women's reproductive difference:

> Liberal feminism works best to defend women's rights to be like men, to enter into men's worlds, to work at men's jobs for men's pay, to have the rights and privileges of men. But what of our rights to be *women?* Pregnancy is distinctive – equal rights does not acknowledge this, or treats pregnancy like a disability. There is actually nothing else like it. (Rothman 1989, p. 248)

Women's health and consumer movements began to address the power imbalance between women and the predominantly male medical profession, providing a counter-discourse to patriarchal medicine, and motivating changes in practice, policy, and legislation (Reiger 2006; Rich 1986, p. xi). Radical feminist debates were the first to identify the political nature of birth, acknowledging the unique reproductive ability of the female body and claiming female traits as empowering (Stone 2007). However, radical feminist discourse can be complicated by ideas of biological essentialism and the tendency for arguments based on innate characteristics of sex to backfire, so despite the temptation to triumphantly claim the 'feminine', it has distinct disadvantages (Gatens 1991, pp. 79–84). Later feminist enquiry that focused on the nature of gender *identity*, rather than *biology*, was also criticised for its essentialist elements and its attempt to provide a unified female experience, thereby denying the simultaneous experiences of race, class, ability, and sexuality, amongst other things.

However, gender binary/fluidity issues aside, the female body does have fundamental differences to the male, if nothing else because of its ability to bear and nourish children (Davis and Walker 2010). Accompanying this are further complexities in relation to how women's position in society has been perceived and how male norms have influenced even our basic understanding of the social world. Rothman (1989) identifies the ambiguities and contradictions of motherhood within a society bound by technology, patriarchy, and capitalism and based on ideals of individualism, within which the liminal nature of the two-in-one body, the interconnectedness between mother and unborn child, cannot comfortably co-exist. More recently, in a discussion about how neoliberal emphasis on individualism, agency, choice, control, and consumerism influences the way women perceive their bodies, Tyler (2011, p. 30) points to the 'fundamental incompatibility of maternity and neoliberalism',[9] reinforcing Rothman's point and highlighting the fact that the relationship between feminism, motherhood, and notions of the individual within contemporary society is still uneasy.

Third-wave feminism emerged from the aforementioned problematic of feminist analysis, recognising the ongoing necessity of a feminist social critique of the diverse influences on women's experience that reflect the globalising, technological, economic, political, sexual, and environmental discourses of late modernity (Budgeon 2011). While they agree that 'women', as an identity group with singular characteristics does not exist, it is acknowledged that these discourses still shape how a woman will experience herself and the world around her, strongly influenced by a flourishing visual, media-heavy culture (Budgeon 2011). Third-wave feminism, positioned precariously between second-wave feminism and the backlash of postfeminist discourse, thus acknowledges the ambiguities, tensions, and contradictions of the female experience, without attempting to reduce this to a homogeneous form: 'third-wave feminism seeks to work with a proliferation of feminine subjectivities and multiplying forms of feminist affiliation' (Budgeon 2011, p. 282). Third-wave feminism is a postmodern critique in that it does not sit comfortably with ideas of structural oppression or binary definitions but identifies with the subjectivity of women's difference (Budgeon 2011; Davis and Walker 2010; Grosz 1994). This emphasis on political self-definition fits loosely with Foucauldian ideas of the 'technology of the self'. While these postmodern/post-structural theories can be viewed as perhaps contradictory to CMA, we propose that a structural focus is still necessary to acknowledge the unequal power relationships that exist in institutions, where resistance is more easily constrained and it is harder to maintain a politics of self-styled empowerment.[10] A final discussion of this triangulation of theory—CMA, Foucault, and feminism—proceeds below.

Merging the Theory

Our intention in bringing elements of Foucauldian and feminist theory into our analysis is to sharpen its focus, enabling an investigation of the nuances of power in order to examine more purposefully the way in which biomedicine has shaped our understanding of birth and how this has carried across to present-day practices and beliefs. CMA attempts to move the attention of analysis away from the phenomenology that accompanied more traditional medical anthropology (the 'sufferer experience') to identify how this sufferer experience is shaped by social and political forces. It links these two levels of analysis by examining the individual micro-experience within the context of the macro-structures that influence political and social life (Singer and Baer 1995).

It is argued that the link between micro-culture and macro-structure has often been left out of analyses (Singer and Baer 1995; Willis, E 2006). Our intention in using the specific combination of theory identified here, as well as recognising the institution as an analytical bridge between macro and micro factors is to acknowledge that link (see Lazarus 1988, p. 47; Singer and Baer 1995, p. 63; Willis, E 2006, p. 429). Therefore, both micro-experiential and macro-structural issues are considered through the CMA lens. However, we also draw on the subtler post-structuralist concerns, explicated above, of perpetuated discourses and their surveillance and discipline of the body. We reiterate that this is commensurate with CMA methodology, which recognises the subtle ways in which hegemonic discourses, or 'webs of significance' (Weber and Geertz, in Singer and Baer 1995, p. 82) maintain power through language, symbolism, and meaning, rather than using overt mechanisms of power or control. This latter point is pivotal because obstetric practices are currently based primarily on biomedical hegemonic discourse that privileges technology and 'complex practices', while evidence that supports midwifery principles has not always been well-implemented (see Newnham 2014). Attention to the micro-sphere is therefore necessary to identify existing practices and experiences, while attention to the macro-sphere is important for unearthing the cultural beliefs and perspectives that perpetuate these practices and experiences. As Iris Young substantiates, 'macro structures depend on micro-level interactions for their production and reproduction, but their form and the ways they constrain and enable cannot be reduced to effects of particular interactions'. Identifying the structural processes and institutional practices that link the two are fundamental to the emancipatory goal of CMA analysis and central to this book.

Conclusion

In this chapter, we have outlined the theoretical perspectives which underpin the rest of the book. We primarily use a CMA approach, which provides a critical focus on the far-reaching influence of medical culture. The CMA lens also proffers a useful perspective on the role of technology within the neoliberal milieu of Western capitalism. In addition to CMA, which is a structuralist methodology, we also recognise the subtle techniques of power as documented by Foucault, and use a number of Foucauldian methodological devices. The impact of scientific culture on the knowledge and history of women's bodies is described utilising feminist perspectives. Our decision to employ these frameworks is to provide a more thorough analysis of culture and power that encompasses both micro-interaction and macro-structure and focuses on the influence of the institution.

Notes

1. Governments have utilised or prohibited the reproductive power of women and the services of midwives, according to needs such as population growth and military requirements, a fact which has been critiqued by feminists (see Rich 1986).
2. While this history has been examined in depth, and is oft-referred to—perhaps even viewed jadedly—it must not be forgotten. That is, although the midwifery and obstetric professions need to find a way to move forward together for the benefit of women, this power imbalance must be transparent in the process, lest it be recreated in a different way.
3. Foucault is primarily discussing sexuality in this text, but the argument he puts forward can also be made for birth as part of the sexual continuum. For example, he says 'at the juncture of the "body" and the "population", sex had become a crucial target of a power organized around the management of life rather than the menace of death' (Foucault 1990, p. 147).
4. In Marxist philosophy, the term 'dialectic' refers to the tension and eventual synthesis of two opposing ideas. As ideas are synthesised, new conflicts arise, leading again to struggle and unification of these dichotomies: 'the social contradictions that are at once creative and destructive' (Waitzkin 1983, p. 5).

5. Waitzkin's terminology could be misconstrued as the 'complex' human birth experience is replaced with the 'mundane' of a mechanical perspective. However, what is meant is that simple and effective practices are often overlooked, or hardly considered by biomedicine, in favour of expensive, machinery.
6. Although caesareans were not solely performed on women who had already died, the operation remained a last resort for many years due to its extremely high mortality rate (Murphy-Lawless 1998, pp. 93–100).
7. It is interesting to note that while medical technologies such as forceps were replacing midwifery practice, midwives such as Elizabeth Nihell, writing in 1760, were commenting on the superiority of midwifery technologies such as patience, labour knowledge and support, and birth facilitation skills, and advocating gentle rather than forceful techniques (Murphy-Lawless 1998, pp. 63, 97).
8. This is meant, as explained, as a historical reference to male influences on birth. It is not to insinuate that all practices are carried out by men. Childbirth is, however, an almost singular experience because it is experienced only by women (we note here the recent instances of transgender men becoming pregnant and giving birth, however maintain that birth has been, and remains, a gendered practice).
9. Late modernity in the West is characterised by those qualities advanced by the agenda of neoliberalism. Although the term neoliberalism has been understood and analysed in various ways, for the purposes of this book, we are referring to the particular values of 'the individual; freedom of choice; market security; laissez faire; and minimal government' (Larner 2000, p. 5). The qualities that are upheld and promoted by these core values now include the constant reinvention of self, amongst endless possibilities of choice and consumerism. There is an emphasis on the observation, reflection, and creation of selfhood as an end in itself (Budgeon 2011). For women, this also affects their self-view and perceptions of pregnancy, birth, and motherhood.
10. Budgeon (2011, p. 285) notes this ambiguity: 'maintaining a coherent empowerment narrative consisting of autonomy, individuality and personal choice requires a denial of the effects that external influences have on the realization of individual success' and observes the potential for 'empowerment' discourse to be co-opted into dominant patriarchal discourse.

References

Akrich, M., & Pasveer, B. (2004). Embodiment and disembodiment in childbirth narratives. *Body & Society, 10*(2–3), 63–84.

Alfirevic, Z., Devane, D., Gyte, G. M. L., & Cuthbert, A. (2017). Continuous Cardiotocography (CTG) as a form of Electronic Fetal Monitoring (EFM) for fetal assessment during labour. *Cochrane Database of Systematic Reviews* (2), Art. No: CD006066. https://doi.org/10.1002/14651858.CD006066.pub3.

American College of Obstetricians and Gynecologists (ACOG). (2017). *Approaches to limit intervention during labour and birth* (Committee opinion, No. 687). https://www.acog.org/Resources-And-Publications/Committee-Opinions/Committee-on-Obstetric-Practice/Approaches-to-Limit-Intervention-During-Labor-and-Birth. Viewed Dec 2017.

Arney, W. R. (1982). *Power and the profession of obstetrics*. Chicago: The University of Chicago Press.

Australian College of Midwives. (2015). Philosophy of midwifery. Viewed 7 Jan. http://www.midwives.org.au/scripts/cgiip.exe/WService=MIDW/ccms.r?PageID=10019. Viewed Dec 2017.

Baer, H., Singer, M., & Susser, I. (1997). *Medical anthropology and the world system: A critical perspective*. London: Bergin/Harvey.

Barger-Lux, M. J., & Heaney, R. P. (1986). For better and worse: The technological imperative in health care. *Social Science & Medicine, 22*(12), 1313–1320.

Baum, F. (2008). *The new public health* (3rd ed.). Oxford: Oxford University Press.

Bohren, M. A., Hofmeyr, G. J., Sakala, C., Fukuzawa, R. K., & Cuthbert, A. (2017). Continuous support for women during childbirth. *Cochrane Database of Systematic Reviews* (7), Art. No: CD003766. doi: https://doi.org/10.1002/14651858.CD003766.pub6.

Budgeon, S. (2011). The contradictions of successful femininity: Third-wave feminism, postfeminism and 'new' femininities. In R. Gill & C. Scharff (Eds.), *New femininities: Postfeminism, neoliberalism and subjectivity* (pp. 279–292). Basingstoke: Palgrave Macmillan.

Campo, M. (2010). Trust, power and agency in childbirth: Women's relationships with obstetricians. *Outskirts Online Journal, 22*. http://www.outskirts.arts.uwa.edu.au/volumes/volume-22/campo. Viewed Dec 2017.

Campo, M. (2014). *Delivering hegemony: Contemporary childbirth discourses and obstetric hegemony in Australia*. PhD thesis, School of Social Sciences and Communications, La Trobe University.

Castel, R. (1991). From dangerousness to risk. In G. Burchell, C. Gordon, & P. Miller (Eds.), *The Foucault effect: Studies in governmentality* (pp. 281–298). Chicago: University of Chicago Press.

Chanter, T. (2006). *Gender*. London: Continuum.

Davies, L., Daellenbach, R., & Kensington, M. (Eds.). (2010). *Sustainability, midwifery and birth*. London: Routledge.

Davis, D. L., & Walker, K. (2010). Re-discovering the material body in midwifery through an exploration of theories of embodiment. *Midwifery, 26*(4), 457–462.

Davis-Floyd, R. (1992). *Birth as an American rite of passage*. Berkeley/Los Angeles: University of California Press.

Davis-Floyd, R. (1994). The technocratic body: American childbirth as cultural expression. *Social Science and Medicine, 38*(8), 1125–1140.

Davis-Floyd, R. (2008). Foreword. In S. Downe (Ed.), *Normal childbirth: Evidence and debate* (2nd ed., pp. ix–xiv). Sydney: Elsevier.

Donnison, J. (1988). *Midwives and medical men: A history of the struggle for the control of childbirth*. London: Historical Publications.

Dove, S., & Muir-Cochrane, E. (2014). Being safe practitioners and safe mothers: A critical ethnography of continuity of care midwifery in Australia. *Midwifery, 30*(10), 1063–1072.

Ehrenreich, B., & English, D. (1973). *Witches, midwives and nurses: A history of women healers*. New York: The Feminist Press.

Engels, F. (1968). *The conditions of the working class in England [1845]*. Stanford: Stanford University Press.

Fenwick, J. (2009). Caesarean section: The ultimate by-product of the One Two Punch Theory. *Women and Birth, 22*, 107–108.

Foucault, M. (1970). *The order of things*. London: Tavistock Publications.

Foucault, M. (1980). Two lectures. In C. Gordon (Ed.), *Power/knowledge: Selected interviews and other writings 1972–1977 by Michel Foucault* (pp. 78–108). London: Harvester Wheatsheaf.

Foucault, M. (1990). *The history of sexuality* (Vol. 1). London: Penguin Books.

Foucault, M. (1991). Politics and the study of discourse. In G. Burchell, C. Gordon, & P. Miller (Eds.), *The Foucault effect: Studies in governmentality* (pp. 53–72). Chicago: Harvester Wheatsheaf.

Foucault, M. (2003 [1963]). *The birth of the clinic*. London: Routledge.

Freund, P., & McGuire, M. (1991). *Health, illness and the body: A critical sociology*. Englewood Cliffs: Prentice Hall.

Gatens, M. (1991). *Feminism and philosophy: Perspectives on difference and equality*. Oxford: Polity Press.

Gramsci, A. (1971). *Prison notebooks*. New York: Columbia University Press.
Grosz, E. (1994). *Volatile bodies: Toward a corporeal feminism*. New South Wales: Allen & Unwin, Crow's Nest.
Hall, S. (1997). The spectacle of the 'other'. In S. Hall (Ed.), *Representation: Cultural representations and signifying practices*. London: Sage.
Harman, T., & Wakeford, A. (dir.) (2014). *Microbirth*. Distrify Media.
Hill, S. (1988). *The tragedy of technology*. London: Pluto Press.
Högberg, U. (2004). The decline in maternal mortality in Sweden: The role of community midwifery. *The American Journal of Public Health, 94*(8), 1312–1320.
Illich, I. (1977). *Limits to medicine. Medical nemesis: The expropriation of health*. Ringwood: Penguin Books.
Johanson, R., Newburn, M., & Macfarlane, A. (2002). Has the medicalisation of childbirth gone too far? *British Medical Journal, 324*(7342), 892–895.
Kincheloe, J., & McLaren, P. (2005). Rethinking theory and research. In N. Denzin & Y. Lincoln (Eds.), *The Sage handbook of qualitative research* (pp. 303–342). Thousand Oaks: Sage Publications.
Kitzinger, S. (1992). *Ourselves as mothers*. Sydney: Bantam Books.
Larner, W. (2000). Neo-liberalism: Policy, ideology, governmentality. *Studies in Political Economy, 63*, 5–25.
Lazarus, E. (1988). Theoretical considerations for the study of the doctor-patient relationship: Implications of a perinatal study. *Medical Anthropology Quarterly, 2*(1), 34–58.
Leap, N. (2000). The less we do, the more we give. In M. Kirkham (Ed.), *The midwife-mother relationship* (pp. 1–18). New York: Palgrave Macmillan.
Lock, M. (2001). The tempering of medical anthropology: Troubling natural categories. *Medical Anthropology Quarterly, 15*(4), 478–492.
Lupton, D. (1997). Foucault and the medicalisation debate. In R. Bunton & A. Peterson (Eds.), *Foucault, health and medicine*. London: Routledge.
Marshall, H. (1996). Our bodies ourselves: Why we should add old fashioned empirical phenomenology to the new theories of the body. *Women's Studies International Forum, 19*(3), 253–253.
Martin, E. (1989). *The woman in the body*. Milton Keynes: Open University Press.
Marx, K., & Engels, F. (2002). *The manifesto of the Communist Party [1888]*. London: Penguin Classics.
McCoyd, J. (2010). Authoritative Knowledge: The technological imperative and women's responses to prenatal diagnostic technologies. *Culture, Medicine and Psychiatry, 34*(4), 590–614.

McLaren, M. A. (2012). *Feminism, Foucault, and embodied subjectivity*. Albany/New York: State University of New York Press.

McNay, L. (2013). *Foucault and feminism: Power, gender and the self*. Cambridge: Polity Press.

Merchant, C. (1980). *The death of nature: Women, ecology and the scientific revolution*. New York: HarperOne.

Murphy-Lawless, J. (1998). *Reading birth and death: A history of obstetric thinking*. Cork: Cork University Press.

Navarro, V. (1986). *Crisis, health and medicine: Social critique*. London: Tavistock Publications.

Newnham, E. C. (2010). Midwifery directions: The Australian maternity services review. *Health Sociology Review, 19*(2), 245–259.

Newnham, E. C. (2014). Birth control: Power/knowledge in the politics of birth. *Health Sociology Review, 23*(3), 254–268.

Oakley, A. (1984). *The captured womb: A history of the medical care of pregnant women*. New York: Basil Blackwell Inc.

Odent, M. (2013). *Childbirth and the future of homo sapiens*. London: Pinter & Martin.

Papps, E., & Olssen, M. (1997). *Doctoring childbirth and regulating midwifery in New Zealand: A Foucauldian perspective*. Palmerston North: The Dunmore Press.

Porter, D. (2006). How did social medicine evolve and where is it heading? *PLoS Medicine, 3*(10), e399.

Purvis, T., & Hunt, A. (1993). Discourse, ideology, discourse, ideology, discourse, ideology…. *The British Journal of Sociology, 44*(3), 473–499.

Ramazanoglu, C. (Ed.). (1993). *Up against Foucault: Explorations of some tensions between Foucault and feminism*. London: Routledge.

Reiger, K. (2006). A neoliberal quickstep: Contradictions in Australian maternity policy. *Health Sociology Review, 15*(4), 330–340.

Rich, A. (1986). *Of woman born: Motherhood as experience and institution [1976]*. New York: W.W. Norton & Company.

Rothman, B. K. (1982). *In labor: Women and power in the birthplace*. London: W.W Norton & Company.

Rothman, B. K. (1989). *Recreating motherhood: Ideology and technology in a patriarchal society*. New York: W.W. Norton & Company.

Sandelowski, M. (1998). Looking to care or caring to look? Technology and the rise of spectacular nursing. *Holistic Nursing Practice, 12*(4), 1–11.

Sandelowski, M. (2002). Reembodying qualitative inquiry. *Qualitative Health Research, 12*(1), 104–115.

Sawicki, J. (1991). *Disciplining Foucault: Feminism, power, and the body*. London: Routledge.

Sinclair, M. (2011). Use of technology in childbirth: The role of the midwife past, present and future. *The Practising Midwife, 14*(9), 34–37.

Sinclair, M., & Gardner, J. (2001). Midwives' perceptions of the use of technology in assisting childbirth in Northern Ireland. *Journal of Advanced Nursing, 36*(2), 229–236.

Singer, M., & Baer, H. (1995). *Critical medical anthropology*. New York: Bayswood Publishing Company.

Stone, A. (2007). *An introduction to feminist philosophy*. Cambridge: Polity.

Tew, M. (1990). *Safer childbirth: A critical history of maternity care*. Melbourne: Chapman and Hall.

Towler, J., & Bramall, J. (1986). *Midwives in history and society*. London: Croon Helm.

Tyler, I. (2011). *Pregnant beauty: Maternal femininities under neoliberalism* (pp. 21–36). Basingstoke: Palgrave Macmillan.

United Nations Population Fund. (2014). *The state of the world's midwifery 2014: A universal pathway. A woman's right to health*. New York: United Nations Population Fund.

Wagner, M. (2001). Fish can't see water: The need to humanize birth. *International Journal of Gynaecology and Obstetrics, 75*(Suppl 1), S25–S37.

Waitzkin, H. (1983). *The second sickness: Contradictions of capitalist health care*. London: The Free Press.

Wajcman, J. (1991). *Feminism confronts technology*. Cambridge: Polity Press.

Walsh, D. (2009). Pain and epidural use in normal childbirth. *Evidence Based Midwifery, 7*(3), 89–93.

Walsh, D. (2012). *Evidence and skills for normal birth*. London: Routledge.

Wendland, C. (2007). The vanishing mother: Cesarean section and "evidence-based obstetrics". *Medical Anthropology Quarterly, 21*(2), 218–233.

WHO. (2009). *Department of making pregnancy safer annual report 2008*. Geneva: World Health Organisation.

WHO. (2015). *WHO statement on Caesarean section rates*. Geneva: World Health Organization. http://apps.who.int/iris/bitstream/10665/161442/1/WHO_RHR_15.02_eng.pdf?ua=1. Viewed Dec 2017.

Williams, J. (1997). The controlling power of childbirth in Britain. In H. Marland & A. Rafferty (Eds.), *Midwives, society and childbirth: Debates and controversies in the modern period*. London: Routledge.

Willis, E. (1989). *Medical dominance* (2nd ed.). Sydney: Allen and Unwin.

Willis, E. (2006). Introduction: Taking stock of medical dominance. *Health Sociology Review, 15*(5), 421–431.

Winkelman, M. (2009). *Culture and health: Applying medical anthropology.* San Francisco: Jossey-Bass.

Zola, I. (1972). Medicine as an institution of social control. *The Sociological Review, 20*(4), 487–504.

4

Institutional Culture: Discipline and Resistance

JADE
Round about 1 o'clock I could feel I was getting contractions,
Which I didn't get really the last time;
I was induced.
So I kind of had a feeling
But I wasn't sure,
So I went to the bathroom and just
Sat in the bath for a while.

They came really quick,
Really hard,
My partner was running around going crazy a bit,
He was trying to pack my hospital bag—
I still hadn't gotten around to it.
It was only about an hour and half til I went to the hospital because
They were about 5 minutes apart
Pretty much straight away.

Yeah I went to the hospital
And then I pretty much asked for the pain relief straight away.
I was very insistent that I got the gas straight away.
I had a heat pack this time around which was lovely

© The Author(s) 2018
E. Newnham et al., *Towards the Humanisation of Birth*,
https://doi.org/10.1007/978-3-319-69962-2_4

That helped so much compared to just the gas.
I think it was a lot more relaxed because
I only had two people in there.

I think it was so late and they were so busy they could only have
one or two people there.
And because it wasn't planned it just made it a lot calmer.
Because I only had two people pretty much in there the whole time,
Which was really nice.
Because the last time
I had interns coming in every 5 minutes,
Or just random people coming in and talking.
And the last time getting the epidural took about 6 or 7 hours
Whereas this time they organised it straight away
So that was really nice.

Until the epidural failed twice
And then I ended up just basically doing it natural at the end.
The epidural fail was horrible.
But in a way I am kind of glad it did because
I was able to feel the urge to push.
I didn't feel that last time.
I had to be told when to push
This time I was like 'Yeah I need to push now, get it out!'
And then the pushing only took 7 minutes.
I wasn't sitting there pushing for an hour because I couldn't feel when I had to.
I actually felt her come out!
I didn't feel that with my son.

It was good, it was good,
But the whole epidural thing wasn't good.
It was just different
Because I could actually feel that I was giving birth
I could actually feel my body doing something
that it was meant to do.
I could feel—
and I knew it would result in her
I don't know,
I think it was just better,
I don't really know how to explain it.

> *Yeah I think because I have had one where I didn't feel anything,*
> *Then a second way, which was positive, because I could feel her*
> *If I could just cut out the contractions, that would be lovely*
> *I wouldn't mind feeling giving birth.*

The Labour Ward Setting

Having delineated our theoretical perspective, we now draw on the observational data to bring us into the centre of the institution. We focus on the dominant cultural beliefs and practices that were seen within the institution, and the ways in which midwives and other clinicians articulated, negotiated, or resisted these norms, as well as the disciplinary mechanisms that were used to promote and uphold them. The hospital in which the fieldwork was conducted is a comparatively large, urban, tertiary hospital in an Australian city that catered for approximately 3500 births a year. It has a large catchment area from surrounding suburbs and is the primary hospital for the local area. The hospital also has general medical facilities, emergency department, theatres and recovery, and mental health services. The maternity section consists of an antenatal/women's health clinic, an antenatal ward for women who needed to be hospitalised in pregnancy, a postnatal ward, and a labour ward (obstetric unit),[1] which is where Elizabeth Newnham, as primary researcher, spent most of her time. There was also a birth centre (midwifery unit) attached to the hospital which was staffed separately. The antenatal clinic of the hospital was staffed primarily by midwives, who ran low-risk antenatal clinics, but there were also concurrent obstetric clinics, where registrars and consultant obstetricians would see women who had pregnancy-related complications. The clinics were very busy and crowded, and women would often have to wait for a long time to be seen.

On entrance to the labour ward, there was a brief walk up a small corridor with the handover room on one side and offices and a corridor that cut through to the tea room, staff toilet, and change rooms on the other. At the top of this corridor was the midwives' station and another corridor from which the labour rooms branched off. There were four antenatal beds, four postnatal/recovery beds, and eight labour rooms in total. One was designated for 'high-risk' births, and this was larger than the others and directly opposite the midwives' station. The other birth rooms were fairly similar in size and layout. There was another corridor leading down to the tea room, which was not accessible or visible to occupants of the ward. Off this little corridor was also the pan room, containing a fridge, a sluice, linen trolleys, a sink, and washer for placenta bowls. The 'dirty' work of midwifery was done here (see Lawler 2006): urine testing, testing pads for the presence of amniotic fluid, checking placentas, and cleaning the bowls and trolleys.

Newnham attended the hospital labour ward for approximately two days a week, across all shifts, for a period of six months. The following are field note excerpts describing the birth room environment.

> *The bed, specialised for labour, is in the middle of the room, its head against the left side of the room as you walk in. The door is closed, and the curtain is also drawn over the doorway. There is an alcove over the bedhead, with the call, staff assist, and emergency bell buttons, and maternal resuscitation equipment which is standard in hospital ward environments: oxygen tubing, adult bag and mask. The N_2O & O_2 is also near the head of the bed. There is a CTG machine tucked under a bench on the side of the bed furthest from the door. In this far corner is a bench with a computer and a stool for the midwife to update her notes. Two chairs are against the wall on the far side of the room opposite the door, and there is a window looking outside. In the next corner is the baby cot, then along the wall facing the bed are cupboards stocked with linen, bedpans, pads and other necessaries. The resuscitaire is folded up against the wall, and on the right of the resuscitaire are stacker boxes with neonatal resuscitation equipment. To the right again is another cupboard and desk space, then a little store room, containing equipment for catheterisation, IV insertion, local anaesthetic, ID tags for baby and adult, cord clamps, etc. There is a sink, then in the corner before getting back to the door, is a small bathroom, with a shower and toilet and handbasin. There is not a lot of room left for walking. (Field notes 4/4/12)*

The excerpt above highlights the lack of space in the room for movement and the centrality of the labour bed. Placing the bed as the central feature in a labour room encourages women to use it simply because it there. However, if beds and furniture are placed differently—the bed is against the wall, for example—before the woman enters the room, then she is less inclined to use it. This does not need to be only within the domain of the 'low-risk' birth centre, and can be achieved within obstetric units (Leap 2012). The use and impact of birth space is being increasingly investigated, showing that it can impact on midwifery behaviours, practice, and birth outcomes (Freeman et al. 2006; Hammond et al. 2013, 2014; Harte et al. 2016; Hodnett et al. 2012).

The midwives' station, located centrally, but visibly, behind glass, in the labour ward, was often occupied, and had a variety of uses.

> The midwives' station is situated in the middle of the labour ward, which is shaped in a kind of L. It is around the corner from the main doors, which are kept locked and need a staff swipe card to access. Guests and patients need to ring a bell to be let in.[2] The midwives' station is enclosed by glass windows, and there is a desk with computers running the whole way beneath the glass window on the inside. On the left past the first doorway is the receptionist's desk, which is open and faces into the entry corridor. In the middle of the midwives' station is a large central island, with cupboards underneath and a bench to stand at and write notes, etc. Behind this is the [patient information] board, another computer, various cupboards and policy/practice folders. The computer on the rear cupboard is often used as the CTG monitor. (Field notes 2/5/12)

This field note excerpt highlights the centrality of the midwives' station, which was used to update computer and written records, such as the birth register (although computers in the birth rooms meant that midwives could also update some records there). It was situated across the corridor from the medication room, so Newnham would often see IV therapy being set up in the furthest doorway of the midwives' station after being checked in the medication room. It was also a gathering place. On night duty, the midwives and registrars might sit and chat if it was quiet, or plates of food were brought in to share. There were thank you cards and messages from women who had recently given birth, and often a box of chocolates from a grateful family. Midwives could come out from the individual birth rooms and debrief or ask their colleagues questions if they were unsure about something. They would also come out to update the team leader (T/L—midwife in charge of that shift) on aspects of the woman's progress, so that the board could be updated and the unit could be managed as a whole. The centrality of the CTG monitor meant that T/Ls and doctors could see what was happening in the room in terms of the monitored heart rate of the foetus. While this acted as a safeguard, it also enabled midwives to leave labouring women for longer periods of time than they otherwise would—monitoring them from the distance of the midwives' station rather than staying in the room—and this was remarked upon by other midwives who saw this as bad practice. The use of technology as a replacement for more traditional midwifery skills has been documented previously and, as we found in our research, there are midwives who align themselves more closely with one or the other (Crozier et al. 2007). The centralised monitoring system offered a disembodied representation of the labour that was occurring in another room. The following excerpt is a more reflective entry from later in the fieldwork stage, showing how Newnham was starting to think about measurement and time in the labour ward.

> *The CTG screen at the rear of the midwives' desk is on in the background, waiting to be looked at. I think about the use of time, the measurement of cervixes, the clocks, clearly visible from the bed in each room, directly above the boxes of gloves on the wall. (Field notes 9/9/12)*

The midwives' station was therefore central in the surveillance of both individual labour and the ward itself, operating as a form of panoptic control by observing, information-gathering, and documenting the bodies of the women in labour (see Foucault 1991b, pp. 200–209). Despite attempts at familiarising the environment, such as posters on the walls and concealing much of the medical equipment in the birth rooms behind pastel coloured curtains, the overall environment of the labour ward was that of a hospital—functional, impersonal, and clinical.

The Institution

Institutional beliefs and practices can impact on the choices that people make within them. Political economy of health theorists have described institutionalised health care in various ways and identified that institutions themselves are not neutral, but are bearers of power relations which determine how work in those institutions is done, by whom, and with what type of instruments. How the work process takes place in those…institutions…is determined by the power relations existent in that society. (Navarro 1986, p. 161)

They therefore have the potential to recreate medical dominance over the birth process. Women, midwives, midwifery practice, and the process of birth have long been at the centre of interactions of power, some of which continue, and which drove, at least in part, the relocation of birth from home to the hospital (Foucault 2003; Murphy-Lawless 1998; Summers 1995; Willis 1989). Health care institutions have been identified as alienating places, for both patients and health care workers, due to increasing fragmentation and reliance on specialisation and technological expertise (Waitzkin 1983, p. 40). Increasing focus on technologies has the effect of decreasing focus on people, and practices can become based on institutional needs rather than the needs of the person. Pertinent to this, Walsh (2009a) has proposed that increasing reliance on epidural analgesia may be due to increasing fragmentation of care, and a resulting fear and alienation in labouring women, rather than an increasing physical need for analgesia. Intrusions that are known to stall women's labours such as too much light, noise, or lack of privacy (Martin 1989; Odent 1999), or that isolate women, such as being left alone or not given adequate information, are nevertheless practised daily because they suit the needs of the institution, with technology used to monitor and speed up any slowing of labour. These behaviours are manifest examples of the above alienation theories, discounting the human and relationship needs of women, and exemplify biomedicine's focus on the mechanical body, the ubiquity of the industrial measurement of time, and a reliance on and idolatry of technological intervention (Deery 2008; Dykes 2005; Szurek 1997).

A Culture of Risk

The centralisation of birthing services in acute-care hospitals within a broader cultural domain that is increasingly preoccupied with risk (Beck 1999), and compounded by a risk discourse specific to childbirth (Skinner

2003; Walsh et al. 2008), means that the overarching focus of these services is largely one of risk, rather one of normality. Where hospital birth is still the norm, women have to fit within this risk model, even if they are classified as having a 'low-risk' pregnancy. Evidence suggests that midwives caring for low-risk women 'adapt their practices according to the context' (Walsh 2010, p. 487). That is, in large, all-risk obstetric units, midwives are more likely to adapt their thinking to cater for high-risk even if the women they are attending are not (Mead and Kornbrot 2004). However, birthing within the context of a risk discourse can lead women to internalise a fear of birth, which can hinder the birthing process (Lupton 1999; Reiger and Dempsey 2006; Walsh 2010). As our 'meaning systems' (Hill 1988, p. 92) of birth have become increasingly fragmented, industrialised, and medicalised with a focus on risk rather than normality, its incorporation into the consciousness of women and midwives is likely inevitable, and it is therefore difficult, yet important, to counter.

Under the Medical Gaze

Hospitals emerged as a plentiful source of material for medical students and practitioners alike to examine bodies and gather information (Foucault 2003, p. 102). In addition, hospitals were increasingly regarded as abundant sites of information for the growing government interest in the body—both individual and social (Foucault 2003, p. 102, 2008, pp. 140–141). The decreasing use of explicit force or coercion and increasing surveillance and regulation of bodies by government is termed by Foucault 'disciplinary power' (Foucault 2008, p. 140). This dual function of hospitals therefore served to reinforce them as 'apparatuses of surveillance' (Foucault 1980, p. 101), offering subjects for the 'medical gaze' (Foucault 1991a, p. 67). During the period of field work, Newnham noted down how the ward was organised, where events occurred, and also much of the dialogue—both that said to her and in front of her. She began to notice the deeply entrenched surveillance that occurred in the ward, and the disciplinary regulation that occurred. Disciplinary power was exerted in the architecture of the rooms and how spaces were used; it was evident in the time impositions on women in labour and the pressure

Bed No	IOL/ SOL LSCS	Gravida/ parity	Membranes SRM/ARM	Cx	Next exam	CTG	Synt	Analgesia
			Time/intact/colour					

Fig. 4.1 The journey board

that midwives were under to 'make time' for women, and it was particularly evident in the primary mechanism of surveillance, the hospital patient *journey board* (Fig. 4.1).

Organisational Technology: The Journey Board as Surveillance

The journey board was a large whiteboard in a central location behind the midwives' desk which included information such as: women's names, status (in labour, antenatal, postnatal), and if in labour, cervical dilatation at what time, when next examination was due, and any review needed. It operated as a mechanism of surveillance in that it not only offered a source of continuous information about the women themselves, but also an overview of the unit more broadly, in terms of staffing needs, bed requirements, and so on.

> *The board is displayed at the back of the midwives' desk, topped with the title 'Improving Women's Journey'. Up the top is the shift coordinator's name, and a key of symbols, e.g. 'seen', 'needs to be seen', 'CTG', etc. At the left hand side is the midwife allocated to care for the woman, the bed number, then the woman's full name, type of labour/birth (IOL, SOL, LSCS), gestation, membranes (time, intact, ARM, SRM, colour), Cx (dilatation and time), next exam due, CTG (yes/no)… Synt, analgesia, remarks (e.g postdates, allergies, gest.diab., Rh neg). Set out as below. (Field notes 2/5/12)*

The use of different colour markers signified if the women were antenatal, in labour, or postnatal. When the women had given birth, the board was marked with a (D) circled indicating 'Delivered'. Figure 4.1 is representative of the journey board, although not an exact reproduction so as to maintain confidentiality of the institution.

The journey board is reminiscent of Foucault's Panopticon—his symbolic description of the way in which people are encouraged to conform simply because of the possibility of being observed, even if they are not under direct observation (Foucault 1991b, p. 200). The disciplinary power invoked by this model, based on Bentham's design for a penitentiary, is founded on indirect observation—for example, the collection of information—and power exerted by manipulation of this knowledge, rather than direct coercion (Foucault 1991b, pp. 214–215). The strength of disciplinary power, Foucault (1991b) argues, is precisely that it requires no coercion, as the techniques of power utilised encourage self-surveillance and self-regulation—where individuals mark and discipline their behaviour according to social norms. Thus, not only did the journey board have a normalising effect on the progress of women's labour, its function was also in disciplining midwives and doctors in their work. The next two excerpts show how the midwives talked about the effects of this surveillance.

> *The doctors stand there and look at the board. If they're 3cm [dilated] they want them to be 7 in four hours. If they [women] don't [dilate fast enough], then they start talking about ARM, Synt. (MW2)*
>
> *I hate examining them. You know, 'cause once they're fully [dilated], then the doctors put a time limit on. The registrars, I know most of them, and they trust my judgement, but then they report to the consultants who don't know the women, and want everything to follow a protocol. (MW4)*

The pressure of 'observation' was a recurring theme in the midwives' talk. Conversely, in Walsh's (2006) ethnography of a free-standing birth centre, he found that the lack of external and medical monitoring was a positive influence on the midwives:

> The reality that escaping surveillance may facilitate nonbureaucratic ways of achieving goals reinforces Foucault's (1973) concept of panopticism and its constraining effects. By being outside the 'gaze', the staff experienced a freedom that, for them, was extremely creative. (Walsh 2006, p. 1336)

Our findings support those by Walsh (2006), as they show the contrast between these models of practice, and identify the specific ways in which medical surveillance curbed and restricted midwifery practices and the space and time in which women laboured.

The journey board was both a mechanism of surveillance of individual women and their progress through labour, as well as the practices of the midwives looking after them, and also worked as an organisational tool for managing the ward and hospital, as shown by the following field note excerpts.

The 'board' appears to be the main focus of attention in the ward. Team leaders, doctors, midwives who come out to the desk, periodically throughout the shift, come and stare at the board. There is discussion about who is doing what, who is coming in, how long they will be here for etc. It seems to be a process of organising…Discussion at the board between T/L and clinical midwife: 'Let's try and get one delivered, then we'll be ok [staffing and bed numbers]. We'll target room 7.' (Field notes 2/5/12)

[I am] discussing the labour [plan of one of the participants, Sophie]. MW 32 says: 'If she wants an epidural with the Synt, we'll get one early. No point making her wait. But she can have her walk, have her shower, then see how she feels.' I know that the board is being watched and they want the Synt up. It is quieter here now, but it goes against the grain of this place [waiting/watching]. The midwife [an agency midwife, who had practised as an independent midwife in New Zealand] is ignoring this, and giving Sophie time. (Field notes 28/6/12)

In addition, medical and midwifery personnel would come from other departments, such as anaesthetics and the neonatal unit, to try and identify their workload, staffing, and potential bed requirements for that shift.

An anaesthetic registrar comes onto the ward, and starts talking to the obstetric registrar: 'You know us anaesthetists, we always plan for the worst. What's going on?' The obstetric registrar responds: 'No high BMIs, nothing complicated.' They are looking at the board. The anaesthetic registrar notices something: Is that a pre-eclamptic? Room 9? The obstetric registrar replies: 'Yes, she's OK, but yes.' (Field notes 28/5/12)

The language in the above excerpt shows an institution-focused, rather than woman-focused mentality; a focus which is known to disrupt the midwife-woman relationship and is unsuited to midwifery philosophies of practice and humanised birthing practices (Behruzi et al. 2010, 2013; Blaaka and Eri 2008; Kirkham 2000; Kirkham and Stapleton 2004). Despite this, there were also many examples of midwives giving woman-centred care within these institutional parameters. One of the main drivers for being institution-focused was to process women through the system quickly, with the aim of avoiding the situation where everyone is unsafe because of the unit becoming over-full.

> *I spoke to a midwife who was on the late [shift] last night. After I left it got messy. They had two MET calls. One for the woman who came in by ambulance yesterday. She had a fainting episode, and 'looked like she was abrupting.' The other [MET call was for] a woman with a massive PPH. These high-risk episodes are surely the kinds of events that cause the 'risk aversion' behaviours previously mentioned. (Field notes 21/6/12)*

While the risk focus of the institution meant that emergencies and complications were managed well, with high levels of clinical expertise, the view through the lens of this research framework brought another perspective. It was as if the institution itself was trying to cast women out in order to keep them safe; as if the longer the women are there, the more likely an error or an intervention or a staffing issue will occur; as if the risk discourse of the institution is a self-fulfilling prophesy.

> *I have been thinking about the staffing issues, and how they affect the way that things happen here. They don't want women here who don't need to be here (eg early labourers) and like to keep things moving along simply so that the labour ward doesn't fill up. It is a safety issue. (Field notes 21/6/12)*

Hunt and Symonds (1995), in their landmark ethnographic study of midwifery, *The Social Meaning of Midwifery*, also observed that women in early labour ('nigglers') would be moved from the labour ward if possible. This was in part because they did not denote the 'real work' of midwifery on the labour ward, but it was also an issue of bed-block (Hunt and Symonds 1995, pp. 98–104). The following excerpt highlights the reality of bed-block in a risk-environment.

The board is full. Two women of 30 weeks gestation are in labour, another woman who is 35 weeks. There is a woman being induced for epilepsy. Two postnatal women on MgSO$_4$ for pre-eclampsia, there are 2 women having elective CS, and one woman due to have a CS for 2 previous CS has come in contracting. Another woman who is scheduled for a CS later in pregnancy with twins has come in with a query of ruptured membranes. The T/L goes through it all with the consultant, then, as there is a mix up with who is covering labour ward that day, goes through it all again with a registrar. If someone else comes in in labour, there will be no bed for her. (Field notes 11/7/12)

Discourses of both risk and safety therefore provide an impetus for moving women through the system. The hospital environment has been fashioned as the site of safety for birth, and yet it behaves as a site of risk. It is structured to process women through quickly in order to mitigate further risk of being held up in—or holding up—the institution, and to keep women 'safe' by discharging them. The aim of keeping women safe within the institution was a very real concern for midwives and the obstetric unit fulfilled its function in alleviating risk in the presence of emergencies. However, rather than viewing the 'processing' of all women through this system as an appropriate solution, we suggest instead, following Dykes (2005), that the situation we describe confirms the unsuitability of large, acute, medical institutions as the appropriate site for all birth.

As well as being a surveillance and organisational tool for managing the ward, the journey board was used as an obstetric management tool.

As the night progresses, the monitoring system is observed, the board attended to, updates given. T/L: 'The woman in Rm 4 is fully, at spines, should have a baby in there soon.' Obstetric registrar 'Oh good' [pause] 'The trace looks beautiful doesn't it?' (Field notes 31/5/12)

The journey board thus represented the functionality of the unit as a whole, not only providing a system of organising staffing and bed numbers, but a visual representation of a 'risky' or 'safe' ward depending on the colour scheme.

The T/L is orientating a new doctor: 'This is our Journey Board…antenates are in orange, labourers in black and postnates in green. Blue is elective section. That way you can always see what you've got.' (27/6/12)

The following comment by a registrar typifies the general relief felt when women have passed successfully though the labour process—as this is where the risk of emergency is greatest—and are now written on the board in green.

> *[There is a] registrar standing at the board with [a group of] new students or RMOs explaining how it works: 'Green is postnatal. They don't cause much trouble, so I like to see a Green board. (Field notes 2/5/12)*

With a 'green board', not only can the doctors relax, as an emergency is now unlikely, it also signals a 'green light' for the unit, as these women can be moved to the postnatal floor or discharged home. This sense of relief is also an example of how pervasive surveillance within a risk culture works equally on doctors and midwives, and is not necessarily imposed by obstetricians themselves but by these systems of power/knowledge and their influence on the institution, as well as practice, that have been produced in relation to medicine, midwifery, and birth (Arney 1982; Downe and Dykes 2009).

The centrality of 'the board' in monitoring and managing labour progress and organising practice has been mentioned in other studies undertaken in the United Kingdom (Hunt and Symonds 1995; Stevens 2009), though without a specific focus on surveillance from a Foucauldian perspective. The disciplinary power symbolised by the journey board in this study was pervasive throughout the unit. For example, a senior labour ward midwife discussed with Newnham how she had attended a conference where an independent midwife had given a talk about a 'midwifery approach' to labour. Sometime after this, at work, while assessing a woman by vaginal examination, the midwife conducted an artificial rupture of membranes (ARM) because she *'knew "they" would want it anyway'* (in order to see the liquor colour, and hasten birth). However, she was now reflecting on and questioning her practice, in part because it had ended up as a ventouse birth. This story was interesting not only because it illustrated the disembodied, panoptic surveillance that was so pervasive that the midwife did not need anyone to tell her directly to do an ARM—she simply knew that 'they' would want one—but, and perhaps more importantly, she only reflected on this practice after being exposed to a less intrusive philosophy of midwifery, one which she described as inspiring but unfamiliar. It was also interesting because it illuminated the power of institutional culture even in very experienced and dedicated midwives.

The impact of this surveillance on midwifery practice is important and requires further investigation. One study has identified how senior labour ward midwives checked up on progress two-hourly because 'the doctors expect it', despite it not being hospital policy nor actually expected by the doctors (Stevens 2009). It has been suggested that midwives, dealing with the dissonance between the ideal of woman-centred care and the reality of institutional birth, have externalised responsibility to the extent that they conform to medicalised practices even when the perceived barriers are not there (O'Connell and Downe 2009). Using the notion of authenticity, O'Connell and Downe (2009) describe how midwives can choose between a range of possible practice options, increasing potential responses and possibilities for woman-centred practices. With awareness of it, and using evidence and midwifery practice that supports normal birth, midwives can take responsibility for challenging medicalised surveillance techniques and exert some influence in normalising birth.

The surveillance and organisational role of the journey board is perhaps understandable in large medical institutions where they are used in part to prevent errors and near misses from occurring, and therefore work as a safety mechanism (Chaboyer et al. 2009; O'Brien et al. 2015). However, although this mechanism may work extremely well for medical or surgical patients, it is not necessarily suited for monitoring labouring women. In an article outlining the implementation of the journey board in one hospital, O'Brien et al. (2015, p. 161) discuss how they 'were also influenced by models used in an industrial setting' and cite *The Toyota Way*, a field-book produced by the Toyota car manufacturing company. Arguably, a safety mechanism designed on industrial factory processing is not going to benefit women undergoing labour and birth; a fluid, psychophysiological human process.

The centrality of the journey board meant that women were under constant surveillance and often placed within time constraints by maternity personnel who also needed to maintain the safety and efficiency of the institution—competing needs, against which the women often lost. We now examine the effects of these time constraints.

Time in Labour

With industrialisation, there was a shift away from a previous experience of the world as a series of cycles—of the sun rising and setting, the moon moving from dark to full, the buds of spring to the chill of winter frost—towards a concept of linear time. Factory rhythm replaced that of agrarian labour and cottage craft, which had been more in step with the those seasonal and other cycles of nature (Hill 1988, p. 114; Walsh 2009b, p. 131), and brought an increasing dependence on 'clock time' with penalisation for breaks, and activities such as smoking, singing, reading, or drinking coffee (Hill 1988, p. 115). Industrial clock time was therefore a symbol of the capitalist mode of production whereby workers' time was equal to profit and not to be wasted. The clock symbolised the new discipline, calculated in seconds and minutes, that represented the 'factory's social relations of production and repressive discipline' (Hill 1988, p. 101).

The change of location to the hospital as the primary site of birth echoed wider social circumstances, such as the movement out of the domestic sphere with increasing industrialisation and factory work, and the corresponding reliance on the regular, systematic, and linear management of time by the clock (McCourt and Dykes 2009, p. 25). Martin (1989, p. 59) equates the phases of labour (in birth) to a production line in a factory whereby deviation from normal 'rates' of labour equals disorder. She observes that women, 'grounded whether they like it or not in cyclical bodily experiences, live both the time of industrial society and another kind of time that is often incompatible with the first' (Martin 1989, p. 198).

Hill (1988, p. 114) identifies that

> Agricultural and craft labour may have involved hard, grinding, bare subsistence labour, but it was organised against the rhythm of nature's harvests and planting times, the rhythms of the day, and against autonomous decisions to work when food or wealth was required but not when economic income was good.

There would be periods of intense activity but also periods of inactivity; waiting for something to grow, or steep, or ripen. Inactivity, inimical to industrialised labour and the creation of profit, was stamped out, as work became routinised, standardised, and set to hourly rates. Factory rhythms, the rhythms of the machine, were therefore more economically productive (Hill 1988, p. 115) and the industrialised world lost its patience for slowness, for *being* rather than *doing*, for idle contemplation and for the process of watching and waiting rather than intervening—many of which also relate to the behaviours that support birthing women. It is apparent from the above quote that the freedom of organising time in a rhythmical or cyclical way, in the way that Martin (1989) mentions might be important to women, was lost with this change in the measurement of time, and this loss was echoed in the words of the midwives in the study.

> *The most frustrating thing about working here is you just want to slow everything down. I mean, just give her a chance, you know? (MW50)*

We do not intend to invoke nostalgic or idealised notions, but the move from home to hospital, the industrialisation of birth and imposition of machinated and linear timing onto the rhythms of birth, has altered the process of birth in ways that we are as yet unaware of the full implications. In many ways it appears that, as a society, we are unaware that these implications even exist. But still, the midwives railed against it.

> *I am not happy with the plan. Assess in two hours, and do an ARM. No way… High head, deflexed OP. She needs to be left alone! (MW27)*

The importance of recognising rhythmic and cyclic time is recognised in an ethnography of postnatal midwifery care by Dykes (2005, citing Kahn), who remarks:

> Linear time, measured by the clock, is pitched relentlessly towards the future and is centred upon the notion of efficient production…In contrast, cyclical time…is a bodily, rhythmic time that is a part of one's ontology and not separate and 'outside' like linear time. (Dykes 2005, p. 249)

Despite a philosophy of 'being with' women, institutional demands and a focus on linear time have been shown to impact midwifery practice (Dykes 2005), sparking a tendency to value being efficient and 'on time', according to the institutional rhythm, rather than being 'in time', or spending relational time with women (Deery 2008). This timekeeping can place another barrier between the midwife and the woman, hindering the potential to build a relationship (Browne and Chandra 2009). Maher (2008) proposes a middle ground to the experience of time, between linear and cyclical. In keeping with Deery's (2008) depiction of being 'in time' with women, Maher (2008) describes a 'time in process', as women appreciate and engage with the embodied 'forward movement towards the birth of the baby' (Maher 2008, p. 136). Walsh (2006) notes how in a free-standing birth centre, without an overarching industrial 'processing mentality', women were encouraged and left to labour within their own time, he writes:

> These events are by their very nature unpredictable. Huge variations exist between the lengths of women's labours, from hours to days…the focus on labour length…is the requirement of large hospitals to keep women moving through the system…These variations from the labour norms are not perceived as deviant if the lens of a 'processing mentality' is removed. (Walsh 2006, pp. 1332–1333)

This idea of normalising the unpredictable progress of labour is important to the normal birth project and there have been calls for 'slow' birth/midwifery, as a response to the perceived detriment at expecting birth to keep up with the furious pace of Western life, in the same vein as other Slow movements, which began in Italy with Slow food several decades ago (Browne and Chandra 2009; Walsh 2005). Obviously, there is a need to ensure safety and ways to identify when labour is not progressing normally for that woman. We applaud the furthering of a slow birth movement and also think, with Maher (2008), that the notion of embodiment may provide a way forward. We return to this idea in Chap. 6.

Institutional Momentum

In order for women to fit within the demands of the institution to run like clockwork, Newnham noticed practices that served to 'push' women through the system. The following excerpts show some examples of this, as well as her thoughts at the time, which contributed to the subsequent analysis.

8am doctors round [standing at board]. The consultant is pleased that the registrar has begun the inductions. Registrar: 'Well, that's what we used to do at hospital X. ARM and Syntoed them all overnight [early hours of morning] and then they'd all be 'going' when the morning staff came on.' (Field notes 10/5/12)

This accentuates the difference in philosophy between midwifery and medicine around birth. There was an understanding between these two doctors that a reduction in workload for the oncoming doctors was a good thing. It also keeps within the lines of the functioning hospital idea, where women left to their own devices are seen as displeasing to medical staff, as if they are making the place untidy. (Analytic memo 10/5/12)

This idea that the needs of the institution come before the needs of the woman has been raised by others (Kirkham 2000; Walsh 2010). Murphy-Lawless (1998, p. 42) writes of the maternity hospital:

> A key element in this organisation is keeping up the throughput of women and, whatever the rhetoric may be about individual choice, the bottom line is to ensure that the individual woman does not upset the system with her own demands or reactions to handling labour…Under such circumstances it is immensely useful to the obstetric system to draw on variants of its own historically grounded argument about the natural unreliability of the female body in labour.

This was certainly played out in the field site, where the pressure to keep up the momentum of the institution meant that women were often pushed to keep up with the pace of institutional time rather being left to follow the rhythms of their labouring bodies. These bodies, the ones that failed to keep pace with the arbitrary rhythm imposed by the institution, were then 'fixed' with interventions such as ARM and Syntocinon (a random field note audit of several days of handover notes show 14 out of 30 women having labour induced or augmented). The obligation to keep the institutional cogs in motion resulted in practices occurring purely because they fell in with institutional rhythm. Practices that were out of synch with this rhythm, those that involved time, waiting, or patience, were obstructed. In the field excerpt below, Newnham had been listening to a conversation between the T/L and a midwife looking after a woman who was being induced for diet-controlled gestational diabetes (GD). As they were looking up the local practice guidelines regarding blood sugar monitoring in labour, Newnham mentioned that women with diet-controlled GD sometimes had their babies in birth centres.

> *'Yes', says the T/L, 'I used to do that in x birth centre, and we didn't do hourly blood sugars'. In fact, this woman shouldn't even be induced – that's what the consultant said when she came on this morning: 'Why is she being induced? It's not necessary. She's 39 weeks and has diet-controlled GD?'*
>
> *T/L: 'It would be different if she was on insulin, then she should be induced at 38 weeks. But oh well, it happens here all the time.' (Field notes 10/5/12)*

Our understanding of this last, throwaway comment by the midwife *'it happens here all the time'* is that women get caught in the smoothly running institutional cogs, which do not stop rolling regardless. Thus, even when an irregularity is discovered—a woman who should not have been induced—the institutional apparatus rolls on as if no-one has the power to stop it. This *institutional momentum* is in fact another entity in an already crowded, and contested, birth space. Stevens (2009, p. 111) observed that although reliance on clock time, including ordering and monitoring labour progress by this mechanism, served to 'create order out of chaotic situations' and give the impression of 'efficiency', it ultimately prohibited any kind of individualised or unique expression of time in labour. The excerpt below shows this same consequence occurring on another occasion:

> *Just heard a long story about an induction that got bumped [postponed]. The T/L explained that two consultants had made the decision. No-one knew why [she was having the induction]. She was bumped because it was busy and the T/L ended up saying to this woman over the phone 'Well, you may not need to be induced now anyway' [she had had a blood transfusion for anaemia on the weekend, and been an in-patient when the decision was made]. Another consultant overheard the midwife's phone call with the woman and berated the midwife for changing the plan decided by consultants. The midwife was following orders from the registrar—no room today—but the issue was her saying that perhaps the induction didn't need to go ahead. The consultant went on to say he had seen the woman in clinic on the Monday, and even he [as another*

consultant] hadn't changed the plan 'even though it's a shit plan'. Both he and the midwife could see that this woman probably didn't need to be induced. The point was, another two consultants had decided she should be, and so changing the plan would 'confuse' the woman, and [therefore] go against her best interests (if doctors couldn't agree on a plan of care). (Field notes 11/7/12)

What is illuminating about situations such as these is they were allowed to go ahead if they conformed to institutional beliefs and practices (such as induction); however, women's 'care plans' could be easily changed if they did not conform to these beliefs, and so women who were planning, for example, a vaginal breech birth, or to birth in water, could have this plan overridden by the midwives or medical practitioners on the day.

In the excerpt below, a midwife expresses the pressure that is exerted in keeping up with the hospital momentum during handover.

The T/L uses [handover] as an opportunity to debrief about the issues with theatres. 'They were going to put a spinal in, with no surgeon even there! And they hadn't even scanned to make sure the babe was still breech! I mean, it's ok to keep things going, but we need to be safe! They get a bit insular round there. I know they're all under pressure. They documented that they rang 3 times for a midwife, but I was ringing them, telling them 'I'm looking for a midwife, I'm looking for a trolley, I'm looking for a paed.' They didn't tell me they were doing two sections at once.' (Field notes 11/7/12)

Pressure from theatres for their elective and non-urgent caesarean section cases was an ongoing impetus for performing at 'institutional time'.

It is difficult for the labour ward staff because when theatres are ready, the labour ward staff have to go. Mostly this is ok, but it creates some stress when it's busy. To accommodate for this need, the theatre preparation (for elective, or as soon as they know, for [non-urgent] emergency) is done early so that they, and the women, are ready to go when called. (Field notes 11/7/12)

This next excerpt sums up the feeling when the unit is full, and in fact is an apt expression describing the underpinning cultural philosophy in general.

> In handover I hear: 'She's a time bomb waiting to happen. There's no point sitting on her' (Previous CS, scar dehiscence, other issues). (Field notes 25/7/12)

And later on, that same phrase: 'She's just a little time bomb' (Field notes 8/8/12). There was an escalating sense of pressure that the midwives articulated: 'We're all under pressure. We are all ready to explode. We are all stressed, all tired, we're all feeling it' (Field notes 15/8/12). And on another occasion: 'I'm over this place [labour ward]. I'm sick of having not enough staff, the board [looks up]…it's not too bad today, but it's always full, you're having to fight…for staff (Field notes 20/6/12).

It appeared that the institution had a momentum of its own; against the ticking of the clock, women were driven through the turning cogs regardless of the views of the practitioners involved, or, in fact, the evidence or best practice guidelines, for example, the continuing induction of labour in women who appeared not to need it. There was a definite sense in which women were 'pushed through' the labour ward, and that midwives also felt 'pushed' in trying to keep up. This contributed to a general feeling of building pressure; a metaphor which was applied to the women who they thought might 'go off' like a time bomb, setting in train the associated chaos and mayhem of an explosion, leading to a situation where the midwives and doctors colluded in 'pushing' the women through, in their efforts to avoid a full board and an unsafe unit. A full board designated a unit that had no free beds for emergency or necessary admissions, and that staffing was stretched. Although 'pushing women through' the system arguably avoids the problems of understaffing, or bed-block, it ignores the knowledge that women's labours have a unique rhythm. This rhythmic dissonance means the labouring woman is by definition 'out of synch' with the institution, and places her at risk of having the requirements of her body's physiology ignored in lieu of reliance on technological intervention.

Playing for Time

The midwives in this study discussed their impressions that they were continually pushing against the rigid parameters of time engaged by the institution.

I do a lot of nights because then I can just do my job. It's hard because you have to fit into the institutional constraints. (MW4)

It's frustrating you know, day in, day out. It depends on the doctor. Some are just worse than others. They jump in too quickly. They don't give them a chance. (MW43)

The fluctuation of labour is evidenced in accounts by independently practicing midwives (see Davis-Floyd and Davis 1997), where labours do not follow predictable patterns—for example, a woman at home might stop labouring and sleep for a few hours, then wake up refreshed and push out her baby (see also Winter and Duff 2009)—and where midwives use a watchful approach towards the unpredictable nature of birth rather than one of control. In a hospital, this same labour, under the 'medical gaze' is likely to be augmented, leading to an increasing need for analgesia and intervention, as the institution imposes an externalised and artificial timeline on a process that is individually and uniquely experienced in cyclical time (Downe and Dykes 2009; Walsh 2009b).

The other thing I've noticed is they do an ARM here, and they'll want to put Synt up in the next hour. And I'm like 'Why?' But no-one gives me an answer. I have a feeling it's about beds, but that's not right. That woman deserves to be given that space for labour. If we do an ARM, she's most likely going to go into labour, she just needs time. (MW34)

'Friedman's curve'—the template for documenting progress of labour by measurement of the cervix—is based on inadequate and outdated research (Downe and Dykes 2009), and there is no real evidence on what a 'normal' length of labour is (Walsh 2012, pp. 40–50). The effectiveness of the partograph at preventing negative outcomes is also under debate (see Lee et al. 2017), and yet there was an institutional demand to 'push women through' the system based on such arbitrary parameters, or, and this is more concerning, not based on any observable parameters at all, but seemingly only to keep pace. Some midwives worked against the institutional momentum, and this is examined later in the chapter. In addition, some doctors would also attempt to give women more time, as shown in the following field note excerpt.

A midwife comes out to discuss the progress of the woman she is caring for in labour with the registrar. She wants to know whether or not Syntocinon will be required and if so, when. The woman has had an epidural in since 9 am. The midwife has done a vaginal examination and the woman is 7–8cms dilated. There is discussion about the contractions. The midwife explains they feel a little less strong than before the epidural but still 3: 10. Moderate? Asks the registrar.

MW35:	Umm yep
REG:	Well, she is a primip, so…let's give her some more time if she is contracting well.
MW35:	So when shall I reassess her?
REG:	Well, in four hours.
MW35:	Ok, great [lets T/L know].
T/L (to registrar):	Good decision.

However, two hours later, during afternoon handover, the consultant came around, and wanted an earlier assessment:

The consultant came and overrode the registrar's decision and wanted a VE in 2 hours (from the 7–8 cms).

T/L: Oh, she's written 'consider' here [ie consider another VE in 2 hours] as a compromise. But Dr [consultant] comes in and she wants, you know, it all to happen, to be fully in 2 hours. (Field notes 11/7/12)

This excerpt shows how at times the doctors and midwives worked together to provide the time and space for women to birth. The midwife is checking to see if the doctor would want to order Syntocinon, given that the woman has an epidural and her contractions are slowing. Although the midwife would have obliged by putting up a Syntocinon drip had the doctor ordered it, she was pleased when the doctor did not. The T/L also reinforced the doctor's decision by giving positive feedback. In this way, inroads into inter-professional collaboration were made, with potential benefits to the women, even though, in this case, the attempt to 'buy' the woman more time was overridden by the consultant obstetrician.

Here is another example of the way in which doctors and midwives collaborated to give women more time.

Institutional Culture: Discipline and Resistance 127

Two doctors and the T/L are at the board, discussing each woman. The woman from earlier today who was fully [dilated] has had her time spent pushing changed, now starting later. It was described as 'effective pushing from quarter past one', giving the woman more time by qualifying the type of pushing being done. (Field notes 11/7/12)

While some midwives appeared quite comfortable working within the institutional culture, other midwives felt it interfered with their own ideas of what it means to be a midwife, and expressed frustration at the intense pressure from the institution to work within a time frame that was external and artificial rather than working with individual women's rhythms of labour. Notably, beneath the surveillance of the journey board, there was often interdisciplinary collaboration to buy women more time.

The lack of capacity within the labour ward (due largely to the effective surveillance engendered by the journey board) to 'allow women time' despite the attempts of various practitioners at 'playing for time', and the way in which the institution's momentum propelled women into interventions even if they did not actually require them, is concerning, and poses questions about the safety of this system. This risk/safety contradiction (putting women at risk in order to maintain their safety) exposed a hidden paradox (see Fig. 4.2) which was further compounded by observations

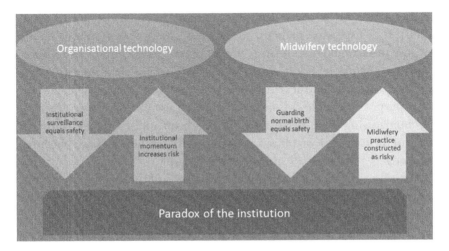

Fig. 4.2 Paradox of the institution

about the midwifery role. This will be discussed later in the chapter, but first we turn to the way in which the midwives negotiated their practice within this system.

Practising the Art of Midwifery: Barriers and Negotiations

How does the valorisation of technology and the institutional apparatus of birth relate to the birth process? And specifically, how does it relate to midwifery—those who are at the coalface of supporting women in labour? First, the assumption that technology is neutral, or an 'independent force that develops according to an autonomous process of evolution and to which we can do nothing but adjust' (Noble, cited in Martin 1989, p. 57) needs to be reviewed, and a critical evaluation of technology needs to occur, particularly since much of it was introduced without good evidence. The focus on technology—for example, cEFM, use of Syntocinon to accelerate labour, reliance on epidural analgesia as a safe and effective pain relief—detracts from other birth knowledge and practices that can benefit labouring women. It also overlooks social relationships of power. As outlined in the previous chapter, many medicalised birth practices were commenced for the benefit of the medical practitioner rather than the woman (Banks 1999; Gélis 1991; Murphy-Lawless 1998; Towler and Bramall 1986). It is necessary, perhaps, to remember here that a critique of the overuse of technology in birth is not an outright rejection of all technology, nor a kind of Luddite reaction to the working environment, but a necessary and thoughtful critical evaluation of how, when, where, and for what purpose technology is used. Considered use of technology is part of the humanising birth perspective. It is 'not an indiscriminate throwing away of the tools. It is an objection to the notion of the world as a machine, the body as a machine' (Rothman 1989, p. 54).

The role of science in fragmenting the body and the mechanistic thinking of the seventeenth and eighteenth centuries has also been doubly influential on women. As the female body was interpreted by science as inherently faulty, deviant, or pathological, medical birth discourse therefore revolved around 'saving' the baby from the trauma inflicted by the woman's body in labour. Martin (1989, p. 64) found that early medical texts propounded the idea 'that even normal labor is intrinsically traumatic to the baby' likening it in one example, to 'falling on a pitchfork'. This discourse not only positions women as inherently dangerous, by virtue of their unruly bodies, it also positions obstetrics as the saviour (see also Reiger 2010), by intervening in the body's natural (dangerous) processes and using science and technology to 'fix' (rescue) birth (Martin 1989), in the way of the one-two punch described in Chap. 3. As we have already described, many of the midwives in the study were opposed to the medicalising and technologising of birth. Midwives (and occasionally doctors) were often conflicted as they attempted to give women more time and space in which to labour while simultaneously working within the panoptic surveillance mechanism symbolised by the journey board.

Hill (1988, p. 82), whose thesis on technology we drew on in the discussion on time, offers another pertinent analogy:

> The introduction of tractors also transforms the rhythms of labour. It changes the regime of planting and harvesting time and practices, and the solidarities and obligations of collective labour. Moreover, the introduction of tractors challenges the wisdom of the old whose authority depended on integrating technical knowledge with all its life and meaning.

Thus, we propose, the introduction of new technologies (labour augmentation, CTG monitoring, epidural analgesia) transforms the rhythms of labour in a way that also transforms the art and knowledge of midwifery. Hill (1988, p. 82) continues:

> Technical knowledge is therefore surgically excised out of the cultural framework into which it was originally set…The culture stays stitched together, but only with dissolving thread. For the central heart of the technique starts to beat to the cultural rhythm of the social and economic assumptions of the invading industrialised culture.

So it appears that the use of an 'invasive' industrial model of birth is eroding midwifery 'technical knowledge'; knowledge that has the potential to be both art and science, and that does not need to compromise safety. The idea of 'progress' for its own sake needs to be re-evaluated, particularly where birth is concerned. We propose that this can be done from a standpoint of midwifery technology.

Midwifery Technology

Holly Powell Kennedy (2002) has described the midwife as an 'instrument' of care. Careful midwifery practice that incorporates support of birth physiology and judicious use of medical technology improves birth outcomes. There were many examples of midwifery practice that conformed to dominant obstetric, institutional, and technological norms, but we want to focus now on the midwives trying to keep the art of midwifery alive. In reality, there is probably a continuum, upon which both midwives and doctors sit, depending on their personal philosophies, their beliefs and principles, their training and experience, as well as their day-to-day energy or enthusiasm for the role.

We have used the word *technology* to describe midwifery practice deliberately. The Greek root for technology, *techne*, refers to the activities and skills of the craftsman but also to the arts of the mind and fine arts. The suffix, *ology*, refers to the *knowledge* about *techne*—literally 'words of knowledge'—or the discourse of art and skill (*Online Etymology Dictionary* 2010; Hill 1988). The linguistic roots of the word 'technology' therefore imply human engagement with the world, and knowledge and art combined, rather than the inflation of science over and above a world that also consists of human meaning (Hill 1988). There was an emphasis in Ancient Greece on the *aesthetics* in science. Hill (1988, p. 81) goes on to say that as new technologies are introduced into traditional cultures, there is an alienation of 'traditional stocks of knowledge'. This knowledge then becomes '"common", useless, and associated with a past order the people are escaping' (Hill 1988, p. 81). For example, we can compare the midwifery art of accepting and sitting with pain, with the ideas portrayed in the biomedical epidural literature, of pain relief as progress, the 'suffering' of which is somehow archaic. There is also no way to account for the loss of knowledge and skills that disappeared with the persecution of midwives during both the witch-hunt era and the medical appropriation of birth.

Midwives in the labour ward who were attempting to hold on to the midwifery technologies that supported normal birth were often put down for their beliefs. The cultural norm of technical dominance constructed midwifery technologies as archaic, quaint, or alternative. One midwife said she was referred to for her 'hippie midwife skills' (e.g., using a 'robozo' sling to help turn a baby). Another midwife divulged that the term 'fish-slappers' was used for the birth centre midwives.[3] A doctor asked a midwife who was going off to work in a midwifery-led birth centre if she was going to 'grow her armpit hair'. The anaesthetist who Newnham interviewed, despite holding fairly balanced views about the role of epidural analgesia in labour, commented:

If you're talking about empowerment and involvement, and all those hairy armpit catchphrases, it's more empowering to someone to have control over themselves.

The two elements of care—empowerment and involvement—which sit at the centre of the midwifery philosophy, were clearly not deemed serious considerations when compared with giving someone 'control' over her experience through the relief of pain.[4] And so there was an underlying discourse that ridiculed and rebuked midwives who attempted to use midwifery technologies—one that was also equated, by its invocation of 'hairy armpits', with the archetype of the non-conformist woman; the hippie, the feminist, the witch.

There was also a belief that supporting techniques of normal birth compromised safety, echoing the dichotomy of scientific thinking, that one has to replace the other completely, rather than the possibility of co-existence.

Midwives working to a 'midwifery model' find it hard in the medical system. Midwives are made to feel that they put women/babies in danger. This is the underlying feeling if [they] advocate for women. (Field notes 25/8/12)

This also preserves the widespread belief that obstetric intervention equals safety, and birth outside of obstetric control equals danger (Campo 2010; Williams 1997). One midwife's response to this was:

'You know what irritates me? Is that midwives who know I'm into natural birth measures equate that with a lack of safety. I would never compromise anyone's safety.' She went on to explain that she found it odd that midwives who *'seemed to like'* using CTG monitoring did not always read it correctly...for example, interpreting an uncomplicated variable deceleration on a CTG as a sign of foetal distress rather than a physiological response to head compression in second stage labour. (Field notes 4/4/12)

As we have already touched on, Waitzkin (1983, p. 33 [emphasis added]) has described how:

> On the ideologic level, there is a contradiction between what one might call the *complex* and the *mundane*. Technologic medicine, grounded in the complexities of scientific technique, carries *symbolic* trappings of effectiveness.

What was observed in this institution was the continuation of the 'symbolic trappings of effectiveness' of medicine. Although the fun poked at these midwives was light-hearted and could easily be brushed aside, it formed part of a deeper cultural undercurrent that placed midwifery technology in the realm of the old-fashioned, fringe, or parochial. More worryingly, it was sometimes constructed as dangerous. In a culture increasingly infatuated with an ideology of new technology, 'mundane and simple' midwifery practices are being driven out; both by policy, as will be discussed in the next chapter, and by an institutional discourse that mirrored the technological imperative more broadly. Within the medicalised institution of hospital birth, midwives as well as doctors are perpetuating this discourse. Those midwives who attempt to resist can be subject to ridicule and criticism.

In Foucauldian terms, midwifery has been constructed as a subjugated discourse (Foucault 1980), initially denigrated and exiled from the dominant knowledge of biomedical birth. It is crucial to the ongoing human experience of birthing and rearing children that midwives (and those others interested in birth) work to uncover, discover, or recreate midwifery technologies of birth (Odent 2013). In another germane perspective from Hill (1988, p. 41), he discusses the difference in experience between the use of tractor technology and manual labour:

With a front-end loader rather than a shovel, our efficiency in digging larger tracts of earth out of the back garden is massively enhanced, but direct sensuous experience is unlikely to be of the earth's texture, coolness and wetness, or of the onion-grass and orchid bulbs that are embedded within the soil, or of the worms and the arachnids that populate it. Our experience of the earth is as one tonne bucket loads of undifferentiated rubble. More importantly however, this experience of the earth is secondary to the more immediate experience of the machine itself.

If we want to keep the humanity, the sensuality, the joy in birth, we need to attend to the matter of midwifery technology. Additionally, if, as Hill (1988) suggests, our understanding is now framed by the technological world in which we live, then it becomes only the more urgent before any more knowledge is lost. There is no reason that technological competence cannot be integrated with traditional midwifery skills; the use of technology in itself does not require a reduction in caring behaviours (Crozier et al. 2007). Crozier et al. (2007) identify the need for a model describing the appropriate use of technology as a way to integrate the benefits of both machines and hands-on midwifery skills. In this study field site, some midwives were clearly trying to keep their midwifery technology alive, by holding on to the concept of the midwifery practice of 'getting women through' labour, and to the midwifery knowledge that labour has a unique pattern for each woman. However, this was a constant struggle for midwives within the confines of institutional birth. One of the ways that midwives achieved this was by taking pleasure in, and passing on stories of, their involvement in normal birth.

Keeping Midwifery Alive: Relishing the Normal

The midwives' talk of normal birth described it as a scarce commodity, rare and something to be enjoyed and shared. This sharing of knowledge provided an oral discourse of 'relishing the normal': keeping normal birth and the art of midwifery alive within the institution.

> *It was beautiful. Crying, we all cried! It's nice we can still do that. Beautiful birth. The mother had had no drugs, so she was doing that [makes breathing sound]…oh she was beautiful…Divine. (MW24)*

> *The midwives seem to be overjoyed, elated, when they get to be present at these kinds of births. This has been a constant theme running through their work discourse. 'I got to attend a 'normal' birth!' [read physiological/non-medicated/non-induced/vaginal with no intervention]. (Field notes 20/6/12)*

The midwives, even while feeling pressure to conform to the hospital protocols, kept their knowledge going by talking about the normal yet unique nature of labour.

> *And if I know anything about labour, it doesn't follow a pattern. Each [labour] is different. It's 'abnormal' to be 'normal'. (MW4)*

This same midwife mentioned the rarity of normal birth in this institution.

> MW4: *'It's not often you get one like this, too!'*
> EN: *'What, spontaneous labour?'*
> MW4: *'Yes, and [points to CTG—implying its non-use]'. (Field notes 4/4/12)*

Other midwives also discussed this, joking that they 'forget' how to manage normal birth, without the usual trappings of technology. The midwives also reminded each other, and therefore themselves, that normal birth was still possible.

> *The other woman in labour, another induction, is also having a CS. [No progress from 5 cm in 2 hours. No progress from 2 hours before that, and thin meconium in the liquor]. Two midwives are talking: 'Well, I had a nice vaginal birth yesterday.' 'Yes, well they got three out this morning [vaginally].' (Field notes 9/9/12)*

This kind of positive reminder between midwives was a way of keeping midwifery going in a system where intervention was the norm. Some midwives would go to great lengths to try and maintain 'normality' in birth, especially if specifically requested by the women.

> *So she was lucky. Very lucky. I was the only midwife on the late [shift] who was accredited [to facilitate waterbirth], and on the night shift as well, so I stayed on. But it was good, because [midwife] got to see her first one for accreditation, and it was the student's first one as well. And it was the first one I had done since becoming accredited. So, it was a lot of firsts. (MW14)*

This midwife was really pleased that she had been able to stay and facilitate this birth. She was pleased that the birth went well for the woman, and that another midwife had had the chance to witness it, a step in the direction towards her becoming accredited to providing waterbirth herself. She was also pleased that the woman had 'got away' with having a waterbirth, as she told me later how close this woman had come to missing out. The woman's body mass index (BMI) was 34 and the cut-off for waterbirth is a BMI of 35.

In 'relishing the normal', by passing on stories of normal birth, the midwives were also holding onto a distinct knowledge and in doing so, attempting to define a midwifery culture that was somehow separate from the temporal and surveillance pressures of the institution (see O'Connell and Downe 2009). This aspect of midwife/institution tension was particularly difficult for midwives to challenge and they expressed deep frustration at trying to 'slow things down' within the institutional demands of throughput and risk management protocols. There were attempts to provide individualised care within (and sometimes pushing through) the barriers of institutional protocol, and midwives drew on this store of knowledge to help substantiate these practices in a potentially hostile environment.

Holding onto this knowledge included building a relationship with the woman and attempting to provide individualised care. They also relied on the midwifery notion of 'getting women through' (Leap 2012).

> *I think that has a lot to do with the midwife in the room, don't you? Some midwives don't know how to get the woman through. They might not offer the woman all of the options. If a woman is in transition and she is asking for an epidural, they'll get them one, or, they won't say 'You're doing really well, let's just see how you go' or offer gas or pethidine first. Most women do really well without one. In my experience, it's up to the midwife to work with them. (MW19)*

They saw their role as 'getting women through' labour in ways that did not involve technology or medication. Ways in which midwives expressed this were not offering pain relief, the 'midwifery mutter' (offering continuous verbal support), delaying tactics/distraction, offering suggestions (e.g., position change), and encouraging women to stay at home as long as possible.

Negotiation and Resistance: Guarding the Normal

Seemingly contradictory to the institutional hierarchy, there were many instances where doctors happily relinquished the responsibility for normal birth to the midwives. Despite the reliance on intervention evident in the labour ward culture, there was an underlying premise that midwives were in fact responsible for 'normal birth' and there were constant references to this in the day-to-day discourse of the doctors. This kind of talk appeared at first as a 'discongruency' in the data,[5] one that showed midwifery practices being supported in an obstetric unit. However, on closer analysis, we found that it joined the *journey board* as another surveillance technique.

MW36: *'As soon as she started pushing the epidural kicked in. Head's on view, she's pushing well.'*
Registrar: *'Station?'*
MW36: *'Well, it was +1 but it seems to have sucked back up again since she started pushing.'*
Registrar: *'Can she have an hour of physiological descent?'*
MW36: *'Well, she's feeling pressure.'*
Registrar: *'Is it OP?'*
MW36: *'No, it's OT, a little bit OT.'*
Registrar: *'Ok. Don't come out until you have a baby, thanks.'* (Field notes 11/7/12)

Paradoxically, the midwives were expected to 'perform' midwifery; facilitate normal birth and prevent instrumental or caesarean birth, which added workload to other members of the hospital team, while correspondingly being ridiculed for practising midwifery technologies and expected to abide by the ever-increasing number of risk-oriented protocols and associated interventions. This, in conjunction with the risk/safety contradiction described above, bared the inherently incongruous paradox of the institution. The pressure of the institution's momentum to 'push women through' exerted yet another pressure on midwives—to be individually responsible for the outcome of the labour.

> *[The woman in room 3] has been fully dilated for 2 hours... They decided to put up Syntocinon earlier, maybe an hour ago. The consultant has just said: 'I don't like it. She has a small baby, a temperature, let's just have a baby. [To midwife, jokingly] What sort of midwife are you? Why haven't you got it out yet?' (Field notes 10/5/12)*

These kinds of comments, commonly interspersed in the daily life of the ward, indicate that in many instances the medical practitioners were quite happy to relinquish 'the normal' to midwives, particularly when there were no risk factors. However, this did not give midwives permission to then use midwifery technologies; the institution still dictated the timetable and the power was still held by doctors, evidenced in the language they used, and the way the midwives discussed these instances of care. Normal birth in the institution, while upheld and supported by the medical staff at times, was therefore still a contested space, where women, then midwives, appeared to hold the least amount of power. Doctors possessed somewhat more power, because of the status of their profession and because it was an obstetric unit based on a medical system (see also Hunt and Symonds 1995). However, overlaying them all was the institutional apparatus, with its self-directed momentum, and overarching even that, were the dominant conceptions and perpetuations of risk and safety, birth and women's bodies, defying the attempts of those individual doctors and midwives grasping for more time and space for women in labour.

But, as Foucault (1980, p. 98) says, every interaction, every site of power is a potential site of resistance, and this was evident in the negotiation and direct resistance from midwives. Midwives negotiated by using the available technologies/systems on offer by the institution to try and 'buy time' or 'resist intervention', as shown in the following field note excerpt:

> *The consultant, registrar and midwife are discussing the CTG of a woman having Syntocinon and the baby is having decelerations. They're discussing the contractions and whether to turn down the Syntocinon. The consultant wants to go straight to theatre ['Let's not sit on this one']. They talk some more and in the time they are talking the CTG normalises a bit (the epidural has gone in and probably taken effect – this slows down the contractions). It is the midwife who points this out. 'Okay' says the consultant, 'Let's give her one hour. If there's no progress we'll go 'round the corner" [to theatre]. (Field notes 25/7/12)*

However, not all of the midwives' negotiating tactics worked, which they found frustrating. Later in this scenario:

> *I come out after handover and there is written on the board for this woman 'for emerg CS'. The T/L and another midwife [MW43] are questioning the need for this, especially as the woman has a BMI of 47. 'Surely they can do foetal blood sampling [to check the wellbeing of the foetus]. She's dilated 1 cm in an hour' [this is an acceptable rate]. The midwife, questioning the decision, asks the registrar why the woman is going to theatre. 'Can't foetal blood sampling be done? She has dilated.' The registrar: 'No, no, because we'd have to do foetal blood sampling every hour. That trace isn't going to get better. No.' (Field notes 25/7/12)*

Most often, the relationships between long-standing staff members allowed for more negotiation, especially with consultants. Midwives often (though not always) had the least success with junior obstetric staff who obviously felt the risk-management policies more keenly, and were perhaps less secure in their practice.

> *The woman had had a longish…labour and towards the end, the baby had a bradycardia, just one, and the registrar had wanted to do a CS, which the woman didn't want, and the midwife didn't think that was necessary, as there was descent of the head into the pelvis with pushing, and she thought the bradycardia was due to normal second stage head compression…The midwife (MW50) was discussing the particular registrar, who she sees as too quick to act. 'Her favourite saying is 'I think it's time to bail on this one''. The consultant who was on call was actually in the hospital and she suggested a forceps delivery instead, which the woman was apparently happier with. (Field notes 25/8/12)*

This midwife also said about a failed negotiation with the junior neonatal registrar, who had been present as a precautionary measure only because it was a forceps birth:

> *I know they're junior, but they should listen to us. If it's not necessary to do a full baby check now, he should listen. We don't put babies at peril. I'm really annoyed, because now skin to skin has been interrupted. (MW50)*

Institutional Culture: Discipline and Resistance

In this example, the midwife believed that the woman was experiencing normal labour and birth. The deceleration that can indicate head compression (and is therefore normal) in second-stage labour was interpreted as pathological by an inexperienced, nervous registrar. While the consultant prevented a caesarean section from occurring, the ensuing forceps birth and presence of another junior (neonatal) registrar meant that the birth and early skin to skin connection was interrupted, potentially unnecessarily.

In the following field note excerpt, a midwife questions a registrar about their decision to use ventouse for a birth:

One of the women who was 2 cms dilated at handover has just had her baby (10.16 am). The epidural was placed, and it turned out she was fully dilated. Baby born by ventouse. Out at the desk midwives are discussing this birth. The epidural had been put in, the woman was feeling pushing urges and was checked for dilatation. That was at 09.45 am—fully dilated. The baby was born by ventouse at 10.06 am. Her midwife (MW6) is unsure why it was felt ventouse was necessary. She explains: 'We have new doctors, they're a bit difficult. It was worse a month or so ago. They're getting better, but they are a bit nervous.'

Later at the board, the T/L (MW7) queried the doctor: 'Did we really need to do that [ventouse] then? It [the CTG] looked like it was coming back up ok, and the head was coming down fine. Do you think we could have waited?'

REG: 'Well it's just because it [the heart rate] went down to 50 [bpm] you see, if it had gone down to 80 I would have waited.'

MW7: 'Yes, it [the heart rate] just seemed to recover quickly. I think it was just because it was happening so quickly, the head was coming down…'

REG: 'Yes, but it was because the heart rate was going down to 50.'

MW7: 'Oh, ok, yes I see.'

The T/L is clearly not wanting to offend the doctor, or tip the balance of power. The woman in question was having a quick labour, and she had had an epidural put in at full dilatation. If the epidural had not been inserted, one could assume that the woman would have had a baby quite quickly. As it was, she had only been pushing for 20 minutes when the new registrar decided to do a ventouse delivery. (Field notes 1/5/12)

Again, the midwives here put the lowered heart rate down to head compression and thought that the birth was occurring quite rapidly on its own. Midwives were less concerned about decelerations in second stage of labour, which they interpreted as part of normal physiology, but which were consistently interpreted by obstetricians as pathological. Though remaining watchful and knowing that intervention might be required, their threshold of 'normal' was higher (see Loghis et al. 1997; Sheiner et al. 2001). The woman ended up having a second-degree perineal tear and a post-partum haemorrhage. The next day, the midwife who had been with this woman said:

> *Well, the CTG wasn't picking up the foetal heart, so I put a scalp clip on, and it was dropping to 50 [bpm], but it was picking up ok, and it is normal, you know, in second stage for the heart rate to drop. And the doctor just said 'Right, I'm doing a ventouse'. I should have just stepped in front and not let her, just got the woman to keep pushing, but I didn't feel comfortable [this MW is a new graduate]. It was only 20 minutes of pushing, and the baby was crowning. She ended up with a 2nd degree tear, which I think could have been avoided [without the ventouse delivery].* (MW6)

Other examples of resistance to protocol have been explored earlier in the chapter with reference to resisting risk culture and institutional throughput. Resistance tactics included delaying vaginal examinations, altering times (flexibility around confirmation of 'active' pushing), delaying Syntocinon use, and advocating against intervention. However, although many midwives attempted to incorporate midwifery technologies, and participated in passing on the stories of 'relishing the normal' at the increasingly rare times that 'the normal' occurred, midwifery practices were consistently ridiculed and maintained as unsafe. Despite the discourse that placed midwives as central to and responsible for 'keeping birth normal', there were many such instances where midwives attempted to negotiate with medical personnel, which failed because the final decision was made within the context of the risk paradigm and the momentum of the institution.

Figure 4.2 illustrates the organisation of data that is explored in this chapter showing how the competing technologies of practice culminated in a *paradox of the institution*.

Conclusion

Hill (1988) describes how industrialisation grew by direct exploitation that involved economic competition with, and the gradual dismantling of, opposing forces, such as artisan guilds. He notes that early factories were initially no more productive than the cottage industries they replaced, but allowed the capitalist classes more control over their labour force. However, as these technologies came to 'frame' Western thought about work, labour, capital, or money generally, it has become impossible to conceive of these things outside of this industrial or corporate frame. This is allegorical to the reframing of birth within the medical model, the way in which biomedicine marked out and attempted to eradicate the competing and rival discourse of midwifery, and situated birth in hospitals with increasing use of technology.

In this chapter, we have described the cultural setting of a hospital labour ward; the set in which the drama of modern birth plays out. We have shown how the institutional 'framing' of birth, with its risk orientation, reliance on technology, and medical understanding of birth as something that requires 'fixing', influenced the hospital birth apparatus. The mechanics of this apparatus were upheld by a panoptic disciplinary power, organisational technology—symbolised by the journey board—that served to maintain an institutional momentum within which women and midwives were expected to conform. This momentum was recognised by both midwives and doctors as having its own impetus and they practised in ways which sometimes resisted it and at other times surrendered. Contradictorily, the momentum of the institution placed women at risk by ignoring both birth physiology and women's individual needs, while purportedly upholding their safety.

While some midwives adapted to the organisational momentum, other midwives felt it interfered with their sense of what it means to be a midwife, and all midwives felt varying degrees of pressure from the institution to work within a time frame that was external and artificial rather than working with individual women's rhythm of labour. Midwives attempted to negotiate the institutional space by sharing and relishing in instances of 'normal birth'. Their upholding of normal birth knowledge—their midwifery technology—was fiercely guarded and was articulated within a context of keeping women safe. Their attempts to negotiate normal birth were sometimes upheld by medical staff but were ultimately under medical control. Ironically, although constituted as 'guardians of normal birth', the practices and knowledge required to truly fulfil this role were not permitted or condoned within the institution. The inconsistencies between setting, expectation, and practice, as well as the contradiction between risk and safety, revealed an institutional paradox that managed to simultaneously expose women to risk while upholding an impenetrable discourse of safety based on the symbolic power of institutional technology.

The organisation of the Western world along parameters of industrial capitalism included the emergence of institutionalised practices that were, for various reasons, also imposed on the birth process. As society moves into a post-industrial age, it is time to rethink some of these practices and the way in which birth is managed. As midwifery technologies were dispersed with no forethought by biomedical discourse, our 'frame' of birth has changed to such an extent as to be almost unrecognisable. The *meaning* of birth needs to enter back into the conversation. This could provide impetus for change both within these settings (for those who need a hospital setting for birth) and also without, supporting the notion that smaller birthing services that cater more fully for the needs of women, and for practising the art of midwifery, are needed.

Notes

1. There are various names for the place in which women give birth in a hospital. The old terminology of 'labour ward' has in many places been replaced with 'birth suite' or other such terminology. In recent studies from the United Kingdom, the current terminology appears fairly consistent, with obstetric unit (or OU) used for hospital labour wards and midwifery unit (MU) for birth centres, or midwife-led units (these can then be prefixed to give context: alongside midwifery unit [AMU], freestanding midwifery unit [FMU]). We decided in this study to stick with the terminology of 'labour ward' because it felt more anonymous to describe it in 'old' terminology and because this term also felt quite accurate in the way it seems to invoke 'the institution'.

2. Note from EN: I was surprised when I noticed my use of the word 'patient' here. I had not consciously used this term, and as a fervent believer in the importance of language, would not normally use it in a midwifery context.
3. This was coined from a health insurance company television commercial advertising their coverage of 'alternative' medicine. While in the hospital it was used as more tongue-in-cheek than outright derogatory, its use highlights the ridiculing of 'traditional' or 'alternative' practices.
4. We agree that relief from unbearable pain in labour can give women a sense of wellbeing and control, but this does not mean that other states, such as feeling empowered or involved in her experience should be belittled.
5. Shown in the following analytic memo:

    Are midwives responsible for 'getting babies out'? Do obstetricians rely on midwives for keeping the normal going? If they do, what does this mean? Does this mean that it is midwives who are perpetuating the medicalisation...not always as I have seen them directly oppose obstetric opinion (Field notes 31/5/12).

References

Arney, W. R. (1982). *Power and the profession of obstetrics.* Chicago: The University of Chicago Press.

Banks, A. C. (1999). *Birth chairs, midwives, and medicine.* Jackson: University Press of Mississippi.

Beck, U. (1999). *World risk society.* Cambridge: Polity Press.

Behruzi, R., Hatem, M., Fraser, W., Goulet, L., Ii, M., & Misago, C. (2010). Facilitators and barriers in the humanization of childbirth practice in Japan. *BMC Pregnancy and Childbirth, 10*, 1–18.

Behruzi, R., Hatem, M., Goulet, L., Fraser, W., & Misago, C. (2013). Understanding childbirth practices as an organizational cultural phenomenon: A conceptual framework. *BMC Pregnancy and Childbirth, 13*, 1–10.

Blaaka, G., & Eri, T. (2008). Doing midwifery between different belief systems. *Midwifery, 24*, 344–352.

Browne, J., & Chandra, A. (2009). Slow midwifery. *Women and Birth, 22*(1), 29–33.

Campo, M. (2010). Trust, power and agency in childbirth: Women's relationships with obstetricians. *Outskirts Online Journal, 22.* http://www.outskirts.arts.uwa.edu.au/volumes/volume-22/campo. Viewed Dec 2017.

Chaboyer, W., Wallen, K., Wallis, M., & McMurray, A. (2009). Whiteboards: One tool to improve patient flow. *Medical Journal of Australia, 190*(11 Suppl), s137–s140.

Crozier, K., Sinclair, M., Kernohan, W. G., & Porter, S. (2007). Ethnography of technological competence in clinical midwifery practice. *Evidence Based Midwifery, 5*(2), 59–65.

Davis-Floyd, R., & Davis, E. (1997). Intuition as authoritative knowledge in midwifery and home birth. In R. Davis-Floyd & C. Sargent (Eds.), *Childbirth and authoritative knowledge: Cross-cultural perspectives* (pp. 315–349). Berkeley: University of California Press.

Deery, R. (2008). The tyranny of time: Tensions between relational and clock time in community-based midwifery. *Social Theory & Health, 6*(4), 342–363.

Downe, S., & Dykes, F. (2009). Counting time in pregnancy and labour. In C. McCourt (Ed.), *Childbirth, midwifery and concepts of TIME*. Oxford: Berghahn Books.

Dykes, F. (2005). A critical ethnographic study of encounters between midwives and breast-feeding women in postnatal wards in England. *Midwifery, 21*(3), 241–252.

Foucault, M. (1980). Two lectures. In C. Gordon (Ed.), *Power/knowledge: Selected interviews and other writings 1972–1977 by Michel Foucault* (pp. 78–108). London: Harvester Wheatsheaf.

Foucault, M. (1991a). Politics and the study of discourse. In G. Burchell, C. Gordon, & P. Miller (Eds.), *The Foucault effect: Studies in governmentality* (pp. 53–72). Chicago: Harvester Wheatsheaf.

Foucault, M. (1991b [1975]). *Discipline and punish: The birth of the prison*. London: Penguin.

Foucault, M. (2003 [1963]). *The birth of the clinic*. London: Routledge.

Foucault, M. (2008 [1976]). *The history of sexuality* (Vol. 1). Melbourne: Penguin Books.

Freeman, L. M., Adair, V., Timperley, H., & West, S. H. (2006). The influence of the birthplace and models of care on midwifery practice for the management of women in labour. *Women and Birth, 19*(4), 97–105.

Gélis, J. (1991). *History of childbirth: Fertility, pregnancy and birth in early modern Europe*. Oxford: Polity Press.

Hammond, A., Foureur, M., Homer, C., & Davis, D. (2013). Space, place and the midwife: Exploring the relationship between the birth environment, neurobiology and midwifery practice. *Women and Birth, 26*(4), 277–281.

Hammond, A., Homer, C., & Foureur, M. (2014). Messages from space: An exploration of the relationship between hospital birth environments and midwifery practice. *Health Environments Research and Design Journal, 7*(4), 81–95.

Harte, J. D., Sheehan, A., Stewart, S. C., & Foureur, M. (2016). Childbirth supporters' experiences in a built hospital birth environment: Exploring inhibiting and facilitating factors in negotiating the supporter role. *HERD: Health Environments Research & Design Journal, 9*(3), 135–161.

Hill, S. (1988). *The tragedy of technology*. London: Pluto Press.

Hodnett, E., Downe, S., & Walsh, D. (2012). Alternative versus conventional institutional settings for birth. *Cochrane Database of Systematic Reviews* (8). Art. No: CD000012. doi: https://doi.org/10.1002/14651858.CD000012.pub4.

Hunt, S., & Symonds, A. (1995). *The social meaning of midwifery*. London: Macmillan.

Kennedy, H. P. (2002). The midwife as an "instrument" of care. *American Journal of Public Health, 92*(11), 1759–1760.

Kirkham, M. (2000). How can we relate? In M. Kirkham (Ed.), *The midwife-mother relationship* (pp. 227–250). New York: Palgrave Macmillan.

Kirkham, M., & Stapleton, H. (2004). The culture of the maternity services in Wales and England as a barrier to informed choice. In M. Kirkham (Ed.), *Informed choice in maternity care*. Basingstoke: Palgrave Macmillan.

Lawler, J. (2006). *Behind the screens: Nursing, somology, and the problem of the body*. Sydney: Sydney University Press.

Leap, N. (2012). *No gain without pain!* North Parramatta: Birth International.

Lee, N. J., Neal, J., Lowe, N. K., & Kildea, S. V. (2017). Comparing different partograph designs for use in standard labor care: A pilot randomized trial. *Maternal and Child Health Journal* (1–9). https://doi.org/10.1007/s10995-017-2366-0.

Loghis, C., Salamalekis, E., Panayotopoulos, N., Vitoratos, N., & Zourlas, P. A. (1997). The effect of early second stage bradycardia on newborn status. *European Journal of Obstetrics, Gynecology, and Reproductive Biology, 72*(2), 149–152.

Lupton, D. (1999). Risk and the ontology of pregnant embodiment. In D. Lupton (Ed.), *Risk and sociocultural theory: New directions and perspectives* (pp. 59–85). Cambridge: Cambridge University Press.

Maher, J. (2008). Progressing through labour and delivery: Birth time and women's experiences. *Women's Studies International Forum, 31*(2), 129–137.

Martin, E. (1989). *The woman in the body*. Milton Keynes: Open University Press.

McCourt, C., & Dykes, F. (2009). From traditional to modernity: Time and childbirth in historical perspective. In C. McCourt (Ed.), *Childbirth, midwifery and concepts of time*. Oxford: Berghahn Books.

Mead, M., & Kornbrot, D. (2004). The influence of maternity units' intrapartum intervention rates and midwives' risk perception for women suitable for midwifery-led care. *Midwifery, 20*(1), 61–71.

Murphy-Lawless, J. (1998). *Reading birth and death: A history of obstetric thinking*. Cork: Cork University Press.

Navarro, V. (1986). *Crisis, health and medicine: Social critique*. London: Tavistock Publications.

Newnham, E., McKellar, L., & Pincombe, J. (2017). Paradox of the institution: Findings from a hospital labour ward ethnography. *BMC Pregnancy and Childbirth, 17*(1), 2–11. Copyright retained by authors under the BioMed Central licence agreement.

O'Brien, L., Bassham, J., & Lewis, M. (2015). Whiteboards and discharge traffic lights: Visual management in acute care. *Australian Health Review, 39*(2), 160–164.

O'Connell, R., & Downe, S. (2009). A metasynthesis of midwives' experience of hospital practice in publicly funded settings: Compliance, resistance and authenticity. *Health, 13*(6), 589–609.

Odent, M. (1999). *The scientification of love*. London: Free Association Books.

Odent, M. (2013). *Childbirth and the future of homo sapiens*. London: Pinter & Martin.

Online Etymology Dictionary. (2010). Dictionary.com website. Viewed 4 June 2015.

Reiger, K. (2010). "Knights" or "Knaves"? Public policy, professional power, and reforming maternity services. *Health Care for Women International, 31*(1), 2–22.

Reiger, K., & Dempsey, R. (2006). Performing birth in a culture of fear: An embodied crisis of late modernity. *Health Sociology Review, 15*(4), 364–373.

Rothman, B. K. (1989). *Recreating motherhood: Ideology and technology in a patriarchal society*. New York: W.W. Norton & Company.

Sheiner, E., Hadar, A., Hallak, M., Katz, M., Mazor, M., & Shoham-Vardi, I. (2001). Clinical significance of fetal heart rate tracings during the second stage of labor. *Obstetrics & Gynecology, 97*(5), 747–752.

Skinner, J. (2003). The midwife in the 'risk' society. *New Zealand College of Midwives Journal, 28*, 4–7.

Stevens, T. (2009). Time and midwifery practice. In C. McCourt (Ed.), *Childbirth, midwifery and concepts of time*. Oxford: Berghahn Books.

Summers, A. (1995). *'For I have ever so much faith in her as a nurse': The eclipse of the community midwife in South Australia*. PhD thesis, School of Nursing and Midwifery, Flinders University of South Australia.

Szurek, J. (1997). Resistance to technology-enhanced childbirth in Tuscany: The political economy of Italian birth. In R. Davis-Floyd & C. Sargent (Eds.), *Childbirth and authoritative knowledge: Cross-cultural perspectives* (pp. 287–314). Berkeley: University of California Press.

Towler, J., & Bramall, J. (1986). *Midwives in history and society*. London: Croon Helm.

Waitzkin, H. (1983). *The second sickness: Contradictions of capitalist health care*. London: The Free Press.

Walsh, D. (2005). What midwives can learn from the slow food movement. *British Journal of Midwifery, 13*(7), 416–416.

Walsh, D. (2006). Subverting the assembly-line: Childbirth in a free-standing birth centre. *Social Science & Medicine, 62*(6), 1330–1340.

Walsh, D. (2009a). Pain and epidural use in normal childbirth. *Evidence Based Midwifery, 7*(3), 89–93.

Walsh, D. (2009b). Management of time and place in a birth centre. In C. McCourt (Ed.), *Childbirth, midwifery and concepts of time*. Oxford: Berghahn Books.

Walsh, D. (2010). Childbirth embodiment: Problematic aspects of current understandings. *Sociology of Health & Illness, 32*(3), 486–501.

Walsh, D. (2012). *Evidence and skills for normal birth*. London: Routledge.

Walsh, D., El-Nemer, A., & Downe, S. (2008). Rethinking risk and safety in maternity care. In S. Downe (Ed.), *Normal childbirth: Evidence and debate* (2nd ed.). Sydney: Elsevier.

Williams, J. (1997). The controlling power of childbirth in Britain. In H. Marland & A. Rafferty (Eds.), *Midwives, society and childbirth: Debates and controversies in the modern period*. London: Routledge.

Willis, E. (1989). *Medical dominance* (2nd ed.). Sydney: Allen and Unwin.

Winter, C., & Duff, M. (2009). The progress of labour: Orderly chaos? In C. McCourt (Ed.), *Childbirth, midwifery and concepts of time*. Oxford: Berghahn Books.

5

A Dialectic of Risk

TESSA
I really, really hated it.
I just—ugh.
Totally overwhelmed
I can't believe that women have been doing it
For thousands, millions of years.
I just think if it was up to me
Civilization wouldn't keep going
Because I think it's,
I can't believe it's normal!
I just can't.

They said 'Go take a Panadol and see how you go'
I said 'Is taking a Panadol necessary?'
And they said
'Well you should go take one'
And they said
'Look, it happens to a lot of women,
Sometimes it goes on for days and then
When they get into labour they
Are just too exhausted to do it'.

© The Author(s) 2018
E. Newnham et al., *Towards the Humanisation of Birth*,
https://doi.org/10.1007/978-3-319-69962-2_5

And then they said
'Well, are you going to take a Panadol?'
And I said 'Look I don't even know if I have Panadol in the house'.
They said
'Give us a call back in 2 hours'
I didn't take Panadol
But I was pretty upset by this stage.
Then he drove me straight to emergency.
They put me straight on the bed
Because I couldn't walk at all
Then brought me to the room,
And I was freaking out.
I was really scared and in a lot of pain.

The student midwife was really good.
I was trying to get her to distract me
I was trying to get her to chat to me.
As soon as I got there they offered me the gas,
Which is fine I guess
But as soon as I got in there they said 'Do you want the gas?'
I'm like 'Oh, yes, yes'
Because I was in so much pain.

I didn't really like the first midwife who was there.
She wouldn't let me get in the bath.
They were drawing a bath for me
And she said 'No turn the water off.
We are not going to use the bath'.
I'd signed a water birth form
(Knowing that I might not get one)
They said 'There isn't a water birth midwife here'
I said 'That's fine I want a bath anyway'
Then I said 'Why aren't we going to use it?'
They said 'We don't think we are going to able to get you out.'
I thought that was a bit strange
Because my partner was there,
He could have carried me out.

So I was just in the shower for as long as I could be
Then eventually went back onto the bed.
I was telling him 'I am scared.

I don't think I am going to be able to do it drug free
I am in so much pain'.
What I found worst about the labour—
The contractions,
Just in my hips.
It felt like it was ripping my body apart,
I couldn't actually feel them in my tummy.
You know, this is a study on what influences pain medication
And it was, for me,
Other than the midwife offering me gas,
The pain.
It was absolutely the pain.

I felt really discouraged by the first midwife.
She was telling me I wasn't pushing hard enough.
I just felt like I was a little kid getting told off.
I didn't like that.
Then the midwife got replaced.
I totally didn't even notice anyone there.
And I felt,
I just felt really discouraged
And broken
From the pain.
But that's it. That was it.
Afterwards I felt good.
Holding the baby I felt good.
I was under no illusion.
I knew it was going to hurt.
But…everything other than the pain was fine.

Realities of Risk

Although some midwives at the field site had been acculturated into a risk culture, and appeared to work easily within these parameters, other midwives were starkly aware of its impact. One midwife described the acculturation of risk as follows:

> *A lot of midwives here are so medicalised. They walk into a room with a woman having a normal physiological labour, and within 10 minutes, they're strapped to the bed. I mean there's no indication for that. The institution is medical. I hate the way [labour ward] treats everyone the same, as high-risk. (MW4)*

Here, the midwife has identified the pervasive push of medicalised risk parameters onto all women, and the effect this can have on healthy women experiencing normal labour. Midwives also found it difficult within this culture to justify less interventionist actions, as outcomes were also measured in terms of risk rather than normality. Therefore, potentially iatrogenic interventions were not questioned, but non-intervention was seen as unsafe and stood out from usual practice. There was a sense of 'getting away with' non-intervention, rather than it being perceived as a legitimate part of midwifery practice when attending normal birth, as described below:

> *The doctor came in and asked if I wanted her to put in [an IV cannula]. I said 'No don't worry—she's about to have her baby'. Then [the woman] has a massive PPH. You try and keep it normal and it all just goes to shit. (MW11)*

The culture of the labour ward was manifestly risk-focused, and although many midwives disagreed with the intense regulation of practice, there was a sense of powerlessness against it, as the hospital policies—some of which the midwives viewed as restricting normal birth processes—were seen as impervious, with no legitimate recourse for resistance. Attempts to defy intervention were occasionally supported, but were more often overturned, as discussed in the previous chapter. The midwives did not necessarily 'believe' in these regulations. The field note excerpt below illustrates the sense of professional detachment that the midwives felt about many new protocols.

> *[The midwives] were talking about the risk assigned to women, because it was a high-risk unit. New rules were being discussed. Two new rules that had just been introduced were that all women had to be weighed on admission to the labour ward [and a BMI calculated], and also given a risk score for blood clots. Although the mood was light, the midwives were ridiculing the new rules,*

wondering what on earth they would have to measure next and there was dismay at the way things were going...one midwife remarks: 'It feels as though we're going backwards.' (Field notes 4/4/12)

However, externally administered policies can alienate midwives from their own sense of clinical expertise, adherence to the midwifery philosophy, and providing individualised care to women (Kirkham 2011; Walsh 2012), leading to midwives' dissatisfaction and attrition from the profession (Ball et al. 2002; Brodie 2002). This problem, raised by Downe (2015) in her Chair address at the *Normal Labour and Birth Conference* as being detrimental to expert practice, has led to an 'unlearning of expertise' that has come with bureaucratic managerialism dominated by risk-averse protocols. An emphasis on relationships, not increased surveillance, is needed, coupled with expertise of practice which recognises that some rules or policies may need to be bent to suit individual women's circumstances (Downe 2015).

Paradoxically, midwives working within an institution are somewhat compelled to follow hospital policy, or put *themselves* at risk if an adverse event ensues (Kirkham and Stapleton 2004; Scamell and Stewart 2014). As documented in the previous chapter, there was some resistance to the medicalised and industrial nature of the birth 'machine' by both midwives and doctors (see Wagner 1994), but these were akin to individual drops in an ocean of intervention. More commonly, the institutional flow was impervious to resistance, and this was compounded by the pervasive view that midwifery technologies, which work towards keeping birth normal, are 'unsafe'. There was a sense of dissatisfaction amongst many of the midwives to medically oriented birth policies, which were imposed hierarchically by the hospital, by obstetric practice guidelines, and government policy documents. Nevertheless, the midwives primarily complied with the 'encoded knowledge'—knowledge that both underpins and defines a profession (Scamell and Stewart 2014, p. 85)—provided by these guidelines because they provide a form of guarantee. If an adverse event were to occur they would be found 'safe' in their practice because they followed policy; highlighting the way in which these policies can lead to the 'unlearning of expertise' described above, as midwives are required to ignore what they believe to be best practice because it does not fit within hospital policy, guideline, or culture.

Risk Rhetoric and Water Restriction

Water in labour and birth is an increasingly common, though still marginal, practice that offers benefits such as increased relaxation and satisfaction, reduced length of labour and intervention, and increased rates of spontaneous vaginal birth (Davies et al. 2015). Research to date has not found any significant adverse effects associated with the use of water (Dahlen et al. 2013; Menakaya et al. 2013; Young, K. and Kruske 2013). Significantly, and perhaps paradoxically, water immersion decreases the use of epidural analgesia in labour (Cluett and Burns 2009) and therefore averts the risks associated with its use. Recent research has identified decreased incidence of neonatal unit admission in babies of women who gave birth in water, whereas the likelihood was increased threefold for the babies of women who had an epidural in labour (Adams et al. 2015). However, choices in the environment of a 'high-risk' obstetric unit are limited both by its 'risk' culture, and wider influences of what constitutes risk. The meanings ascribed to particular practices as described by hospital policies tended to normalise intervention and marginalise non-medical practices. This influenced the behaviour and individual practices of the midwives, affecting the culture of the site as a whole. As one midwife put it:

> *The thing is, here, is that there aren't that many options. There's pethidine or there's epidural. They don't use TENS here, which is really good for early labour. And they don't really use the baths.* (MW19)

Another midwife identified:

> *I wouldn't ever recommend an epidural to anyone. No, I sometimes push the TENS because it really works for back pain, and in some OP labours… Although it's [TENS] not used much here.* (MW30)

There was a lot of discussion by the midwives about the restrictions on labour and birth in water. There was a process underway to 'accredit' midwives to practise waterbirth. This involved an online education package, observation of three waterbirths, and facilitation of three more waterbirths under supervision of another accredited midwife. It had been exceedingly difficult in the day-to-day running of the ward for midwives to gain accreditation. Women were not even supposed to get into the bath unless the midwife who was caring for her was accredited to provide waterbirth. This created more restriction than before the accreditation process began, as most women then could opt for a bath in labour, albeit under the expectation that they would get out for the actual birth. This created frustration for the midwives:

> *I had all this experience, I'd done it in my previous jobs, but here, I had to go through the whole process again. In case I hadn't learned how to do it properly!* (MW10)

Another barrier to the use of water in this facility was the increased paperwork. One midwife, discussing this difficulty, said:

> MW13: *They are good pain relief. I think they should have more [water birth].*
> EN: *Do many women ask for it?*
> MW13: *No, and we don't volunteer the information, even down in clinic. Just like today, [we] could use water therapy for her, but it's a bit late in labour to talk about water therapy. There's so much involved now, whereas in the old days [women used to just get in the bath, it was simple]. When we're all 'qualified' I think we'll offer it more…It's just all the paperwork.*

Midwives were vocal about the lack of perceived support for waterbirth by senior management, who they saw as delaying the process by not having it as a priority and by the imposition of other restrictions. Institutional restrictions to implementing the practice of waterbirth are not uncommon, probably due to the fact it is considered an alternative practice (Cooper, M. et al. 2013; Keirse and Andrews 2006; Russell 2011). In order to manage the limitation of water use and facilitate choice for women in labour, some midwives used subtle techniques of resistance. As other midwifery researchers have found, midwives who feel bound by highly regulated policies that they consider too stringent, often find more covert resistance mechanisms (Dove and Muir-Cochrane 2014; Kirkham 2000; Kirkham and Stapleton 2004; Scamell and Stewart 2014). In the next example, a midwife uses the protocol of the journey board to work in favour of the woman.

MW8 (coming out of a labour room): Well, I didn't see that...
EN: Didn't see what?
MW8: She's in the bath. We're not really supposed to use them yet, until 80% of the staff are accredited. But who knows how long that'll take? She's in orange [on the board – signifying antenatal – not active labour] so she's technically not in labour yet.

Despite some midwives attempting to offer water as a viable choice, the culture of the site—including the midwives' perceived lack of support for waterbirth by the senior management—as well as state-wide policy documents, discussed below, had the potential to affect the options offered to women in labour and therefore the choices that women were able to make. Whether a woman could access water was ultimately dependent on the midwife that the woman had on the day, and whether she was willing to undertake extra paperwork, turn a blind eye to hospital policy, or find an accredited midwife to support her through a waterbirth—if there was one available.

Risk Culture and Epidural Endorsement

The cultural emphasis on risk meant that it was far easier to get an epidural than it was to get into a bath, but this was not only due to the risk orientation of the labour ward. Despite the capability for the government (Health department) policies about labour and birth in water to 'legitimise' the practice of waterbirth, one of the effects of the introduction of the *Waterbirth Policy* was the potential control and restriction of this practice (see Newnham 2010).

Women who were contemplating a waterbirth had to read a pamphlet based on the *Waterbirth Policy*, which they then signed. A waterbirth consent form also needed to be signed and a copy went into the case notes. The amount of paperwork clearly deterred some midwives from introducing the idea, particularly if the woman had not been informed about the policy antenatally. The introduction of the *Waterbirth Policy* therefore led to a situation where an essentially low-risk, effective form of analgesia for labour now has inordinate restrictions for use, even if women are not planning to birth in water. Simply getting into the bath in labour is no longer an option. And, by contrast, there is no corresponding health department policy requiring women to be fully informed antenatally about epidural risk factors, despite the fact that many women may not be completely cognisant of the risks of epidural.

In the fieldwork site, there were two main documents pertaining to epidural administration: a hospital-specific *Epidural information sheet* and an anaesthetic checklist. The women would also sign a *Consent to medical treatment* form. The *Epidural information sheet* is what was available to women in terms of the information they received. The *Epidural information sheet* is discussed below in contrast with the *Waterbirth policy pamphlet*. The following field note excerpt captures the inherent contradiction between the requirement that women need to be fully informed and sign a document before accessing water in labour, and the consent process to getting an epidural.

EN: *What about epidurals? Do they sign a consent?*
MW13: *Yes, they sign a 'Consent to treatment' form.*
EN: *Why is it easier for women to sign an epidural consent than a waterbirth consent?*
MW13: *Because they have to understand the [waterbirth] policy and all that. I don't think they can do a true informed consent if they're in labour. I suppose the same goes for epidural. I don't know.*

However, in practice, the 'same' did not apply to epidural consent; specifically, there was no policy handout for a woman to read and sign. There was also no way of gauging how much information women had received about epidural antenatally. In fact, midwives discussed the fact that consent for epidural insertion was often only gained verbally prior to the epidural being placed, with the woman not signing the *Consent to medical treatment* form until the epidural had taken effect and the woman was more comfortable.

Documenting Risk: Discourse Analysis

Table 5.1 contains section titles and information given in the two leaflets. It is evident that there is a strong difference in language between the two handouts—how each practice is framed—that perpetuate mainstream discourses of risk and safety. The language in the *Waterbirth policy pamphlet* handout signals restrictions and conditions. For many women, the fact that 'hospitals, doctors and midwives…generally do not advocate waterbirth' (column 1, row A) would be enough to deter them in making this choice as they negotiate mainstream ideas of risk and responsibility. Although the *Waterbirth policy pamphlet* does not give the source of this information,[1] it does later appeal to the lack of evidence to support the practice of waterbirth (column 1, row C). However, the evidence actually cited (column 1, row C) identifies promising outcomes with water use, resulting in an incongruity between the evidence and the claim that this practice is not supported by midwives and doctors. Still under the 'Evidence' section, rare events such as drowning are discussed, leading to the conclusion that it 'demands extra care both of who can give birth in water and how'. It then follows with who is allowed access to water and the conditions for using a bath. In this section (column 1, row D) there is a reiteration of the need for safety; implicitly reinforcing the 'dangerousness' of water use as well as appealing to the woman's sense of responsibility in the face of such risk. There is not such a call to consider safety concerns within the *Epidural information sheet*.

The *Epidural information sheet*, which is a hospital-specific document but also carries a Health Department logo, has none of the cautious tone adopted for waterbirth. Epidural analgesia almost appears to be recommended (column 2, row A) as a common and effective analgesic choice. The obstetric risks associated with epidurals are acknowledged, but downplayed, and possible negative effects on the baby are completely ignored; in fact, having an epidural is discussed as potential benefit to the baby (column 2, row E). The anaesthetic risks (column 2, row F) are quite comprehensive, listing rare complications. What is surprising, given the identification of these risks, is that the overall tone of the *Epidural information sheet*—compared to the *Waterbirth policy pamphlet*—is pleasant, conciliatory, and formulated to facilitate the process.

As can be seen throughout Table 5.1, the overall language of the *Epidural information sheet* is that of safety while the *Waterbirth policy pamphlet* is couched in terms of risk. There are no 'conditions' for who can use an epidural (see column 1, row F). Particularly telling is the language used in row G: 'You can only give birth in water if…' as compared to 'Can I definitely have an epidural?'—these women are only advised if an epidural is not 'recommended', whereas the women choosing water are 'told' if they have a condition that 'prevents' them from using water (see column 1, row D). The epidural pamphlet emphasises access—who can have one, while the water birth pamphlet emphasises restriction—who cannot. This reflects the 'safety and necessity' of the medical epidural discourse already described and reveals the way that dominant discourses are recreated even in the absence of 'evidence', despite biomedicine's claim to superiority precisely because of its proximity to scientific knowledge. This shows a clear example of how biomedical discourse is created and maintained, according to Foucault's theory of power/knowledge (see Gordon 1980), whereby the construction of knowledge is mediated and constituted by those discourses that are already, and seek to remain, powerful; situating, as Foucault (1991a, p. 79) suggests, 'the production of true and false' as the focus of 'historical analysis and political critique'.

Policy and Practice

Restrictions on the use of water in labour and birth may be reasonable, for example, if a woman has just had pethidine, or indeed an epidural—two of the conditions for not using a bath. But this judgement, as with much midwifery practice, has usually been left to the midwife's discretion, in consultation with the woman, and forms part of safe and competent practice in line with a multitude of professional practice and ethical guidelines provided by the professional regulatory bodies, in this case, the Nursing and Midwifery Board of Australia (NMBA 2015). Government health policy has not usually intervened at this level of practice. Meanwhile, there is no corresponding concern about epidural use despite the rare complications that can occur,[2] which cast a potential 'cloud' over its use. In addition, at this site, midwives are not required to undertake

Table 5.1 Comparison of main headings and content: waterbirth policy pamphlet and epidural information sheet

Row	Column 1 Waterbirth policy pamphlet	Column 2 Epidural information sheet
A	**Background** Hospitals, doctors, and midwives in South Australia generally do not advocate waterbirth. Those who allow the use of water need to adhere to the policies of the Department of Health for labour and birth in water to occur safely	**Introduction** Epidurals are commonly used in labour for pain relief. Nearly one in two women in South Australia has an epidural during labour. Epidurals provide very good pain relief, and you may want one when you are in labour
B	**Arguments for and against the use of a bath** Enthusiasts for baths in labour and birth argue that it enhances relaxation, reduces pain, and promotes supportive care Critics are concerned about the potential harm to the baby mainly through getting water in the lungs and the risk of infection	**What is an epidural?** An epidural is a special form of pain relief. A thin plastic tube called an epidural catheter is inserted into your lower back...Local anaesthetic and other drugs are given into the epidural space via the catheter. The drugs help take away the pain from the uterus, cervix, and birth canal by numbing the nerves to these areas
C	**Is there good evidence on the use of a bath?** There is a lot of opinion and anecdote on the use of baths, but little is substantiated by good scientific evidence...Studies have shown...less pain and fewer epidurals. No effects on the duration of labour or on the condition of the baby have been demonstrated Giving birth in water has resulted in some serious incidents that do not occur outside water, including drowning....While these situations have been rare they have cast a cloud over waterbirth	**How is my epidural put in? Does it hurt?** First your anaesthetists will assess you to make sure there are no reasons why you should not have an epidural, and to make sure you understand the risks and benefits involved You will feel a sting as some local anaesthetic is put into the skin at the area of your lower where the epidural needle will be inserted. You might feel a dull pressure as the epidural needle is inserted, but this is usually not painful

A Dialectic of Risk 161

D **Who can use a bath?**
In or outside the bath, safety for you and your baby are the main concerns. You should not use the bath at all:
If there is a state of altered consciousness....
If you have an epidural...
If either you or your baby need a level of monitoring that is difficult to achieve in a bath...
Your doctor or midwife will tell you if there is a condition that would prevent you from using the bath during labour or for the birth

Conditions for using a bath during labour

E You must not have a condition that makes use of the bath too risky
You must never be alone in the room when using the bath...
You can leave the bath at any time you wish
You must leave the bath to urinate
You must also leave the bath when advised to do so for safety reasons
You cannot have pain killers or an epidural when using the bath

Will I be completely numb? Does an epidural always work?
Different strengths of local anaesthetic solution can be used. Stronger solutions used to relieve stronger pain will cause more numbness, heavy legs, and less pushing sensation. About 1 in 20 women may not get adequate pain relief. You may feel some pain in the second stage of labour if the epidural is allowed to wear off for pushing

Will I be able to push my baby out? Will the epidural affect my baby?
Having an epidural can make the second stage of your labour longer, and there is a slightly higher chance you will need help delivering your baby, either with forceps or the suction cup (Ventouse). Some studies suggest you have a slightly higher chance of needing Caesarean delivery, but this is not definite
As long as your blood pressure is well maintained during labour there is little effect on your baby from an epidural. In fact an epidural may be better for your baby than other types of pain relief as it minimises the effects of painful labour

(continued)

Table 5.1 (continued)

Row	Column 1 Waterbirth policy pamphlet	Column 2 Epidural information sheet
F	**Conditions for giving birth in a bath** All conditions for using a bath during labour must be met There must be no medical reasons against giving birth in water You must be prepared to leave the bath when necessary for reasons of safety You may need to stand up to facilitate the birth The baby must be brought to the surface as soon as it is born… The baby's cord must not be cut underwater After birth the baby must be protected against heat loss (a wet baby loses heat 25 times faster than a dry baby) You must leave the bath for the delivery of the placenta after the baby is born	**Are epidurals safe? Can I be paralysed?** Epidurals are very safe, but there are some common minor side-effects. Serious problems do occur, but are very rare. Common side-effects include discomfort…a drop in blood pressure, and occasionally the need for a catheter in the bladder…If the epidural needle is unintentionally inserted too far it can puncture the membrane containing the spinal fluid, causing severe headache…less common side-effects include the epidural working too high up your body, leading to some difficulty breathing. Rarely, local anaesthetic gets into your circulation and can cause problems with your heart, or directly affects your brain, leading to a fit or convulsion….with prompt medical attention should cause no long-term harm Temporary nerve injury…happens about 1 in 1000 deliveries Nerve damage causing permanent paralysis can also happen after an epidural, but is extremely rare (less than 1 in 100,000 epidurals). Infection or bleeding around the spinal cord…are very serious problems, but both are very rare If you are worried about any of these side-effects you should discuss them with an anaesthetist well before your delivery day

A Dialectic of Risk 163

G **You can only give birth in water**
If you have a normal pregnancy and normal labour
If you explicitly ask for a waterbirth
If you accept to leave the bath when advised to do so....
You have been informed of the Department of Health policies on the use of water for labour and birth
If you have read this leaflet, understood it, and discussed it with your midwife or doctor and signed the consent form below; and
If you are attended throughout by a midwife or doctor who is confident and experienced in conducting waterbirths

Can I definitely have an epidural?
Your epidural will be difficult to insert if you are overweight or have certain back problems....
If you have a bleeding problem or are taking medication to thin the blood, you might be advised not to have an epidural

What about forceps delivery or caesarean birth?
If you need help with the delivery of your baby, the epidural you had during labour can be used to provide anaesthesia for forceps delivery, Ventouse, or Caesarean section

Concluding comment
If you ask for an epidural when you are in labour you will be asked to sign a consent form to show that you have read and understood this information

H

I **Concluding comment**
I confirm that I have received a copy of the Labour and Birth in Water information, have read it, understood it, and discussed the management of labour and birth with the person whose signature appears below

extra training or accreditation to monitor and maintain birth with an epidural, although it is likely as necessary, given the complexities introduced by this intervention. Women are not informed that they 'must be attended throughout by a midwife or doctor who is confident and experienced in conducting' epidural management (see column 1, row G) despite this surely being optimal; neither are they required to read a policy document which outsets the practice they are desiring for their labour in clear terms of risk and restriction, and have it signed before labour.

In comparing these two documents we have drawn attention to the way in which practices are framed as risky or safe depending on their acceptance by biomedical and hospital culture, rather than their actual level of risk. In Beck's (Beck 1999) description of risk society—a self-reflexive, secondary era of modernity where ideas of certainty are no longer possible—he identifies the 'power game of risk' acknowledging that power rests with whomever gets to define risk in the current environment of 'manufactured uncertainties' (Beck 1999, pp. 4–5). While risk analysis may contribute to the diminishment of certain real dangers, the construction of particular practices as risky—and certain individuals as 'at risk'— also serves to maintain existing authoritative social structures (Beck 1999). As we move increasingly towards a risk-driven society, it becomes more important to critically assess our cultural meanings and understandings of particular practices and the way in which risk is assigned. In the example above, the 'manufacturing' of waterbirth as a risky practice is evident. The inculcation of this risk discourse into the everyday language and practice of midwives is of concern. As seen by the field note excerpts, it impacts on midwifery practice, even for those midwives who see themselves as coming from a midwifery philosophy, and it restricts choices for women in ways that are imperceptible, or at least not necessarily overt, exampled by the difference in language between the two pamphlets.

Theorising Risk

Smith, Devane, and Murphy-Lawless (2012) argue that risk as a concept is both abstract and unstable. Its changeable boundaries mean what is constituted as 'risk' varies over time and is not always based in evidence

(Murphy-Lawless 2012; Pitt 1997), and it is therefore an inexact frame of reference. The placement of evidence and anecdote within the two leaflets demonstrates how the language of risk in this case is manufactured to uphold acceptable medical practices and discourage the 'alternative'. Anecdotal evidence suggesting catastrophic possibilities are included in the information on waterbirth to further dissuade women from this choice, while severe adverse epidural events are not mentioned.

However, despite society's current obsession with risk, its use as a management tool is fallible primarily because its chief deductive methods—statistics and probability—are abstract concepts which are inexact predictors of pregnancy outcomes; women designated at low-risk may have an acute, emergency event, and women designated as high-risk can birth without experiencing a complication (Bryers and van Teijlingen 2010; Possamai-Inesedy 2006). And this is the final dilemma: risk factors as identified through probability, mediated by guidelines, and internalised by women, can inspire fear and alienation (Reiger and Dempsey 2006) without necessarily safeguarding against the uncertain event, which in any case may never happen.

Risk analysis in maternity care is therefore a fragile science. While the science of risk is essentially based on probability, Lane (1995) observes that in the case of obstetrics, the assignment of risk to individuals, instead of to populations, has legitimised medical intervention. The paradoxical nature of how risk constitution and management can work *against* individuals is lucidly illustrated in the following example:

> Formal risk management schedules too frequently protect the interests of hospitals, health authorities, and ultimately, the state through its regulatory bodies. If, for example, a woman wants to birth at home because the birth of her previous baby in an overcrowded, understaffed public hospital, with too few midwives experienced in sustaining the birth process without intervention, and a heavy reliance on routine CTG as part of the local protocols, leading to an emergency caesarean section, a common enough occurrence, that event itself now precludes the woman from giving birth at home as a VBAC. The woman has already sustained a traumatic and damaging outcome physically and psychologically. The state and its institutions will take no responsibility whatsoever for the lack of 'best practice' leading

to this outcome; indeed the woman may well have been told or been encouraged to infer that the emergency Caesarean section 'saved' her baby, yet the conditions of care and poor clinical management of her labour will not be 'seen', as problematic, let alone documented as 'risk factors'. Her decision to have a subsequent baby at home will be blocked because of the obstetric belief that any birth which happens beyond the borders of a hospital constitutes a greater 'risk' compared with birth inside a hospital simply because it lies beyond that border, and therefore beyond its control. (Murphy-Lawless 2012, p. 70)

The issue demonstrated in the above example is the same as that expressed by the midwives in this study and illustrated in the constitution of waterbirth as a risky practice.

Risk society encourages the constitution of the self as an 'individual'; the responsibility to avoid risk is placed firmly on the self rather than on societal factors (Beck 1999, p. 9). Women are therefore positioned as choosing agents; there is pressure to succumb to social norms and avoid risk-taking behaviours, and there was an appeal to this sense of responsibility throughout the *Waterbirth policy pamphlet*. Women can participate in 'purchasing' freedom from risk (Smith et al. 2012) by utilising private obstetricians, or consenting to intervention, and this is the main thrust of obstetric discourse in Australia (Campo 2014; Donellan-Fernandez 2011). Disciplining the individual and regulating the social body are techniques of power that provoke self-regulating behaviour and conformity to dominant discursive norms, techniques that formed the practice of 'governmentality' (Foucault 1990, pp. 139–147, 1991b). Direct medical coercion is often not required, as most women will engage in self-surveillance and monitor their own behaviour according to the incentives of the discourse—in this case, medical safety/approval. The irony of this circumstance lies in the fact that the obstetric model is an unreliable safeguard against risk, because interventionist practices can increase the risk of adverse outcomes (Bryers and van Teijlingen 2010; Dahlen et al. 2014; Donellan-Fernandez 2011); though it is obscured behind a convincing discourse of 'safety' (Newnham 2014) while midwifery models and non-interventionist practices are still framed as occupying a position of risk despite increasing evidence to the contrary (Brocklehurst et al. 2011;

de Jonge et al. 2009, 2013; Janssen et al. 2002, 2009; Olsen and Clausen 2012; Wiegers et al. 1996).

Bryers and van Teijlingen (2010) raise the concept of tolerable risk, whereby individual perceptions of what constitutes a risky practice are weighed up and some freedoms or compromises are made in order to feel safe. These individual meanings of risk differ according to prior experience and beliefs about birth practices, and will vary depending on whether one is committed to a model of childbirth as inherently risky, or inherently normal. Women therefore make their own interpretation of risk and safety according to their own parameters, which may differ from those of the medical establishment (Chadwick and Foster 2014; Dahlen 2010; Smith et al. 2012). Operating from a 'risk management' perspective, women's understanding and experience of pregnancy and birth is often overlooked by the medical model. The use of the risk model of birth serves to maintain medical authority and control over birth processes, often working against current evidence (Bryers and van Teijlingen 2010; Campo 2014; Donellan-Fernandez 2011; Murphy-Lawless 2012). Interestingly, Bryers and van Teijlingen (2010, p. 493) use the very example of water use and epidural to illustrate their point of how tolerable risks come to be accepted:

> For example, when a woman who has had a previous caesarean section chooses to have a waterbirth, the midwife is put in a difficult position: she may wish to support the woman, but to do so will mean that she (in some maternity units) is practising outside the agreed clinical guidelines. Both the midwife and the woman will face considerable pressure from the dominant obstetric ideology; that this is not safe. However, the medical approach to this case is likely to see an epidural in labour as an acceptable risk because this is perceived as a technology which can be controlled by continuous monitoring; it is arguable whether this is 'an optimum level of care' but this is how it will be perceived as it is supported by the authoritative knowledge.

This example illustrates perfectly the central concern of this chapter: the ubiquity of the authoritative medical standpoint on risk, and the way that practices are then framed, both by health care practitioners, and also by women, as risky. The acceptance of medically tolerable risks over risks that are tolerable to women potentially create suboptimal clinical situations. In the above quote, medical risk tolerance overlooks the evidence that points to significant risk associated with introducing epidural into labour, such as those outlined in Chap. 2. What is more, in the instance of a vaginal birth after caesarean (VBAC), epidural analgesia can mask the pain that identifies uterine rupture (Archer 2014), while cEFM increases the risk of another caesarean section (Alfirevic et al. 2017). There is no reason why a woman would not, in considering these risks, decide that her idea of tolerable risk involves the rejection of this technology and that water use, with its associated positive benefits such as shorter labours and a reduction in the need for analgesia, would present a rational choice. However, this places the midwife in a 'risky' position of supporting the woman outside of recommended guidelines and taking responsibility for any professional, legal or clinical consequences (Bryers and van Teijlingen 2010), again highlighting the conflict for midwives of following risk-driven hospital policy and still providing woman-centred care (Edwards 2004).

Documenting Risk: What the Women Heard

Having established how hospital and policy documents served to recreate the pervasive medical discourse of epidural as 'safe and necessary', echoing the broader biomedical epidural discourse demonstrated in Chap. 2, we now examine the effects of this discourse on the information received or understood by the women in the study.

The Pros and Cons of Epidural

The women in general did not have a comprehensive understanding of the potential risks and side-effects of epidural analgesia. In concert with medical and social views, it was broadly perceived as safe. One participant, Rose, who was having her first baby, and who was not planning an epidural, said:

I don't really know what the cons of having an epidural would be… there is a small possibility of something going wrong which probably isn't…worth worrying about. (Rose, interview 2)

Kate, who had had an unplanned epidural after a long posterior labour with her first baby, and who was not necessarily planning on having one with this labour said:

I mean, they say there is a very slim chance anything can go wrong but there is always a chance, as with anything, particularly something going into your spine. (Kate, interview 2)

The idea of a needle being placed into the back was unappealing, even frightening, to many of the women. Anna, having her third baby, was more aware of the obstetric risks, including instrumental birth:

I don't like the idea of forceps or ventouse and…the pain relief that you can probably get from an epidural I guess it's probably counteracted by the fact that you've had other interventions…Apart from being scared of needles, I guess from what I've heard from a lot of people who are more pro-epidural versus those who are anti- is the fact that you can't move around, from what I understand, and that you need to be monitored. (Anna, interview 2)

The women described the need for epidural analgesia if labour became intolerable, but fear of risks and being unable to move detracted its appeal as an option:

I think it's great if you are in pain and you can't tolerate your pain and if the labour has gone on too long…I have just heard horror stories as well…just about no feeling for couple of days in your legs and I had a friend who had headaches for almost two years after because of the positioning of the needle. (Bella, interview 2)

I would say, the pros – that you can't feel…the pain. But the cons are that once you've had an epidural you can't move around, you're kind of limited as to how you can give birth, all of that. (Emma, interview 2)

Then there were the women who had decided that they would opt for an epidural, and this too was expressed quite decisively and without much discussion of the pros and cons. Recent studies looking at women's experiences of epidural have found that women can feel ambivalent about their decision, even if they choose epidural analgesia (Hidaka and Callister 2012; Jepsen and Keller 2014). The women in this study were also ambivalent about epidural, whether or not they were choosing to use it.

> *I have, I've had thoughts about it. Because when my mum had me, this is going back 29 years ago though, she lost control of her body from up here [chest]— right down… So that sort of freaks me out about it. But then I've also spoken to people who—because the drugs have come a long way since then, who have had nothing but praise for it. I'm not a huge fan of pain, so I would take it, but I just don't want to lose control of my legs and stuff like that, too early. (Arkadia, interview 2)*

> *I would say, the pros – that you can't feel it. Like the pain, you can't feel the pain. But the cons are that once you've had an epidural you can't move around, you're kind of limited as to how you can give birth, all of that. I think if you're in that much pain, an epidural is really, really beneficial but if you can manage the pain and keep moving around—that's what I hated about having an epidural. That was the main personal thing for me. But the instant relief was just [laughs] amazing. (Emma, interview 2)*

However, the women described their attempts at finding out the right information as not always satisfactory, as they thought the effects of medication were minimised.

> *It doesn't seem like it affects the baby at all and according to the midwives—I said 'You know what about blocking the natural endorphins?' they said 'No it doesn't block it, it actually promotes it because when your body is relaxed you're promoting more of the endorphins' and I thought 'That doesn't sound right to me'…I ask questions like 'Will it affect my ability to be able to produce milk and the baby's ability to be able to suckle?' and they are 'No, no, no that's all fine' and I thought 'Oh okay. I just can't just imagine how it could possibly be absolutely fine but if that's what you are saying then that's what you're saying.' (Tessa, interview 2)*

Nina outlined her confusion and frustration at the presentation of information, particularly in her observation of the way particular practices were presented:

> *Even in the birthing classes it's up to you to ask what the negatives might be especially of things like pethidine on the baby…I was quite shocked that it is a narcotic and that it goes into the baby and then they kind of say off-hand, 'Oh yeah [baby] comes out and if it's a bit non-responsive they can give it a different drug to pep it up' or something and I was like 'Not having that one.'* (Nina, interview 2)

The women were more likely to want to '*start with the gas*' because the side-effects are fewer. The effects of pain relieving drugs on their unborn babies was a big concern for the women, and pethidine was not proposed by any of the women as an option because they had all heard that it 'goes through to the baby'. Some women also knew that it was an opiate and the stark contradiction between the ever-increasing need to monitor and restrict intake in pregnancy (e.g., soft cheese, cured meats, coffee, alcohol) to then '*shoot yourself up with some pethidine*' in labour seemed anomalous. Unanimously, the women agreed that pethidine was a bad choice, epitomised in the following quote:

> *I was adamant I didn't want the pethidine and I never would have had it, you could have ripped me apart and I wouldn't have had it because it was all about the baby…I just said 'Oh does pethidine go to the baby?' and they were like 'Oh the epidural doesn't really' and I am like 'Give it to me, give it to me right now.'* (Tessa, interview 3)

Despite Tessa being able to choose epidural in this instance, as demonstrated in Bella's quote below, the hesitancy of women to have pethidine conflicted with the knowledge and practice of the midwives who would often suggest pethidine as a way of avoiding epidural, seeing it as a 'trade-off' if women were requesting epidural analgesia. The midwives saw pethidine as far less invasive, and without the attendant interventions (and therefore risks) of epidural analgesia, such as IVT, Syntocinon, and cEFM.

I didn't want the pethidine because I knew it would go through to the baby but she said 'We will examine you and if you are further along or if you are not too far along then the pethidine will be ok for the labour and it won't affect her when she is coming out because it would have worn off by then.' (Bella, interview 3)

Although aware of some of the risks of epidural, the women were not fully informed of all of the potential effects of epidural analgesia. This was in part due to women's not wanting to know too much, but it was also perceived by the women as a playing down of risk in the information they received from midwives. Participants described feeling patronised by the way information was presented or that it was '*sugar coated*', as if they needed to be protected somehow. As well as being considered less of a risk to the baby than pethidine, epidural analgesia was also demarcated as the better option because it allowed the women to be present mentally, unlike the gas or pethidine which they saw as being more likely to affect their thinking. The knowledge conveyed by the women in the study reflects the dominant discourse—of epidural as safe—from within which they made their choices about what kind of analgesia to use during their labour and birth.

Informed Consent

Informed consent is based primarily on the biomedical principal of autonomy (Braun et al. 2010; Beauchamp 2007)—authority over the decision-making that happens about one's body and characterised by 'threshold' elements of competence and voluntariness, 'information' elements, including disclosure of factual information and explanation of alternative treatments, and 'consent' elements, essentially the consent or refusal of the recommended plan (Braun et al. 2010, p. 814). The process of informed consent is therefore 'characterized by … disclosure, understanding (or competency), and decision-making' (Gerancher et al. 2000, p. 171). However, in a society where intervention-free birth is presented as 'risky' and medicalised birth as 'safe', the process of information giving and receiving is so tainted that it is difficult to see how women have genuine choice to any significant degree. As a responsible agent within risk society, the individual is encouraged to avoid risk (Beck 1999); women are positioned as autonomous decision-makers within neoliberal discourse, without an acknowledgement of the powerful and persuasive effect of dominant discourses in influencing these decisions (Bacchi 1999). The current focus on 'informed choice' supports the neoliberal philosophy of individualism and undermines critical examination of the context within which decisions are made (Budgeon 2011), although it is argued that the contradictions and pluralism of neoliberalism also offers room for challenge and resistance (Larner 2000).

The obstetric recommendation that epidural analgesia should be provided at maternal request whenever indicated (Gaiser 2005, p. 13) raises concerns, because women's requests for analgesia may coincide with the transitional phase of labour—that time between late first stage and the bearing down sensations of second-stage labour; a time, midwives well know, that women can sound irrational or frightened, can want to 'go home', can want it to end, can demand pain relief or a caesarean section. Some women sleep (if in an environment that allows this to occur). While many midwives see this as a normal part of labour progress and a time to increase their support and 'talk women through' to the birth of their baby, now there is the potential for an 'informed consent' mandate, whereby requests for an epidural must not be dissuaded, even if the midwife ascertains that it is indeed transition, and the birth of the baby is imminent (Klomp 2015; Walsh 2009). Correspondingly, women may not realise that they are in transition when making this request, which raises questions as to the 'informed' aspect of this decision (Martin 1989, p. 74). Postnatally, particularly if women had planned not to have an epidural, women report relief that these transitional demands were not met and they were instead offered continued support to birth their babies (Leap 2012). The rhetoric of informed consent, and what this translates to in practice, remains contested in maternity care (Kirkham 2004; Kitzinger 2005; Marshall, J. et al. 2011). Questioning the wisdom of epidural analgesia as a routine analgesic option, given the risks it poses, May (2017, p. 94, original italics) writes,

> There appears to be a disconnect between theory and practice in the case of informed consent. Without true informed consent, where *all* pertinent information is provided, there can be no true autonomy.

In the section above, women's information reflected the ideology of mainstream discourses of risk and safety regarding the safety of epidural analgesia. However, despite the obstetric 'epidural on demand' mandate and anaesthetic 'pain relief as a human right' agenda, epidural and 'pain-free' labour does not necessarily increase women's satisfaction with the birth process (Cooper, G. et al. 2010; Kannan et al. 2001; Ross 1998). One comprehensive discussion of maternal satisfaction with analgesia identified that satisfaction with birth is multidimensional and possibly more related to control, choice, and a woman's 'sense of mastery of her birthing experience' (Ross 1998, p. 509).[3] A recent literature review of women's experience of pain in labour also noted the complexity of childbirth pain, observing that the need for continuous support and acceptance of pain were the two most common findings across the qualitative literature (Van der Gucht and Lewis 2015). In Cooper, G. et al.'s (2010) study, looking at various methods of epidural dosage, satisfaction rates were significantly increased when women experienced a spontaneous vaginal birth, regardless of method of analgesia. If, as indicated by the literature, there is a risk of instrumental delivery with epidural analgesia (Amin-Somuah et al. 2011), and this is known to decrease women's satisfaction with the birth process, midwives should be making this risk absolutely clear to women. Why then is epidural analgesia presented as just another choice on the 'pain relief menu' (Leap and Anderson 2008, p. 39), instead of as a potentially complicating intervention that should only be considered for specific circumstances such as a protracted, painful labour or the presence of high blood pressure? In order to answer this question, we will first discuss the way that epidural analgesia was presented to women in the antenatal classes.

Information Received

It may be that epidural information is disparate because no-one claims ownership of the task of informing pregnant women, specifically about epidural analgesia. Women are not usually exposed to anaesthetists in pregnancy, obstetricians could feel comfortable in promoting epidural in labour and midwives might cover epidural and other analgesic agents in classes or clinics, but it may not be in depth, or cover all of the risks. Midwives might not consider providing comprehensive information, specifically about epidural to be a primary objective of their role. This conundrum prompted the question:

> *Also, who tells women [about epidural]? There is clearly this idea from labour ward midwives that women aren't aware of 'all of the ins and outs' but no discussion about who provides this information, or who should provide it. (Field notes 31/5/12)*

Although the midwives on labour ward did think that women were not prepared enough antenatally (some of these midwives were attempting to remedy this, also running antenatal classes), it was not clear who they thought should be giving women the information about epidural analgesia. This was one of the questions in mind when designing the research in the first place, as it was a problem we had noticed in practice. During the fieldwork, there were a few examples of women speaking to anaesthetists, and Newnham also had the opportunity to interview a senior anaesthetist while in the field.

It appears—and this, for us, was an incongruity of the study—that anaesthetists themselves are far more willing to discuss the adverse effects of epidurals, particularly antenatally. By the time the anaesthetist is called in labour, the woman has already requested it, in which case, although they give a cursory informed consent, it is unlikely that the woman will weigh up the options and refuse at that moment. When Newnham interviewed a consultant anaesthetist on labour ward, he acknowledged the intrusion of having an epidural:

> *Epidurals are fantastic. They're valuable in obstetrics as analgesia and as a tool, but you're still better off not having one. It's an invasive procedure. It's risky—not very, or we wouldn't do it, but it is still risk involving more people [in the room], more strangers, more equipment, which if you don't need is nicer not to have around. It's nicer to come in, have a few contractions, push a baby out, cuddle the baby. It's better not to have strangers involved. But the risks are overstated. Ask any woman coming in in labour if she knows the risks of paralysis, she'll have heard of it.*

Discussing the benefits of epidural, he noted that they can prevent caesarean section at times by providing adequate analgesia in a dystocic labour. He makes the point—the same one we make in the introduction—that when used judiciously, epidurals can be beneficial.

> *If she's stuck at 7 cm, if she gets an epidural, it takes away the pain. Otherwise, she could go to section if left at 7cm. It gives the baby a chance to rotate and come out vaginally, instead of abdominally. Epidurals can be therapeutic. The nice thing about it is if a woman has an enormous amount of pain and worked hard—they're...out of energy. Not interested in the baby. [With an epidural she is] not totally wasted, can sensibly have a part in pushing out her baby, she knows what's going on. (Field notes 18/7/12)*

In other instances, participants described how anaesthetists provided detailed information regarding epidural risks:

> *I spoke the anaesthetist and she was great, she was really honest...what it can do to your body and the baby in particular, which is so fragile...she was just really honest, she took me through all of the pain—basically there were four options—in detail and if it can go through the placenta, and if it goes through to the baby, and if the baby can break it down or not. I just thought it was really good... being educated about what the painkillers are. (Tessa, interview 1)*

Or were more effective than midwives in simply calming the woman down:

> *When the anaesthetist came in, because I didn't realise he would come so quick, he said something like—I was breathing from my—like up here, and he showed me properly how to breathe. Which I had been practising with the book, but it just went out the window when I was in that much pain. And straight away it felt better, and so I was like... 'Why couldn't someone...a midwife done that at the start?' She surely should have known that I wasn't breathing properly. Why couldn't she have said that, and I would have got through those first few hours, probably longer. (Lily, interview 1)*

Contrastingly, in the three antenatal classes that were observed—each run by a different midwife and with a different group of women and partners—the midwives were not forthcoming with all of the effects of analgesia, and worked within the pain relief menu model as described by Leap and Anderson (2008). In addition, they echoed the institution's reticence at providing water for childbirth in the way they conveyed information about this practice.

> *[The midwife] goes on 'So, we've tried distraction [squeezing stress balls, stamping feet] but for those women who choose other forms of pain relief, what can you have in the hospital?'*
> *'Gas' a woman calls out. 'Epidural' [calls another]. The midwife brings up pethidine. 'Those are pretty much your options. Some will choose none of them, some will choose all of them, and it really doesn't matter, you can have what you want.'*

And later:

> *'An epidural needs to be put in by an anaesthetist, in a sterile procedure.' She explains how the woman needs to sit, with back curled, how the epidural is inserted, and the needle removed, that there is an initial test dose, then a full dose given. Ideally it 'will make you extremely comfortable'. She goes on to tell them that it is not guaranteed to work 100%; that it can be more effective on one side than the other; that it may need to be re-sited; that the level of block should ideally be from the 'belly button down'. She talks about the side-effects: the possibility of a headache; that it might not work; risk of nerve damage; how the anaesthetist will explain the risks and get consent. An epidural means the end of active labour though. 'We don't really do walking epidurals here…you [will] have a bladder catheter, along with having to stay on the bed. Epidural and catheter nearly always go hand in hand. The other thing that goes with an epidural is the little hand-held Doppler, and you'll need to be connected to a monitor. Dads love these, and pushing buttons. It's a bit of a boy toy. You have a print out of your contractions and the baby's heart rate.'*

There is no discussion here of the obstetric risks of epidural such as longer labour, hypotension or pyrexia in labour, or instrumental birth. Although women who are informed about the 'cascade of intervention' would recognise that some of these interventions can increase their risk of assisted birth, this is not explicitly referred to by the midwife. The use of cEFM is also downplayed; the midwife's description of the monitor as something that 'dads love' omitted the fact that its use increases the risk of caesarean section. Similarly, although this midwife mentions waterbirth, it is in the context of being 'eligible' and not a lot of detail is given:

> *Whatever pain relief you choose to use, whether it is more natural or more physiological, if you're eligible for a waterbirth, that's great.*

Water was not brought up again until one of the women asks a question:

> *'Do all the rooms have baths in them?'*
>
> MW: *Three rooms have a bath, but all rooms have bathrooms with showers.*
>
> *'So should you ring and ask for one of those rooms [if you want to use a bath?]'*
>
> MW: *Yes, but you must have a signed consent form, have done all the paperwork before you come in, and not only do you need to meet all of the criteria, but there needs to be midwife on who is accredited, and there needs to be a bath free. (Field notes 25/8/12)*

Here, the midwife reiterates the lack of access that is the standard approach of the institution. While in the second antenatal class, the midwife articulates the access available with epidural analgesia:

> *'Women use epidurals quite regularly upstairs. They are placed by an anaesthetist.'* She goes on to explain how a needle is placed into the back, which numbs the lower half of the body. There is still some feeling, she says, but the contractions are now like a pressure, not pain. It can lead to more intervention. Women usually end up with a catheter to drain urine, because the 'legs aren't working' and the [midwives] want the bladder to empty. *'Epidurals do work well with posterior babies and can give women 'time' in a difficult labour for babies to move into the right position. Epidurals can affect pushing. Women don't feel that involuntary pushing. The midwife needs to examine you and may wait for the epidural to wear off in order to push in second stage. The positive side of an epidural is that if you do need to go to theatre, it can just be topped up.'* (Field notes 27/8/12)

While all of the midwives attempted to describe the pain of labour in encouraging terms, such as being '*positive*' or '*good*' or urging the women to '*trust their bodies*', the rules of the institution were constantly being referred to: '*we don't like you to eat*', '*you can only bring two support people*', '*we expect you to progress one centimetre an hour*', '*there is a time we will need you to have your baby by*'. The midwives were attempting to espouse the midwifery philosophy of normal birth, but this was moderated by a need to convey the fact that the institution does not tolerate any real trust in the birth process (Healy et al. 2016). The need to disclose institutional requirements—knowing that women are expected to comply—therefore undermined the positive language that the midwives used to try and promote women's empowerment ('*it's your body*').

In the second antenatal class, waterbirth was again not discussed seriously as an option until someone asked about it:

A woman asks:	'*You don't do water births here?*'
MW:	'*Yes, we do. [Hospital] has quite a strict policy on waterbirth. You need to have signed the consent, and you need to have a midwife on who is accredited. You have to stay under the water. I think it's great… buoyancy, warm water…providing you have no complications and there is an accredited midwife. You need to be well informed*'. [She] goes on to say that 3rd stage is not allowed to occur in the water.
The woman asks:	'*Can you get out if you want? If you've signed?*'

> *It is interesting to notice the language of the class. The woman is asking for permission and testing what the hospital will allow. The question is telling of this relationship, of the power manifest by the midwives, the policies and the hospital itself – as the woman asks if she is allowed to get out of the bath. The midwife replies 'It's your birth. You can do what you like. For example, you don't need to get on the bed. But it is also good, if things don't go to plan, to say "That's okay too."*' (Field notes 27/8/12)

The rhetoric continues here, as the midwife follows her explanation of the '*strict policy*' on water use with the statement: '*It's your birth. You can do what you like*'; an incongruity, as the latter assertion clearly contradicts the former.

At the third antenatal class, yet another midwife gave the technical details of epidural insertion, but no real information about the effects:

The midwife explains clearly about the catheter, how it is put in, and the needle withdrawn, which part is left inside the back, how it is taped and where the drug goes in, that there is a filter. 'Anaesthetics will talk to you about it at the time, but...you are unlikely to be in the space to talk to anybody at that stage, so do your research now and look at your pain relief options now.' She then talks about needing to sit in a 'funny position' to have it put in, and the need to communicate with the midwife and anaesthetist if having a contraction.

Once again, water use had to be raised by a participant of the class.

Question (another man): *If you don't have much of a birth plan, and you are in a room with a bath, can you have a waterbirth?*

MW: *'If you even think you might have an inkling about a waterbirth, then you need to have a talk to your midwife next clinic visit, because there are all these restrictions and all this paperwork to do. In my clinic, I get most women to fill it out just in case they want to get in the bath. You need to have a room with a bath. Are many of you considering waterbirth?'* Two or three women raise their hands. *The midwife goes on to say: 'I've never heard a bad thing about it.'* (Field notes 12/9/12)

This midwife was obviously proactive in her clinic about getting the women to fill out the paperwork for waterbirth 'just in case'. In none of the antenatal classes was water raised as a realistic option until it was asked about. There was also no information given about epidural analgesia increasing the risk of instrumental birth, decreasing breastfeeding rates, or affecting the newborn. We propose that this reflects institutional culture more than it does the individual midwives' knowledge or beliefs.

Analysing this data, also drawing on our own experiences of midwifery, leads us to consider that these midwives were led by an attempt to somehow protect women in the event their birth did go as planned. This is shown by the positive language that midwives used to promote women's empowerment ('*it's your body*') while also feeling compelled to disclose the institutional requirements—to be honest about the needs of the institution. In doing so, they (probably unwittingly) discussed epidural analgesia with a sense of access and entitlement and water with a sense of restriction and prohibition, even while simultaneously promoting its benefits—exposing yet another aspect of the paradox of the institution. The lack of acknowledgement of obstetric risk with epidural acts as another protective effort, as the midwives were attempting to give some information—the practicalities of having an epidural—while at the same time wanting to normalise the procedure for those women who would choose it. Midwives are all too aware of the sense of the failure that some women experience when their birth experiences do not go to plan and these midwives were trying to give permission for all the options. However, the outcome of these intentions was to reinforce institutional needs and undermine their own efforts at using empowering language.

Discursive Practices: The Consent Process

Having tracked the discourse of epidural analgesia through the perpetuation of medical knowledge, policy implementation, and the information given to and received by women, we now turn to the way in which these discourses were operationalised at the level of the informed consent process.

In the second antenatal class, the midwife told the women: '*You need to be well informed*' about birthing in water. In the section *Risk culture and epidural endorsement* above, we quoted a midwife who mused: '*I suppose the same goes for epidural. I don't know*' about the need for information to be given before labour begins. The reality was that there were very different processes for the giving and receiving of informed consent with regard to the two practices. Below are some examples of the consent process as experienced by the study participants, either in this labour or their memory of previous labours.

EN: *So no one has sort of sat down and gone through that with you?*
Lily: *It's probably not ideal really, you just sign the consent form in the hospital but I guess you are not sure what you are signing off to, are you?*
EN: *What do you remember last time of that consent form?*
Lily: *I think I signed something, I think I signed something! [laughs]*
EN: *So you don't remember what they said to you at that point, or…*

Lily: *There wasn't a lot said because I would remember if—he [anaesthetist] wasn't in the room for a long time so I would have remembered...I just remember he helped me breathe a bit better...yeah there is not a lot said. (Lily, interview 2).*

In this case, Lily highlights the lack of information given about epidural analgesia during the 'informed consent' process, observing '*maybe they presume that you've done some wider reading and understand the risk*'; clearly not an acceptable option for women choosing water.

Emma describes her previous experience with epidural analgesia as something she regrets, in part, because she was not aware of the risks:

At the time it didn't affect me, but looking back, I said to my midwife, I wish that I could have tried it a little bit differently. But with a first-time baby you just don't know. When I had the epidural I was just in that much pain that I didn't even think about how it would affect the pushing and everything...I remember signing a form, and he was kind of talking to me but I don't really remember. I knew that it would make me go a bit numb though. (Emma, interview 2)

Jade had had a failed epidural and several attempts at resiting it in her first labour, and although planning an epidural if she felt she needed pain relief for the coming labour, she describes being disconcerted at the lack of information she was given:

Even after you've had an epidural, if you have a catheter or if you need stitches or anything, because I have never had any of that explained to me. I didn't even think they would do that and then I ended up with a whole heap of stitches and I was in pain for months and I wasn't prepared for it because...I didn't really think about it as an option. (Jade, interview 2)

Bella joked about the informed consent process in her labour, as she just wanted the pain relief:

He was blabbing on and I just went 'Yep, just put it in' and he did say something. Obviously there are risks, so he went through the risks...and I went 'I don't care, just put it in!' Kind of a joke but...at that time it was irrelevant.

I was like 'Just give it to me' and I remember I said 'I can still feel my legs' and he goes 'I haven't put it in yet' [laughs]. (Bella, interview 3)

The next interview excerpt describes Nina's experience with informed consent about having a waterbirth:

EN: *Have you gone through the water birth policy and signed it?*
Nina: *Yeah…I guess it's just the system covering itself which is fair enough but I don't think—they go on about risks of water birth and not the risk of epidurals and a lot of the other more medical interventions. I think it's a bit unbalanced, you kind of read between—because you know the midwives can't say explicitly 'It's fine, you have just got to sign it' but—you can read between the lines that it's kind of what they think. (Nina, interview 2)*

Rose had a similar sentiment about having to sign the consent forms for waterbirth.

EN: *How did you find signing the waterbirth policy?*
Rose: *I thought it was a bit—I thought it was a bit ridiculous, really, that you can give verbal consent to have drugs and yet you have to sign this huge form just to be in water. It makes it seem really dangerous and scary, I think. Not so much for me because I wasn't—I already knew a lot about it, but I think if you didn't know much about it and they're like 'Here sign this form', you would be like 'Oh well, why? What is going to happen to me while I am in the water?' It was a bit full on. (Rose, interview 3)*

Rose also noticed the reticence of midwives to offer this option:

I felt like there was a big lack of information about waterbirthing. Everyone just kept telling me 'Well you might not be able to do it because there might not be someone there or there might not be a room.' (Rose, interview 3)

These excerpts show how obstetric discourse affects women and their opportunities to make choices in labour. In this section, we have outlined how the discourses of epidural and waterbirth, as fashioned and maintained by the biomedical model, influence the way that these practices are fashioned and maintained within the hospital. The women were ambiguous towards epidural analgesia use and were not completely versed in the risks. The midwives were explicit in their identification of the barriers to accessing waterbirth but not in their delineation of the obstetric risk of epidural analgesia. However, it was presumed, because of the existence of the waterbirth policy, that women needed to be more informed about this practice than they did about any other. In a discourse analysis on waterbirth policies and guidelines, Cooper, M. et al. (2017) have also shown how the existence of water birth policies negatively influences the practice as it is then only offered when requested. The midwives in the study reflected this, with several commenting that they would more freely offer the bath before the policy. The obvious conflict for midwives is that this directly counters their professional requirement to promote normality in birth. The informed consent process for epidural analgesia was far removed from the stringent consent criteria for the use of water for labour and birth. Foucault (1991a, p. 75) identifies that power can be observed in 'regimes of practice': those interactions and occurrences where the daily re-creation of power/knowledge resides. It is in recognising these practices, which illustrate what is allowed, through discursive techniques, to be seen as 'truth', that the disruption of the dominant discourse occurs, and the veneer of self-evidence is peeled away revealing the underlying forces at play (Foucault 1991a, p. 76).

Clinicians are in positions of power and can pass on ideological assumptions in their responses to clients. However, they are also constrained by the institution to varying levels, which can result in a deferment of power to the institution itself (Lazarus 1988). It might be more beneficial to women as well as more politically appropriate (see Walsh et al. 2015) if midwives were honest with women about the risks of epidural and the reasons why water is so inaccessible, and perhaps even—at a stretch—the fact that the institution has a disciplining effect on women's labouring bodies that can diminish women's autonomy and control. We suggest that not to do so might actually constitute a breach of professional ethics in that it is otherwise upholding medicalised risk-focused philosophy of birth and may contribute to a lack of true informed consent for women. However, we are taking the position of devil's advocate here, and recognise that this is a complex area, with midwives balancing the need to follow policy, to fulfil women's expectations and not undermine their confidence in their chosen place of birth as well as uphold professional relationships. In addition, in order to do this, the midwife must first be aware that s/he is upholding the dominant discourse in the first place.

Conclusion

In the analysis of guiding policy documents, we have shown how the practice of waterbirth was constructed and presented to women as risky, even dangerous. Employing current risk theory, we have argued that dominant conceptualisations of risk are commonly perpetuated by medical authority rather than evidence. In this case, perceptions of risk, as defined by others, and underpinned by a medical model that valorises intervention as a 'tolerable risk', led to the strict control of the use of water in labour and birth, by restricting access and limiting midwifery practice. In addition, the information given to women in the two hospital leaflets identified epidural analgesia as a normal, acceptable, accessible, and relatively safe option while insisting on caution if contemplating the use of water. However, when looked at in terms of danger rather than risk, the evidence points to the epidural as the more 'dangerous' of the two practices. Essentially, epidural analgesia 'fits' within medical interpretations of safety, which allowed this practice to slip more easily into the flow of the institutional apparatus described in the previous chapter.

The consequence of the way these two practices were approached—one with a policy and one without—was that this affected both the content and the style of information given to women. The midwives reflected the lack of access to water and the availability of epidural analgesia in their antenatal classes, and women had to ask to find out that water was an option. Correspondingly, the informed consent process for epidural was fairly lax, whereas the waterbirth informed consent process was laborious in terms of midwives' work, and perceived by the women as excessive and potentially frightening. The construction of these practices as risky or safe therefore affected how midwives were able to talk to women about them in the antenatal classes and how women themselves also viewed these options and weighed up their choices. In deconstructing these 'regimes of practice' (Foucault 1991a, p. 75) we have demonstrated how the broader biomedical discourse of the epidural as 'safe and necessary' is perpetuated at the practice level.

Notes

1. If the authors of the pamphlet are relying on anecdote, it depends who you listen to. Most midwives we know support the practice. If they are citing evidence, then it should be referenced. Either way, this is not a balanced statement.
2. Two cases of extremely rare complications from epidural have occurred in the last decade in Australia alone. In one case, a woman died of bacterial meningitis following an infection at the epidural site. In the other, chlorhexidine was mistakenly inserted into the epidural, leading to paralysis. Adverse events have also occurred in the United States and the United Kingdom.

   http://www.smh.com.au/lifestyle/diet-and-fitness/call-for-ban-follows-horrific-epidural-error-20110330-1cgb9.html. Viewed Dec 2017.

   http://www.smh.com.au/articles/2004/03/09/1078594364666.html?from=storyrhs. Viewed Dec 2017.

   http://www.nbcnews.com/id/9818616/ns/dateline_nbc/t/routine-epidural-turns-deadly/#.VEJC2BZ0a4k. Viewed Dec 2017.

   http://www.dailymail.co.uk/health/article-506607/Mother-died-epidural-injected-arm-instead-spine.html. Viewed Dec 2017.
3. This paper was even more interesting given that it was written by the head of an Anaesthetics department. Contradicting the dominant epidural discourse, Ross proposes that the pain relief mission of medicine is too simplistic in the case of childbirth.

References

Adams, J., Frawley, J., Steel, A., Broom, A., & Sibbritt, D. (2015). Use of pharmacological and non-pharmacological labour pain management techniques and their relationship to maternal and infant birth outcomes: Examination of a nationally representative sample of 1835 pregnant women. *Midwifery, 31*(4), 458–463.

Alfirevic, Z., Devane, D., Gyte, G. M. L., & Cuthbert, A. (2017). Continuous Cardiotocography (CTG) as a form of Electronic Fetal Monitoring (EFM) for fetal assessment during labour. *Cochrane Database of Systematic Reviews* (2), Art. No: CD006066. doi: https://doi.org/10.1002/14651858.CD006066.pub3.

Anim-Somuah, M., Smyth, R., & Howell, C. (2011). Epidural versus non-epidural or no analgesia in labour. *Cochrane Database of Systematic Reviews* (12), Art. No: CD000331. doi: https://doi.org/10.1002/14651858.CD000331.pub3.

Archer, T. (2014). Unrecognized uterine hyperstimulation due to oxytocin and combined spinal-epidural analgesia. In J. L. Benumof (Ed.), *Clinical anesthesiology* (pp. 273–283). New York: Springer.

Bacchi, C. (1999). *Women, policy and politics: The construction of policy problems*. London: Sage.

Ball, L., Curtis, P., & Kirkham, M. (2002). *Why do midwives leave?* London: Royal College of Midwives.

Beauchamp, T. (2007). The 'four principles' approach to health care ethics. In R. E. Ashcroft, A. Dawson, H. Draper, & J. Mcmillan (Eds.), *Principles of health care ethics*. Chichester: John Wiley and Sons.

Beck, U. (1999). *World risk society*. Cambridge: Polity Press.

Braun, A. R., Skene, L., & Merry, A. F. (2010). Informed consent for anaesthesia in Australia and New Zealand. *Anaesthesia and Intensive Care, 38*, 809–822.

Brocklehurst, P., Hardy, P., Hollowell, J., Linsell, L., Macfarlane, A., McCourt, C., Marlow, N., Miller, A., Newburn, M., & Petrou, S. (2011). Perinatal and maternal outcomes by planned place of birth for healthy women with low risk pregnancies: The Birthplace in England national prospective cohort study. *BMJ, 343*(7840), d7400.

Brodie, P. (2002). Addressing the barriers to midwifery – Australian midwives speaking out. *The Australian Journal of Midwifery, 15*(3), 5–14.

Bryers, H. M., & van Teijlingen, E. (2010). Risk, theory, social and medical models: A critical analysis of the concept of risk in maternity care. *Midwifery, 26*(5), 488–496.

Budgeon, S. (2011). The contradictions of successful femininity: Third-wave feminism, postfeminism and 'new' femininities. In R. Gill & C. Scharff (Eds.), *New femininities: Postfeminism, neoliberalism and subjectivity* (pp. 279–292). Basingstoke: Palgrave Macmillan.

Campo, M. (2014). *Delivering hegemony: Contemporary childbirth discourses and obstetric hegemony in Australia*. PhD thesis, School of Social Sciences and Communications, La Trobe University.

Chadwick, R. J., & Foster, D. (2014). Negotiating risky bodies: Childbirth and constructions of risk. *Health, Risk & Society, 16*(1), 68–83.

Cluett, E. R., & Burns, E. (2009). Immersion in water in labour and birth. *Cochrane Database of Systematic Reviews* (2). Art. No: CD000111. doi: https://doi.org/10.1002/14651858.CD000111.pub3.

Cooper, G., MacArthur, C., Wilson, M., Moore, P., & Shennan, A. (2010). Satisfaction, control and pain relief: Short- and long-term assessments in a randomised controlled trial of low-dose and traditional epidurals and a non-epidural comparison group. *International Journal of Obstetric Anesthesia, 19*, 31–37.

Cooper, M., Warland, J., & McCutcheon, H. (2013). Diving in: A dip in the water for labour and birth policy debate. *Essentially MIDIRS, 4*(9), 32–37.

Cooper, M., McCutcheon, H., & Warland, J. (2017). A critical analysis of Australian policies and guidelines for water immersion during labour and birth. *Women and Birth, 30*(5), 431–441.

Dahlen, H. (2010). Undone by fear? Deluded by trust? *Midwifery, 26*(2), 156–162.

Dahlen, H., Dowling, H., Tracy, M., Schmied, V., & Tracy, S. (2013). Maternal and perinatal outcomes amongst low risk women giving birth in water compared to six birth positions on land. A descriptive cross sectional study in a birth centre over 12 years. *Midwifery, 29*(7), 759–764.

Dahlen, H., Tracy, S., Tracy, M., Bisits, A., Brown, C., & Thornton, C. (2014). Rates of obstetric intervention and associated perinatal mortality and morbidity among low-risk women giving birth in private and public hospitals in NSW (2000–2008): A linked data population-based cohort study. *BMJ Open, 4*(5), e004551.

Davies, R., Davis, D., Pearce, M., & Wong, N. (2015). The effect of waterbirth on neonatal mortality and morbidity: A systematic review protocol. *JBI Database of Systematic Reviews and Implementation Reports, 13*(10), 180–231.

de Jonge, A., van der Goes, B. Y., Ravelli, A. C. J., Amelink-Verburg, M. P., Mol, B. W., Nijhuis, J. G., Gravenhorst, J. B., & Buitendijk, S. E. (2009). Perinatal mortality and morbidity in a nationwide cohort of 529,688 low-risk planned home and hospital births. *BJOG: An International Journal of Obstetrics & Gynaecology, 116*(9), 1177–1184.

de Jonge, A., Mesman, J. A., Manniën, J., Zwart, J. J., van Dillen, J., & van Roosmalen, J. (2013). Severe adverse maternal outcomes among low risk women with planned home versus hospital births in the Netherlands: Nationwide cohort study. *BMJ, 346*, f3263.

Donellan-Fernandez, R. (2011). Having a baby in Australia: Women's business, risky business, or big business? *Outskirts Online Journal, 24*. http://www.outskirts.arts.uwa.edu.au/volumes/volume-24/donnellan-fernandez

Dove, S., & Muir-Cochrane, E. (2014). Being safe practitioners and safe mothers: A critical ethnography of continuity of care midwifery in Australia. *Midwifery, 30*(10), 1063–1072.

Downe, S. (2015). Chair address. In *Normal Labour and Birth Conference*. University of Central Lancashire/Australian College of Midwives, Sydney.

Edwards, N. (2004). Why can't women just say no? And does it really matter? In M. Kirkham (Ed.), *Informed choice in maternity care* (pp. 1–30). Basingstoke: Palgrave Macmillan.

Foucault, M. (1990). *The history of sexuality* (Vol. 1). London: Penguin Books.

Foucault, M. (1991a). Questions of method. In G. Burchell, C. Gordon, & P. Miller (Eds.), *The Foucault effect: Studies in governmentality* (pp. 73–86). London: Harvester Wheatsheaf.

Foucault, M. (1991b). Governmentality. In G. Burchell, C. Gordon, & P. Miller (Eds.), *The Foucault effect: Studies in governmentality* (pp. 87–104). London: Harvester Wheatsheaf.

Gaiser, R. (2005). Labor epidurals and outcome. *Best Practice & Research. Clinical Anaesthesiology, 19*(1), 1–16.

Gerancher, J., Grice, S., Dewan, D., & Eisenach, J. (2000). An evaluation of informed consent prior to epidural analgesia for labor and delivery. *International Journal of Obstetric Anesthesia, 9*, 168–173.

Gordon, C. (Ed.). (1980). *Power/knowledge: Selected interviews and other writings 1972–1977 by Michel Foucault*. London: Harvester Wheatsheaf.

Healy, S., Humphreys, E., & Kennedy, C. (2016). Midwives' and obstetricians' perceptions of risk and its impact on clinical practice and decision-making in labour: An integrative review. *Women and Birth, 29*, 107–116.

Hidaka, R., & Callister, L. (2012). Giving birth with epidural analgesia: The experience of first-time mothers. *The Journal of Perinatal Education, 21*(1), 24–35.

Janssen, P. A., Lee, S. K., Ryan, E. M., Etches, D. J., Farquharson, D. F., Peacock, D., & Klein, M. C. (2002). Outcomes of planned home births versus planned hospital births after regulation of midwifery in British Columbia. *Canadian Medical Association Journal, 166*(3), 315–323.

Janssen, P. A., Saxell, L., Page, L. A., Klein, M. C., Liston, R. M., & Lee, S. K. (2009). Outcomes of planned home birth with registered midwife versus planned hospital birth with midwife or physician. *Canadian Medical Association Journal, 181*(6–7), 377–383.

Jepsen, I., & Keller, K. D. (2014). The experience of giving birth with epidural analgesia. *Women and Birth, 27*(2), 98–103.

Kannan, S., Jamison, R. N., & Datta, S. (2001). Maternal satisfaction and pain control in women electing natural childbirth. *Regional Anesthesia and Pain Medicine, 26*(5), 468–472.

Keirse, M., & Andrews, C. (2006). Development of statewide policies for alternative birth options: The water birth option. *Birth Issues, 15*(1), 5–9.

Kirkham, M. (2000). How can we relate? In M. Kirkham (Ed.), *The midwife-mother relationship* (pp. 227–250). New York: Palgrave Macmillan.

Kirkham, M. (Ed.). (2004). *Informed choice in maternity care*. Hampshire: Palgrave Macmillan.

Kirkham, M. (2011). Sustained by joy: The potential of flow experience for midwives and mothers. In L. Davies, R. Daellenbach, & M. Kensington (Eds.), *Sustainability, midwifery and birth*. London: Routledge.

Kirkham, M., & Stapleton, H. (2004). The culture of the maternity services in Wales and England as a barrier to informed choice. In M. Kirkham (Ed.), *Informed choice in maternity care*. Basingstoke: Palgrave Macmillan.

Kitzinger, S. (2005). *The politics of birth*. Sydney: Elsevier.

Klomp, T. (2015). Management of labour pain: Perceptions of labour pain by Dutch primary care midwives. Conference presentation. *Normal Labour and Birth conference*, University of Central Lancashire, Preston.

Lane, K. (1995). The medical model of the body as a site of risk: A case study of childbirth. In J. Gabe (Ed.), *Medicine, health and risk: Sociological approaches*. Oxford: Blackwell Publishers.

Larner, W. (2000). Neo-liberalism: Policy, ideology, governmentality. *Studies in Political Economy, 63*, 5–25.

Lazarus, E. (1988). Theoretical considerations for the study of the doctor-patient relationship: Implications of a perinatal study. *Medical Anthropology Quarterly, 2*(1), 34–58.

Leap, N. (2012). *No gain without pain!* North Parramatta: Birth International.

Leap, N., & Anderson, T. (2008). The role of pain in normal birth and the empowerment of women. In S. Downe (Ed.), *Normal childbirth: Evidence and debate* (pp. 29–46). Sydney: Elsevier.

Marshall, J., Fraser, D., & Baker, P. (2011). An observational study to explore the power and effect of the labor ward culture on consent to intrapartum procedures. *International Journal of Childbirth, 1*(2), 82–99.

Martin, E. (1989). *The woman in the body*. Milton Keynes: Open University Press.

May, M. (2017). *Epiduralized birth and nurse-midwifery: Childbirth in the United States*. Amazon: Sampson Book Publishing.

Menakaya, U., Albayati, S., Vella, E., Fenwick, J., & Angstetra, D. (2013). A retrospective comparison of water birth and conventional vaginal birth among women deemed to be low risk in a secondary level hospital in Australia. *Women and Birth, 26*(2), 114–118.

Murphy-Lawless, J. (2012). Empty promises: The dangers of risk discourses. In *Human Rights in Childbirth: International Conference of Jurists, Midwives & Obstetricians*.

Newnham, E. C. (2010). Midwifery directions: The Australian maternity services review. *Health Sociology Review, 19*(2), 245–259.

Newnham, E. C. (2014). Birth control: Power/knowledge in the politics of birth. *Health Sociology Review, 23*(3), 254–268.

Newnham, E., McKellar, L., & Pincombe, J. (2015). Documenting risk: A comparison of policy and information pamphlets for using epidural or water in labour. *Women & Birth, 28*(3), 221–227. Copyright permission obtained from Elsevier under pre-existing licence terms.

Newnham, E., McKellar, L., & Pincombe, J. (2017). It's your body, but…' Mixed messages in childbirth education: Findings from a hospital ethnography. *Midwifery, 55*, 53–59. Copyright permission obtained from Elsevier under pre-existing licence terms.

NMBA. (2015). *Nursing and midwifery Board of Australia*. Viewed 20 July 2015.

Olsen, O., & Clausen, J. A. (2012). Planned hospital birth versus planned home birth. *Cochrane Database of Systematic Reviews* (9), Art. No: CD000352. doi: https://doi.org/10.1002/14651858.CD000352.pub2.

Pitt, S. (1997). Midwifery and medicine: Gendered knowledge in the practice of midwifery. In H. Marland & A. Rafferty (Eds.), *Midwives, society and childbirth: Debates and controversies in the modern period*. London: Routledge.

Possamai-Inesedy, A. (2006). Confining risk: Choice and responsibility in childbirth in a risk society. *Health Sociology Review, 15*(4), 406–414.

Reiger, K., & Dempsey, R. (2006). Performing birth in a culture of fear: An embodied crisis of late modernity. *Health Sociology Review, 15*(4), 364–373.

Ross, A. (1998). Maternal satisfaction with labour analgesia. *Baillière's Clinical Obstetrics and Gynaecology, 12*(3), 499–512.

Russell, K. (2011). Struggling to get into the pool room? A critical discourse analysis of labor ward midwives experiences of waterbirth. *International Journal of Childbirth, 1*(1), 52–60.

Scamell, M., & Stewart, M. (2014). Time, risk and midwife practice: The vaginal examination. *Health, Risk & Society, 16*(1), 84–100.

Smith, V., Devane, D., & Murphy-Lawless, J. (2012). Risk in maternity care: A concept analysis. *International Journal of Childbirth, 2*(2), 126–135.

Van der Gucht, N., & Lewis, K. (2015). Women's experiences of coping with pain during childbirth: A critical review of qualitative research. *Midwifery, 31*(3), 349–358.

Wagner, M. (1994). *Pursuing the birth machine: The search for appropriate birth technology*. Camperdown: Ace Graphics.

Walsh, D. (2009). Pain and epidural use in normal childbirth. *Evidence Based Midwifery, 7*(3), 89–93.

Walsh, D. (2012). *Evidence and skills for normal birth*. London: Routledge.

Walsh, D., Christianson, M., & Stewart, M. (2015). Why midwives should be feminists. *Midirs Midwifery Digest, 25*, 154–160.

Wiegers, T., Keirse, M. J., Van der Zee, J., & Berghs, G. (1996). Outcome of planned home and planned hospital births in low risk pregnancies: Prospective study in midwifery practices in the Netherlands. *BMJ, 313*(7068), 1309–1313.

Young, K., & Kruske, S. (2013). How valid are the common concerns raised against water birth? A focused review of the literature. *Women and Birth, 26*(2, 6), 105–109.

6

A Circle of Trust

ROSE
It was fantastic!
It was exactly as I wanted.
So I had the waterbirth that I wanted,
And had an amazing midwife who was very helpful
And also left me alone most of the time,
Which was nice because that is what I wanted as well.

And, it was just good, it was good.
After I had him I went 'Oh yeah I could do that again!'
I had all my music and my oils burning and it was just lovely!
I was very lucky.
When I first went into labour I called up and I said 'Oh I want
to have a water birth,'
And they were like 'Umm, okay we will see what we can do.'
And when I got there they were like 'We had to move someone out of this
room so that you could
Have the tub.'
Then the midwife was supposed to finish at 9 but she ended up staying on
Because
She was the only accredited water birthing midwife

© The Author(s) 2018
E. Newnham et al., *Towards the Humanisation of Birth*,
https://doi.org/10.1007/978-3-319-69962-2_6

So she just, like, stayed on over time for me,
So I could stay in the water and it was just
Really good.

The water was amazing!
It was so calming.
I was having,
I was getting pretty tense before I got in the water,
Thinking 'Oh I don't know if I can do this
It's all a bit too much!'
But as soon as I got in the water, I could
Just relax in between contractions
And it was just so much nicer
And warm!
Because
I was really cold before I got in the water.
And private!
It feels more private when you are in the water,
Cause, you know
You don't have everyone staring up your vagina the whole time,
Cause the water sort of makes it feel like you are a bit more covered up.

Painful—it was weird
At the same time a lot worse and a lot less than I had expected.
I hadn't expected to feel so normal in between contractions
All of a sudden you are just 'Lalalalala' chatting away
Like everything's normal
I wasn't really expecting that.

When my contractions started I was like 'Oh yeah wow this really hurts!'
When it got to the point where I was ready to push I thought,
'Oh isn't it supposed to get worse before the pushing starts?'
Once I'd kind of gotten used to the pain,
I just expected it to keep getting worse and worse and worse and worse,
And then it sort of didn't get as bad as I thought.
But, I mean it was still pretty bad.
Yeah, man the contractions are so much worse than the pushing!
Cause you just think
There's just no end in sight.
You just think
'How many hours am I going to have to go through this for?'

Even up until the very end I was still ten minutes in between contractions,
Then all of a sudden it was all happening.
I probably would have brought a pack of cards or something because it just—
It would have been less scary,
If you knew that you had that rest time.
Because although the pain is really bad
When you've got that little break to rest you can sort of
Revitalise yourself,
Eat something.
I was eating grapes the whole time, yep.
Because they all said there is going to be a gap in between contractions
But then didn't really say you are going to feel totally normal.

Birth Ideology

In their study about pain relief choices and beliefs about childbirth, Heinze and Sleigh (2003) found that women's birth ideology was a motivating factor for specific choices determining analgesia use in labour. Women's ideologies of birth were in turn influenced by the psychological factors of locus of control (internal or external), seeing themselves as active or passive participants in the process of childbirth, and fear of childbirth (Heinze and Sleigh 2003). Levels of fear about birth were more significant in women's choices than actual experience of pain in labour—in fact 'no relationships were found between epidural use and ratings of pain' (Heinze and Sleigh 2003, p. 330)—and this showed most specifically in the difference between women having their first babies and those having subsequent babies. These findings indicate that social and cultural childbirth norms may have a larger influence over women's sense of being able or not able to birth than the physical reality of labour itself. Similarly, fear of birth has also been linked to an external locus of control, as well as low self-esteem (Fisher et al. 2006). However, circumstances such as support and prior experience, and expectations of birth as either easy or difficult, can also affect how women anticipate and experience birth. Conversely, a woman's sense of achievement can also be compromised by the expectation that birth will be easy if they go on to experience it as difficult (Halldorsdottir and Karlsdottir 1996). Hodnett (2002) identifies that women's personal expectations, the support she receives, her relationship with her care provider, and contribution to decision-making are more influential on women's overall satisfaction with childbirth than pain, continuity of care, physical environment, or intervention. The focus moved to pain and/or its relief only if expectations were not met (Hodnett 2002). Clearly the minutiae of experience and personality that coalesce to form women's personal birth ideologies are intricate (Fig. 6.1).

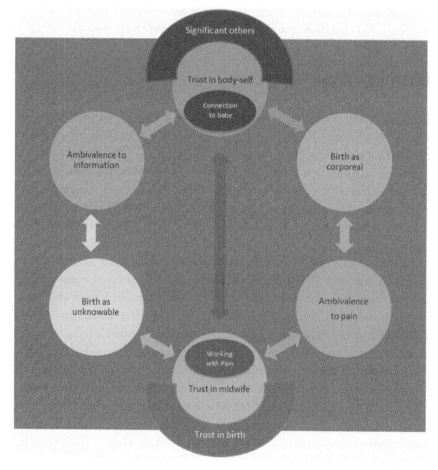

Fig. 6.1 The circle of trust

The first theme that we discuss is the idea of a woman's *Trust in her body-self*, that her body will 'know what to do' in labour and birth, leads to a sense of the corporeality—the physicality—of birth. This, in turn, relates to an ambivalence to pain, rather than the requirement to avoid pain relief at all cost, which is a major premise of the biomedical literature. The woman thus turns to the midwife for guidance; she trusts the midwife because of her understanding that birth is corporeal, that pain is necessary or significant, and also because birth is an unknowable event. The unpredictable nature of birth leads the woman not to seek excessive information, but turns, full circle, to trust in her body-self, which also has a direct relationship with *trust in the midwife*, signified by the central arrow (all of the arrows are double-headed, as each theme is shaped by but also shapes the ones on either side) showing that this trust needs to be reciprocated. Trust in body-self strengthens the connection between woman and child and the woman is also supported by her significant others. Midwives, in order to reflect trust back to the woman ideally approach birth with an acceptance of pain, or 'working with pain' (Leap and Anderson 2008, p. 40) approach, and this is supported by a sense of trust in the birth process as a whole. For the circle of trust to develop, the environment must be there to support it; it therefore dovetails with the theory of birth territory and midwifery guardianship (Fahy et al. 2008) which identifies the midwife's role (midwifery guardianship) in supporting the appropriate space (the sanctum) in order to facilitate 'mind–body integration and enhanced embodied sense of self' (integrative power) in women to give birth (Fahy and Parratt 2006, p. 49). We now elaborate on each of these themes, providing supporting data from interviews and field notes.

Trust in the Body-Self

The ambiguities between biology, gender, and experience have been pondered over decades of feminist theory, and none of these concepts are without complexity. Postmodernist feminism, with its focus on discourse and body-as-text, eventually found itself with the loss of the physical body (Davis and Walker 2010; Marshall, H 1996). This led to a focus on phenomenological concerns of the lived body that then attempted to incorporate theory and corporeality (Marshall, H 1996).[1] Embodiment theory is utilised by third-wave feminists to focus on personal experience of the lived body (Budgeon 2011, p. 282; see Grosz 1994), thereby doing away with the problematic idea of a shared, or in some way homogeneous, female identity. Moving away from both identity politics and the more abstract gender-as-discourse, feminism of the lived body was first introduced through phenomenological existentialism and utilised by Simone de Beauvoir (Stone 2007, p. 175; Young 2005, p. 15). More grounded than discursive theory, it can overcome the complications associated with categorising sex and gender, while simultaneously bringing the body back into view. Additionally, it adds subjective experience to the otherwise scientific concept of a biological or physiological 'sexed' body, enabling a philosophical shift away from both reductionism (to just a body) and dualism (of a particular—male or female—body). With regard to gender construction, the influence of discourse, norms, and beliefs and their effect on the body is acknowledged, but gender identity as intrinsic to a woman's selfhood is left behind. Young (2005, p. 17) comments:

> it is a mystification to attribute the ways of being associated with the category "gender" to some inner core of identity of a subject, whether understood as "natural" or acquired.

Additionally, embodiment theory provides an antithesis to Cartesian dualism by embedding experience firmly back into the lived body, uniting Descartes' mind-body split. A focus on embodiment also interrupts the prominence of 'the individual' passed down from classic liberal philosophy by acknowledging the blurred boundary between the physical bodies of the woman and the foetus (Young 2005, pp. 5, 15, 48). In this study, the women made frequent references to their bodies as knowing entities in their own right.

> *I don't like being in pain, obviously…but I think as far as pain in labour goes, I don't feel worried that I can't handle it. I think—I'm very trusting that my body will have the ability to handle that. (Rose, interview 1)*
>
> *I mean, your body knows what it's doing and to be able to experience those muscles doing what they are doing and your body just knows what to do…It's*

just an amazing feeling. As much as I was in shock this time round with everything happening so fast, I was able to feel what my body was doing and my body was doing it all on its own, it knew what it was going to do…to be able to experience that, you know, that your body just naturally knows what it is meant to do…it knows what it needs to do. It's an amazing experience. (Kate, interview 3)

I think, after experiencing two births and seeing what your body does, you go 'Yes, definitely…my body knows what it's doing'…you've had this experience that totally solidifies that understanding that is what our bodies are designed to do and supported to do. (Juno, interview 1)

Murphy-Lawless (1988) has suggested that in focusing on the male suppression of midwives and childbirth, critique of the concurrent control and construction of women's birthing bodies has been left lacking, and she calls for a discourse of the body in which women's invisibility is counteracted. Since this observation, the birthing body has become more central in midwifery theory (Akrich and Pasveer 2004; Davis and Walker 2010; Kelpin 1992; Lupton and Schmied 2013; Walsh 2010). For similar reasons that embodiment theory is used within feminism, as a way of transgressing the mind-body split and bringing women's lived bodies to the foreground, we are suggesting, with these authors, the use of embodiment theory to better understand and support women during birth, to focus attention on the meaning of birth, as well as transgress the medical/midwifery divide.

Traditionally, the scientific view of women's bodies has tended not only to ignore women's subjective experience but deny it altogether, placing medicalised and pathological standards onto pregnant women's bodies and overruling women's experiential knowledge with 'expert' opinion and various technologies (Young 2005, p. 47; Martin 1989); perhaps because the experience of pregnancy and birth challenges Western concepts of mind-body dualism, bodily boundaries, and individualism (Young 2005; Rothman 1989; Rich 1986). More recently, neoliberal constructions of the individualised pregnant form, as well as the commodification of maternity, also 'marks the disavowal of any recognition of the maternal as a relation *between* a mother and a child' (Tyler 2011, p. 30, italics in original). Medicine, remaining firmly androcentric, has failed to acknowledge the connection—physical or otherwise—between a pregnant woman and her unborn baby (Rothman 1989), and while negating women's experience of this relationship on the one hand, medical science has sought to negotiate directly with the foetus—thus maintaining this separation and failing to acknowledge the embodied union inherent in the mother/baby dyad (Duden 1993; Maher 2002). This has a double effect. It operates both as a mechanism of control, whereby medical knowledge is placed above the woman's own knowledge of her baby and provides further scope for the identification of the pregnant woman as a site of risk (Martin 1989), juxtaposing mothers and babies and regarding their interests as being in conflict (Davis and Walker 2010).

The idea of being present to the pain of birth reflects an engagement with their bodies by the women. This engagement—the corporeal connection to pain in childbirth—presents an opportunity to reconnect the mind and body as well as to connect with her child during the exquisite and inimitable experience of bringing her baby from the inside of her body to the outside world:

> The essence of women's experiences of pain during childbirth can be expressed as 'being one's body', which includes a non-objectified view of one's body, a presence in the delivery process, and a meaning connected to the process of motherhood. (Lundgren and Dahlberg 1998, p. 108)

Emily Martin's (1989) work *The woman in the body* details the effects of various institutions on women's bodies. She maintains that women themselves do not necessarily accept these interpretations, and use subjective versions of the body/self both as forms of resistance, and as a way of making sense of their experience in the world. Although medicine may make claims about women's bodies, and gendered discourse may influence the way a woman is treated, or the information she is given, she will invariably construct her own reality based on her own *knowledge of her body* (Martin 1989).[2] Young (2005, p. 26) notes that, '[g]ender as structured is also lived through individual bodies, always as personal experiential response and not as a set of attributes that individuals have in common' and proposes that gender as a concept is still expedient, even necessary in the description of social institutions, in feminism's role in social criticism (Young 2005, p. 19). She states:

There is no situation…without embodied location and interaction. Conversely, the body as lived is always layered with social and historical meaning and is not some primitive matter prior to or underlying economic and political relations or cultural meanings. (Young 2005, p. 7)

In agreement with Young's proposal, we offer that the biomedical system is a gendered institution, and that a 'male' bias is evident, with current dictates and norms based in historical gender inequities.[3]

Embodiment theory has the capacity to develop understanding because it captures the experience of 'women' as differentiated persons, not a representative of a homogeneous gender, and can lead the discussion away from the dichotomous discourses of medical/natural, while still examining power constructs; the use of a 'gender' construct is still relevant (even if classifications of gender are no longer useful in categorising women's experience) and can be utilised at an institutional level (Walsh 2010).

Despite the various medical interpretations, social pressures, or institutional restrictions, the women in this study came back to their bodies, time and again, as a site of trust and knowing.

> *And no chemicals, drugs, nothing…So yes, let the body do what it does. (Annie, interview 1)*
>
> *I'm really looking towards having a natural, painkiller-free birth and hoping that my body does what it's meant to do and hope that emotionally I'll be able to get through it. (Tessa, interview 1)*
>
> *I'm a big believer in just letting your body do—what it knows how to do, basically… Trying not to think about the actual process so much, because your body's going to know what it's going to do anyway. (Kate, interview 1)*
>
> *I tell myself I can. I just say 'yeah I can do it'…it's about having faith in your own body being able to do it and trying not to worry about things that haven't happened yet. (Rose interview 2)*

However, not all women had this sense of trust in their bodies, and this reflects other findings (Heinze and Sleigh 2003; Davis-Floyd 1992). It has been proposed that since birth is a culturally mediated event, dominant discourses (e.g., of what constitutes a 'safe' birth) have already been assimilated into women's understanding of birth, and who therefore actively co-create the medicalised birth experience (Akrich and Pasveer 2004; Campo 2014; Davis-Floyd 1994; Lazarus 1994; Maher 2003). For these women, fear of birth can be reconciled by the knowledge that medical intervention is close at hand.

> *I think [my thoughts] have changed—not sure—because I am getting bigger and its getting closer and reality has set in more but I am exhausted enough as it just with having this virus and the pregnancy…I am just more scared…I still want to do it as naturally as possible but I am just doubting my strength and ability to be able to do that now. And it's not because I'm less informed because I absolutely was—at our first interview—but I am just more—scared and doubtful in myself. (Tessa, interview 2)*

Also, some women do not want to take ownership of the birth process, and prefer to remain passive (Marshall et al. 2011). Arguably, this is when midwifery knowledge and support become even more crucial.

Birth as Corporeal

The women had differing conceptualisations of birth and they were influenced by their life philosophies, such as whether they resorted to orthodox or alternative medical models outside of pregnancy, social representations of birth (including the media and wider social beliefs), as well as the 'birth stories' that were told to them by friends and family, particularly their mothers (see Kay et al. 2017 for an excellent discussion on the way birth stories shape and co-create social meanings of birth). However, despite having these individual ideologies, the women, by and large, saw labour as a natural process, something that their bodies were designed to do, including two of the four women who had epidural analgesia in their birth plan.

> *In a nutshell, I think our bodies are meant to deliver babies, so I think birth is just one of those parts of human nature. (Anna, interview 1)*
>
> *I don't really have any beliefs as such. It's natural, but yeah, I don't know [laughs]. (Arkadia, interview 1)*

They also acknowledged a trust in their body; that it would know what to do. This exposed a deeper 'ideology' of birth: one that acknowledged the reality of following in the footsteps of millennia of birthing women, and that identified the physiological normality of birth. As Rose said:

> *I think the fact that people have been doing it for a long, long time, for me, I just think 'well, if they can all do it, then I probably can too'…I think that is one of the reasons why I feel so able to deal with it. (Rose interview 2)*

> *I know that I'll get through it and I know that I'm going to come out the other end just fine…knowing that I've come out the other end okay and other women have done it and I'm built to do it probably will keep me focused. (Tessa, interview 1)*

While some women focused on the immediacy of the body's role in birth, other women echoed similar thoughts in relation to their role as mothers.

> *I think [childbirth] is kind of the extension of life…the nature for me to be a mother, to express a life. (May, interview 1)*

> *Trying to be relaxed as possible [about birth]…when I went in to give birth to my first child, I went in with that aspect and I think that's what made me a very relaxed, first time mother. I was very, very comfortable with her, right from the word go…yes, just basically being as relaxed as possible and trying to enjoy it as much as I can. (Kate, interview 1)*

With a comprehension of birth as natural came an understanding that the natural world is not necessarily a safe one. There is a view—associated perhaps with birth at its most idealised—that because women see birth as a normal, physiological function, they think nothing will go wrong. However, both birth and death are 'natural' life events, and—as midwives are well aware—at the moment of birth, both life and death hang in the balance. Rather than meaning that *all* birth therefore needs to be interfered with, as portrayed in the one-two punch theory discussed in Chap. 3 and exemplified in a risk model of birth, according to a midwifery philosophy this means that along with the quiet watchful waiting—the non-interference—comes a specific vigilance. This midwifery vigilance assumes that any birth can become complicated, not simply those designated as 'high-risk', and it is herein that the safety of this model lies: in the knowledge that risk can attend any birth, but that until it does, every birth should be treated as a normal physiological event. Likewise, the women in the study were under no ideological illusions in their description of birth as something their bodies *could* do, that their bodies *would* do it.

> *It is a natural process…we're designed to birth, you know, as women…it's natural but it's also dangerous as well, you know. And…just being aware of the miracle of it and the many things that could go wrong within the process of birth…the fine line between life and death…becomes a lot more real. (Juno, interview 1)*

> *I think it's an individual thing, everyone has their own beliefs, like as in what they want out of birth. But as a general rule I think that if everything is normal, everyone can do it without intervention, but I think we're lucky we live in a world where if it isn't normal there is intervention available for them. (Sinead, interview 1)*

Therefore, in their understanding of birth as natural, and as potentially risky, they placed faith in the midwives who would be able to support their bodies to birth well if all was going well, and intervene if they or their babies were in danger. It also contributed to women's fear of birth.

The Birthing Body: Fear, Pain, and Control

It is argued that fear of birth is located both in the social dimension, where it is associated with the unknown quantity of labour, the 'horror stories' of birth and generalised fear for the baby's wellbeing, as well as in the personal dimension, where it takes the form of a fear of pain, of losing control, and the unique nature of each birth (Fisher et al. 2006). The findings of Fisher et al.'s (2006) study are supported by our own findings; corresponding themes include the unknown and unknowing of labour, and a focus on control and pain. However, we found that women identified some of these factors as ways of reconciling and alleviating fear, rather than as only contributing to increasing fear; pain and the unknown were viewed ambiguously, rather than solely negatively. Some of the women that Newnham interviewed communicated a fear of birth, although in many cases this was not overwhelming to the point where they wanted any kind of intervention. In some cases, it revealed itself as a fear of intervention or physical damage rather than a fear of pain.

May's excitement about birth and her fear are intertwined with her imagining of how the actual process of birth happens:

> [I] still panic because [it's] really painful I think…I heard they will cut you in the vagina or something and it makes me…shiver but they say you can't feel it at all because it is too painful inside the body, so it's more like the bone has been moved and opened—oh its horrible, because your bones—it's such a small hole and you have to push the whole baby out. Oh my god, I think it is quite—I think it is a miracle. (May, interview 2)

In some cases, this fear was expressed by first-time mothers more as a fear of the unknown—discussed later in the chapter as a separate concept.

> Scared…I don't think it's going to be a walk in the park. You know I have had challenges in my life…but…I think I am pretty healthy and fit and pretty tough so, I have no idea what to expect, I don't how intense it will be but I am just hoping that I can do it. (Bella, interview 2)

Women who had already had a baby were more able to draw on their past experiences in order to cope with any fears they may have in this pregnancy, and did so frequently. Although—as will be shown in that section—the 'unknown' quality of birth remained present with multiparous women. Fear of intervention, and early experiences were a factor for Anna, below:

> A long time ago probably talking about ten years ago now, I volunteered to do some telephone counselling for a pregnancy support line. And as part as that, they brought in some of the tools that can be used in delivery just to give us an understanding so if we were talking to clients on the telephone we would know

what they were. So…I'm looking at the size of, you know, the ventouse and the forceps, probably gave me a bit of a fright. And maybe that's lingered a little bit, because I'm not the kind of person who wants a mirror, I don't want to touch the baby's head when it comes out. I'm not interested in what goes on in that zone, so! [laughs]. (Anna, interview 2)

Fear of pain was also a consideration for some women, and this was a reason for those women who considered having an epidural.

I know—the process is painful. I can't help worry[ing] about the pain. Everyone told me it's painful so I get ready for it. I want to take the epidural if I can't stand that pain. (Isobel, interview 2)

My thing is why be a hero if…I just was worried about losing the plot and being distressed myself that would then cause the whole experience to be horrible. I'd do it again, the epidural, because it just—I don't know—that thought of getting to the point of no return and being in some world that technically you don't have to be there. (Lily, interview 1)

However, fear of pain was not the only reason for wanting an epidural. Reasons also included prior experience of long labour or complications and wanting an epidural in case these were to reoccur, wanting to retain some physical control (not being 'out of control' with pain) and long-standing fear of birth.

I've always had a fear of childbirth. It's just always been something that I've feared. So when I first fell pregnant I had to get my head around how I was going to do it, because there was this big fear. (Lily, interview 1)

The idea of giving birth always freaked me out. I couldn't watch it on TV, I had to change the channel and whatnot. So I always thought yes, planned C-section just because the idea of the pain really did scare me quite a lot…I always wanted to have a caesarean just because pain freaks me out. (Tessa, interview 1)

Tessa's pregnancy was spent coming to grips with her fear of birth pain. She went from initially wanting an elective caesarean to planning a labour and birth with no pain relief. She sought out advice from an anaesthetist, quite early in her pregnancy, and was also influenced by a good friend, a chiropractor and holistic practitioner. (Interestingly, Tessa's visit with the anaesthetist was a turn-around for her, and provides one of the discongruities of the study—see below.)

> *It's also, in a way, vanity, because you know your body changing and your vagina not being as tight as it once was kind of thing. That's probably—honestly and embarrassingly—that's another thing. I just don't know—just the idea of it—pap smears have always really scared me, just the idea of something going inside you and, very well knowing it isn't painful at all, but it's just—I don't know, the idea of it—there's blood and it's dirty and it's obviously painful, no-one ever lies to you or even sugar-coats it, and that's—to be honest I'm not sure why I had to change the channel when I saw a women giving birth when I was watching it on TV, but yes I think—probably just thinking the idea of pain—no-one likes pain and neither do I. (Tessa, interview 1)*

Tessa did end up having an epidural in labour, and in her final interview, she attributed this to the pain, however, she also described a lack of support in labour that may also have contributed to her feeling overwhelmed by pain.

> *They said 'Well, are you going to take a Panadol?' and I said 'Look I don't even know if I have Panadol in the house', they said 'Give us a call back in 2 hours' and I didn't take Panadol but I was pretty upset by this stage…I was freaking out, I was really scared and in a lot of pain at this stage…I didn't really like the first midwife who was there. I thought she was—she wouldn't let me get in the bath. (Tessa, interview 3)*

It was probable that Tessa's experience was tainted by her lack of feeling supported and the fear that this provoked. Not being allowed to access the bath, when she had it in her plan and had signed the form antenatally would almost definitely have affected her labour experience and increased her need to instead access epidural analgesia. Caregiver support is now well documented as having a positive influence on women's experience of birth and how she copes with pain (Halldorsdottir and Karlsdottir 1996; Hodnett 2002; Leap et al. 2010; Lundgren and Dahlberg 1998; Parratt and Fahy 2003; Van der Gucht and Lewis 2015). Women in our study also described feeling supported—by birth partners and by midwives, antenatally and during labour—as important to them.

Some women described a fear of *loss of physical control*, which included the idea of being observed in this state, highlighting again the importance of the midwife's role and how vulnerable women can feel about labour.

> *I guess the thing that's the most worrying is just like the loss of control of your body, from being in so much pain, and you know, having people around to see you like that. That I guess is probably what I'm more worried about, in a vain kind of way, than the actual labour itself. (Rose, interview 1)*

> *Oh, just the loss of body control as well. Like, I found that one out before I was pregnant. Like you lose control of your bowels and things like that, and it's not like you feel it or do anything about it, it's going to happen. But still, I'm a very private person, and—I just don't like losing control in public and things like that, so it's sort of that issue that freaks me out the most I think. (Arkadia, interview 1)*

Some women saw the epidural itself as a contributing factor to a sense of lack of control over the process.

> *I didn't have a lot of confidence around what might happen with an epidural. Without an epidural I pretty much know what's going to happen, it's going to be painful but at least I'll be able to tell what's going on. But with the epidural, you know, people were sort of neither here nor there on what the experience was going to be like, it's not guaranteed. (Anna, interview 2)*

> *I just cannot handle the idea of someone putting a big needle in my spine, or cutting me open, because you're out of control then. It frightens me to be at the mercy of such an experience…Seems like it's being inflicted upon you and you don't have any control or choice or anything. (Nina, interview 1)*

Control and empowerment, or their loss, appear as important considerations in other studies about women in labour (Larkin et al. 2009; McCrea and Wright 1999; Parratt and Fahy 2003). Loss of control has been found to be a major fear in childbirth (Fisher et al. 2006) and lack of control is a 'strong predictor of a negative birth experience' (Waldenström et al. 2004, p. 25). Indeed, feelings of being 'in control' or 'out of control' are probably central to the woman's experience of labour (Ross 1998). Women who feel out of control describe the importance of kind, caring, and connected midwifery presence, described by midwives as 'being with' women, to support them (Halldorsdottir and Karlsdottir 1996; Hunter et al. 2008; Parratt and Fahy 2003; see also Walsh 2010). In addition, although intense pain can plunge women into feeling out of control (Halldorsdottir and Karlsdottir 1996), this is not significantly correlated to pain, but related to these other multifarious factors (Waldenström et al. 2004). Parratt and Fahy (2003) found that women had a heightened sense of self when they were able to trust in their midwives, relinquish control, and surrender their bodies to the unknowable process of labour, and similar findings have been reported in other studies (Leap and Anderson 2008). This was reflected in our research. While in some ways, women knew they would not be able to control the process of birth, and this was reflected in their discussion of trust in the body and ambivalence to information, they did discuss ways of managing the experience in other ways. The women described the importance of feeling supported by the midwife, both antenatally and during childbirth, whether or not they had met them beforehand. It was easier for women to trust in their midwife if they did have a relationship, but this was not essential. Other ways of maintaining control included control over the environment (who they invited into the birth space, choosing the setting), maintaining privacy (e.g., staying in the bath), and control of self (knowledge and preparation).

For the participants in this study, losing control also referred to losing emotional control, and therefore their sense of self as controlled/controllable.

And I don't know how I'm going to be emotionally—I don't want to be a cow to everyone and I'm really scared—from what I hear, midwives give you the go ahead to swear at them and stuff. But I don't want to be that person. (Tessa, interview 1)

Women who had had babies before could draw on past experience to take them past the fear of giving birth.

I'm very happy just to take it as it comes, and just to see what happens and do what I need to do. I'm not stressed [laughs]…I was to start to with, I remember saying at my first appointment, 'I'm freaking out about giving birth again, because I know what I'm in for'. But I've got my head around that since then, and yeah, I think, I'm feeling good about it. (Emma, interview 1)

I do feel like I had much more control this time than the last time… The pain was really familiar and so in my head… it wasn't so much like 'Oh this is just really hurting' it was like 'Oh this is the same experience.' (Anna, interview 3)

Fear of pain, and a loss of control caused by intense pain, was a reason for choosing epidural. However, like in Tessa's case above, women who described intense, 'uncontrollable' pain in labour also described feeling scared and unsupported. This is how Lily described her first birth:

My memory from that is a dark room, reasonably dark room because it was 2 o'clock in the morning. And I'd asked for the ball, the medicine ball and a mat, and the medicine ball came out and it was flat and it was useless. So that was one of my strategies gone, and then all I wanted to do was just count, like I was counting. But yes, I just felt really like I needed someone to step up and go 'This is what you need to do'. And in the end I said to the midwives 'These contractions are full on, why? Am I weak, because this is just the start of labour?' I'm thinking maybe it's just that I can't handle this pain. She goes 'No they're pretty intense'. Because I was already 3cms when I got to the hospital. And then I called for the…the epidural came at 7 o'clock or something. Because…I just felt I can't deal—I can't do this by myself. I seriously felt like I had no support. (Lily, interview 1)

Fear of birth was therefore associated with pain, but pain was not an exclusive or primary cause of birth fear. This coincides with other findings that identify the complexity of women's attitude to birth (Waldenström et al. 2004). Fear of birth was also associated with fear of intervention, fear of physical damage, and triggered by past experiences or loss of control. It was related to the privacy and intimacy that the vagina represents, and the invasion or disruption of that privacy. Women also described 'always' having had a fear of birth. It is probable that women's early life experiences of birth or related events, as well as our cultural 'story' of birth, influence women's perceptions and expectations of birth as either something to be feared or welcomed. Understanding birth as a corporeal experience not only allowed women to put faith and trust in their bodies to 'know' how to birth, it also brought up long-standing or deep-seated fears about pain, and loss of physical, emotional, or environmental control. It is therefore as important to turn our attention to the portrayal of idealised or socialised bodies and, using embodiment theory, identify how childbirth can be reintegrated as a powerful, rather than a powerless, experience.

Ambivalence to Pain

Pain has been defined as 'an unpleasant sensory and emotional experience associated with actual or potential tissue damage or described in terms of such damage' (International Association for the Study of Pain [IASP] in Mander 1998, p. 17). Pain, or the management of pain, has been placed at the centre of birthing practices. It is a major focus of the technocratic birth philosophy, with its emphasis on the relief of pain, and of biomedicine as a rescuer of women (Mander 2000). As outlined in Chap. 2, the underlying premise of biomedical research concerning pain and analgesia is that labour pain is abnormal, that it should be avoided, and that it is a woman's right to labour without pain. Pain in labour has also been described, by women, midwives, and researchers, as a transformative function of birth as a rite of passage (Davis-Floyd 1992; Leap & Anderson 2008). Women describe a contradictory relationship with labour pain, but along with the negative descriptors that might be expected from descriptions of pain are words that describe it in terms of intense positivity, such as power, energy, strength, and ecstasy (Lundgren and Dahlberg 1998, p. 107). It appears that the emphasis on pain and pain management may have always been more important to biomedicine than to women. As Lundgren and Dahlberg (1998, p. 108) point out, 'there is a risk that we compare and treat pain during childbirth as we do pain caused by illness', and it is important to acknowledge the difference.

Mander (1998, p. 5) contends that labour pain was not prioritised prior to the nineteenth century, and that historically, pain in childbirth only became significant as medical men began to penetrate the realm of birth. Pain (relief) became a focus because the relief of pain with anaesthesia could only be provided by a medical practitioner, thus occasioning him to be present at more births. Midwives were often blamed for causing pain in labour, and doctors, by hastening the length of labour, claimed that they facilitated less painful births (Mander 1998, p. 5; Murphy-Lawless 1998, pp. 72–74, 84). As described in Chap. 2, midwives did use herbs and other techniques to aid labour and help with pain. It was believed that fear of death—and with much higher rates of maternal mortality, this was probably a real concern for women—was detrimental to the labour process, and so the labouring woman would be supported by local, experienced mothers, the 'god-sibs' (Mander 1998, p. 6). As medicalisation increased, and man-midwives replaced midwives and god-sibs, this crucial element of support to stave off fear of pain, or fear of death, was largely removed from the birth experience. Support in labour has now been shown to increase women's likelihood of a spontaneous vaginal birth, decrease their likelihood of needing analgesia, and increase their overall satisfaction with the experience of birth (Bohren et al. 2017). Importantly, the god-sib tradition was not about relieving pain, which would have been expected by women, but about alleviating *fear* which is arguably worse than the actual experience of pain in a straightforward labour, and may complicate labour and increase the experience of pain (Foureur 2008).

Some women would have actively sought out pain relief; however, considering the perspective offered in Chaps. 2 and 3, we argue, with others (see Fisher et al. 2006), that fear of birth was increased by its medicalisation, as women were removed from their families, social supports, and midwives, and left to labour alone in hospital beds, often with no explanation of what was happening to them. In addition, the medical childbirth position, lithotomy, where a woman is on her back with her feet up in stirrups only serves to increase pain. Practices known to reduce pain, such as walking, being upright, immersion in water, and having continuous support in labour, were not available to most women in Western countries throughout most of the nineteenth and twentieth centuries (Wagner 2001). Two hundred years of labour practices that are now known to increase both pain and fear in women have left a scar on our collective understanding of birth and pain, as particular 'truths are given to, and derived from, the female body in a male social order' (Shildrick 1997, p. 15). These truths affect women directly on a physical level (Akrich and Pasveer 2004; Shildrick 1997). As Lundgren and

Dahlberg (1998, pp. 109–110) ask, within the context of negative body image and media representations of the 'ideal' body, how can we expect women to 'be able to trust their body during childbirth?'

Labour pain is therefore a site of contestation whereby biomedicine has staked a claim in both the understanding and control of women's labouring bodies, and women have the opportunity to recreate the meaning of pain in labour for themselves (Maher 2010; see also Martin 1989). Investigations into pain do not only recognise pain as a destructive influence. Pain is also potentially productive as it produces a new subjectivity—a new sense of self—by eliminating that old distinction between mind and body (Maher 2010; Mander 2000). Pain can thus bring about a unique sense of 'being one's body' and also reduces the distinction between the bodies of mother and baby, increasing the feeling of connection (Lundgren and Dahlberg 1998). Kelpin (1992, p. 98) says:

> The work, exertion, effort, is not just the physical power of the uterus, nor is it just the intellectual power of the mind, but the unity of self which calls us to use all our resources.

Perhaps then, pain does influence how women transition to motherhood, as the physical embodiment of pain allows them to reconstitute ideas of self-as-mother. This process, described by Walsh (2006) as 'matrescence', is also greatly influenced by midwifery approaches. Scarry's (1985) seminal work on pain describes the destructive and isolating nature of pain, the way in which pain can obliterate a sense of selfhood. However, and this argument is taken up by Maher (2010) in describing feminist accounts of pain and subjectivity, pain is also constitutive of self. Pain in labour requires a constant re-assembling of the body-self, producing new subjectivities, so a focus on childbirth pain can offer a new perspective of birthing women's bodies to 'resituate authority with the birthing woman' (Maher 2010, p. 5). If pain is seen as constitutive of, rather than destructive of body-self, birthing women can no longer be constructed as 'less than', as 'non-subject', as controllable or needing to be controlled. The power that was disrupted by medical attempts to control the birthing body is returned. Maher (2010, p. 6, italics in original) argues that:

If pain is relocated as constitutive of birth experience, if pain is understood as encompassing all the complex, troubling and challenging aspects of birthing and asserted as an active process of interpretation and transformation, as the *work of birthing*, pain becomes a vital ground for knowledge and agency, rather than a potential threat.

The women in this study were curiously ambivalent in their approach to labour pain. Most of the women preferred to either 'wait and see' how they coped with their labour, or wanted to avoid epidural altogether. Four of the sixteen women had epidural in their birth plan antenatally. Pain was talked about in contradictory terms. In asking Emma what her plans would be in a third pregnancy, after having an epidural in her first birth, and no pain relief for her second, she said:

> *I don't know to be honest. With my pregnancy with him I didn't want any drugs and then on the way to the hospital—I remember the pain now like 'I don't know if I can do'—because I didn't know I was so far into it—and I'm like 'If I am going to be doing this for another 5 hours I want pain relief'. It just happened that way. I just don't know. I honestly don't know [what I would choose next time]. It was pretty cool telling people I had no drugs. It was very cool, but yeah, I honestly don't know what I would do with a third. I guess during the pregnancy I would say not to have drugs but you never know in the heat of the moment. (Emma, interview 3)*

A few women described an absolute fear of pain, and this was a reason given by those women who chose epidural. Most of the women, while apprehensive about the pain, or rather, how they would cope with it, described pain as a natural part of the labour process; necessary but potentially bearable. Others described the pain as something they *wanted* to feel, as part of the process of becoming a mother. So the women described their relationship to pain in as one of fear, apprehension, or significance. Certainly labour pain was not something to be avoided at all costs for most participants. Our findings are in accord with Lundgren and Dahlberg's (1998) study of women's experience of pain during childbirth, although we have a slightly different emphasis.[4] Our theme *pain as significant* corresponds to their theme of transition to motherhood, while trust in the body and trust in the midwife are expanded and become the two overarching premises as illustrated in Fig. 6.1.

Pain as Necessary

Many of the women displayed a pragmatic approach to the pain of labour.

> *I don't really get that, because I think it's a natural process giving birth and you're meant to have pain. So why would you not go—okay this is what's meant to happen. (Sinead, interview 1)*

> *Yes. It's just…It's normal. It's normal pain, I suppose…I don't find it's like a scary pain because it's just something that's supposed to hurt, it's supposed to. (Rose, interview 2)*

> *It's kind of a healthy pain…it's all for a positive end. And it's your body naturally doing what it's supposed to do. So while I don't love the idea of having to go through a painful experience, I guess I can cope with it. The damage and the pain that could be associated with…an epidural is I think, doesn't outweigh, that says more of a negative pain than the positive pain of a muscle doing it's natural work. (Anna, interview 2)*

Lily, who was definite that she wanted an epidural, still expected to experience some pain in labour, saying:

> *At least I know what to expect. I think I can handle the pain, the contractions more than—with the right breathing—can't say I'm looking forward to that. (Lily, interview 1)*

Sinead was planning on a natural birth with her first baby, but ended up with an epidural after a long, malpositioned labour. She describes the difference in pain:

> *I guess—the pain was different, I just knew it wasn't right, and it was just when I had a contraction…which is hard to describe anyway…But you know when you feel that pain and that pressure and all that kind of stuff, that didn't bother me, but I had this acute stabbing pain right on my pubic bone, and like I could hardly stand up. Before that I was swaying, I was fine, I felt absolutely fine, felt really, really good, so it's hard to sort of tease out. But it was a feeling of 'This isn't right.' (Sinead, interview 1)*

Bella expressed the ambivalence that was also common with this realistic perception of labour pain:

> I'm a little bit nervous. But it sort of has to happen. So I guess I'm a little bit excited as well. It's just weird. I'm looking forward to the baby, so I guess that's just what I have to go through to get that experience...But I'm interested to see what happens, and I'm also interested to see how I handle it. (Bella, interview 1)

Emma had had a posterior labour with her first baby, and had ended up having an epidural. In our first interview, she described how she needed to change her approach because of the pain she experienced.

> It's weird with labour, because it's like the most painful thing you ever do, but you forget about it so quickly. I broke my arm however many years ago, and I still remember the pain from breaking my arm like it's weird—but I don't have a very high pain threshold, not really. I think in labour there's a point that you can handle. I think it's a lot of mental preparation as well, as to how much you can handle. (Emma, interview 1)

Despite this, and her admission that the first time she had wanted to be a 'hero', and that there was social pressure on women not to use drugs in labour, on my querying about the coming labour, she stated:

> I want to be a hero again! [laughs] I don't know—I still keep telling myself that with my first if she wasn't posterior I would have got through it okay. Even after an epidural I could still feel that grinding back pain and all of that. I couldn't feel anything when she was coming out. I figured I could still do it without drugs, but if I needed something I would do it. (Emma, interview 1)

The attitude of these women belies the biomedical preoccupation with pain relief at all costs. The women in the study, even those planning an epidural, expected to feel a level of pain. While they were not necessarily overjoyed about this, most were not overly concerned about it either. This could be because of their belief in birth as a natural process, and the knowledge of all of the women who had given birth before them, described above. The fact that women expect some pain in labour and are not necessarily fearful is now acknowledged in the literature (Van der

Gucht and Lewis 2015). It is possible that maternity systems now need to catch up to the women to provide what they need antenatally in order to better prepare for coping with childbirth pain.[5]

Pain as Significant

While the women often discussed pain as simply a necessary part of the labour process, even if they were choosing to have pain relief, there was also an emphasis on the significance of giving birth, and its place as a rite of passage into motherhood. Bella identified that the whole experience was something to be cherished, and she did not want it diminished into the banality of everyday. The pain of labour added to its significance:

> It's not like going to the shop and buying a baby, it's what women are meant to do and I think our bodies are built that way, to give birth so…I guess it is something that I just want to treasure forever and it's my experience…I don't want to be…like something that you could go do on any Sunday of the week. (Bella, interview 2)

Kate also described this sentiment, as motherhood had not come easily to her.

> I think from experiencing the feeling of possibly never having children, it was important to me to savour every bit of that…facing a world without possibly having that is what really spurred me on to enjoying every moment of it because, you don't appreciate it otherwise and I think it's that appreciation of 'Oh my gosh! I am actually going to be a parent'. Something—I never thought that was going to happen, but every bit of it was important even the pain. (Kate, interview 3)

Annie described a fear of the pain, but nonetheless was looking forward to it in a kind of 'feel the fear and do it anyway' approach, because of its significance to her experience as a woman.

> Terrified, absolutely terrified! I'm such a wuss, but part of me can't wait to experience it. I think giving birth to a baby, and going through that pain, I that it's actually giving birth to yourself as well. So part of me goes—bring it on! And

the other part of me goes 'Oh shit—I'm terrified', but I don't want to numb any of that...I don't think there could be anything more raw or you know, real, earthy and feminine and yes—so bring it on [laughs]. (Annie, interview 1)

And later in the interview process:

I need to feel it. I think it is part of becoming a mum and going through that, I think why numb that? I think it's like—it's an initiation, I think for me, into motherhood. (Annie, interview 2)

This idea is echoed in Sinead's words, below:

For one thing...I think you are meant to feel pain, I think you are meant to actually feel the contraction and I think the baby is meant to feel the contraction, I think that is a part of what it is to give birth and to labour...I think we have been doing it for 40,000 years...so I just think it's an empowering thing to be a woman and to go through labour and to actually feel some of it. (Sinead, interview 2)

Emma described it as an experience she wanted to feel, especially since she had required pain relief in her previous birth.

I don't know it's weird. I think it's a more of a personal thing than me being worried about the baby, because with the first one, she was perfectly healthy when she came out. But yes, I think it's just a personal choice, of me wanting to just give it a go. Like the whole experience of labour without drugs, which I obviously didn't do before. (Emma, interview 1)

To sum up, the women in this study were practical in their approach to labour pain. The idea of birth as a natural event that women have been doing for millenia, and that women draw on this knowledge, has been found in another study (Karlsdottir et al. 2014). In keeping with our findings of women seeing pain not only as necessary but as absolutely significant to the process of labour and birth and becoming a mother, the women in their study also discussed the transformative power of labour pain, with women describing themselves as changed; as now being capable of anything (Karlsdottir et al. 2014). The results of this research therefore support Karlsdottir et al.'s (2014, p. 8) idea that pain in labour is concomitant with the *meaningfulness* of having a child and is therefore also associated, in many cases, with joy. These authors suggest that this represents a third paradigm of labour pain—that of the birthing woman—remarking that previous understandings of pain in labour stemmed from either a midwifery or a medical paradigm (Karlsdottir et al. 2014); a valuable advance in the argument that seeks to reposition the woman and her labouring body as central to the birth process. In addition, other studies support the finding that women primarily view labour pain as part of the normal process, that is, *pain as necessary*, and that the pain of birth is not necessarily *the* primary consideration for women (Karlsdottir et al. 2014; Mander 2000; Van der Gucht and Lewis 2015). In their study, Karlsdottir et al. (2014, p. 9) found that

> very little of the women's attention was focused on the management of pain by pharmacological means…Nonpharmacological measures for relief of labour pain are relatively neglected in the…medical literature, and often too much attention is paid to pain management with medication when pain in labour and birth is discussed. The conventional medical approach to the management of pain in labour and delivery has increasingly come to rely on the use of anaesthetic and analgesic drugs, in spite of reservations within the medical establishment itself.

This is consistent with our findings: both our reading of the medical literature and the interview themes. Research such as this, with the addition of our finding that women see birth as a corporeal event, with its embedded ideas of pain as necessary or significant, allows an alternative to the medical interpretation of birth, one where women reintegrate the conceptual Cartesian duality of mind and body and recreate themselves as mothers.

Trust in the Midwife

There is much research now to support the idea that the care provider's role in labour is of paramount importance. Lundgren and Dahlberg (1998) identified that women expressed a trust in their bodies to cope with pain, and our findings also support this. There is a correlation between a woman having a caring and understanding midwife and her ability to cope with the pain of labour (Halldorsdottir and Karlsdottir 1996). The trust shown by the midwife in the woman is vital, as women need to know that all is well; midwives are critical in holding the space for women to follow their bodies' cues (Halldorsdottir and Karlsdottir 1996; Maher 2010; Leap et al. 2010; Mander 2000). This is particularly important given that some women do not necessarily want to be decision-makers during their labour, and rely upon the expert opinion of their caregiver (Marshall et al. 2011, p. 95). A relationship with a supportive midwife, preferably in a continuity of care model, was one of two mediating factors that protected women against fear of birth (Fisher et al. 2006). In their review of the qualitative literature on women's capacity to cope with the pain of labour, individualised and continuous support was identified as the first of two major contributing themes (Van der Gucht and Lewis 2015). The other key theme in their study was the acceptance of pain during childbirth. The women in our study also recognised that birth would be painful and although they had conflicting feelings about pain, it was not necessarily to be avoided; pain was described as both 'necessary' and 'significant'. The women who described 'out of control' pain also described feeling unsupported; a significant finding that reflects comparative literature (Van der Gucht and Lewis 2015). Van der Gucht and Lewis (2015) identify that coping with labour pain was in effect a universal practice amongst women across all socioeconomic or cultural groups. Although support during labour was the absolute key factor in this, women showed an acceptance that pain was an inevitable part of the labour experience, as with our findings, a natural or normal or expected thing—if somewhat bittersweet. These authors also suggest that there is a need for maternity care providers to also show an acceptance of pain (Van der Gucht and Lewis 2015), a major principle of Nicky Leap's (Leap and Anderson 2008; Leap et al. 2010) 'working with pain' thesis.

The women echoed this view as they discussed their ideas about birth. Seeing birth as uncharted territory and something they did not want to over-prepare for, as their bodies would know what to do, they expressed a reliance on the midwife who would be there on the day of labour. Anna said:

> *To be honest I get a bit confused when it comes to which drug does what…I understand gas…so I'm quite comfortable with that. Then, you know, in terms of the epidural being like the highest one at the other end. The ones that are in between, the self-administered options and whatever, I get a bit mixed up about what crosses the placenta and if you have to be monitored or not. So my plan would be that if I really wasn't coping using non-drugs or just gas that I would ask the midwife at the time to clarify for me what those drug options did…Like 'Will I have to lie down? What are the chances of it crossing over to the baby?' Because if I think about it now, I'm probably going to get it mixed up, but if I can ask at the time. (Anna, interview 2)*

Meanwhile Rose talked about receiving the advice to trust the experts on the day:

> *And my partner's mum…said, you know, 'Just don't get too caught up in what you have to do', like 'I will not have a caesarean' or anything like that, because when it comes down to it, you may not have, you know—it might not be the best idea. So just try and be a little bit more relaxed, and listen to the people around you. The midwife and the doctors, and yeah, so I think that's all pretty solid advice. (Rose, interview 1)*

The way that information and options are discussed and presented makes a difference to women. In discussing her previous labour in a different public hospital, Anna said:

> *I've heard…some friends that have used it [water], and most of them have actually birthed in the pool…they were saying the pain relief is quite significant in the pool—just the gravity and the water—quite different to having a shower, or standing under running water, which is what I did last time. There was a big bath there, but I didn't ask and it wasn't offered. So I don't know whether it was able to be used or not. I hadn't ever—I didn't know that there was a difference. I hadn't heard of them, like the difference between floating in a birth versus standing under running water. It was just the idea of warm water, so I didn't…I didn't question that angle. Nobody offered it. So I didn't use it last time. I guess reliance is on the advice that was coming from the staff that were on that day. And I figured if they thought it was a good idea, that they would offer it I guess. I was very much being led by what they were saying, so I didn't really…think about it. (Anna, interview 2)*

The situation that Anna describes here highlights the fact that many women are not being offered water as a realistic option in labour. In her current pregnancy, Anna was booked to the birth centre, and was confident in the advice that might be offered or suggested to her in labour because she believed that it would align with her own ideology of birth:

And at the end of the day, if something happens and the advice is that I need some stronger analgesics, then because I'm in the birth centre, I know that the philosophy these people come from is not—that that wouldn't have been their first option…I guess because they come from a similar philosophy I'm not too worried if it ends up being stronger. But I will just take their advice. At the end of the day, they're the medical professionals and I'm not. So I'm comfortable. (Anna, interview 2)

In another example Emma discusses her previous labour experience:

But with the first one, the midwife looked at me, and she just said 'You're not coping; I think you should think about something'. And that did influence the first time. And I guess it'd be the same this time, but I think I'm in a better position to know whether or not I am going to need anything. (Emma, interview 2)

Leap and colleagues (Leap and Anderson 2008; Leap et al. 2010) have discussed the need for midwives to be prepared for this trust in their expertise and to reflect back a sense of confidence in the woman's ability to cope with birth in their 'working with pain' approach to labour. Women in labour are vulnerable. If midwives suggest pain relief, invariably, women will take it (Leap 2012), not necessarily because they need it, but because they are relying, as the women in this study articulate, on the midwife's knowledge. Conversely, if the woman looks at the midwife and the midwife reflects back a calm and a trust in the process, implying to her 'This is normal, you are doing fine, I trust that you can do this', then the woman is encouraged and her belief in her body to birth is restored (Halldorsdottir and Karlsdottir 1996; Leap and Anderson 2008). What this means, according to Leap, is that midwives need to explore their own attitude to pain in labour (Leap et al. 2010), because 'the attitudes of caregivers and labour companions or doulas play an important role in how women are supported to cope with pain in labour' (Leap et al. 2010, p. 240).

I was hysterical. I'd tried gas and hot showers and just anything before that, and I was just not coping. And I didn't think that at the time, but she said it and I kind of thought 'Yes, maybe she's right.' And she was. I wasn't coping at all! [Laughs] I think she did the right thing. Like she didn't tell me that I had to have it, she just said maybe you should think about it before it's too late. And because my partner was stressing out as well, he just didn't know what to do with me. I think maybe that had a little bit to do with it. (Emma, interview 2)

Although in hindsight, Emma thinks she was not coping, and that the midwife was right, she also identifies the influence of both the midwife and also her partner in how she came to make the decision to use pain relief. In the above quote she also discusses the fear, also brought up by other women in the study, of being 'too late' for an epidural. The apprehension about running out of available time to access epidural analgesia was not prominent, but was raised by other participants and led to at least one other woman asking for an epidural before she actually felt like she needed it.

Leap et al. (2010) quote from the National Institute for Health and Care Excellence (NICE) guidelines, which identify that maternity care providers should 'consider how their own values and beliefs inform their attitude to coping with pain in labour and ensure their care supports the woman's choice' (NICE, in Leap et al. 2010, p. 240). Although a useful idea, the trouble with this particular wording—and the problem with using the word 'choice' in general—is that firstly, it obfuscates the fact that 'choice' is not necessarily as it seems (see Kirkham 2004). As we have shown—to co-opt a familiar Orwellian maxim—*All choices are equal, but some are more equal than others*. Likewise, not all that is manufactured as 'choice' is, in actuality, a real option; moreover, it assumes that women have a defined set of expectations or choices set out for labour (which some women might, but as we show here, many do not and want to 'go with the flow' on the day). This first point was revealed in the discourse analysis in Chap. 5, showing how practices and options are thickly wrapped in language and meaning that influence their presentation and uptake. The second point—the misconception that women have mostly pre-determined their labour choices—was commonly held by the midwives in the study.

Trusting the Midwives

The midwives had varying views on their requirement to actually provide support to women in labour. Many did feel it was up to them to support and guide women through their labour, and not offering analgesia formed a part of this practice.

> *The midwife [MW42] tells me that she goes through the options (of pain relief: gas, pethidine, epidural—what Nicky Leap calls the pain relief menu) at the beginning of labour. She tells them that the gas is 30 seconds away, the pethidine somewhat longer, and the epidural takes the longest (in terms of time). So this midwife puts it in terms of 'time 'til the drug effect' or time until availability of the drug, but won't offer it again. She says that the partners often say 'Can't you give her something?' and she tells them that as she has gone through it at the beginning, she won't offer it after that. It's up to the woman to ask. (Field notes 25/7/12)*

However, others did not see support as a major requirement of their professional role.

> *I can't handle this sitting in a room the whole time. I don't think it's my job and I don't do it, sitting and talking through each contraction. It's the support people's job. If they just sit in a corner and don't participate, I pull the partner over and give them the cream and say 'You do this, do that' and they quite enjoy it. (MW2, Field notes 2/4/12)*

In addition, numerous midwives mentioned the belief that women had already decided on their plan (or should have decided) before they came into labour ward. As has been found in other studies (Marshall, J et al. 2011), the midwives did not see labour ward as an appropriate place for discussing options for labour and also thought that women had 'already made up their minds'. However, this is in direct conflict to the finding from this study—discussed below—that women were overwhelmingly undecided in their approach to the unknowable territory of labour, preferred to 'wait and see', and were relying on the midwives' expertise.

> *When someone comes in in labour, it's too late to talk to them about active birth. But I'm old school. Women get resentful in the end because [midwives] try and talk them out of it [pain relief]. You know, 'Get in the water, try this, try that.' Then you go in and they say 'Thank god you came in', and you get them sorted. (MW2, Field notes 2/4/12)*

There was a view that most women occupied either side of a dichotomy, and that most had internalised a medicalised view of birth:

> *[If] they're really 'natural' in their thinking, they'll think waterbirth, but if they're general medicalised society, then they're just 'gas, epidural'. Two different cultures—alternative, natural type thinking and medicalised thinking. (MW13, Field notes 10/5/12)*

It is likely that rather than being committed to one end of the birthing ideology continuum or the other, most women have views of birth that are complicated by ideologies, social norms, and ideas about risk and safety (Coxon et al. 2014). While it may be the case that many women subscribe to a 'medicalised' birth perspective, and this is backed up in the midwife-participants' descriptions of antenatal classes, where they felt most women were interested in hearing about the options for analgesia, it also assumes that women need to come in demanding a 'natural' or a 'water' birth if they think that birth is a natural process or that they want to avoid pain relief. This was not the case for the women interviewed and other research has also found that women's birth ideologies are richly informed by various, sometimes competing, discourses (Coxon et al. 2014). The analysis showed a dissonance between what the midwives thought and what the women expected. Below is an excerpt of an analytic memo from the field notes regarding the view expressed in the quote above.

> *Two thoughts here: 1) that women are thinking about having epidural in pregnancy (which a lot probably are, but many of the women I talked to weren't) and 2) that women have to be 'natural' ideologues to want a natural birth, which seemingly they don't either. Many of the women I interviewed talked about seeing birth as natural process, and that they would accept guidance from the midwives. Whereas, many midwives I spoke to seemed to think that women had already decided before they came in. But…the women I interviewed*

seemed to want to take advice on the day. Is it because [midwives] are not telling women about waterbirth that they don't choose it? Not because they're not 'natural' [in their thinking] women? What if they had all of the information? Had to sign an epidural form as well? Were aware of all of the problems, if they saw these side by side with water, what would they choose? (Analytic memo, Field notes 10/5/12)

More important than how many women choose epidural, or how many women think birth is natural, is the assumption that women will be knowledgeable and prepared for this option when they come into labour ward. Despite this, midwives were aware that women were not always fully informed about epidural analgesia, and this was one of the reasons they attempted to use Pethidine as a trade-off.

I would say to the woman, 'You should never feel guilty for the choice you make. If you're too stressed it's not good for the baby, so there is no guilt about having an epidural'. But, I think a lot of women aren't really aware of all the ins and outs of them. They just think it's an easy option. No pain. (MW19, Field notes 31/5/12)

Midwives could get frustrated with the fact that they tried to offer the information that women would need to succeed in having a normal birth, but that it was not what the women wanted to hear.

I am sitting with one of the midwives in the tea room before handover…She has just started holding antenatal classes. MW13: It's been really interesting. They [the women] don't seem to want to know about other birth methods, using focus, or anything. They all want to know about pain relief. I think it's society driven. What can we do? I offer resources and recommend books, but they don't want to know. (Field notes, 11/6/12)

However, on balance, what it did seem to come down to was '*the midwife in the room*' (MW19, in Chap. 4). A couple of midwives thought the TENS machine worked well and would advocate for its use, but other midwives would say things like 'I don't use the TENS'. These kinds of practices become part of the accepted culture, and can be difficult to change. For example, there was also a strong cultural belief in this labour ward that if labours was being induced or augmented with Syntocinon then women would need epidural analgesia because it made labour too painful. Newnham had some interesting conversations with midwives who had recently begun working at the hospital which also emphasised the relativity of many practices, as they identified clear differences in culture (and therefore practice) between this site and others they had worked in.

> *Talking to two different midwives today about the way things are done here. Both of them are agency midwives, and one had worked in New Zealand, one in a rural hospital. Both of them talked about their lower CS rates (23% in NZ). The New Zealand midwife talked about their different method of induction (gels, x2 or 3, no Synt) and the rural midwife about the different 'headspace' of women birthing there:*
>
> *MW15: Most [women in the country] do not want an epidural for example. It's to do with the antenatal education, I think. We have a lot of midwives who are really for natural childbirth, so this is just passed on. And the women talk together, there's a strong sense of community and they hear each other's birth stories. And if we do augment birth with Syntocinon, we don't push epidural. I think about 30% of women who have Synt don't have an epidural, but in some places, they are almost given together. And as soon as a midwife says that [that a woman will need an epidural with syntocinon] then you ruin their mojo, and they think they can't [go without it] (Field notes 16/5/12).*

In the next excerpt, the effect of a midwife's view on whether an epidural is needed with Syntocinon is illustrated:

> *MW17: [looking after a woman being induced] Well, apparently she doesn't want any pain relief, so we'll see how that goes. She may do OK.*

Then later on:

> *The MW did a VE on the woman being induced. She was 3 cms dilated. She's going to increase the Synt. MW17: She still doesn't want pain relief. I asked her directly. I told her she'd be having a breakfast baby [meaning she still had hours to go].*
>
> *This midwife is clearly not comfortable with this woman choosing not to have pain relief. The midwife not only asked the woman directly...but in a way*

almost tried to scare her into it…telling her she still had a long time to go. These things could easily influence a women teetering on the edge to opt for pain relief. (Field notes, 28/5/12)

On another day, Newnham was sitting in handover. There were five midwives on for the night shift and four women on the ward, two of them being induced. In her field notes, she wrote:

[From handover report] A woman in labour—induction, Synt from 5pm, not using any pain relief.

A midwife (MW21) rolls her eyes and looks sideways, as if to say 'We'll see about that'. The T/L who is handing over says: 'She's doing all right. Her contractions feel ok.'

The midwife (MW21) who rolled her eyes was allocated to the woman in labour, the one being induced with Syntocinon, and no pain relief. She gave an earful to the outgoing T/L about how this woman may have been awake all night, she'd be tired, why didn't they start the Synt earlier? In the 'old days' with nulliparous women they started Synt straight away, none of this waiting business. Then the baby would be born before the early shift went home.

It will be interesting to see if this woman ends up with an epidural.

Not long afterwards, she wrote:

The anaesthetist gets here at 9.40pm to insert an epidural!

I ask the midwife later whether the woman had asked for the epidural fairly quickly, as the T/L handing over from the late shift had seemed to think the woman was doing fairly well without pain relief, and she had not asked for anything.

MW21: Well, I went in there, and I said 'It's up to you, but we are interfering with the process [of birth] and so it is a bit more intense' and her mum said 'You don't have to put yourself through that. I had an epidural.' So she decided fairly quickly to have one.

Another midwife (MW22) joins the conversation: Yes, but when we talk about informed consent and autonomy and women-centred care, it all goes out the window in labour anyway. Women in the throes of labour are not going to hear all of the pros and cons, or they say afterwards, 'I wouldn't have cared', or 'I don't care, just give it to me!' So it's either a yes or no question. 'Do you want pain relief or not?' But I don't see many women come in here really prepared, with good support, to have a natural birth. (Field notes 11/6/12)

Some midwives expressed a practice philosophy that left a great deal up to the women. This was often explained from a standpoint of facilitating informed consent or women's empowerment. Although the midwives might not leave every decision to the woman, they suggested that they would 'follow the woman' rather than taking the lead, which is the reverse of what the women in this study expected.

MW30:   *Well, I would never tell a woman what to do in labour. I would never recommend anything. It has nothing to do with me…I leave it to the women, what position they want to be in. Some midwives, all of their women seem to be on all fours and I wonder if they are encouraging that. I mean if I had a choice, I would have them lying in left lateral…but it's not up to me. A woman in OP labour is going to get on all fours to get the pressure off her back. Women know what to do.*
EN: *Do you think most women have an idea what they want when they come in?*
MW30:   *Yes, because they've talked to their friends, gone to classes. Most have already made up their minds when they come in here. [NB this is not what I have found in my interviews. Women want guidance in labour because of the unknown, and also do not all feel prepared information wise]. The only time I hesitate is if a woman comes in and says 'I don't want an epidural under any circumstances' and then changes her mind. You want to be sure it's what she really wants.*
EN: *Would that normally be in transition then?*
MW30:   *Yes, but I will get them an epidural if they've asked for it. Even if they're 9cms [dilated]. Because with a primip, you just don't know. They might have another 3 hours to go yet. The last thing you want is to hear, 'The midwife told me to'. That's not right. (Field notes 27/6/12)*

There are a couple of different points illustrated by this long excerpt. It illustrates the midwife wanting to *'leave it to the woman'*, who *'knows what she wants'*. There are benefits to midwives taking that 'watchful waiting' role in labour, and not interfering with, or disturbing, the birth process too much (Leap 2000; Leap and Anderson 2008). However, as shown in the memo [NB] to herself in this field note, Newnham noticed a discrepancy between what some of the midwives were saying and the interview data from the women, who appeared to expect more guidance. Michel Odent (see 1999; 2013) has spent several decades researching and writing about how women in labour are operating primarily from their limbic system, a part of the brain that is ancient and autonomic, switching on the cascades of birth hormones and leading to the instinctive movements and altered state of mind that is evident in undisturbed birth. It is this system that can be interrupted if women are frightened, interrupted, or spoken to too directly in labour, as well as by bright lights and noise. The switching on of the neocortex, the 'thinking' part of the brain, can lead to release of adrenaline and cortisol which halt the progress of labour (Odent 1999, 2013). There is a need for a supportive presence, knowledge of how to actually support the process of normal birth, and quiet reassurance with suggestions about how to get through the next stage, rather than either expecting women to be fully cognizant, respond to constant questions or make too many decisions, or leave them completely to their own devices (though this may be appropriate for some women, especially if they have other support). Perhaps there is a fine balance between watchful waiting and providing more demonstrated direction—which many midwives might already do, but this did not come across in the study.

It also shows the propensity, discussed above, for the 'informed consent' mandate to overtake the midwifery adage of 'getting women through' even if the woman had expressly stated she did not want an epidural. This is of course also complex and situation-dependent. We are not faulting the requirement for informed consent in most circumstances, nor are we implying that a woman who said she did not want an epidural cannot change her mind, but there is also the common situation where women ask for an epidural during the transitional phase of labour, who on reflection (after being supported through this phase) are very pleased they did not receive one (Leap et al. 2010). It means that although in some cases the woman asking for the epidural at nine centimetres dilation will want one, in many cases, she will not.

Birth as Unknowable

The reason that such faith was placed in the midwife is that labour was described as a complete unknown—as uncharted territory—that had to be navigated in real time. Although preparation was potentially useful, it was also seen as somewhat superfluous, as the women had no idea what to expect. There was usually an accompanying optimism and excitement about the birth, and that everything would go well.

> *I want to feel like I can do it, and I can handle the pain. That's how I feel, but at the same time—I'm not really sure if I actually can. It's really hard 'cause I have no idea what to expect. I really don't know…It's really hard to know how you are going to feel about it until it's happening. (Rose, interview 1)*

> *It's funny, when people say 'You have no idea until you are there', you have no idea until you are there! I had no idea…You can't explain it. (Bella, interview 3)*

Women who were having their second or third babies were not immune to this feeling, and were well aware that each labour and birth is different. This was described in terms of the unique quality of each labour, with a different body (older, more experienced, already birthed) and a different baby:

> *It definitely is different this time around knowing what you could expect…my body feels a lot different this time around, so you have got to expect that it is possible that your body could react completely different. (Kate, interview 2)*

> *But we'll just…you don't know. I've got a friend who had—both her babies were posterior so she was in quite a lot of pain. So we don't know what's going to happen with this one. (Anna, interview 1)*

Or it was described in terms of a comparison to the previous labour:

> *I have always been scared of labour but I think that having [first baby] didn't really help the situation. Just knowing my recovery and what obviously went on*

just doesn't make me feel confident at all. So, the only thing is that I'm thinking that the second labour, they say that your body is a bit more prepared for it so it may be easier, but it's just the unknown…you don't know. (Lily, interview 2)

I'm trying not to think about it too much. I just get in a frazzle when I do. So just—cruise—I am freaking out more this time because I'm kind of expecting to go into labour the same way I did with the first. Which is very unlikely… That's probably my biggest thing, the second time round, is like—the not knowing, you don't the first time either, but I've got so much to compare it to now. (Emma, interview 2)

Sometimes it was fear that put women off thinking too much about the coming labour.

I think it has changed dramatically from my first birth to my second because I found it so extraordinarily overwhelming that I think that I actually don't want to focus on it coming up…there is a lot of focus on preparing yourself mentally and whatever but I actually think this time round I want to just relax and I want to just coast as much as I can. (Sophie, interview 1)

Isobel was openly scared of the pain of labour, and talked about having an epidural. Even so, there was still uncertainty at the end of her second interview, late in pregnancy:

I still don't know too much about that [pain relief]. I know the process and the consequence [but]…I don't know how it works. Well I will see during the labour if I need it. (Isobel, interview 2)

Emma brought up another reason that labour could not really be planned—that of birth outcomes and emergencies being unpredictable events:

No, because it can go from one extreme to another. At one point there were people putting drips in my arms—he went into foetal distress—I think his heart rate went really low and you know at one point anything could have happened and then half an hour later he was sort of out. So yeah, you just don't know. (Emma, interview 3)

What the women then relied upon, due to the uncertainty of the impending experience that would be the labour and birth of their baby, was trust in their bodies.

Going with the Flow

A recurring theme coming out of the interviews and underpinned by the unknowable experience that is childbirth was the sense of needing to *go with the flow* of labour. Combining their mediation of information and trusting in their bodies was this idea that they would wait and see what happened on the day; planning birth was not only impractical, it was unrealistic and even naïve.

> *I mean, admittedly, I didn't have a massive plan when I went in there. I was going to take as it comes because, it's just so different and you don't know how you are going to react. (Kate, about her first labour, interview 2)*
>
> *I've just sort of said 'Oh look, first of all, I'll just see how we go doing non-medical stuff and then if we need some gas—like I'll probably have the gas I think [laughs]. Let's just see how we go.' (Anna, interview 2)*

In some respects, this followed the pain relief menu approach (Leap and Anderson 2008) presented by the midwives in the antenatal classes, but there was also a sense of literal 'unknowing', being unable to plan for this unknowable event, and that to surrender to a state of 'flow' was the way to accept this unknowableness in a positive way.

> *So yeah—It's still unknown but, because every experience is going to be different…but, you know, I think I'm just happy to just walk in with—not a plan as such, I'm just going to…go with the flow. (Lily, interview 1)*
>
> *Now that I am going to be staying home, probably a lot more relaxed and free-form I think, just going to go with the flow. A friend said to me this morning 'You've got so no idea how much pain you're in for' and I said 'Yeah but I'm not going to know that until I am there'. I am not going to worry about it I am just—It will be what it will be.' (Annie, interview 2)*

Even those women who described having a plan of sorts also described alternate events that could possibly occur and the subsequent requirement to be ready for a change in this plan.

> *I still have that in my mind as well, if I am doing all that prep work and it does happen before the induction date, then there goes all those sort of plans that I have got in my head and it might be completely different to that and I still might end up with a completely natural birth without any drugs at all, who knows... Yeah then we just go with the flow. (Sinead, interview 2)*

There was also the acknowledgement, particularly amongst first-time mothers, that they would not know the intensity of labour pain, or how they would cope with it, until they were experiencing it for themselves.

> *I have no...firm views against anything. And I'm more than happy, if I cry in the first contractions [laughs], I'll be like 'Give me an epidural!' I'm not against that. (Bella, interview 1)*

The other reality for women regarding 'going with the flow' was the recognition that labour does not always progress normally, and that there might be circumstances where they would need to undergo intervention for their own sake, or the sake of the baby.

> *When I was pregnant with [first baby] I wanted the whole pain free, natural birth and it didn't happen that way. I think you just need to go with the flow with it all and if something's going wrong you need to do—whatever you need to do to get the baby out, regardless of what pain relief you need or anything like that. (Emma, interview 1)*

The women then, although holding views, predominantly, that childbirth is essentially a corporeal experience that their bodies could be relied upon to do, approached labour with this sense of pragmatism and reason.

> *I'm still kind of just going with the flow. I'd like not to have as much pain relief as I did last time. But if I have to I will. (Emma, interview 2)*

> *I would really like to avoid any drugs or intervention if I possibly can. At the same time, I'm not, like, dead against it. If it happens it happens. (Rose, interview 2)*

Parratt and Fahy (2003) also discuss the way that the unpredictability of birth causes women to surrender to the physical process of birth and focus on her body's cues. Hauck et al. (2007) identify that women, in the wake of an unsatisfying birth experience, adapt their expectations for future births in an attempt to forego the cognitive dissonance of keeping high expectations in these circumstances. They warn that a focus on 'being flexible' or 'having a healthy baby' can be read as the incorporation by women of medicalised expectations and demands and caution that these need to be 'framed within an approach that values, trusts and supports the natural birth process' (Hauck et al. 2007, p. 245). The women's descriptions of their experiences in pregnancy—of fragmented information, of keeping information at bay, and putting the physical role of their bodies foremost, as well expressing the uncharted territory of labour as needing not to plan as such, but to go with the flow of labour—culminated in the need to put their faith in the midwife to guide them on the day of labour itself.

Ambivalence to Information

Within these contexts—the need to place trust in the midwife, the understanding of labour as unpredictable—described by the women, many participants talked about deflecting the barrage of information and advice on pregnancy and birth that came at them.

> *People just say oh you've got do that and you can't do this, and it's like yeah, nah, yeah. I have a really strong resonance when I hear something and it goes 'Yes that's what I need.' Then I can just grab it and the rest of it I go, 'Nope, it's not for me.' So I haven't actually done a lot of research on anything, other than the bits that I think I need to know about. (Annie, interview 1)*

I guess it's just sort of life experience…and I don't want to be overloaded. You can research and get as much gory details as you want, or you can research and get good stuff. So it's sort of like…I'm happy to make it my experience instead of someone else's. (Bella, interview 1)

This became a theme in the data that we tentatively titled 'I don't want to know' and it puzzled us because the women also described in detail about how they searched around for specific information when they wanted to.

Yes, obviously, know what's going to happen, but I don't—like, with all the other stuff I don't want to know too much detail in case it just freaks me out too much. To be prepared yes, because to be unprepared would just be foolish, but not to be over prepared. (Arkadia, interview 1)

Trawling through the interview transcripts one time, Newnham found the following quote, which put this phenomenon into a slightly different light. The women were not 'not wanting to know'. They had demonstrated this by the way they accessed particular information. It seemed, rather, that the women did not want to *overthink* the whole process, and by not overthinking they were avoiding an emphasis on the *mind* and maintaining a connection to *body*.

I'm a great believer in not thinking too much about what I was actually doing, and just letting your body do it…I feel for the people who do it every day, and do help people give birth, because it's a very scary thing, I think, to look at anyway. When you go through it, you're not thinking about that—you're just thinking 'I want the baby out.' (Kate, interview 1)

Sometimes, even third time around you don't ask too many questions, sometimes when you are actually in the zone…it's better to know less—there is that fine balance, isn't there? Knowing too much or not knowing enough so you can't make an informed decision. (Juno, interview 3)

This connection to the body in labour creates the possibility of reconciling the conceptual Cartesian dualism between mind and body, rendering a new cohesion or holism to the way birth is approached. Women also picked the kinds of information that they wanted or needed to process or deal with at the time. For some women, this led to a lack of information seeking about epidural—because they did not want to use it, and therefore had no interest.

> *I actually don't know anything about birth, um pain relief, that they try and offer you. I don't know anything about what they do. I'm just like 'Nup, don't wanna know.' (Annie, interview 1)*

> *I think the information [about epidural] has always been available. I haven't delved into it because it's not something that I am interested in, if it has to happen on the day then it has to happen on the day, yeah I don't want to read anymore horror stories about it. (Bella, interview 2)*

Tessa had, early on, sought advice from an anaesthetist about the effects of labour drugs, and was probably more informed that she appears to be in the quote below. However, as discussed in the previous chapter, she had been confused by the conflicting advice given by midwives in an antenatal class, who she understood as saying there were no effects on the mother in terms of hormone production/milk production or the baby suckling.

> *Cons? I know a couple of cons. There might be a little bit more but I don't really feel the need to know them because I don't really want one. (Tessa, interview 2)*

Another participant described herself as knowing enough because she knew she was going to use epidural analgesia, and whatever the risks were, they were worth it to counteract her fear of pain in labour. As Lily describes here:

> *I mean I'm aware that there are risks but…the other scenario is just not doable for me so I just don't think I have a high pain tolerance or labour just scares the hell out of me so I don't have any intention to do it naturally. (Lily, interview 2)*

Lily acknowledged her decision not to look into the information too closely, as essentially she felt she had no other choice. If an epidural appeared too dangerous, her plan to manage labour pain would no longer be an option and she would have to manage her pain and fear some other way.

I guess—that's really bad because I actually—I guess by choice haven't done a lot of reading into it because then that would provoke more fear which I don't need. But I guess there are some issues with semi paralysis, permanent paralysis…but besides that I must admit I don't have enough information—but that's by choice. (Lily, interview 2)

Maher (2003) has similarly described such information-filtering in pregnant women and concluded that women were preparing themselves as 'informed consumers'. While this analysis is synergistic with current theory that women co-create themselves as good consumers (Tyler 2011), we found the constant reference to the body provided a new insight; despite the inevitability of internalising aspects of medicalised discourse, women have also kept their own version of events (Hales, in Maher 2003, p. 150; Martin 1989). Although not all of the women referred to a sense of bodily connection when talking about disregarding particular topics of information, it was a constant reference throughout the interviews. This closes the analytic circle (Fig. 6.1) by a conceptual return to trust in body-self. As acknowledged in the opening discussion, recent midwifery research has identified embodiment as a way of re-engaging the mind-body connection, of replacing the woman back in the centre of the maternity equation and therefore bridging the divide between midwifery and obstetrics (Davis and Walker 2010; Walsh 2010).

Conclusion

The women in this study were not as a group either particularly fearful of birth, or wanting to avoid pain. Although they cannot be considered as a representative sample of the population in the way of quantitative studies, in utilising 'thick description' (Geertz 1973)—rich data coupled with incisive analysis—it is plausible to consider that other women could hold similar beliefs. In addition, there are relationships between the findings of our study, and the extant midwifery research, as discussed throughout this chapter. The women in this study showed a pragmatic and ambivalent approach to pain. A few demonstrated a deep fear of birth. However, this was not necessarily fear of pain, but of being out of control, or being injured, or having intervention. Women were also ambivalent about cerebral knowledge, expressing the need to protect themselves against too much information. Due to the unpredictability and unknowableness of birth, women needed to be flexible in their approach, preferring to 'go with the flow' and relying on the guidance of the midwife. As shown in the circle of trust, the primary finding—and the one that buttresses the other themes in a cycle of trust—was the faith that the women described in their bodies to 'know what to do' in labour. This highlighted a trust in body-self that serves as a connection to the baby, and the process of becoming a mother, and essentially overcomes the artificial and conceptual Cartesian dualism that plagues Western understandings of the body. This trust is also placed in the midwife, and this was a crucial point in the women's dialogue—the centrality of the midwife's role. It is of significance that many midwives did not express the same view, articulating that women had decided what they wanted before they came in. Midwifery practices need to focus on supporting women fully through labour in the understanding that most women will have a sense of trust in their bodies, and this trust needs to be reflected back by the midwife. Rather than seeing women as dichotomised into 'medical' or 'natural' paradigms, it might be better for midwives to assume that although women have complex and competing input into their individual ideologies of birth, many women hold that birth is a fairly normal corporeal experience, and that their bodies will (eventually, somehow) manage it, and that unless they specifically have epidural in their birth plan, then midwives should assume that women want to be supported through the process of giving birth.

Notes

1. Grosz' (1994) 'mobius strip' where physical and cultural turn in on each other in a helix-type structure is often cited as a clear description of the synergistic relationship between subjective experience and social construct.
2. Although Foucault's (1991, p. 138) concept of 'docile' bodies has been criticised by feminists for dispensing with the possibility of agency and

resistance (see Davis and Walker 2010, p. 4), it has also been argued, and it is our position, that a Foucauldian analysis of power allows for agency and resistance, at the micro-level of interaction.
3. While an increasing number of obstetricians, and most midwives, are women, we are not referring here to practitioner gender. Men can operate from a more holistic perspective, and women operate from a biomedical one (see Young 2005, p. 24–25; Pitt 1997).
4. Lundgren and Dahlberg's (1998) findings were as follows: Pain is hard to describe and is contradictory; Trust in oneself and one's body; Trust in the midwife and the husband; Transition to motherhood.
5. Several women in interview mentioned the book *Birth Skills* by JuJu Sundin, a Sydney physiotherapist and antenatal educator. They specifically referred to the description of birth pain as positive, and the analogy between the contracting uterus and the contraction of any other working muscle (e.g., during exercise). This normalised the pain of birth, and in combination with an explanation of the birth hormones that contribute to the body coping with pain, was seen as useful knowledge for approaching birth.

References

Akrich, M., & Pasveer, B. (2004). Embodiment and disembodiment in childbirth narratives. *Body & Society, 10*(2–3), 63–84.

Bohren, M. A., Hofmeyr, G. J., Sakala, C., Fukuzawa, R. K., & Cuthbert, A. (2017). Continuous support for women during childbirth. *Cochrane Database of Systematic Reviews* (7), Art. No: CD003766. doi: https://doi.org/10.1002/14651858.CD003766.pub6.

Budgeon, S. (2011). The contradictions of successful femininity: Third-wave feminism, postfeminism and 'new' femininities. In R. Gill & C. Scharff (Eds.), *New femininities: Postfeminism, neoliberalism and subjectivity* (pp. 279–292). Basingstoke: Palgrave Macmillan.

Campo, M. (2014). *Delivering hegemony: Contemporary childbirth discourses and obstetric hegemony in Australia*. PhD thesis, School of Social Sciences and Communications, La Trobe University.

Coxon, K., Sandall, J., & Fulop, N. (2014). To what extent are women free to choose where to give birth? How discourses of risk, blame and responsibility influence birth place decisions. *Health, Risk & Society, 16*(1), 51–67.

Davis, D. L., & Walker, K. (2010). Re-discovering the material body in midwifery through an exploration of theories of embodiment. *Midwifery, 26*(4), 457–462.

Davis-Floyd, R. (1992). *Birth as an American rite of passage.* Berkeley/Los Angeles: University of California Press.

Davis-Floyd, R. (1994). The technocratic body: American childbirth as cultural expression. *Social Science and Medicine, 38*(8), 1125–1140.

Duden, B. (1993). *Disembodying women: Perspectives on pregnancy and the unborn.* Cambridge, MA: Harvard University Press.

Fahy, K., & Parratt, J. (2006). Birth territory: A theory for midwifery practice. *Women and Birth, 19*(2), 45–50.

Fahy, K., Foureur, M., & Hastie, C. (Eds.). (2008). *Birth territory and midwifery guardianship: Theory for practice, education and research.* Sydney: Elsevier.

Fisher, C., Hauck, Y., & Fenwick, J. (2006). How social context impacts on women's fears of childbirth: A Western Australian example. *Social Science and Medicine, 63*, 64–75.

Foucault, M. (1991 [1975]). *Discipline and punish: The birth of the prison.* London: Penguin.

Foureur, M. (2008). Creating birth space to enable undisturbed birth. In K. Fahy, M. Foureur, & C. Hastie (Eds.), *Birth territory and midwifery guardianship: Theory for practice, education and research* (pp. 57–77). Sydney: Elsevier.

Geertz, C. (1973). Thick description: Toward an interpretive theory of culture. In G. Geertz (Ed.), *The interpretation of cultures: Selected essays* (pp. 3–30). New York: Basic Books.

Grosz, E. (1994). *Volatile bodies: Toward a corporeal feminism.* New South Wales: Allen & Unwin, Crow's Nest.

Halldorsdottir, S., & Karlsdottir, S. I. (1996). Journeying through labour and delivery: Perceptions of women who have given birth. *Midwifery, 12*, 48–61.

Hauck, Y., Fenwick, J., Downie, J., & Butt, J. (2007). The influence of childbirth expectations on Western Australian women's perceptions of their birth experience. *Midwifery, 23*(3), 235–247.

Heinze, S., & Sleigh, M. (2003). Epidural or no epidural anaesthesia: Relationships between beliefs about childbirth and pain control choices. *Journal of Reproductive and Infant Psychology, 21*(4), 323–333.

Hodnett, E. (2002). Pain and women's satisfaction with the experience of childbirth: A systematic review. *American Journal of Obstetrics and Gynecology, 186*(5 Suppl 1), S160–S172.

Hunter, B., Berg, M., Lundgren, I., Ólafsdóttir, Ó. Á., & Kirkham, M. (2008). Relationships: The hidden threads in the tapestry of maternity care. *Midwifery, 24*(2), 132–137.

Karlsdottir, S. I., Halldorsdottir, S., & Lundgren, I. (2014). The third paradigm in labour pain preparation and management: The childbearing woman's paradigm. *Scandinavian Journal of Caring Sciences, 28*(2), 315–327.

Kay, L., Downe, S., Thomson, G., & Finlayson, K. (2017). Engaging with birth stories in pregnancy: A hermeneutic phenomenological study of women's experiences across two generations. *BMC Pregnancy and Childbirth, 17*, 283–294. https://doi.org/10.1186/s12884-017-1476-4.

Kelpin, V. (1992). Birthing pain. In J. M. Morse (Ed.), *Qualitative health research* (pp. 93–103). London: Sage Publications.

Kirkham, M. (Ed.). (2004). *Informed choice in maternity care.* Hampshire: Palgrave Macmillan.

Larkin, P., Begley, C. M., & Devane, D. (2009). Women's experiences of labour and birth: An evolutionary concept analysis. *Midwifery, 25*(2), e49–e59.

Lazarus, E. (1994). What do women want: Issues of choice, control, and class in pregnancy and childbirth. *Medical Anthropology Quarterly, 8*, 25–46.

Leap, N. (2000). The less we do, the more we give. In M. Kirkham (Ed.), *The midwife-mother relationship* (pp. 1–18). New York: Palgrave Macmillan.

Leap, N. (2012). *No gain without pain!* North Parramatta: Birth International.

Leap, N., & Anderson, T. (2008). The role of pain in normal birth and the empowerment of women. In S. Downe (Ed.), *Normal childbirth: Evidence and debate* (pp. 29–46). Sydney: Elsevier.

Leap, N., Sandall, J., Buckland, S., & Huber, U. (2010). Journey to confidence: Women's experiences of pain in labour and relational continuity of care. *Journal of Midwifery and Women's Health, 55*(3), 234–242.

Lundgren, I., & Dahlberg, I. (1998). Women's experience of pain during childbirth. *Midwifery, 14*, 105–110.

Lupton, D., & Schmied, V. (2013). Splitting bodies/selves: Women's concepts of embodiment at the moment of birth. *Sociology of Health & Illness, 35*(6), 828–841.

Maher, J. (2002). Visibly pregnant: Toward a placental body. *Feminist Review, 72*, 95–107.

Maher, J. (2003). Rethinking women's birth experience: Medical frameworks and personal narratives. *Hecate, 29*(2), 140–152.

Maher, J. (2010). Beyond control? Resituating childbirth pain in subjectivity. *Outskirts Online Journal, 22.* http://www.outskirts.arts.uwa.edu.au/volumes/volume-22/maher. Viewed Dec 2017.

Mander, R. (1998). Analgesia and anaesthesia in childbirth: Obscurantism and obfuscation. *Journal of Advanced Nursing, 28*(1), 86–93.

Mander, R. (2000). The meanings of labour pain or the layers of an onion? A woman-oriented view. *Journal of Reproductive and Infant Psychology, 18*(2), 133.

Marshall, H. (1996). Our bodies ourselves: Why we should add old fashioned empirical phenomenology to the new theories of the body. *Women's Studies International Forum, 19*(3), 253–253.

Marshall, J., Fraser, D., & Baker, P. (2011). An observational study to explore the power and effect of the labor ward culture on consent to intrapartum procedures. *International Journal of Childbirth, 1*(2), 82–99.

Martin, E. (1989). *The woman in the body.* Milton Keynes: Open University Press.

McCrea, H., & Wright, M. (1999). Satisfaction in childbirth and perceptions of personal control in pain relief during labour. *Journal of Advanced Nursing, 29,* 877–884.

Murphy-Lawless, J. (1988). The silencing of women in childbirth or 'Let's hear it from Bartholomew and the boys. *Women's Studies International Forum, 11*(4), 293–298.

Murphy-Lawless, J. (1998). *Reading birth and death: A history of obstetric thinking.* Cork: Cork University Press.

Odent, M. (1999). *The scientification of love.* London: Free Association Books.

Odent, M. (2013). *Childbirth and the future of homo sapiens.* London: Pinter & Martin.

Parratt, J., & Fahy, K. (2003). Trusting enough to be out of control: A pilot study of women's sense of self during childbirth. *Australian Journal of Midwifery, 16*(1), 15–22.

Pitt, S. (1997). Midwifery and medicine: Gendered knowledge in the practice of midwifery. In H. Marland & A. Rafferty (Eds.), *Midwives, society and childbirth: Debates and controversies in the modern period.* London: Routledge.

Rich, A. (1986). *Of woman born: Motherhood as experience and institution [1976].* New York: W.W. Norton & Company.

Ross, A. (1998). Maternal satisfaction with labour analgesia. *Baillière's Clinical Obstetrics and Gynaecology, 12*(3), 499–512.

Rothman, B. K. (1989). *Recreating motherhood: Ideology and technology in a patriarchal society*. New York: W.W. Norton & Company.
Scarry, E. (1985). *The body in Pain: The making and unmaking of the world*. Oxford: Oxford University Press.
Shildrick, M. (1997). *Leaky bodies and boundaries: Feminism, postmodernism and (bio) ethics*. Hove: Psychology Press.
Stone, A. (2007). *An introduction to feminist philosophy*. Cambridge: Polity.
Tyler, I. (2011). *Pregnant beauty: Maternal femininities under neoliberalism* (pp. 21–36). Basingstoke: Palgrave Macmillan.
Van der Gucht, N., & Lewis, K. (2015). Women's experiences of coping with pain during childbirth: A critical review of qualitative research. *Midwifery, 31*(3), 349–358.
Wagner, M. (2001). Fish can't see water: The need to humanize birth. *International Journal of Gynaecology and Obstetrics, 75*(Suppl 1), S25–S37.
Waldenström, U., Hildingsson, I., Rubertsson, C., & Rådestad, I. (2004). A negative birth experience: Prevalence and risk factors in a national sample. *Birth, 31*(1), 17–27.
Walsh, D. (2006). Nesting' and 'Matrescence' as distinctive features of a freestanding birth centre in the UK. *Midwifery, 22*(3, 9), 228–239.
Walsh, D. (2010). Childbirth embodiment: Problematic aspects of current understandings. *Sociology of Health & Illness, 32*(3), 486–501.
Young, I. (2005). *On female body experience: "Throwing like a girl" and other essays*. Oxford: Oxford University Press.

7

Closing the Circle

ANNIE

No pain relief apart from squeezing him really tight.
And yeah it was amazing
The most painful thing
I have ever experienced in my life,
But just gorgeous,
Yeah, it was beautiful.
I went really quickly into active labour
Then that was it, game on, 'Right fill that pool!'
Four o'clock in the morning she came out and perfect,
She was perfect,
It was all just perfect.

Yeah, I mean it hurt like hell
I am so glad I didn't do anything remotely to take that away,
That's the whole point of it.
The pain is there for a reason.
That whole experience of
Honouring her and me,
And just the whole journey of her birth
And my becoming a mum.
I can't imagine not feeling that pain

Even though
While I was half way through it
I was like 'I don't think I can handle this,
I don't think I have got what it takes
To go through this'
But then you do,
Next contraction,
You are in it,
And you just do.

For me, to not experience that pain
Is cheating
You've got to feel pain to grow.
I don't think
I would have bonded with her
Anywhere near as much
If I didn't feel that,
Feel her coming through,
Coming out.
Yeah I loved it.

You can't explain that joy of feeling that pain.
You know what I mean.
Afterwards,
We just sat here,
Completely elated,
Blissed out, totally blissed out,
and the pain was just gone, gone, gone.

In this book, we have used epidural analgesia as a device for exploring hospital birth culture, taking a critical perspective of institutions as purveyors and arbitrators of cultural norms. As the macro-culture of Western birth ideology has influenced what is known about birth and birthing practices, the discourses of science and technology have influenced medical knowledge of, and therefore practices surrounding, women's birthing bodies. These same discourses maintain the safety of epidural analgesia, even while outcome debates are still ongoing. The message from a biomedical perspective is that despite the complications associated with epidural, it is nevertheless safe; it provides the most effective analgesia and should therefore be available to all women who request it. Epidural analgesia also fits within the technorationalist culture, exemplified by the 'pain relief as progress' theme in the literature. Epidural use, along with its health sequelae such as the need for cEFM and Syntocinon and increased rates of instrumental birth, conforms to biomedical principles of control, technology, and intervention. Although we have contributed a critical assessment of the biomedical positioning of epidural analgesia as 'safe', there is a need for further research and informed debate regarding the appropriateness of epidural analgesia in low-risk labour.

Fleshing out the historical and political influences on health knowledge and practice, we have illustrated how medicine is positioned as a powerful social discourse in Western culture. This, coupled with the far-reaching influence of technological rationalism and the technological imperative, means that it is ever more crucial that technology use is subject to critical evaluation that includes, where possible, addressing the underlying power relationships. However, despite this, women maintain the ability to negotiate and experience their bodies within these discourses. Embodiment theory is an important tool with which to capture women's experience, bypassing the midwifery/obstetric dichotomy, focusing on the meaning of birth and the mother-baby dyad, and resituating women in the centre of the birth space.

The influence of Western birth ideology on birth practices was evident in the hospital culture, where biomedical discourse was perpetuated, facilitated by a strong surveillance apparatus, epitomised in the panopticism of the journey board. This surveillance, operationalised within a risk culture, enforced strict temporal restrictions on the birth process. Although practitioners—midwives and doctors alike—attempted to resist these restrictions, they were confounded by the self-regulating momentum of the institution, which sometimes put women at risk in its attempt to keep them safe; revealing an inherent institutional paradox—mirroring the risk/safety paradox in the wider medical discourse—that persisted throughout other areas of the hospital. This paradox was also distinguished by the way that midwives were nominally positioned as guardians of normal birth, yet ridiculed or criticised if they actually practised according to a midwifery philosophy. Despite this, midwives found ways to try and perpetuate midwifery technology.

Despite midwives' efforts to incorporate midwifery philosophy, the biomedical discourse of epidural safety was nonetheless recreated in practice, in part due to hospital and other policy documents. Comparing the documents surrounding epidural analgesia to those pertaining to the use of water in labour and birth, we have delineated how the paradox was maintained and how the relatively safe procedure of water use in labour and birth was constructed as risky, yet the potentially risky procedure of epidural analgesia use, was constructed as safe. Midwives were caught in this paradox, recreating it in the way they managed information giving in antenatal classes, leading to a situation whereby midwives were attempting to provide woman-centred care and fulfil women's right to bodily autonomy using a 'your body, your choice' rhetoric, which they then had to contradict as they warned women of the demands of the hospital culture, policy, and practices.

When women were deciding about whether or not to have an epidural, influences included their own ideas about pain or fear of birth and past experience or concern about birth intervention. Rather than having a definitive birth ideology (either 'natural' or 'medicalised', as perceived by the midwives, and also found in other research, e.g., Davis-Floyd 1994), we found that women were multifaceted in their approach to birth, influenced by different experiences. While this is not such a surprising finding, it does raise questions about midwifery approaches to birth within hospital labour wards. Our findings correspond with Coxon et al.'s (2014) assertion that:

> The assumption that women's birth place decisions are polarised between preference for either 'natural' or 'medical' birth has rested largely unchallenged in the sociological literature since the early 1970s, and this dichotomy increasingly fails to capture the nuances of women's experiences, or the breadth of contextual influences upon their decisions. (Coxon et al. 2014, p. 53)

This approach provides a novel, paradigm-shifting platform from which to develop new areas of research.

By writing about the multiplicity of women's influences and experiences, we hope to have captured some of these nuances of these within the pages of this book, which drew us, ultimately, to the finding that despite the institutional flow of risk and intervention, and dominant discourses of safe technology, women maintained a belief in their bodies to birth (see also Lundgren and Dahlberg 1998) and a sense of birth as a corporeal experience, as neither 'natural' nor 'medicalised' but placed within their bodies, highlighting the deep connection between woman and baby, no longer positioning mother and baby as competing forces but reintegrating them. Drawing on feminist theory that seeks to make the birthing body visible (Davis and Walker 2010; Murphy-Lawless 1988; Walsh 2010), we also further this position, identifying the various competing influences on women's bodies and emphasising the importance of individual, experiential knowledge.

Birth is both a universal and intimately individual experience. The poems we placed at the beginning of each chapter illustrate some of the tensions that have been revealed throughout this book and provide texture—a layer of richness—to the conclusions we have drawn from the study. Themes show their features in the women's words. There is joyful embracing of the birth process and there are exclamations of fear, pain, and loneliness. They show that the women who were discouraged early on, or who felt unsupported and afraid, described more pain and fear than those who were supported and encouraged. Even when viewed by the women themselves as 'not coping with the pain', from the perspective of our analysis, the lack of support appears to have initiated the fear and pain rather than the other way around. It is also interesting to note the impact of the access or denial of water in the experiences of pain in these poems. The poems also illustrate the effect of self-esteem and (internal or external) locus of control as discussed in Chap. 6 (see Heinze and Sleigh 2003). Rather than seeing women's internal psychology as static or predictive of a negative or passive birth experience, it emphasises the need for every woman to be given the opportunity for a positive birth experience and it is in the changing of culture that this can occur. As Rich (1986, p. 182) argues:

> To change the experience of childbirth means to change women's relationship to fear and powerlessness, to our bodies, to our children; it has far-reaching psychic and political implications.

Women who do have low self-worth or past trauma can have the opportunity to start to turn this around, beginning with an empowering and supportive birth environment.

Humanising Birth

Humanised birth practices place the woman at the centre of care (Wagner 2001) and are based on tenets of compassion, relationship, connection, shared responsibility, and considered use of technology (Davis-Floyd 2018). In her recently published book of selected writings, Davis-Floyd (2018) provides new insight from her decades-long work in this area. She presents humanism as a useful middle ground between the technocratic and holistic paradigms that she found in her early work. Humanised childbirth provides a possible platform for the continuum of care that we proposed to replace the midwifery/obstetric dichotomy. She points out a vital difference between 'superficial humanism' (such as more homely décor, permitting attendance of birth partners)—which is important, and better than the dehumanising alternatives, but does not get to the crux of the matter—and 'deep humanism' (such as providing flexible spaces to support freedom of movement, eating and drinking, use of water and other comfort measures, choice of caregiver)—which provides real attention to the woman's needs. In this sense, deep humanistic care balances the needs of the woman with the needs of the institution in a way that prioritises birth physiology and the woman's experience (Davis-Floyd 2018).

The paradox of the institution provokes questions as to the relevance and safety of institutional birth in a postmodern age. Critique of the industrial nature of maternity institutions is not new and has been much debated (Oakley 1984; Martin 1989; Murphy-Lawless 1998; Rothman 1989). However, although the institution has been identified as alienating and depersonalised, and thus unappealing to women, it's identification as a *risk* to women is relatively recent. It came to global attention in late 2014 when, following the UK Birthplace study (Brocklehurst et al. 2011), updated National Institute for Health and Care Excellence (NICE) guidelines for antenatal care (NICE 2014) recommended that women in labour be informed of the increased risk of intervention when birthing in a labour ward compared to a midwifery-led unit. We submit that the paradox of the institution, as identified throughout this book, demonstrates how the risk discourse behaves in some measure as a self-fulfilling prophesy. Our ideas for change now follow.

Antenatal education needs to support women's trust in their body and normalise the physiology of labour. Currently, hospital antenatal education can perpetuate the risk/safety paradox as the midwives feel bound to relay to women the hospital policies and practices. It might be that antenatal education is better provided by external educators. If it is important to the women or the hospital to have familiarisation with the site (including policies and practices) or the staff, then a separate orientation day could be run. It is also important that women are fully cognisant of the risks and side-effects of epidural analgesia and it would appear that this information is delivered more comprehensively—at least in the antenatal period—by anaesthetists. Informed consent processes for epidural should be at least as robust as policies or informed consent requirements relating to water use.

The women in this study appreciated the view that pain in labour is physiological, akin to running a marathon. It put pain in perspective and framed it in a way they could relate to and not be afraid of. Lundgren and Dahlberg (1998) suggest training the body for birth by incorporating relaxation and breathing exercises. Van der Gucht and Lewis (2015) identify how the acceptance of labour pain is a crucial coping strategy, Leap et al. (2010) describe how they normalised birth pain by facilitating the sharing of birth stories and photographs in antenatal groups and Levett et al. (2016) were able to show reduced epidural rates, as well as increased vaginal birth rates, with a tailored antenatal education package that included teaching women about birth physiology and tools for labour based on complementary therapy approaches. All authors suggest more research is needed in this area, and our findings support this suggestion.

Women's satisfaction is strongly associated with their expectations of birth and support in labour (Hodnett 2002). Midwives should be aware that women do not necessarily come into labour with a specific plan; they expect support, comfort, suggestions for coping, and identification of the abnormal. Unless a woman specifically requests an epidural in an antenatal birth plan, she probably does not really want one. That is not to say that women should be refused epidural analgesia or that they cannot decide later in labour that they need one. It is important not to be blind to women's real need for pain relief when necessary (Lundgren and Dahlberg 1998; Mander 2000). A woman's request for analgesia might signify labour dystocia, but feelings of vulnerability, loneliness, and doubt are common, and can be exacerbated if a woman feels unsupported (Nilssen and Lundgren 2009; Van der Gucht and Lewis 2015). Women's experiences of birth are strongly influenced by the attitude of the midwife and how the trusting relationship is developed (Fisher et al. 2006). This is complicated when institutional culture perpetuates ridicule or derision of normal birth practices because it puts midwives in a position where they are attempting to facilitate a trusting relationship on one hand and work within hospital policy on the other—a conflict that has been noted by others (Kirkham 2000; Kirkham and Stapleton 2004; Scamell and Stewart 2014). It also undermines women's expectations—as they are expecting to be offered choices that actually do encourage normal birth. This disruption of the midwife-woman relationship by the institution can be detrimental to both women and midwives (Kirkham 2000).

The midwife-woman relationship has been identified as a significant influence on women's birth experience (Dove 2010; Halldorsdottir and Karlsdottir 1996; Hunter et al. 2008; Parratt and Fahy 2003). The importance of this relationship was highlighted again here as women described the reliance they felt on the midwife who would care for them in labour, whether or not they knew them (most did not). There was an inherent trust that the midwives would let them know what they needed to do. Birth was seen as unknown territory and the women intently distilled or disregarded information, preferring to rely on their body's knowing. This led to the circle of trust diagram, a visual representation which we hope is useful not only in illustrating the interconnection of themes identified in the women's interviews but in changing the way that labour (and women's labouring bodies) is understood. The circle of trust model places the body-self back into the centre of the process and highlights the centrality of the midwife-woman relationship. Trust (between women and midwives) has been recognised as a primary mechanism for overcoming obstetric risk discourse, with the midwife-woman relationship described as 'one of the most effective responses midwives have to obstetric power' (Dove 2010, p. 194). Once this is used as the starting point, then other problems can be solved; the body in time, intervention, use of space, all refer back to the woman in her body and the relationship with her midwife.

Midwives can harness this trust by embracing a 'working with pain' (Leap et al. 2010) approach that acknowledges the circle of trust between women and midwives, and moving birth culture beyond old dichotomies of medical/natural and mind/body. Bear in mind the circle of trust represents fundamental practice philosophy at the micro-level. Trust also needs to extend outwards from the midwifery profession to include recognition of pathology and obstetric transfer and inwards from obstetrics to endorse midwifery practices and environments that support the process of birth (Dahlen 2010; Walsh 2010, p. 494). However, this remains contested territory under dominant discourses of risk and safety. If represented visually, professional trust and cultural trust would form two outer concentric circles within which the circle of trust is either developed or constrained. Even if intervention is required, the circle of trust remains pertinent, to allow the facilitation of information and decision-making between the midwife and woman. This is not just about 'normal' birth—not simply about outcomes—it is about maximising the potential for normal birth and focusing on the process (Akrich and Pasveer 2004; Maher 2010; Walsh 2010). Dahlen (2010, p. 160) notes that 'keeping birth normal is at the heart of building trust—building trust keeps birth normal'. This is the beginning of a humanised birth culture that attributes trust, power, and respect to women's bodies. It places women at the centre of the birth process and prohibits actions based on the current hollow rhetoric of 'informed consent' and 'bodily autonomy' that does not acknowledge the power of the discourse within which it is operating.

This now brings us to the conclusion of the book. We reiterate that ethnography can only present a version of the story, not *the* version. In this version of the story, we have illustrated how despite the lack of conclusive evidence, the primary assertions in the biomedical literature are that epidural analgesia is safe, should be universally available, and is modern and progressive. Childbirth pain is painted as part of a bygone era, and practices that support normal birth are construed as risky. Policies that restrict 'normal' birth practices and facilitate 'medical' ones further embed these discourses. The paradox of the institution—the entrenched surveillance and momentum that sought to keep women safe by pushing them through—potentially put women at risk and juxtaposed midwives both as guardians of normal birth and as risky practitioners. These discourses, together with the misunderstanding by many midwives about women's sense of the 'unknown' in their approach to birth, culminated in a situation whereby a woman's chances of having an epidural were more dependent on the midwife she happened to get on the day, staffing levels, and hospital protocol and capacity, than her desire or need for one. The influence on women of whether or not to use epidural in labour is therefore complex and multifaceted and not simply related to levels of pain.

The finding of the paradox of the institution demands a revision of the hospital labour ward as the primary birthplace for women. The risk/safety paradox under which it operates, that reproduces dominant discourse and contradicts current evidence, places women at unnecessary risk. We recommend that alternative settings, such as alongside or free-standing birth centres, should be implemented as a matter of priority. In instances where women need to birth in hospital labour wards, practices that support normal birth, such as continuous labour support or the use of water, should be implemented and viewed as best practice. Where normal birth is not possible, supportive trusting relationships should still be facilitated. To this end, we suggest that midwives practise with an understanding of the circle of trust. We hope that this model can provide a useful way of understanding the relationships and influences described by women and required of midwives and a template for humanised birth practice. Incorporating a 'working with pain' approach, two specific points that we accentuate are that women should be supported through birth without an epidural unless specifically requested, and that women should be offered the opportunity to use water as a matter of course unless there are absolute contraindications for its use.

There is much still to learn about women's experiences of pain and corporeality in labour. Coupled with embodiment theory, the exploration of the role of pain can provide new directions in how birth is understood, that could transcend old dichotomies and resituate the woman at the centre of the birth space. There is scope for more research in this area.

For the midwifery profession, we see the next steps as needing to include a renewed focus on midwifery technology—with an emphasis on the continuing importance of research, education, documentation, dissemination, and support of knowledge and practice that facilitate normal birth. More significantly, we suggest that midwives acknowledge their disruptive potential, being at the nexus between women and medical discourse, and consider how they use their interactions with women to either uphold or resist dominant biomedical discourse.

We finish with a quote from Adrienne Rich, both as a vision for the future and a reminder of those who have already walked the path and paved the way for change:

> But taking birth out of the hospital does not mean simply shifting it into the home or into maternity clinics. Birth is not an isolated event. If there were local centers to which all women could go for contraceptive and abortion counselling, pregnancy testing, prenatal care, labor classes, films about pregnancy and birth, routine gynaecological examination, therapeutic and counselling groups through and after pregnancy, including a well-baby clinic, women could begin to think, read about, and discuss the entire process of conceiving, gestating, bearing, nursing their children, about the alternatives to motherhood, and about the wholeness of their lives. (Rich 1986, p. 184)

SOPHIE

My brain was just pain, pain, pain!
There is just nothing like that pain.
Now if I had a midwife who had coupled with me the whole way through,
I think that just the comfort of knowing someone intimately
Is going to help you when you are in pain.

You need that emotional connection,
Because my brain nearly fell out of my head because my mum didn't come,
you know,
I was really distraught because I thought maybe, maybe,
Because I had called her at 4 o'clock
And I called her at 6 o'clock
And 8 o'clock.
And then in the end she just didn't bother.

I was just so grateful for my auntie to be there,
Who said 'Oh I did nothing.'
But when she was speaking to other people about, like
'Oh she doesn't like to be touched'
Just hearing someone sticking up for me,
Being on my side, was so important.

It's just too much.
It's just frying your head that you are in this much pain
And you still haven't passed out, you know.

Every problem that I had
Could have pretty much been solved by
Being coupled with a midwife from the beginning
And right through.

It's a long-term thing.
People sort of think it only one day of your life,
But it's not.
There is a lot of healing that you have to do.
It's not just having a wonderful baby.
It's trauma to your body.
You just can't have grief over all,
You have just got to deal with it.
You know, if I was pregnant again I would just be really, really
Actually dreading the birth,
It's not a nice experience for me.

I know some people think that it's pleasant
But the point where I broke down in tears and then you know,
The midwife was saying 'You're stronger than that'
And I thought 'If I was stronger than that I would punch you in the head'
I really thought 'Fuck off',
I thought 'That is not helping! Help me', you know
And I just thought I needed to cry,
That is what I needed to do.
I was exhausted.
It is underestimated how much
Pain is influenced by your emotional state.
Fear is a big one.
This interview might be providing something that makes a change,
That sows a seed,
When I am an old grandma and say
'Back in my day, the medical system', you know.
If when we wave our magic wands,
I would like to be a part of supporting women and I feel like this is a step
towards it, you know,
Just being heard, and acknowledging
Women feel like they have got an entitlement
And a right to choose about their own body.

References

Akrich, M., & Pasveer, B. (2004). Embodiment and disembodiment in childbirth narratives. *Body & Society, 10*(2–3), 63–84.

Brocklehurst, P., Hardy, P., Hollowell, J., Linsell, L., Macfarlane, A., McCourt, C., Marlow, N., Miller, A., Newburn, M., & Petrou, S. (2011). Perinatal and maternal outcomes by planned place of birth for healthy women with low risk pregnancies: The Birthplace in England national prospective cohort study. *BMJ, 343*(7840), d7400.

Coxon, K., Sandall, J., & Fulop, N. (2014). To what extent are women free to choose where to give birth? How discourses of risk, blame and responsibility influence birth place decisions. *Health, Risk & Society, 16*(1), 51–67.

Dahlen, H. (2010). Undone by fear? Deluded by trust? *Midwifery, 26*(2), 156–162.

Davis, D. L., & Walker, K. (2010). Re-discovering the material body in midwifery through an exploration of theories of embodiment. *Midwifery, 26*(4), 457–462.

Davis-Floyd, R. (1994). The technocratic body: American childbirth as cultural expression. *Social Science and Medicine, 38*(8), 1125–1140.

Davis-Floyd, R. (2018). *Ways of knowing about birth: Mothers, midwives, medicine, and birth activism.* Long Grove: Waveland Press.

Dove, S. (2010). *Desire versus safety and the negotiation of risk in a continuity of care midwifery program: A critical ethnography.* PhD Thesis, School of Nursing and Midwifery, University of South Australia.

Fisher, C., Hauck, Y., & Fenwick, J. (2006). How social context impacts on women's fears of childbirth: A Western Australian example. *Social Science and Medicine, 63*, 64–75.

Halldorsdottir, S., & Karlsdottir, S. I. (1996). Journeying through labour and delivery: Perceptions of women who have given birth. *Midwifery, 12*, 48–61.

Heinze, S., & Sleigh, M. (2003). Epidural or no epidural anaesthesia: Relationships between beliefs about childbirth and pain control choices. *Journal of Reproductive and Infant Psychology, 21*(4), 323–333.

Hodnett, E. (2002). Pain and women's satisfaction with the experience of childbirth: A systematic review. *American Journal of Obstetrics and Gynecology, 186*(5 Suppl 1), S160–S172.

Hunter, B., Berg, M., Lundgren, I., Ólafsdóttir, Ó. Á., & Kirkham, M. (2008). Relationships: The hidden threads in the tapestry of maternity care. *Midwifery, 24*(2), 132–137.

Kirkham, M. (2000). How can we relate? In M. Kirkham (Ed.), *The midwife-mother relationship* (pp. 227–250). New York: Palgrave Macmillan.

Kirkham, M., & Stapleton, H. (2004). The culture of the maternity services in Wales and England as a barrier to informed choice. In M. Kirkham (Ed.), *Informed choice in maternity care*. Basingstoke: Palgrave Macmillan.

Leap, N., Sandall, J., Buckland, S., & Huber, U. (2010). Journey to confidence: Women's experiences of pain in labour and relational continuity of care. *Journal of Midwifery and Women's Health, 55*(3), 234–242.

Levett, K. M., Smith, C. A., Bensoussan, A., & Dahlen, H. G. (2016). Complementary therapies for labour and birth study: A randomised controlled trial of antenatal integrative medicine for pain management in labour. *BMJ Open, 6*(7), e010691.

Lundgren, I., & Dahlberg, I. (1998). Women's experience of pain during childbirth. *Midwifery, 14*, 105–110.

Maher, J. (2010). Beyond control? Resituating childbirth pain in subjectivity. *Outskirts Online Journal, 22*. http://www.outskirts.arts.uwa.edu.au/volumes/volume-22/maher. Viewed Dec 2017.

Mander, R. (2000). The meanings of labour pain or the layers of an onion? A woman-oriented view. *Journal of Reproductive and Infant Psychology, 18*(2), 133.

Martin, E. (1989). *The woman in the body*. Milton Keynes: Open University Press.

Murphy-Lawless, J. (1988). The silencing of women in childbirth or 'Let's hear it from Bartholomew and the boys. *Women's Studies International Forum, 11*(4), 293–298.

Murphy-Lawless, J. (1998). *Reading birth and death: A history of obstetric thinking*. Cork: Cork University Press.

NICE. (2014). *Intrapartum care: Care of healthy women and their babies during childbirth [CG190]*. National Institute for Health and Care Excellence. https://www.nice.org.uk/guidance/cg190. Viewed Dec 2017.

Nilssen, C., & Lundgren, I. (2009). Women's lived experience of fear of childbirth. *Midwifery, 25*, e1–e9.

Oakley, A. (1984). *The captured womb: A history of the medical care of pregnant women*. New York: Basil Blackwell Inc.

Parratt, J., & Fahy, K. (2003). Trusting enough to be out of control: A pilot study of women's sense of self during childbirth. *Australian Journal of Midwifery, 16*(1), 15–22.

Rich, A. (1986). *Of woman born: Motherhood as experience and institution [1976]*. New York: W.W. Norton & Company.

Rothman, B. K. (1989). *Recreating motherhood: Ideology and technology in a patriarchal society.* New York: W.W. Norton & Company.

Scamell, M., & Stewart, M. (2014). Time, risk and midwife practice: The vaginal examination. *Health, Risk & Society, 16*(1), 84–100.

Van der Gucht, N., & Lewis, K. (2015). Women's experiences of coping with pain during childbirth: A critical review of qualitative research. *Midwifery, 31*(3), 349–358.

Wagner, M. (2001). Fish can't see water: The need to humanize birth. *International Journal of Gynaecology and Obstetrics, 75*(Suppl 1), S25–S37.

Walsh, D. (2010). Childbirth embodiment: Problematic aspects of current understandings. *Sociology of Health & Illness, 32*(3), 486–501.

Index

A

Abstract, 79
Acceptance of pain, 174, 220
Alienating, 109
Ambivalence to Information, 235–238
Ambivalence to pain, 211–219
Anaesthesia, 26
Analgesia, 26
Anodyne, 26
Antenatal classes, 178, 225
Artificial timeline, 125
Art of midwifery, 133
As a transformative function, 211
As constitutive of, 213
Assembly-line care, 38
Augmentation of labour, 46
Aura of facticity, 33
Authenticity, 117
Autonomy, 10

B

Bacon, Francis, 31
Best practice guidelines, 43
Biological essentialism, 91
Biomedical model, 5
Biomedicine, 7
    acts as an agent of social control, 75
Bio-power, 86
Birth, 233
    as corporeal, 202–211
    ideology, 4, 29, 54, 195–197
    intervention, 23
    as a normal physiological process, 1
    as a rite of passage, 211
    room, 106
    technologies, 4
    territory and midwifery guardianship, 197
    as uncharted territory, 220
    as unknowable, 231–235

Birthing body, 199
Birth Wars, 3
Bodies as knowing entities, 198
Body-self, 213
Breastfeeding, 24
Brown, S., 48

C

Caesarean section, 23, 45
Capitalism, 91
Capitalist economic system, 73
Caregiver support, 207
Cartesian dualism, 31, 32
Cascade of intervention, 46
Chestnut, 45, 46
Chloroform, 26
Circle of trust, 195
Clinical expertise, 153
Clock time, 118
Collectivism, 76
Consent to medical treatment form, 157
Constructionist, 33
Continuity of midwifery care, 12
Continuous electronic foetal monitoring (cEFM), 84
Continuous labour support, 84
Continuous support, 174, 220
Contradictory relationship with labour pain, 211
Control, 10, 208
Critical discourse analysis, 13
Critical ethnography, 6, 8
Culture of birth, 8
Cyclic time, 119, 125

D

de Beauvoir, Simone, 198
Decision-making, 172
Dehumanised, 38
Depersonalised, 38
Descartes, 31
Desire, 5
Determinants of health, 77
Disciplinary power, 110, 112
Discourses, 88
　of power, 82
　of risk and safety, 13
Discursive Practices
　The Consent Process, 181–185
Disembodied representation of the body, 84
Disempowerment, 9
Dualism, 198

E

Ecologically sustainable, 75
Emancipatory, 70
Embodied knowledge, 2, 83
Embodiment, 13
　of pain, 213
　theory, 198, 199
Empowerment, 9, 131
Endogenous oxytocin, 47
Engels, Friedrich, 73
Epidural information sheet, 157
Epigenetic, 80
Ethnography, 8
Evidence-based medicine (EBM), 42
Evidence-based practice, 81
Exogenous oxytocin, 47
Experience of pain, 212
Experiential knowledge, 199

F

Fear
of birth, 29, 42, 110
of childbirth, 195
of intervention, 205
of *loss of physical control*, 208
of pain, 206
Feminism, 90
Fieldwork, 105
Folk practices, 40
Foucault, M., 86–88
Panopticon, 112
Fragmentation, 109
of care, 29
Free-standing birth centre, 120
Friedman's curve, 37, 125

G

Galenic theory, 40
Gender inequity, 51
God-sibs, 28, 212
Go with the flow of labour, 233
Gramsci, A., 70

H

Health care
arena model, 6
institutions, 8, 109
Hegemony, 70
Holistic discourses, 82
Hormones of labour, 37
Hospital protocols, 134
Humanised birth, 13
Humanised birthing practices, 114
Humanising, 250–255
Humanising the birth process, 23

I

Iatrogenic interventions, 3, 74, 152
Identity politics, 198
Ideological discourse, 70
'In case' syndrome, 80
Individualised care, 153, 220
Individualism, 199
Industrial capitalism, 32
Industrialisation, 36
Information received, 174–181
Informed choice, 11, 173
Informed consent, 11, 172
process, 181
Institutionalised health care, 108
Institutionalised midwifery, 10
Institutional momentum, 120–130
Institutional restrictions, 155
Institutional rhythm, 119
Institutional time, 123
Institution-focused, 114
Instrumental birth (ventouse and forceps), 24, 44
Inter-professional collaboration, 126
IV oxytocin, 45

J

Journey board, 111

L

Labour
analgesia, 29
companionship and support, 29
dystocia, 44
progress, 116
ward, 105, 108
Labouring bodies, 121

Lack of control, 208
Laudanum, 27
Limited in the choices, 89
Linear, 118
Lithotomy, 212
Lived body, 198
Losing emotional control, 209

M

Man-midwives, 38
Marxist, 70
Maternal mortality, 212
Matrescence, 213
Meaning in birth, 39
Meaning of pain, 213
Mechanisms, 32
  of control, 200
  of power, 87
Mechanistic thinking, 32
Medical anthropology, 7
Medical dominance, 4, 39
Medical gaze, 13, 110, 111
Medicalisation, 74
  of childbirth, 29, 89
Medicalised birth, 2
  ideology, 29
Medicalization, 7
Medical/midwifery divide, 199
Medical technologies, 80
Microbiome, 80
Midwifery, 70
  emancipatory philosophy, 53
  as a feminist praxis, 53
  has been constructed as a subjugated discourse, 132
  model, 1
  philosophy, 1, 153
  practice, 10
  'technical knowledge', 129
  technology, 83
Midwife-woman relationship, 13, 114
Midwives' station, 106
Mind/body connection, 238
Mind-body dualism, 199
Mind/body split, 199
Morphine, 27
Mother/baby dyad, 200
Motherhood, 39, 90
Mother–newborn dyad, 49

N

National Institute for Health and Care Excellence (NICE), 223
'Natural childbirth' movement, 39
Needs of the institution, 121
Needs of the woman, 121
Neoliberal, 73, 199
  ideology, 75
Nihill, Elizabeth, 38
Nitrous oxide, 26
Non-intervention, 152
Normal birth, 1, 133
Normalising birth, 70
Nursing and Midwifery Board of Australia (NMBA), 159

O

Obstetric technologies, 77
One-two punch, 203
Opium, 27
Organisational and midwifery technologies, 13

Organisational technology, 111–120, 141
Organising practice, 116
Oxytocin, 24

P

Pain, 54, 213
 avoidance, 79
 definition of, 211
 in labour, 211, 213
 necessary, 215–217
 relief as progress, 52
 relief menu, 174
 relief paradigm, 52
 as significant, 214, 217–219
Pain-free labour, 27
Panoptic surveillance, 13
Partnership, 1
Pathologising of pregnancy, 82
Pethidine (meperidine), 27, 172
Pharmaceutical analgesia in labour, 27
Phenomenological existentialism, 198
Philosophy of 'being with' women, 119
Policy and practice, 159–164
Political economy, 70
Postfeminist discourse, 92
Post-industrial capitalism, 34, 51
Post-structuralist, 93
Power/knowledge, 13, 86
Power of institutional culture, 117
Power relationships, 7
Practice guidelines, 153
Practice philosophy, 229
Primary health care principles, 77

The Pros and Cons of Epidural, 168–172

R

Randomised-controlled trial (RCT), 42
Reductionism, 198
Reflexivity, 6
Regulation of practice, 152
Relief of pain, 49
Renaissance, 31
Resistance, 39
Rhythms of labour, 127
Rich, Adrienne, 255
Risk analysis, 165
Risk culture, 10
 and epidural endorsement, 156–157
 of the institution, 13
Risk discourse, 109
Risk paradigm on birth, 29
Risk rhetoric and water restriction, 154–156
Risk society, 164
Rite of passage into motherhood, 217
Rituals, 89

S

Safety, 4
Scientific paradigm, 33
Scopolamine, 27
Second-wave feminism, 90
Self-regulation, 112
Self-surveillance, 112
Simpson, James Young, 27

Social medicine, 73
Spontaneous vaginal birth (SVB), 46
Subjective experience, 199
Support in labour, 212
Surveillance and self-surveillance, 86
Surveillance techniques, 10
Syntocinon, 126

T

'Techniques' of power, 87
Technocratic birth, 79
Technological determinist, 51
Technological imperative, 52, 79
Technological imperialism, 51
Technological intervention, 124
Techno-rational, 29
Techno-rationalism, 55, 79
Technorationalist, 77–86
Theorising risk, 164–168
Thesis of the 'one-two punch', 85
Thick description, 6, 238
Third paradigm of labour pain, 219
Third-wave feminism, 92
Time, 13, 118
Transformative power of labour pain, 218
Transition to motherhood, 54, 213

Trust, 1
  in body-self, 197–202, 238
  in their bodies, 233
  in the process, 222
Trusting relationships, 10
Trusting the midwives, 197, 219–231
Twilight sleep, 27

U

UK Birthplace study, 250
Uncertainty of, 233
Unpredictable nature of birth, 125

W

'Watchful waiting' role in labour, 230
Waterbirth policy pamphlet, 157
Water immersion, 13, 154
Western birth culture, 25
Witch hunts, 40
Woman as a site of risk, 200
Woman-centred care, 1
Woman-focused, 114
Woman's choice, 223
Working with pain, 197, 220

CPI Antony Rowe
Eastbourne, UK
November 23, 2019